In The National Interest

In The
National Interest

The Road to Nigeria's Political, Economic, and Social Transformation

Olu Fasan

Penguin Publishers

First published in the United States by Penguin Publishers, 2025

www.penguinpublishers.org

Copyright © Olu Fasan 2025

A CIP catalogue record for this book is available from the British Library

OLU FASAN-Luminari Books

eBook ISBN: 979-8-89795-744-6
Paperback ISBN: 979-8-89795-870-2
Hardcover ISBN: 979-8-89795-746-0

For enquiries about bulk orders for this book, please contact:

Penguin Publishers
info@penguinpublishers.org

Contents

Forewords

Rudyard Kipling famously wrote a novel titled *Two Forewords*. One unique feature of this book is that it contains two forewords, which is necessitated by its nature: a book about the political economy of Nigeria, which draws insights from a large body of knowledge internationally. It is thus fitting that the first foreword is written by a world-renowned economist and expert on Africa, and the second by a famous Nigerian political economist.

Professor Sir Paul Collier, the first foreword writer, is the author of several award-winning books, including *Bottom Billion* and *Left Behind,* and co-author of the seminal report on state fragility titled *Escaping the fragility trap*. He is a Professor of Economics and Public Policy at the Blavatnik School of Government, Oxford University, Director of the International Growth Centre, and former Director of the Research Development Department of the World Bank. In 2014, Professor Collier, a Fellow of the British Academy, received a knighthood for services to promoting research and policy change in Africa. His foreword reflects a deep understanding of Nigeria as well as an empirical perspective on Africa.

The second foreword writer, Professor Pat Utomi, is a Brown Capital Management Fellow and International Policy Scholar at the Wilson Centre, Washington DC, an Adjunct Lecturer at the School of Advanced International Studies at John Hopkins University, and a Professor of Political Economy and Management at the Lagos Business School in Nigeria. Professor Utomi is the current Chair of the African Union Pan-African Private Sector Trade and Investment Committee (PAFTRAC). A former presidential aide,

Professor Utomi has been actively involved in Nigeria's political, economic and social developments for several decades. He is the Founder and CEO of the Centre for Values and Leadership, based in Nigeria, and has authored numerous books, including *Why Not? Citizenship, State Capture, Creeping Fascism and Criminal Hijack of Politics in Nigeria.* His foreword provides an insider perspective.

Sir Paul Collier FBA

This is the book that Nigerians have long needed: an agenda for root-and-branch renewal based on a profound historical understanding. I am honoured to have been invited to write this Foreword: before going further, I will allay suspicions. Far from being one of my former students or colleagues, Dr Fasan is someone who wrote to me 'out of the blue.' I have never met him, though reading his book I most certainly wished that I had. Without further ado, I turn to why you should read it too.

Nigerian émigré communities succeed everywhere in the world: manifestly, the society has talent in abundance. Yet despite that raw talent, plus the good fortune to have had 50 years of huge revenues from oil, Nigeria remains one of the world's poorest societies. This is unambiguous evidence of misgovernance on a staggering scale. Sadly, it is sufficiently common in resource-rich societies that academics have a pejorative term for it: the resource curse. It describes a syndrome in which the vast revenues flowing directly into government coffers induce an intense contest to win control over them. Control comes from the authority conferred by the political office and from opportunities for misappropriation conferred by pertinent administrative roles in a bureaucracy. Both prospective politicians and prospective bureaucrats devote money and effort to gaining these positions in a costly and wasteful scramble of rent-seeking. This is a global, not an African problem, but some resource-rich societies have built robust defences against it. Botswanans have used their revenues from diamonds to escape the deep poverty they suffered until Independence and are now more than twice as well-off per person as the average Nigeria. Norwegians, with oil like Nigeria, are now nearly twenty-times as well off as Nigerians.

The pressures of the oil curse can be countered, and Dr Fasan wisely sees a start to remedy by means of constitutional reform. The first step in curtailing abuse is to establish institutional checks and balances on how power can be used. Alone, they are unlikely to be sufficient, but without them, any society is vulnerable.

He then turns to economic restructuring. The Nigerian economy lacks the key industrial sectors by which, within living memory, some other societies have lifted themselves out of poverty: key examples are South Korea, China and now, within Africa, Ethiopia. The industrial sectors that drove these transformations have been labour-intensive and needed predominantly modest levels of skill. When South Korea and China were still very poor, this gave them a competitive advantage in the global market over the same industries in Europe and America, where wages were far higher. As clusters of firms grew and the workforce developed more experience, wages rose, so people were not trapped into low-paying jobs, but that initial phase was vital in enabling the process of take-off to get started. The same engine of growth is currently driving Ethiopia forward, and it could do the same for Nigeria with its huge young workforce initially willing to work for modest wages. However, it is urgent to get the process ignited because as global technology advances, robotics are likely to reduce the need for workers in these industries. Dr Fasan explains the past failure to diversify the Nigerian economy away from its three big sectors of oil, small-scale agriculture and bureaucracy by a mindset in which protection from foreign competition is regarded as necessary for establishing a new manufacturing enterprise. His favoured model is openness to global markets, with the objective of establishing firms that are oriented towards being competitive in those markets. This is what Ethiopia is already achieving despite being landlocked. Nigeria is geographically far better positioned for those same markets.

The third part of the book brings us to the nub of the matter. It focuses on rebuilding the capabilities of governance. Rightly, Dr Fasan dismisses the conventional capacity building of individual skills: what Nigeria lacks are well-motivated teams across the critical functions of governance, such as the protection of street crime, and the critical institutions of governance, such as those responsible for taxation. Nigeria has too many institutions of governance, some established as means of rent-seeking. Some are redundant, others are fragile but have the potential to be restored to functionality. However, building functionality is not primarily a technocratic matter. As the author emphasises, it depends upon the motivation of the teams tasked with critical functions. We cannot expect public officials to be saints working for peanuts, but we can and should expect them to take pride in contributing to the purpose of their institution. For this, Nigeria indeed needs moral and cultural renewals that expand the horizons of public officials far beyond the narrow objective of personal enrichment. Working in a nationally crucial institution, members of a team need to be motivated beyond not just selfishness, but beyond the limited horizons of family, tribe, state, region and religion. The title, *In The National Interest*, reflects this vital need to build a shared identity around which all Nigerians can rally. Nor is it infeasible: Julius Nyerere, the great founding president of Tanzania, did just that, forging fifty tribes into a larger common identity. It is his great legacy to his country.

Demographically, Nigeria is set to be one of the most important countries of the future. By the end of the 21st Century, it may well overtake China to be the second most populous country in the world. Currently, and for much of this century, it will have an overwhelmingly young workforce and electorate. Once that youthful electorate starts to cohere around a shared identity – 'the Nigerians of the Future' instead of being fragmented into the moribund little identities of their parents and grandparents, that transformation achieved from the top by President Nyerere can happen even without unifying political leadership. In another vast society, Bangladesh, whose population is not far short of Nigeria, students came together to protest patronage governance. There, the government refused to listen and was swept away. Nigeria has wiser leadership, and so renewal can come about without such disruption. But the winds of change, which once swept colonialism into history's dustbin, are again a force to be reckoned with.

Paul Collier,

Professor of Economics and Public Policy,
The Blavatnik School of Government,
Oxford University,
October 2024.

Professor Pat Utomi

The promise of Nigeria and the failure to quickly realise it has bred an army of contemplatives who have captured their explanations of the apparently inexplicable in books. Some have been spewing anger at failure, and others have burrowed into theories in politics, economics and even sociology to offer lamentations. They include elder statesmen and academics like Senator Femi Okunrounmu, Dr Uma Eleazu and Chinu Achebe, who blamed leadership failure. Others use the approach of history, like Max Siolum and Dele Ogun, to lay bare the facts.

So, how should we categorise Olu Fasan's *In the National Interest*? It is a thoughtful but simple analysis of political economy that avoids the trap of being emotional yet manages to depict passion. What Fasan offers is, in my view, a manifesto and call for action to change course. From an analytic but fair and balanced commentary on the historical evolution of politics, governance and development practices in Nigeria, he puts forward what can be called a Federalist agenda. It is a manifesto that keeps from being a polemic that eulogises his preferred way and demonises the other.

With his narrative of the chiselling out of a country from the scramble for Africa, with girlfriends of colonial officers naming territory, you are made ready for a future rigged for trouble.

The book is designed evidently to be an easy read for a general audience; so, while the ideas of leading authors are pointed to, the book does not turn into the language of the disciplines of academic areas covered here is a way that could make it turgid for a person without a certain background.

This strength manages to limit explanation. But narrative style should commit to a target readership and so the book reads like a good Sunday column baking fresh history as it is happening. The mountains of evidence needed to justify the explanation are not as high as may be justifiable in a few cases, but the clarity of thought makes meaning crystalise as he desires it. Each of the dozens of issues, from the June 12 election annulment to the embrace of six- geopolitical-zones-based restructuring for true federalism, could be a book running into several times the size of this volume.

But he provides a quick insight into matters like Dutch disease, import substitution industrialisation and Trade as a pathway to growth. This makes the volume a useful manual for elected politicians and Civil Servants. His lucid explanation of issues of current history, like fuel subsidy removal, the floating of the Naira and multiple exchange rates under Tinubu, makes this book beneficial for the economic education of politicians and business leaders trying to understand the environment of business.

I encourage this quick read for the advance of citizenship.

Patrick (Pat) Okedinachi Utomi
Professor of Political Economy and Management,
Lagos Business School,
Nigeria.
November 2024

Introduction

Nigeria is a mix of contradictions: blessed with sprawling natural resources, yet one of the world's poorest nations; endowed with enormous human talents, yet unable to govern itself well. Nigeria goes by the sobriquet 'Giant of Africa' principally because of its size and economic importance. But the best metaphorical description of the country is a *sleeping giant*. And being *asleep*, Nigeria is not fulfilling its potential. Yet, it is not hard to imagine what Nigeria could become if it were awake. Napoleon famously said of China: 'Let China sleep. For when she wakes, the world will tremble.'[1] Of course, the world will not tremble at the rising of Nigeria, not least because it will not be a nuclear power and a threat to world peace. But if, as the United Nations projects, Nigeria could become the second most populous country on Earth after India, overtaking China, by 2100, then the world cannot ignore Nigeria; rather, it needs Nigeria to be politically stable, economically prosperous and socially cohesive and to be a force for good, not only for the sake of its own people and for the sake of Africa, to which it matters hugely, but also for the sake of the world at large.

Yet, the challenges are daunting and, with the way things are, the omens are not good. A multiethnic country with over 350 ethnic groups, each with a distinct language, Nigeria continues to suffer from the legacy of colonisation. Cobbled together by Britain in 1914, Nigeria remains today, 110 years later, a deeply fractured society, lacking internal cohesion and a shared purpose. The core ethnic identities compete with, and often trump, the national identity. The original artificial construct, with its inherent conflicts, and the overcentralised political and governance structures later created and entrenched during decades of military rule are sources of deep-seated ethnic tension and resentment and of continuing disharmony and instability in the country, often threatening to split it at its seams.

On the economic front, Nigeria is one of the world's most volatile and fragile economies. While it was economically diverse, with a vibrant manufacturing sector, at the time of independence in 1960, Nigeria later became almost totally oil-dependent, with crude oil accounting for nearly ninety per cent of its total exports and eighty per cent of its foreign exchange earnings. Being oil-dependent, Nigeria's economy is thus subject to the vagaries of world oil prices. At independence, Nigeria's level of development was on a par with that of South Korea, Taiwan, Thailand, Indonesia, and Malaysia. But today, Nigeria lags far behind each of these countries. Indeed, in 2025, the World Bank classified Nigeria as a Lower-Middle Income Economy (LMIE) behind Libya and Gabon.[2] Socially, Nigeria is ravaged by endemic corruption, widespread unemployment, extreme poverty and inequality, and debilitating insecurity. Put simply, Nigeria is a sick 'giant', all because it lacks the right political, economic and social institutions that can engender stability, progress and prosperity.

The foregoing is the context in which this book is written. It is a book about the political economy and sociology of Nigeria; a book that analyses Nigeria's political, economic and social challenges and offers ideas on the way forward. The book's analytical approach is based on the premise that there is a symbiotic relationship between the political, economic, and social factors shaping Nigerian society and that political governance, economic performance, and social well-being are interdependent. For instance, the right political institutions that positively shape the character and efficiency of democratic governance are a prerequisite for successful economic governance and management, and both political stability and economic prosperity are critical to state capacity, social progress, and internal cohesion, which, in turn, can affect the operation and performance of the political and economic systems. As a result of this analytical standpoint, the book is structured in five sequential but interrelated parts, each consisting of chapters that address specific themes. Part 1 deals with political and democratic governance; Part 2 focuses on economics and economic governance; Part 3 addresses state capacity and institutional development; Part 4 focuses on Nigeria's ability to tackle social challenges, such as poverty, inequality, and insecurity; and, lastly, Part 5 concludes and offers final thoughts on the way forward.

The core argument in the book's political chapters is that Nigeria's political and governance structures are deeply flawed and hindering development. To govern its economy and society well and achieve maximum economic and social benefits, a country needs, in the first place, political institutions and governance structures that work. Without a stable political environment, economic progress is impossible. Therefore, it is futile to talk about economic governance without, as a starting point, political governance. Thus, this book's central political argument is that Nigeria needs political restructuring, which must lead to an inclusive and enduring political and constitutional settlement and a new constitution that ensures that the country is governed in a pluralistic, unity-inducing and prosperity-engendering manner.

Complementing the political chapters are the economic ones, which deal with economic, trade, and industrial issues. Following on from the political argument, it is submitted that once Nigeria has had a negotiated political and constitutional settlement and a new constitution, it would need to restructure its economy. Without economic progress, even a stable political environment will begin to unravel. So, economic restructuring must follow from political restructuring, and the book's central economic argument is that Nigeria must be an open, competitive, market economy, and an export-led industrial nation. That requires abandoning the age-old mindsets of protectionism and import substitution, removing all barriers to private sector development, and turbocharging Nigeria's productive and trade capacities. Nigeria must diversify away from dependence on oil-based exports into value-added non-oil exports. Adam Smith's immutable words are worth remembering: 'No nation is ever rich by the exploitation of the crude produce of the soil but the exportation of manufactures and services.'[3]

As mentioned earlier, Part 3 addresses a significant issue in Nigeria: the shortage of governmental capabilities. This deficiency hinders Nigeria's ability to manage various societal challenges—Part 4 explores these challenges, including joblessness, poverty, inequality, and insecurity. The issue isn't due to a lack of skilled individuals; Nigerians are recognised for their leadership on global stages. Instead, the root of the problem lies in ineffective governance, fragile institutions, and a deficit of crucial moral and cultural standards. But Nigeria cannot be an effective state unless it is first a strong nation where leaders and citizens, regardless of ethnic, regional, or religious differences, have a sense of shared purpose and common interests. As Professors Paul Collier and Tim Besley put it in their joint report entitled *Escaping the fragility trap*, 'State building requires nation building.'[4] That means that Nigeria must first be restructured to create a new political and governance system that is fair, just, and equitable, ensuring that the right values, norms, and incentive structure underpin that system. Only when Nigeria is united and stable, only when there is a sense of shared belonging and purpose, will an effective state emerge and state capacity and progress with it.

Thus, my deeply held conviction, which informed the writing of this book, is that it is impossible for Nigeria to achieve the much-needed political, economic, and social transformations and fulfil its great potential without a negotiated political and constitutional settlement and a new constitution, followed by the revamping of its economic model. The book rejects the argument that Nigeria does not need to be restructured, that what it needs are good leaders and good citizens. While the success of all institutions depends, in large part, on those who run them, it is also true that institutional structures can constrain behaviour and shape outcomes. Besides, no serious nation puts its faith solely in the goodness of its leaders, rather than in the robustness of its institutions. For instance, if a country's constitution concentrates and over-centralises power and lacks effective checks and balances but, instead, allows a determined government to do what it will without let or hindrance, as Nigeria's Constitution does, it is inconceivable that the country will be run well simply because its leaders are good. The truth is that bad institutions incentivise bad behaviour and bad outcomes. All that said, leadership matters, and the attitudes of citizens matter, but the right institutional structures, underpinned by the right values and norms, are powerful incentives in driving behaviours, performance and outcomes.

The overarching appeal of this book is to the national interest. It is not beyond human ingenuity and creativity to produce for a country an enduring political and constitutional settlement and create a fit-for-purpose economic and governance structure. However, it requires acting in the national interest to do so. Acting in the national interest means reacting as every group with a shared identity does in the face of real and present danger and putting the best interests of a nation and its people above sectional and myopic considerations. The truth is that Nigeria's current political and governance structures cannot ensure or guarantee its unity, stability and progress, and maintaining the status quo is not sustainable; it is even dangerous. Nigeria must, therefore, chart a new path forward. My greatest hope is that this book, which is a call to action for critical reforms to ensure Nigeria's stability and progress, will contribute to that process and that it will lead to a national consensus to restructure Nigeria and create a new political and constitutional settlement, and a new constitution, both of which are preconditions for economic and social transformations.

This book draws heavily on my diverse experiences: first, as a researcher and academic at the London School of

Economics, where I obtained my PhD and taught International Political Economy, International Trade, and Economic Diplomacy; second, as a senior policy adviser in the UK Government for nearly 20 years, during which I developed policies and advised ministers in a range of areas, including trade policy and negotiation, energy and climate change, industrial strategy and regulatory reform; and third, as an immersive journalist, writing a weekly column for two of Nigeria's most popular newspapers, *Vanguard* and *BusinessDay*, for over ten years, analysing and commenting on political, economic and social developments in Nigeria. Weaving together my academic, journalistic, and policy experiences with extensive research and meticulously sourced evidence, I have put together a book that, I believe, addresses the subject matter comprehensively and holistically.

The book takes both reductionist and systems views of the issues. The former dissects each theme into its parts to better understand the issues; the latter takes a top-down holistic view and looks at the connections and linkages between the themes and how they affect Nigeria's political, economic, and social development. To that extent, the book is comprehensive. Yet, as Wayne Booth says in his book *The Rhetoric of Fiction*, 'To write a book at all – any book – one must rule out *almost* everything that is potentially interesting.'[5] Thus, some subjects that probably deserve separate chapters of their own are inevitably compressed within chapters, but, hopefully, without doing too much injustice to them.

The specific focus of this book is Nigeria. However, it is intended to reach a wider audience. By dissecting historical events and current issues in Nigeria, the book provides in-depth insights that help readers understand the root causes of Nigeria's ongoing challenges, making it an ideal read for those interested in the complexities of Nigeria's situation. And by offering practical ideas on the way forward, the book is a valuable resource for those looking for thoughtful solutions to Nigeria's ongoing struggles. Thus, alongside Nigerians who are concerned about the continuing challenges of their country and the way forward, the book should resonate with a broader audience outside Nigeria, especially those interested in Nigerian and African affairs or in the political economy of development and the management of diverse, multinational states in general, as Nigeria offers great lessons for other countries in similar situations.

PART ONE

Politics, Democracy and Governance

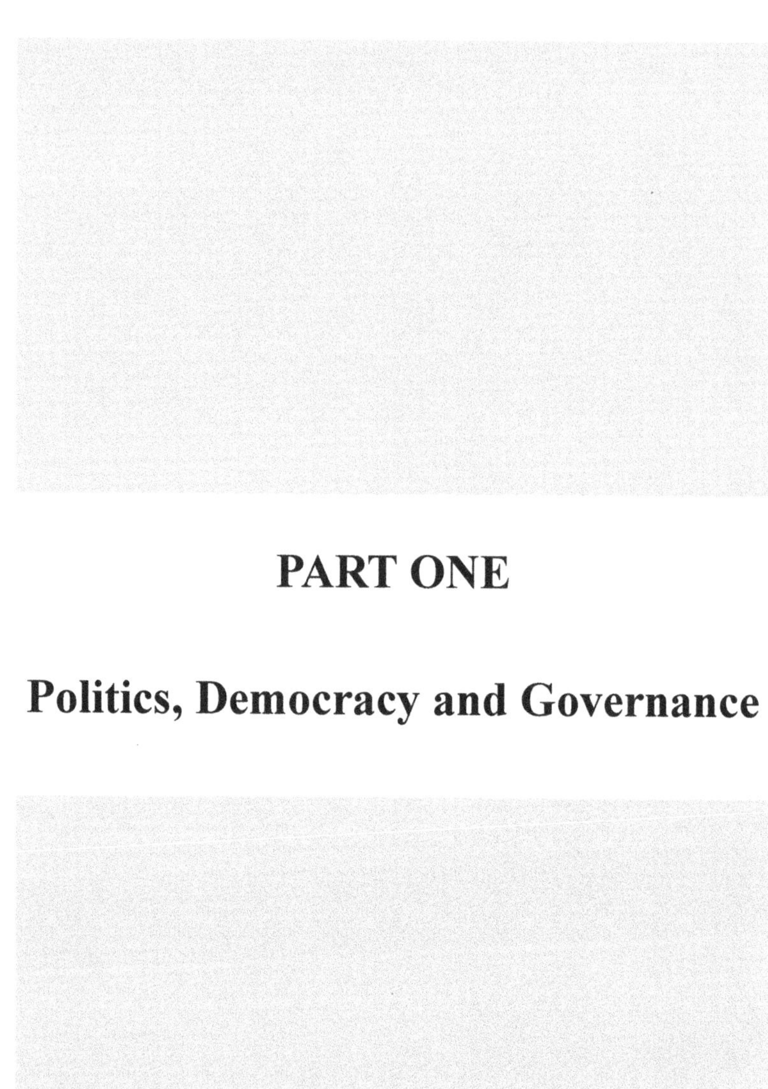

1

A Political History of Nigeria

The political entity called Nigeria owes its existence to annexation by European powers and colonisation by Britain. After the Berlin Conference of 1885, which triggered the Scramble for Africa, the European powers sliced up Africa and handed the geographical territories that would later become Nigeria to Great Britain. The territories were not barren lands. They were owned and inhabited by ancient kingdoms that had existed independently as distinct nations for centuries. However, the ancient kingdoms were cobbled together to create Nigeria without consultation or agreement. As Part 1 of this book will argue, the challenges of nationhood and development that Nigeria still faces today, well over one hundred years after its creation, are mostly traceable to the circumstances of its birth, called here 'birth defects', and Nigeria's continued failure to *recreate* itself and evolve into a strong and united nation-state. To better understand the history, it is necessary to narrate it chronologically from the beginning.

From Annexation to Colonisation

In the late 1880s, after taking ownership of the vast territories in West Africa that later became known as Nigeria, the British government granted a royal charter to George Goldie, a British merchant, to run the territories as a trading monopoly under his Royal Niger Company. Goldie met resistance from the Yoruba, Igbo, Hausa/Fulani, Efik, and Nok kingdoms, among others. But with just over 500 men armed with the lethal Maxim gun[1], he defeated the large armies of those kingdoms and forced their rulers to sign away their territories. Goldie's military exploits in Bida, Ilorin, and many of the kingdoms in what is now Nigeria are narrated in John Flint's book titled *Sir George Goldie and the Making of Nigeria*.[2] The author portrays Goldie as a 'great merchant adventurer' who personally and through his commercial entity, the National African Company, both agents of the Imperial Power, dominated the West African territories politically and economically for almost a quarter of a century, from 1886 onwards.[3] Goldie divided the conquered territories into Northern and Southern entities for trading and administrative conveniences. However, in 1900, he handed the entities to the British government as protectorates. That marked the beginning of formal colonial rule in Nigeria.

The British government appointed Frederick Lugard, later Lord Lugard, as the first High Commissioner of Northern Nigeria in 1900. Fourteen years later, in 1914, Lugard merged the two protectorates into one entity named Nigeria and became its first Governor-General. Lugard's girlfriend, later wife, Flora Shaw, a colonial editor for The Times of London and a staunch advocate of imperialism[4], invented the name 'Nigeria.' Thus, neither Nigeria's creation nor its name is indigenous to the people called 'Nigerians.'

More importantly, as a seed for future disunity, Nigeria was a forced union of disparate ethnic nationalities, each with a proud history. As the literary icon, the late Chinua Achebe put it, the ancient kingdoms were 'held together by a delicate artificial lattice.'[5] Chief Obafemi Awolowo, one of Nigeria's independence leaders, described Nigeria as a 'mere geographical expression,' saying: 'There are no "Nigerians" in the same sense as there are "English" or "Welsh" or "French."'[6] For Professor Wole Soyinka, Africa's first literature Nobel laureate, Nigeria is just a 'nation space' because it lacks the 'coherent philosophy of reproducing our existence, of harmonizing co-existence, or integrating the constituent parts into a discernible, functional whole, all of which transforms a mere nation space into a true nation state.'[7]

The above views simply point to the fact that Nigeria, as constituted, lacks nationhood and internal cohesion. Today, Nigeria has a population of about 230 million people and more than 350 ethnic groups, each with a different language. But each of the main ethnic groups lives in mutual suspicion of each other and believes Nigeria is not working. This is how a Nigerian journalist and columnist, Fola Ojo, captures the tension.

> Ask regular northerners, they will tell you that severing their entire region from Nigeria is a welcome idea. Ask the same question in the South-West, its people are just waiting for a signal to leave the fold and flag off the Oduduwa Republic. Take a trip to the South-South and conduct an opinion poll among its people. They feel cheated and robbed by

Nigeria, and they prefer to stay independent in steering their crude oil ship. There is no breathing being in the world that does not know where the South-East stands. The Igbo consider Nigeria an entrapment and a starkly unfair and unjust overlord. They want out of what they call a contraption like yesterday.[8]

In truth, most Nigerians, if only for reasons of pragmatism and realism, have accepted the existence of Nigeria, regardless of how it came about, as a fait accompli. However, the structural imbalance and tension embedded in Nigeria's creation and ongoing existence have engendered the absence of national unity and cohesion that Ojo accurately describes. That disunity, that lack of a shared purpose, played out at significant moments in Nigeria's history, including, as discussed below, the struggle for independence, the civil war, and the perennial inter-ethnic struggles over power and resources.

The Divisive Struggle for Independence

The 1950s were a period of intense agitation for independence in British colonies across Africa. In most countries, rival political parties and ethnic groups put their differences aside and united in demanding independence from Britain. But in Nigeria, unity was elusive. The two southern regions, East and West, vociferously called for an independent Nigeria, but the North viscerally opposed it. As James Hubbard puts it in his book, *The End of British Colonial Rule in Africa*, 'Southern agitation was unsettling political leaders in the northern region, worried that their region would lose out in an independent Nigeria.'[9]

The British government exploited the division, arguing that if it acceded to the South's demand, the North would secede, and Nigeria would disintegrate. But the South was undeterred. In 1953, Chief Anthony Enahoro of the Action Group political party introduced a resolution in the House of Representatives, calling for Nigerian independence in 1956. The northern representatives proposed an alternative resolution calling for independence 'as soon as practicable.'[10] At the next Federal Council of Ministers meeting, the four northern ministers joined the six British ministers to form a majority, which then voted to bar all ministers from participating in the parliamentary debate. The Action Group ministers resigned in protest. In March 1953, northern votes in parliament defeated Enahoro's resolution.

The backlash was fierce. In May 1953, four days of fighting between northerners and southerners in Kano, a northern city, left 36 people dead and 241 injured. Riots also broke out in Lagos. The Northern Region's assembly and house of chiefs adopted a programme that, according to one British official, 'amounted to call for the dissolution of Nigeria.'[11] In a speech in May 1953, Dr Nnamdi Azikiwe, leader of the National Council of Nigeria and the Cameroons (NCNC), urged the North to 'weigh the advantages and disadvantages of secession'[12] but said they were 'perfectly entitled to consider whether or not they should secede.'[13] Nigeria was teetering on the verge of a breakup.

Britain responded by appeasing the South without betraying the North. It agreed to grant self-government to the Western Region and the Eastern Region in 1954 but insisted that Nigeria itself would not become independent unless the North first agreed to self-government. This effectively gave the North a veto over Nigeria's independence since Nigeria could not be independent unless the North first agreed to their own self-government. Given that the North had enjoyed *indirect rule* since the creation of Nigeria, with indigenous rulers controlling local governance, it seemed strange that the northerners did not want self-government. But considering that self-government for the North would mean independence for Nigeria, it was understandable why the North continued to reject self-rule for itself in order to forestall independence for Nigeria.

However, two events conspired to accelerate Nigeria's independence. The first was the demonstration effect of self-rule in the West and in the East. Self-rule was a huge success in both regions. Chief Obafemi Awolowo, premier of the Western Region, governed the West wonderfully well, spurring significant economic and social development in the region.[14] Dr Nnamdi Azikiwe, premier of the Eastern Region, also did well. Indeed, some British parliamentarians later cited the success of self-rule in Western and Eastern Nigeria as a reason Britain was more confident that Nigeria could govern itself and, thus, deserved to be granted independence.[15]

The second contributory factor was the political development in the Gold Coast, later known as Ghana, which caused reverberation in Nigeria, and triggered a chain of events. In March 1957, Ghana became Britain's first African colony to achieve full independence. There had been something akin to a sibling rivalry between Nigeria and Ghana, and political leaders in Southern Nigeria always wanted political developments in Nigeria to keep pace with, if not outpace, those in Ghana. Thus, in May 1957, the Nigerian House of Representatives voted to demand independence in 1959. Interestingly, this time, the northern legislators did not oppose the resolution. With Ghana gaining independence, it would have seemed odd if the North continued to filibuster and oppose independence for Nigeria. So, the North had a change of heart, and Northern members of the House of Representatives supported the independence motion. Crucially, the North went on to accept self-government for itself in 1959. With the last British condition met, Nigeria's independence was inevitable: it happened on October 1, 1960.

But while the positive effects of successful self-rule in the East and the West, as well as Ghana's independence, eventually persuaded the North to accede to Nigeria's independence, the inter-ethnic divisions and self-interest that underpinned the struggle for Nigeria's independence continued to dog the country after independence, even stronger than they did before it. The manner in which Nigeria gained independence and formed its first indigenous government contributed to the inter-ethnic tensions. For instance, it wasn't unity-engendering that the North, which had vehemently opposed Nigeria's independence, ended up being its chief beneficiary. The North formed Nigeria's first post-independence government.

In his book *There Was a Country*, Chinua Achebe argues that the British manipulated the pre-independence elections in favour of the North's Abubakar Tafawa Balewa, 'who had been tapped to become Nigeria's first prime minister.'[16] Achebe states: 'The British made certain on the eve of their departure that power went to that conservative element in the country that had played no real part in the struggle of independence.'[17] Britain's preferential treatment of the North, which was a pattern throughout its colonial rule in Nigeria, contributed in no small measure to the inter-ethnic tension and resentment that have remained deep-seated in the country.

Another evidence of the continuing inter-ethnic tension is the fact that just as the North rejected the South's call for independence for Nigeria, the same North today opposes the South's call for the political restructuring of Nigeria. However, just as the North eventually came round to support Nigeria's independence, it must be hoped that the North will also come round to support the restructuring of Nigeria because the future stability, even existence, of Nigeria rests squarely on it being restructured to become a true nation-state.

The Short-Lived Independence Euphoria

On July 14, 1960, the British Government introduced the 'Nigeria Independence Bill' in the House of Commons. During the Bill's second reading, the Secretary of State for the Colonies, Iain Macleod, hailed Nigeria's progress towards independence as a 'model' for Africa.[18] Speaker after speaker wished Nigeria well and expressed confidence that it would succeed as an independent nation. They said that the success of self-government in the western and eastern regions for six years, from 1954 to 1960, showed that Nigerians could govern themselves. In Nigeria itself, the excitement was indescribable. As independence approached, the general feeling in the air was extraordinary, as everyone looked to freedom.

Yet, after the much-celebrated independence on October 1, 1960, things went so badly wrong that, within six years, there were two military coups and a devastating civil war. Why did things go so badly wrong so soon? The first reason was maladministration. However unacceptable colonialism was, the British ran Nigeria well administratively, with order, discipline and professionalism defining the civil service under British rule.[19] But that order, discipline and professionalism soon disappeared after independence as the new indigenous political masters corrupted, politicised, and manipulated the civil servants.[20] The casualty was a strong and effective administration needed to undergird governance in newly independent Nigeria, meaning the country lacked a robust bureaucratic foundation.

But a more important cause of the post-independence decline was the behaviours of the Nigerian politicians in power. Their excesses had been restrained under colonial rule. But following the departure of the colonialists, the politicians were off the leash. Corruption and abuse of office was rife, resulting in the distortions of everything ranging from census to elections and the administration of justice. The inter-ethnic tensions discussed earlier, a by-product of Nigeria's birth defects and Britain's lack of even-handedness, reared their heads in deadly ways and led to a succession of crises, including ethnic riots, two military coups and eventually a civil war.

The Civil War: A Monumental Tragedy

Much has been written about the Nigerian Civil War, but this chapter on Nigeria's political history cannot be complete without a mention of the war, one of the world's bloodiest civil wars. The war is estimated to have claimed the lives of about 100,000 combatants on both sides, while over two million Igbo civilians, many of them children, died of starvation and disease. In addition, between two million and five million people were displaced during the war.[21]

A chain of major events led to the war. First, on January 15, 1966, a group of young officers carried out a failed military coup but succeeded in killing several prominent politicians, notably Sir Tafawa Balewa, the prime minister, Sir Ahmadu Bello, the premier of Northern Region, Chief Samuel Ladoke Akintola, the premier of Western Region, and several prominent senior military officers, such as Brigadier-General Samuel Ademulegun. The coup plotters, led by Major Chukwuma Kaduna Nzeogwu, blamed their intervention on corruption and misrule by the political class, as well as the rigged federal election of 1964 and, particularly, that of the Western Region in 1965 that provoked massive violence. The coup was foiled in Lagos, and Major-General Johnson Thomas Aguiyi-Ironsi became Nigeria's first military head of state. He immediately issued a Unification Decree No. 34 of 1966, abolishing Nigeria's federal structure and replacing it with a unitary system, while the four semi-autonomous regional governments were replaced with 35 provinces. The unification decree was unpopular with the political class, particularly in the North, and further fuelled distrust after the January 15 coup.[22]

However, the coup itself had taken the genie out of the bottle, and its aftermath became molten lava before a volcanic eruption. Northern officers were spoiling for revenge. They were under huge pressure from the northern politicians and, indeed, the northern populace to retaliate the January 15 killings of prominent northern politicians. For instance, the northern officers were publicly ridiculed and called 'big fools and cowards'[23] for dithering over what most northerners regarded as an ethnic 'Igbo' coup, targeted at the Hausa/Fulani North.[24] However, in his memoir, *A Journey in Service*, General Ibrahim Babangida, a combatant during the civil war, attempted to debunk the claim of ethnic motivation, saying: 'Ethnic sentiments did not drive the original objective of the coup plotters.'[25]

For evidence, Babangida cited the fact that: a) Major Kaduna Nzeogwu, the head of the plotters, was only 'Igbo' in name; born and raised in Kaduna, he spoke fluent Hausa and was as 'Hausa' as any! b) the coup plotters wanted to release Chief Obafemi Awolowo, a Yoruba, from prison and make him 'the executive provisional President of Nigeria', which would be strange if the coup was Igbo-centric; c) some non-Igbo officers, such as Major Adewale Ademoyega, a Yoruba, took part in the coup; d) some senior officers of Igbo extraction were also victims of the coup; and e) it was an Igbo officer, Major John Obiena, who crushed the coup.[26]

Babangida, however, acknowledged that the plotters' handling of the coup gave it 'an unmistakeably ethnic coloration', especially with the 'heinously callous' murder of Sir Ahmadu Bello and his wife, Hafsatu, 'compounded by the fact that there were no related coup activities in the

Eastern Region.[27] However, other accounts, especially the one by Major Adewale Ademoyega, one of the coup leaders, in his book *Why We Struck*, suggests that the coup was driven by idealism, to right the wrongs in Nigeria, and not ethnicity.[28] In truth, the 'ethnic colouration' was more of perception than reality. The plotters were idealistic young officers who strongly detested the status quo in Nigeria and genuinely wanted to bring about a change and, thus, were not motivated by ethnic considerations.[29]

However, that notwithstanding, the northerners were not persuaded that coup was not an Igbo coup. Northern officers and politicians, and indeed the northern populace, insisted the coup was ethnic and wanted revenge against the Igbos. The distrust was accentuated and aggravated by the feeling that General Aguiyi-Ironsi, the new military head of state, who was himself an Igbo officer, treated the coup plotters with kid gloves.[30] For instance, despite a promise, after the coup was quashed, to try the coup plotters, none was ever brought to trial. Instead, a few of the coup plotters were promoted.[31] A revenge coup was, thus, in the offing.

On July 28, 1966, six months after the January 15 coup, several Igbo officers were killed by northern officers during a mutiny in the Abeokuta Garrison, and the next day, on July 29, a group of young northern officers executed a countercoup and assassinated General Aguiyi-Ironsi and Lieutenant Colonel Adekunle Fajuyi, the military governor of Western Region, who had been hosting Aguiyi-Ironsi in Ibadan, capital of Western Region. Following the assassination of General Aguiyi-Ironsi in the July 29 countercoup, the expectation was that Brigadier Babafemi Ogundipe, a Yoruba, who was the next most senior officer, would be the next head of state. However, a group of 'headstrong' northern officers, led by Lt-Colonel Murtala Muhammed, refused to accept Ogundipe's leadership, and 'were spoiling for a fight and even toying with the idea of a secession.'[32] In the end, a negotiated compromise, involving the adamant northern officers, led to the emergence of Lt-Col Yakubu Gowon, a Northerner, as the new head of state.

If the North wanted revenge, they, arguably, had it with the killings of several Igbo officers in the Abeokuta Garrison on July 28, and with the countercoup of July 29, during which General Aguiyi-Ironsi was assassinated. However, despite those retaliations, they were not appeased. Northern politicians continued to whip up anti-Igbo sentiments, endlessly goading their people to attack the Igbos. The consequence was a bloodbath that, more proximately, triggered the civil war. Between May 29, 1966, when the killings started, and September 29, when they peaked, no less than 213 predominantly Igbo officers and other ranks were killed, according to Official Army Records.[33] In what became known as a 'pogrom', over 30,000 Igbos were massacred and several thousand wounded in the North[34], while some 50,000 Igbos were forced to flee northern Nigeria for the eastern region by the end of July 1966.[35]

In his memoir General Babangida blamed General Gowon, the then head of state, for failing to protect the Igbos in the North[36], and seemed to justify the reactions of Lt-Col Chukwuemeka Odumegwu Ojukwu, the military governor of Eastern Nigeria. Babangida wrote: 'Faced with this intolerable situation, Ojukwu, *understandably* (emphasis added),'[37] concluded that the Igbos and the Easterners, in general, were not safe in Nigeria. Consequently, Ojukwu began to prepare the Eastern Region to secede from Nigeria.

However, apart from the ethnic hatred and killings of the Igbos, personal war and collision of egos between Gowon and Ojukwu was probably a contributory factor, albeit a minor one, in triggering the war. Both Gowon and Ojukwu were trained at the Royal Military Academy Sandhurst in England, with Ojukwu, also educated at Oxford University. It was speculated that Ojukwu had little regard for Gowon and did not recognise his authority as head of state.[38] Indeed, earlier, Ojukwu had rejected the emergence of Gowon as head of state, insisting that it was Brigadier Ogundipe, the most senior military officer in Nigeria, not Gowon, who should succeed Aguiyi-Ironsi.[39]

It is conventional wisdom to cite the January 15 coup and July 29 countercoup as the direct causes of the civil war. However, the reality is somewhat different. A deeper analysis would show that it was the northern politicians' endless and insatiable braying for revenge against the Igbos, and General Gowon's failure to protect the Igbos in the North, that triggered the pogrom, the attempted secession and the war, while the persona animus between the two protagonists, Gowon and Ojukwu, probably made it harder to avert the war. A peace deal brokered in Aburi, Ghana, famously called the Aburi Accord[40], which both Gowon and Ojukwu interpreted differently[41], as well as other well-meaning attempts[42], failed to prevent the war.

On May 30, 1967, with the endorsement of the Eastern Nigeria Consultative Assembly, Ojukwu declared the secession of Eastern Nigeria, now called the Republic of Biafra, from Nigeria. To weaken Ojukwu's power base,

Gowon split Nigeria's four regions into 12 states, dividing the eastern region into three states, namely, South-Eastern, East-Central and Rivers. But that did not stop the war, which started on July 6, 1967. However, thirty months later, with nearly100,000 soldiers and 2 million civilians dead, Biafra fell on January 15, 1970. Ojukwu fled, leaving his second-in-command, Philip Effiong, to lead Biafra's formal surrender to General Gowon and his military council. Gowon immediately declared a 'no victor, no vanquished' policy and launched the three Rs – Reconstruction, Rehabilitation, and Reconciliation – to reintegrate the Igbos into Nigeria. However, while the Igbo have been integrated economically, the question of their political integration remains a thorny issue, considering the political marginalisation of the Igbos, evidenced by the structural obstacles to an Igbo becoming president of Nigeria.

Why Has the Civil War Not United Nigeria?

Former Nigerian military leaders often invoke memories of the civil war and their roles when discussing Nigeria's unity. They often say that they fought the civil war to unite Nigeria. For instance, General Ibrahim Babangida, a civil war combatant, who later became Nigeria's military head of state, once said: 'I still carry a bullet of the Civil War as a permanent reminder in me; so, any time someone talks about Nigeria's unity, I get impassioned about it.'[43] However, the problem is that victory in a civil war alone cannot engender unity in a country. After winning a war, a nation must win the peace. All over the world, whether the civil war in America, apartheid in South Africa, or ethno-nationalist conflict in Northern Ireland, there eventually were negotiated settlements that brought all parties together to achieve lasting peace and unity.

But the Nigerian civil war ended with the defeat and surrender of the Igbos, without any attempt to learn real lessons from the war, excavate the historical trouble spots, and reorganise Nigeria to make it workable as a multi-ethnic country. As a result, the issues that caused the Civil War still linger today. Nigeria's ethnic nationalities co-exist in entrenched mutual suspicion and hostility; they eye one another with utter incomprehension and distrust. The civil war has not engendered nationhood. Rather, Nigeria remains a disunited, polarised state with deep-rooted schismatic tendencies.

In his book, *Because I Am Involved*, the former Biafran leader, Odumegwu-Ojukwu, said: 'An impossible federation was created in which all cards were stacked in favour of one component of it.'[44] He described two types of unity, 'the unity of Jonas inside the belly of the whale and the unity of marriage,' saying that 'the unity we seek is the latter.'[45] In other words, Ojukwu advocated that Nigeria should be remade to become an inclusive and fair partnership among its constituent parts, not a skewed union favouring some and disadvantaging others.

A strong strand of opinion holds that if the military had not intervened in 1966 and imposed a unitary system on the country, Nigeria was closer to near-perfect management of its diversities and better power- and resource-sharing under the 1960 Independence Constitution or the 1963 Republican Constitution. Indeed, when it comes to constitution-making, it is evident that the British colonialists and the Nigerian independence-era politicians understood Nigeria far better than the country's present-day political leaders.

For instance, during the debate on the Nigeria Independent Bill in the British House of Commons, Ian Macleod, Secretary of State for the Colonies, said that, given Nigeria's extraordinary diversity, 'it is not the least surprising that the political development it has chosen is that of a Federation in three regions, with each region self-governing in its own concerns.'[46] Later on in the debate, another MP remarked that the Bill 'records the culmination of a tremendously difficult and complex exercise in constitution-making,' adding that 'It is a constitution of great delicacy where various interests have had to be reconciled.'[47] Three years later, Nigerians themselves negotiated the 1963 Republican Constitution, which gave the regions even greater autonomy. But the military jettisoned this notion of federalism and a constitution in which each of Nigeria's regions self-governed in its own concerns in favour of a centralised political system, an oxymoronic *unitary federalism.*

To date, 65 years after independence, Nigeria has been governed by military regimes for 29 years and by civilian administrations for 36 years. But nothing has changed structurally and in the characters of the political institutions and the characters of democratic governance in Nigeria from what the military created and imposed on the country. The constitution of Nigeria, the system of government – presidential – and the governance structure – an overpowerful centre with multiple peripheral states that are mere appendages of the centre – are all military impositions. Thus, thirty-six years of civilian rule have had no impact on the political structure and character of the Nigerian state. What follows is an overview of Nigeria's military and civilian administrations since the first military intervention in 1966.

From Military to Civilian Rule: Between Soldiers and Politicians

Nigeria had its first military government under General Aguiyi-Ironsi following the January 15, 1966 coup. A few months later, after the July 1966 countercoup, which toppled Aguiyi-Ironsi, the country had its second military regime under General Gowon, who was in control throughout the civil war. Shortly after the war ended in January 1970, General Gowon promised to return Nigeria to civil rule but reneged on the promise. On July 29, 1975, Gowon was overthrown in a bloodless coup while he was attending a summit of the Organisation of African Union (OAU), now called the African Union (AU), in Kampala, the capital of Uganda. Thereafter, General Murtala Muhammed became Nigeria's third military head of state. But just about six months later, on February 13, 1976, General Muhammed was assassinated in a bloody military coup. That assassination ushered in the regime of General Olusegun Obasanjo, who was chief of staff and second-in-command under General Muhammed. General Obasanjo kept the promise made by the Muhammed regime to hand over power to a democratically elected civilian government. Thus, on October 1, 1979, General Obasanjo handed over to Alhaji Shehu Shagari, a schoolteacher and former minister who won a controversial presidential election, finally settled in his favour by the Supreme Court.

The Shagari administration was buffeted by many crises, mostly economic, as well as allegations of widespread corruption. The August 6, 1983, election that won Shagari a second presidential term was believed to have been massively rigged. On December 31, 1983, the military overthrew the Shagari government, citing 'economic collapse and political chaos'[48] as well as accusing the Shagari administration of 'inept and corrupt leadership.'[49] Decades later, in his memoir, General Babangida, who played a key role in overthrowing the Shagari government, revealed that some senior military officer in the Obasanjo regime had opposed a return the civil rule in 1979 and wanted the military to stay on much longer in the power. Babangida himself referred to the Obasanjo regime's handover to civilians as 'the errors of the military's sudden and rapid departure in 1979'.[50] That view that Nigeria was not ready for civil rule in 1979 became a self-fulfilling prophecy and must have fuelled the soldiers' sense of rightness as they toppled the Shagari government in 1983 after four years in power.

Following the December 1983 coup, Major-General Muhammadu Buhari became Nigeria's fifth military head of state. The focus of the Buhari regime was on fighting corruption and what it believed was a general decline of morality in society. As a result, the regime launched the War Against Indiscipline (WAI), a draconian policy in which even the failure to queue in public spaces attracted corporal punishment, including public caning by soldiers. Around 500 politicians, officials, and businessmen were jailed for corruption, some for up to 100 years.[51] Fela Kuti, the famous musician and government critic, was imprisoned for five years for allegedly attempting to export foreign currency. The regime clamped down on the media, closing newspaper houses and jailing journalists. The authoritarian grip on political and social life created enormous tension, while the regime's dirigiste policies caused economic decline. The 'economic collapse and political chaos' that the military cited for overthrowing the Shagari government in December 1983 worsened under the Buhari regime, exacerbated by the social tensions created by the regime's brutal dictatorship.

Barely two years after General Buhari came to power, he was overthrown on August 27, 1985. In a coup speech read by then Brigadier Joshua Dogonyaro, General Buhari's military colleagues accused him of 'stubborn and ill-advised unilateral actions' and said that his regime 'distanced itself from the people and ignored their yearnings and aspirations.'[52] Years later, General Babangida expanded on that allegation, saying that Buhari and his deputy, Brigadier Tunde Idiagbon, 'had separated themselves from the mainstream of the armed forces by personalising what was initially a collective leadership', adding that the military administration 'came to be seen as the private personal autocracy of a stubborn few.'[53] However, Buhari later accused his colleagues of overthrowing him because he was fighting corruption, including within the military.[54]

General Babangida, who succeeded Buhari and became Nigeria's sixth military head of state, styled himself 'president', rather than head of state, the title used by previous military rulers in Nigeria. He argued that being called president was necessary to reinforce the institutions of the state along the best lines the presidential system, which he strongly favoured over the parliamentary system.[55] In truth, using the title 'president' was a self-aggrandising, megalomaniacal, decision. However, as a military president, Babangida was a benevolent dictator. He reversed the draconian decrees and policies of the Buhari regime and made overtures to the wider society, including academia and the traditional institutions. However, on the political front, Babangida took Nigeria through a self-serving experimentation that ended badly, and which deserves attention here for its consequential and ripple effects.

Babangida's Ill-Fated Political Transition

As early as 1986, barely six months after he became Nigeria's military ruler, General Babangida indicated his intention to return Nigeria to civil rule. To that end, in January 1986, he set up a 17-member Political Bureau to kick off a national debate on the political future of Nigeria. In July 1987, the regime announced a detailed timetable for the return to civil rule; and after receiving the report of the Political Bureau in September 1987, it established appointed a 10-member National Electoral Commission (NEC) headed by Professor Eme Awa, who was later removed and replaced with Professor Humphrey Nwosu, who the regime believed was 'a more dynamic and less dogmatic person better suited for the job'.[56] Subsequently, on May 3, 1989, the regime lifted the ban on political activities, and invited the politicians to form political parties.

However, while 80 political associations expressed interest in becoming political parties, NEC recommended that only six were suitable. But even so, the regime rejected the six associations, saying it favoured a two-party political system. Consequently, it decreed into existence two political parties: Social Democratic Party (SDP) and National Republican Convention (NRC). Babangida was a strong believer in the two-party system, arguing that it suited Nigeria better than a multi-party system.[57] One of the two parties would be 'a little to the left, the other a little to the right'[58], and, according to the regime, the SDP was the *left-leaning* party, while the *NRC, the right-leaning one.* However, despite the purported attempt to create two parties based on ideologies, the politicians only joined the party they felt offered them or their candidates a better chance of getting elected, not because of the party's ideological orientation.

In their desperation for power, the politicians rode roughshod over universal democratic values. They followed every dictate of General Babangida, who was called, and relished being called, 'Maradona' and 'Evil Genius' because of his uncanny ability to manipulate the politicians and string them along. Indeed, at every stage of his 'transition' programme, Babangida strung the politicians along. For instance, the military did not only create the two parties, but it also wrote their constitutions and manifestos and appointed administrators to run them. Yet, the politicians unquestioningly rushed into the two parties like sheep being led to the slaughter. They ignored President John F. Kennedy's famous words in his inaugural address in 1961 that 'those who foolishly sought power by riding the back of the tiger ended up inside.'[59]

Another curious feature of the regime's transition programme was its decision to operate a diarchy, under which soldiers and politicians governed together, with the politicians being shepherded by the military like sheep, as the best route to a return to civil rule. Thus, Babangida, whose decision to style himself 'President' began to make sense, was the head of state, supported by the Armed Forces Ruling Council (AFRC), the highest decision-making body, while, at the state level, politicians were governors and legislators, and, at the federal level, federal legislators. On December 12, 1991, state governors and legislators were elected across Nigeria, and were sworn in on January 2, 1992. The National Assembly elections took place on July 4, 1992. About six months later, on January 2, 1993, General Babangida set up a civilian-dominated cabinet called the Transitional Council and appointed Ernest Shonekan, former chairman of the United Africa Company (UAC) in Nigeria, as Head of the Transitional Council. The diarchic arrangement was supposed to pave the way for a successful presidential election and a return to a full-fledged democracy with a civilian president. But, alas, things went badly awry in quick succession.

First, the regime cancelled the two parties' presidential primary elections conducted on August 1, 1992, on grounds of 'widespread rigging and corruption'.[60] The parties conducted fresh primaries, which were won by Major-General Shehu Yar' Adua for the SDP and Alhaji Adamu Ciroma for the NRC. However, the regime said the elections were also marred by allegations of rigging and bribery and cancelled the results on October 16, 1992. It went further, and banned Yar' Adua, Ciroma and all 23 presidential aspirants who had participated in the presidential primaries 'from further participating in the Transition Programme'.[61]

With the defenestration of the 23 prominent aspirants, doubts and distrust, which had existed almost since the start of the 'transition' programme, began to crystalise as the integrity of the programme was questioned. Even retired senior military officers, such as former chief of army staff, Lt-General Theophilus Danjuma, and former military head of state, General Olusegun Obasanjo, cast aspersions on the Babangida regime's transition programme, with Obasanjo deriding it as 'silly experiments and gimmicks.'[62] Babangida rejected Danjuma and Obasanjo's characterisation of the transition programme, saying 'as decorated officers like them, our honour meant a lot to us.[63]

But the widespread doubts and distrust did not go away, especially after the sudden emergence of a clandestine group called 'Association for Better Nigeria (ABN)', led and funded by the maverick Igbo billionaire, Arthur Nzeribe. The group called for the elongation of military rule and the termination of the transition to civil rule. Babangida later said in his memoir that 'figuring out the real forces behind this shadowy organisation took a long time'[64] and claimed the regime 'had no hands in the group's activities'[65]. Yet, it was widely known that the group's leader, Nzeribe, had strong ties with the military and with Babangida himself.[66] As a result, the regime's failure, indeed refusal, to rein in the ABN and curtail its activities fuelled speculations about its real intentions regarding the transition programme.

Meanwhile, the two political parties plunged ahead in blissful indifference as if everything was normal. While the sign 'caveat emptor', or buyer beware, was visible to the naked eye, the politicians ignored it and continued to engage actively with the military regime. The two parties held fresh presidential primaries in August and September 1992, with Chief Moshood Kashimawo Olawale (MKO) Abiola, a billionaire business and media magnate from the southern state of Ogun, emerging as the SDP candidate, while Alhaji Bashir Tofa, a businessman from the northern state of Kano, became the NRC candidate. Despite the doubts and speculations, the stage, it seemed, was set, and the path cleared for the presidential election, scheduled for June 12, 1993, and for a new civilian president to emerge. Alas, it was not to be.

The 'June 12' Annulment

Two days before the June 12, 1993, presidential election, the ABN secured a court injunction to stop the election. The electoral body, however, ignored the injunction and went ahead to hold the election, widely believed to be free and fair. However, barely three days after the election, the ABN obtained another injunction to stop the announcement of the results. This time, on June 16, the NEC obeyed the court injunction and did not declare the results, although unofficial results filtered out and indicated that Abiola won. General Babangida later said in his memoir that the decision of the NEC to suspend the announcement of the results took him by surprise. Babangida wrote: 'Then, on June 16, without my knowledge or prior approval, NEC chairman, Professor Nwosu, announced the suspension of the June 12 election results "until further notice"'.[67]

The cancellation of the announcement of the election results created widespread anxiety and confusion across the country. However, a week later, on June 23, instead of averting the looming national crisis, General Babangida gave a national broadcast, in which he announced the annulment of the election. In the statement, Babangida said: 'In view of the spirit of litigation pending in various courts, the government is compelled to annul the election to protect our legal system and the judiciary from being ridiculed and politicised.'[68] Babangida said the regime wanted 'to rescue the judiciary from intra-voyaging'[69] and cited widespread electoral malpractices, including vote-buying. However, few people believed that Babangida annulled the election to protect the judiciary or because of some irregularities.

The annulment provoked local and international outrage, so intense that General Babangida's carapace of invincibility cracked. He hastily left power or 'stepped aside,' as he put it, and made Chief Shonekan head of the 'National Interim Government.' But the political class considered Shonekan, seen as a military stooge by the wider society, as illegitimate. This was buttressed by a decision of a Federal High Court judge, Dolapo Akinsanya, who, on November 11, 1993, declared the interim Government 'illegal'.[70] The court's decision gave impetus to the pressure on Shonekan to resign and hand over to Abiola. But squeezing water from a stone was easier than getting Shonekan to step down for Abiola.

Amid the furore and the standoff, General Sani Abacha, who always had his eyes on the highest seat, seized power from Shonekan on November 17, 1993, and became Nigeria's seventh military head of state. Always hiding his eyes behind a large pair of dark glasses, Abacha was a brutal dictator. He unleashed a reign of terror, sending secret agents and hired assassins after those agitating for the reversal of the 'June 12' annulment. He jailed Abiola for treason after he proclaimed himself president. Abiola died in custody on July 7, 1998. Apart from his brutality, Abacha also plundered the national treasury, with an estimated $5 billion of Nigeria's national assets believed to have been looted by him, his family, and their associates.[71] In the years that followed, the Nigerian government reached agreements with foreign governments, such as Switzerland, the United States, the United Kingdom, and France, to recover the stolen funds, which the Nigerian media tagged 'Abacha loot.' According to one estimate, $4 billion in cash and $2 billion in assets were recovered from 1999 to 2023.[72]

General Abacha announced a transition to civil rule, with a presidential election scheduled for August 1, 1998. But he intended to run for election and transmute himself into a civilian president. He corralled and pocketed the politicians, who sang his praises and coerced the five political parties into endorsing him as the sole presidential candidate. But he died in mysterious circumstances on June 8, 1998. Following Abacha's death, the military swiftly named General Abdulsalami Abubakar as Nigeria's eighth military head of state. A genial officer, General Abubakar returned the country to civil rule. But before coming to the civilian dispensation, it is worth dwelling more on the annulled presidential election, particularly the reason behind it, as that singular event shaped subsequent political developments in Nigeria,

Why Was the June 12 Election Annulled?

In June 2018, President Buhari, who became a civilian president 22 years after the annulment of the presidential election of June 12, 1993, named June 12 as Nigeria's 'Democracy Day,' replacing the earlier date of May 29, to immortalise the annulled election. President Buhari also conferred Nigeria's highest national honour, Grand Commander of the Federal Republic (GCFR), on Abiola but fell short of officially declaring him the winner of the annulled election. The Buhari government claimed that 'the unjust annulment was a huge elite conspiracy'[73] and acknowledged the 'clamour for a probe'. However, the administration did not probe the annulment, leaving rife speculations to continue as to the real reason behind the decision.

One popular view was that the military did not want Abiola to become president and that Babangida was under pressure from junior officers, who held a gun to his head and forced him to annul the election. In his national broadcast annulling the election, General Babangida had said: 'There were cases of documented and confirmed conflict of interest between the government and both presidential candidates that would compromise their positions and responsibilities were they to become president.'[74] Abiola was a military contractor and the idea that his business transactions with the military regime may have contributed to the annulment of the June 12 election was given some validity by Sule Lamido, a former governor of Jigawa State who said that the military annulled the election to avoid paying the ₦45billion they owed Abiola's company, International Telephone and Telecommunication (ITT) Corporation. During the launch of his autobiography his autobiography, *Being True to Myself,* in May 2025, Lamido said: 'They (military) said they cancelled the June 12 elections because if they made him

President, he would take his money, and the country would become bankrupt.'[75] He added that General Babangida confirmed to him that Abiola was owed ₦45 billion.[76] Lamido's intervention suggested that Abiola fell out of favour with the top echelon of the military regime, with it had a cosy relationship as a contractor.

Indeed, years later, in August 2021, General Babangida himself appeared to give credence to the view that the military did not want Abiola to be president. In an interview with the Arise TV journalist Ngozi Alaegbu, General Babangida was asked why he annulled the election. He replied: 'You want me to be honest with you? If it materialised [that is, if Abiola had become president], there would have been a coup d'etat which would have been violent.'[77] The implication was that the military strongly objected to Abiola becoming president. Yet, in all his public statements on the annulment, General Babangida denied that his military colleagues held a gun to his head and forced him to annul the election. He said the decision was entirely his own and that he took responsibility for it. However, that narrative changed dramatically when Babangida published his memoir in February 2025, to which attention must now turn.

Babangida's memoir: The shocking annulment story

On February 20, 2025, General Babangida launched his long-awaited memoir, titled *A Journey in Service: An Autobiography*, in Abuja amid great fanfare, with the current president, Bola Tinubu, and all living former presidents/heads of state, except President Buhari, who later died on July 13, 2025, aged 82, in attendance. The public expectations of Babangida's memoir were extremely high. Everyone wanted to know what he had to say about several issues, including, notably, the annulment of the presidential election of June 12, 1993. Indeed, Babangida did not avoid the subject in the memoir. He devoted a whole chapter, titled 'Transition to Civil Rule and the June 12 saga', to the matter. Specifically, on the annulment, Babangida gave the impression that he was helpless and was outsmarted and outmanoeuvred by some of his military colleagues and their civilian collaborators who were determined to frustrate the return to civil rule.

On the civilian front, there was, as mentioned earlier, the ABN, led by Arthur Nzeribe, which publicly called for the continuation of military rule in Nigeria. There was also the attorney-general and minister of Justice, Clement Akpamgbo, who supported a court injunction, granted by a former lawyer in his chambers, Justice Ikpeme, 'in the dead of night, in clear violation of Decree 13, which barred any court from interfering with NEC's conduct or scheduling of the elections.'[78] Then, there was the head of NEC, the electoral body, Professor Humphrey Nwosu, who Babangida said announced the suspension of the June 12 election results 'without my knowledge or prior approval'.[79]

But despite the shenanigans of those civilians, Babangida did not say in his memoir that he ever confronted them, which would suggest he tacitly supported their behaviours; in which case, he was complicit and duplicitous in the June 12 annulment. Indeed, bizarrely, Babangida justified his decision not to rein in the ABN, saying: 'If we didn't stop the torrent of abuse and opposition to us, why should we stop the only ray of "approval" that came our way?'[80] This is a false equivalence, given that the so-called 'opposition' was aimed at pressuring the regime to keep its promise to return Nigeria to civil rule, while the ABN's 'approval' was intended to get the military to remain in power. So, it was perverse that Babangida treated both groups as if they were the same: they were not!

However, the shenanigans of the civilians apart, it was fractionalisation within the military and opposition from top military officers that General Babangida ultimately blamed for the June 12 annulment. Babangida wrote: 'One of my biggest mistakes was failing to firmly secure the support and firm commitment of my military colleagues to the Transition programme from the beginning. We completely underestimated the deep opposition to civil rule within the military's top hierarchy.'[81] For the first time, General Babangida revealed that the June 12 election was not his original idea or decision, but that it was forced on him and he had to go along with the decision to avoid a split in the military that could lead to bloodletting. It is worth quoting verbatim how Babangida described the annulment decision.

On the morning of June 23, I left Abuja for Katsina to commiserate with the Yar' Adua family over the death of their patriarch, Alhaji Musa Yar' Adua. The funeral took place, and as I got ready to leave, a report filtered to me that the June 12 elections had been annulled. Even more bizarre was the extent of the annulment because it terminated all court proceedings regarding the June 12 elections, repealed all the decrees governing the Transition and even suspended NEC! Equally weird was the shabby way that statement was couched and made. Admiral Aikhomu's press secretary, Nduka Irabor, has read out a terse, poorly worded statement and from a scrap of paper, which bore neither the presidential seal nor the official letterhead of the government, annulling the June 12 presidential elections. I was alarmed and horrified.[82]

Thus, according to Babangida's version of the story, the annulment was forced on him by his military colleagues. How could a presidential election be annulled extrajudicially without the prior knowledge and approval of the Head of State and Commander-in-Chief of the Armed Forces? It was effectively a coup. But who was really behind it? Babangida named General Sani Abacha, then-Chief of Army Staff.[83] General Babangida said:

> I remember saying "These nefarious *inside* forces opposed to the elections have outflanked me!" I would later find out that the "forces" led by General Sani Abacha annulled the elections. There and then, I knew I was caught between "the devil and the deep blue sea"!! From then on, the June 12 elections took a painful twist for which I regrettably take responsibility.[84]

General Babangida said that having been outsmarted by the 'Abacha-led forces', he had no choice but to acquiesce to the annulment and support it. Three days later, on June 26, Babangida addressed the nation and declared that the election had been annulled. He gave several reasons in the national broadcast for the annulment, including widespread rigging and irregularities, but admitted in his memoir that those reasons were tepid and disingenuous, especially as the election was 'deemed the freest and fairest in our country's history'.[85]

> The polarisation within the military was so fraught with danger that the best I could do in the circumstances was to project a united front as government in the face of the stiff opposition I faced as President. Although the annulment took me by surprise, as Commander-in-Chief, I took responsibility for it. In my speech on June 26, tepid and disingenuous as it may seem, I attempted to "justify" the annulment in the face of supposed national "widespread electoral malpractices during the election!"[86]

Babangida went on to say what he had not publicly said before, namely, that Abiola won the annulled election. He said that, based on 'all the available facts, particularly the detailed election results ... there was no doubt that MKO Abiola won the June 12 elections.'[87] However, he added: 'Unfortunately, the forces gathered against him [Abiola] after the June 12 elections were so formidable that I was convinced that if he became President, he would be quickly eliminated by the same forces.'[88]

General Babangida's 'revelations' were shocking and stretched credulity. They provoked strong criticisms and accusation of cowardice.[89] To be sure, if the story told by General Babangida, that he was completely helpless and led by the nose by his subordinates, and even civilians, is indeed true, then it shatters his public image that had endured for decades; it busts the myths, tarnishes the mystique, around him as a brave and fearless officer imbued with courage and conviction.[90] Babangida gave the impression throughout the narrative that he was always behind the curve, that he was always taken by surprise. For instance, he said 'it took a long time to figure out' who was behind the ABN, and that he 'would later find out' that Abacha was behind the annulment. Yet, Babangida was a famed military strategist, an aficionado of military intelligence, who was widely known as 'Evil Genius'. What happened to those attributes? Was he too afraid of General Abacha and his other military colleagues that he could not confront them and nail his colours to the mast?

Babangida's apparent cowardice and fearfulness fuelled speculation that the annulment was part of a game to which he himself was privy. For instance, was there a power transfer deal between Babangida and Abacha that went awry? In an interview with Channels Television in February 2025, retired General Ishola Williams, the Nigerian Army's former Head of Operations, Training, and Planning, suggested that there might have been such a deal. General Williams said: 'In my conversations with General Babangida before he stepped aside, I spent several nights in Minna. I asked him directly, "Did you have a deal with Abacha that he was going to succeed you?" He could not answer the question.'[91] General Williams said that during Babangida's regime, General Babangida frequently referred to Abacha 'as caubar, a term that suggested he was positioning him as his successor.'[92] If General Williams' narrative is true, then it perfectly explains why Babangida made no attempt to counter Abacha's alleged opposition to the June 12 election and to the return to civil rule.

However, it does not help that Abacha is not alive to defend himself or give his own version of the story. In a statement, General Abacha's family accused General Babangida of tarnishing the late dictator's image, saying it was Babangida, not Abacha, who annulled the election.[93] The statement adds: 'Any attempt to shift this blame onto General Sani Abacha is a deliberate distortion of historical facts.'[94] Indeed, one of the major criticisms of Babangida's accounts of the annulment of the June 12 election is that virtually everyone he accused of being behind the annulment is dead, leaving them no chance to give their own accounts of the events. In an article titled 'June 12, IBB and the Missing Persons' Simon Kolawole, a popular newspaper columnist, said: 'Curiously, Babangida did not blame any living person in his entire annulment story. There are too many missing persons in the picture. IBB only named dead military officers such as Abacha and Dogonyaro — who cannot defend themselves. Admiral Augustus Aikhomu, Babangida's former second-in-command, is also not alive to tell us the story behind THAT statement issued by his media aide. Akpamgbo died in 2006. We can't ask him why he supported the out-of-order injunction issued by his former employee.'[95]

The inevitable conclusion must be that General Babangida did not tell the whole truth about the inside, behind-the-scenes story of the June 12 annulment. This is because aspects of Babangida's narrative came across as cunningly devised fables, which is not helped by his failure to name any living person even though some of those who took part in the annulment are still alive. As stated earlier, the Buhari administration said that the annulment 'was a huge elite conspiracy'. Some of those who played critical roles in the 'elite conspiracy' continue to parade themselves as true democrats, some of them occupying high political offices in the current administration. The failure of successive civilian governments to probe the annulment means that the real lessons of the epochal event have not been learned. One of such lessons is the duplicity, opportunism, and unscrupulousness displayed by politicians during the ill-fated 'transition programme'. Sadly, those behaviours have become deeply ingrained in Nigeria's political and democratic cultures, as discussed in the following sections.

Nigeria's Endless Cycle of Undemocratic Elections

Nigeria's democratic dispensations are described as 'Republics'. So, the First Republic covered the period from October 1, 1960, to January 15, 1966; the Second Republic (October 1, 1979, to December 31, 1983); the Third Republic (January 2, 1992, to August 26, 1993); and the Fourth Republic (May 29, 1999 to date). Between the *republics* were military interregnums (1966 to 1979 and 1983 to 1999). Preceding each *republic* was a general election. However, all the negative elements that can be associated with elections have long been present in Nigerian elections. These include ethnic politics, election rigging, political violence, monetisation of politics, lack of ideological orientation and godfatherism.[96] For instance, regarding election rigging, John Campbell and Matthew Page said in their book *Nigeria: What Everyone Needs To Know*: 'Massive election rigging by rival elites has been characteristic of Nigeria since independence.'[97] This is indeed true. All the elections have, to varying degrees, been rigged and marred by violence. The federal elections of 1964 and the Western Nigeria elections of 1965 were so massively rigged and violent that the January 1966 coup plotters cited them, particularly the latter, which triggered the 'Wild, Wild West' conflagration, as one of the reasons for their intervention.

In August 1979, the Obasanjo military regime conducted a general election that ushered in the *Second Republic*. Shehu Shagari emerged as president with 33.77 per cent of the vote, beating second and third places Obafemi Awolowo, who scored 29.18 per cent, and Nnamdi Azikiwe, with 16.75 per cent. The controversial election ended at the Supreme Court, which ruled in favour of Shagari. But four years later, the presidential election of August 6, 1983, in which Shagari was re-elected president, was widely regarded as massively rigged, so much so that the military gave the rigged elections as a reason for overthrowing the Shagari administration on December 31, 1983. That intervention led to sixteen years of continuous military rule until power returned to a civilian government in May 1999.

1999 To Date: Nigeria's Longest 'Democratic' Rule

Since the start of the *Fourth Republic* on May 29, 1999, Nigeria has had the longest period of continuous civilian rule since its independence. Since May 1999 to March 2025 (the time of writing this book), Nigeria has had nearly 26 years of uninterrupted civilian rule. During this period, it has had six presidential elections (2003, 2007, 2011, 2015, 2019 and 2023), all conducted by a civilian government, and it has had five civilian presidents: Olusegun Obasanjo (1999-2007), Umaru Yar' Adua (2007-2010), Goodluck Jonathan (2010-2015), Muhammadu Buhari (2015-2023) and Bola Tinubu (2023-).

The military fixed the 1999 presidential election that birthed the *Fourth Republic* in favour of General Obasanjo, a former military head of state. In his book, *Vindication of a General*, Ishaya Bamaiyi, chief of army staff under the regime of General Abdulsalami Abubakar, said that General Abubakar entered into a pact with Generals Ibrahim Babangida, T Y Danjuma and Aliyu Gusau to hand over to General Obasanjo.[98] Indeed, General Babangida confirmed the military's backing for the People's Democratic Party (PDP), the party under which General Obasanjo ran for president. In one statement, Babangida said: 'From the foundation stage, I saw PDP as the IRA [the Irish Republican Army]. We are the military wing of the PDP. When I say *we*, I mean my boss, TY Danjuma, Obasanjo, General Aliyu Mohammed, and others. I term us as IRA – the military wing of PDP.'[99] Evidently, the retired generals, who constituted themselves as the 'military wing' of the PDP, ensured that the 1999 presidential election was fixed in favour of one of their own: General Obasanjo.

Subsequently, Obasanjo, the beneficiary of the military's manipulation of the 1999 presidential election, went on to conduct two massively rigged elections himself. The April 19, 2003, presidential election was so massively rigged that Obasanjo, who was seeking re-election, got 99.9 per cent of the votes cast in his home state of Ogun. The Supreme Court found the outcome so outlandish that it annulled the entire results for the state. President Obasanjo did not personally contest in the 2007 presidential election, held on April 27, after his attempt to seek a third term in office, which he denies, failed. However, he hand-picked a presidential candidate, Umaru Yar' Ardua, then governor of Katsina State, for his party. But the election was so flawed that international observers described it as 'a charade'.[100] Even the beneficiary, Yar' Adua himself, admitted the election 'had shortcomings'.[101]

For the first time in Nigerian electoral history, the Supreme Court was close to voiding a presidential election and removing a sitting president from office. The Supreme Court only affirmed Yar' Adua's election by a startlingly close 4 to 3 majority decision, but all the seven justices were united in saying that the poll was marred by gross non-compliance with the electoral laws. President Yar' Adua responded by setting up the Electoral Reform Commission on August 28, 2007, headed by Justice Mohammadu Uwais, a former Chief Justice of Nigeria. The commission submitted its report in December 2008. However, many of the report's key recommendations have not been implemented, leaving Nigeria's electoral system acutely defective, a subject addressed in Chapter 3.

The 2011 presidential election, held on April 16, triggered a deadly violence. The incumbent President, Goodluck Jonathan, secured 58.87 per cent of the vote to beat General Buhari, who scored 31.97 per cent. Following Buhari's rejection of the results, violence broke out in North, his political base, leaving over 800 people dead. Against the backdrop of the 2011 conflagration and to prevent an apocalypse, the international community showed an unusual interest in the 2015 presidential election, held on March 29. Jonathan of the PDP again faced Buhari of the newly formed All Progressives Congress (APC). President Barack Obama addressed Nigerians directly in a broadcast, invoking the civil war slogan: 'To keep Nigeria one is a task that must be done.'[102] World statesmen like former UN Secretary-General Kofi Annan and former Commonwealth Secretary-General Emeka Anyaoku, supported by the United Nations, United States, and European Union, got the candidates to sign a peace deal in which they promised to eschew violence and rein in their supporters.

In the end, Armageddon was averted: the 2015 presidential election was largely peaceful. An incumbent president lost a re-election bid for the first time in Nigerian history. President Jonathan conceded defeat and congratulated General Buhari. In her book *Fighting Corruption Is Dangerous,* Dr Ngozi Okonjo-Iweala, Minister of Finance in President Jonathan's administration, said the president resisted pressure from prominent members of his cabinet and party not to concede[103]; instead, Jonathan instructed his spokesperson and speechwriter, Rueben Abati, to draft a concession speech.[104] The concession earned Jonathan, whose government had been unpopular, a post-defeat fame. However, a few years later, Jonathan blamed President Obama for his defeat, saying that Obama and his officials 'made it very clear to me by their actions that they wanted a change of government in Nigeria and were ready to do anything to achieve that purpose.'[105]

Yet, the consensus was that the election was credible, and much of the credit for that rightly went to Professor Attahiru Jega, the chairman of the Independent National Electoral Commission (INEC). In November 2015, Jega was invited to the London School of Economics to 'give the inside story of Nigeria's first successful transfer of power in the contentious 2015 elections that brought the country back from the brink'.[106] He was hailed worldwide for how he and the INEC he led successfully managed the 2015 elections.

However, if the 2015 presidential election was relatively peaceful, free, and fair, the one of 2019 was anything but. President Buhari was seeking re-election, with former Vice President Atiku Abubakar as his main opponent. INEC also had a new chairman, Professor Mahmood Yakubu, an Oxbridge-educated historian. But everything that could go wrong with elections went wrong with the 2019 general elections. For instance, despite Buhari, Abubakar, and other presidential candidates signing a peace deal, more than 500 people were killed during the elections. In its final report on the 2019 general elections, the European Union Election Observer Mission (EOM) said: 'Nigeria's 2019 general elections were marked by severe operational and transparency shortcomings, electoral security problems, and low turnout', adding that 'Instances of the misuse of state resources and vote-buying were evident and remained generally unaddressed.'[107]

Buhari won the election with 55.6 per cent of the vote, while Abubakar came second with 41.22 per cent. The latter rejected the results but lost his appeal at the Supreme Court. Many were, however, disappointed that Nigeria could not sustain the progress it had achieved in the 2015 general elections in the 2019 polls. But things got even worse.

2023 Presidential Election: A Monumental Betrayal

There were high hopes locally and internationally about the 2023 general elections. This was because, in 2022, President Buhari signed a new electoral bill into law. The Electoral Act 2022 introduced two new technologies intended to make Nigerian elections more transparent and credible. The first technology was the Bimodal Voter Accreditation System (BVAS), designed to ensure the electronic accreditation of voters and the transmission of results. If properly utilised, the BVAS would drastically reduce, if not eliminate, over-voting and human tampering with election results. The second technology was the Independent National Electoral Commission (INEC) Result Viewing portal, known as IReV. This technology would ensure that election results were transmitted in real-time from polling units to a central portal so that voters and other interested parties could monitor and view the results as they were being released. In a country where the manipulation of election results is rife, the IReV would significantly enhance the transparency of the electoral process.

In its Elections Regulations and Guidelines, INEC said it 'shall' transmit election results 'electronically' and 'upload' them 'to the INEC Result Viewing Portal (IReV).' Furthermore, in several public statements before the elections, including in a Chatham House speech[108] in January 2023, Professor Yakubu, the INEC chairman, said that the new technologies would be deployed in the presidential election. Those commitments, both in the INEC regulations and in public statements, created legitimate expectations and raised hopes about the polls.

However, INEC blatantly broke the commitments. The results of the presidential election were not transmitted electronically and were not shown on the IReV portal. INEC blamed 'technical glitches,' although both the BVAS and the IReV worked smoothly for the National Assembly elections conducted on the same day as the presidential poll on February 25. Many were suspicious. International observers said the failure to transmit the votes electronically and post them on the IReV portal severely eroded the election's credibility. Former President Obasanjo called for the cancellation of some of the election results, saying most of the results announced outside BVAS and IReV 'are not true reflection of the will of Nigerians.'[109] He said it was 'no secret that INEC officials have been allegedly compromised to make what should work not to work.'[110]

Nevertheless, Bola Tinubu, a former governor of Lagos State and candidate of the ruling APC, was declared winner of the presidential poll with 8.8 million votes (36.6%), while Atiku Abubakar of the PDP came second with 7 million votes (29.1%) and Peter Obi of the Labour Party, a surprise but formidable Third Force, came third, with 6 million votes

(25.4%). In its final report, the European Union Election Observation Mission (EU EOM) said: 'The 2023 general elections did not ensure a well-run, transparent, and inclusive democratic process as assured by the Independent National Electoral Commission (INEC).'[111] According to the EU EOM, 'only 31 per cent of the presidential election results' uploaded on the IReV system 'were formally and mathematically correct'.[112] However, the US Bureau of Democracy, Human Rights and Labour said the presidential election 'reflected the will of voters, despite technical and logistical difficulties, and some irregularities.'[113]

In truth, the election was marred by significant irregularities and failed basic transparency tests, which undermined its credibility. Ultimately, though, the courts had the final say. The Presidential Election Petition Tribunal and later the Supreme Court rejected the petitions of Atiku Abubakar and Peter Obi and validated Bola Tinubu's victory in controversial rulings.

The Judicialisation of Elections in Nigeria

A common feature of Nigerian elections is that they almost always end up in the courts. As a result, there have been several judge-made federal and state legislators and judge-made state governors in Nigeria. When Nigeria started the current *Fourth Republic* in 1999, all the country's 36 state governors were elected on the same day. However, only 28 governorship elections are currently held simultaneously; the remaining eight are held on different dates. This is because, in those eight states, the courts removed their governors in some cases after two years in office on the grounds of rigged elections. Their replacements would then be entitled to complete their own constitutionally allowed first term of four years, starting from when they were sworn into office. The result is what is known as 'staggered' or 'off-season' elections in Nigeria.

But the judicial interventions in electoral matters are not always popular because they are often based on mere legal technicalities and are frequently viewed as politically driven and favouring the ruling party at the centre. As a result, judicial interventions in elections often tend to subvert the will of the people. For instance, in 2019, the Supreme Court, based on some convoluted technicalities, removed Emeka Ihedioha as governor of Imo State, even though he came first in the election, according to INEC, and replaced him with Hope Uzodinma, who came fourth. In the same year, the Supreme Court nullified the election of David Lyon as governor of Bayelsa State simply because his deputy, Biobarakuma Degi-Eremienyo, presented forged certificates to INEC. The court's logic was that if the deputy must be sacked for violating an electoral law, the governor, too, must go since they were both on a joint ticket.

Given that electoral malpractices are prevalent in Nigeria, it is hard to argue that the courts have no role to play. In his BBC Reith Lectures in 2019, Lord Sumption, a former Justice of the UK Supreme Court, said that 'the decline of politics leads to the rise of law to fill the void,' adding that 'law inevitably rises where politics fails.'[114] But the court's role as the final arbiter in political and electoral matters places a huge responsibility on judges to ensure that mere technicalities do not replace substantive justice, that the courts are not the continuation of politics by other names, and that the judicial processes do not become a tool for subverting the will of the people, severing the electoral links between the governed and the governor that are at the heart of a true representative democracy. This is why it is far preferable for a court to order a rerun of a disputed election instead of simply substituting one candidate with another, as if they are fungible, purely on grounds of legal or procedural technicalities.

Interestingly, while the Supreme Court has nullified the elections of several governors, it has never voided the election of any president. The fact that the Supreme Court hears presidential election petitions suggests that, in principle, it could remove a sitting president from office on the grounds of a materially flawed election. Indeed, as stated earlier, the Supreme Court came close to sacking an incumbent president when it affirmed President Yar' Adua's controversial election by a 4 to 3 decision in 2007. If one of the four judges had switched the other way, Yar' Adua would have been removed from office. But the fact that the four judges validated Yar' Adua's election despite agreeing with the three dissenting judges that the election was deeply flawed confirms the widely held view that the Supreme Court will never remove a sitting president from office, however fraudulent his election.

The logic is simple. While it is less disruptive to remove a state governor, it would be hugely disruptive to public administration to remove an incumbent president who has already consolidated himself in power and surrounded himself with loyal military and security chiefs. The situation would probably be different if, as is the case in countries such as Kenya and Ghana, all presidential election petitions were concluded and finalised before a new president was sworn into office. But in Nigeria, the courts are being asked, in presidential election petitions, to remove a president who has already been sworn into office, a president who has already formed a government months after the election, and who has received congratulatory messages from several world leaders. Pragmatically, that is an impossible ask, a tall order. As a result, the Supreme Court merely resorts to technicalities to affirm the election of a president.

For instance, in the election petitions against President Tinubu, the Presidential Election Petition Court and later the Supreme Court used all conceivable procedural technicalities to reject the evidence and arguments provided by Atiku Abubakar and Peter Obi, while the courts held that INEC was not obliged to honour the commitments it made regarding the use of the BVAS and IReV technologies. But if the courts do not nullify the election of a sitting president, however materially flawed, and if the electoral body enjoys an irrebuttable presumption of regularity, then presidential elections in Nigeria will always favour whichever party and candidate can obtain 'victory' most fraudulently. As discussed in more detail in Chapter 3, that would undermine the integrity and credibility of Nigerian presidential elections and the legitimacy of Nigerian presidents.

What Kind of Democracy Is Nigeria Anyway?

The Economist Intelligence Unit (EIU) annual 'Democracy Index' has four categories: Full Democracies, Flawed Democracies, Hybrid Regimes and Authoritarian Regimes. In its 2024 index, as in previous indexes, the EIU put Nigeria under the 'hybrid regimes' category. According to the EIU, hybrid regimes have the following characteristics: 'Elections have substantial irregularities that often prevent them from being both free and fair. Government pressure on opposition parties and candidates may be common. Serious weaknesses are more prevalent than in flawed democracies—in political culture, functioning of government, and political participation. Corruption tends to be widespread, and the rule of law is weak. Civil society is weak. Typically, there is harassment of and pressure on journalists, and the judiciary is not independent.'[115] According to the EIU, Nigeria is even worse than a 'flawed democracy,' which is why it is classified as a 'regime', not a 'democracy'. Indeed, with its overall score of 4.16 (on a 0-10 scale), Nigeria only marginally escaped being classified as an 'authoritarian regime,' which has the highest score of 4.00 points.[116]

In truth, electoral democracy is in a terrible state in Nigeria. Its practice defies universal standards. In their book *Political Systems of the World*, Denis and Ian Derbyshire list seven basic criteria for credible elections.[117] They are:

1. All adults should have the right to vote.
2. The ballot should be cast freely without intimidation.
3. Elections should be held within prescribed time limits and in accordance with constitutional rules.
4. All candidates should be free to openly campaign.

5. All parties and candidates should be able to get their messages across, and there should be equity in media access and coverage.
6. The campaign and vote counting should be supervised by an impartial electoral body.
7. All parties and candidates should accept the adjudged results, and power should be handed over to the successful party within a prescribed timetable.

All the above criteria sound reasonable and practicable. But they are blatantly violated in Nigerian elections. For instance, millions of adult Nigerians who are eligible to vote are disenfranchised in every election either because of a) the electoral body's failure to distribute voter cards efficiently and start voting promptly or b) voter intimidation caused by political violence and the militarisation of elections. As a result, turnouts in Nigerian federal and state elections are abysmally low. For instance, in the 2019 presidential election, there were 82 million registered voters, 73 million collected Permanent Voter Cards (PVCs), but only 29 million, about 36 per cent, voted. Things got worse in the 2023 presidential poll. There were 93.4 million registered voters; 87 million collected their PVCs, but only 24 million, about 26.7 per cent, voted, the lowest turnout in a presidential poll since Nigeria returned to civil rule in 1999.

Vote buying gives power to the highest bidder

Linked to the problems of moneybag politics and godfatherism is the prevalence of vote-buying in Nigerian elections. In the 2019 general elections, 26 foreign missions in Nigeria said, 'We were gravely concerned over widespread incidents of vote-buying during the recent gubernatorial elections.'[118] According to a survey by the National Bureau of Statistics (NBS), 22 per cent of Nigerians reported that they were personally offered money in exchange for a vote before or during the 2023 general election, while nine per cent said they were offered another favour.[119] In February 2025, Achike Udenwa, former governor of Imo State, told the broadcast journalist Edmund Obilo on his State Affairs podcast that elections were usually bought in Nigeria and always went to the highest bidder.[120] The conversation went thus:

> **Udenwa**: Elections in Nigeria are such that even if I don't vote for you, you can buy your way through if you have the right amount of money.
>
> **Obilo**: How do they do that? Can you buy INEC?
>
> **Udenwa**: Ask the courts.
>
> **Obilo**: You can buy the voters, but can you buy INEC, buy the police, buy the army?
>
> **Udenwa**: Yes, you can buy everybody.
>
> **Obilo**: So, our elections are about buying.
>
> **Udenwa**: Yes, and that's the thing we must curb because if we curb it, we will get the correct leadership.

Of course, former Governor Udenwa was saying the obvious. Nigerian politicians acquire vast amounts of wealth through corruption and use the money to muscle their way into power by buying votes and corrupting the electoral bodies, the security agencies and, even, the courts. But beyond that, once they are in power, either as a governor or a president, they abuse their incumbency to stay in power. In Nigerian elections, the incumbents flagrantly misuse state resources to their electoral advantage and their opponents' disadvantage, thereby distorting the playing field. Then, there is the actual rigging and manipulation of election results. The British playwright Tom Stoppard once wrote, 'It is not the voting that makes a democracy; it is the counting.'[121] In Nigeria, vote counting is not sacrosanct; it is often subject to blatant manipulations.

Finally, Nigeria lacks an impartial electoral body. Given that the president appoints the chairman of INEC as well as the national and resident electoral commissioners, there is a strong perception that INEC is not an independent electoral body. Because the first six criteria of credible elections are not achieved in Nigerian elections, the seventh is never fulfilled: parties and candidates never accept the adjudged results, which are often adjudicated upon by the courts based on allegations of rigging, which are often true as the following evidence shows.

The Confession of Election Riggers

In 2018, Ibrahim Mantu, a former Deputy Senate President, told *Channels TV* how he helped rig elections. Esther Ogun-Yusuf, the interviewer, was incredulous and sought clarification.

Ogun-Yusuf: Can I just clarify one thing? Did I hear you say you helped to rig elections before now?

Mantu: Yes, I did.

Ogun-Yusuf: Really?

Mantu: Yes, I am now confessing the truth because I am a born-again politician.

Ogun-Yusuf: How did you rig elections?

Mantu: The rigging did not always involve tampering with ballot boxes   but giving money to INEC boys to help if they can see any chance that they can favour you and providing money to security agencies.[122]

Mantu went on to say that 'all our elections in the past' had involved rigging, adding: 'I've been in this game for about 20 years.'[123]

In 2024, another politician, Tony Okocha, chief of staff to the then governor of Rivers State, Rotimi Amaechi, also confessed to rigging elections in the following interview with Chamberlain Usoh on *Channels TV*.[124]

Usoh: Mr Okocha, let me ask you, were you really rigging elections while you were chief of staff?

Okocha: On the issue of whether I rigged elections, yes, I didn't hide it.   I should be praised as a whistleblower.

Usoh: Praise for rigging elections? You should be behind bars.

Okocha: That's not correct. If you were an armed robber yesterday, and today you confess that you stole something somewhere, are you saying that the law will now take a retrospective effect? The answer is no.

Usoh: Who was giving the orders to rig elections? I assume you were not alone.

Okocha: Yes, all of us were together.

Nigeria is infested with too many election riggers, past and present, who, unlike Mantu and Okocha, will not publicly confess their sins. But ballot fraud is iniquitous; it is illegal, immoral, and deleterious. Rigging is illegal because it violates all conceivable constitutional and electoral rules and norms. It is immoral because it undermines the key requirement for legitimate government: the consent of the people, as expressed by votes in free, fair, transparent, and peaceful elections. If someone secures power by electoral fraud, the fundamental doctrine of consent of the governed is breached, and the emergent government lacks the legitimacy and moral right to govern. Election rigging also impairs democratic and political accountability. If any politician gains power by bribing electoral officers and/or voters, he will not be answerable to the people or serve their interests. Rather, he is likely to enrich himself and his acolytes and secure re-election, regardless of his performance, by repeating the well-honed practice of buying votes, co-opting security agencies, and influencing electoral officers.

But all of this is a product of the rottenness of politics in Nigeria. That rottenness is also reflected in the fact that politics in Nigeria is not based on ideologies, values, and issues but is driven by personalities and crude self-interest. In theory, Nigeria is a multi-party democracy. In the 2019 general elections, 74 registered parties contested the elections. This number was reduced to 18 in the 2023 general elections after INEC deregistered most of the parties. However, despite the mushrooming of political parties, Nigeria, in practice, resembles a one-party state. This is because political parties are mere vehicles for winning elections as politicians move seamlessly between them.

For instance, in 2025, as politicians anticipated the 2027 general election, several prominent opposition political figures, including governors and members of the National Assembly, defected from their parties to the ruling APC. President Tinubu hailed the defections and called on more opposition politicians to join his party[125], while the national chairman of the APC, Abdullahi Ganduje, advocated for a one-party state in Nigeria. He said: 'Too many cooks spoil the soup; too many political parties spoil governance,' adding: 'Today, China is one of the strongest countries in the world and is a one-party system.'[126] Indeed, the fluidity and fickleness of party loyalty already makes Nigeria look like a one-party state as politicians frequently 'forum-shop,' looking for which party can best advance their ambitions. This is easier because no ideology or policy distinguishes the political parties; they are mere 'special purpose vehicles' for capturing power.[127]

Yet, as Will Hutton points out in his book *The State We're In,* 'democracy depends on parties being able to develop distinctive policies that correspond to some coherent political vision.'[128] He adds that if there are no ideological differences or choices between political parties, 'then political debate becomes a charade.'[129] There is no semblance of credible issue-based political debate in Nigeria. Given the opportunistic and self-serving nature of Nigerian politics, it is defined by personalities, elite horse-trading, monetisation, and corruption. It serves only the interests of the political class. As one former Nigerian minister puts it, 'Nigeria is more a government by the political class, of the political class, for the political class.'[130]

***

This chapter is a whistle-stop tour of Nigeria's checkered political history, from its creation to the present. Its main themes are Nigeria's birth defects and convoluted evolution, including its deeply flawed political and governance structures, which are the main sources of its disharmony and instability. Others are Nigeria's broken politics and troubled democracy. The chapter provides the context and background for the discussions and arguments in the next two chapters, namely that, given Nigeria's acute political and structural challenges, the country's future rests squarely on political restructuring, which must lead to a negotiated political and constitutional settlement, and the creation of a new constitution.

2

The Restructuring Debate: Why Nigeria must be restructured

As argued in the preceding chapter, Nigeria was, at birth, an artificial construct. Its creation was not organic in the sense that Nigeria did not emerge, as many nations did, from autochthonous people who had the same language, culture, or ethnic origin. Two or more distinct nations can come together as one country in two ways. One is by conquest, whereby one nation conquers another, such as when England colonised Ireland in 1169 and conquered Wales in 1277; the other is by agreement, such as when England and Scotland signed the Treaty of Union in 1707. However, the creation of Nigeria did not follow either of those patterns.

Although the Fulani Jihad of 1804, led by Usman dan Fodio, resulted in the Fulanis conquering the Hausas and bringing certain parts of the North, known as the core North[1], together under the Sokoto Caliphate,[2] the rest of the territories that later became known as Nigeria were inhabited by definable and independent ethnic nations that had not conquered or signed a treaty with one other to create a country. Rather, they were forced into a 'union' by a foreign power. In his book *Empire*, Professor Niall Ferguson, a renowned historian, describes the colonialists' modus operandi as follows: 'Chiefs were hoodwinked, tribes dispossessed, inheritances signed away with a thumbprint or a shaky cross and any resistance mown down by the Maxim guns.'[3] The creation of Nigeria in 1914 was, in that manner, a unilateral act in which a colonial power forced disparate nations into a marriage of convenience.

Perfecting an Imperfect Union

But the Nigeria that emerged from that external imposition lacks nationhood and internal cohesion, with intense distrust and divisiveness prevalent among the different ethnic groups. In the book *Political Restructuring in Europe*, Professor Chris Brown argues that in multi-national states, politics 'at best takes the form of group bargaining and compromise and at worst degenerates into a struggle for domination'[4]. In Nigeria, the latter is the case: politics is defined by a struggle for domination or a struggle to avoid domination. This is because, as Professor Chinua Achebe puts it in his book *There Was a Country*, 'The structure of the country was such that there was an inbuilt power struggle among the ethnic groups.'[5] That structure, which makes it possible for one or two ethnic groups to dominate others and, thus, denies equal opportunities and fair material treatment for all the constituent parts of Nigeria, is the major cause of disunity and instability in the country. While most Nigerians may have accepted Nigeria's creation as a fait accompli, they are not willing to live with its deeply flawed structure. Those structural flaws are precisely at the roots of many separatist agitations and the disharmony and instability that continue to dog Nigeria.

Undoubtedly, the legacy of British colonialism is, broadly speaking, one of brutality and exploitation. Britain not only regarded its colonies as sources of natural resources to be extracted and as captive markets for its domestic products, but it also artificially created countries or states where none hitherto existed by merging previously independent nations. However, destiny is not set in stone; destiny is not immutable. Several countries have altered the unfavourable trajectories of their futures through bold actions. For instance, former British colonies such as India, Malaysia, and Singapore restructured themselves internally after Britain's departure and are now stable and prosperous nation-states. This internal restructuring, this remodelling of a nation, is what Nigeria has yet to undertake. For the avoidance of doubt, the call for restructuring does not advocate for the disintegration of Nigeria – far from it. Rather, it seeks to refine an imperfect union and secure the future of Nigeria as a functioning nation-state that serves all its citizens. Restructuring is a critical pre-condition for Nigeria's unity, stability, and progress.

Britain, too, Struggles with Nationhood

All heterogenous states face challenges of nationhood and unity. It should, therefore, come as no surprise that Britain, which created Nigeria, is itself grappling with its own problems of disunity. To some extent, Britain and Nigeria are both artificial constructs; they are not nation-states but political unions in the sense that they are made up of entities that retain their own national identities.[6] As stated above, Britain or, more broadly, the United Kingdom emerged after

England conquered Wales, colonised Ireland, and signed a treaty with Scotland, while Nigeria emerged after Britain conquered and cobbled together several ancient and hitherto independent kingdoms. But reading or hearing what British newspapers and politicians say about the country's union, the inevitable question must be: If Britain is struggling with nationhood, why won't Nigeria its flawed creation? Take a few examples.

In 2021, the Sunday Times in Britain published a report titled 'Revealed: Our Disunited Kingdom.'[7] The report showed 'rising support for a break-up of the UK.'[8] When asked in a poll, 56 per cent in Scotland said they were more Scottish than British; 45 per cent in Northern Ireland were more Irish than British; 36 per cent in Wales were more Welsh than British; and 27 per cent in England were more English than British. The Times columnist Alex Massie wrote: 'The UK is, in a quite literal sense, dying.'[9] The Financial Times also asked: 'Is the UK heading for a break-up?'[10]

Britain's former prime ministers also warned of dangers ahead. Gordon Brown put it starkly: 'I think the UK could end unless it fundamentally changes.'[11] Another former prime minister, John Major, wrote in the Financial Times: 'Scotland cannot be kept forever in an arrangement if her people wish to end it,' adding: 'If the Union is to be kept together, it must be as a true partnership.'[12] Indeed, in 2014, Scotland only marginally lost an independence referendum by 45 per cent to 55 per cent. A prominent Scottish politician, Lord Owen, former British Foreign Secretary, was later to say: 'Many Scottish people are ready to vote for separation unless they are presented with a new constitutional federal structure for the UK that allows Scotland to feel the fullest autonomy of nationhood within a federal state.'[13] Not to be left out, Mark Drakeford, then First Minister of Wales, said: 'The Union, as it is, is over. We must create a new Union. We must recraft the UK as a voluntary association of four nations.'[14]

The point of bringing up the above is that centuries after Britain was forged together, the British identity is still weaker than the core ethnic identities of English, Scottish, and Welsh. Why, then, should it be different for Nigeria? Ethnic identities cannot be wished away. The solution is to manage a nation's diversity well. But Nigerian leaders constantly say that Nigeria's unity is non-negotiable while doing nothing to strengthen the country's fragile union. By contrast, Britain does not take its unity for granted. Since 1973, there have been more than 12 referendums in the UK, most of them in response to pressure to restructure the country politically, which resulted in the creation of devolved governments in Scotland, Wales, and Northern Ireland in the late 1990s, and later the devolution of power to the regions through big city mayors, called Metro Mayors. Yet, there are demands for more radical solutions, for more decentralisation and devolution of powers.

Indeed, there have been calls for a 'full constitutional convention to agree new relationships between the nations of the UK.'[15] Agreeing on a new relationship between Nigeria's ethnic nationalities is, in large part, what restructuring and a new political and constitutional settlement would achieve. Yet, Nigeria continues to ignore the need to forge such a new relationship. British politicians refer to the UK as 'a country of nations'; in fact, the UK

Prime Minister's website used the phrase 'countries within a country'[16] to describe the UK, referring to England, Scotland, Wales and Northern Ireland. But Nigerian politicians will never describe Nigeria in such a language; rather, they pretend as if the ethnic nations do not exist. They deliberately ignore the complex realities of Nigeria's diversity and, in fact, mismanage the country's diversity.

Mismanagement of Nigeria's Diversity

One of the immediate challenges to Nigeria's unity is the mismanagement of its diversity by its political leaders. There is a near-total insensitivity to the fact that Nigeria is a diverse country, which requires managing that diversity well with a strong commitment to the principles of fairness, justice, equity, and inclusivity. As discussed below, there are three main areas where Nigeria's diversity is being mismanaged: ethnicity, religion, and resource control.

Ethnicity

The 2022 Nigeria Social Cohesion Survey (NSCI), published by the Africa Polling Institute (API), found that 36 per cent of Nigerians were comfortable with being both Nigerian and members of their ethnic groupings, while 35 per cent identified more with their ethnic groups. More strikingly, however, only 10 per cent felt more Nigerian than ethnic.[17] Those findings show that ethnic identity is an inescapable reality in Nigeria. However, Nigerian politicians do little to promote inter-ethnic harmony but rather exploit ethnicity for political advantages.

For instance, in 2015, General Muhammadu Buhari won the presidential election with the votes of his Northern Hausa/Fulani base (12 million votes) and those of the Yoruba in the South-West (2.4 million votes). He got fewer than 300,000 votes from the Igbos in the South-East and just 418,590 votes from the Ijaw/Niger-Delta people in the South-South geopolitical zone. It was an election defined by ethnic bloc voting, in which the different ethnic nationalities *spoke with one voice* in favour of one candidate or another.

After the election, Buhari famously said at a press conference, when asked whether he would treat all Nigerians fairly as president: 'Constituencies that gave me 97 per cent cannot, in all honesty, be treated equally, on some issues, with constituencies that gave me five per cent.'[18] Indeed, throughout his eight-year presidency, Buhari gave most of the prominent national positions to people from his ethnic Fulani group. He decidedly discriminated against the Igbos. For instance, in his eight years in power, President Buhari found not a single Igbo good enough to be one of Nigeria's security chiefs. Asked in a TV interview why there was no Igbo security or service chief, he said: 'You can't just pick people to balance out; the positions have to be earned.'[19] The implication was that no Igbo was qualified enough in the armed forces or in the police to reach the top. And asked why there very few Igbo heads of federal government parastatals and agencies, Buhari replied: 'They have to go through the mill.'[20]

In an open letter published in Nigerian newspapers in May 2020, Abubakar Dangiwa Umar, a highly respected retired army colonel and former military governor of Kaduna State, accused President Buhari of mismanaging Nigeria's diversity with his administration's 'lopsided appointments, which continue to give undue preference to some sections of the country over others.'[21] He added: 'Nowhere is this more glaring than in the leadership cadre of our security services.'[22] Such inequity does not engender a sense of belonging and inclusion, which is a condition for unity and cohesion in any diverse, multinational country.

Like President Buhari, but even more so, his successor, President Tinubu, blatantly mismanaged Nigeria's ethnic diversity by filling critical offices of state with people from his Yoruba ethnic group in what became known as the *Yorubanisation* of his government. The list of his appointments to the critical economic, security and criminal justice positions is outrageously lopsided. Take the economic offices. A Yoruba is the Central Bank governor, Minister of Finance, Coordinating Minister of the Economy, Minister of Blue Economy, Minister of Digital Economy, Minister of Solid Minerals, Minister of Trade, Industries and Investment; Minister of Petroleum (Tinubu himself!); Head of Bank of Industry; Head of the Federal Inland Revenue Service; and Accountant General of the Federation. In the security fields, a Yoruba is the Chief of Army Staff, Inspector-General of Police, Head of the State Security Services, SSS, Head of Immigration, and Head of Customs. Indeed, a Yoruba is Tinubu's Chief Protocol Officer, Aide-de-Camp, Chief Security Officer and Commander of Brigade and Guards. And a Yoruba is the Attorney-General and Minister of Justice, Head of Economic and Financial Crimes Commission, EFCC, and Chief Justice of the Federation. While appointments to chairmanship and board-membership of federal agencies were fairly balanced,[23] those to the critical offices of state listed above were not; they were dominated by the Yorubas.

Those blatantly lop-sided appointments ignore the fact that Nigeria is a multi-ethnic country whose government should reflect the country's diversity.[24] The Vanguard columnist, Ugoji Egbujo, accused Tinubu of 'going full throttle in installing an ethnic hegemony.'[25] Even the Yoruba socio-cultural group, Afenifere, under the leadership of Chief Ayo Adebanjo, now late, considered the lopsided appointments inequitable, describing them as 'a threat to the age-long inter-ethnic relationship and peaceful co-existence in Nigeria.'[26] Unfortunately, such exclusionist, zero-sum politics defines inter-ethnic relations in Nigeria.

The fact that no Igbo has become president of Nigeria since the country returned to democratic rule in 1999 is a proof of such exclusionist politics and a major source of ethnic grievance in Nigeria. Between 1999 and 2023, a Yoruba, an Ijaw, and a Hausa/Fulani have been presidents of Nigeria, but no Igbo has reached the highest office. Consequently, the country that allowed a contest between only two Yoruba presidential candidates in 1999 and the country that allowed a contest between only two Northern presidential candidates in 2019 should have been willing to support the Igbos from the South-East to produce the president in 2023. But the Yoruba insisted it was their turn to produce the next president, despite having produced president for eight years and vice-president for another eight years. Eventually, Tinubu, a Yoruba, became president with the help of the Hausa/Fulani, with whom the Yoruba entered a political alliance that resulted in General Buhari, a Fulani, becoming president in 2015.

But with the emergence of Tinubu as president, the Igbos could remain in the political wilderness for as long as the Israelites were in the physical wilderness, if not more. This is because if Tinubu did two terms in office, power would return to the North after the expiry of his second term in 2031. A Northern president would then also serve for two terms, ending in 2039. Thus, by 2039, there would have been no president of Igbo extraction for 40 years since 1999. What is more, if the above scenario plays out, when power returns to the South in 2039, after a two-term South-West presidency, followed by a two-term Northern presidency, power may still not go to the Igbos because the Ijaw/Niger-Delta people of the South-South could lay a claim to the presidency, and, if supported by the North, their traditional ally, they could have it. Thus, the presidency of Nigeria may elude the Igbos for the unforeseeable future. The truth is, there is an intense inter-ethnic struggle for power in Nigeria, and the Igbos are disadvantaged in that struggle. That condemns them to a subordinate political status, which is a source of disharmony and instability.

Religion

Nigeria is a deeply religious country, with Christianity and Islam being the two dominant religions. The official consensus is that Christians and Muslims each account for about half of the population, and thus, neither religion is dominant over the other. That consensus owes its origin to the former military head of state General Murtala Muhammed (1975-76), who famously propounded the fifty-fifty formula as conventional wisdom.[27] Consequently, since the Murtala Muhammed regime, there has been a heightened sensitivity to honouring the convention such that a Muslim head of state always has a Christian deputy, and vice versa.

For instance, when General Murtala Muhammed was assassinated in a failed military coup in 1976, his deputy, General Obasanjo, a Christian, became the head of state. The next most senior officer to Obasanjo was General Theophilus Yakubu Danjuma, a northern Christian. But to honour the conventional wisdom, General Danjuma did not become Obasanjo's deputy. Instead, a much junior officer, then Lt Col Shehu Musa Yar' Adua, a northern Muslim, was made Obasanjo's deputy and promoted two steps up to the rank of Brigadier.[28] General Danjuma, a patriot, clearly did not want to create a situation where both the head of state and his deputy would belong to the same faith. Consequently, he, a northern Christian, declined to be deputy to Obasanjo, a southern Christian, but, instead, nominated as Obasanjo's deputy Yar' Adua, a northern Muslim officer, who was promptly promoted to Brigadier, and then Major-General.[29] However, there were two exceptions to that rule. The first was when General Muhammadu Buhari, a northern Muslim, became military head of state in 1983, with his deputy, Brigadier Tunde Idiagbon, also being a northern Muslim. The second instance was the Muslim-Muslim ticket of MKO Abiola, a southern Muslim, and Baba Gana Kingibe, a northern Muslim, in the annulled presidential election of June 12, 1993. But the two exceptions were aberrations.

For instance, in his memoir, *A Journey in Service*, General Ibrahim Babangida, who was the military president during the presidential election of June 12, 1993, specifically remarked that 'Abiola, a southern Muslim, defied conventional wisdom by picking another Muslim as his running mate for the June 12 presidential election.'[30] That remark confirms that it was, indeed, conventional wisdom that the president and his vice president should not belong to the same faith. That conventional wisdom also influenced the decision of General Buhari, a northern Muslim, to not pick Tinubu, a southern Muslim, as his running mate for the 2015 presidential election. In his autobiography, *Participations*, former Governor Bisi Akande, a Tinubu ally, revealed that the party's Northern governors also insisted that it would not be appropriate for Buhari to have a fellow Muslim as his running mate.[31] Consequently, General Buhari ran with a Christian, Professor Yemi Osinbajo, who became Nigeria's vice president after they both won the election in 2015.

However, Tinubu turned the conventional wisdom on its head in the 2023 presidential election when he chose Kashim Shettima, a fellow Muslim, as his running mate. He did so as a political calculation, believing it was the only way he could secure the support of the Muslim North and win the election. Indeed, as Nasir El-Rufai, a former governor of Kaduna State and an Islamic zealot, put it in a viral video, Tinubu 'had no option'[32] but to pick a Muslim running mate; otherwise, 'he would lose the election.'[33] Thus, Tinubu's Muslim-Muslim ticket was a self-serving political consideration that rode roughshod over Nigeria's religious diversity. But if a long-cherished conventional wisdom was to be overturned, it should be done with massive support. Yet, Tinubu secured only 36.6 per cent of the popular vote, with about 90 per cent of his votes coming from the Muslim North, and Muslim voters generally.

But beyond the exclusionist Muslim-Muslim presidency, which relegated Christianity to a second-class status, Tinubu's emergence as president violated the fifty-fifty conventional wisdom in another respect. In line with the convention, the Nigerian presidency, under democratic rule, would normally alternate between Christians and Muslims. Thus, President Umaru Yar' Adua (a Muslim) succeeded President Olusegun Obasanjo (a Christian); President Jonathan (a Christian) succeeded President Yar' Adua; President Buhari (a Muslim) succeeded President Jonathan. However, Tinubu upended that convention; he is the first Muslim civilian president to succeed another Muslim civilian president, and his presidency could entrench Islamic leadership in Nigeria for at least two decades. If he served for two terms as president, power would return to a Northern-Muslim president in 2031 for two terms. Thus, by 2039, Nigeria would have been under a Muslim president for 24 consecutive years, counting from Buhari's first term in 2015. Such a prolonged Islamic leadership would raise fears of Islamic domination and fuel tension in a country where Christians and Muslims traditionally view each other with suspicion. It would be another mismanagement of Nigeria's diversity.

Resource control

Besides ethnicity and religion, another major source of tension in Nigeria is the subject of resource control, namely, to what extent should a community control natural resources derived from its territory? This debate came to a head at the end of 2021, with heated altercations between three of Nigeria's most prominent elder statesmen. In December 2021, former President Obasanjo, Chief Edwin Clark, leader of the Pan Niger Delta Forum (PANDEF), who died in February 2025, and Cardinal Anthony Olubunmi Okogie, the archbishop emeritus of Lagos, exchanged open letters in which they strongly espoused their views on ownership of the oil wells in the Niger Delta. For context, here is a summary of the arguments.

At a summit on December 13, President Obasanjo said that the oil found in the Niger Delta belonged to Nigeria, not to the Niger Delta. Enraged by that statement, Chief Clark fired off an open letter[34] to Obasanjo on December 22, questioning his position on the issue and accusing him of showing hatred towards the Niger Delta people. Obasanjo fired back. In an open letter[35] to Chief Clark on December 28, he reasserted his position on the issue. 'The territory of Nigeria is indivisible, inclusive of the resources found therein,' he said, adding: 'No territory in Nigeria, including the minerals found therein, belongs to the area or location.'[36] He said it was 'the most basic constitutional fact' that 'you cannot have two sovereign entities within a state.'[37] Cardinal Olubunmi Okogie joined the fray. On December 31, he issued a statement titled 'Who owns the oil?' in which he challenged Obasanjo's view on the ownership of the Niger Delta oil wells. 'The owner of the land owns whatever is on the land or under the land,' Cardinal Okogie said, adding that 'to deprive them of that right is to be patently unjust.'[38] He concluded: 'Contrary to President Obasanjo's declaration, the oil in the Niger Delta does not belong to Nigeria.'[39]

This debate on resource control pivots back to the wider issue, discussed earlier, about the origin of Nigeria and the fact that the ancient kingdoms, such as the Ijaw, that the British cobbled together to create Nigeria do not want to subsume their ethnic identities and interests under the Nigerian identity and interest, especially as they believe that the country is not built on principles of fairness, equity, and justice. And there are few issues of equity and fairness more important than who controls the resources found in one's ethnic land, which borders on indigenous rights. President Obasanjo anchored his position on positivism or *what is*, namely, as described under Nigeria's current Constitution, saying that his stance was the legal and constitutional position. However, Chief Clark and Cardinal Okogie based their arguments on normativism or *what ought to be*, and, indeed, on what used to be before Nigeria's independence and under the 1963 Constitution. Thus, to better understand the argument, it is worth considering how resource control was treated before Nigeria's independence and under the 1963 Republican Constitution and how it is treated under the current 1999 Constitution.

Resource control pre-independence and under the 1963 Constitution

During the pre-independence era, each of the three regions in Nigeria had control over resources derived from their territory. They had control over revenue accruing from the export of their produce – the North (groundnut), the East (palm oil), and the West (cocoa) – and made contributions to the centre for the maintenance of common services. When

Nigeria became independent in 1960, the same arrangement was maintained under the 1960 Independence Constitution and the 1963 Republican Constitution. Under those constitutions, the Federal Government controlled no resources but acted as *agent* of the regions concerning export and the collection of export duties, given that only the Federal Government controlled customs and, thus, export trade. However, once the Federal Government collected the export duties, it was required under section 139 of the 1963 Constitution to pay the duties, after deducting drawbacks and refunds, to the region where the export commodity was derived. In return, the regions contributed a sum towards the running of Customs and Excise, a federal agency.

The key point is that the Federal Government did not own or control the commodities derived from any of the regions. For instance, section 139(4) of the 1963 Constitution says: 'For this section, any amount of a commodity that is derived from the federal territory shall be deemed to be derived from Western Nigeria.' At the time, the federal territory was in Lagos. But as Lagos was part of Western Nigeria, any commodity derived from there belonged to Western Nigeria. This shows the regionality of resource control and deference for indigenous rights.

However, the situation was slightly different with respect to mineral resources. Only the Federal Government could grant licences and extraction rights and collect royalties and rents. Extractions of mineral resources often involved foreign companies and fell within foreign affairs, a matter within the exclusive remit of the Federal Government. As a result, the 1963 Constitution put minerals on the exclusive legislative list. However, under section 140, the Federal

Government was required to pay fifty per cent of royalties and rents to each region for minerals extracted from that region. This significant amount – fifty per cent – was a recognition of the regions' ownership of natural resources derived from their territories.

Thus, there were two arrangements in relation to resource control pre-independence and under the 1963 Constitution. In one, the regions owned and controlled their agricultural commodities but made contributions to the Federal Government for maintenance of the centrally controlled Customs and Excise department, which collected export duties on their behalf. Under the second arrangement, relating to mineral resources, the Federal Government was responsible for granting licences and extraction rights for minerals as well as collecting royalties and rents. However, in recognition of the indigenous rights of the regions, a substantial amount of the royalties and rents collected – fifty per cent – was paid to the regions from which the minerals were extracted.

Resource control under the current 1999 Constitution

The above arrangements were jettisoned after the military coup of January 1966 when General Aguiyi-Ironsi abolished Nigeria's federal structure and regional autonomy and imposed a unitary system on the country. The subsequent military-imposed 1979 and 1999 constitutions gave the Federal Government ownership of natural resources. In 1978, the Obasanjo military regime enacted the Land Use Decree, which later became the Land Use Act. But while the act vests lands in state governments, it gave ownership of any minerals found under those lands to the Federal Government. Currently, all revenues accruing from oil and gas, from all exports and imports, from corporate and other income taxes and from Value Added Tax (VAT) first go into the Federation Account. Then, the revenues are shared monthly according to the following formula: the federal government (52.68 per cent), Nigeria's 36 state governments (26.72 per cent), and the country's 774 local governments (20.60 per cent). However, under section 162 (2) of the Constitution, before allocations are made to the three tiers of government – federal, state, and local – 13 per cent of the revenue accruing to the Federation Account directly from any natural resources must be set aside for the nine oil-producing states, based on the principle of derivation, that is, in recognition that the natural resources, such as oil, are derived from those states.

The overriding question around resource control, including the controversial VAT distribution formula,[40] is that it is a symptom of the north-south divide that has long been a bitter element of Nigeria's politics since its colonial creation. It is also a consequence of the long-standing divergence in economic performance and social outcomes between the more populous and poorer northern states and the less populous but more economically dynamic southern states. Sharing resources, including power, between the North and the South has always been a major flashpoint in the history of Nigeria.

Yet, the overriding question, in the wider context of the management of Nigeria's diversity, is whether the Federal Government should control revenues from resources, including commodities, derived from the regions or states and just hand some percentage of the revenues to them. That is the question at the heart of the agitation for resource control. This question becomes pertinent given that revenues from resources, such as oil, derived from the regions are used to fund the Federal Government, while the regions from whose lands those resources are derived, particularly the oil-rich Niger Delta, suffer acute economic and social deprivations. The resource control agitation is not about having multiple sovereign entities within Nigeria, as President Obasanjo suggested. Rather, it is about recognising property and indigenous rights within a federal system. While it is sensible to share revenues from oil and gas and other natural resources with all the states of Nigeria, it cannot be right that the states or regions that produce those resources, and thus predominantly fund the Nigerian state, do not benefit significantly from the revenues.

There are two possible solutions. One is for the federating units to control all the resources within their territories and make contributions to the Federal Government. The other is for the Federal Government, if it must control those resources, to pay a substantial percentage of the revenues – probably between 17 and 20 per cent derivation payment – to the regions that produce the resources. This would incentivise the sub-national entities to become more productive and focus on how best to harness their resources rather than waiting for handouts from the central government.

Furthermore, the current revenue-sharing formula, which gives the Federal Government 52.68 per cent of all revenues accruing to the Federation Account, is wrong. The Federal Government's disproportionate share is a consequence of the fact that too many responsibilities and powers are centralised, whereas a lot of those responsibilities, with accompanying resources, should be devolved to the federating units, which are closer to the people, a subject discussed in Chapter 3. Nigeria needs an ownership or a derivation system that allows each region to benefit meaningfully from resources within its area. The failure to address the issue of resource control or revenue-sharing satisfactorily is one form of the mismanagement of Nigeria's diversity, and a major source of tension, particularly the incessant militancy in the Niger Delta, as well as separatist agitations.

Nigeria Must Be a Strong Nation to Be an Effective State

The above discussions around the management of Nigeria's diversity in relation to ethnicity, religion, and resource control lead inevitably to the question of whether Nigeria's current political and governance structure is fit for purpose and whether it allows Nigeria to be a functioning state. From a functionalist perspective, every structure exists because of the functions it performs and because of the needs it meets. If a structure fails to perform those functions or meet those needs, it must be changed. That is a great insight from the theories of regime formation and regime change.[41] As Professor Chris Brown argues in the book *Political Restructuring in Europe*, no political structure has an ethical reason to survive unless it is working, and thus, every political structure should be open to reconstruction.[42] So, the question is whether Nigeria's current political and governance structures are working for Nigeria and whether they make Nigeria a functioning state.

In theory, Nigeria is a state to the extent that it has the physical elements of statehood: a settled population, a defined territory, a government, instruments of state coercion, and the ability to formalise relations with other states. However, in practice, Nigeria is a dysfunctional state, as discussed in later chapters. But if Nigeria is not a functioning state, the question is why? The answer lies in the fact that Nigeria is not a nation or a nation-state. Although the British created a country or a state, they did not forge Nigeria into a nation, to enable all the constituent parts to have a shared sense of purpose and pull in the same direction. The Nigerian identity is far from being a unifying one. Nigeria is like a big tent under which every group inside the tent fights for their group interest instead of fighting towards a common goal. This is because Nigeria's structure engenders recurrent inter-ethnic conflict over power and resources, fuelled by the overconcentration of power at the centre and the structural imbalance between the North and the South, which creates a perception of Northern hegemony. Thus, Nigeria has not attained nationhood; it is not a *nation* with a shared purpose and internal cohesion.

But nationhood matters because it is impossible to have an effective state without a nation. As Professors Paul Collier and Tim Besley, co-authors of a seminal report on state fragility, put it: 'State building requires nation building, and nation building requires actions by the state.'[43] They added that 'shared identity across something as large as a country can only be built by the state, and in doing so, the state strengthens its own capacity to achieve other national goals.'[44] This means that a country cannot be a functioning state unless it first becomes a nation. But a country cannot become a nation unless the state, represented by the government, forges a nation out of deeply polarised peoples. Both statements are at the heart of the restructuring debate: Nigeria must achieve nationhood to be a successful state, but to attain nationhood, it must be restructured through a process led by the state, that is, the government, so that its constituent nations can live together in harmony instead of perpetual inter-ethnic struggles.

The truth is that Nigeria should be a multinational union of consent, which should not be held together by fear or force. But Nigeria is a product of two perverse rules: colonial rule and military rule. The colonial rulers created and held Nigeria together with lethal force; and, for decades, the military kept the country together with brutal force. Unfortunately, successive civilian presidents have used military force to suppress separatist agitations, thus perpetuating a vicious circle. Yet, in the end, Nigeria can only be held together through dialogue and by restructuring the country to engender a sense of fairness and inclusion among its ethnic regions or nations.

Anyaoku Is Right on Political Restructuring

Many prominent Nigerians have repeatedly called for the political restructuring of Nigeria. But Chief Emeka Anyaoku is the most laser-focused on the issue. Furthermore, as the Secretary-General of the Commonwealth of Nations for ten years, from 1990 to 2000, he is the only one who brings the best qualifications and experience to the debate. It is, therefore, important to hear his views, as articulated in many interventions he has made over the years.

In 2012, at the launch of Dr Ngozi Okonjo-Iweala's book *Reforming the Unreformable*, Chief Anyaoku argued that the over-concentration of power in the Federal Government was the driver of the inordinate struggle for power at the centre, which fuelled ethno-religious tensions. He called for a return to regionalisation and devolution of power to the regions.[45] In October 2015, as chairman of the Akintola Williams Distinguished Lecture Series, he argued that 'unless Nigeria goes back to regional government, it may be embarking on an endless, fruitless search for meaningful development.'[46] In 2017, both at the inauguration of the Ibadan School of Government and Public Policy and a public symposium to mark the 50th anniversary of the Bible Society of Nigeria, he urged Nigeria to adopt the current six geo-political zones as the country's new federating units, saying that the 36 states were not viable.[47] In 2021, as the special guest of honour at the Obafemi Awolowo Annual Lecture, he remarked that 'in constitutional governance, the model for Nigeria should be India, not the USA, with its immigrant population,' saying that 'in contrast, India is a country of a diverse population, whose component parts have lived in their separate areas for centuries.'[48]

More recently, in 2023, while delivering the Convocation Lecture of the Afe Babalola University, Ado Ekiti, Chief Anyaoku said Nigeria was undergoing an 'unprecedented level of divisiveness and a declining sense of national unity'[49] and called for a new constitution that would, 'in recognition of the crucial principle of subsidiarity in every successful federation, involve a devolution of powers from the central government to fewer and more viable federating units.'[50] In March 2024, at a national dialogue, Chief Anyaoku laid out two routes for restructuring Nigeria. One was to adopt the report of the 2014 National Conference; the other was a delegate option, not elected on a party basis for a fresh national dialogue.[51] In August 2024, Chief Anyaoku led a group called 'The Patriots' to meet President Tinubu at the State House, asking him to convene a National Constituent Assembly that would draft a new constitution for the country.[52] Then, in July 2025, the group, in partnership with the Nigerian Political Summit Group (NPSG), held a three-day conference in Abuja to discuss the political and constitutional future of Nigeria.[53]

Every rhetorician knows the Aristotelian modes of persuasion. To sound persuasive on any subject, the speaker must successfully appeal to authority or credibility (ethos), emotion or feeling (pathos), and logic or reason (logos). Chief Anyaoku ticks all the rhetorical boxes in his advocacy for the political restructuring of Nigeria. First, he is eminently qualified to speak on the subject. As the Commonwealth Secretary-General for ten years, and even before then, a high-ranking diplomat in the Commonwealth, he helped to steer many countries towards political settlements, including, most significantly, the end of apartheid in South Africa and the post-apartheid political and constitutional settlement. He knows from his extensive experience with Commonwealth countries that no country with the ethnic diversity and make-up of Nigeria has the kind of centralised political culture that Nigeria has.

In his remarks at the Obafemi Awolowo Annual Lecture, Chief Anyaoku said: 'After my over thirty-four years of close association with governance in the fifty-four diverse Commonwealth member states, I can say with reasonable confidence that from the experiences of other countries whose national attributes are comparable to Nigeria's, there is abundant evidence to show that a federal system based on more economically and socially viable federating units with a less dominant centre is what will restore Nigeria to the path of greater political stability and a more assured economic growth.'[54] It is hard to fault such a statement by someone who worked closely with ethnically diverse Commonwealth countries like India, Canada, and South Africa for more than ten years.

The logic and emotional appeal of Chief Anyaoku's advocacy is also unassailable. He described the current structure of 36 states and the Federal Capital Territory as too expensive, with huge recurrent expenditure and leaving only a meagre percentage for the badly needed capital development. Indeed, the structure also leaves virtually all the states overdependent on the Federal Government, unable to develop their own independent sources of revenue but, rather, supplementing their federal allocations with heavy borrowings to run their affairs. Chief Anyaoku is right in saying that the multiplicity of government administrative structures at the federal and state levels drains the country's limited resources and stifles its growth. Nigeria runs an expensive presidential system, with a behemothic presidency sheltered in opulence in Aso Rock and having more than 900 parastatals and agencies, many with overlapping functions, as well as a bicameral federal legislature with legislators whose salaries and operating expenses are among the highest in the world.[55]

Chief Anyaoku also rightly argues that Nigeria's history and pluralistic character call for truer federalism. Nigeria is a country consisting of nations and a political and governance structure that does not recognise that multi-nationality is bound to fail. Several decades earlier, in his famous book entitled *Path to Nigerian Freedom*, published in 1945, Chief Obafemi Awolowo argued that Nigeria should have a federal structure based on ethnic and linguistic affinities. Later, in 1968, he predicted in another book entitled *The People's Republic* that every multi-lingual or multi-national country 'must either have a federal constitution based on the principles which I have enunciated, or disintegrate, or be perennially afflicted with disharmony and instability.'[56] Awolowo said he came to this view after studying the constitutions of virtually all countries in the world and was convinced that a federal system based on ethnic and linguistic lines best suited Nigeria's diverse population.

Indeed, as Chief Awolowo and Chief Anyaoku posited, based on research and experiential evidence, there is virtually no other country with the same diverse nationalities as Nigeria that has a centralised political culture. For instance, India, Australia, New Zealand, and Canada do not have an excessive concentration of power at the centre. In 1956, India enacted the State Reorganisation Act, which reorganised India's 29 states along linguistic lines. Similarly, as part of its post-apartheid political settlement, South Africa created nine provinces based on ethnic and linguistic lines, and in 1997, the country abolished its Senate and replaced it with the National Council of Provinces (NCOP), which consists of representatives of the provinces, as the upper house above the National Assembly. In Canada, the provinces enjoy the fullest autonomy of nationhood within a federal state. The experiences of India, Canada and other ethnically diverse countries have shown that Nigeria will be stronger when its federating nations are strong, hence the need to return to regionalism.

Chief Anyaoku's views and this book's arguments are aligned on the need to wind up the current mostly unviable 36 states and return Nigeria to regional powerhouses. Autonomous and self-sustaining regional governments would engender regional economic development. Evidence from the pre-independence era and from the post-independence First Republic (1960 to 1966) shows that the three, and later four, regions were economically viable as competitive regionalism facilitated rapid development. In his book *Left Behind*, Professor Collier argues that regions often fall far behind in highly centralised countries and calls for the devolution of powers and resources to regions, which, through shared agency and rapid learning, have the capacity to become powerhouses.[57] The truth is that devolving power to regional governments is a key to driving up growth and productivity. In his first King's Speech, written by his government, Sir Keir Starmer, UK's new prime minister, said: 'My Government believes that greater devolution of decision-making is at the heart of a modern dynamic economy and is a key driver of economic growth.'[58] That is the view around the world: devolution of powers to regional and sub-regional entities is a driver of economic growth and prosperity. Thus, returning Nigeria to regionalism does not only have political benefits, but it also has economic advantages. And, as discussed next, it will also strengthen Nigeria's unity.

Separatist Agitations: Regionalism As an Antidote

There are regular drumbeats for secession in Nigeria, with separatist agitations by Yoruba, Igbo, and Niger Delta youths. The desire for self-determination is at the heart of all separatist agitations. According to Wolfgang Danspeckgruber, founder of the Liechtenstein Institute on Self-Determination at Princeton University, 'No other concept is as powerful, visceral, emotional, unruly, as steeped in creating aspiration and hopes as self-determination.'[59] The Unrepresented Nations and Peoples Organisation (UNPO) had only 15 members at its founding in 1991 but now has 43 members, all of which want to exercise the right to self-determination. Around the world, there have been active demands for self-determination, with groups seeking the right to rule over their own affairs. In September 2018, the Kurdish people in Iraq ignored international pressure and held a referendum on independence from Iraq. Similarly, in October 2021, Catalonia in Spain held an independence referendum in defiance of the ruling of Spain's Constitutional Court and opposition from both the Spanish government and the European Union. Quebec voted unsuccessfully for separation from Canada in 1995, and Scotland lost a referendum on independence from the UK in 2014. All of this shows that agitation for self-determination is a global phenomenon.

The right to self-determination has long been recognised as fundamental by the United Nations and in international law, so fundamental that it is regarded as a rule of *jus cogens*, a hard law from which there can be derogation. It is embodied in Article 1 of the Charter of the UN, affirmed by the International Court of Justice in, for example, the cases of Namibia, Western Sahara, and East Timor, and recognised by several Resolutions and Declarations of the UN General Assembly.[60] Crucially, international law imposes a duty on states to refrain from any forcible action calculated to deprive a people from exercising the right to self-determination. Some countries, such as the UK and Switzerland, respect this duty by allowing self-determination, including full independence, subject to a referendum; others, such as China and Spain, both with authoritarian histories, have anti-secession clauses in their constitution. Nigerian Constitution contains a similar clause, declaring Nigeria 'as one indivisible and indissoluble sovereign state' (section 2(1)).

The Harvard economist Alberto Alesina argues that 'If country size were determined by economic rationality or democratic preferences of national communities, the map of the world would look completely different.'[61] For instance, why are small entities like Timor-Leste (population: 1.3m), Montenegro (629,000), and the Pacific Island of Nauru (11,359) independent states while the Kurds (45m) or the Catalan (7.5m) are denied statehood? The answer lies in how low or high the strategic stakes are.[62] In other words, if a region is strategically important within a country, its demand for independence would be resisted. By that logic, Iraq will not let the Kurds go, as it won't be the same without them. Equally, Spain won't release Catalonia, its richest region.

The same strategic calculations are at work in Nigeria. By their sizes and resources, the Yoruba (approximately 40m), the Igbo (34m), and the Ijaw (14m) are viable enough to be independent countries, not to mention the Hausa/Fulani (approximately 50m). But the stakes are too high for Nigeria. The British refused to support the break-up of Nigeria during the civil war because it saw the value of a big, regional power in West Africa, which is borne out by the fact that Nigeria accounts for about 60 per cent of the population ECOWAS (Economic Community of West African States) and 78 per cent of its GDP. Nigerian political leaders, despite pandering to ethnic, regional, and religious interests, often stress the benefits of keeping Nigeria as one, given its size, economic importance, and regional strategic relevance.

But if Nigeria is too important to disintegrate, why is its diversity not managed in such a way as to engender internal cohesion and inter-ethnic cooperation and harmony? Why should the conditions exist that fuel separatist or secessionist agitations? If the Igbo cannot produce a president because the Yoruba and Hausa/Fulani can easily gang up against them, would they have faith in Nigeria? Chinua Achebe said that 'Nigerians will probably achieve consensus on no other matter than their common resentment of the Igbo.'[63] But how can that seeming national resentment of the Igbo engender national unity? Furthermore, if power is so concentrated at the centre such that the sub-national units cannot deploy their own resources and develop at their own pace, would they be happy in Nigeria?

For instance, one of the initial key drivers of the agitation for Scotland's independence from Britain was that, for many years, particularly in the 1980s and 1990s, regardless of how Scotland voted, the Conservative Party under Margaret Thatcher, whose values the Scots detested, always formed the government in Westminster mainly with the English votes, without winning a single seat in Scotland.[64] In other words, the Scottish votes did not count. This was considered an affront to Scottish sensibilities and left many Scots feeling alienated.[65] Such a situation would exist in Nigeria if one or two ethnic groups were so dominant that they could deny others the presidency, making their votes irrelevant in choosing Nigeria's president. It is utterly naïve to expect that, in a multi-ethnic state, any ethnic group would subordinate its core identity to the 'national' identity without equity, justice, and fairness.

Yet, secession is not the solution. Rather, the solution is to return to regionalism and create regional powerhouses. Francis Ellah, who helped to set up the Biafran mission in London and served Biafra in several capacities during the civil war, reportedly said that the war would probably have been avoided or ended sooner if the two protagonists, Gowon and Ojukwu, had turned Nigeria into a confederation, as agreed in the Aburi Accord. According to him, instead of 'insisting that Biafran sovereignty was not negotiable, Ojukwu should have worked towards achieving a confederation,' adding that 'this country would have been much better if we had a confederation of four to six states.'[66]

A similar argument applies today. What Nigeria's various ethnic nationalities need is not secession but strong and powerful regional governments with a significant degree of political and economic autonomy within a federal structure. Considerable self-government at the regional level is needed to enable each region to mobilise its resources and develop at its pace. That way, with each government enjoying significant self-rule, separatist or secessionist agitations in Nigeria might just end or be reduced to non-threatening fringes.

The Mismatch of Power and Identity in Nigeria

Political stability is a critical precondition for economic and social progress in any country. But at the heart of political stability is the relationship between power and identity. A mismatch of power and identity in any country would severely undermine its stability and progress. Power refers to the ability of a government to direct the internal affairs of the state, such as the ability to raise and collect taxes, maintain law and order, and ensure national harmony and social cohesion. Identity is about group characteristics that people attach to themselves, how people define themselves culturally, historically, linguistically, etc, in relation to others. Here is a simple test. If push comes to shove and people must choose, which takes precedence for them: their ethnic identity or their national identity? The evidence from surveys in the UK and in Nigeria, shown earlier, is that the majority will choose their ethnic identity over their national identity, that is, if they must choose only one of the two.

In an interview with the Spectator magazine in December 2024, Kemi Badenoch, the new leader of the UK Conservative Party, who is of Nigerian parentage, said: 'I find it interesting that everybody defines me as being

Nigerian. I identify less with the country than with the specific ethnicity (Yoruba).'[67] The statement provoked strident criticisms from some Nigerians[68], including the country's vice president, Kashim Shettima, who suggested Badenoch could 'remove the Kemi from her name' if she was not proud of her 'nation of origin'[69]. Yet, there are many in Nigeria who will say they identify with Yoruba, Igbo, Hausa, Fulani, Ijaw or any other ethnic group more than with Nigeria. That's the reality of ethnic nationalism in Nigeria, proof that Nigeria is not (yet) a true nation-state.

Given the above, power and identity are deemed to be misaligned if power lies at the centre and identities lie at the subnational levels. Several studies have established that when there is such a mismatch, it is difficult to turn power into authority. As Professor Collier of Oxford University put it in a course titled *From Poverty to Prosperity*, 'authority is where people choose to obey without a lot of effort, where compliance becomes semi-automatic.'[70] But where power is concentrated at the centre while identities remain at the subnational levels, citizens may not regard the state as legitimate and may not willingly comply with it. This often manifests in the rise of insurgencies and other organised non-state violence at the subnational levels and the inability of the central government to tackle them.

To be sure, there is a mismatch of power and identities in Nigeria, with power so hugely concentrated at the centre. Inevitably, with the mismatch of power and identities comes the failure of the state to turn power into authority. The Nigerian state simply cannot generate voluntary compliance with its authority, whether in terms of tax collection or maintenance of law and order. As a result, the state often resorts to repression to force compliance. For instance, in 2017, the federal government used military force under the so-called *Operation Python Dance* to suppress militant agitations by the Indigenous People of Biafra (IPOB). Indeed, successive Nigerian governments have used repression to force compliance with authority. Often, people pushed back, resulting in open conflict and the deaths of thousands. In other instances, the state simply gives up, thus creating a state of anarchy, such as with the rise of inter-ethnic conflicts and the incessant violent clashes between herders and farmers. Without voluntary or semi-automatic compliance with authority, no state can achieve stability and progress. However, without the alignment of power and identities, such voluntary compliance won't exist. The result will be either repression, open conflict, or both.

But how can power and identity be aligned? There are two approaches. One is to move the structure of identities towards the structure of power. This means building a shared national identity, where the people, regardless of their ethnic identities, define themselves primarily in terms of a common identity. However, this approach usually only succeeds when adopted at the birth of a multi-ethnic nation rather than when separate identities are fully entrenched. Julius Nyerere of Tanzania and Lee Kuan Yew of Singapore followed this route in meshing together their ethnically diverse countries. Tanzania was a medley of distinct tribes arbitrarily put together by the colonialists. But as the founding native president, Nyerere set out to create a common national identity. He introduced a common national language, Swahili; created a national curriculum that taught a common narrative history; changed the capital from Dar es Salam to

Dodoma to bring it to the middle of the country; and decreed that civil servants must not work in their ethnic areas. Lee Kuan Yew did similar things in Singapore, a country that was, at its creation, blighted by racial, religious, and language divisions. The result is that Tanzania and Singapore have a sense of common national identities and are relatively peaceful, stable countries devoid of malign ethnic tensions.

By contrast, neither the British nor their Nigerian successors created a sense of shared national identity for Nigeria. At independence in 1960, Nigeria's founding fathers owed primary allegiance to their ethnic groups. Nigeria later tried to do some of what Nyerere did to promote national unity. For instance, it introduced the National Youth Service Corps, under which tertiary education graduates are required to serve for one year outside of their ethnic areas; it also moved its capital from Lagos to Abuja to locate it in the middle of the country. But none of these has worked. Nigeria is as ethnically divided today as it was in 1960. It is hard to see a common symbol that unites the disparate ethnic groups, all of which see their coexistence in terms of zero-sum struggles for domination rather than cooperation.

But, in truth, the Tanzanian and Singaporean examples offer little help. First, Tanzania and Singapore were, at independence, small countries. Tanzania, a collection of small kingdoms, was, at its independence in 1961, about 8 million, while Singapore had a population of 1 million at its independence from Britain in 1963. By contrast, Nigeria's population was 45 million at its independence in 1960, with large, pre-existing ancient kingdoms. Second, Nigeria did not have independence-era leaders of the kinds of Nyerere and Lee Kuan Yew with a post-independence national vision that resonated across ethnic and religious divisions. Third, Nyerere and Kuan Yew forged common identities with the use of force; they operated a repressive one-party state. This would have been impossible in Nigeria.

Put simply, it is not possible in all multinational states to move the structure of identities towards the structure of power, whereby ethnic identities are subsumed under the national identity. For instance, as noted earlier in this chapter, despite being forged together as a union centuries ago, Britain's shared identity is still weaker than the underlying ethnic identities. There is no British national football or rugby team but English, Scottish and Welsh teams. A lawyer or a medical doctor who qualifies in England must re-qualify in Scotland to practise there. The education, legal, and social systems in Scotland are starkly different from those in England and Wales. The same situation exists in Canada, where its ethnically based provinces have unique identities and separate education, legal and social systems. Thus, not every multinational country can build a shared identity by moving the structure of identities towards the structure of power, which requires a problematic unitary system. That necessitates the second route to internal cohesion.

The second approach to aligning power and identities is to move the structure of power towards the structure of identities. Basically, this means decentralisation or devolution of power. Radical decentralisation, with significant autonomy and power devolved to regional governments, is the route followed by developed countries, such as Switzerland, Belgium, and Canada, and by countless other multi-ethnic countries. This approach has guaranteed peace, stability and progress worldwide, and it is the approach Nigeria must adopt to align power and identities and ensure that the central government has legitimacy in the eyes of the people.

A Condition for Nation-Building: Nigerians Must Own Nigeria

The political restructuring of Nigeria must be underpinned by three things: First, ownership; second, decentralisation; and third, regionalism. The last two are commonly understood and have been discussed earlier in this chapter. Decentralisation has been, as John Naisbitts put it in his book *Megatrends*, the 'revolutionary global trend'[71] since the 1980s. So, to reiterate, the political restructuring of Nigeria must involve radical decentralisation of powers. A meaningful restructuring must also result in regionalism. Where decentralisation and devolution of powers have been successful, it is because they have been linked to regional development. Nigeria's federal government should do significantly less than it is currently doing and control a significantly smaller share of the national resources than it currently does. More responsibilities and resources should be devolved to regional governments.

But what about ownership? The idea here is that the people of Nigeria, whose ancestors had no say in Britain's cobbling together of the country, should now have a say about the country's future. David Pilling, the Africa Editor of the Financial Times, was right when he said that 'Africa's so-called tribes are better seen as mini-nations, with mutually unintelligible language as distinct as French,

English and German'.[72] By that logic, the Yoruba could as well be the English, the Hausa/Fulani, the Germans, and the Igbo, the French, just to mention Nigeria's three main ethnic nations. If the French, the English, and the Germans could not be in a loose union together, let alone be in one country, without a negotiated order, why would Nigeria's diverse ethnic nationalities be in the same country without a negotiated political pact?

As stated earlier, Nigeria did not emerge through internal conquest or by agreement; rather, it was imposed externally. Nigerian ethnic nationalities have lived together in mutual distrust since they were forced into a marriage of convenience. The only way they can live peaceably together in the imperfect union called Nigeria is to perfect the flawed union through a negotiated political settlement sealed by a referendum. This means that all the ethnic nationalities must come together, with other critical stakeholders, to negotiate, in good faith, the terms of their co-existence in Nigeria. The terms of the settlement should be legitimised through a referendum and translated into a People's Constitution. Only the recreation of Nigeria in that way will give Nigerians ownership of the country.

The legal theorist HLA Hart talks about the 'internal point of view,' which makes people feel a sense of legitimacy about an institution. Most Nigerians don't currently feel that way about Nigeria. There is a widespread sense of unfairness, injustice, and inequity. Only with the recreation of Nigeria through a negotiated settlement, a referendum and a new constitution can Nigerians have a true sense of ownership of Nigeria. The 1960 Independence Constitution and the 1963 Republican Constitution both included provisions for referenda, but the military removed a provision for referenda from the constitutions they created and imposed on Nigeria. The current constitution should be amended to allow for referenda so that a negotiated political and constitutional settlement and a new constitution can be subjected to a national referendum to give Nigerians ownership of the country's future.

Responding to Critics of Restructuring

Finally, to end this chapter, it is important to address the opposition to restructuring. Those opposed to the political restructuring of Nigeria have two main arguments. First, some say that it is not a system or a structure that matters but the people operating the system. In other words, it is not Nigeria that needs to be restructured but the *minds* of Nigerians, both leaders and citizens alike. To those people, the problem is cultural, not structural. Second, some opponents of restructuring taunt proponents of the idea with the question: 'What do they mean by restructuring?' But these contrary views are mischievous and misguided, as discussed below.

Culture versus structure

Those who argue that what needs to be restructured is not Nigeria, but the minds of Nigerians, attempt to shift the focus away from structure to culture. They say the type of political system or constitution that Nigeria operates doesn't matter; rather, what matters is the attitude of the operators of the system or the constitution.[73]   Another version of this argument posits that Nigeria's problems are artificially contrived; they are not structural; therefore, there is nothing to restructure. In his speech to mark Nigeria's 60th independence anniversary, the theme of which was *Togetherness*, the late President Buhari said: 'An underlying cause of most of the problems we have faced as a nation is our consistent harping on artificially contrived fault-lines that we have harboured and allowed unnecessarily to fester.'[74] On that, as discussed throughout this chapter and the preceding one, the simple response is that Nigeria's problems are structural, not artificial.

To be sure, culture matters, and patriotic leadership matters too. For instance, President Buhari provided appalling leadership, demonstrating unbelievable levels of nepotism, tribalism, and religious bigotry.[75] He appointed fourteen of the country's seventeen security chiefs from just one section of the country and gave over 67 per cent of his top appointments to Muslims.[76] This was certainly a leadership problem, but it arose because Nigeria's constitutional structure did not restrain him. Societies that have strong institutions and norms can constrain a bad leader. As discussed in more detail in Chapter 3, the right institutions, the right governance structure, and the right political system are necessary to shape behaviours and drive political, economic, and social progress.

Furthermore, those who blame culture for everything cannot explain why the same Nigerians who would not respect traffic rules in Lagos obey traffic rules in London or in New York. Why do the same Nigerians who behave rowdily at Nigerian airports act orderly at Heathrow Airport in London or JF Kennedy International Airport in New

York? The answer is that they are constrained by the institutions or systems in the UK or the US, whereas there are no institutional incentives for them to behave properly at home. In other words, their culture is amenable to institutional or structural constraints shaped by the right incentives.

It is trite to say that human beings are the same everywhere. However, institutions differ, and good institutions can make a huge difference in shaping how people behave. For instance, determined politicians can attempt to undermine democracy and good governance, but strong institutions of checks and balances, such as an independent judiciary, can act as guardrails, constraining the bad behaviour of those in power. Furthermore, public officers who want to do the right thing are better incentivised when they can cite the constitution, the law or other regulatory requirement to back their action, rather than merely relying on moral arguments. In that sense, strong institutions can embolden and enable good people.

Steven Levitt and Stephen Dubner, authors of the fascinating book entitled *Freakonomics*, gave probably the best insights on the power of incentives. They said: 'Incentives are the cornerstones of modern life – and understanding them is the key to solving just about any riddle,' adding: 'An incentive is a bullet, a lever, a key, an often-tiny object with astonishing power to change a situation.'[77] The idea is that every individual ultimately responds to incentives; thus, changing the incentives that people face would change their behaviour. But the most powerful incentives that can shape human behaviour and trigger cultural change are institutions, systems, or structures.

In their best-selling book, *Why Nations Fail*, Daron Acemoglu and James Robinson, both economics Nobel laureates, disagreed with the culture hypothesis. They argued that while culture, such as social norms, matters, it is the nature of a country's political and economic institutions that makes the difference between success and failure: 'As institutions influence behaviour and incentives in real life, they forge the success or failure of nations.'[78] They studied several countries with the similar characteristics, such as the same geographical area or same cultural attributes, and found that those with the right political and economic institutions were more successful, while those without such institutions were less successful. Simply put, countries become more prosperous or less prosperous because of the different political and economic institutional choices they make. The authors distinguished between two types of institutions: inclusive and extractive. Inclusive political institutions decentralise political governance; they devolve power, create effective checks and balances and embed accountability in the exercise of centralised power. By contrast, extractive institutions concentrate power in the hands of a narrow elite and place few constraints on the exercise of executive power.

So, both culture and structure matter. However, structure creates the framework within which culture exists and operates. Therefore, the right institutional structure, underpinned by the right values and norms, can both constrain and incentivise human behaviour and shape culture. However, Nigeria's current political and governance structure incentivises the wrong culture and the wrong behaviour. It is wrong to blame the operators of a flawed system when they are simply exploiting the perverse incentives that the system itself creates. Nigeria is an extractive state, where political and economic powers are concentrated and centralised, benefitting few at the expense of many. Thus, Nigeria must be restructured to create the right institutional incentives for its unity, stability, and progress.

What restructuring really means

In his eight years in power, President Buhari scoffed at the idea of restructuring Nigeria. While his predecessors set up political and constitutional conferences, even though they didn't implement their recommendations, Buhari did not even attempt to convene any political or constitutional convention or consider the reports of the previous conferences. Instead, he was derogatory about restructuring and those advocating it, describing such advocates as 'ignorant and naïve.'[79] In one TV interview, he said: 'Those who talk of restructuring, I want them to define what they mean,' adding: 'If you ask many Nigerians what they are going to restructure, you will find that they have nothing to talk about.'[80] And speaking in France in November 2018, Buhari said: 'There are too many people talking lazily about restructuring in Nigeria; they couldn't define what they meant.'[81]

But those questioning what restructuring means are being mischievous because the term defines itself. Restructuring simply means that an entity's structure is flawed and that it needs to be restructured. Many countries in the world have reformed their governance systems to make them fit for purpose. For instance, in 2002, France reduced its presidential term from seven years to five years because 'seven years is too long' and 'five years is more modern.'[82] Later, in 2008, the French constitution was amended to impose a two-term limit on the president. Those are political restructurings. In the UK, before 1997, powers were centralised in Westminster. However, devolved governments were later established in Scotland, Wales, and Northern Ireland, and powerful mayoralties were created in the English regions. And since then, every successive UK government has extended the devolution of powers from the centre. For instance, in his first King's Speech as prime minister, Sir Keir Starmer introduced the English Devolution Bill to give new powers to Metro Mayors and combined authorities in the regions.[83] He also established a new Council of the Nations and Regions[84] so that the prime minister, heads of devolved governments, and mayors of the regional combined local authorities could collaborate with each other. These are all examples of restructurings, and other examples abound worldwide.

Indeed, Nigeria itself is not a stranger to political restructuring. Throughout its history, it has had *restructurings*, some good, some bad. In 1951, the British introduced the Macpherson Unitary Constitution, which overcentralised powers. However, the constitution was so unpopular that the colonial authority abrogated it three years later and replaced it in 1954 with the Lyttleton Federal Constitution, which established three autonomous regions. The 1960 Independence Constitution mirrored the Lyttleton Constitution and was based on a Federation of three regions, 'with each region self-governing in its own concerns',[85] as Iain Macleod, Britain's Secretary of State for the Colonies, put it. Similarly, the 1963 Republican Constitution was based on a Federation of autonomous regions, each controlling huge resources and self-governing in its own concerns. Nigeria's founding fathers and leaders of Nigeria's ethnic groups led those pre-independence and immediate post-independence restructurings. The complex but inclusive negotiations culminated in great political and constitutional settlements that reconciled various interests and defined the relationships between the regions and the federal entity in the true spirit of federalism.

However, the military introduced bad *restructurings*. From 1966 to 1999, the military orchestrated *political restructurings* in Nigeria. First, General Johnson Aguiyi-Ironsi imposed a unitary system following the January 1966 coup. Then, in 1967, at the start of the civil war, General Yakubu Gowon introduced the 12-state structure, more an attempt to decapitate the Eastern Region, led by Ojukwu, and render it landlocked than anything else.[86] The Murtala Muhammed/Olusegun Obasanjo regime added seven states to bring the number up to 19 in 1976; the Babangida regime raised the number of states to 30 in 1991; and the Abacha regime created additional six states in 1996 to raise the number to the current 36 states.

In his speech in May 1967, Gowon said he split Nigeria into 12 states from four regions 'as a basis for stability to remove the fear of domination.'[87] But splintering Nigeria into multiple states – from 12 states to the current 36 states – has not united Nigeria, made it stable, or stopped the fear of domination. The truth is that deep concerns about structural imbalance remain, and Nigeria is more disunited and more unstable today than it was before 1966, when it had four regions. Furthermore, instead of the strong and economically viable regions of the pre-1966 era, Nigeria now has weak state governments that are mere appendages of an over-powerful Federal Government, with all the states borrowing heavily to run themselves.

But good restructuring is possible in Nigeria. First, there is already a template for a nation-transforming restructuring. The template is the current six geo-political zones. Today, all federal political offices and appointments are based on the six geopolitical zones, namely: North-West, North-East, North-Central, South-West, South-East, and South-South. Indeed, section 5(1) of the Federal Competition and Consumer Protection Act 2018 explicitly states: 'All Board Members … shall be appointed … from the six geopolitical zones of Nigeria.' Furthermore, the National Assembly has legitimised the six geopolitical zones by creating regional development commissions that mirror them. However, while acts of parliament recognise the geopolitical zones, the Constitution itself does not. In other words, the six geopolitical zones do not exist constitutionally, but via statutes. That is anomalous, as statutes usually derive their primary authority from a constitution.

Regional commissions are not substitutes for regional governments

Since then-President Obasanjo's government established the Niger Delta Development Commission in 2000, regional 'development' commissions have proliferated in Nigeria, with each of the country's six geopolitical zones having its own. In 2020, then-President Buhari signed the bill creating the North-East Development Commission, NEDC, into law. His successor, President Tinubu, assented to the bill establishing the North-West Development Commission and the South-East Development Commission in July 2024. As of the time of writing, the bill creating the North-Central Development Commission and the bill establishing the South-West Development Commission are awaiting the president's signature.

Interestingly, legislators from the South-South geopolitical zone sponsored a bill to establish the South-South Development Commission (SSDC), despite the existence of the Niger Delta Development Commission.[88] One of the bill's sponsors, Senator Seriake Dickson, a former governor of Bayelsa State, argued that 'NDDC is a resource-based commission, which includes all oil-producing states in the South-South, South-East and South-West geopolitical zones, unlike the zonal-based commissions which the proposed South-South Commission, falls under.'[89] In other words, the South-South federal legislators want the zone to have its own 'development' commission like other geopolitical zones. However, given that the Niger Delta is another name for the South-South and considering that most of the oil-producing states are in the South-South, it would be hard to justify having the NDDC and the SSDC, if created, existing side by side with each other, as both will largely have overlapping roles and memberships.

But why are regional 'development' commissions created in Nigeria? The simple reason is that the federal lawmakers and the presidents who created the commissions believe they are game-changing and would radically transform regional development in Nigeria. Indeed, the establishment of the regional 'development' commissions is a tacit recognition of the imperative of regionalism in Nigeria, a recognition that the six geopolitical zones would be better developed if the states within those regions were encouraged to work more closely together and if funds allocated to the regions by the Federal Government and foreign donors were managed and used by a federal agency to develop the regions. As a result, all the regional 'development' commissions have the same functions. For instance, under the acts establishing the commissions, each is required to 'conceive, conceptualise, plan and implement projects and programmes for the sustainable development' of its region and to 'identify factors inhibiting the development' of its region 'and assist the member-states in the formulation and implementation of policies to ensure a sound and efficient management of the resources' of that region.

However, while, at face value, the commissions are about regional development, being top-down federal agencies, they are not credible, efficient and effective ways of promoting regional development. All over the world, the tried-and-tested way of promoting regional development is to devolve powers to the regions through democratic, transparent and accountable regional governments. The idea that a federal agency can replace a regional government is a perversion of true regionalism, which is about regional autonomy. Indeed, evidence from the long-existing regional 'development' commissions shows that they are mere extractive institutions created to serve the interests of a small elite and have done little to advance regional development in Nigeria; rather, they are mired by massive corruption.

In his 2025 budget proposals, President Tinubu, who seemed to be using regional development commissions as a substitute for proper restructuring based on regionalism, allocated huge sums to the regional development commissions. The proposed allocations were as follows: ₦290.99 billion for the North-East Development Commission; ₦341.27 billion for the South-East Development Commission; ₦498.40 billion for the South-West Development Commission; ₦585.93 billion for the North-West Development Commission; and ₦776.53 billion for the Niger Delta Development Commission. In an incisive article, the columnist and policy analyst Waziri Adio rightly noted: 'Beyond being conduits for elite settlement, these commissions have done little to uplift the material conditions of the people in their respective zones.'[90] Indeed, as pointed out earlier, the regional development commissions have failed abysmally to deliver any tangible development for their individual regions.

Take the Niger Delta Development Commission, which was established in 2000 and is believed to have received nearly ₦6trillion between 2000 and 2021.[91] The NDDC says on its website that its mission is 'to facilitate the rapid and sustainable development of the Niger Delta into a region that is economically prosperous, socially stable, ecologically regenerative and politically peaceful.' Yet, the NDDC did not remotely achieve any of those goals 24 years after its creation. In 2019, President Buhari instituted a forensic audit of the NDDC 'to get to the root of the problem undermining the development of the Niger-Delta region.'[92] The audit report, submitted in September 2021, found, among other things, that more than 13,000 projects by the NDDC were either abandoned or incomplete.[93] In 2022, then-EFCC chairman Abdulrasheed Bawa said that 'the statistics of NDDC abandoned projects in the region is very alarming,' adding that 'some NDDC staff identified to have mismanaged and embezzled government resources have been prosecuted, convicted and proceeds of crime forfeited.'[94] Today, the NDDC represents a classic case of how so-called regional 'development' commissions can become a drainpipe on public funds.

Beyond corruption, there is also institutional failure. The North-East Development Commission, NEDC, established in 2020, is a perfect example of that. According to a World Bank report published in 2022, there was 'a major gap in terms of the availability of necessary quality systems and processes that would enable the NEDC to achieve its statutory mandate.'[95] The report added that the NEDC was not 'a strong and functioning body' and faced many 'areas of capacity shortfall that are currently bearing on it', in addition to 'weak bottom-up accountability and transparency.'[96] In other words, NEDC was not institutionally, strategically and functionally capable of advancing genuine development of the North-East region.

So, regional 'development' commissions have failed in Nigeria. At the heart of the problem is the fact that regional 'development' commissions, which are federal government agencies, lack the transparency, accountability and democratic element to genuinely advance regional development. Such a top-down intervention cannot serve the purpose of a full-fledged regional government with political legitimacy and holistic economic and developmental agendas. In October 2024, President Tinubu abolished the Ministry of Niger Delta Affairs and replaced it with the

Ministry of Regional Development. According to the presidency, the new ministry would 'supervise' all the regional 'development' commissions, not just the NDDC.[97] But the Niger Delta Development Commission was supposedly supervised by the Ministry of Niger Delta Affairs, while the North-East Development Commission was under the supervision of the Ministry of Humanitarian Affairs and Poverty Alleviation. Yet, that did not stop the NDDC and the NEDC from being corrupt or underperforming.

The truth, which is worth repeating, is that a federal agency or ministry purportedly advancing regional development is a poor substitute for a regional government that exists primarily for that purpose. Of course, the Federal Government should have a ministry, a commission or an agency to ensure collaboration between the centre and the regional governments. For instance, the UK government established a Council of the Nations and Regions 'to renew opportunities for the Prime Minister, heads of devolved governments and mayors of combined authorities to collaborate with each other.'[98] However, the council does not replace the governments of the nations and the regions; it merely ensures collaboration between them and the centre.

Therefore, the way forward is a new constitution that recognises the six geopolitical zones as Nigeria's federating units and that turns them into regional governments. As stated earlier, the six geopolitical zones are already used to allocate federal political offices and appointments and to promote regional economic development, albeit unsuccessfully. Thus, it should not be impossible, as part of the political restructuring of Nigeria, to constitute them into regional governments. There have been suggestions that the geopolitical zones should be increased to between eight and ten. For instance, a prominent traditional ruler, the Asaba of Asaba, proposed dividing Nigeria into ten regions.[99] Eight or even ten regions are reasonable. Significant powers, resources, and responsibilities, including policing, should be devolved to the regions, which should have their own constitutions and be able to organise themselves administratively to achieve economies of scale, prioritising their internal security, economic growth, and the prosperity of their people. Nigeria's future lies in having regional powerhouses, not an overpowerful centre and vassal states.

***

In sum, this chapter responds to the challenges that the preceding one posed, namely, how to address the problems of Nigeria's birth defects and deeply flawed political and governance structures, which are the root causes of the deep-seated tensions in the country. It discusses those challenges and their manifestations, ranging from Nigeria's lack of nationhood to the mismanagement of the country's diversity, from separatist agitations to the mismatch of power and identities, which weakens the authority of the state. To all these challenges, the chapter argues strongly for the political restructuring of Nigeria, underpinned by the three goals of decentralisation and devolution of power, return to regionalism, and ownership of Nigeria's future by Nigerians through a referendum. The next chapter takes the discussion further on a more practical level of what a political restructuring should entail, that is, what its essential elements should be.

3

The Imperative for a New Political and Constitutional Settlement

The focus of Chapter 2 was on the *why* of restructuring, that is, why there is a need for political restructuring in Nigeria. This chapter, however, focuses on the *what* and the *how*, that is, what to restructure and how to do it. The subjects are wide-ranging, but the overarching message is that Nigeria needs a new political and constitutional settlement. The starting point, therefore, is to explain what a political and constitutional settlement means.

What Is a Political and Constitutional Settlement?

There are those who scoff at politics and think that every discussion should focus on the economy. For instance, a prominent business newspaper editorialised that Nigeria needed economic restructuring, not political restructuring.[1] A former vice president, Yemi Osinbajo, made the same point, saying 'Nigeria needs economic diversification, not political restructuring'.[2] But politics and political institutions matter. First, political institutions determine how politics works: what kind of constitution a country has, what form of democracy and party system a country operates, what system or form of government a country has, and whether there are genuine checks and balances in the governance of a country, and whether political power is centralised or distributed in society. The character of a state's political institutions shapes the democratic character and the efficiency of governance.[3]

Second, as the economics Nobel laureates Daron Acemoglu and James Robinson make clear in *Why Nations Fail*, it is the political process that determines the economic institutions a country will have.[4] For instance, politics determines who gains power, and who gains power shapes the economy. If a country elected a socialist president, it would have a socialist economy; if it elected a market-oriented president, it would have a market-oriented economy. Douglass North, another economics Nobel laureate, also strongly linked institutions and economic performance in his book *Institutions, Institutional Change and Economic Performance*.[5] Indeed, economic performance and political governance are inextricably linked. If a political process facilitates the emergence of corrupt politicians who will abuse their powers and pursue their own agendas at the expense of the common good and national welfare, the economy will suffer, undermined by corruption, patronage politics and abuse of power.

Furthermore, the economy and business respond to external stimuli, and one of the most potent is how politics and institutions work and the incentives they create. It is not for no reason that 19th-century economists such as Adam Smith, David Hume and John Stuart Mill were called political economists, not just economists. This is because they were interested in the interactions between economics and politics, that is, how politics affected the economy and how the economy affected politics. Put simply, they were concerned with how political, economic and institutional factors interact to shape how a country is managed or governed. As Will Hutton argues in *The State We're In,* 'the attempt to isolate economics from other disciplines – notably politics, history, philosophy, finance, constitutional theory and sociology – has fatally disabled its power to explain what is happening in the world.'[6] So, politics and political institutions matter. Political settlements are the preconditions for politics; they also influence institutions' form, nature, and performance. But political and constitutional settlements must flow from negotiation, consensus, and agreement if they are to succeed and endure.

However, since the collapse of the *First Republic,* Nigeria has not had a political settlement. There has never been a negotiated political arrangement about how the people of Nigeria should live peaceably together, how power should be organised and exercised to generate political stability, and how the institutions and the economy can work harmoniously to promote sustainable growth and development. The immediate post-independence political settlement, negotiated by Nigeria's independence-era leaders and which resulted in the 1963 Republican constitution, collapsed within three years following the 1966 military coup that eventually led to the civil war. Nigeria won the war; it defeated the Biafran rebels. But winning a civil war is one thing; winning peace is another. However, although Nigeria won the civil war, it did not win the peace through a post-war negotiated political settlement. Hence, over fifty years after the civil war ended in 1970, there are still secessionist and separatist agitations.

There is a body of scholarship that puts political settlements at the heart of development. One study by the then UK Department for International Development (DFID) said: '... the political settlement is central to all development'[7], adding that 'political settlements explain the difference in performance between countries with apparently similar endowments or disadvantages.'[8] In other words, political settlements are central to explaining the degree of economic and political stability and institutional performance in a country. Indeed, in many countries, political stability, a precondition of economic progress, was only achieved after a negotiated political settlement. Such countries include South Africa, which, after the collapse of apartheid, negotiated a political settlement that produced a constitution universally praised for devolving significant powers to the provinces, guaranteeing individual rights, and creating and strengthening critical state institutions. After decades of conflicts, the peace in Northern Ireland is also due to a negotiated political settlement. The truth is political settlements tend to remove the sources of internal tension and, thus, structural obstacles to progress. Nigeria needs and must have a political and constitutional settlement that will guarantee its unity, stability and progress, at the heart of which must be true federalism and a pluralistic political system.

Political and Economic Imperatives of True Federalism

According to the *Encyclopaedia Britannica*, a true federal system must have the following characteristics: non-centralisation, local autonomy and elements that promote common nationality.[9] Nigeria's federalism fails the three tests. In their book *Nigeria: What Everyone Needs To Know*, John Campbell and Matthew Page state: 'Nigeria's federalism is quite flawed and aspirational than real in many areas.'[10] They add that 'power flows from the top down, not from the bottom up'[11] and that 'the Nigerian president is freer of constraints than any American president could ever be.'[12] What they are saying, which is true, is that there is overconcentration and over-centralisation of power in Nigeria. The Nigerian president is extremely powerful, as the veteran journalist Eric Teniola brilliantly explained in a multi-part article titled 'The supreme powers of the President'.[13]

In his book, *Reclaiming the Jewel of Africa*, Dr Olusegun Aganga, a minister under President Goodluck Jonathan's administration, said President Jonathan once remarked that 'the Nigerian president was invested with so much power that it was best to check oneself in the exercise of those powers.'[14] Aganga adds: 'The Nigerian presidential constitution vests so much power in the president that only conscious and conscionable exercise of these powers can save the holder of the exalted office from themselves.'[15] The implication is that there are no real checks on presidential power in Nigeria. The political system allows a determined president to do what he will without let or hindrance.

For instance, the Nigerian president can declare a state of emergency in any state and remove its democratically elected governor and house of assembly members from office. In 2004, President Obasanjo used a state of emergency to remove Governor Joshua Dariye of Plateau State from office, and in 2006, invoked a state of emergency to remove Governor Ayo Fayose of Ekiti State from office. Chief Rotimi Williams, who chaired the committee that drafted the 1979 Constitution, from which the current 1999 one was derived, described Obasanjo's decisions as 'illegal and unconstitutional', saying: 'There is no provision contained in any part of our Constitution which confers such a power on the President. It is a contradiction of all known principles of true federation operating in a democratic society.'[16] Yet, that did not stop President Tinubu from proclaiming a state of emergency to remove Governor Siminalayi Fubara of Rivers State, his deputy, and members of the House of Assembly from office. In his reaction, the Nobel laureate Wole Soyinka said the president's decision was 'against the federal spirit of association.' He added: 'The government is over-centralised. The constitution has put too much power in the hands of the president. That's against the federal imperative.'[17]

In 2024, President Tinubu got a compliant National Assembly to change the Nigerian national anthem back to the one bequeathed to the country by the colonial rulers and did so within seven days without consulting Nigerians.[18] That such a fundamental decision could be taken without consultation by a president who won just 36.6 per cent of the popular vote shows how powerful the Nigerian president is. The truth is, Nigeria's constitution overcentralises powers and invests excessive and unconstrained powers in the president, which undermines the true meaning of federalism.

But beyond creating an overpowerful president, the Nigerian constitution concentrates so much power at the centre at the expense of the subnational units. For instance, the Exclusive Legislative List in the constitution contains 67 items, including '(a)ny matter incidental or supplementary to any matter mentioned elsewhere in the list' (Schedule 2). Then, there is the Concurrent Legislative List, which contains items on which both the federal and state governments can legislate. However, where any state law clashes with a federal law on any item on the Concurrent List, the federal law prevails. Thus, taken together, the Exclusive List and the Concurrent List give the federal government the power to do virtually everything. Every nation needs a sufficiently centralising system to maintain order and coordinate the economy, but Nigeria overconcentrates and over-centralises power in a way that undermines true federalism.

In addition to the over-centralisation of power and the lack of local autonomy, Nigeria's 'federalism' lacks strong elements that promote common nationality. Nothing binds together the country's strongly divergent ethnic nationalities. For instance, Nigeria's federal capital was moved from Lagos to Abuja in the middle of the country, purportedly to promote common nationality. But out of the 17 Ministers of the Federal Capital Territory since 1979 to date, only two have come from the South, the rest have been Northerners. If Abuja is a symbol of national unity, then it should belong to all Nigerians and every eligible Nigerian, regardless of their ethnic origin, should be eligible for appointment as a Minister to run Abuja. However, the presumption is that the FCT Minister should be a Northerner because, in the views of some prominent Northerners, Abuja belongs to the North.[19]

Furthermore, Nigeria's 'federalism' does not guarantee equal opportunity for political power. The *Encyclopaedia*

Britannica says that, in a true federal system, no part of the federation should be 'so dominant that others have little opportunity to provide national leadership'.[20] However, the political structure of Nigeria is such that two powerful ethnic groups, notably the Hausa/Fulani and the Yoruba, could gang up and rotate power between each other to the exclusion of other ethnic groups. For instance, as noted in Chapter 2, the Igbos have always lost out in the inter-ethnic struggle for power. Yet, there can be no true federalism if there is no balance and equality of opportunities among the constituent entities.

So much for the politics of federalism; what about its economics? Central to the economics of federalism is economic efficiency, namely, which level of government is best suited to manage governmental functions more efficiently. According to the Tiebout model of decentralisation, developed by the economist Charles Tiebout, public activities should be decentralised unless where there are possibilities of significant inter-jurisdictional externalities or spillovers.[21] This is similar to the ideas behind fiscal federalism, a concept developed by another economist, Richard Musgrave, who argued that the federal government should be responsible for economic stabilisation and income redistribution. In contrast, state and local governments should have significant responsibilities and resources as they are closer to the people and best able to meet their needs.[22] It is also similar to the European Union idea of subsidiarity, the principle that a central authority should have a subsidiary function, performing only those tasks which cannot be performed at a more local level.[23] But Nigeria's federalism fails the economic efficiency test. The federal government does much of what the subnational units and local governments should be doing. It controls huge resources, which creates a bloated central government and the acute cost-of-governance problem in Nigeria, as discussed below.

Nigeria Is Over-governed: Oronsaye's Report Is Not the Solution

In 2011, then-President Jonathan set up the Presidential Committee on Restructuring and Rationalisation of Federal Government Parastatals, Commissions and Agencies, headed by a top civil servant, Stephen Oronsaye. The committee submitted its report, known as the Oronsaye Report, to the government in 2012. The report identified 541 federal parastatals, commissions and agencies. It recommended eliminating or merging 220 of them, including reducing the number of statutory agencies from 263 to 161. However, for nearly 12 years, no government implemented the committee's recommendations. During that period of inaction, the number of ministries, departments and agencies (MDAs) in the Federal Government budgetary structure rose from 541 to 929.[24] In February 2024, President Tinubu ordered the 'full implementation' of the Oronsaye report.[25] However, at the time of writing, near the end of 2024, the presidential order has been dogged by dithering. The reality is that even if the Tinubu government eventually decided to act on its promise, it is almost impossible that it would significantly reduce the number of MDAs, which has grown beyond the original 541 and may grow even more. Furthermore, implementing the Oronsaye report alone will not tackle Nigeria's acute cost-of-governance problem, which is far more structural.

The truth is that Nigeria is administratively over-governed. To address the problem, key shibboleths must be slain. For instance, does Nigeria need an expensive presidential system? Does it need a bicameral or full-time federal legislature whose members are among the highest-paid legislators in the world? Does Nigeria need 36 mostly unviable states, each with its own sprawling administrative structure? These questions and the related cost-of-governance problem cannot be addressed within the narrow scope of the Oronsaye report. They can only be addressed within the wider context of restructuring Nigeria. True federalism will reduce the cost of governance by consolidating administrative structures, including reducing unnecessary duplications between federal and state governments and between states within the same geopolitical zone. Streamlining the federal government and reducing the current 36 states to six regional governments, based on the current six geopolitical zones, or, at most, ten regions, should be a key element of restructuring Nigeria.

Local Governance as a Catalyst for Development

It is impossible to talk about restructuring Nigeria without mentioning the role and place of local governments. This is not only because there is no philosophical understanding of the value of local government in Nigeria, particularly the role it can play in fostering a healthy democracy and engendering social and economic development at the grassroots, but also because the treatment of local governments in Nigeria defies global trends.

Take the philosophical point first. John Stuart Mill, a strong defender of local governance, warned that the concentration of power in central hands is dangerous to a free society and posited that local government is valuable because it promotes local democracy.[26] Indeed, the values that justify democracy also justify strong local government. Thus, as Gissur Erlingsson and Jorgan Odalen put it in a paper titled *A normative Theory of Local Government*, 'if we value democracy, we must also value strong local government'.[27] But besides the normative justification, local government also serves an important expediential role: it provides local public goods in a way that state and central governments cannot. According to Alexis de Tocqueville, another 19th-century champion of local autonomy, this local specificity, as opposed to the uniformity of central or state government's provision, is the clearest functional rationale for the existence of local government.[28] And nowhere is this more pertinent than concerning local economic development and poverty reduction. As the tier of government with local proximity and knowledge and the one closest to local bodies and the people most in need, local government has the potential to stimulate the local economy and help reduce poverty. Indeed, the World Bank said in one report that 'poverty is best tackled at the local level.'[29] Furthermore, local governments can tackle insecurity by strengthening the social fabric through empowering communities and social entrepreneurs, such as charities, which can transform lives by getting young people into productive activities and endeavours.

Beyond the philosophical arguments, there is also empirical evidence of how local governments are given pride of place as a critical tier of government worldwide. In many countries, power is widely dispersed to the lowest practical level. For instance, in the US, where local government is a matter of state law under the Dillion Rule, ten of the fifty states have constitutionally granted 'home rule' to their local governments, allowing them to govern themselves as they see fit, within the bounds of state and federal constitutions. Another 29 states operate a dual system, whereby they grant 'home rule' to their local governments in some matters and limited authority in others.[30] In 2011, the UK introduced the Localism Act, which grants significant freedoms and flexibilities to local governments; the act devolved significant powers away from central government into local councils and communities.[31] In developing countries, localism is central to the development efforts of many countries, such as Chile, Bolivia and China. The South African constitution protects the rights of municipalities to administer specific matters.

By contrast, local governments are reduced to irrelevance in Nigeria. Paradoxically, while the Nigerian Constitution concentrates power at the centre and leaves states with little autonomy to develop themselves, it also confers huge executive powers on state governors. Indeed, as John Campbell and Matthew Page put it in their book *Nigeria: What Everyone Needs to Know*, 'Nigerian state governors are more powerful than their American counterparts.'[32] But how do the governors exercise the untrammelled executive power? Among other abuses of power, they strangulate the local governments in their states.

First, politically, they make sure that there is no local democracy. In Nigeria, the party of the state governor automatically controls all the state's local governments because governors control the state electoral commissions and have always ensured that their party secured all the contested positions in local government elections. In some cases, elections were delayed indefinitely, allowing the state governor to appoint his cronies as 'interim' chairmen of 'caretaker' committees.[33] In May 2024, the Vanguard newspaper published a story titled 'Undemocratic LGAs: 19 states run 433 councils with caretaker committee'.[34] According to the story, written by the newspaper's Politics Editor, Clifford Ndujihe, 'no fewer than 19 state governors are running their local councils with transition or caretaker committees.'[35] That is the extent to which state governors damaged local democracy in Nigeria.

Local governments are also crippled administratively and financially. Although the Constitution reserves for local governments the residuary functions under Schedule IV, such as the provision of primary, adult and vocational education, the construction and maintenance of certain roads and streets, the provision and maintenance of markets, motor parks and public conveniences, state governments usually encroach on these functions to raise revenue. Furthermore, state governors had free rein over federal allocations to local governments, which were paid into the State Joint Local Government Account. For many years, Nigerian state governors opposed constitutional amendments to grant full autonomy to local governments, asserting a right to exercise close oversight over the operations of the local governments in their domains. That resistance, however, somewhat ended with, as discussed below, the Supreme Court ruling granting financial autonomy to local governments.

Local Government Autonomy: The Supreme Court Ruling

In 2019, President Buhari accused state governors of crippling local governments by 'stealing' their federal allocations.[36] The National Assembly took a similar view, stating that governors were 'killing' the local government system by denying them financial and administrative autonomy.[37] Consequently, both President Buhari and the National Assembly attempted to grant financial autonomy to local governments. In May 2020, Buhari signed Executive Order 10, empowering the Accountant General of the Federation to deduct local government allocations from the state's allocations and pay them directly to the local councils.[38] However, in October 2021, the 36 state governors went to the Supreme Court to challenge the constitutionality of the executive order, arguing that the president acted unconstitutionally in introducing it. In February 2022, the Supreme Court nullified the executive order on the basis that it violated the principles of federalism and separation of powers set out in the Constitution.[39] Subsequently, in March 2022, the Senate passed a bill to grant local governments full financial and administrative autonomy.[40] But such a constitutional change required ratification by at least two-thirds of the 36 state assemblies, most of which would not ratify it. So, the bill stood no chance of success, and it failed.

The situation changed dramatically following a lawsuit instituted in May 2024 against the 36 state governors by the federal government under the new president, Tinubu. In the suit, the federal government accused the state governors of 'gross misconduct and abuse of power' in their treatment of the local governments. It asked the Supreme Court to allow federal allocations for the local governments to be paid directly to them and not through the state governments.[41] In July 2024, the Supreme Court gave its ruling and granted financial autonomy to local governments.[42] The court held that the monthly allocations to local governments from the Federation Account should no longer be paid into the State Joint Local Government Account but directly into each local government's account.

However, while the Federal Government and many public figures welcomed the Supreme Court judgement, it contradicted the express provisions of the Constitution and undermined the principles of federalism. Section 162 (5) says that the amount due to local governments from the Federation Account should 'be allocated to the State for the benefit of their Local Government Councils.' Section 165(6) states that 'Each State shall maintain a special account to be called "State Joint Local Government Account" into which shall be paid all allocations to the Local Government from the Federation Account and from the Government of the State,' Then, section 162(8) provides that 'The amount standing to the credit of the Local Government Councils of a State shall be distributed among the Local Government Councils of that State on such terms and in such manner as may be prescribed by the House of Assembly of the State.' The recurring word 'shall' leaves no room for alternative interpretations.

It is clear from the above provisions that the framers of the Constitution wanted to achieve two objectives. First, they wanted to uphold a principle of federalism by making local governments the responsibility of state governments; hence, they a) used the words 'their Local Government Councils'; b) said local government allocations should be paid to the states through the State Joint Local Government Account; and c) mandated the State House of Assembly to prescribe how the funds should be 'distributed among the Local Government Councils of that State.' These provisions accord with the spirit of federalism. However, the second objective of the framers of the Constitution was to ensure the financial viability of local governments. Hence, they required States to pass on the allocations 'for the benefit of their Local Government Councils.' Unfortunately, most state governors betrayed that second objective by refusing to pass on the federal allocations 'for the benefit of their local governments', as the Constitution requires, thereby strangling them financially.

Therefore, the task before the Supreme Court was to correct the anomaly in a way that achieves the dual intentions of the framers of the Constitution. However, the Supreme Court tilted the balance the other way. It granted financial autonomy to the local governments but upended the Constitution and undermined the principle of federalism. The Supreme Court did not deny the existence of the constitutional provisions but argued that they were not working because state governors were not passing federal allocations on to the local governments 'for their benefit'. To address this mischief, the Supreme Court adopted a broad interpretation of the Constitution, saying: 'Demands of justice require a progressive interpretation of the law.'[43] It added: 'Since paying [the local government allocations] through states has not worked, justice of this case demands that local government allocations from the Federation Account should henceforth be paid directly to the LGAs.'[44]

But by overriding, without constitutional amendments, section 162 (5) which explicitly says that local government allocations *shall* be paid through states and section 162(6) which creates the State Joint Local Government Account for that purpose, the Supreme Court simply indulged in judicial constitution-making. Furthermore, the court arbitrarily took away the function given to the State House of Assembly under section 162(8) to prescribe how the local government allocations should be distributed among the local government councils of the state. Without constitutional amendments through the process prescribed by the Constitution, the Supreme Court was wrong to amend the Constitution through judicial activism. What the court should have done was to declare the intentions of the framers of the Constitution and order the governors to adhere to them. As Lord Hodge, Deputy President of the UK Supreme Court, put in a paper titled *The scope of judicial law-making in constitutional law and public law*, 'a judge's task is to make decisions that are justified by the law as it is.'[45] However, the Nigerian Supreme Court replaced the explicit words of the Constitution with its own, thereby undermining the Constitution and the little semblance of federalism existing in Nigeria.

In any true federal system, local government is a matter of state law as it is in the US under the Dillion Rule. Nigeria claims to model its constitution and system of government on those of the US. But the US Federal Government will never sue the state governors on any matter concerning local governments. This is because local governments are entirely the responsibility of the states. Each US state has its own constitution and grants its local governments either full or partial autonomy. Any dispute under the constitution goes to the state Supreme Court, not the federal Supreme Court. But in Nigeria, the Federal Government and the country's Supreme Court can determine who runs local governments. That is not federalism; it is a unitary system.[46]

One of the principles of judicial remedies is that they must be effective[47]; that is, they must be capable of producing the right relief, and judges should do a consequential analysis of their proposed rulings. Unfortunately, the Supreme Court ruling may have either of two adverse consequences. One is that the judgment may be ineffective because it would be circumvented by state governors. The second is that, even if it were effective, it could cause real tensions between local and state governments instead of a cooperative relationship, thereby further undermining local governance because it is inconceivable that any local government can function well without the support of its state government.

Take the first point. The Supreme Court verdict gives local governments financial autonomy, but it does not, and cannot, give them administrative and political autonomy. In the ruling, the Supreme Court prohibited governors from appointing caretaker committees to run the local governments, saying that local governments should be run democratically. As a result of that ruling, all the state governments which ran their local governments through caretaker committees rushed to conduct local government elections. But in each of the states, the governor's party won all the chairmanship elections in all the local governments, prompting the Senate to condemn the local government elections across the country, describing them as 'a serious breach of democratic principles.'[48]

Thus, while the Supreme Court's ruling requiring caretaker committees to be replaced by democratically elected councils was welcomed, it omitted the fact that state governors control the political process and that there is no such thing as local democracy. In the US, it is common for one party to control the state government and another party to control most of the local governments. However, in Nigeria, the party that controls the state government also automatically controls all the local governments in the state because state governors have control over, and have hijacked, the State Independent Electoral Commission such that local government elections are never free and fair.

Furthermore, state governors always handpick loyalists to run for elections as local government chairmen and even councillors. In those circumstances, local government chairmen and councillors lack independence in the running of their councils. Thus, the 'financial autonomy' that the Supreme Court granted to the local governments may be meaningless as it is not accompanied by administrative and political autonomy. State governors will continue to exercise direct political control over local government chairmen and councillors and indirect control over their councils' purse strings. But even if the Supreme Court ruling worked and local government chairmen could act independently because of their *financial autonomy*, a hostile relationship would develop between them and the governors, who would loathe the new-found independence of the local government chairmen. And, as stated above, it is inconceivable that any local government can succeed if it is locked in a hostile relationship with the state government.

Ironically, as governor of Lagos State from 1999 to 2007, Tinubu, now president, strongly believed that local governments were under the jurisdictions of state governments and the Federal Government had no power to interfere in their running. This was the subject of a dispute between Lagos State and the Federal Government in 2004. As governor, Tinubu created 37 local governments, in addition to the 20 recognised by the constitution, and held elections into them. The Federal Government, led by President Obasanjo, withheld Federation Account allocations to local governments in Lagos State on the ground that Tinubu had no power to create local governments additional to those recognised in the Constitution. However, Tinubu sued the Federal Government at the Supreme Court, arguing that by virtue of Section 162, subsections 5-8, a state government, not the Federal Government, was the channel for passing federal allocations to the LGAs and that a state government, not the Federal Government, was the trustee of the funds on behalf of the local governments. In December 2004, the Supreme Court held that the president had no power to suspend or withhold the statutory allocation due and payable to the Lagos State Government under section 162(5) of the Constitution.[49]

It is thus ironic that Tinubu, who, as governor, sued the Federal Government to claim that local governments were state affairs, later, as president, sued state governors to assert the Federal Government's 'right' to interfere in local government affairs. It is also ironic that the Supreme Court, which, in 2004 and 2022, protected the links between state governments and their local governments, later, in 2024, severed those links by saying that federal allocations to local governments should be paid directly to them, not through the states. The fact that the Senate later said that a constitutional amendment might be needed to give full effect to the Supreme Court ruling[50] suggests that the ruling might not by itself be fully effective or implementable. Indeed, several months after the Supreme Court verdict, the Federal Government did not implement it, as local governments' allocations were still being paid into the Joint State-Local Government Accounts. As The Punch newspaper puts it, 'Supreme Court's judgment fails to seal Local Government autonomy seven months after verdict.'[51] According to the Attorney General of the Federation and Minister of Justice, Lateef Fagbemi, this was because the government 'acknowledged the need to establish certain frameworks before full implementation'.[52] He added: 'We do not want to rush into implementation that could lead to legal complications or nullification by the courts.'[53]

The difficulties with the implementation of the judgement and the constant warnings by the Federal Government that the state governors must not circumvent the ruling both suggest the complex relationship between state governments and local governments cannot simply be addressed by judicial activism but through a political solution. According to Professor Charles Soludo, the governor of Anambra State, 'absolute autonomy for the 774 local government areas in the country is unrealistic and could cause disorder if not carefully structured.'[54] While that sounds like a special pleading, it reflects the views of most state governors in Nigeria and suggests that the issue cannot be handled through judicial or federal arm-twisting of the states. Yet, in December 2024, the Attorney General of the Federation and Minister of Justice threatened state governors that tried to circumvent the Supreme Court judgment with a contempt of court suit, describing the failure to fully comply with the Supreme Court ruling as 'gross misconduct' that could justify an impeachment.[55] In response, the governor of Oyo State, Seyi Makinde, said that 'when two elephants are fighting, it is the grass that will suffer,'[56] suggesting that the legal tussle between the federal and state governments over local government autonomy would only hurt the local governments. All of this reinforces the point made above that the issue is politically sensitive and requires careful handling.

The Way Forward

There is a universal recognition and abhorrence of the problem created by state governors' emasculation of local governments in Nigeria. However, this problem cannot be tackled through judicial activism and judicial constitution-making. Rather, it must be tackled through a negotiated political and constitutional settlement that results in the restructuring of Nigeria and in the creation of a new constitution that clearly and properly defines the powers and responsibilities of the constituent units of Nigeria within a federal system underpinned by regionalism and localism. The best form of restructuring for Nigeria is to create between six and ten regional governments from the present thirty-six states and devolve significant political and economic powers to the regions. In the First Republic, a regional structure allowed each of the four regional governments, spurred by competitive regionalism[57], to exploit their comparative advantages, economies of scale and agglomeration and to develop at their own pace. The theory of agglomeration[58] says that several firms (and states) may be viable if they are together, but none may be viable if it is on its own. That is a powerful economic argument for regionalism. The truth is, hardly any of Nigeria's thirty-six states can achieve the feats of any of the regional governments in the First Republic, even if power were devolved to them. They simply lack the economies of scale and agglomeration necessary to become economic powerhouses and generators of economic prosperity.

The way forward is to convert the current thirty-six states into metropolitan areas headed by mayors within six or eight regions, run by governors or premiers. There is no state government in Nigeria that is bigger or richer than the New York Metropolitan Area (population: 20m; GDP: $2 trillion) or the London Metropolitan Area (population: 12 million; GDP: $978 billion). Yet, neither is a state, but each is a strong metropolitan area with a powerful mayor. So, there is no reason why there cannot be Lagos Metropolis, Ibadan Metropolis, Kaduna Metropolis, etc, each headed by a mayor and each as part of a regional government. In turn, each metropolitan area will consist of viable local governments, strong enough administratively and financially to support job creation, poverty-reduction and crime reduction through empowering community organisations and social entrepreneurs. Regionalism will create regional economic regeneration and development in Nigeria, while viable localism will unleash local-level political and institutional dynamics that will promote local democracy and governance as well as stimulate the local economy.

The only obstacle to achieving this regional system is the ambition of politicians who want to be state governors and have unfettered executive powers while failing to generate economic prosperity, stimulate job creation and improve the living standards of the people. But if Nigeria must make progress, it cannot be held hostage by self-interested political calculations: the national interest, the greater good, should trump self-interest. In June 2024, a member of the House of Representatives, Akin Fapohunda, drafted an 18-page bill to return Nigeria to a regional system of government`, based on eight regions.[59] Although the bill was not listed for debate in the House, it generated a lot of interest in the Nigerian media[60], and several other prominent Nigerians support the call to return Nigeria to a regional structure[61], although there are other prominent Nigerians who oppose the proposition.[62]

However, in a bizarre development in February 2025, the House of Representatives Constitution Review Committee proposed the creation of 31 new states, which would bring the total number of state governments in Nigeria to 67.[63] In a striking front-page headline, The Guardian newspaper put it thus: 'Lawmakers push for 31 new states amid N11.47tr debt by existing ones.'[64] In other words, the ridiculousness of the proposal is reflected in the fact that the existing 36 states are not financially viable but debt-ridden. The truth is that Nigeria has not benefitted from being fragmented into a multiplicity of states. The current 36 states, with the exception of two or three, are unviable. Therefore, the idea of creating additional 31 states is utterly misguided. It is thus surprising, but welcomed, that the House of Representatives Committee on Constitutional Amendments later rejected the 31 proposed new states, saying none of them met the constitutional requirements for state creation.[65] Yet, the battle of wits between proponents of regionalism and those calling more states continues. But, as argued in the foregoing, logic is on the side of regionalism. Nigeria needs regional powerhouses, not multiple and unviable states.

Nigeria Should Return to the Parliamentary System

Restructuring Nigeria and creating a new political and constitutional settlement must involve looking at whether its current system of government – presidentialism – is fit for purpose. All over the world, countries choose a system of government that suits them, and many readily change their form of government if it is not working. In their paper entitled *Determinants of Constitutional Change: Why do countries change their form of government?* Bernd Hayo and Stefan Voigt identified 123 changes in the form of government in 169 countries from 1950 to 2003.[66] They argued that political considerations were important drivers of these changes to achieve internal cohesion, increase political participation and strengthen the process of democratisation.[67]

At its independence in 1960, Nigeria inherited the parliamentary system and practised it for six years until the military intervention in January 1966. However, about thirteen years later, when the military regime, headed by

General Murtala Muhammed, and later, after his assassination in 1976, by General Olusegun Obasanjo, decided to return Nigeria to civil rule, they instructed the 49-strong constitutional drafting committee, dubbed the '49 Wise Men', to shun the parliamentary system and adopt the US-style presidential system of government. In his memoir, *A Journey in Service*, General Babangida, a former military head of state, said: 'A presidential system with a head of state and government vested with ultimate executive powers was the best option for the nation.'[68] The logic, based on the military command-and-control unitary model, was that, instead of having, separately, a ceremonial president as head of state and a prime minister as head of government, both powers should be vested in one person, who, as a powerful executive president, could act as a unifying figure and have the authority and power to coral the country's multiple ethnic groups to ensure unity.[69]

However, Nigeria has never had a president that could be described as a unifying figure. This is because politics in Nigeria is largely a zero-sum game whereby a president is deemed to represent his ethnic group while other ethnic groups wait eagerly for their own turns to assume national leadership. Indeed, each president has favoured one or two sections of the country over the others in key national appointments. For instance, as noted in Chapter 2, most of the key security positions in President Buhari's administration were held by people from his Hausa/Fulani ethnic group, while most of the economic, security and criminal justice system positions in President Tinubu's government were held by people from his Yoruba ethnic group. As a result of such inherent nepotism or sectionalism, no president has really been a unifying figure. Furthermore, it is impossible to govern a multi-ethnic country with a strongman mentality by vesting excessive power in one person from one ethnic group. Instead of an authoritarian utopia, where strong leaders bring people happily together, what Nigeria has had under the presidential system is a totalitarian dystopia, where supposedly unifying leaders use military force to suppress ethnic agitations and enforce elusive unity. So, the presidential system has not produced a unifying president in Nigeria and has not guaranteed political stability.

The truth is that the presidential system, with an all-powerful executive president, is not suitable for a multi-ethnic, multinational country. Indeed, most countries have prime ministers and not executive presidents. For instance, of the 193 United Nations member states, only about forty-six have a presidential system, where full executive powers are vested in one person. Out of the fifty sovereign states in Europe, thirty-four are parliamentary systems; so are nearly forty of the fifty-four member states of the Commonwealth, including Canada, Australia, India and Singapore. It is hard to imagine Canada, a multi-ethnic country, to have a centralised political system with ultimate executive powers vested in an 'executive president'

Those who cite the United States as a model of presidentialism ignore the fact that America is a country of immigrants, where every 'ethnic' group emigrated from another country. For instance, Irish Americans claim Ireland as their origin; Jewish Americans regard Isreal as their root, and Arab Americans have long-standing affinity with the Arab nations. Furthermore, America's 'ethnic' groups are not concentrated in specific geographic areas but, rather, spread across the country. By contrast, in Nigeria, the Yorubas, the Igbos, the Hausa/Fulani etc are not only concentrated in specific geographic locations but are indigenous owners of their respective territories which predate Nigeria itself. Finally, the American presidential system is underpinned by true federalism, with the states enjoying significant power and autonomy, whereas the Nigerian presidential system is combined with a centralised political system. Thus, Nigeria is an outlier not only in being a multi-ethnic country with a powerful executive presidency, but also in having so much power concentrated at the centre. Thus, rather being pluralistic, it is absolutist in nature.

Besides the presidential system being unsuitable for Nigeria as a multiethnic country, there is also a broad consensus that it breeds corruption in Nigeria. At the launch of her book *Fighting Corruption Is Dangerous* in 2018, Dr Ngozi Okonjo-Iweala, a two-time Finance Minister of Nigeria and currently Director-General of the World Trade Organisation (WTO), said there were two root causes of corruption in Nigeria. The first was weak institutions, and the second was 'Nigeria's costly presidential system and its impact on elections.'[70] The excessive monetisation of politics in Nigeria, which is a consequence of the presidential system, fuels corruption and erodes Nigeria's democracy. Furthermore, the presidential system is too expensive to run. In his book *Reclaiming the Jewel of Africa*, Olusegun Aganga says: 'The consensus is that the American-style presidential system has proven too expensive for Nigeria.'[71] He argues that while the presidential system is effective for a large economy like the US, it is too expensive and less effective 'for a country with a small economy and high rate of poverty, such as Nigeria.'[72] It is thus an incontrovertible fact that the presidential system is not only too expensive for Nigeria, contributing significantly to the cost of governance, but also that it is a major cause of corruption in Nigeria, in addition to eroding democracy through encouraging the excessive monetisation of politics.

But the foregoing apart, there is also the argument about government effectiveness and economic performance. In the 2022 Trust in Government survey by the OECD, the top 20 of the 41 countries surveyed have a parliamentary system of government.[73] The United States, which is the standard bearer of presidentialism, scores only 31 per cent and ranks 35 in the survey. In a research paper entitled *Who does better for the economy? Presidents versus parliamentary democracies*, economists Richard McManus and Gulcin Ozkan argue that parliamentary systems produce superior economic outcomes than presidential systems.[74] Using data from 119 countries across the period 1950 to 2015, they found that, on average, annual GDP growth is up to 1.2 percentage points higher in countries governed by parliamentary systems; inflation is 6 percentage points lower, and income inequality is up to 20 percentage points lower. They found that 91 per cent of the best performers on growth and income inequality are parliamentary governments. By contrast, the study found that presidential regimes are consistently associated with less favourable economic outcomes, such as slower output growth, higher and more volatile inflation and greater inequality.

Why do parliamentary systems deliver better economic outcomes? The authors argue that this is because parliamentary systems consistently feature higher scores on democracy, more extensive media freedoms, a stronger rule of law and greater checks and balances. Robust legal, political and administrative institutions, which are more associated with parliamentary systems than presidential ones, explain why parliamentarism has produced greater democratic and economic progress than presidentialism. The US bucks this trend in economic performance; it is a presidential system yet economically successful. The authors argue that this is because of America's inherent checks and balances, saying that the US system 'is checked and balanced to a fault.'[75]

A country's system of government can determine its political and economic progress. The preponderance of evidence shows that the presidential system is not suitable for a multi-ethnic country and is generally not conducive to government effectiveness and economic performance. In contrast, parliamentarism is a better route to political stability, government effectiveness and economic progress. Evidently, the presidential system has not served Nigeria well. Twice within eight years, some members of the Nigerian House of Representatives have tabled a bill to amend the constitution and return Nigeria back to a parliamentary system of government on the basis that the parliamentary system would make 'governance accountable, responsible, responsive and ultimately less expensive.'[76] Many other prominent Nigerians[77] have also voiced support for replacing the current presidential system with a parliamentary system of government.

However, some critics point to the fact that the parliamentary system and regionalism were terminated following the military coup of January 15, 1966, and, thus, argue that both systems were tried and failed in the First Republic. For instance, in an interview in June 2024, the Emir of Kano, Sanusi Lamido Sanusi, said that regionalism and the parliamentary system were not solutions for Nigeria. As he put it, 'We had a parliamentary system in the First Republic. What happened? We had a regional system in the First Republic. How did it end?'[78] The vice president, Kashim Shettima, and a former governor of Lagos State, Babatunde Fashola, made the same point at a public event in 2024.[79] Fashola said: 'Let's think deeply about why the parliamentary system failed in the First Republic. Have we overcome those reasons?'[80]

But the argument that the presidential and regional systems failed in the First Republic is a red herring. As the statistical saying goes, correlation does not imply causation. There is no causal link between the practice of parliamentarism and regionalism and the January 1966 coup. The coup plotters did not blame the parliamentary system or the regional system for the coup. In any case, if the 1966 coup discredits regionalism and the parliamentary system in Nigeria, then the December 1983 coup equally discredits the presidential system, given that the military terminated the Shehu Shagari presidency just after four years in office. The truth is that coups did not discredit regionalism and the parliamentary system any more than they discredited the multiplicity of states and the presidential system.[81] Evidently, parliamentarism recommends itself as a far better system of government for Nigeria than presidentialism. The latter has proved to be too expensive, too corruption-prone, too economically inefficient and too divisive for Nigeria, a multi-ethnic country. Thus, for those functionalist arguments alone, Nigeria should return to the parliamentary system.

Strengthening Electoral Democracy in Nigeria

Besides the question of which system of government best suits Nigeria, there are also questions about the integrity of Nigeria's democracy and the inclusivity of its democratic governance. The former relates to the independence of the electoral body, the Independent National Electoral Commission (INEC); the latter concerns issues like rotational presidency, the winner-take-all system and the first-past-the-post or plurality of votes electoral system. The restructuring of Nigeria and the creation of a new political and constitutional settlement must address these issues. They are discussed below.

The Independence of INEC

In their final report on Nigeria's 2023 general elections, the European Union Election Observation Mission (EU-EOM) raised concerns about the independence and impartiality of the electoral body, INEC, saying that 'the selection process of INEC commissioners and Resident Electoral Commissioners leaves the electoral institution vulnerable to the perception of partiality.'[82] However, concerns about the perceived lack of independence of INEC are not new. They formed parts of the analyses and recommendations of the Election Reform Commission set up by then-President Umaru Musa Yar' Adua after the controversial 2007 presidential election. As the Commission noted in its final report, submitted in December 2008, 'the independence and impartiality of INEC have been questioned by the generality of Nigerians'[83], saying that the electoral bodies, both at the national and state levels, 'have generally been adjudged as operating as appendages of the ruling party and Executive arms of government.'[84] This perception stems from the fact that the president is wholly responsible for appointing the chairman of INEC as well as the Resident Electoral Commissioners, albeit subject to the approval of the Senate, and some presidents have allegedly appointed some people loyal to their parties into those positions.[85]

In response to such concerns, the Election Reform Commission, chaired by a retired Supreme Court Justice, Muhammadu Lawal Uwais, recommended in its final report, widely called the Uwais Report, that 'the 1999 Constitution should be amended to ensure that INEC becomes truly independent, non-partisan, impartial, professional, transparent, and reliable as an institution and in performance of its constitutional functions.'[86] In order to remove the perception of INEC's alignment with the government, the Uwais Report recommends that section 153 of the Constitution should be amended 'to remove INEC from the list of Federal Executive Bodies.'[87] The commission did not mince words about the president's role in the selection of the electoral body, saying: 'The continuing involvement of the President in the appointment of the INEC chairman and members of the commission as well as Resident Electoral Commissioners deprives the electoral body of the autonomy it requires to conduct free and fair elections.'[88] Thus, it recommended that the appointment of the INEC chairman and members should be handled by 'a neutral and non-partisan agency, subject to the approval of the Senate.'[89] However, while some recommendations of the Uwais Report were implemented in the Electoral Act 2010 and through some constitutional amendments, those relating to the independence and impartiality of INEC have not been adopted.

Yet, if Nigeria's general elections are to pass the credibility and integrity tests, the independence and impartiality of the electoral body must never be in doubt. Given the prevalence of the abuse of incumbency and the absence of a level-playing field in Nigerian elections, incumbent presidents and governors mustn't be able to control and manipulate the electoral bodies, and, indeed, the security agencies are also critical during elections. Thus, the recommendations of the Uwais report on the independence and impartiality of INEC should be fully implemented. There should be, as the EU-EOM similarly recommended, 'a robust operational framework for the independence, integrity, and efficiency of electoral administration through an inclusive and publicly accountable mechanism for selecting candidates to the posts of INEC commissioners and RECs based on clear criteria of evaluation of merits, qualifications, and verified non-partisanship.'[90]

Election Petitions: Shifting the Burden of Proof

Apart from questions about INEC's independence from the Executive Arm of Government, there is also concern about the presumption of regularity it enjoys in election petition matters before tribunals and the courts. In election petitions, especially those involving presidential elections, the odds are stacked heavily against the petitioners as the Presidential

Election Petition Court (PEPC) and the Supreme Court tend to presume that INEC did everything right and that the onus is on the petitioner to prove otherwise, and the evidential burden is extremely heavy. For instance, the petitioner must file his petition with detailed pleadings and relevant documents within 21 days of the declaration of election results of a presidential election. Anything that is not filed or 'frontloaded' within 21 days will be rejected. With 176,846 polling units across Nigeria, it is nearly impossible for a presidential candidate making allegations of electoral malpractices nationwide to gather evidence from all the polling units and agents within 21 days.

Furthermore, the petitioner has two additional evidential burdens. First, he must prove irregularities and non-compliance with the electoral law. Second, he must prove that the irregularities and non-compliance substantially affected the results.[91] There is no burden on INEC or the respondents to prove anything. The heavy burden of proof placed on the petitioner is partly blamed for why no presidential election has been upturned by the Supreme Court in Nigeria, even when there were widespread irregularities.[92]

The Uwais Report addressed this issue and recommended reversing the burden of proof and placing it on INEC and the respondents. It said: 'The burden of proof should be shifted from the petitioners to INEC to show, on balance of probability, that disputed elections were indeed free and fair and candidates declared winners were truly the choices of the electorate.'[93] It added: 'Rules of evidence should be formulated to achieve substantive justice rather than mere observance of technicalities.'[94]

The Uwais committee's recommendations are significant for the integrity of Nigeria's electoral system and democracy. If a presidential election cannot be upturned, regardless of how materially flawed it was, simply because the election petition process is unfairly skewed against the petitioner or because the courts resort to technicalities, confidence in Nigerian presidential elections and the election petition process would evaporate, causing irreparable damage to the integrity of Nigerian democracy. By contrast, shifting the burden of proof to INEC would ensure that the electoral body pays meticulous attention to conducting credible elections as it may subsequently need to justify its actions and decisions before the courts. The recommendations of the Uwais Report should, therefore, be implemented to restore confidence in the election petition process.

Zoning and Rotational Presidency

There is a broad consensus that the presidency should rotate between northern and southern Nigeria, such that if a northerner is president for the constitutionally allowed two terms of eight years, a southerner should succeed him, and vice versa. This consensus has been honoured since Nigeria returned to civilian rule in 1999, and any attempt to violate it has been resisted.[95] For instance, in 2022, President Buhari, a northerner who was completing his second term in office, wanted to manipulate his party's presidential primary to enable another northerner, Ahmed Lawan, then Senate President, to succeed him.[96] But he was stoutly resisted by some governors in his party who insisted that power must return to the South. However, while there is a consensus to rotate power between the North and the South, there is no such consensus to rotate the presidency within the South or within the North. The implication is that in a plural and diverse country made up of over 250 linguistic groups, power could, in theory, be permanently controlled by the dominant ethnic group in the North, the Hausa/Fulani, and the dominant ethnic group in the South, the Yoruba.

In 2007, President Obasanjo handpicked Umaru Musa Yar' Adua, then governor of Katsina State, as his party's presidential candidate and handpicked Goodluck Jonathan as his running mate. By picking Jonathan, an Ijaw, as Yar' Adua's running mate, Obasanjo paved the way for him to become Nigeria's president after the death of President Yar' Adua in 2010, following which he successfully won the presidential election of 2011. Without Obasanjo's affirmative action in facilitating Jonathan's emergence as president, there was no way someone from a minority ethnic group would have become president of Nigeria. But that raises the question of whether anyone from any ethnic group outside of the dominant Hausa/Fulani and Yoruba ethnic groups could ever become president of Nigeria in their own right.

For instance, on the grounds of equity, fairness and justice, the Igbos should have produced the president in 2023. This is because between 1999, when Nigeria returned to civil rule, and 2023, the Hausa/Fulani had governed Nigeria for eleven years, the Yoruba for eight years and the Ijaw for five years, while the Igbo had not produced a president. So, the Igbo should have produced the president in 2023. However, that argument did not sway Tinubu, a Yoruba, from running for the presidency, which he won with the support of the Hausa/Fulani in the North. Thus, an alliance between the Hausa/Fulani and the Yoruba kept the Igbos out of national leadership. That would not have happened if there had been an arrangement to rotate power among the six geopolitical zones rather than just between the South and the North.

In a speech at the Sixth World Igbo Summit in December 2020, Pius Anyim, a former Senate President and former Secretary to the Government of the Federation, said: 'For such critical national office as the Office of the President of the Federal Republic of Nigeria not to be rotated among the zones can only breed discontent and disharmony.'[97] There are, however, those who argue that the presidency of Nigeria should be based strictly on competence and not on geography. For instance, in 2021, Mamman Daura, a prominent Northern leader, told the BBC that the presidency 'should be for the most competent and not for someone who comes from somewhere.'[98] Both Anyim and Daura have a point, but the political imperative and moral force of power rotation in Nigeria favour Anyim's position.

The main argument against zoning is that it undermines the principle of political competition and choice, which is at the heart of a representative democracy. The idea is that democracy is strengthened when there is real contestation for power and when voters can choose among several candidates. By zoning the presidency to one part of the country at a particular time, that contestation is limited, and that choice is constrained. However, the reality is that zoning or power rotation is a political imperative in a multi-ethnic country, where there is a recurrent inter-ethnic conflict over power and where the fear of ethnic domination is rife. As

Professors Paul Collier and Tim Besley pointed out in their report on state fragility, 'The purpose of power-sharing is primarily to allay mutual fears.'[99] Without power sharing, tension-prone multi-ethnic countries will experience more political instability.

Ironically, those who oppose zoning or power rotation on the grounds that it undermines meritocracy and competence in the selection of Nigeria's presidents are strong defenders of the Federal Character Principle under which a quota is set for the number of public servants to be appointed from each state in Nigeria. The Constitution states: 'The composition of the Government of the Federation or any of its agencies and the conduct of its affairs shall be carried out in such manner as to reflect the federal character of Nigeria and the need to promote national unity and also to command national loyalty thereby ensuring that there shall be no predominance of persons from a few States or from a few ethnic or other sectional groups in that government or in any of its agencies' (section 14(3)).

Evidently, while meritocracy should be considered in the application of the Federal Character Principle, it is not the main rationale behind the principle. Rather, its aim is to prevent ethnic domination in the public service and to *promote national unity*. And despite concerns that the Federal Character Principle has not always led to the recruitment of the most meritorious or most competent people, there is no clamour to abolish it simply because of the overriding need to promote national unity and command national loyalty. Why, then, is there opposition to zoning and rotating the presidency, which would prevent ethnic domination and promote national unity?

Yet, a rotational presidency cannot continue in perpetuity. Once each of the geopolitical zones has produced a president, the race should then be thrown open to the whole country. Furthermore, a rotational presidency would become unnecessary once Nigeria is restructured and returned to the parliamentary and regional systems of government, with strong regions and a less powerful centre. It is because the centre is too powerful, with an overpowerful president who controls virtually everything in the country, that every ethnic group wants to gain power at the centre and control the presidency. Regional powerhouses would reduce, even remove, the cut-throat inter-ethnic struggle for power.

Towards a Truly Representative and Accountable Democracy

There are two models of democracy. One is a direct democracy; the other is a representative democracy. In the former, citizens elect people as 'delegates' to the legislature to formulate laws and policies but retain the powers to decide directly themselves what laws and policies they want. One notable example of a direct democracy is Switzerland, where all major laws and policies must be approved by the people directly in a referendum. By contrast, in a representative democracy, the citizens elect people to represent them and govern on their behalf, that is, to make laws and formulate policies without going back to the citizens to seek their approval in a referendum. Most democratic countries in the world operate a representative democracy. Nigeria is, in theory, one of them.

However, a representative democracy is a unique system of governance with several characteristics[100], and it is predicated on two fundamental assumptions. One is that the government that emerges from such a democracy reflects the genuine will and consent of majority of the electorate, freely expressed in credible elections. The second assumption is that, in a representative democracy, there is an agency relationship between those governing and those being governed, under which the elected government acts as the agent of the people, works faithfully for the citizens, and is accountable and answerable to them. The relationship between citizens and governments is also rooted in the concept of social contract. Indeed, several great philosophers, such as Thomas Hobbes and John Locke, have long argued that governments have their origins in an implied social contract between citizens and their governments whereby citizens surrender to the authority of government in return for the state protecting their lives, property and general wellbeing. It thus follows that, in assessing whether a nation's democracy is truly representative and accountable, it is important to ask: 1) whether the government that emerges from such a democracy is based on the popular and genuine consent of the people freely expressed in credible elections and 2) whether the government works as the agent of the people, pursuing policies that reflect the wishes of the people. In other words, is there a meaningful social contract between the government and the citizens?

The first question as to whether elected governments in Nigeria reflect the genuine will and consent of the citizens in free and fair elections has been answered in Chapter 1 and earlier in this chapter: elections are never free, fair, transparent and credible in Nigeria. What's more, the 'government' that emerges may not even reflect the will of the majority of voters. Indeed, as stated above, the Nigerian Constitution allows a president to emerge by winning a narrow victory after ruthlessly deploying the wedge issues of ethnicity and religion as Tinubu did in 2023 when he won with votes from a tiny segment of the Nigerian population, having aggressively played the ethnic/regional card ('Yoruba lokan' or 'It's Yoruba's turn') as well as the religious card (Muslim-Muslim ticket) during the election campaign. In the end, he became president with just 36.6 per cent of the popular votes, which came overwhelmingly from the Muslim North and the Yoruba South-West. Such a narrow mandate, devoid of broad-based national support, distorts the true meaning of representative democracy.

Regarding the second question as to whether Nigeria is an accountable democracy where governments act as the agents of the citizens, the truth is that there is no agency relationship or a social contract between those governing and those being governed in Nigeria. In true representative democracies, elected politicians are servants of the people. But in Nigeria, the governing are masters, the governed are servants; the governing are feudal lords, the governed are serfs. As a former Nigerian minister put it, democracy in Nigeria is 'a government by the political class, of the political class, for the political class'.[101] Evidence of widespread unemployment, poverty and insecurity, and the absence of basic necessities of life, show that the Nigerian government does not serve the interests of its citizens. Ordinary Nigerians live in appalling conditions, with no access to basic things of life like good healthcare, good education and good sanitation. For instance, according to the

World Bank, nearly 50 per cent of Nigerians have no access to electricity[102], and UN data shows that only 29 per cent have access to sanitation.[103]

The foregoing suggests that politics and governance in Nigeria are broken, and that Nigeria's democracy is not truly representative or accountable. The key characteristics of a representative democracy are either absent or impaired in Nigeria, including accountability, transparency and, indeed, a social contract. Nigeria is not a genuine representative democracy, let alone an effective and inclusive state. In her book *Fighting Corruption Is Dangerous*, Dr Ngozi Okonjo-Iweala lists the following as factors undermining governance in Nigeria: inappropriate policies, inefficient and non-transparent institutions, corruption, capture by leaders and rent-seeking elite.[104]   All of this makes Nigeria what Acemoglu and Robinson call in their book *Why Nations Fail* an 'extractive' state, that is, a state where political and economic powers are concentrated in the hands of small group of elites who dominate and exploit the people. It also means that Nigeria lacks the ideals of inclusive and representative democracy, which partly explains why it is struggling to become an effective state that can generate prosperity for its people.

The theoretical analysis points to strong links between healthy representative democracy, government effectiveness and economic prosperity. This is because a true representative democracy necessarily entails having inclusive political institutions and norms, such as a liberal constitution, political accountability, transparency in government, liberty and the rule of law, all of which strengthen state capacity and engender the right economic institutions and policies to generate growth and prosperity. The need to ensure that policies reflect the wishes of the people, and the societal and political pressures that come with the failure to do so, are key factors driving government effectiveness and pro-growth policies in genuine representative and accountable democracies.

It is thus possible to deduce from the foregoing analysis that in order to engender a true representative democracy that enhances state capacity and enables economic growth and prosperity, the following critical institutions and norms of governance and democracy must be present in a society, namely:

- **A liberal, inclusive and people-oriented constitution** that devolves power from the centre, limits the power of the state and guarantees basic rights for the citizens

- **Genuine political competition and choice**, including through allowing independent candidacy in elections, regulating election financing so that power doesn't go to the highest bidder, and ensuring free and fair elections that genuinely reflect the will of the people.

- **Robust institutions of checks and balances** through guaranteeing the independence of critical institutions of governance and democracy, such as the judiciary, the electoral commission, security agencies and anti-corruption bodies.

- **Transparent, responsive and accountable government** through greater openness of the policy process, promoting meritocracy in the bureaucracy and supporting the flourishing of an independent media and a robust civil society.

The starting point in tackling Nigeria's governance problems is to recognise that the citizens have little faith in the country's democracy and governance and have absolutely no trust in its politicians. Given that economic performance is inextricably linked to the political process and political institutions, the priority is to undertake critical political and constitutional reforms in order to create the political institutions that will engender faith and trust in politics and governance, enhance state effectiveness and give rise to pro-growth policies. Thus, to ensure Nigeria's democracy is truly representative and accountable, the following measures are imperative:

Electoral democracy

- Nigeria's Constitution and electoral laws should promote credible elections, including through strict enforcement of prohibitions on the abuse of incumbency and misuse of state resources to gain an electoral advantage.

- Independent (non-party) candidacy will make Nigerian elections more competitive and address the situation where Nigeria has a multi-party system but operates a de facto one-party state, with indistinguishable registered parties that are mere elite patronage machines for capturing the state.[105]

- Nigeria's election should be based on the absolute majority, not the plurality of votes, so that the winner in a presidential election is required to secure more than 50 per cent of the total vote cast. This will be more reflective of a true representative democracy than a situation where a candidate can become president with just 35 per cent of the vote

- Vote buying and financial inducement of officials of electoral bodies and security agencies during elections should be serious criminal offences. Where electoral offences exist in statutes, they should be strengthened and strictly enforced; their violation must not go unpunished.

- Godfatherism should be actively discouraged in Nigerian politics. This could be achieved by promoting mass-based parties, with thousands of subscription-paying members, rather than cadre parties that are dominated by a relatively small number of party adherents, special interest groups and influential people. This also requires strengthening internal party democracy by giving real voice and power to all party members in selecting candidates for elective offices. In addition, party constitutions should prohibit godfatherism and ensure that parties are not hijacked by moneybags.

Political participation, Transparency and Public Disclosures

- Nigeria should create citizens' assemblies at various levels of government to encourage a deliberative democracy. Citizens' assemblies are one way of diffusing power and ensuring citizens are involved in governance between elections.

- Every major government policy and legislative proposal should be accompanied by an Impact Assessment that considers the potential social and economic impacts of such a proposal. The Impact Assessment should be signed off by the Auditor-General, while the proposed policy or legislation should be subject to a statutory public consultation that is open, transparent and inclusive before it is adopted and implemented.

- All government contracts should pass the value-for-money and social-value tests to ensure that public funds are properly used and that projects benefit society. There should be strictly enforced transparency and public disclosure requirements for all public contracts, licences and permits with a value above ₦10 million regarding their awardees, recipients and value. Furthermore, there should be an annual audit of budgetary implementation and performance, and the audit report should be publicly available and accessible. The statutory obligations of ministries, departments and agencies (MDAs) to publish their financial information should be strictly enforced.

Institutions of checks and balances

- A new Constitution should guarantee the absolute independence of, and non-interference with, the institutions of checks and balances such as the judiciary, the Central Bank, the office of the Auditor-General, the electoral commissions, the anti-corruption agencies, security agencies, etc. Non-compliance with court rulings should be constitutionally declared an abuse of office.

- Independent non-governmental organisations and think tanks like the UK's Institute for Fiscal Studies and Institute of Government, should be empowered and encouraged to research and publish evidence-based studies on government practices, policies and performance and should be given reasonable access to official documents and personnel.

- Nigeria should enact and strictly enforce laws incentivising and protecting whistle-blowers and witnesses.

For far too long, the patronage and corruption of Nigeria's political class have held the country hostage and stunted its development. Power flows from the top down, not conversely, with the will and consent of the people counting for little in elections, while the emergent government is never accountable to the citizens, whose interests are hardly represented in the process of political decision-making. Yet, if Nigeria must have a true democracy, it must be one that is truly representative and accountable, where elected leaders have genuine legitimacy and are willing to sacrifice their self-interest for the greater good of the nation and its citizens.

The Imperative of a Free, Unfettered Press

The foregoing discussion on the need for a true representative and accountable democracy in Nigeria cannot be complete without a specific mention of the role of the press and the need for a free, robust and unfettered press. This is because democracy and good governance need guardrails, and two of the most critical are a feisty press and a vibrant civil society. They act as bulwarks against bad governance and can be a powerful check on the excesses of government. The media is called the 'fourth estate of the realm' precisely because, after the legislature, the executive and the judiciary, they play a critical role in governance; they act to expose abuse of power. The Nigerian Constitution guarantees freedom of expression and of the press. Specifically, Section 22 says that the press, and the media generally, 'shall at all times be free to uphold the responsibility and accountability of the Government of the people', while Section 39 stipulates that 'Every person shall be entitled to freedom of expression, including freedom to hold opinions and to receive and impart ideas and information without interference.'

However, despite the constitutional guarantees of a free press and freedom of expression, there are constant attacks on the media by government officials and agencies in

Nigeria, with frequent reported cases of intimidation and violence against journalists and other individuals who publish stories or circulate information on social media that are unfavourable to the government.[106] Successive governments have also attempted to constrain the media through draconian regulation. For instance, in 2021, some members of the National Assembly, with the acquiescence of the Buhari government, proposed amendments to the Nigerian Press Council Act and the National Broadcasting Commission Act to give the president free rein to appoint their boards, including their chairmen, without the Senate's approval, thus allowing the president to fill the boards with his loyalists. The bills would also vest the minister of information with unrestrained powers to control the media, including powers to approve the establishment, ownership and operation of newspapers.

The proposed amendments provoked unprecedented protest from Nigerian newspapers which jointly, on the same day, published on their front pages the same bold headline: 'Information Blackout'.[107] The bills were later withdrawn. However, the urge to regulate the media has not gone away, with, for instance, the Tinubu administration's proposal to regulate social media, which it described as a 'societal menace', and its regular use of the Cybercrime Act of 2015 to suppress freedom of expression and of the press.[108] At its conference in November 2024, the Nigeria Guild of Editors (NGE) expressed concern over 'the rise in harassment and violence against journalists' and called for 'stricter enforcement of journalist protection.'[109]

The Financial Times said in one editorial: 'Good journalism, and by extension society, relies on leaks that expose abuses of power', adding: 'The fourth estate must be free from threat of prosecution simply for doing its job. That includes holding the government to account.'[110] That message is also true for Nigeria: journalists must not be treated like criminals for performing their constitutional duty of holding the government up to scrutiny. Thus, violence against media personnel must stop, and must not go unpunished where it occurs. Of course, the press must ensure journalistic integrity, but the media must be free, vibrant and uncensored. As Martin Bright, editor of Index on Censorship, put it, 'legislation that allows no public interest defence, even when a whistleblower is acting in the best patriotic interests of the country, has no place in a modern democracy.'[111]

The absence of public interest journalism or public interest defence for journalistic practices is a major reason why real investigative journalism is rare in Nigeria. Yet, in countries where anti-corruption and integrity systems have worked, investigative journalism has been a critical factor. For instance, the Watergate scandal in America would not have been exposed without investigative journalism. It is thus imperative that public interest journalism, underpinned by robust investigative practices to hold the government to account and expose abuse of power, flourishes in Nigeria.

Nigeria Needs a New Constitution

Having discussed what a new political and constitutional settlement for Nigeria should entail, this chapter ends with how to do it. Essentially, this is about consensus-building and constitution-making. The constitution is a central determinant of how a country is governed. Therefore, restructuring Nigeria and creating an enduring political and constitutional settlement must involve giving the country a new constitution. Indeed, the history of constitution-making in Nigeria shows that every constitution since the colonial era replaced the one before it. Rather than tinkering with an existing constitution, a new one was often created. Nigeria's first-ever constitution, the Amalgamation Constitution, came into effect on January 1, 1914. During the subsequent colonial period, there were four other constitutions, namely the Clifford Constitution in 1922, the Richards Constitution (1946), the Macpherson Constitution (1951), and the Lyttleton Constitution (1954). Each of these constitutions replaced the one before it. Britain imposed all the colonial-era constitutions on Nigeria, but Nigeria's ethnic nationalities, led by their political leaders, negotiated the 1960 Independence Constitution and the 1963 Republican Constitution. However, since the coup of January 1966, which ushered in a prolonged period of military rule, the military imposed all the subsequent constitutions on Nigeria. The General Obasanjo regime created the 1979 Constitution, while General Abdulsalami Abubakar's regime enacted the current 1999 Constitution.

Yet, all the military-era constitutions lied about their provenance and legitimacy. For instance, the preamble to the 1999 Constitution says: 'We the people of the Federal Republic of Nigeria – Do hereby make, enact and give to ourselves the following Constitution.' First, 'the people' did not make the constitution; second, the constitution is not truly 'federal'; and third, it is not truly 'republican'. Although the military always set up a constitutional committee led by a civilian, the emergent constitution ultimately reflected the preferences of the military leaders and never involved national deliberations, consensus or popular ratification.

For instance, while the Obasanjo regime set up a constitutional drafting committee chaired by the legal icon Chief Rotimi Williams, it did not only set boundaries on what should and should not be included in the constitution, it also introduced nearly 20 amendments in the final draft constitution.[112] Furthermore, the regime did not put the draft constitution to the people via a referendum to ensure wider popular ratification; rather, the final draft of what became the 1979 Constitution was approved by the military council and foisted on the country.

In his memoir, *A Journey in Service*, General Babangida, who was the military head of state between August 1985 and August 1994, said that after his regime set up a 46-member Constitution Review Committee in September 1987, they 'barred its members from reviewing some "no go areas" of the 1979 Constitution, which, in our view, constituted "agreed ingredients of Nigeria's order."'[113] The Draft Constitution that the committee submitted to the regime in April 1989 was 'critically amended by the Armed Forces Ruling Council'[114] but was not put to the people in a referendum. The military's approach to constitution making involves setting boundaries or limits around constitutional deliberations and unilaterally amending and approving draft 'constitutions' without popular ratification. Indeed, the current 1999 Constitution was enacted by the General Abubakar regime under Decree 24 of 1999, which was later annexed to an act. Thus, Nigeria is governed by a military decree termed a constitution. That is not how constitutions are made. For instance, the making of the US Constitution in 1787 shows that it was a product of negotiated political and constitutional settlement, which went through a process of wider popular ratification.[115]

The second claim of the 1999 Constitution is that Nigeria is 'federal'. But this, too, is false because Nigeria is anything but a true federal state. As argued in the preceding chapters and this one, the key characteristics of a federal system are non-centralisation and local autonomy, with subnational entities being able to pursue policies different from those of the centre. But power is overcentralised in Nigeria, with the constitution reserving more issue-areas exclusively to the federal government than any other federal constitution around the world. Section 5 of the Constitution specifically states: 'If any Law enacted by the House of Assembly of a State is inconsistent with any law validly made by the National Assembly, the law made by the National Assembly shall prevail, and that other Law shall, to the extent of the inconsistency, be void.' The Tenth Amendment of the US Constitution provides that all powers not delegated to the federal government are reserved to the states, and the drafters of the US Constitution retained significant residual powers for the states.[116] By contrast, the Nigerian Constitution provides for an Exclusive Legislative List and a Concurrent Legislative List that both give the federal government the power to do virtually everything. As a result, the state and local governments lack the ability to become autonomous and self-sustaining. That is not a true federal system.

The third claim is that Nigeria is a 'republic'. But republicanism is about the people. As Will Hutton argues in his book *The State We're In*, a key characteristic of a republican state is that political power and authority are firmly rooted in the people, with the state ruling *for* the people rather than *over* them.[117] However, that is not the case in Nigeria. In their book *Nigeria: What Everyone Needs to Know*, John Campbell and Matthew Page said that 'politics is an elite game largely played without reference to the Nigerian people.'[118] Dr Segun Aganga made the same point in *Reclaiming the Jewel of Africa*, describing Nigeria as 'more a government by the political class, of the political class, for the political class'.[119] Despite the façade of elections, power flows from the top down, not from the bottom up. Nigeria is an 'extractive' state where a small elite dominates and exploits the people. Furthermore, while the Nigerian constitution creates certain rights for the citizens, such as the rights to life and economic self-determination, those rights are not justiciable or enforceable. A test of a good constitution is the extent to which it constrains executive power. But the Nigerian state is too powerful, and its unfettered powers trump the *rights* of the citizens, which makes a mockery of the claim that Nigeria is a republic, where power supposedly belongs to the people.

So, Nigeria lacks a constitution that has gone through popular ratification through a referendum and lacks a constitution that is truly federal and truly republican. Therefore, Nigeria needs a new constitution rather than merely tinkering with the current deeply flawed, military-imposed one. However, the focus of each of the nine National Assemblies since Nigeria returned to civilian rule in 1999 has been to tinker with the Constitution through piecemeal amendments that, despite the huge costs expended, have resulted in no meaningful change to the Constitution.

In a column titled 'Back Again to the Unending Search', Abraham Ogbodo, a former Editor of the Guardian newspaper and now a columnist for the Nigerian Tribune, captures the charade pungently thus: 'One estimate puts the cost of amending the 1999 Constitution at five billion naira per an amendment committee. Nine Assemblies means Nine Amendment Committees. The maths comes to N45 billion, which is enough to build and equip, let me be conservative, two teaching hospitals. We can as well say that the National Assembly has used two teaching hospitals and 26 years to introduce just five alterations in the 1999 Constitution. It gets really annoying if a value is attached to these alterations. They are cosmetic applications that do not speak to the fundamental fault lines and are, therefore, incapable of providing answers to national questions. It has been an unbroken legislative merry-go-round, to say the least.'[120] That reflects a lack of political will to go beyond constitutional tinkering.

In 2022, the then Deputy Senate President, Ovie Omo-Agege, who was leading the constitutional review exercise, said that section 9 of the Constitution only allowed the National Assembly to amend and not to replace it.[121] Another senator, Opeyemi Bamidele, then chairman of the Senate Committee on Judiciary, Human Rights and Legal Matters, said: 'We cannot have a totally new Constitution because the law does not grant us the power to do that.'[122] But section 9(3) allows for amending section 9 itself, albeit with a higher threshold: four-fifths of the 109 Senators and four-fifths of the 360 members of the House of Representatives, plus two-thirds of state assemblies. That shows that section 9 is not an obstacle to creating a new constitution. Indeed, Senator Bamidele later admitted that section 9 was not necessarily an obstacle, saying: 'A new Constitution is possible, but we have to amend section 9 for the process to be activated.'[123]

Given that admission, what the legislators should do is amend section 9 to allow for a new Constitution and a referendum so that the process of creating a new Constitution could begin. The renowned constitutional lawyer, Professor Ben Nwabueze SAN, now late, proposed a better option. He said that it was not necessary to amend section 9. Rather, given that the current Constitution is not an act, but a schedule attached to an act, there should be a constitutional replacement whereby the National Assembly would invoke sections 4(1) and 4(4) of the constitution to detach the schedule from the act and replace it with a new constitution. That view was echoed by another senior lawyer, Dr Olisa Agbakoba SAN, at a public election in January 2024.[124]

What the foregoing shows is that the 'barriers' to restructuring Nigeria and creating a new Constitution are not constitutional but political. President Buhari demonstrated a lack of political will throughout his eight-year presidency as he repeatedly passed the buck and insisted that the responsibility for constitutional amendments lay with the National Assembly. But restructuring Nigeria requires more than some constitutional amendments; it requires giving Nigeria a new Constitution, and giving Nigeria a new constitution is not a role solely for the legislature. It must start as a political process, which only the president can initiate and lead before it morphs into a legislative process. As the leader of a country, the president has a convening power as well as a narrative power. This is because leaders are first and foremost communicators: they have a unique power to be heard by their citizens.[125] However, President Buhari failed throughout his eight years in power to use the convening, communicative and narrative levers to bring Nigerians together and forge a national consensus for restructuring the country.

Some believe that Buhari's successor, President Tinubu, is quietly restructuring Nigeria, albeit focusing on low hanging but vital fruits. For instance, Muyiwa Adetiba, a senior journalist, listed the Tinubu administration's initiatives on local governments' financial autonomy, tax reforms and state police, and said: 'If these are not forms of restructuring, then I don't know what the word means.'[126] But the truth is that these are haphazard and half-baked 'reforms' that do not fundamentally address Nigeria's deeply flawed political and governance structures. Rather, the top-down 'reforms' risk deepening the centralisation of governance in Nigeria. For instance, as stated earlier in this chapter, the Supreme Court ruling on local government autonomy undermines true federalism, while state police, unless properly thought through, could be counterproductive and produce unintended consequences, as discussed in Chapter 12. What Nigeria needs is a coherent and holistic restructuring of the polity based on a national consensus. Truth be told, Tinubu cannot whimsically and unilaterally 'restructure' or 'remake' Nigeria from Abuja. He must deploy his convening and communicative powers as president to lead the restructuring process by building cross-party, cross-ethnic and cross-societal consensus for a negotiated political and constitutional settlement that will result in a new constitution.

To be sure, Nigeria has had many constitutional conferences, and there may be no appetite for another expensive one. Therefore, the president should constitute a reasonably sized group of respectable Nigerians across political parties, across ethnic groups and across the wider society and task them to pore over the reports of previous conferences, learn from other countries, pull together constitutional proposals, consult nationally on them and put the final proposals to Nigerians in a referendum. The National Assembly should legislate for a referendum and endorse its outcome, translating it into a new constitution. Restructuring Nigeria and giving it a new political and constitutional settlement that will engender enduring unity, stability and progress for the country is an imperative. Nigeria's political leaders, led by the president and the legislators, must show the political will to build a national consensus for a new Nigeria. It is greatly hoped that this book will make a valuable contribution to the consensus-building and constitution-making processes that will help hugely transform Nigeria.

***

This chapter concludes the political part of this book. It takes forward the discussions in Chapter 1 on the historical and political contexts of Nigeria's structural challenges and in Chapter 2 on why Nigeria must be restructured. The focus of this chapter has been on what to restructure and how to do it. The list is not exhaustive, but it covers the essentials: the imperative for true federalism, underpinned by the decentralisation of power, regionalism and local governance; the need to replace Nigeria's current presidential system with the less expensive, less corruption-prone, less divisive and more economically efficient parliamentary system or a hybrid system; and the need to reform and strengthen Nigeria's electoral system so that Nigeria's elections can be credible and its democracy truly representative and accountable.

The chapter concludes by calling for a negotiated political and constitutional settlement and a new constitution that is genuinely federal and republican and that goes through a process of wider popular ratification through a referendum. Good political governance is a pre-condition for good economic governance. But without economic prosperity, no political arrangement can be sustainable. Thus, Part 2 of this book, the economic part, is as important as Part 1, the political part, because while the right political institutions and environment are a prerequisite for economic success, a robust and resilient economy is critical to sustain political stability, social cohesion and national security.

PART TWO

Economics and Economic Governance

4

Nigeria's Economic History

In his treatise *Of the Jealousy of Trade* (1758), David Hume argued that every country is specially endowed with resources and geniuses such that no nation should lack manufactured goods to export provided they 'preserve the spirit of industry and remain civilised.'[1] Then, he added: 'and if, notwithstanding these advantages, they lose such a manufacture, they ought to blame their own idleness or bad government, not the industry of their neighbours.'[2] Herein lies the issue at the heart of Nigeria's economic history. The country is endowed with abundant natural and human resources. Yet, despite these advantages, it has been unable to transform its economy and become a prosperous nation. The fault evidently lies, as Hume put it, with 'bad government' and, by extension, bad economic management.

Nigeria's Economy at Independence

At independence in 1960, Nigeria had a diversified economy and export base. It exported multiple agricultural commodities, including a substantial share of the world's cocoa, palm oil, ground nuts, cotton hides, rubber and coffee. It also exported minerals such as tin and coal. However, no sooner had Nigeria discovered crude oil in the 1960s than it slipped from its diversified export base into a monoculture economy that became almost entirely dependent on oil export. The statistics are staggering. While agriculture as a share of the value of exports was 75 per cent in 1965, it declined to 3 per cent in 2010. By contrast, oil went from 25 per cent of export by value in 1965 to 96 per cent in 2010.[3] Thus, in four decades, oil became Nigeria's main export product, accounting for about 90 per cent of total exports and the primary source of government revenue, averaging more than 75 per cent.

But how did Nigeria move from having a diversified export base to becoming an oil-dependent, monoculture economy? The analysis often turns on what is called 'Dutch Disease'.[4] With the influx of oil money (foreign exchange) in the 1970s, the value of the Nigerian currency, the naira (₦), became too high, making agricultural exports expensive and agricultural imports cheaper. Consequently, the focus shifted away from producing and exporting agricultural products to importing them, such that, as stated above, agriculture's export value share declined precipitously from 75 per cent in 1965 to 3 per cent by 2010. The rise of oil also created a large population of rent-seekers and arbitragers, who were simply buying and selling crude and refined products instead of engaging in productive activities that could grow the economy, create jobs and generate tax revenues for the country.

But besides Dutch Disease, rent-seeking and arbitrage, there is also the 'resource curse' argument, which is predicated on the corruption and mismanagement often associated with resource-rich countries. For instance, an estimated $400bn of Nigeria's oil revenues is believed to have been stolen since 1960.[5] Leaving aside the massive corruption, successive governments also mismanaged

Nigeria's oil wealth and failed to use it to diversify the economy. In the early 1970s, the then-Nigerian leader, General Yakubu Gowon, famously said that money was not the country's problem but how to spend it.[6] By contrast, many other oil-producing countries used their petrodollars to diversify and industrialise their economies.

In his book *The Wealth and Poverty of Nations*, David Landes said: 'In 1965, Nigeria (oil exporter) had higher GDP per capita than Indonesia (another oil exporter); twenty-five years later, Indonesia had three times the Nigerian level.'[7] Indonesia, like many of the Persian Gulf states, invested their oil wealth in developing flourishing non-oil sectors. However, Nigeria dissipated its oil wealth on white elephant projects. As Olusegun Aganga, a former finance and trade minister, points out in his book *Reclaiming the Jewel of Africa*, there are many abandoned or uncompleted projects across Nigeria. These include the four moribund state-owned oil refineries, the moribund Ajaokuta Steel Mill, built in 1979, abandoned hydroelectric power projects, redundant national satellites in space and several uncompleted buildings, stadia and roads.[8] In 2020, it was reported that 17 federal government airports were unviable and incurring losses.[9] Another report in 2023 said that 15 state government airports were unsustainable as they were underused and operating at huge losses.[10]

Nigeria's failure to realise its economic potential can also be blamed on its pursuit of the wrong economic philosophy. For decades, Nigeria followed a failed development path. While countries like Indonesia and Malaysia moved towards the East Asian growth model of export-led industrialisation, Nigeria pursued a protectionist import-substitution economic policy. The allure of protectionism has always been strong in Nigeria especially when there is an economic downturn. Nigeria's first major economic crisis of the oil era hit the Shehu Shagari government in the early 1980s. That government's response, as set out in the Economic Stabilisation (Temporary Provisions) Act of 1982, had at its core the curtailment of imports. When the Buhari military regime replaced Shagari's government in December 1983, it escalated the import-restriction policy by placing all imports under licensing and closing Nigeria's borders. As Jeffrey Herbst and Adebayo Olukoshi put it in their paper titled *Nigeria: Economic and Political Reforms at Cross Purposes*, 'the Buhari regime rejected fundamental structural and institutional changes that could allow Nigeria to adjust to the changing oil market.'[11]

The Babangida regime that replaced Buhari's was, broadly speaking, economically liberal. It accused the Buhari regime of running a Soviet-style centralised economy and expressed a preference for an open, free-market economy.[12] To that end, it introduced the pro-market Structural Adjustment Programme (SAP), backed by the IMF and the World Bank. The key elements of the SAP included fiscal tightening, deregulation of the foreign exchange market, trade liberalisation and privatisation and commercialisation of public enterprises. However, even with the scrapping of the notorious import-licensing system, the regime still introduced a tariff system that raised tariffs almost every year, sometimes up to 100 per cent for some products[13], and banned imports of consumer products such as wheat, vegetable oil, textiles and 'other items with available local substitutes.'[14] Even so, the SAP reform led to massive devaluations of the Naira and to high inflation, which made the reform very unpopular with Nigerians.[15] As

BusinessDay put it in an editorial, 'experience showed that SAP led to inflation, widespread job losses and economic hardship', adding that the reform 'did not help the economy much, but led to rising unemployment, currency devaluation and worsening poverty.'[16]

In 1994, General Sani Abacha succeeded Babangida. His regime reversed much of the SAP reforms and introduced wide-ranging regulations and controls. However, in 1995, to assuage the concerns of foreign investors, Abacha announced what he called 'guided deregulation'[17] and reversed some of the existing controls. But, as Abacha became increasingly dictatorial and unpopular internationally, his economic and trade policies became very restrictive. The situation did not improve under the civilian dispensation that started with the Obasanjo administration in 1999. Indeed, President Obasanjo once vowed that 'We are certainly going to ban more products', adding that 'the idea is to protect our local industries and boost our manufacturing capability substantially'[18]. Yet, despite the bans, powerful individuals were always able to bypass Ministry of Trade officials and secure import waivers directly from the president himself.[19]

In the UK, the government introduced the 'Tariff Suspensions Window', a scheme that allows any UK business to apply for a temporary suspension of import tariffs for specific goods normally used in domestic production. The aim of the suspension is to help UK companies benefit from lower input costs, that is, lower costs for products which are not produced in sufficient quantities within the UK, supporting their competitiveness in the global marketplace. Although domestic producers of substitutable products could object to such applications, the

UK government would accept applications to suspend import tariffs unless there is strong evidence that the products concerned are produced sufficiently at home. The overriding aim is to lower the costs of intermediate products for UK manufacturers, thereby supporting their competitiveness. However, in Nigeria, even if a product used in domestic production is not produced in sufficient quantities at home, the government would still ban it just to protect a few import-competing industries, ignoring the inevitable consequences.

For instance, when the central bank placed foreign exchange restrictions on the importation of 43 items in 2015, it claimed that the policy was intended to spur local production. However, when the same central bank, under a different leadership, lifted the forex restrictions in 2023, it said that removing the restrictions would benefit local production. In a statement after lifting the restrictions, the CBN said: 'Local production will benefit from cheaper imported inputs, and consumers will benefits from cheaper retail products,' adding: 'It is expected that employment generation will be boosted as closed factories re-open.'[20] Thus, the CBN, under one leadership, introduced the forex restrictions to spur local production; yet, the CBN, under another leadership, lifted the restrictions to achieve the same aim. That cannot be right as two diametrically opposed policy instruments cannot serve the same purpose. The truth is that protectionist tools, such as import prohibitions or restrictions, do not have the capacity to transform an economy or make a country self-sufficient. If they do, Nigeria would have been an economic powerhouse after decades of pursuing the import substitution industrialisation policy. Protectionism creates an extractive system that enriches a few producers but penalises consumers and the wider society and harms the economy. The argument in this chapter, and the remaining chapters in Part 2 of this book, is that Nigeria needs an open and competitive market economy that is export-oriented to unlock its economic potential and generate prosperity for its people.

'Buharinomics': Economic Failures of the Buhari Presidency

It is almost impossible to discuss Nigeria's economic history without a special mention of President Buhari's civilian administration from 2015 to 2023. As a military head of state from 1984 to 1985, General Buhari pursued a dirigiste economic policy that had at its heart capital, exchange and price controls, import licensing, indiscriminate import bans and other forms of state intervention.[21] The result was a collapsed economy with high levels of unemployment and poverty. About 30 years later, in 2015, Buhari returned to power as a civilian president. Learning nothing from the past, he pursued the same failed command-and-control economic policy that he implemented as a military ruler.

First, although he inherited an economic crisis caused by oil price shocks in 2014, he did not see the urgency to form a cabinet for the first six months of his administration.[22] His failure, amid an economic crisis, to appoint a finance minister for nearly seven months spooked the market and further sapped international confidence in Nigeria's economy. Second, he pursued misguided economic policies that made the bad economic situation he inherited a lot worse. Specifically, he pegged the naira to the dollar, refusing to allow its price to adjust in the face of the terms of trade shocks, against economic wisdom. According to the Mundell-Flemming trilemma, a theory propounded by two famous economists, Robert Mundell and Marcus Fleming, a government cannot do three things simultaneously. It cannot fix the exchange rate, control interest rates and allow free movement of capital. The three together would trigger capital flight.[23]

That was exactly what happened with the Buhari government's pegging of the exchange and interest rates while capital moved freely. Yet, as Nigeria haemorrhaged foreign exchange, Buhari stubbornly refused to scrap the currency peg, accusing those calling for the liberalisation of the exchange rate regime of wanting 'to kill the naira.'[24] In 2016, the economy went into a recession for the first time in two decades. Nigeria exited the recession in 2017 but slipped back again in 2020. Although the economy stayed out of recession since then, growth remained anaemic, hovering between 2 and 3 per cent. Buhari's aversion to economic expertise – he once referring to economists as 'the so-called economists'[25] – meant that he did not have economic advisers during his first term in office (2015 to 2019), and although he eventually constituted an economic advisory council at the start of his second term in 2019, he largely ignored their advice,[26] with the following policies being the key components of his economic philosophy, the so-called 'Buharinomics'.

Indiscriminate import bans

One of the defining characteristics of the Buhari administration's economic policy was the indiscriminate prohibition of imports. President Buhari said the 'underlying philosophy' of his government's economic policy was 'to promote import-substitution and self-sufficiency'[27], adding that 'under my watch, we will grow what we eat and consume what we make.'[28] As a result, his government imposed several import bans. For instance, in 2015, the Central Bank of Nigeria (CBN) published a list of 43 product groups deemed 'ineligible for foreign exchange', meaning that the importers of those products could not access foreign exchange through the official window. The CBN forex-ban list affected over 936 product lines, ranging from food items, such as rice, tomatoes, and meats, to manufactured goods, such as certain steel and wood (including toothpicks, textiles, plastics and cosmetic products. The list also included several intermediate products used in domestic production.[29]

As discussed later in this chapter, to ban food imports when Nigeria could not produce enough food items at home and in the face of acute food scarcity was a misguided, ideologically driven policy. Similarly, banning intermediate products or input raw materials that domestic industries needed to produce more efficiently undermined the intended policy aim of 'spurring local production.' Even the trade minister, Okechukwu Enelamah, admitted in an interview with the BBC that the CBN forex ban had 'unintended consequences'[30]. Yet, President Buhari refused to scrap the list throughout his eight years in power; rather, his administration added to it, including more items used in domestic production.

The reasoning behind the entrenched policy of import prohibition is that Nigeria is import-dependent and, therefore, must ban or restrict imports to conserve foreign exchange and protect local industries. But the argument is flawed. First, contrary to a widely held view, Nigeria is not exceptionally import-dependent. According to an analysis[31] by BusinessDay, Nigeria's and West Africa's topmost business newspaper, Nigeria's import-to-GDP ratio, a measure of how much a country imports relative to its economic size, was 11.8 per cent in 2022, which was far lower than those of its peers in Africa, as shown by figure 1 below. Compared with countries with similar economic size, Nigeria also imports significantly less, as Figure 2 shows.

Figure 1:

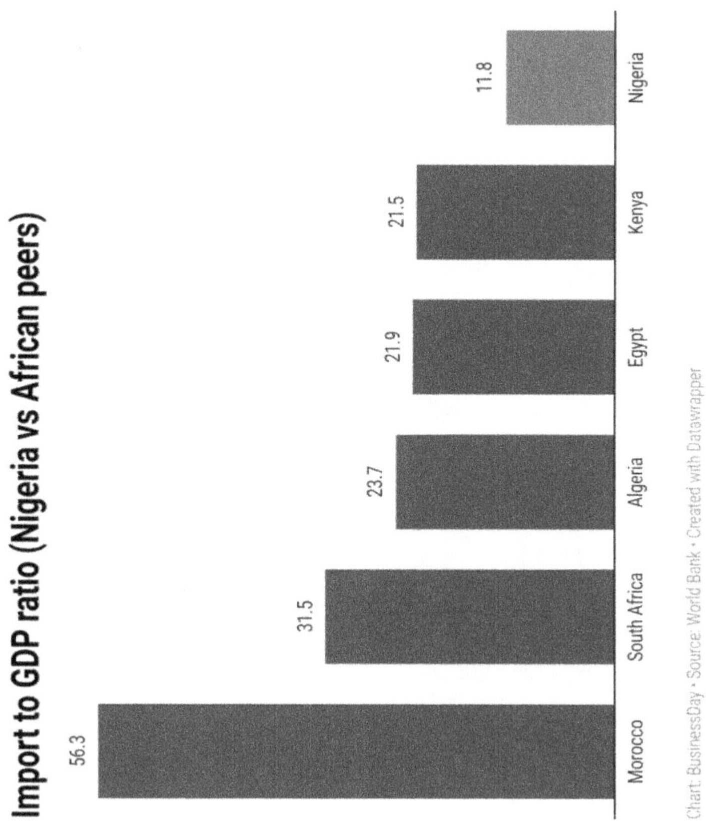

Figure 2:

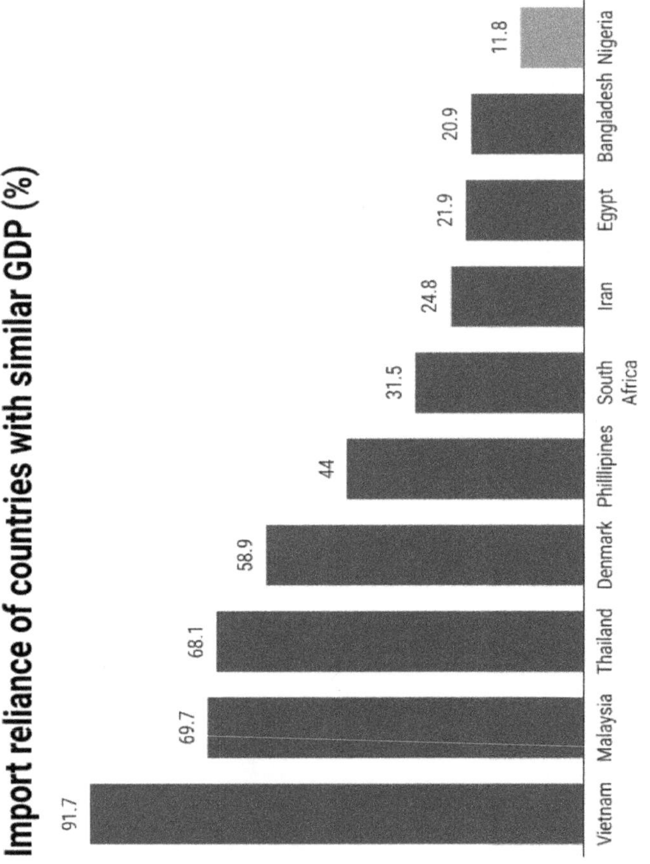

The above figures show that Nigeria is nowhere near being import-dependent compared with many other countries. Indeed, an earlier World Bank analysis also confirmed this, showing that Nigeria's import of goods and services as a percentage of its GDP was 12.9 per cent in 2012, dropping to 10.8 per cent in 2015, while that of South Africa was 33 per cent in 2013 and 32 per cent in 2015.[32] Furthermore, the World Bank ranked Nigeria only 34th out of 137 major importing nations in 2015[33], and the position has barely changed. Indeed, according to the WTO, imports as a share of Nigeria's GDP was around 11 per cent in 2023, with refined petroleum imports accounting for 38.3 per cent of total imports in 2023.[34] Thus, taking out refined oil imports, Nigeria is not import-dependent, and its policy of indiscriminate import restrictions cannot be justified on grounds of import dependency.

The problem is not that Nigeria is import-dependent but that it is not export-oriented. Exports are crucial to pay for imports, and when a country is not exporting enough, it will face a serious terms-of-trade problem as it will not have sufficient foreign exchange to fund its imports. But Nigeria is not a major exporter of goods beyond crude oil, which is subject to supply constraints, such as oil theft and pipeline vandalism, as well as the vagaries of the world oil market. As noted above, imports as a share of Nigeria's GDP were just around 11 per cent in 2023, and 38 per cent of that was refined petroleum imports. If Nigeria were really generating foreign exchange from exports, particular valued-added non-oil exports, concerns about being import-dependent would not arise, as exports would be paying for the imports.

The truth is that most of the world's top importing countries are also top exporters, as a BusinessDay analysis, conducted by Lolade Akinmurele, Wasiri Alli and Eniola Olatunji, shows. Figure 3 shows the top five import-dependent countries, while Figure 4 shows their export orientation. The statistics show that Nigeria's problem is low exports, not high imports. With imports accounting for about 12 per cent of GDP, Nigeria is certainly not an import-dependent country. If Nigeria were a major exporting country, it would not be fretting about the relatively small volumes of goods it imports, which, in any case, is dominated, as stated above, by refined oil imports.

Figure 3

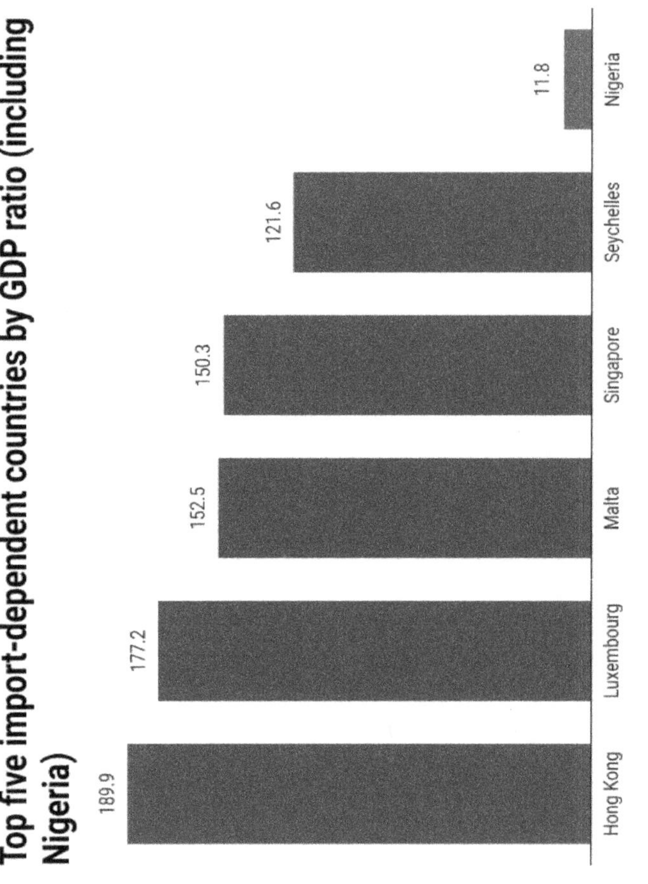

Figure 4

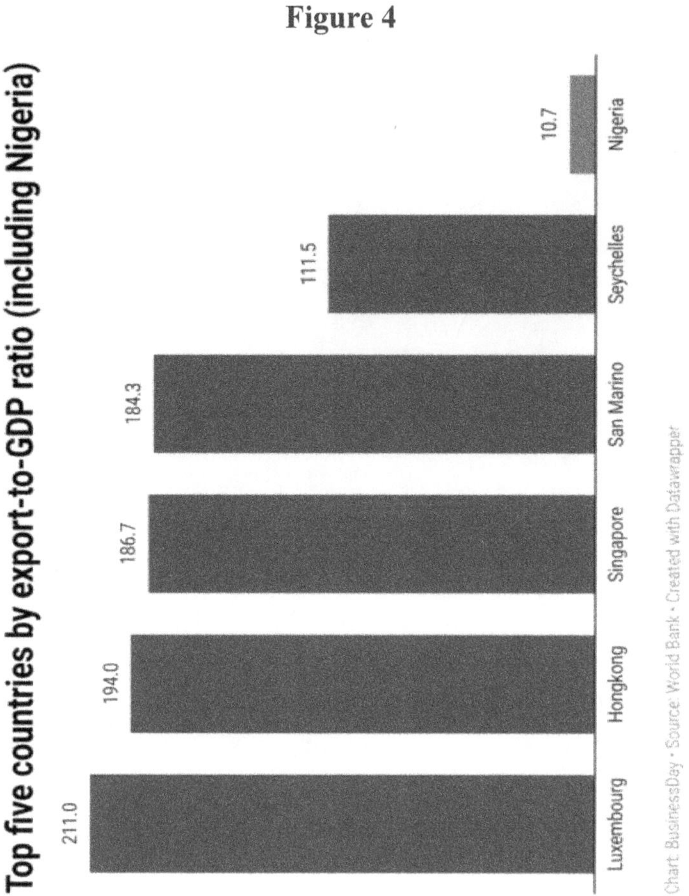

But faced with the shortage of foreign exchange, Nigeria tends to blame imports as the primary cause, ignoring the fact that it is simply not generating enough foreign exchange from non-oil exports and foreign investment. Foreign exchange shortage can be viewed either as a demand problem or a supply problem. If it is viewed as a demand problem, a government may want to reduce demand for foreign exchange by reducing the demand for imports through import bans, high tariffs and other trade restrictions.

However, if it is viewed as a supply problem, the aim would be to increase the supply of foreign exchange by attracting more of it. In the case of the latter, the solution is not to ban imports and fix the exchange rate. Rather, it is to allow the exchange rate to adjust and regulate imports, while also encouraging the inflow of foreign capital.

Floating a currency could lead to its devaluation, dictated by market forces. Such a devaluation would not only make imports more expensive, thereby reducing the demand for imports, but it would also make a country's exports less expensive and, thus, more attractive internationally, which would favour the export-oriented sector and, potentially, spur domestic production. In his adjustment theory, known as the *price-specie-flow mechanism*[35], David Hume argued that if a local currency is overvalued, it would encourage imports and discourage local production; but if it is devalued, it would discourage imports and encourage local production and, potentially, exports. That market-based mechanism is the best way to address foreign exchange shortages rather than pegging a currency and artificially fixing its value or banning/restricting imports to reduce demand.

Furthermore, a floating exchange rate would incentivise the inflow of foreign capital as foreign investors know that the value of a country's currency is market-determined and that they can bring money in and take money out without the government interfering in the process. By contrast, a fixed and overvalued currency will simply make imports cheaper and worsen the foreign exchange shortage while also discouraging exports and foreign investment inflows. Thus, a weak currency that incentivises domestic production and, possibly, exports is better than an overvalued currency that disincentives domestic production and harms export potential. However, these were not the considerations in the exchange rate and import policies of the Buhari administration.

In his eight years in power, President Buhari pursued a dirigiste economic policy. He imposed indiscriminate bans on imports, fixed the exchange rate of the naira, propped it up with scarce foreign exchange, and distorted the macroeconomic environment with massive spending and borrowing, allowing inflation and unemployment to grow uncontrollably. Billions of dollars of investment in unproductive and economically unsustainable infrastructure and wasteful spending on agriculture did not lift the economy out of the doldrums. Economically, the Buhari presidency was a failure. Under President Buhari, Nigeria was a closed and uncompetitive economy, and investor confidence was extremely damaged, resulting in a dwindling inflow of foreign capital.[36] According to one report, 70 firms exited Nigeria in seven years under President Buhari's government due to foreign exchange problems and poor power supply.[37] In 2014, a year before Buhari became president, Nigeria was Africa's biggest economy, but by 2023, when Buhari left office, Nigeria had slipped into fourth place in dollar terms. Buhari's successor accused his administration of 'bankrupting' Nigeria[38], of leaving behind 'a totally ruined economy.'[39]

'Tinubunomics': President Tinubu's Economic Approach

President Bola Tinubu succeeded President Buhari on May 29, 2023. Sensitive to some of the issues highlighted above, and particularly the concerns of foreign investors and foreign governments about them, Tinubu moved swiftly to abolish some of the Buhari administration's most controversial policies. For instance, on his inauguration on May 29, he veered from his written speech and declared: 'Subsidy in gone', referring to the decades-old petroleum subsidy. With that surprise announcement, the fuel subsidy was immediately scrapped. On the same day, his government announced the end of the pegged and multiple exchange rate systems. A few months later, the Central Bank of Nigeria scrapped the controversial list of 43 import items deemed ineligible for foreign exchange in the official forex market. These three policies – the removal of the fuel subsidy, the scrapping of the currency peg and the withdrawal of the CBN forex-ban list – were critical economic reforms of the Tinubu administration and defined its more liberal and market-oriented approach as opposed to the Buhari government's dirigisme.

However, while President Tinubu's economic reforms moved Nigeria's economy away from the acute instability and volatility of the Buhari years into some form of stabilisation, they also produced some perverse consequences. In particular, they triggered soaring inflation and massive devaluation of the naira and inflicted unbearable levels of poverty and misery on millions of ordinary Nigerians.[40] The following sections discuss two of the reforms – the subsidy removal and the scrapping of the currency peg – and attempt to explain the reasons for their perverse consequences.

The Fuel Subsidy Removal

Fuel subsidies were introduced in Nigeria in the 1970s. Although the world's thirteenth-largest oil producer, Nigeria lacked sufficient capacity to refine its crude oil. As a result, it imported refined petroleum products, which it sold to the public at below-market prices. Hence, the intervention was called a fuel subsidy. However, the financial cost of the subsidy became increasingly unsustainable, accounting for about 15 per cent of government expenditure in 2022.[41] Thus, successive Nigerian governments attempted to remove the subsidy. However, this proved challenging both because of economic realities and hostile public reactions. For instance, the Obasanjo administration abolished the fuel subsidy in 2004 but restored it two years later, in 2006, when world oil prices went up.[42] The ordinary cost of fuel subsidy is linked to the landing costs of imported refined petroleum products, but the landing costs are linked to the price of crude oil in the world market as well as the exchange rate of the local currency, the Naira. Where world oil prices are rising, and the naira loses its value, importing refined petroleum products would be very expensive. Without a subsidy, the high landing costs of imported refined petroleum would push up the pump price of petrol and the costs of other things like food and transport. It was thus difficult to remove the fuel subsidy in the face of rising world oil prices or the naira's devaluation.

But at other times, fuel subsidy removal was politicised. Most Nigerians have not benefitted from the country's enormous oil wealth. Even though being a national asset, Nigeria's oil should benefit every segment of Nigerian society, that's not so, as the country's oil wealth has long benefitted its elites.[43] Thus, to most ordinary Nigerians, the fuel subsidy was the only thing the state had ever done for them or, as Dr Okonjo-Iweala put it, 'the only direct benefits they enjoyed from their country's oil resources.'[44] This made attempts to remove the fuel subsidy politically difficult as it was bound to provoke public protests. However, the difficulty was doubly increased by the fact that opposition politicians always seized on government plans to remove the fuel subsidy to gain political advantage.

For instance, in January 2012, President Jonathan announced the removal of the fuel subsidy. However, the policy was immediately withdrawn after nationwide protests. Although the labour unions led the protests, it was the backing of the opposition political parties, which seized the opportunity to play politics against the government, that increased the political salience. The then Action Congress of Nigeria (ACN), led by Bola Tinubu, Nigeria's current president, was the brain and force behind the *Occupy Nigeria* protests that spread across many Nigerian cities, opposing the subsidy removal.

Indeed, Tinubu himself wrote an article titled 'Removal of oil subsidy: President Jonathan breaks social contract with the people'[45] in which he strongly condemned the government's plan to remove the subsidy, saying that it 'will destroy more jobs than it creates,'[46] adding: 'For every job it creates in the capital-intensive petroleum sector, it will terminate several jobs in the rest of the labour-intensive economy.'[47] Tinubu described the proposed subsidy removal as 'the Jonathan tax' that 'will increase the price of petrol, transport and most consumer items.'[48] The article, published on January 11, 2012, resurfaced in 2023 after President Tinubu scrapped the fuel subsidy and prompted allegations of hypocrisy. In September 2023, Kayode Fayemi, a former governor of Ekiti State and chieftain of the then ACN, publicly apologised to former President Jonathan, saying that his then party's opposition to Jonathan's planned subsidy removal was political. 'We in ACN at the time, in 2012, we know the truth, Sir, but it is all politics,'[49] he told Jonathan at a public event.

In 2023, former President Buhari also revealed how he played politics with the subsidy removal. Buhari said he amended the Petroleum Industry Act 2021, which mandated the removal of the fuel subsidy, to delay its implementation so as 'to allow Tinubu to win the election.'[50] According to him, 'polls after polls showed that the party would have been thrown out of office if the decision as envisaged by the new Petroleum Industry Act was made.' [51] So, Buhari manipulated the law and policy on fuel subsidy removal to 'allow Tinubu to win the election'. But once Tinubu won, he scrapped the fuel subsidy on his first day in office. Such politicisation of the fuel subsidy removal by Tinubu, who stridently opposed it in 2012, and by Buhari, who delayed it to gain an electoral advantage for his party in 2023, did not inspire confidence that the Tinubu government's withdrawal of the fuel subsidy in May 2023 was done with conviction, thoughtfulness and consideration of its potential consequences.

The intended aim of the fuel subsidy removal was to allow market forces to determine the pump price of petrol, which could then have other outcomes, such as ensuring efficient allocation of state resources and encouraging profitable investment in the liberalised downstream sector.[52] However the withdrawal of the fuel subsidy had two major problems. The first was the failure to consider whether the circumstances were right for scrapping the subsidy immediately or whether there were better alternatives to scrapping it altogether. The second problem was, assuming the subsidy removal was inevitable, the failure to put in place a robust mitigation plan to alleviate the impact on the living standards of poor and vulnerable Nigerians. The problems are considered further below.

Reliance on imported refined petroleum

At the heart of the fuel subsidy issue is the failure of Nigeria to refine its crude and produce consumable fuels. Nigeria is the world's sixth-largest oil-producing country and yet one of the largest importers of refined petroleum products. Although Nigeria has four state-owned refineries, they were moribund and unable to produce consumable fuels like petrol, kerosene, and diesel to meet growing downstream demand. As a result, Nigeria had to import almost all the refined petroleum products it consumes. Rationally, the Nigerian government should have privatised the state-owned refineries if it cannot make them work. However, the government continued to spend billions of dollars on so-called 'turnaround maintenance'. For instance, although Nigeria spent $25billion between 2013 and 2023 on fixing the refineries, it still spent, during the period, about $28billion per annum to import refined petroleum products.[53]

In November 2024, the Nigerian National Petroleum Company (NNPC), the state-owned oil company, announced that the Port Harcourt Refinery, one of the state-owned refineries, had become operational and was capable of refining crude.[54] The NNPC also announced that the Warri Refinery was 60 per cent operational.[55] However, due to the lack of government transparency in Nigeria, with citizens' trust in government virtually non-existent, doubts were cast on the claims. For instance, a community leader said that the Port Harcourt Refinery was only operating skeletally and was not processing refined petroleum[56], although the NNPC disputed the statement.[57] A newspaper also claimed that the Port Harcourt Refinery was only blending finished or semi-finished petroleum products and not refining crude[58], to which the NNPC responded that blending was not a crime.[59] Former President Obasanjo described the claims that the refineries were working as 'lies', saying they were still not working despite the $3bn spent to rehabilitate them.[60] The NNPC responded by inviting Obasanjo to 'tour the rehabilitated refineries' and see things by himself.[61] Yet, in July 2025, the new CEO of NNPC, Bayo Ojulari, said the government was considering selling the state-owned refineries because efforts to revive them were becoming 'a bit more complicated'.[62] That was despite the fact that, at the time, over $2.8bn had been spent on so-called Turnaround Maintenance.[63] The NNPC later ruled out selling the refineries, but that did not remove the fact that they were not functioning, despite years of 'maintenance'.

The point here is that, at the time Tinubu abruptly scrapped the fuel subsidy, none of the state-owned refineries nor any private refinery was refining crude, and Nigeria was still heavily importing refined petroleum products to meet domestic demand. This was contrary to the commitment in Tinubu's election manifesto, which said: 'We shall phase out the fuel subsidy.'[64] Indeed, the manifesto went on to link the removal of the oil subsidy to the Dangote Refinery, saying: 'By the time we took office, the Dangote Refinery would have been fully operational, nullifying the need to import refined petroleum.'[65] But at the time Tinubu took office and announced the withdrawal of the fuel subsidy, the Dangote Refinery was nowhere near being fully operational, and Nigeria was still importing refined petroleum, which made the abrupt scrapping of the fuel subsidy seem impulsive.

Dangote Refinery: Is it a game-changer for Nigeria?

In 2023, Aliko Dangote, reputed to be Africa's richest man, opened his $20 billion refinery in Lagos. The refinery was expected to receive 650,000 barrels of crude oil per day and produce between 25-30 million litres of petrol daily.[66] At the launch of the first output of the Dangote Refinery's refined petrol in September 2024, Dangote said his refinery would end petrol queues in Nigeria.[67] Indeed, it was reported in February 2025 that the refinery was already producing 33 million litres of refined petroleum a day and that the plant had reached a capacity of 550,000 barrels a day.[68] However, those achievements masked the fact that, since its opening, the Dangote Refinery has had a topsy-turvy relationship with the state-owned oil company, NNPC, on the one hand, and the oil sector's statutory regulator, the Nigerian Midstream and Downstream Petroleum Regulatory Authority (NMDPRA), on the other.

In July 2024, a rift broke out between Dangote and NMDPRA when the regulator said that the refinery's products were inferior to imported ones[69] and accused Dangote of seeking to monopolise the domestic market for refined products, which Dangote denied.[70] As for the NNPC, it initially made a downpayment of $2.7bn for a 20 per cent stake in the refinery but later inexplicably whittled its stake down to 7.2 per cent, which suggested a cooling in the relationship between the Dangote Refinery and the NNPC. Indeed, much of 2024 was dominated by sniping between Dangote and the NNPC over the supply of crude and on what terms, as well over the role of NNPC in the purchase of the Dangote Refinery's refined petroleum and its pricing. Although NNPC was supposed to supply 650,000 barrels of crude a day to the Dangote Refinery, the refinery said NNPC was not delivering all the crude it was supposed to deliver, forcing it to turn to suppliers in places like Brazil and the US. Amid the dispute between NNPC and the Dangote Refinery, President Tinubu ordered NNPC to sell crude to the Dangote Refinery on the local currency, naira, rather than in dollars. According to Tinubu's spokesperson, Bayo Onanuga, this was a 'game-changing intervention[71] as it would save the Dangote refinery the pressure of competing for scarce foreign exchange.

However, Dangote later said that the government's plan to sell crude in local currency was not working as the NNPC was unable to supply the crude his refinery needed. 'We need 650,000 barrels per day, NNPC agreed to give a minimum of 385,000 bpd, but they are not even delivering that,' Edwin Devakumar, head of the Dangote refinery, said, according to a report by Reuters.[72] Indeed, it was reported that the Dangote Refinery was importing one-third of its crude from the US as domestic supply was not meeting its needs.[73] Dangote himself blamed the shortage of domestic crude supply to his refinery for the surge in imports from the US, saying in a statement: 'Due to a shortage of domestic crude oil, the refinery has increasingly relied on imports from the United States to meet its needs.'[74]

The foregoing raises the key question of whether the Dangote Refinery would, indeed, be a game-changer for Nigeria. First, would the existence of the Dangote Refinery stop Nigeria from importing refined petroleum? Second, even if Nigeria stopped importing refined petroleum products, would local production bring down the pump price of fuel? On the first question, the government's assumptions are that the Dangote Refinery and other local refineries would not only lead to the reduction of refined petroleum imports but also result in the export of refined petroleum. Indeed, the revenue projections in President Tinubu's 2025 budget proposals were, in large part, based on 'reduced importation of petroleum products alongside increased export of finished petroleum products.'[75] However, there is no sound basis to assume such positive future projections due to, as discussed above, uncertainties around domestic crude production and supply.

To be sure, Dangote had long accused the NNPC, the NMDPRA and the international oil companies (IOCs) of attempting to sabotage his refinery either by importing refined petroleum, despite local production, or by refusing to supply his refinery with enough crude oil.[76] But if the importation of refined petroleum continues, despite local refining, and if domestic refineries cannot access crude locally but have to import much of it, then the Dangote Refinery may turn out not to be the much-touted game changer for Nigeria. As of the time of writing, the situation with the Dangote Refinery, particularly regarding its relationship with the NNPC, the oil sector regulators and the oil marketers, is in a state of flux. The question of whether the Dangote Refinery is a game-changer for Nigeria would very much turn on how those relationships develop, and whether the early challenges become transient or entrenched.

Above all, however, the real question is whether the arrival of the Dangote Refinery would lead to sustained reduction in the pump price of petrol. This is important because continued fuel price rises, despite supposed local refining, would jar with the public. Following the withdrawal of the petrol subsidy in 2023, the price of petrol at the pump tripled from ₦197/litre to ₦620/litre. However, in September 2024, Dangote petrol sold for between ₦950 and ₦1,200 in most filling stations in Nigeria. In that month, the *Daily Trust* newspaper published a story titled 'Nigerians: Our hopes dashed over Dangote fuel price',[77] reflecting the disappointment expressed by many Nigerians that Dangote Refinery had not resulted in the lower pump price of petrol. However, it should be said that, sometimes, the pump price dropped because the Dangote Refinery reduced its ex-depot petrol price[78], while, at other times, fuel price fell because of so-called 'price war' between the Dangote Refinery and the NNPC, which had started to sell refined petrol from its partially revived Port Harcourt and Warri refineries.[79]

Yet, despite Dangote's occasional generosity in lowering the prices of his fuel and the so-called 'price war', the truth is that the pump price of petrol was still about ₦900 per litre in March 2025, nearly five times the price before the removal of the fuel subsidy in May 2023. Tinubu said in his election manifesto that 'there will be no need for a subsidy because supply will come from local refineries.' But with the pump price of petrol potentially rising above ₦1,000/litre, despite local production, it would be hard to ignore the impact on ordinary Nigerians, especially as rising fuel prices are a major driver of Nigeria's persistently high inflation and cost-of-living crisis, which erode household budgets and deepen poverty.

Subsidy Corruption

The second problem with the subsidy removal is that there was a better alternative, namely, to tackle the massive corruption around the subsidy instead of eliminating it altogether. In her book *Fighting Corruption Is Dangerous*, Dr Ngozi Okonjo-Iweala devotes a chapter to what she calls 'Confronting the Oil Scammers'.[80] It is clear from her analysis that corruption probably accounted for half of the $10 billion that the government spent annually on the fuel subsidy. As Okonjo-Iweala puts it, 'The story of Nigeria's oil and gas sector is ugly.'[81] According to the findings of a House of Representatives committee in 2012, the subsidy regime 'was fraught with endemic corruption and entrenched inefficiency.'[82] The corruption took the forms of 'subsidy claims for products not delivered; overcharging of the government by oil marketers; requisition of foreign exchange for imports of refined products, with the foreign exchange diverted to other uses; unauthorised deductions by the Nigerian National Petroleum Corporation (NNPC) to itself; and mismanagement by government officials.'[83] Furthermore, the fuel subsidy created arbitrage whereby subsidised petrol was bought in Nigeria and sold expensively in other West African countries.

In 2023, Isa Yuguda, a former governor of Bauchi State, told a TV station that a friend of his in the oil industry told him that he told President Buhari: 'Mr President, please remove this subsidy. We are tired of making money!'[84] In his book titled *The Shadow of Loot and Losses: Uncovering Nigeria's Petroleum Subsidy Fraud*, the former chairman of the Economic and Financial Crimes Commission (EFCC), Abdulrasheed Bawa, revealed that Nigeria lost $450 million to fuel subsidy fraud between 2006 and 2012.[85] Indeed, in June 2025, two fuel subsidy fraudsters were each jailed for 14 years for fraudulently collecting ₦2.2 billion ($13 million) in subsidy payments for claiming to have imported 20 million litres of refined petroleum, which they did not import.[86]

The truth is that the fuel subsidy created several billionaires overnight, and successive governments did nothing to stop the corruption. Therefore, there is a valid argument that, on the ground of corruption alone, the subsidy should be scrapped. But there is also a credible argument that the government should have tackled the corruption and inefficiency around the fuel subsidy, including recovering public funds from subsidy fraudsters and targeting the subsidy more effectively to ensure that it is paid for petroleum products consumed and not for fictitious claims. But while it scrapped the subsidy, the government did nothing to prosecute and recover money from those who fraudulently enriched themselves through the scheme. Thus, the policy allowed the oil scammers to enjoy their stolen billions but subjected ordinary Nigerians to the inflationary pains of the subsidy removal.

Failure to Mitigate the Impacts of Subsidy Withdrawal

The last problem with the abrupt removal of the fuel subsidy was the failure to put in place the right mitigation plans. One of the arguments in favour of scrapping the fuel subsidy was that it benefitted only the rich. As the IMF put it, the fuel subsidy was 'highly regressive, benefitting people that are driving large cars and not the poorer people.'[87] However, when the subsidy was removed, the immediate impact was felt by poor Nigerians. The pump price of petrol tripled from ₦197/litre to ₦620/litre, fuelling a surge in food and transport costs. The government did not heed the IMF's call for 'adequate compensatory measures for the poor and efficient and transparent use of the saved money.'[88] Although the government repeatedly said that it saved trillions of naira from the subsidy removal, the savings were not used to alleviate the cost-of-living pains of ordinary Nigerians beyond some paltry palliatives, such as handing out bags of rice and cash stipends to a small proportion of the population. For instance, it was reported that the Federal Government would give ₦50,000 ($32) to 100,000 homes across Nigeria[89], potentially benefitting fewer than 15 million people in a country where more than 100 million people live below the poverty line.

That said, there continued to be speculations that the government had restored some fuel subsidy payments. In a report titled 'Petrol subsidy nears N1trn monthly, bigger than when Tinubu came,' *BusinessDay* said the government had started to pay some subsidies as the naira's devaluation pushed up the landing cost of petrol.[90] Former Kaduna State governor Nasir El-Rufai also said the subsidy was back, adding that 'right now, the government is paying a lot of money for subsidy, even more than before.'[91] The IMF, too, believed there was the quiet reintroduction of 'an implicit subsidy'.[92] According to the IMF, the government introduced a subsidy-like instrument at the end of 2023 by capping fuel prices at the pump, which are lower than actual costs.[93] The IMF estimated that newly introduced price caps could amount to 2.8 per cent of GDP in 2024.[94] However, the government continued to deny that it had reintroduced, in any form, the fuel subsidies.

To be sure, removing the fuel subsidy could be justified on many grounds, such as costs, corruption, the need to incentivise investment through a market-based price mechanism, and the need to mitigate climate change through a reduction in fossil-fuel energy use. However, as discussed in the foregoing, the policy had major weaknesses. First, at the time the subsidies were removed, Nigeria still relied heavily on imported petroleum products instead of producing them at home. Second, subsidy scams, rather than subsidies themselves, accounted for much of the cost of the subsidies. Given that there is no country without some form of social subsidies, the government should have tackled the subsidy corruption and streamline and targeted the subsidies instead of scrapping them altogether. And third, even if the subsidies were to be removed, the government should have put in place effective mitigation to alleviate the pain on the poor. In truth, until Nigeria can refine its crude oil and produce affordable consumable fuels locally or until it can put in place adequate relief measures for the poor, the fuel subsidy removal would remain problematic for the country.

Scrapping of the Currency Peg

As discussed earlier, President Buhari introduced the fixed currency regime, pegging the naira to the dollar. When he campaigned for the presidency in 2015, he vowed to ensure the naira's parity with the dollar so that one dollar would sell for one naira. However, on becoming president, he abandoned the campaign pledge and settled for pegging the naira at the then prevailing rate of 198 naira to one dollar. That administrative fiat entrenched the overvaluation of the naira and inevitably led to capital flight. In 2016, as Nigeria haemorrhaged foreign exchange and struggled to defend the pegged currency from a depleted foreign reserve, the government introduced a multiple exchange rate system, with different rates, some fixed, others floating, applying to different segments of the economy. For instance, there was the fixed (official) rate of ₦305 per $1 used for government imports, there was also the fixed (official) rate of ₦320 per $1 available to favoured importers, and there was the black-market rate of up to ₦500 per $1 for everyone else.[95]

Inevitably, the multiple exchange rates distorted the market and acted as restrictions on capital mobility as foreign investors could not access foreign exchange and repatriate their profits, especially as the government rationed foreign exchange, which created a backlog of $7 billion dollars of unrepatriated revenues. Consequently, the multiple exchange rate regime discouraged foreign investment. Furthermore, the system boosted the black market and encouraged rent-seeking behaviour through roundtripping, whereby powerful individuals bought dollars at fixed or official rates and sold them at the black market, making a profit of billions of naira as a result. That was the exchange rate system that President Tinubu inherited, and it was hardly surprising that he was widely hailed, especially internationally, for scrapping the currency peg and replacing it with a floating exchange rate system.

However, the predictable, if not intended, effect of floating the naira was its immediate and sustained rout against the dollar. When President Tinubu took office on May 29, 2023, the naira's exchange rate was 465.07 naira per dollar. But as soon as he scrapped the multiple exchange rates, the naira's value dropped to 900 naira per dollar and continued its downward spiral, reaching 1,650 naira per dollar about nine months later in March 2024. Thus, by March 2024, the official exchange rate had lost around 70 per cent of its value in US dollar terms. Coupled with the withdrawal of the petroleum subsidy, which itself fuelled inflation, and a loose fiscal policy, the naira's steep devaluation pushed up the rate of inflation to a three-decade high of 34 per cent by March 2024, deepening poverty and misery in the country.

The collapse of the naira's value and the high inflation prompted aggressive responses by the central bank. First, it raised interest rates six consecutive times in 2024. For instance, the CBN raised the interest rates to 22.75 per cent in February 2024, then to 24.75 per cent in March 2024, then 27.25 per cent in September 2024 and 27.50 per cent in November 2024. To be sure, the combination of naira's massive devaluation and the big hikes in interest rates, resulting in yields of 20 per cent to 25 per cent, made Nigerian assets cheaper and attractive to foreign portfolio investors, leading to significant foreign portfolio investment flows into Nigeria's bond markets.[96] However, while high interest rates may attract foreign portfolio investors, they are damaging to manufacturers by increasing the cost of borrowing and reducing the profitability and competitiveness of businesses. Therefore, the central bank's orthodox response to the naira's devaluation and the high inflation, through the hiking up of interest rates, would, if it continued, severely damage the economy.

There were also allegations that the central bank was using Nigeria's foreign reserves to defend the naira.[97] In February 2025, the economist Bismark Rewane said the CBN had spent $8bn to stabilise the naira.[98] Indeed, to stem the naira's continuing devaluation, the government frequently intervened in the forex market by selling dollars cheaply to the 1,588 Bureau De Change (BDC) operators.[99] However, using the country's limited foreign reserves to defend the naira would be counterproductive. As the IMF said in its 2024 Article IV Consultation report on Nigeria, 'such interventions should not be used as a substitute for required macroeconomic policy adjustment needed to restore internal and external stability.'[100] The value of a country's currency is determined by the strength of its economy. If the economy is strong, the currency will be strong; if the economy is weak, the currency will be weak. Therefore, trying to prop up a weak currency artificially, instead of allowing its value to reflect demand and supply conditions, would undermine market confidence and could trigger capital flight.

Thus, having floated the naira, which was a good policy, the government should know that the naira's performance relative to foreign currencies, particularly the dollar, will depend on the macroeconomic environment, especially low inflation, and the ability of Nigeria to attract significant foreign exchange through exports and foreign investment, particularly foreign direct investment ('sticky money'), as opposed to foreign portfolio investment ('hot money'). But Nigeria lacks a diversified export base, which is oil dominated. Indeed, manufacturing exports went down 62 per cent in four years.[101] Furthermore, the long-running shortage of foreign exchange and a sharp devaluation of the naira forced many multinational companies to leave Nigeria.[102] According to a report published by the Vanguard newspaper in July 2024, sixteen multinational companies exited Nigeria in three years.[103] These included popular names like Unilever, Procter and Gamble, Kimberly-Clark and Diageo.[104]

The floating of the naira was a necessary but insufficient measure to revive the Nigerian economy. Floating the naira was an *enabler* that removed a barrier, namely, the pegged currency that discouraged foreign investment. But to attract large and sustained foreign exchange, the economy needs *drivers*, which must include a strong macroeconomic environment, notably low inflation and low interest rates, a conducive business environment that makes investing in Nigeria attractive, and a diversified export base and other sources of foreign capital inflows. Unfortunately, instead of spurring local production and incentivising significant non-oil exports, the naira's devaluation led to an acute shortage of foreign exchange and further devaluations. This is because Nigeria lacks the supply-side incentives to boost local production and exports, and boost forex earnings. One of the key solutions is to aggressively promote non-oil exports.

However, as evidenced by an investigative report in the Vanguard newspaper titled 'Why exporters are struggling,'[105] Nigerian exporters face huge obstacles, including the high cost of inputs, which increased their working capital by 350 per cent within one year; high interest rates, which constrained their ability to raise funds to sustain or increase production; and restrictions on exporters' repatriation of foreign exchange earnings.[106] Yet, unless Nigeria can attract significant foreign exchange in a sustainable way, rather than mainly through foreign portfolio investment inflows, which are easily reversible, the naira's value would always be at risk, and the benefits that should accrue from floating the currency would not be realised. Depleting Nigeria's foreign reserves or aggressively raising interest rates to defend the naira would be counterproductive and extremely damaging to the economy.

Finally, it would be misleading to think that the elimination of the pegged and multiple exchange rates has made Nigeria an open and competitive market economy. This is because the government still maintains several interventions, known as capital flow management measures (CFMs), that restrict the outflow of foreign exchange. For instance, in June 2024, the Central Bank required international money transfer operators to quote exchange rates based on the official exchange rate while prohibiting the payout of inward US dollar transfers in foreign exchange as well as outward transfers by them.[107] The CBN also lowered the limits on the immediate repatriation of oil export proceeds of international oil firms from 80 per cent to 50 per cent, allowing remaining proceeds to be repatriated only after 90 days.[108] There are also payment limits on naira-denominated credit and debit cards for overseas transactions.[109] The IMF considered such CFMs to be inconsistent with its 'Institutional View on Liberalisation and Management of Capital Flows' and urged the Nigerian government to remove them.[110] The existence of such foreign exchange restrictions suggests that Nigeria's new foreign exchange regime is not fully liberalised and, thus, it is suboptimal. Furthermore, such restrictions, if sustained, could undermine investors' confidence, especially as it limits the abilities of foreign investors to access foreign exchange and repatriate their profits.

Other Major Fault Lines in Nigeria's Economy

This chapter on Nigeria's economic history will be incomplete without mentioning other key fault lines in Nigeria's economy. These fault lines and the need to tackle them are briefly highlighted below.

Lack of Resilience to Oil Price Shocks

There are few certainties in life. External shocks are among them. They can be anticipated but hardly prevented. The question is whether a country is well-positioned to withstand them when they come. Adverse growth shocks from developed economies affect resource-dependent states more than other countries because of the inherent nature of their economies. Oil-dependent African countries are particularly sensitive to global economic spillovers because monetary or fiscal tightening in a major economy transmits, for these countries, primarily through trade and commodity price channels, and the inevitability of oil price volatility leaves oil-dependent economies vulnerable to perennial price shocks.

Thus, at best of times, oil is problematic for most oil-dependent countries as they are at the mercy of the vagaries of the oil market and buffeted by oil price and oil revenue volatilities. Oil is a fickle asset: its prices are among the most volatile of commodity prices. But no country is more at risk of such volatility than Nigeria, a country where oil accounts for 96 per cent of exports and over 75 per cent of government revenues, a country that has absolutely no resilience to oil price shocks. In her book *Reforming the Unreformable*, Dr Ngozi Okonjo-Iweala, Nigeria's two-time finance minister, said: 'The Nigerian economy earned the dubious distinction of being rated one of the world's most volatile'[111], adding that 'Nigeria's volatility was more than twice the median volatility for almost all the important economic variables'[112], such as terms of trade and per capita real GDP.

But even without the volatilities in the international oil market, Nigeria faces domestic challenges that make it difficult to maximise the production and sale of its crude oil despite having the second-largest crude oil reserves in Africa, estimated at 37,500 million barrels. The first challenge is crude oil theft and pipeline vandalism. It is estimated, for instance, that up to 80 per cent of Nigeria's crude oil is stolen, and pipeline vandalism causes further leakages.[113] As a result, Nigeria has often failed to meet its OPEC-allocated production quota of 1.776 million barrels a day, with production dropping by 50 per cent from its peak in 2015.[114] Indeed, Nigeria has experienced the most dramatic oil production decline in Africa, dropping from about 2.5mn barrels of crude oil a day in 2010 to 1.26mn barrels per day in 2023.[115] One major reason for the decline in output is the curtailment of investments in upstream development, especially as Western companies and multilateral institutions have stopped financing oil and gas projects in developing countries in line with the energy transition and global decarbonisation agenda.[116] Other related reasons are maturing fields and ageing infrastructure.[117]

But the most cited reason for the output drop is security-related, with the prevalence of oil theft and pipeline vandalism, which are estimated to have caused the loss of over 37 million barrels in 2021, amounting to $1.63bn.[118] The phenomenon of oil theft is particularly curious because of alleged state complicity. In July 2024, the Financial Times wrote in an editorial that 'the state is implicated in the wholesale theft of oil, depriving the nation's coffers of billions of dollars.'[119] This suspicion about state involvement in the oil theft was shared by Tony Elumelu, a Nigerian oil magnate, who told the Financial Times in an interview that Nigeria was losing over 95 per cent of its oil to theft. 'This is oil theft we are talking about,' he said, adding: 'The government should know; they should tell us. Our security agencies should tell us who is stealing our oil.'[120] Thus, Nigeria is short-changing itself by failing to produce enough oil for sale due to pipeline vandalism and crude oil theft.

However, there is also the challenge of high production costs. While Saudi Arabia has a production cost as low as $5 per barrel, without capital expenditure, or $7.50 a barrel, with capital expenditure, Nigeria's production cost is as high as $17 per barrel. As Mele Kyari, the then Group Managing Director of NNPC, put it, 'There are countries whose cost of production is classified at $30 per barrel, and we [Nigeria] are one of them.'[121] He added: 'If the oil price is $30 or $32 and you are producing at the cost of $30, you are out of business'.[122] Nigeria is the second most expensive place to produce a barrel of crude among major oil producers.[123] Thus, unless Nigeria can keep its production costs down, the country will be unable to maximise the production and sale of its crude oil.

Yet, nothing can disguise the real challenge of falling international demand for crude oil. For a start, the shale revolution, which made the US the world's largest oil producer in 2018, dramatically reduced American imports of Nigerian crude oil. Indeed, the US went from the largest importer of Nigerian oil in 2012 to the tenth largest in 2015 as the 'shale boom' reduced its demand for Nigerian oil.[124] Furthermore, the value of Chinese oil imports from major

African oil producers, including Nigeria, declined by around 28 per cent between 2018 and 2023.[125] In 2020, the IMF warned that 'global demand for oil will peak by 2040'[126] and that 'oil-exporting countries must be ready for a post-oil future sooner rather than later'.[127] Indeed, according to an analysis published by the oil giant BP in 2023, demand for crude oil may have peaked.[128] The reality is that as Western countries tackle climate change by investing heavily in green sources of energy, such as wind and solar power, as well as electric cars and other fuel-efficient vehicles, the global demand for oil would fall.

In his book *Material World: A Substantial Story of our Past and Future*, Ed Conway noted that the Wesseling oil refinery in Germany, which used Nigerian crude oil, would be shut off by 2025 and would begin to make fuel out of green alternatives.[129] He added: 'Plants, vegetable oils, municipal waste and even cow dung will replace the flows of light, sweet Nigerian crude.'[130] This peak demand and the shift towards renewable energy are a major challenge for Nigeria's oil dependence. Added to that is the fact that increased oil exploration in the face of falling demand will lead to a supply overhang that would further dampen the prices of oil. Indeed, the International Energy Agency foresees a potential glut of oil and gas, which means that while hydrocarbon-producing countries may continue to produce and sell crude oil and natural gas, they would, in a world with more renewables and electric vehicles, get paid less for them.[131] These global trends will put Nigeria under enormous pressure as an oil-dependent country.

According to the IMF, Nigeria's break-even prices are far above projected prices, giving rise to external and fiscal vulnerabilities.[132] For instance, the IMF estimates that Nigeria's fiscal break-even price, that is, the price at which the overall deficit would be zero, is at $156 per barrel, while Nigeria's current account break-even price, i.e. the price at which the current account is in balance, is $80 per barrel.[133] Yet, the IMF projects that medium-term oil prices range from $79 per barrel in 2024, declining to $67 per barrel in 2028.[134] Even worse, Goldman Sachs analysts estimated that Brent crude oil might trade at an average of $50 a barrel in 2026, while President Trump said he would like to get oil price down to $50 per barrel.[135] Nigeria generates almost 90 per cent of its export revenues from oil, with over a third of those revenues flowing out through profit repatriation.[136] Thus, it follows that, with declining oil prices, Nigeria's economic future is dire if it is based mainly on hydrocarbon production and exports.

A key test of a country's strength is its resilience to external shocks. But Nigeria lacks such resilience. It does not ensure self-insurance through reserve accumulation and investments. Saudi Arabia and other Gulf state producers build up large foreign reserves as well as investments in foreign assets, which bring them additional income. Norway is another country that has used its oil money well. Norway's Norges Bank Investment Management is the world's largest sovereign wealth fund. It was set up almost 30 years ago to manage Norway's oil wealth; although it started with just $200 million, it is today an investment behemoth with $1.2 trillion in assets, with equity holdings equating, on average, to 1.4 per cent stake in every listed company globally.[137] But Nigeria is unwilling to save, let alone invest in foreign assets to boost earnings. Nigerian state governors resisted attempts to create an Excess Crude Account and Sovereign Wealth Fund, insisting that all revenues accruing to the country should be shared among its constituent units and not saved.[138]

In the long term, the only sustainable way to ensure resilience to global oil shocks is to end Nigeria's heavy dependence on volatile oil revenues by diversifying its export base. This requires boosting the manufacturing sector, including attracting investment into Nigeria's budding petrochemical industry and ensuring that Nigeria can export significant amounts of non-oil products and even services by exploiting markets in Africa and in other trading regions and nations, a subject discussed in detail in Chapter 5. Currently, agriculture and manufacturing account for 2.6 per cent and 1 per cent of Nigeria's total exports, respectively. It is impossible to develop resilience to the economic impact of peaking global crude demand with such a narrow export base that is dominated by oil-based exports. Unfortunately, Nigeria seems to have tied its economic future to hydrocarbons. One evidence for this is that under the Petroleum Industry Act (PIA) 2018, 30 per cent of profits accruing to the Nigerian National Petroleum Corporation, NNPC, would be used for further oil exploration. Thus, Nigeria's growth model is based on a hydrocarbon-led economy, while its energy generation is tied to fossil fuels.

Evidently, Nigeria lacks the will to build buffers for its extremely volatile oil-based economy, but it is also doing little to prepare for a post-oil future. Oil has been a curse rather than a blessing for Nigeria. First, it spurred massive corruption and a rentier economy. Then, due to the Dutch Disease, it shifted attention away from the non-oil sectors, such as agriculture and manufacturing. But global peak oil demand is a real threat, and Nigeria must develop resilience to such threats by building buffers, diversifying away from its oil-based exports and diversifying its revenue base.

Climate Change Mitigation and Adaptation

Linked to the discussion on Nigeria's dependence on fossil fuels is its feeble response to the risks of climate change. Yet, Nigeria is extremely vulnerable to, and already being impacted by, some of the devastating effects of climate change. Indeed, nearly a quarter of the Nigerian population lives in areas highly exposed to climate change, such as droughts and flooding, including rising sea levels.[139] President Buhari put it accurately in his speech at COP 26, the United Nations Climate Conference held in Glasgow, UK, in 2021. He said: 'I do not think anyone in Nigeria needs persuading of the need for urgent action on the environment. Desertification in the North, floods in the centre, pollution and erosion on the coast are enough evidence. For Nigeria, climate change is not about the perils of tomorrow, but what is happening today.'[140]

Indeed, desertification, coastal erosion and extreme weather conditions continue to pose great danger to Nigeria's economic and social life. The Economist Intelligence Unit (EIU) said in its 2024 Business Environment Rankings that one of the most debilitating impacts on growth and the overall business environment in the long term will be from climate change, especially with extreme heat events and severely disruptive storms. Those economic risks are evident in Nigeria. In its report titled

Climate Change and Socio-Economic Development, Agora Policy, a consultancy outfit, noted that Nigeria risked losing $ 446 billion to climate change unless urgent actions were taken.[141] In Lagos, which is perched high at sea level, 3.2 million people would be exposed to flood by 2050.[142] Droughts, soil erosion, famines, pest attacks and poor crop yields are climate change consequences that seriously threaten food security in Nigeria.

Yet, despite the enormous damage that climate change is already causing in Nigeria and the greater danger it poses for the future, the Nigerian government is not doing enough to tackle the problem. Nigeria makes shallow international climate change commitments that it is not even faithfully implementing at home. Two years after the COP21 Agreement in Paris in 2015, Nigeria submitted its Nationally Determined Contributions (NDCs) in which it pledged to reduce its greenhouse gas emissions unconditionally by only 20 per cent by 2030 and conditionally by 45 per cent if it received international support. Nigeria pledged to reduce its emissions by ramping up the rollout of solar energy production, improving energy efficiency and ending gas flaring.

However, Nigeria made little progress on these pledges. For instance, on gas flaring, a report by Daisy Dunne for Carbon Brief, a UK-based organisation, noted that an estimated 7.4bn cubic feet of gas was flared in Nigeria in 2018.[143] On solar, Nigeria's first NDC committed the country to installing 13,000 MW of solar power, but, to date, solar has made virtually no contribution to Nigeria's energy generation. In 2021, 74 per cent of Nigeria's electricity was provided by fossil fuel sources, with hydroelectricity accounting for 25 per cent. However, solar, wind, biomass and waste accounted for less than 1 per cent.[144] So, Nigeria is not embracing renewables despite all the pledges. The result of the broken pledges was that, according to the International Energy Agency (IEA), GHG emissions from fossil fuel production and use in Nigeria increased by 16 per cent since 2015.[145]

Yet, against the backdrop of the broken climate pledge in its first NDC, Nigeria submitted an updated NDC in May 2021, ahead of COP26. In the revised pledge, Nigeria promised to reduce GHG emissions by 20 per cent unconditionally and by 47 per cent conditionally by 2030. However, it nearly halved the original baseline projections, making the potential impact of the targets seem significant. It pledged to improve the electricity grid, increase the use of buses rather than cars, eliminate kerosene lighting by 2030, and reduce crop residues burnt by 50 per cent by 2030.

It is almost impossible to eliminate carbon emissions without addressing the use of petrol cars, as more than a fifth of the world's greenhouse gas emissions are traceable to fossil fuel vehicles; hence the pledge by many countries to replace vehicles powered by internal combustion engines with electric cars powered by batteries. Nigeria has an estimated 11.8 million petrol-powered vehicles on its roads. But despite the government's pledge to roll out electric vehicles, there is hardly any evidence that it intends to keep the promise, as the Tribune newspaper noted in an editorial titled 'FG's unfulfilled EV promise'.[146] This contrasts with countries like the UK, whose zero-emission vehicles mandate requires all new cars sold in the UK to be electric by 2035 and set a target of a minimum of 28 per cent of new car sales in 2025, rising from 22 per cent in 2022.[147]

The credibility of Nigeria's international climate change commitments has always been questionable. For instance, despite pledging to end gas flaring, the practice has continued. According to the World Bank, Nigeria is the ninth-highest natural gas-flaring country by volume, with 5.318 cubic metres of natural gas flared in 2022.[148] While section 104 of the Petroleum Industry Act 2021 prohibits gas flaring, the act also creates conditions, such as 'emergency', under which gas flaring is permitted, which means that gas flaring is not completely outlawed, making the pledge to 'end' gas flaring meaningless. Nigeria has the highest rates of deforestation in the world; yet, instead of taking steps to reverse deforestation, the government is building projects like the Cross Rover superhighway, which are rainforest destroying.[149] In July 2024, the United States Agency for International Development (USAID) said that 'Nigeria lost over 60 per cent of its mangrove cover since independence and about 35 per cent in the last 20 years'[150], adding that 'with only six per cent of Nigeria's mangrove forest under protected status, Nigerian mangroves face further loss and degradation.'[151]

At COP 26, Nigeria pledged to achieve net zero carbon by 2060, but President Buhari immediately undermined the pledge when he said that Nigeria would continue to burn gas to generate electricity because it 'has huge reserves of the fuel, about the ninth largest in the world, that remains largely untapped'.[152] Nigeria also has largely untapped coal reserves, about the eighteenth largest in the world, and is committed to building more coal-fired power plants.

Unfortunately, while Nigeria is rich in dirty fossil fuels –
coal, oil and gas – it is not rich in energy-transition minerals
such as cobalt, lithium, manganese and copper, which are
increasingly in demand globally. In truth, Nigeria cannot
abandon its fossil fuels overnight. The question is whether it
is serious about energy transition. The truth is that Nigeria is
unwilling to wean itself off fossil fuels; as such, it is not
taking the bold actions needed to tackle man-made climate
change.

In 2022, while campaigning for the presidency, Tinubu
described climate change as a 'poisoned holy communion,
saying 'it is a question of how you prevent a church rat from
eating poisoned holy communion.' He then added: 'We need
to tell the West, if they don't guarantee our finances, we are
not going to comply with their climate change.'[153] Tinubu
used the metaphors of a 'church rat' and 'the poisoned holy
communion' to suggest that fossil fuels were both bad and
good, both useful and destructive; that, as a poor country,
Nigeria needed to burn fossil fuels to accelerate its
development even though the resultant carbon emissions are
poisonous. Thus, he threatened that unless the West funded
energy transition in Nigeria, the country would not 'comply
with their climate change', a view criticised by some
commentators as unrealistic.[154]

To be sure, Nigeria, like most other developing countries,
needs international finance in order to realistically achieve
energy transition, and there were, rightly, criticisms of the
'paltry' $300 billion by 2035 promised by the rich countries
at COP 29 in Azerbaijan in November 2024.[155] However,
even if international finance was available, only the
developing countries that have specific and measurable

plans to decarbonise would be able to access it. For instance, South Africa secured $8.5 billion in 2021 from developed countries as part of a landmark deal to fund its climate transition, leading to the closure of its Komati coal-fired power plant in 2022.[156] Thus, Tinubu's statement that Nigeria would not 'comply with their climate change' unless the developed countries funded its energy transition, without concrete plans as to how it would wean itself off fossil fuels, would cut no ice with the rich countries.

That said, once he became president, Tinubu rowed back from the campaign rhetoric and made symbolic gestures towards climate change mitigation. For instance, in 2023, he led a delegation of 1,411 people to COP28 in Dubai. The large delegation, the third largest at the climate summit, raised eyebrows among Nigerians, but government officials argued that it was in recognition of the fact that Nigeria was Africa's biggest economy and, by implication, Africa's biggest emitter.[157] But that explanation would only be credible if it meant Nigeria would take the tackling of climate change seriously. However, so far, there is little evidence of that beyond some symbolism.

In May 2024, President Tinubu established the Presidential Committee on Climate Action and Green Economic Solutions and appointed his then spokesman, Ajuri Ngelale, as the Special Presidential Envoy on Climate Action.[158] In August 2024, the Presidency announced that a German company, PANA Holdings, had expressed an interest in building renewable energy and allied decarbonisation technology manufacturing facilities in Nigeria with the support of the German government.[159] Such announcements are common in Nigeria but rarely amount to anything. Besides, tackling climate change requires holistic measures that would lead Nigeria to end its dependence on burning fossil fuels and replace that with renewable or low-carbon energy generation. In other words, measures that would help Nigeria to transition to a net zero carbon economy. This seems far-fetched at the time of writing, given how much Nigeria is wedded to burning fossil fuels and deepening oil and gas explorations.

At COP28, held in Dubai in December 2023, Nigeria was among the 200 countries that agreed to transition away from fossil fuel energy systems by 2050 and to triple renewable energy capacity and double energy efficiency by 2030.[160] However, Nigeria continues to indulge in *both-wayism*, holding two contradictory positions: claiming to be committed to tackling climate change but deepening its burning and use of fossil fuels. Nigeria is building oil refineries, big polluters, and increasing hydrocarbon exploration. For instance, apart from the Dangote Refinery, the government licenced the Edo Refinery[161] in 2024 and announced that South Korean investors would build four refineries in Nigeria.[162] All these private refineries are in addition to the four moribund state-owned ones that the government still hoped to revive. Then, there are the artisanal crude oil refineries, that is, illegal refineries that refine stolen crude and which contribute hugely to environmental pollution. Add to all that what is known as Scope 3 emissions, that is, emissions generated by consumers burning oil and gas in cars as well as in cooking and heating at home. Simply put, Nigeria is addicted to fossil fuel use, defying global trends whereby many oil producers and polluters are accelerating the green transition.

However, President Trump's return to power in January 2025 and his eulogisation of fossil fuels has adversely affected the global push to tackle climate change. Just as he did in his first term, President Trump announced a policy of 'drill, baby, drill', intended to ramp up fossil fuel production, and withdrew the US from the Paris Agreement on climate change.[163] Both actions amount to a repudiation of global efforts to curb climate change. However, most other oil producers and polluters remain committed to the green energy transition. For instance, China is the world's biggest polluter. Yet, according to a Financial Times report, the scale and pace of China's transition away from fossil fuels 'has smashed international forecasts', with about two-thirds of all new solar and wind power projects worldwide taking place in China.[164] Brazil is the world's eighth largest oil producer, but it generated 89 per cent of its electricity from renewables in 2023.[165]

At COP 29 in Azerbaijan in November 2024, Saudi Arabia said it was committed to making the transition to a green energy system. Khalid Almehaid, the Saudis chief climate negotiator at the summit, said his country wanted to the 'part of the train,' adding: 'If Saudi Arabia can transition, I think anyone in the world can transition.'[166] Nigeria needs to be part of the train, too. However, President Tinubu has embraced President Trump's 'drill, baby, drill' philosophy as he is determined to boost crude oil exploration and production in Nigeria. For instance, in January 2025, he announced his government's plan to resume oil drilling in Ogoniland, one of the most environmentally devastated parts of the oil-rich Niger Delta, after a three-decade halt.[167] Thus, despite the rhetoric about tackling climate change, Nigeria appears to be turning its back on the green energy transition.

That said, in 2021, Nigeria enacted the Climate Change Act. The act commits Nigeria to reaching net zero greenhouse gas emissions between 2050 and 2070. The act mirrors the UK's pivotal Climate Change Act of 1998 and establishes the National Council on Climate Change, with powers to set carbon budgets and formulate the National Climate Change Action Plan. However, the act is a weak instrument that will be ineffectual. First, it is not enforceable against the government, unlike the UK Act, which constrains government actions and has successfully been legally invoked by NGOs to challenge government policies. For instance, in May 2024, based on an action brought by some NGOs, the High Court ruled that the UK government's climate action plan was unlawful for failing to demonstrate how it would meet the legally binding commitment to reach net zero carbon under the Climate Change Act.[168] However, Nigeria's Climate Change Act is not justiciable and thus not legally enforceable against the government. Secondly, while the UK's Climate Change Committee, CCC, created under the 1998 act, independently polices the UK government's policies and actions on climate change, Nigeria's National Council on Climate Change is part of the government and, thus, subject to the Federal Government's policy choices.

Above all, the challenges in Nigeria are not the absence of laws but of their enforcement. For instance, existing environmental laws in Nigeria are not properly enforced, and environmental agencies are mismanaged, while funds allocated for environmental purposes, such as the Ecological Fund, are misappropriated and embezzled.[169] Yet, as James

Lovelock argues strongly in his book *The Revenge of Gaia*, climate change poses a real and present danger, and nations must wean themselves off fossil fuel consumption and stop natural habitat destruction.[170] Nigeria must heed the advice and stop paying lip service to climate change mitigation. It must move away from burning hydrocarbons and embrace renewable energy sources, electric cars and forestation. Nigeria cannot be a fossil fuel economy in a world moving towards net zero carbon and biodiversity and environmental net gains, as well as embracing nature-based solutions in general.

Admittedly, Nigeria might be emboldened by the Trump administration's stance on energy transition. For instance, at the 10th edition of the annual 'Powering Africa Summit' in March 2025, the US Energy Secretary, Chris Wright, said that the US would not pressure African countries to move away from fossil fuels and towards renewables, thereby reversing the policy of the Biden administration.[171] Secretary Wright described the Western countries' policy of discouraging African countries from developing coal as 'just nonsense, hundred per cent nonsense', saying: 'Coal has been the largest source of global electricity for a hundred years. Coal transformed our world and made it better.'[172] The US policy shift on climate change and energy transition could incentivise Nigeria to remain wedded to burning fossil fuels. However, that would be a mistake. As the economists Adrien Bilal and Diego Kanzig argue in their paper titled 'Does Unilateral Decarbonisation Pay For Itself?' there are rational reasons to 'act locally' and decarbonise without international agreement or pressure because the local damage from global warming is enormous, given the high social cost of carbon.[173] Furthermore, as the IMF points out, implementing the policy commitment to achieve net zero by 2060 'would help spur growth in green technology, increasing employment opportunities and boosting economic growth.'[174] That economic rationale, in addition to the social imperative of tackling climate change, based on the wider benefits of a low-carbon society[175], is why Nigeria should decarbonise and diversify away from its hydrocarbon economy. It must stop paying lip service to tackling climate change.

The Fiscal Quagmire and Low Tax Base

In August 2019, the Buhari government issued a query to Dr Tunde Fowler, then chairman of the Federal Inland Revenue Service (FIRS), asking him to explain why there were 'significant variances between the budgeted tax collection and the actual collection for the period 2015 to 2018'[176] and why 'the actual collections for the period 2015 to 2017 were significantly worse than what was collected between 2012 and 2014'.[177] Subsequently, in December of that year, the government refused to reappoint Fowler for another term in office. Fowler's query and eventual removal from office reflected the anxiety within the government about the perennial low tax mobilisation amid deep fiscal challenges, which the IMF has repeatedly highlighted.

In its Article IV consultation with Nigeria in 2019, the IMF said Nigeria suffered from 'low tax mobilisation,' adding: 'The revenue base is simply too low to address the current challenges.'[178] In April 2024, while presenting the regional economic outlook for Sub-Saharan Africa, the IMF made the same point, saying: 'In a country like Nigeria, Africa's most populous country with all of those development spending needs, we think it's problematic that tax revenue to GDP is only 8 to 9 per cent when it should be much higher, so that more resources can be spent on building universities, on building infrastructure.'[179]

The problem is twofold. First, the economy is not growing enough to generate more tax revenues, and second, most Nigerians that should be paying tax are simply not doing so, while a lot lack the productive capacity to even pay tax. With a tax-to-GDP ratio of 9 per cent, worse than sub-Saharan Africa's average of 18.6 per cent, Nigeria has acute and chronic problems with revenue mobilisation. According to one analysis, 67 million of Nigeria's labour force of 77 million are not registered taxpayers.[180] Less than 6 per cent of the registered taxpayers are active in the corporate income tax category, and Nigeria raises less than 1 per cent of GDP in VAT revenue, according to the IMF.[181] In a newspaper article in 2017, Nigeria's then finance minister, Kemi Adeosun, said 'only 241 people paid more than N20 million in personal income taxes in 2016'[182], while the then head of the Federal Inland Revenue Service told journalists that 'over 6,772 billionaires don't pay tax'.[183] Certainly, there are weaknesses in the system of tax collection and administration in Nigeria, as well as the problem of systemic non-compliance with tax obligations.

In July 2023, President Tinubu inaugurated the Presidential Committee on Fiscal Policy and Tax Reforms, headed by Taiwo Oyedele, a tax expert at the accounting firm PwC. President Tinubu said his administration aimed to increase Nigeria's tax-to-GDP ratio to 18 per cent by

2026.[184] The committee submitted its report in October 2023, highlighting what it described as 'quick wins', including through the simplification and digitalisation of the tax regime. At the World Economic Forum held in Saudi Arabia in April 2024, President Tinubu and Bill Gates, the Microsoft founder, both discussed how to use digital technology to ease tax collection in Nigeria. Gates told Tinubu he would work with his administration to create a digital identity platform to ensure payment efficiency and make tax collection easier.[185]

But while tax administration is extremely weak in Nigeria, the absence of a digital payment system is not the reason most rich people don't pay tax or pay the requisite amount of tax. The problem is corruption. A lot of wealthy Nigerians avoid and evade tax and get away with it, aided and abetted by complicit tax officials. So, if Nigeria wants to increase tax revenues from the rich, it must tackle the corruption within the tax administration. There is no reason why the wealthy, who are easily identifiable, are not paying enough tax in Nigeria.

Yet, the tax-dodging billionaires are not the only problem. In most countries, the middle classes, micro, small, and medium enterprises, MSMEs, the employed, and the self-employed collectively account for the largest proportion of tax payments. For instance, in the UK, while the top 1 per cent of taxpayers, that is, the billionaires, contribute 30 per cent of income tax, the rest, which includes the middle classes and the lower classes, account for 70 per cent of income tax receipts.[186] However, the strength of the economy determines the strength of the different categories of taxpayers and, thus, the robustness of the tax intakes. Economic growth is the only sustainable source of higher tax revenues and higher living standards. For when the economy is growing, resulting in business expansion and more and better jobs, company income tax, personal income tax, VAT, etc will generate more revenue, enabling the government to fund its budgets and raise living standards for everyone. As Martin Wolf, the chief economics commentator of the Financial Times, rightly put it, 'the main source of greater prosperity and higher fiscal revenue must be faster economic growth.'[187]

The truth, however, is that the Nigerian economy does not produce enough high-income taxpayers. The middle class is disappearing, and most of those still in that class are only managing to eke out a living. According to an estimate by the International Labour Organisation (ILO), 93 per cent of all employment in Nigeria is in the informal sector.[188] It is well known that most of those in the informal sector do not pay taxes. First, because they earn a very low income and depend on a daily income to survive. Second, because the state cannot even track them for tax purposes.

In his book *Reclaiming the Jewel of Africa*, Dr Olusegun Aganga, a former Minister of Finance and later Minister of Industry, Trade, and Investments, said that MSMEs accounted for about 48 per cent of Nigeria's GDP, but added: 'Most MSMEs are nano, micro, and small businesses that do not make sufficient profit to pay high tax or they are not in the tax net.'[189] With such an economic structure, Nigeria will struggle to generate sufficient taxes. At 3 per cent of GDP, Nigeria's non-oil revenue is one of the lowest in the world. Thus, a key solution to Nigeria's low tax revenues is the diversification of the revenue base. Nigeria needs a robust economy, it needs businesses of all sizes to flourish and create well-paying jobs, and it needs to incentivise those in the informal sector to join the formal, tax-paying sector.

But even with all that, there is, as mentioned earlier, the problem of systemic non-compliance with tax obligations. This problem stems from the breakdown of the social contract. The Magna Carta established the principle of 'no taxation without representation', which means that taxation is predicated upon representation. But representation is more than just elections; elected governments must meet the basic needs of the people. However, most Nigerian cannot see what the government has done with the country's oil revenue. The Nigerian state has failed woefully to improve the lives of ordinary Nigerians, to provide the basics of life, such as electricity, clean water, motorable roads, good schools and hospitals and, indeed, protection of lives and property. This acute failure is a violation of the social contract between the state and the citizens, and it has engendered a deep distrust, which translates into a lack of voluntary tax compliance.

Nigeria's New Tax Laws

In October 2024, President Tinubu submitted four tax reform bills to the National Assembly. The bills were the Nigerian Tax Bill, aimed to 'simplify' the tax regime by merging various rules into a single, easier-to-understand code and eliminates more than 50 small, overlapping taxes.; the Nigeria Tax Administration Bill, which aimed to set common rules for how taxes are collected across federal, state, and local governments; the Nigerian Revenue Service (Establishment) Bill, which sought to change the name of the Federal Inland Revenue Service (FIRS) to the Nigerian

Revenue Service 'to better reflect its mandate as the revenue agency for the entire federation, not just the Federal Government'[190]; and the Joint Revenue Board (Establishment) Bill, which aimed to create a Joint Revenue Board to replace the Joint Tax Board, covering federal and all state tax authorities.

The Government said the tax reform proposals were 'pro-poor' and 'pro-business, while simplifying and harmonising the cumbersome tax regime in Nigeria. On the 'pro-poor' claim, there is some justification in the sense that Nigerians earning ₦800,000 ($520) and below per annum would be exempt from paying income tax, while the Value Added Tax (VAT) would no longer be payable on essential goods and services, such as food, healthcare, education, power and baby products, thus helping families better able to afford basic needs.[191] Yet, while the tax reform proposals would grant some relief to the poor, the pass-through costs of the removal of fuel subsidies and increases of other levies, such as electricity tariffs, coupled with the inflation-induced cost-of-living crisis, would still reduce the disposal incomes of poor Nigerians in a country where there is no social security. The pro-business claim also has some justification, given that small businesses with annual turnover below ₦50m ($32,400) will no longer pay company income tax, while large businesses will benefit from reduced corporate tax rates, dropping from 30% to 27.5% in 2025 and 25% in subsequent years.[192] The proposal was however undermined by the government's intention to raise the VAT from 7.5 per cent to 15 per cent by 2030, given the impact of such VAT hike on the production costs of businesses.

Judged against the goal of streamlining Nigeria's tax system, the bills were also broadly positive. For instance, it proposed to repeal 11 existing tax laws and bring them under the omnibus Nigeria Tax Bill; it also proposed to make a newly created Nigeria Revenue Service (NRS) the sole collector of all federal taxes, including those currently collected by agencies like the Nigeria Customs Service. Yet, the scale of the problem is such that it would be premature to describe the harmonisation proposals as a game changer. For instance, according to the WTO, 'companies make about 60 official tax payments per year and about 200 unofficial tax payments'[193] in Nigeria. It is doubtful that the proposed tax reforms would radically change that. Second, it is also doubtful that concentrating the tax-collection powers of all federal agencies in the NRS would end the endemic inefficiency and corruption that bedevilled all the agencies; instead, consolidating tax-collection powers in the proposed NRS might simply consolidate inefficiency and corruption in one powerful agency, instead of many. Finally, there must be doubts about whether the agencies that would be stripped of their tax-collecting powers would go quietly or whether they and the vested interests entrenched in them would fight back through informal routes, such as extracting unofficial taxes and levies from businesses.

The Legislative process and controversy

Even if the tax reform bills were sensible, they suffered from being crafted without consensus building. Although Nigeria's federalism is deeply flawed, as discussed in Part 1 of this book, critical decisions with nationwide impacts still usually require consensus among the federal and state governments. However, President Tinubu introduced the tax reform bills without building such consensus and without securing the buy-in of other critical stakeholders. In November 2024, after the meeting of the National Economic Council (NEC), which consists of Nigeria's 36 state governors and is chaired by the vice president, the governors unanimously urged the president to withdraw the bills from the National Assembly to allow for 'more comprehensive consultation and consensus-building among key stakeholders.'[194] It was clear that, given the polarisation across the country, especially opposition from the state governors, the tax reform bills would not survive without fundamental changes.

In January 2025, after a meeting with the Presidential Tax Reform Committee, the Nigeria Governors' Forum issued a communique supporting 'the comprehensive reform of Nigeria's archaic tax laws', saying they acknowledged 'the importance of modernising the tax system to enhance fiscal stability and align with global best practices.'[195] However, they rejected the Federal Government's proposal to reduce the corporate income tax from 30 per cent to 25 per cent and raise the VAT from 7.5 per cent to 15 per cent by 2030. The governor's communique said: 'We agreed that there should be no increase in the VAT rate or reduction in Corporate Income Tax (CIT) at this time, to maintain economic stability.'[196] Furthermore, while the Federal Government had included a terminal clause for tax-collecting bodies like the Tertiary Education Trust Fund (TETFUND), the National Agency for Science and Engineering Infrastructure (NASENI) and the National Information Technology Development Agency (NITDA), the governors said in their communique: 'The meeting recommended that there should be no terminal clause for TETFUND, NASENI, and NITDA in the sharing of development levies in the bills.'

Interestingly, in a statement issued by Bayo Onanuga, President Tinubu's special adviser on information and strategy, the president thanked the governors for 'their unanimous endorsement of the four Tax Reform Bills currently under consideration by the National Assembly'.[197] In other words, the presidency accepted the governors' proposals in order to save the tax bills, even though that meant abandoning key planks relating to the VAT increase, CIT reduction and the termination of some tax-collecting bodies. The presidency's acquiescence to the governors' and the legislators' changes to the proposed tax reform bills facilitated their passage in the National Assembly. In May 2025, the National Assembly passed the four tax bills, making several amendments to the version sent to them by the President. On June 26, 2025, President Tinubu signed the new tax bills into law.[198] Thus, Nigeria has new tax laws, namely: the Nigeria Tax Act; the Nigeria Tax Administration Act; the Nigeria Revenue Service (Establishment) Act; and the Joint Revenue Board (Establishment) Act, all of which the president said were 'pivotal to the success of the administration's reforms and the country's prosperity.'[199]

Yet, the foregoing suggests that, while Nigeria's tax system is in deep crisis and in dire need of fundamental reform, the new tax regime may not fundamentally tackle the multifaceted problems facing Nigeria's tax administration. The new tax laws are a product of compromises in which several vested interests forced the president to accept several amendments to his original version. This raises concerns about their implementation as entrenched interests might undermine the smooth operation of the new laws. However, if faithfully implemented, the new tax laws, while not perfect, should bring some positive improvement to the tax system in Nigeria. Yet, Nigeria still has a long way to go to significantly boost the share of tax revenue in its GDP, despite the Tinubu administration's aggressive revenue mobilisation.[200] In the end, if Nigeria wants to increase its tax revenue intake, it must grow the economy, broaden the tax base, overhaul the tax collection and administration system, and, crucially, induce voluntary tax compliance among Nigerians by honouring the social contract.

Avoiding Another Debt Overhang

Despite an oil windfall of $300 billion between 1970 and 2001, resulting from two oil price hikes in 1973-74 and 1979-1980, Nigeria found itself trapped in unsustainable debt because of the mismanagement and embezzlement of the oil windfall.[201] When General Obasanjo became Nigeria's elected president in 1999, he made it a personal and a national priority to obtain international relief for Nigeria's $35 billion official government (Paris Club) debt that he inherited. As Obadiah Mailafia, a former deputy governor of the Central of Nigeria, put it, 'Obasanjo took a political decision to free our country from that kind of debt peonage.'[202] To achieve this, Obasanjo brought back Ngozi Okonjo-Iweala from the World Bank into his government as finance minister and tasked her with leading the negotiations for debt relief. After two years of negotiations, the details of which Okonjo-Iweala chronicles in her book *Reforming the*

Unreformable[203], Nigeria received $18 billion, or 60 per cent, write-off on its Paris Club debt and cleared the remaining $12 billion owed to the Paris Club in 2006. By the time President Obasanjo left office in May 2007, Nigeria's external debt burden had fallen from $35 billion to approximately $5 billion.[204] However, since then, Nigeria's external debt has grown astronomically. As of December 2023, it stood at $43billion, while domestic debt was $70billion, according to the Debt Management Office. In August 2024, the World Bank announced that Nigeria had become the third largest debtor in its International Development Association, owing $16.5bn.[205]

While the Nigerian government borrows heavily externally, it also does so domestically. Successive Nigerian presidents have forced the central bank to print money to fund their insatiable appetite for debt. For instance, the central bank advanced ₦30trillion Ways and Means[206] lending to the Buhari government. The Nigerian central bank is far from being independent as presidents frequently 'ordered' the bank to take one action or another. As long ago as 2015, Charles Soludo, a former governor of the Central Bank of Nigeria, complained about the common diktat 'Presidency directs central bank to …', saying that 'When the market knows or believes that the central bank is merely an extension of the Presidency and takes daily 'directives' from there, the Bank loses credibility.'[207] But that practice continued, especially under the government of President Buhari. In all, over a few decades, Nigeria's domestic debt surged dramatically, rising from ₦4.14 trillion in 2005 to ₦134.3. trillion by the third quarter of 2024.[208]

The truth is that Nigeria's fiscal policy is extremely expansionary, leading to massive budget deficits that are funded through borrowings. Furthermore, temperamentally, Nigerian leaders have a relaxed approach to borrowing and debt. For instance, before he became president, Tinubu defended President Buhari's government's borrowing spree, saying: 'If borrowing is a crime, the entire America should be in jail'[209]. Within six months of becoming president in May 2023, Tinubu took an external loan of $8 billion. In an article titled 'Banking on Borrowing', SBM Intelligence, a highly respected research and strategic communications firm, shows, with a cgraphical illustration (see below), that Nigeria's external debt rose from $10.71bn in 2015 to $43.03bn by the end of 2024.[210] In July 2025, the National Assembly approved a new loan of $21bn[211], pushing Nigeria's external total debt to about $65bn, and the country's total debt, in naira terms, to ₦183 trillion, from ₦145trn in 2024.[212] Indeed, in July 2025, the government sought legislative approval for additional $347mn external loan[213], insisting that 'there is no sin in borrowing'.[214]

Nigeria's external debt: 2015 to 2024

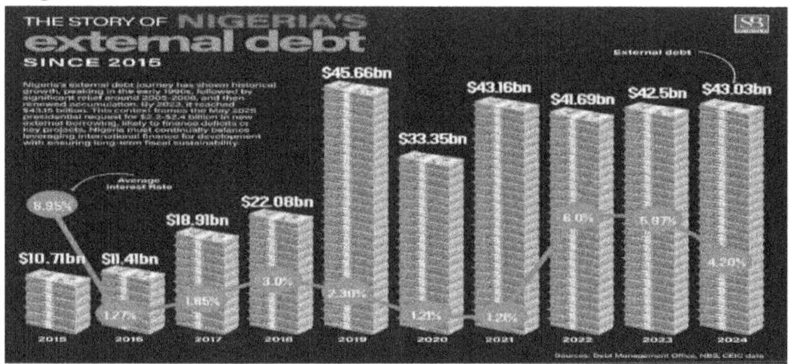

Source: SBM INTELLIGENCE

But it is a false equivalence to compare America's debt status with that of Nigeria. First, America is the world's economic superpower, with a GDP of $29.17 trillion in 2024, compared to Nigeria's $199.72.8 billion, according to the IMF. Second, America's currency, the dollar, is the world's reserve currency, meaning that America enjoys the advantage of borrowing at interest rates that are lower than in the rest of the world[215], whereas Nigeria's US-denominated debt is vulnerable to US interest rate rise. Third, America's debt-service-to-revenue ratio is about 6.8 per cent, whereas Nigeria's was 162 per cent in the first half of 2024[216], rising from 99.2 per cent in July 2023.[217]

Indeed, the most potent argument against Nigeria's debt accumulation is the debt service to revenue ratio. The problem is not necessarily the debt-to-GDP ratio. Although Nigeria's debt-to-GDP ratio reached the highest level ever, at 52.9 per cent in July 2024[218], that ratio is below the African average of about 85 per cent. That said, as Dr Ngozi Okonjo-Iweala pointed out at a public lecture, Nigeria, given its stage of development and vulnerability, should have a debt-to-GDP ratio 'well below 40 per cent'.[219] However, the real problem is Nigeria's debt service-to-revenue ratio, which, as noted above, was 162 per cent in 2024, well above the benchmark of 23 per cent.[220]

The debt service-to-revenue ratio is susceptible to interest rate hikes in creditor nations, particularly the US. Thus, the ratio could potentially rise to 150 per cent. When a country spends most or nearly all its revenue to service its debt, it has virtually nothing left to spend on critical areas, such as education, health and infrastructure. Nigeria borrows heavily to fund recurrent expenditures and unproductive infrastructure that contributes little to economic growth and that are not revenue-generating. Nigeria has learned nothing from its first debt overhang, and the Western nations are unlikely to be sympathetic to another request for debt relief. Therefore, Nigeria must stop its borrowing spree, fuelled by uncontrolled public expenditure and the mismanagement of its resources.

Unemployment: The Phenomenon of Jobless Growth

When the economist Simon Kuznets came up with a system or metric of national accounts known as the Gross Domestic Product (GDP) in the 1940s, he argued that growth would benefit everyone. The Kuznets theory is captured in the mantra: 'Growth is a rising tide that lifts all boats.'[221] However, not everyone agrees that growth should be measured solely by the Gross Domestic Product (GDP), which is the sum of the value of all goods and services produced within a country. In his acclaimed book *The Growth Delusion: The Wealth and Well-being of Nations,* David Pilling, the Africa Editor of the Financial, argues that the GDP does not measure everything that matters, such as activities that are not monetised and things that really contribute to the wellbeing of people.[222] Indeed, such concerns led to the development of alternatives to the GDP, such as the Human Development Index (HDI), the Genuine Progress Indicators (GPI) and the Gross National Happiness (GNH).[223]

However, notwithstanding the reservations about the GDP[224], it remains the best available quantitative measure of how an economy is performing.[225] As Daniel Susskind put it in his book *Growth: A Reckoning*, 'GDP is correlated with almost every measure of human flourishing.'[226] A quicker economic expansion will not only improve the public finances through higher tax intakes but will also improve living standards. The assumption is that if a country is experiencing a high GDP growth rate, which reflects the fact that its economy is expanding, then such a country should also be experiencing high levels of job creation and poverty reduction. Growth should translate into more and better jobs and poverty reduction. Indeed, the examples of China and India prove it. Over the past four decades, both countries, together, lifted an astonishing 1.1 billion people out of poverty as they enjoyed a step-increase in GDP growth, and the superlative economic dynamism lifted all boats. As Shekhar Aiya put it in an article in the Financial Times, 'The steep fall in the number of people living in absolute poverty in China and India must count as one of the most dramatic improvements in human welfare in the history of the world.'[227] The driver was economic growth.

That said, growth does not always lead to job creation and poverty reduction. There is the phenomenon of 'jobless growth', where, despite a growing economy, people cannot get jobs or make ends meet. This phenomenon exists in Nigeria. Over the past ten years, Nigeria's economic growth has flatlined at an average annual growth rate of 2.5 per cent. But before then, up to around 2014, the economy grew at about 6 or 7 per cent annually. Yet, even in those halcyon years, the growth did not create many jobs and did not reduce poverty.

The World Bank identified this problem some years ago in its 2014 Nigeria Economic Report. At that time, Nigeria's economy was growing at about 7 per cent, yet unemployment was very high, while the poverty rate was at more than 60 per cent. The World Bank called it 'the poverty/growth puzzle', saying this posed two major economic questions: 1) 'Why has the rapid economic growth in Nigeria not generated greater poverty reduction?" and 2) 'How could the economy of the size and wealth of Nigeria have such high poverty rates?'[228] The World Bank's answer was that 'the quality and quantity of the growth has proved insufficient to generate the productive jobs needed by a rapidly growing population'.[229] In her book *Reforming the Unreformable*, Dr Ngozi Okonjo-Iweala highlighted the same problem. She noted that while the economy had been growing 'at a respectable 7 per cent average annual rate, it's clear that it is not yet creating the number of jobs needed to absorb the youth', adding that 'the need to create jobs is the most important problem confronting the Nigerian economy now and for years to come.'[230]

So, even when the economy grew at an average annual rate of 7 per cent, it was jobless growth. But the problem is not with the Kuznets theory: growth should benefit everyone. The problem is with the quantity, quality and spread of growth in Nigeria. First, the economy needs always to grow faster than the rate of population growth to ensure that Nigeria attains higher per capita income, which is the real measure of prosperity. But since 2015, the population growth rate, at about 3 per cent, has level-pegged with, or even outstripped, the average economic growth rate at about 2.5 per cent, which implies a low per capita income. Second, even when the economy is growing, it should grow fast enough (at over 10 per cent annually) and grow in the right sectors. The oil sector is over-privileged in Nigeria. It contributes just 5.8 per cent to the size of the economy but accounts for over 90 per cent of Nigeria's exports and 85 per cent of Nigeria's foreign exchange. Yet, according to the ILO, the oil sector creates about 65,000 direct jobs in Nigeria and more than 250,000 jobs in indirect employment.[231] That is less than 5 per cent of Nigeria's labour force. The oil sector is not creating a lot of jobs because it is largely capital-intensive, not labour-intensive.

By contrast, the non-oil sector, which contributed 94.52 per cent to the total GDP in 2023, is usually labour-intensive and accounts for the largest number of jobs. For instance, agriculture, notably small-scale farming, accounted for about 40 per cent of jobs in 2022, while industry accounted for 15 per cent. Services, the biggest sector by GDP, accounted for 44 per cent of jobs.[232] However, these sectors are not productive or competitive enough to create large amounts of jobs or significantly reduce poverty. It is interesting that the sectors that dominated the Nigerian economy in 2023 – services (44%), agriculture (23%) and industries (18%) – are not export-oriented, with all of them together accounting for less than 10 per cent of Nigeria's total exports. Yet, export-oriented sectors are usually the most competitive and productive sectors. As a World Bank study put it, 'exporters on average are more productive, larger and pay higher wages than non-exporters'[233] In other words, sectors that produce for export experience higher productivity and create more and better-paid jobs than those that do not.

So, growth is not enough. Nigeria needs productive and competitive sectors that can create quality jobs and create them in large numbers. This requires supply-side incentives, as discussed in Chapter 6, to boost industrial productivity and competitiveness. Furthermore, Nigeria needs to attract foreign direct investment into the dynamic real sectors, with huge capacities to export non-oil products and services. Currently, almost all direct investment flows into Nigeria are concentrated in the oil sector, which, though accounts for the bulk of Nigeria's total exports and foreign exchange earnings, is a minuscule source of GDP growth, job creation and poverty reduction. For growth that is job-creating and poverty-reducing, Nigeria needs a productive, efficient and internationally competitive real sector – the non-oil sector – the subject of the next two chapters.

A Low-Productivity Economy

There are few topics in economics more important than productivity, the ability to produce more with the same, or even fewer, labour. Indeed, the economist Ed Conway describes productivity as 'the most important of all economic forces,' saying that 'it is about humanity's ability to create ever more value out of ever less input.'[234] If the purpose of economic management is to generate prosperity and improve the welfare of citizens, then productivity growth is the answer. While the size of the economy, the GDP, is important, it is how well-off people are, measured by GDP per head, that really matters. But how well-off people are depends on how productive the economy is. Paul Krugman, the renowned economics Nobel Laureate, puts it this way in his book *The Age of Diminished Expectations*: 'Productivity isn't everything, but, in the long run, it is almost everything. A country's ability to improve its standard of living over time depends almost entirely on its ability to raise its output per worker.'[235] So, productivity matters.

But what is productivity? Economists talk about labour productivity and Total Factor Productivity (TFP). Labour productivity is the 'output per hour worked', that is, the value of the output generated by a single worker per hour. In contrast, TFP measures how efficiently all inputs – land, labour and capital – are used in producing goods and services. Whichever way productivity is measured, the main interest is how it promotes economic prosperity and general welfare. So, how does productivity improve living standards? The simple answer is that because higher productivity means a more efficient way of producing goods and services, the efficiency gains translate into better salaries for workers and lower prices of goods and services, both of which increase household incomes – thereby raising living standards.

For any sector, if productivity is rising, one should expect rising wages and falling prices of goods and services. For instance, growing productivity in the agricultural sector should lead to higher income for farmers and lower food prices; equally, higher productivity in the industrial sector should mean industrial workers are paid well and the prices of industrial products are falling. All this leads to higher living standards as workers and consumers can see their incomes rising, and firms can grow and make more profits. But, in Nigeria, the government fails to distinguish between production and productivity. It often talks about increasing local production, i.e., producing more of a product, such as rice, but hardly about increasing productivity, about producing things more efficiently.

According to the IMF, labour productivity in Nigeria has remained low outside the oil and mobile telecommunications sectors, on average significantly lower compared with the median of oil exporters.[236] In its 2019 'Nigeria Economic Update', the World Bank laid bare the nature and extent of the productivity crisis in Nigeria. In the report, the bank says, 'Nigeria's growth and jobs challenges stem from its low levels of productivity,' adding that Nigeria's economic productivity is 'low by international standards.'[237] In September 2016, Nigeria's labour productivity reached a record low of -3.82 per cent; since then, it has not grown much beyond the 1.14 per cent it reached in September 2018, while labour productivity is 5.85 per cent in Egypt, 4.74 per cent in South Africa and 4.15 per cent in Ghana.[238] The average productivity of a worker in Nigeria is US$3.24/hr, compared to US$19.68/hr in South Africa and US$29.34/hr in Turkey.[239]

However, it is somewhat misleading to talk about measuring labour productivity in Nigeria when only about 10 per cent of the working-age population is employed in formal labour, and over half of that is employed in the public sector. According to the World Bank, 'Nigeria has the largest installed manufacturing base in West Africa, yet wage employment in industry is rare, while the manufacturing sector employs just 8 per cent of Nigerian workers.'[240] The World Bank warned: 'Without robust productivity growth, poverty in Nigeria will continue to rise, and living standards will continue to deteriorate', adding: 'If labour productivity remains on its current path, workers will not be able to earn enough to reduce the number of Nigerians living below the poverty line.'[241]

But why is productivity so low in Nigeria? The starting point is to recognise the three components of productivity, namely, labour quality, capital deepening and total factor productivity. Increases in labour quality, such as through improved skills and better healthcare, can raise productivity by enabling workers to perform more, or more complex, tasks. Capital deepening, as represented by public and private investments, drives productivity growth by providing firms and workers with the capital they need to produce output efficiently. Total factor productivity, generated through innovation and the diffusion of ideas, as well as the efficient allocation of resources, can help improve the efficiency with which inputs are combined. Put simply, productivity growth can be achieved through higher stocks of human and physical capital and through an open and competitive environment that results in innovation and diffusion and better resource allocation in an economy. However, hardly any of these exists in Nigeria: the stocks of human and physical capital are extremely low; Nigerian industries and the whole economy are not exposed to the competitive pressures; there is little genuine attempt to boost private-sector dynamism, reduce investment risk and, generally, create an enabling environment that is conducive for productivity growth; and there is little attempt to embrace cutting-edge technology, including Artificial Intelligence.

Take human capital. In his book *Capital in the 21st Century*, the French economist Thomas Piketty said, 'Knowledge and skill diffusion is the key to overall productivity growth.'[242] Basically, the more educated, knowledgeable and skilful workers are, the more productive they will be. But Nigeria ranked 161 out of 193 in the 2024 Human Development Index. Most of Nigeria's labour force is low-skilled, with about 50 per cent of workers having only primary education or less and 30 per cent never having attended school, while just 20 per cent of Nigerian adults aged 18–37 years who completed primary school can read.[243] Then, there are the well-known supply-side constraints: non-existence of basic infrastructure, lack of access to finance, including foreign exchange, lack of policy transparency and predictability, and excessive government intervention and regulatory discretion. All of these are barriers to productivity growth. For instance, as the World Bank noted, Nigeria's productivity hinges, in large part, on improved electricity.[244] Yet, Nigeria suffers 4,600 hours of blackouts a year.[245]

Then, take digital infrastructure. There is a view that AI can help poorer societies 'leapfrog' whole phases of development, enabling them to close the development gap.[246] But while Nigeria is a regional tech hub, its average download speed of wired internet is a tenth of Denmark, and most broadband users in Nigeria are limited to mobile internet, which is even slower.[247]

Above all, productivity is low in Nigeria because, both at the firm and wider-economy levels, there is a lack of competitiveness and allocative efficiencies. As Piketty argues in his book, 'autarky has never promoted prosperity.'[248] Openness to foreign competition and influences helped the Asian countries to catch up with the West. But Nigeria has not really embraced economic openness. Yet, Nigeria won't leap forward in productivity unless it adopts best practices in human and physical capital development, governance and economic openness. Nigeria must tackle its abysmally low productivity level by creating the right policy and institutional environment for productivity growth.

Nigeria's diaspora as an economic asset

Two pejorative terms are commonly used to describe the phenomenon of Nigerians emigrating to other countries. One is 'japa', a word that became so popular it was adopted by the Oxford English Dictionary in January 2025. According to the OED, 'japa' means 'to leave Nigeria for another country (esp. one in Europe or North America) in search of further education, employment, or economic opportunity.' More generally, it also means 'to escape, to flee.' The other pejorative term is 'brain drain', a well-worn phrase describing a situation where a country loses its highly trained or qualified people to other countries through emigration.

To be sure, both 'japa' and 'brain drain' are, at face value, not positive things. For instance, 'japa' is symptomatic of a deeper malaise that can perpetuate the spiral of decline in a country. The economics Nobel laureates Daron Acemoglu and James Robinson said in their famous book *Why Nations Fail* that good governance often requires pressure from the people. In other words, without societal pressure, good governance may not happen. Surely, then, when citizens choose to flee or escape rather than stay and fight for good governance, there is little pressure on those in power to govern well. Thus, from the perspective of citizens' role in ensuring good governance, 'japa' is bad. As for 'brain drain', it goes without saying that a country that loses its best brains to other countries will be left with fewer competent people and, thus, less human capital at home to run its affairs. For instance, in 2013, the president of the Nigerian Medical Association estimated that of 71,740 medical doctors registered with the Nigerian Medical and Dental Council, only 27,000 were actually practising in Nigeria.[249] Nigerian medical doctors and other medical professionals, such as nurses, are major contributors to the health sectors of the UK and the US. The same is true of teachers and other highly skilled individuals. Some would argue that those talented Nigerians should be in Nigeria developing the country, rather than abroad developing other countries.

However, the issues are more complex for two reasons. First, in a study on poverty trap, two World Bank economists Aart Kraay and David McKenzie found that 'the strongest evidence for a poverty trap at an individual level is the one based on country of residence.'[250] In other words, many people will remain poor if they stay in their country of origin. To tackle what the authors described as 'geographic poverty trap', they called for policy efforts to lower the barriers to international mobility.[251] Thus, on the ground of escaping the geographic poverty trap, it is perfectly rational for Nigerians who sees no prospects for themselves at home to 'japa', if they can, in search of better opportunities abroad. In any case, no country can expect its people to stay if it doesn't provide the right environment for them. Thus, a country that wants to keep its young people and best brains at home must provide the right environment for them to stay; otherwise, as rational human beings, they will seek to minimise their losses and maximise their gains by exploring better opportunities abroad.

The second reason why the negative attitude to emigration is wrong is that the narrative about brain drain has changed. Instead of 'brain drain', scholars now talk about 'brain gain', which refers to a growing phenomenon where individuals who left their country eventually return home, bringing new skills, experiences and capital, to contribute to their country's development.[252] For instance, some successful Nigerian emigrants, such as Dr Ngozi Okonjo-Iweala and Dr Segun Aganga, returned to serve as government ministers, and many other emigrants have returned to contribute in other ways. However, as Dr Aganga said in his book *Reclaiming the Jewel of Africa*, gifted and accomplished Nigerians in the diaspora 'do not have to return to the homeland to make valuable contribution.'[253] Indeed, Nigerians who have found success abroad often want to 'give back' to Nigeria[254], and many frequently do so without returning home.

So, it is worth stressing that 'brain drain' can become 'brain gain'. For that reason, the renowned Indian-born, US-based, economist Jagdish Bhagwati called for a 'Diaspora Model' on the basis that it works to the advantage of developing countries to have their own people in the rich countries.[255] Professor Bhagwati is right. For instance, remittances have contributed significantly to the economies of many developing countries. In 2024, remittances hit $685bn, dwarfing aid flows of $212bn that year, and, over a period of 10 years to 2024, remittances rose 57 per cent while FDI fell 41 per cent; indeed, in 2019, remittances overtook foreign direct investment to developing countries for the first time.[256] Nigeria is one of the major remittance recipient countries. According to a World Bank estimate, the Nigerian diaspora remitted over \$65bn to Nigeria between 2018 and 2020, accounting for four per cent of GDP.[257] The Nigerian government itself said that diaspora remittances in 2019 amounted to \$25bn, which was six per cent of the GDP.[258] It is hard to underestimate the extent to which many households in Nigeria are relieved from excruciating poverty and misery because of the money that Nigerians abroad regularly send home as gifts, payment of school fees, settlement of hospital bills and upkeep allowances. It is also hard to underestimate the effect of such remittances in shoring up the exchange value of the Nigerian local currency, the Naira. Put simply, the naira would suffer far steeper devaluation against the dollar without the billions of dollars of diaspora remittances. While it is unwise for any country to base its development strategy on remittances[259], diaspora remittances cannot be ignored. And Nigeria must do everything to incentivise the increase of such remittances given its large and economically valuable diaspora.

But beyond remittances, there is export trade. In theory, given Nigeria's population of about 230 million people, it can be described as a large consumer market, with domestic demand driving economic growth. However, in practice, given the level of poverty and the abysmally low disposable income and, thus, purchasing power of the people, Nigeria is not a strong consumer society and, as such, it cannot build its economy on a domestic demand-led growth model. As a result, while Nigeria must stimulate domestic demand, its future lies in pursuing an export-led growth strategy based on significant non-oil exports, as argued in Chapter 5. In that regard, Nigeria's large diasporic communities around the world, particularly in Commonwealth countries, the US, Europe and China, represent significant export markets and, thus, a significant trade advantage that Nigeria can leverage. It is estimated that there are over 20 million Nigerians in the diaspora.[260] If Nigeria is serious about diversifying its economy and promoting non-oil exports, its diaspora is a market it must target because Nigerians abroad have a craving for Nigerian products, such as Nigerian foods, clothing, music, and films.

Given the foregoing, the Nigerian government should do everything possible to leverage the economic advantages of the Nigerian diaspora. However, policies are often not in tandem with such an imperative. For instance, as stated earlier in this chapter, despite the liberalisation of the foreign exchange market, the central bank imposes several foreign exchange restrictions, known as capital flow management measures (CFMs), that adversely impact remittances. In June 2024, the CBN ordered that dollars remitted to Nigeria must be exchanged at the official rate and that they must only be paid out in naira, not in dollars, thus preventing recipients from getting a market-determined value for the remittance. This is not a market-based mechanism, and it is not a great incentive to attract significantly more remittances. With respect to harnessing the Nigerian diaspora for non-oil exports, Nigeria lacks the capacity to track, monitor and cultivate its diaspora so that it can be more easily reached by Nigerian exporters.

In 2017, the Buhari administration established the Nigerian Diaspora Commission, NiDCOM. Since then, NiDCOM's Chairman and CEO, Abike Dabiri-Erewa, has raised its profile. However, the commission's impact is not felt beyond the issues of human trafficking and the treatment of Nigerians in foreign countries, as well as occasional congratulatory messages sent to Nigerian achievers abroad. In its National Diaspora Policy, published in 2021, NiDCOM itself admitted that it faces 'obstacles to effective deployment of the Diaspora to the country's national development'.[261] Some of the obstacles listed by the commission include the following: continuing inadequate skills and expertise in the country; inadequate data on the Diaspora to support evidence-based interventions; high cost of remittances; obtaining relevant data and lack of an effective information portal.[262] Yet, until Nigeria can successfully tackle these institutional and policy challenges, it would not be able to harness the huge economic advantage of its diaspora.

However, the Nigerian diaspora must not be seen only as an economic asset; it can also contribute to the political and social development of Nigeria. Interestingly, NiDCOM defines its mandate thus: 'To provide for the engagement of Nigerians in Diaspora in the policies, projects and participation in the development of Nigeria and to utilise the human capital and material resources of Nigerians in Diaspora towards the overall socio-economic, cultural and political development of Nigeria for related matters.'[263] However, typical of policy-making in Nigeria, there is a wide gap between the policy intention stated in the mandate and policy delivery; rhetoric is not matched by action or reality. The truth is that there is no mechanism for actively engaging with Nigerians in the diaspora, let alone systematically ensuring their participation in policy development. One long-lasting issue is successive governments' unwillingness to allow Nigerians in the diaspora to vote remotely in Nigerian elections. As Aganga rightly put it in *Reclaiming the Jewel of Africa*: 'The advances in technology of today are such that no excuse is tenable for not allowing Nigerians in the diaspora to exercise their franchise,' adding that 'Nigeria needs to have a mechanism for giving full franchise and citizenship rights to all Nigerians in the diaspora as well as at home.'[264] That, it goes without saying, is beyond dispute. If Nigeria is to fully harness the enormous advantages of its highly successful diaspora, it must not see the diaspora as being useful for remittances alone, or as an export market. Nigeria must adopt a holistic approach to engaging with and leveraging its diaspora.

Subsistence Farming Won't Feed Nigerians

Another subject worth discussing as part of the fault lines in Nigerian economy is the impact of subsistence farming. As stated earlier, Nigeria is a country of micro, small and medium enterprises (MSMEs), which account for 48 per cent of the country's GDP. But they are nano, micro and small businesses that merely enable their owners to eke out a living, not to earn enough to live well and pay taxes. Similarly, Nigeria is a country of smallholder farmers who cannot grow enough to keep their families properly fed, let alone feed the nation. The agricultural sector accounts for roughly 30 per cent of Nigeria's GDP and employs more people than any other sector. But while Nigeria's agricultural sector is vast, its productivity is very low. This is because the sector is almost entirely dominated by small, rain-fed farms with minimal physical capital. There are very few mechanised, well-irrigated industrial farms in Nigeria.

Throughout history, incremental improvements in agriculture have increased productivity in food production. These improvements have included better-growing techniques (cultivation), the availability of fertilisers (fertilisation) and ever-better tools (mechanisation), such as moving from wooden ploughs to iron ploughs and then to steel ploughs, with progressive reductions in the hours of labour needed to produce more food.[265] But none of these improvements have taken place in Nigeria. For instance, growing techniques are still largely rudimentary, while fertilizer, which has transformed farming worldwide, is often subject to fraud in Nigeria. Between 1980 and 2010, several billions of dollars budgeted to buy fertilizer for struggling farmers were reportedly embezzled by corrupt officials.[266] And despite government efforts to tackle fertilizer fraud, official corruption remains a major obstacle to modernising agriculture in Nigeria.[267] As for better tools, the truth, as noted earlier, is that farming in Nigeria is predominantly manual, with the result being extremely low productivity.

Nigeria provides domestic support for agriculture through tax-related incentives, subsidised farm inputs, tariff concessions for machinery, subsidised credit schemes and, above all, import prohibitions and high tariffs.[268] The government of President Buhari prided itself on promoting agriculture through the Anchor Borrowers' Programme (ABP), whereby the central bank provided loans to smallholder farmers. In 2019, the CBN said it had disbursed nearly 1 trillion naira to over 4.5 million smallholder farmers, although, according to a BusinessDay report in 2020, 'many rural/small-holder farmers and cottage agri-businesses criticised the programme as they were unable to benefit from it.'[269] One international report says of the ABP: 'In the rice sector, government incentives have benefitted *political farmers* who use political connections to access loans and vouchers and distribute these onward for profits.'[270]

However, despite all its domestic support for agriculture, Nigeria has not been able to produce enough food to feed itself, with small farmers producing 90 per cent of agricultural output.[271] While the sector suffers from multiple logistical, skill-related, climatic and economic challenges[272], the main problem is that Nigeria has always viewed agriculture through the prism of subsistence farming. For instance, President Buhari said that 'only 2.5 per cent of Nigerian arable land is being used' and that 'we have to go back to the land.'[273] But what he really meant was that there should be a proliferation of small-scale farmers. Indeed, successive governments have urged most Nigerians to take up farming. But where more food can be produced per hour of labour, thanks to productivity, only a few people would be needed to work in fields and feed the nation while the rest engage in other jobs to grow the economy.

However, the Buhari government was fixated on subsistence farming. The administration's mantra was 'We will grow what we eat and eat what we grow', a self-sufficiency slogan backed by protectionist measures such as import bans and high tariffs. Yet, despite the gimmick of unveiling the 'the world's largest rice pyramids'[274] in

January 2022, with 15 pyramids, each purportedly containing 1 million bags of paddy rice, Nigeria has never been able to produce enough rice to feed its people. For instance, in 2019, rice consumption in Nigeria was 7.0mmt as against the production of 4.79mmt.[275] The result was smuggling and food inflation.

Any sensible agricultural policy must lead to 1) agricultural and economic growth, 2) job creation and poverty reduction, 3) availability and affordability of food items and 4) agricultural exports. But agriculture is not driving economic growth in Nigeria; it is not creating well-paid jobs; it is not feeding the people; and it is not boosting non-oil exports. This is because, with over 80 per cent of farmers being smallholders, agriculture in Nigeria is too subsistence-based to yield sophisticated outcomes. Historically, nations that started their development journey with subsistence agriculture moved up to the value chain through mechanised, large-scale farming. However, agriculture in Nigeria is characterised by labour-intensive manual farming. But peasant farming won't feed Nigeria's burgeoning population, won't grow the economy, and won't generate export earnings. Only mechanised and commercial farming can achieve those outcomes.

The truth is that Nigeria can't be a serious agrarian economy through peasantry; it must transition from smallholder farming to large-scale commercial agriculture. David Pilling, the Africa Editor of the *Financial Times*, wrote: 'Africa must jettison the romantic notions that smallholder farmers and micro-entrepreneurs are the route out of poverty. They are not. Their existence in large numbers is the definition of poverty itself.'[276] That wisdom applies to Nigeria: it must escape 'the cult of the small', of micro-entrepreneurs, of smallholder farmers. It must embrace mechanised farming and support micro-businesses, usually stuck in the informal sector, to grow into viable enterprises in the formal sector.

Nigeria Can't Ban Food Imports Amid Food Insecurity

The subject of subsistence farming leads inevitably to a discussion of the related subjects of food insecurity in Nigeria and the government's penchant for banning food imports. The truth is that Nigeria suffers from severe food scarcity, with food insecurity believed to have affected 23 million Nigerians in 2023, according to the United Nations Children's Fund (UNICEF).[277] The primary reason is, as argued in the preceding section, the subsistence nature of farming in Nigeria, which means that, without mechanised, large-scale agriculture, farming in Nigeria lacks the productivity and efficiency to produce something close to enough food to feed the population. The second reason is the supply shocks that come from violent conflicts and insecurity where, for instance, marauding herdsmen displace farming communities across Nigeria's Middle Belt, the country's main food-producing areas. Such violence disrupts food production and raises production costs. The consequence for a country of over 200 million people is food insecurity and food inflation. According to an analysis by the consulting firm SBM Intelligence in November 2024, the average Nigerian spent roughly 97 per cent of their income on food[278], yet food inflation was running at 40.7 per cent.

Amid that acute food problem and related widespread hunger, Nigeria has always banned food imports in the misguided belief that it can achieve food sufficiency through subsistence farming. Throughout history, nations have responded to poverty and hunger by removing or reducing tariffs on imports. For instance, the Irish potato famine in 1845 prompted Britain to repeal the Corn Law, which protected landowners and raised the prices of imported food items. In 2000, African leaders pledged to reduce or waive tariffs on mosquito nets and drugs needed to tackle malaria. No serious nation responds to poverty, hunger and food insecurity by restricting access to cheap imports. Even agriculturally efficient countries, such as Brazil and Britain, still import food items to meet supply gaps. For instance, in 2020, the UK imported 46 per cent of the food it consumed.[279] In March 2025, Brazil, a major producer and exporter of agricultural commodities, announced that it would scrap import duties on several food items, such as meat, coffee, sugar, corn, sardine and pasta, in a bid to control rapidly rising food prices.[280] That is what every country must do to tackle hunger. Ensuring low food prices, thereby reducing the cost of living, must be a priority of any government.

However, Nigeria continues to ban food imports even as food insecurity and high food prices force most of the citizens to skip basic foods and go hungry. In July 2024, President Tinubu's government announced that it would grant a 150-day suspension of duties, tariffs and taxes on the importation of certain food items to address food insecurity and the cost-of-living crisis in the country.[281] However, several months after the announcement, indeed as of April

2025, the government failed to implement the policy.[282] Yet, even if the policy was implemented, Nigeria needs more than ad hoc interventions. It should move away from the ideological mindset of banning food imports when it cannot produce enough food at home to feed its people. As Alan Beattie argued in the Financial Times, open markets have delivered unmatched levels of food security[283], with nations being able to get basic food commodities from around the world at reasonable prices. Nigeria should not let its domestic policies stop it from importing food to feed its people.

***

The foregoing economic history of Nigeria shows that the country's economic journey has been defined by costly unforced policy errors and persistence in pursuing misguided policies over several decades. From the failure to use Nigeria's oil wealth to develop the country's economy and diversify its export base to the culture of borrowing rather than saving to create buffers and resilience to oil price shocks, from protectionism that undermined the competitiveness of Nigeria's industries to dependence on subsistence farming and food import bans that exacerbate food insecurity, Nigeria has followed the wrong economic and developmental paths.

The government of President Buhari (2015 to 2023) marked a defining period in Nigeria's economic history in that it deliberately pursued policies that were damaging to the Nigerian economy and shunned those that could boost its competitiveness, productivity and growth. President Buhari's successor, President Tinubu, followed a more liberal path, with the withdrawal of the central bank's list of products deemed ineligible for foreign exchange (an effective import ban), the removal of the fuel subsidy and the scrapping of the currency peg and floating of the naira. However, the planning for and implementation of these policies, particularly the withdrawal of the fuel subsidy, have left much to be desired, creating some perverse consequences. While the economic reforms moved Nigeria away from the acute instability and volatility of the Buhari years, with the exchange rates stabilising at 1,535 naira per dollar in September 2025, as opposed 1,650 naira per dollar in March 2024, they also pushed tens of millions of already impoverished Nigerians deeper into misery, with no social safety nets.

The government described the drastic measures, such as the abrupt removal of the fuel subsidy, as a 'shock therapy' needed to fix Nigeria's economy in the long term.[284] But, as the Financial Times rightly pointed out in an editorial, 'Shock therapy alone will not cure Nigeria's economic ills.'[285] The truth is that while the Tinubu government's reforms are necessary, they are not sufficient. The macroeconomic environment is not conducive with excessive spending and massive money supply that fuel skyrocketing inflation; with uncontrolled borrowing sprees that threaten Nigeria's debt sustainability; and with endless interest rate hikes that harm the industrial sector. Above all, the Nigerian economy is massively underperforming, failing to generate growth and economic prosperity.

In July 2025, the Nigerian National Bureau of Statistics (NBS) announced that it had rebased the country's GDP, as it did ten years earlier, in 2014. The latest GDP recalculation, undertaken in 2024, accounted for previously excluded sectors, such as digital activities, pension funds and the informal sector activities, and pushed Nigeria's GDP from $187.76bn, as estimated by the World Bank, to $244bn (₦372.82tn), a 30 per cent increase.[286] When Nigeria's GDP was rebased in 2014, its economy became the largest in Africa, overtaking that of South Africa, although it slipped into the fourth largest in 2023.[287] However, despite the latest rebasing of the GDP in 2024, Nigeria's economy remained the fourth largest in Africa, behind South Africa, Egypt and Algeria.[288] The truth is that, as the World Bank said in 2025, Nigeria is stuck among Lower-Middle Income Economies (LMIEs) and among heavily indebted poor countries.[289]

The core lesson from Nigeria's economic history is that its economic model is not working and must be radically overhauled. Too often, Nigerians blame 'interventions' by the IMF and the World Bank for their country's economic woes.[290] But Nigeria's problems are endogenous,[291] and Nigerians must hold their government and leaders accountable for the mismanagement of the country's economy instead of blaming the IMF and the World Bank for Nigeria's self-inflicted economic woes. Truth is, Nigeria must tackle the supply constraints created by its weak macroeconomic conditions, including excessive debt and high inflation. Above all, Nigeria needs far-reaching economic restructuring based on prioritising the growth of high-value non-oil exports, which requires robust industrial and private sector development, as discussed in detail in the next two chapters.

5

Towards a Welfare and Prosperity Trade Agenda

Every great nation is a trading nation. As Charles Molloy, the 17th-century Irish maritime lawyer, famously said of his country: 'What would this island be without foreign trade. It is foreign trade that renders us rich, honourable and great, that gives us a name and esteem in the world'.[1] Trade, both exports and imports, are drivers of economic growth, job creation and poverty reduction – and, thus, sources of welfare and prosperity. However, Nigeria is not a serious trading nation. Apart from crude oil and natural gas, which both account for 91 per cent of its total exports, Nigeria sells very little non-oil merchandise goods or services to the rest of the world. Expectedly, the political economy of Nigeria's trade policy is shaped by that lack of non-oil export orientation.

The near-total absence of non-oil exports is responsible for Nigeria's resistance to negotiating meaningful trade agreements and drives the heightened protectionist interests in Nigeria. Dr Ngozi Okonjo-Iweala, Nigeria's two-time finance minister, put it this way: 'In Nigeria, the trade regime is politicised, with different business groups and their political backers interfering in the setting of tariffs and even asking for the implementation of non-tariff barriers to benefit their businesses'.[2] This is to be expected in a country with predominantly import-competing industries. Trade liberalisation creates winners and losers. While free trade benefits a country in terms of ensuring efficient resource allocation and benefits consumers through the combination of choice, quality and lower prices, it adversely affects industries that cannot compete with foreign producers. The losers from free trade are always more able to organise and exert political influence than the winners, namely consumers and export-oriented firms. As a result, free trade runs counter to political currents in Nigeria, and the protectionist idea of import substitution is widespread among political leaders and government officials.

For instance, in 2017, President Buhari said: 'We remain committed to economic diversification through import substitution and export promotion'.[3] The logic behind that statement, for a country that routinely prohibits imports, is mercantilist: export is good, import is bad. As Buhari put it in his 2017 Budget Speech, 'When we import things, we provide jobs for people in the countries that produce what we import, while our people are jobless.'[4] But the logic runs the other way as countries buying Nigeria's products can also argue that they are exporting jobs to Nigeria and importing unemployment and poverty from the country. However, the incongruency of simultaneously pursuing export orientation and import substitution, that is, simultaneously aiming to increase exports and restrict imports, is not understood by Nigerian politicians and officials and deserves some attention here.

Import Substitution: A Tried and Failed Policy

Import substitution means substituting imported goods with those produced at home. Its aim is to shift demand away from imported goods to similar domestic products. This is not wrong if such substitution results from the voluntary choices of consumers. In their paper titled *The ineffectiveness of 'Buy-British' campaigns*, David Clayton and David Higgins argued that 'consumers generally prefer domestic to foreign products, but when price, quality and product-country images are taken into account, the country-of-origin effect is weakened considerably.'[5] In other words, they are saying that trying to get citizens to choose locally made goods over foreign ones would only work if it is based on voluntary decisions influenced by price, quality and taste. However, by contrast, import substitution as a deliberate policy implies the use of government interventions to influence consumer choices, which is a throw-back to the 1950s and 1960s when most developing countries, particularly those in Latin America, pursued inward-looking industrial policies that drove them into an economic cul-de-sac.[6] A government that pursues import substitution as a policy will need to introduce a range of protectionist measures, including import bans, prohibitive tariffs and exchange controls, all of which will harm domestic industries' ability to be competitive, make consumers poorer and, probably, provoke tit-for-tat retaliations from other countries. Thus, 'economic diversification through import substitution and export promotion' is oxymoronic because import substitution and export promotion cannot go together; it is either one or the other.

Import substitution is particularly harmful for three specific reasons. First, as stated above, the policies needed to support it – import bans, prohibitive tariffs and other protectionist measures – will undermine the objective of export orientation. According to the Lerner symmetry theorem, imports and exports are the flip sides of the same coin, and restrictions on imports act as restrictions on exports.[7] When a country restricts imports, particularly of raw materials, it raises production costs for domestic industries that use the input materials and harms their productivity and ability to compete and export. Import substitution policy tools, such as high tariffs, impose a 'home-market bias'.[8] This is because import restrictions if they work, may lead to less demand for imports and thus less demand for foreign exchange, which will strengthen the local currency and make exports more expensive and less attractive. In consequence, therefore, import substitution policies protect producers of uncompetitive import substitutes at the expense of competitive export-oriented producers.[9]

Second, shielding domestic industries from international competition creates anti-export bias. Few firms would have the incentive to produce quality goods for export markets when they can easily take advantage of a protected home market. As a World Bank study noted, 'A major impediment to export growth is the strong anti-export bias of Nigeria's trade regime'.[10] Finally, import prohibitions have adverse distributional effects in that they harm consumers while benefitting import-competing producers. As tariffs are a tax levied on goods that cross borders, they are paid by importers, which pass the costs on to consumers. So, tariffs are ultimately taxes on consumers.[11] Trade protections thus cause higher prices of consumer goods and reduce real incomes for households, particularly poor ones. Inevitably, a tax on consumption means less consumption and less consumption means less jobs. Furthermore, while domestic import-competing industries benefit from high import tariffs, which shield them from international competition, their workers do not. This is because workers in sheltered domestic industries are likely to be condemned to low-productivity jobs and poor wages. Without competitive pressure, protected industries lack the incentives to innovate and generate higher productivity and efficiency that lead to higher wages and better living standards. A former British trade secretary, Vince Cable, once said regarding Britain: 'Protectionist self-sufficiency makes no sense to small states or medium-sized economies like Britain.'[12] If protectionist self-sufficiency makes no sense to Britain, how can it make sense to Nigeria, which needs greater integration into regional and global markets? The answer is: It doesn't.

Nigeria's Economy Is Diversified; Its Export Base Is Not

Overall, based on economic structure, Nigeria's economy is diversified, but its export base is not. As the World Bank noted in its 2014 Nigeria Economic Report, Nigeria's economy 'is more diversified and complex than previously documented', adding that 'the more diversified structure of Nigerian GDP and the sectoral growth rates imply a more complex story of GDP growth in Nigeria.'[13] According to the National Bureau of Statistics' GDP report for the third quarter of 2023, the following sectors are the top contributors to Nigeria's GDP: agriculture (29.31%), trade (15.19%), ICT (15.97%), manufacturing (8.42%), mining and quarrying (5.64%), real estate (5.58%) and finance and insurance (4.58%). This wide range of sectors shows that Nigeria's domestic economy is diversified, even though the sectors lack strong productive capacities.

However, in terms of revenue and trade structure, Nigeria's economy is extremely concentrated and not diversified. According to the 2024 Global Economic Diversification Index, 'Nigeria's economy remains among the least diversified even for its level of income or compared with other commodity-dependent countries, in particular when measuring diversification in terms of revenues or trade structure (looking at goods and services and imports as well as exports)'.[14] Thus, Nigeria's main challenge is trade and export diversification. As stated earlier, oil and gas accounted for 91.4 per cent of Nigeria's total exports in 2023, while services exports, dominated by transport and travel services as well as predominantly digitally traded business/financial services, accounted for 6 per cent.[15] This shows that non-oil goods exports account for less than 3 per cent of Nigeria's total exports.

Given that Nigeria's main economic challenge is export diversification, the question then is whether the government has the right response to it. Olusegun Awolowo, former chief executive of the Nigerian Export Promotion Council (NEPC), claimed that Nigeria 'has over 100 globally export-ready commodities'[16] and projected that Nigeria could earn $100bn annually from non-oil exports.[17] However, as argued above, protectionist import-substitution policies are not compatible with such export-oriented ambition. Export-led industrialisation requires export orientation and industrial competitiveness. In his book, *Made in Africa: Learning to*

Compete in Industry, Finn Tarp, a professor of Development Economics, argued that export orientation and competition help to raise industrial productivity, improve firm capabilities and facilitate exposure to innovation and technology.[18]

However, Nigeria ranks very poorly on the Economic Complexity Index. For instance, in the 2022 index, Nigeria scored -1.67 and ranked 119 out of 124 on trade, while it scored -1.94 and ranked 95 of 96 in the technology category. Yet, it is only through export orientation and industrial competitiveness that Nigeria can increase the sophistication and complexity of its trade and technology and, thus, diversify its export base. By contrast, protectionism and fixation with import substitution will harm Nigeria's industrial and export potentials. In its 2017 Trade Policy Review report, the WTO noted that protectionist measures in Nigeria 'have more significantly reduced exports than imports, and the importance of trade for Nigeria has decreased, with a trade (in goods and services) to GDP ratio of 21.1% in 2015, down from 52.8% in 2011.'[19] With merchandise trade as a share of GDP being only 29 per cent in 2023, Nigeria is still a very closed economy.[20]

Capacity Challenges to Non-Oil Exports in Nigeria

Besides protectionism and anti-export bias, there are other obstacles to non-oil exports in Nigeria. One is a weak productive capacity; another is the lack of quality infrastructure to ensure that Nigerian products meet international standards. Regarding the former, Nigeria's poor rankings on the Economic Complexity Index in the trade and technology categories, as cited earlier, expose the very low-value addition to the products that Nigeria exports. Nigeria is not adding value to its agricultural products and is not producing quality manufactured goods for exports. Simply, Nigeria has a narrow production base, and hence a narrow non-oil export capacity. Economies that experience strong GDP growth depend on strong growth in their manufacturing outputs and exports.[21] Yet, manufacturing accounted for 15.7 per cent of Nigeria's GDP in 2023 and under 1 per cent of its total exports.

However, added to the weak industrial capacity are problems with standardisation and quality control. International trade is now affected less by tariff barriers than by standardisation and all other factors relating to quality. As a result, exporters need to meet stringent quality and packaging requirements. However, the EU has persistently rejected Nigerian agricultural exports for failing to meet its food safety standards.[22] Nigerian exporters of agri-based products are also failing to take advantage of the preferential US African Growth and Opportunity Act (AGOA) to export to the huge US market because of standardisation problems. So, even if there are products to export and there are international markets for them, Nigeria is unable to export non-oil commodities because of its inability to comply with international standards. For a country that wants to boost non-oil exports, tackling the quality problems should be a priority. This requires establishing world-class laboratories, securing the certification of major trading partners and educating exporters to pay attention to standardisation and quality control to comply with sanitary and phytosanitary measures.

Yet, there is a third problem. Even if Nigerian manufacturers have productive capacities and can produce products that meet international standards, they lack the necessary market access and export-promotion support. The Nigerian Export Promotion Council (NEPC) and the Nigerian Export-Import Bank (NEXIM) are not doing enough to facilitate export opportunities for Nigerian businesses despite the existence of incentives such as tax relief on interest income and currency retention schemes. In some other countries, governments support businesses in a more direct way by helping firms to identify and exploit export opportunities. For instance, the UK's Department for Business and Trade (DBT) has experts in all UK missions abroad who carry out research into potential markets for UK exporters and help them to make valuable contacts in those markets. DBT actively encourages UK firms to export and helps them develop their export plans. Japan's 'JETRO' and South Korea's 'KOTRA' also proactively support their industries' abilities to access international markets.

The NEPC claims to provide support to Nigerian exporters in the form of advisory services, coaching and training, as well as providing information through sponsoring trade fairs and establishing contacts with buyers.[23] NEXIM, on the other hand, claims to provide support in the form of export finance, insurance and guarantees, including direct lending and trade finance facilities.[24] However, these measures have not significantly advanced non-oil exports simply because they are not effective. Nigerian officials stated in Nigeria's new trade policy, published in January 2023 that 'a major challenge facing trade development in Nigeria has been the inability of

Nigerian firms to effectively utilise market access negotiated in the global trading system'.[25] But this is somewhat disingenuous as it ignores two problems. First, as will be discussed later in this chapter, Nigeria is not negotiating meaningful free trade agreements to create market access for its businesses. Second, as discussed earlier, decades of protectionism have created a strong anti-export bias among Nigerian firms. Prohibitive tariffs and import bans protected Nigerian domestic producers without making them globally competitive, which fostered a strong anti-export bias. Based on the entrenched import-substitution policy, import-competing industries are far more favoured, through deliberate policy choices, than export-oriented ones, which face several obstacles, including those relating to customs procedures and requirements as well as, in some cases, export prohibitions, restrictions and licensing.[26] The way forward starts with having the right trade policy regime.

Imperatives of an Export-Oriented Trade Policy

For nearly two decades, Nigeria did not have a trade policy since the last one was published in 2002. During that period, Nigeria took ad hoc trade decisions without a coherent policy framework, leading to criticisms, perfectly justified, that the country's trade regime was complex, opaque and unpredictable.[27] One consequence of that opaqueness is that trade policy is used as a tool for political patronage and for extending favours to influential and politically connected people. For instance, while Nigeria has always had import prohibition lists and restrictive tariff systems, waivers and concessions are granted to very select enterprises and politically connected individuals. According to the WTO, "each year, broadly around 120 waivers for these goods [on the prohibited for import list] were issued'[28] under a non-transparent process. Indeed, the nature of a protectionist and opaque trade policy is that it breeds corruption and disregard for the rule of law as influential individuals who seek to avoid the trade protection curry favours from those in authority who, in turn, exercise wide discretionary powers.[29] However, Nigeria has always had problems with formulating any trade policy, regardless of its nature, owing to a lack of interministerial coordination necessary for reaching a consensus on policies. Graham Allison's bureaucratic politics model shows that policymaking is a push-and-pull game of influence, bargaining and competition among government actors.[30] Nowhere is this more evident, undermining policy development, than in Nigeria.

For instance, a trade policy document produced in 2001 was abandoned, according to one senior official, 'because of disagreements among the relevant ministries as to the appropriate policies.'[31] However, in 2018, the newly established Nigerian Office for Trade Negotiations (NOTN) launched a 'nationwide' call for inputs into what it dubbed 'A 21st-century trade policy for Nigeria'. Thus, the NOTN promised to overcome the age-long interministerial coordination problem and produce a long-awaited trade policy for Nigeria, with the involvement, unusual in Nigeria, of civil society and research institutes. Sadly, a year later, in September 2019, the inaugural chief executive of NOTN, a renowned trade expert and former Director at the WTO, Dr Chiedu Osakwe, died. It fell to his successor, another trade expert and former Deputy Director-General at the WTO, Dr Frederick Agah, to lead in developing the trade policy.

In January 2023, a 59-page document entitled 'Trade Policy of Nigeria 2023-2027' was published. The document confirms the view that trade policy is an intellectual or ideational issue. In his book *Pop Internationalism*, Paul Krugman puts it this way. 'If top government officials are strongly committed to a particular economic doctrine, the commitment inevitably sets the tone for policymaking'.[32] Put differently, trade policy choices do exist outside the conceptual or cognitive framework of policymakers. The liberal tone struck in Nigeria's new trade policy document certainly owes so much to the ideational position of Agah, a liberal economic thinker who traversed the world as a Deputy Director-General of the WTO, advocating trade openness, arguing that 'open and predictable markets are key to fostering economic recovery.'[33] It is, therefore, not surprising that Agah presided over the drafting of a trade policy for Nigeria that attaches a strong role to trade as 'a catalyst for the development of a diversified and competitive economy.'[34]

However, there is a major problem with the draft trade policy document. Rhetoric is one thing; action is another. In Nigeria, there is always a gap between policy statements and policy actions. For instance, despite the trade policy document's objective to 'increase the competitiveness of Nigeria's products and services in the domestic and international markets'[35], there are no explicit commitments to dismantle the tariff and non-tariff barriers that have long defined Nigerian trade policy, such as import bans, prohibitive tariffs and the incessant border closures. Rather, the document stresses safeguarding the interests of domestic industries, including using tariffs.[36] Yet, import prohibitions and tariff barriers have been identified in every successive trade policy review of Nigeria by the WTO.

Under the WTO, Nigeria's trade policy is reviewed every six or seven years. Since the WTO was created in 1994, it has reviewed Nigeria's trade policy six times: first in 1994, then in 1998, 2005, 2011, 2017 and 2024. After each review, Nigeria's trade policy was found to be more protectionist than in the previous review. For instance, following Nigeria's trade policy review in 2005, the WTO noted: 'Since its last Trade Policy Review (TPR) in 1998, Nigeria's trade regime has become more protective', with 'a 10-fold increase in products covered by import bans'.[37] Before the 2017 trade policy review was conducted, other WTO members sent 270 advance written questions to Nigeria. These questions related to the complexity, restrictiveness and opacity of Nigeria's trade regime.[38] The fact that 270 written questions were sent to Nigeria ahead of its trade policy review shows how concerned other WTO members were about its trade policy regime.

The result of the fifth review showed that Nigeria remained a protectionist country: it maintained high tariff rates and imposed numerous additional duties and charges on imports; it kept longstanding import prohibition lists and imposed local content requirements, in addition to several other non-tariff barriers. The draft Trade Policy said nothing about whether and how Nigeria would dismantle the tariff and non-tariff barriers, which makes the document's commitment to 'increase the competitiveness of Nigeria's products' doubtful, given that domestic industries can only be competitive when they are exposed to competition.

The sixth and current trade policy review[39] acknowledged the reforms being undertaken by President Tinubu's government, including the elimination of the multiple exchange windows and the scrapping of the CBN restrictions, imposed since 2015, on the use of foreign exchange for the imports of 43 groups of products affecting more than 900 tariff lines. However, while the WTO welcomed these reforms, it noted that several restrictive measures were still in place, including the fact that Nigeria 'continues to ban the import and export of certain goods.'[40] Furthermore, the WTO highlighted the arbitrary and opaque use of duty concessions that 'benefit large and politically connected enterprises in particular.'[41] In sum, the WTO concluded that 'some restrictive and interventionist policies seem to counteract broader government strategies to support economic diversification and the integration of more productive manufacturing enterprises into global value chains.'[42] If the *Trade Policy of Nigeria 2023-2027* document is the country's new trade policy, then it fails to address the key issues raised by the WTO in Nigeria's sixth trade policy review and cannot ensure that trade plays a critical role in promoting non-oil export growth and of creating jobs and reducing poverty.

The truth is that Nigeria needs the right trade policy, one that ensures the productivity and competitiveness of its industries and their export orientation. International trade widens the geographical extent of the market, enabling local enterprises to export more, reap economies of scale and increase productivity. It is also, as David Hume put it, 'a conveyor belt for the transmission of ideas and technology across the borders'.[43] Thus, a country's trade policy should enable it, through openness, to take advantage of the diffusion of technologies and ideas to increase the productive and trade capacities of its domestic firms. Furthermore, beyond the dynamic efficiency gains from the transmission of ideas, a good trade policy will enable a country to exploit the static efficiency gains of accessing quality goods at competitive prices from all over the world, thereby increasing the welfare and prosperity of the people. Nigeria cannot begin the journey to becoming a serious export-led industrial nation unless it stops being fixated on restricting imports and instead has a trade policy that focuses on increasing the productive and export potentials of its industries.

Yet, the trend and policy preference are towards trade restrictions. For instance, in February 2025, the Nigerian government imposed a four per cent Customs Administration Charge on the Free on Board (FOB) value of all imports into Nigeria,[44] while the Nigeria Ports Authority (NPA) introduced a 15 per cent tariff increase at the ports.[45] The Nigeria Employers' Consultative Association (NECA) said the new customs levy would devastate the economy and increase the misery of ordinary Nigerians[46], while the Manufacturers' Association of Nigeria (MAN) warned that the NPA's tariff hike would force the closure of many businesses.[47] The truth is that tariff escalation, including increases in customs levies and port charges, has long formed part and parcel of Nigeria's trade policy regime. But, as the WTO pointed out in its sixth Trade Policy Review report on Nigeria, such measures undermine Nigeria's economic diversification and the integration of more productive manufacturing enterprises into global value chains.[48] The impacts of protectionism on productivity and output growth are hardly appreciated in Nigeria. Yet, Nigeria's economy cannot develop without an open and competitive operating environment.

Nigeria Needs the Capacity to Tackle Unfair Trade

The foregoing argument in favour of trade openness must be balanced with an argument in support of a strong defence against unfair competition or trade practices. Free trade is good, but certain trade practices can be unfair and injurious to domestic industries. Thus, any rounded trade policy will include legal and institutional frameworks for tackling unfair trade practices, such as injurious dumping and subsidies. The WTO Agreement describes dumping as a practice that is 'to be condemned if it causes or threatens material injury to an established industry or materially retards the establishment of a domestic industry'[49] and provides for anti-dumping measures to deal with it.[50] The WTO also frowns on injurious subsidies and allows for the imposition of a subsidy countervailing duty where a subsidy causes or threatens injury.[51] These measures are known as trade remedies. But a trade remedy measure can only be imposed in a rules-based manner, requiring an independent national authority to thoroughly investigate allegations of dumping or subsidised exports and establish injury to domestic industries and causation. Thus, a country's trade policy regime must include a sophisticated trade remedies system.

However, Nigeria does not have a trade remedies mechanism even though it always complains about dumped and subsidised imports. During its WTO Trade Policy Review in 1998, Nigeria admitted that its trade remedy laws were inconsistent with WTO rules but also pointed out that it did not have the institutional and regulatory capacity to investigate anti-dumping issues.[52] Twenty years later, during its TRP in 2017, Nigeria was still citing 'the difficulty in the domestication' of its WTO commitments as a reason for not having a trade remedy legislation.[53] Nigeria's contingency measures laws are outdated and still governed by the Customs Duties (Dumped and Subsidised Goods) Act 1958. According to the WTO, Nigeria's last semi-annual notifications relating to anti-dumping and countervailing duty action were both 'nil notifications' submitted in June 2012 and October 2009, respectively, while Nigeria indicated that it had not imposed any such duties since its trade policy review in 2017.[54] The implications are that Nigeria had either not imposed any antidumping or countervailing duties or had imposed them without following the due process required under WTO law. Whatever the case, Nigeria cannot have a proper trade policy without a trade remedy system. Yet, while the draft Trade Policy of Nigeria 2023-2027 document refers to trade remedies, it says nothing about establishing a trade remedies system. However, Nigeria is said to be introducing an International Trade Authority Act that would also cover anti-dumping and countervailing measures.[55]

Nigeria needs a robust and rules-based trade remedies regime to deal with concerns about unfair competition or trade practices. While Nigeria should not shield its domestic industries from international competition, it must ensure a level playing field for them by tackling, in a WTO-consistent manner, unfair and injurious trade practices. However, given the potential for industry lobbyists to hijack a trade remedy system, it is important to ensure that any trade remedies authority is independent and distinguishes between cheap imported products, which benefit consumers, and predatory and injurious dumping, which unfairly undermines domestic industries. For instance, in creating its trade remedies authority after leaving the European Union, the UK built the system around the principles of impartiality, proportionality, efficiency and transparency. At the heart of the UK's trade policy is a commitment to free and fair trade. So, trade remedies are not a protectionist tool but a means of levelling the playing field for all economic actors. In sum, Nigeria cannot have a credible trade policy regime without a robust, rules-based trade remedies system.

Nigeria Frets About Smuggling, but its Trade Policy Fuels It

Few things agitate Nigerian officials about international trade more than smuggling. In 2019, the then-Buhari government closed Nigeria's borders for nearly one year, in part to stop the smuggling of goods into the country. Smuggling is, indeed, a prevalent problem in Nigeria, so prevalent that even the big smugglers are known. As former finance minister Ngozi Okonjo-Iweala wrote in her book *Reforming the Unreformable*, 'Nigeria must be one of the few countries in the world where smugglers are known and talked about openly, and where these same big-time smugglers walk around freely in the corridors of powers'.[56]

The scale of the problem is also huge. For instance, a World Bank report notes that 'The total amount of potential smuggling from Benin is estimated at close to $5bn, nearly 10 per cent of Nigeria's official imports'[57], adding: 'Tackling this would lead to an estimated gain of $1.2bn in government revenue.'[58]

Yet, the Nigerian government's response to the smuggling challenge, notably through incessant border closures, ignores the real issue. There is a large body of knowledge on the relationships between trade policy and smuggling, but Nigeria is fretting about smuggling without facing the fact that its economic policies, particularly its trade policy, create huge incentives for the phenomenon.

First, take the economic theory of smuggling. The economists Jagdish Bhagwati and TN Srinivasan posit in a paper entitled *Smuggling and Trade Policy* that smuggling could be a welfare-enhancing activity because it constitutes (partial or total) evasion of high tariffs and import bans that represent a suboptimal policy.[59] Put another way, smuggling is a response to severe policy distortions and an attempt to alleviate those distortions. Thus, to reduce smuggling, there is a need to have a trade policy that makes it unattractive. Smuggling involves a real cost: the hazards of avoiding the legal channels, the risk of being caught, the cost of bribing customs officials, the risk of losing the smuggled imports, etc. Thus, if smuggling is pervasive in a country, despite the risks and hazards involved, it must, from an economic rationality perspective, be because the costs are lower than the benefits.

That theory applies to Nigeria because the country's import barriers are among the highest in the world. Indeed, as discussed above, Nigeria has made protectionism in the forms of prohibitive tariffs and import prohibitions the core of its trade and industrial policies. There would be little or no smuggling in the first place if there was no demand for smuggled goods. However, there is a high demand for smuggled products in Nigeria because they are cheaper than local ones. For instance, a rice retailer told the Financial Times: 'Cotonou (rice) is cheaper than Nigerian rice — it is not supposed to be like this.'[60] It defies economic logic to expect rational actors to voluntarily adjust to a policy distortion that worsens their welfare. If a government policy makes a domestic product very expensive, rational people would prefer the cheaper, probably better-quality, foreign one, smuggled or not. Once there are large differentials in the retail prices of local products and like-foreign ones, which create demands for foreign products, there would be incentives for smuggling unless the cost of smuggling is prohibitive.[61]

However, to make the cost of smuggling prohibitive, the government must invest heavily in border enforcement. However, few developing countries have the resources to spend on effective border control and detection. Nigeria is noted for its extremely porous borders and lacks the financial resources, the technology and the disciplined officials to ensure efficient and effective border control. Nigerian customs officers are reputedly among the most corrupt in the world. Yet, the biggest incentive for smuggling is not porous borders but economic and trade policy distortions. That is where the solution to smuggling in Nigeria must start. Unless Nigeria reduces the incentives for smuggling by significantly lowering its extremely high rates of protection, it will continue to experience pervasive smuggling, which would mean that its desired policy objectives will not achieved and that it will suffer an unnecessary decline in the optimal tariff revenues that should have accrued from legal imports.

Yet, no country is an island. So, having a good domestic trade policy is not enough. It is important for a country to harmonise trade policies with its neighbours through regional integration because divergent economic policies between neighbouring countries increase smuggling.[62] This is why Nigeria should be actively involved in ECOWAS and the African Continental Free Trade Area (AfCFTA). Indeed, according to one study, Nigerian customs officials argued that smuggling into Nigeria would increase if Nigeria did not participate actively in AfCFTA.[63] Thus, to tackle smuggling, Nigeria must do the right things domestically, in terms of its own trade policy, and regionally, in terms of harmonising and integrating its policies with those of its neighbours.

The Need for a Stronger Commitment to Trade Facilitation

The Trade Facilitation Agreement is the first major WTO agreement since the conclusion of the Uruguay Round Agreement in 1993. It is widely seen as a 'win-win' deal for developing and developed countries because of its potential to bring down trade transaction costs, increase customs productivity and revenue collection, help attract foreign direct investment, and help make supply chains work well. Yet, many developing countries were sceptical about a trade facilitation agreement. Among other issues, they expressed concerns about its implementation costs and its impact on their policy space.[64] Nigeria was not an enthusiastic supporter of the agreement during its negotiation. In the months leading up to the Ninth WTO Ministerial Conference (MC9) in Bali, Indonesia, in December 2013, where the agreement was concluded, Nigeria was a strong voice within the Africa Group, citing domestic concerns, such as policy priorities and balance of trade issues, as well as implementation challenges, as the reasons to 'move very cautiously' on negotiating the agreement.[65] However, thanks to compromises, such as flexibility in implementing the agreement as well as promises of technical assistance and support for capacity building by the developed countries, developing countries, including Nigeria, withdrew their opposition to the agreement in Bali.

Yet, concluding the agreement was one thing. The actual commitments that each country made under the agreement were another. The Trade Facilitation Agreement consists of three categories. Category A covers commitments that a member state would start implementing immediately after the agreement entered into force. Category B includes provisions that must be implemented after a transitional period following the agreement's entry into force. Category C covers provisions that must be implemented after a transitional period following the agreement's entry into force and require assistance and support for capacity building. Nigeria notified the WTO of the indicative and definitive dates for measures under Categories A, B and C in 2017 and 2019. However, according to the WTO in its sixth trade policy review of Nigeria, carried out in 2024, only about 15 per cent of the provisions had been implemented under Category A, and only 42 per cent were designated under Category B, while only 25 measures were notified in

Category C requiring technical assistance.[66] Indeed, Nigeria did not accept commitments relating to the following areas: transparency, general or specific disciples on fees and charges, except penalty disciplines, release and clearance of goods, border agency cooperation and the simplification of formalities and documentation on import and export. Furthermore, Nigeria submitted an incomplete notification regarding the use of customs brokers in November 2022, prompting a call for full notification by some of its trade partners, such as the US.[67]

In 2023, Nigeria enacted the Nigeria Customs Service Act 2023, which replaced the old Customs & Excise Management Act, and earlier, in 2022, passed the Business Facilitation Act 2022. These measures suggest a commitment to customs and trade facilitation, and, indeed, the acts mandate the authorities to facilitate trade. However, in reality, trade facilitation remains problematic in Nigeria, first, because nearly all consignments undergo physical inspection prior to customs clearance despite risk management being in place[68], and second, because Nigeria's external trade costs, caused by factors other than tariffs, such as transport costs, port congestion and complex regulatory requirements, remain very high.

In its 2025 National Trade Estimate Report on Foreign Trade Barriers, the Office of the United States Trade Representative, USTR, noted concerning customs barriers and trade facilitation in Nigeria: 'The Nigeria Customs Service's practices continue to present major obstacles to trade. Importers report inconsistent application of customs regulations; lengthy clearance procedures, often due to outdated manual processing systems; and corruption.'[69] The reports added that despite the customs authority's attempt to automate its processes, 'many basic customs procedures are still paper-based and require an unreasonably long time to complete.'[70] Indeed, as the WTO put it, 'Nigeria continues to lag other lower-middle-income economies in relation to trade facilitation measures and significantly lags OECD high-income economies.'[71] This is borne out by the table below.

Nigeria's trade facilitation performance, compared to middle-income/OECD economies

	Nigeria 2017	Nigeria 2019	Nigeria 2022	Lower - middle income	OECD high income
OECD Trade Facilitation Indicators (0 - 2 (best)					
Average trade facilitation performance	0.824	0.893	0.93	n.a.	n.a.
A – Information Availability	1.05	1.05	1.05	1.25	1.85
B – Involvement of the trade community	1	1.14	1.14	1.25	1.81
C – Advance rulings	0.571	0.571	0.571	1	1.806
D – Appeal procedures	1.33	1.44	1.44	1.2	1. 57
E – Fees and charges	1.36	1.46	1.46	1.45	1.85
F – Documents	0.63	0.88	0.88	1.33	1.8
G – Automation	0.62	0.7	0.7	0.95	1.85
H – Procedures	0.94	1	1	1.34	1.71
I – Internal border agency cooperation	0.46	0.46	0.55	0.78	1.62
J – External border agency cooperation	0.46	0.46	0.55	0.63	1.6
K – Governance and impartiality	0.67	0.67	0.89	1.2	1.93

Source : WTO (2024), TPR, Nigeria, viewed at https://www.wto.org/english/tratop_e/tpr_e/s462_e.pdf

The above table shows that Nigeria underperforms other middle-income countries on nearly all indicators of trade facilitation, including information availability, involvement of the trade community, advance rulings, availability, involvement of the trade community, advance rulings, documents, automation, procedures, internal and external border agency cooperation and governance and impartiality. And, of course, it lags far behind the OECD high-income economies. Trade transaction and logistics costs are high in Nigeria, according to the Logistics Performance Index.[72] With cumbersome cargo handling, the near absence of automation, multiple border agencies, not to mention corruption, importing and exporting goods in Nigeria are extremely costly. Nigeria has always stressed its commitment to trade facilitation, but despite the rhetoric and, indeed, the existence of some legislation, the reality is different.

A stronger, binding international commitment under the WTO Trade Facilitation Agreement would lock in deeper reforms and send a more powerful signal about its intentions, in addition to enabling it to take advantage of technical assistance and support for capacity building under the agreement to transform its weak customs infrastructure. Nigeria certainly needs to remove burdensome port and customs operations and procedures, which significantly constrain terminal operators and, thus, foreign trade.

Economic Diplomacy: A Growth Strategy for Nigeria

In his book *Negotiating the World Economy*, Professor John Odell defines economic negotiations as those in which 'parties' demands, offers and related actions refer to the production, movement or exchange of goods, services, investments, money, information or their regulations.'[73] As Odell points out, all the subjects of economic negotiations are 'sensitive to concrete markets'[74]; that is, they shape market behaviour and investor confidence. Thus, economic diplomacy, which is the process of negotiating and concluding trade and economic agreements, must be integral to the trade and economic policies of every country. This is important because even if a country has productive and export capacities, it still needs market access overseas to create export opportunities for its companies. Furthermore, active economic and commercial diplomacy can boost productive capacity by locking in, through meaningful trade and other economic agreements, critical reforms that can attract significant and quality foreign direct investment; it can also create overseas market access that removes anti-export bias and thus increase exports. Finally, boosting trade abroad is essential to deliver a strong economy at home, which is why economic diplomacy, encompassing trade and market access negotiations, is a critical growth strategy for any country.

In its 2014 Business Environment Rankings, the Economic Intelligence Unit (EIU) listed Vietnam as the country that has seen the biggest improvement in its business environment in the past 20 years, and one of the reasons for this steep rise in the index, according to the EIU, is Vietnam's adoption of several free-trade agreements, which led to the adoption of liberal trade policies and declining operational costs for foreign businesses.[75] The EIU added that 'strides made in strengthening relations with the West have also helped Vietnam deepen economic ties with major export markets, such as the US and the EU.'[76] To be sure, President Trump's decision to impose a 46 per cent 'reciprocal' tariff on imports from Vietnam as part of his tariff blitz on other trading partners, on the ground that Vietnam had a trade surplus with the US and also allowed China to evade US tariffs by trans-shipping exports through its country[77], raised questions about Vietnam's export-based economic model[78] and about the value of free trade agreements, especially between small countries and large ones. However, it should be noted that President Trump's hostile attitude to tariffs and disregard for the rules of global trade is exceptional and widely frowned upon.[79]

In truth, most countries honour free trade agreements with one another, and many are keen to negotiate more trade deals to lock in market access with their trading partners. For instance, in January 2025, the Financial Times reported that several countries were seeking to increase bilateral trade deals with major trading partners as a safeguard against US protectionist policies under President Trump.[80] More than 75 countries already have FTAs with the EU, which, in 2024, signed an FTA with Mercosur, the Latin American trading bloc with 400 million people.[81] Most countries prioritise FTA negotiations in their economic diplomacy because FTAs don't only help in improving the business environment at home but also in securing strong market access abroad.

Trade, Not Aid

Trade and economic diplomacy become even more important for developing countries as the developed world tightens the noose around international aid or make it a more explicit tool of their commercial and geopolitical interests.[82] For instance, at the start of his second term in January 2025, President Trump shut down the US Agency for International Development (USAID),[83] created by President John F Kennedy in 1961, and subsequently announced the cancellation of 83 per cent of the agency's programmes.[84] In the UK, the prime minister, Sir Keir Starmer, cut the aid budget from 0.5 per cent of gross national income to 0.3 per cent to fund an increase in defence budget.[85] The UK's aid budget was 0.7 per cent of gross national income until Prime Minister Boris Johnson reduced it to 0.5 per cent of GNI in 2021, citing fiscal constraints.[86] The West's retreat from international aid raises the salience of the longstanding argument that what developing countries, particularly African countries, need is more trade and less aid. In a statement, Ngozi Okonjo-Iweala, Director-General of the WTO, said: 'In Africa, we really need to change our mindset. Access to aid? I think we can really begin to think of it as a thing of the past.' [87] That means 'Trade, not aid' must go beyond a mantra and become a reality. Yet, the only way to guarantee trade and market access with other countries is through reciprocal trade negotiations, through economic diplomacy.

However, if economic diplomacy is measured by the number of trade and other economic negotiations that a nation engages in, Nigeria is a laggard and seems averse to serious trade negotiations. This is ironic, given that Nigeria has prominent economic diplomats, such as Yonov Agah, who was a Deputy Director-General of the WTO and Ngozi Okonjo-Iweala, who is the current Director-General of the

WTO. Yet, despite these individual-level achievements, Nigeria itself is not a serious player in economic diplomacy. This is understandable because when a country is a commodity-based monoculture economy, with predominantly import-competing rather than export-oriented industries, it is unlikely to be active in economic and commercial diplomacy, which is mainly about negotiating market access for trade in manufactured goods and services. It is interesting, for instance, that while Nigeria is not active in WTO negotiations and in negotiating FTAs, it is an active member of OPEC, the oil cartel, simply because it is a major oil-exporting country. The following subsections discuss Nigeria's economic relations with major trading blocs and nations.

ECOWAS and AfCFTA: Embracing Regional Integration

The biggest economic development in Africa since the start of its post-colonial era is the creation of the African Continental Free Trade Area (AfCFTA), which is potentially the world's largest common market, given Africa's current population of about 1.47 billion and projected population of 2.5 billion by 2050. The logic of AfCFTA is unassailable. Africa trades less with itself than any other continent. For instance, over 80 per cent of African trade is with the rest of the world, while intra-Africa trade accounts for just over 10 per cent of its total trade, compared with nearly 70 per cent in Europe, 54 per cent in North America, 51 per cent in Asia and 15 per cent in Latin America.[88] Yet, a legacy of the colonial era, Africa's exports to the developed world remain dominated by primary goods such as coffee beans, cocoa, and raw minerals while the continent imports back from the West those primary goods but as refined, processed and manufactured products, which locks African countries to the colonial-style trading relationships in which they export raw materials and import finished goods.[89]

However, if AfCFTA worked and became a single integrated market, African countries could process and manufacture goods that are traded among themselves, thereby unlocking labour-intensive industrialisation throughout the continent and potentially increasing intra-African trade to more than 42 per cent.[90] Furthermore, a single African market could give Africa a bigger clout in international negotiations, enabling the continent to strike better deals that tie commodity deals with foreign economic powers to the domestic processing of raw materials in Africa.[91] Indeed, it is estimated that foreign investment in Africa, as a single integrated market, could surge as much as 159 per cent[92] because a vast integrated African market would cast a wider net for global capital, mitigating the risk of investing in individual countries and enabling economies of scale.[93] However, all of these are, so far, in the realm of potential rather than reality as AfCFTA, launched in 2018, is still mostly a theoretical free trade area, facing huge obstacles to fully taking off, let alone becoming a functioning single market.[94] For instance, while AfCFTA has eliminated tariffs on 90 per cent of goods, non-tariff barriers, such as customs procedures, standards regulations and transport logics, as well as corruption and bureaucratic red tape, continue to hinder intra-Africa trade.[95]

One other major weakness of the AfCFTA is the absence of a free movement of people agreement, given that free movement is a prerequisite for a single market. Yet, as Aanu Adeoye, the West Africa correspondent for the Financial Times, wrote in an article titled 'Unfree movement – Why can't Africans travel around Africa?'[96], the failure of a free movement agreement is a major obstacle to AfCFTA's success as it hinders the ability of African investors, businesspeople and citizens to move freely around the continent, thereby limiting intra-Africa trade and cultural ties. The Free Movement of Persons Protocol of the African Union was codified in 2018 to allow African citizens to move visa-free across the continent for up to 90 days. However, only 32 of Africa's 54 countries have, so far, signed up to the agreement, and only four – Mali, Niger, Rwanda and Sao Tome and Principe – have ratified it, falling short of the 15-nation minimum required to bring the agreement into force.[97] Furthermore, as of the time of writing, only Benin, Gambia, Rwanda and Seychelles guarantee visa-free travel for all Africans.[98] Yet, if AfCFTA must succeed, it must truly mimic the EU's single market, on which it is modelled, and allow the free movement of people.

Nigeria and AfCFTA

The history of AfCFTA is not complete without mentioning the pivotal role of Nigeria in creating it. First, the idea behind AfCFTA was mooted at a summit of African leaders in Abuja, the capital of Nigeria, in 1991, where they signed a treaty, the Abuja Treaty, that established the African Economic Community (AEC), which laid the foundation for the creation of a continental free trade area. Nearly 25 years later, in 2015, the AfCFTA negotiations were launched but stalled for two years. Then, in June 2017, at their summit in Niamey, capital of Niger, African leaders elected Dr Chiedu Osakwe, a Nigerian and former director of the Doha Development Round at the WTO, as chairman of the AfCFTA Negotiating Forum. Osakwe led the negotiations to a conclusion at the technical level, while the then Nigerian Trade Minister, Dr Okechukwu Enelamah, was responsible for the completion of the negotiations at the ministerial level of the African Union (AU).

The AfCFTA Agreement was launched in Kigali, the capital of Rwanda, on March 21, 2018, and signed by 44 of the 54 member countries of the AU. However, despite effectively helping to create the AfCFTA, Nigeria refused to sign the agreement in Kigali. President Buhari later justified Nigeria's refusal to sign the deal in Kigali, thus: 'We need the full support and buy-in of our private sector and civil society stakeholders and the public in general.'[99] But this was strange from an economic diplomacy point of view. In his book *Diplomacy and Domestic Politics: The Logic of Two-Level Games*, Robert Putnam argues that any international economic negotiation is a two-level game, played at the domestic and the international tables and involving alignment of the domestic and international processes and interests. The fact that the Nigerian government did not secure domestic stakeholder support and buy-in for the agreement during its negotiations and only sought to do so after the negotiations had been concluded and the agreement could not be changed defied the principles of economic diplomacy, which must involve domestic stakeholders at the outset.

Eventually, after much international pressure, Nigeria signed the agreement in July 2019 and established the AfCFTA National Action Committee Secretariat to, among other things, facilitate the development and implementation of the domestic AfCFTA plan and facilitate AFCFTA trade capacity building. Yet, concerns remained in the country about the agreement's potential impact. For instance, in 2019, the then Minister of Finance, Zainab Ahmed, warned that 'the AfCFTA could create a nightmare situation for Nigeria'.[100] This would indeed be the case unless Nigeria developed the productive and trade capacities to exploit the market access opportunities created by AfCFTA. However, Nigeria could benefit from AfCFTA. Indeed, writing in the Financial Times in August 2024, Wankele Mene, AfCFTA's secretary-general, said Nigeria was among the African countries that had exported products under the AfCFTA regime.[101]

Yet, the general view, as of 2025, was that Nigeria had had little to show for its membership of AfCFTA beyond creating administrative structures, such as the AfCFTA National Coordination Office, headed by Olusegun Awolowo, former Executive Director and Chief Executive Officer of the Nigerian Export Promotion Council (NEPC). In January 2025, The Guardian newspaper published a front-page report titled 'Four years on: Why AfCFTA impact on Nigeria's trade, integration, economic growth remains lean.'[102] According to the report, although many companies were given certificates of origin to export under AfCFTA, only a few shipments were made in four years. Nigeria's challenges in leveraging the AfCFTA opportunities are frequently blamed on infrastructure deficiencies, such as inadequate transport networks, limited shipping facilities as well as complex and inefficient regulatory environments that hinder export sectors in Nigeria. However, Chinyere Almona, Director-General of the Lagos Chamber of Commerce and Industry (LCCI), argued that the problem was also cultural. 'We have a wrong culture as far as export is concerned,' she said. 'We don't have an export culture.' She cited Nigeria's failure to take advantage of preferential export opportunities in Europe and the US, saying: 'So, AfCFTA is not likely to be different unless we become intentional and change our strategies.'[103]

Indeed, there are challenges ahead. Nigeria can only benefit from AfCFTA if it can produce efficiently and penetrate other African markets with high-quality goods and services. If Nigeria fails to develop its productive and trade capacities, it could be the biggest loser as it would be unable to sell to the rest of Africa while more competitive AfCFTA members would seek to penetrate Nigeria's large market. Nigeria's response to such a perceived surge of African imports would be to impose import restrictions against AfCFTA rules. In 2019, Nigeria's then central bank governor, Godwin Emefiele, said that 'AfCFTA won't stop us from adding more items to the forex restriction list'[104], referring to a policy that banned importers of certain products from accessing foreign exchange through the official window. AfCFTA is also unlikely to stop Nigeria's penchant for closing its borders. Going by its typical behaviour, Nigeria would not be constrained by its AfCFTA commitments, as shown by the case of ECOWAS below.

Nigeria and ECOWAS

The evidence with ECOWAS shows that Nigeria is doing extremely poorly in terms of intra-African trade. Although neighbours and near-neighbours tend to dominate trade destinations, Nigeria is not good at exporting to its neighbours. For instance, in 2022, Nigeria accounted for 50.1 per cent of ECOWAS population and 62 per cent of its GDP. However, Nigeria only accounted for a meagre 4.6 per cent of ECOWAS intra-regional trade in terms of exports in 2023.[105] Nigeria is a reluctant and perfidious member of ECOWAS when it comes to trade openness, despite the existence of the ECOWAS Trade Liberalisation Scheme, which aims to eliminate tariff and non-tariff barriers on intra-ECOWAS trade. Although Nigeria eventually signed the ECOWAS Common External Tariff (CET) agreement, it was the last country to do so and has never fully implemented it.[106] Nigeria implements the ECOWAS CET, but with a lot of deviations, such as Import Adjustment Taxes, added to nearly 200 tariff lines in 2023, up from 97 in 2017.[107] The WTO said in its 2024 report of Nigeria's sixth trade policy review: 'Nearly every year, the Federal Government issues fiscal policy measures that create changes to the IATs, duty rebates and import prohibitions.'[108] As one scholar put it, Nigeria has 'displayed an absence of leadership and has in the past behaved in an obstructionist fashion'[109] in relation to the ETLS and ECOWAS CET. Thus, with respect to Africa, be it on ECOWAS or on AfCFTA, Nigeria's economic diplomacy leaves much to be desired and needs a radical change.

The Commonwealth: Leveraging a Trade Advantage

In 2015, the Commonwealth Secretariat published a report titled 'The Commonwealth in the Unfolding Global Trade Landscape: Prospects, Priorities, Perspectives'.[110] The report also called the Commonwealth Trade Review, tells an interesting story about a phenomenon known as the 'Commonwealth effect' and how it is positively influencing trade and investment between Commonwealth members, thereby creating a 'Commonwealth trade advantage'. This is interesting because the Commonwealth is not a typical trading bloc but a voluntary organisation of 54 former British colonies. But, despite being an unnatural trading hub, the report notes that 'when two countries are both Commonwealth members, they trade and invest significantly more with each other than they would otherwise have done.'[111] According to the report, 'when two countries are both Commonwealth members, their bilateral trade in goods and services is about 10 per cent and 42 per cent higher respectively, and bilateral foreign direct investment (FDI) is 10 per cent higher.'[112] What this means is that trade and investment between Nigeria and, say, Canada or India should be higher than between Nigeria and Japan or Russia, based on the 'Commonwealth effect'.

The factors that drive the 'Commonwealth effect' are not just the usual suspects – a common language, colonial links, etc. It is more than these factors. First, the analysis draws on the 'gravity model of trade', which says that bilateral trade can be explained by the economic mass of countries, captured by their combined GDP and the distance between them. But the model also includes other variables, such as sharing a common language, belonging to the same trading bloc, having a past colonial linkage, and having common administrative and legal systems. However, after accounting for these variables, the analysis suggests that they cannot fully explain the Commonwealth trade advantage. So, there must be something additional to the variables. And that additional factor is the cause of the 'Commonwealth effect'. This factor, the report says, is the large Commonwealth diasporic community. This is explained using the concept of 'psychic costs.' According to this concept, when firms want to expand to international markets, they typically begin in countries that are culturally similar. Where such similarity exists, the 'psychic' costs are low, and where it doesn't, the 'psychic' costs are high. The report concludes that 'the *psychic* costs of international trade are lower in the Commonwealth'.[113] This is what creates the 'Commonwealth effect' and, in turn, the Commonwealth trade advantage.

But if there is a Commonwealth trade advantage, how can Commonwealth members leverage it? The report sets out four key recommendations. First, countries should build productive and trade capacities. This must involve reducing barriers to trade, promoting private-sector development and tackling supply-side bottlenecks. Second, they should improve trade logistics. For instance, the report notes that if each Commonwealth country achieves the same level of Logistics Performance Index (LPI) score as Singapore (4.00 in 2014), the combined Commonwealth GDP would increase by $501 billion. Indeed, even if each country with a lower LPI score than South Africa can achieve the same score as that country (3.43 in 2014), the combined Commonwealth GDP would increase by $177 billion. Third,

Commonwealth developing countries should strengthen regional integration and take advantage of preferential trade agreements with the developed countries. Finally, they should exploit the potential of their Commonwealth diaspora 'to catalyse innovation and investment and bridge into new markets.'[114]

Nigeria is an active member of the Commonwealth politically. A Nigerian, Chief Emeka Anyaoku, was the Secretary-General of the Commonwealth for ten years, from 1990 to 2000. However, Nigeria is not active in the Commonwealth economically. For instance, Commonwealth countries accounted for small percentages of Nigeria's total exports between 2015 and 2021. South Africa accounted for the highest share at 5.37%, followed by the UK (1.76%), India (1.62%) and Canada (1.55%).[115] Nigeria should be exporting more to other Commonwealth countries, based on the Commonwealth effect, particularly the diasporic factor. It is interesting that the *Trade Policy of Nigeria 2023-2027* document identifies the 'Diaspora market' as a key target for diversifying Nigeria's export base, putting the number of Nigerians living in the diaspora at 'over 15 million' and saying that 'the diaspora population constitutes a huge market for Made-in-Nigeria products.'[116] As argued in Chapter 4, Nigeria's diaspora constitutes a significant economic asset, not only in terms of diaspora remittances and investment, but also in terms of market access for non-oil exports. Nigeria should, therefore, fully harness the economic value of its huge diaspora communities worldwide, not least in Commonwealth countries.

However, to benefit from the 'Commonwealth effect' and diasporic advantage, Nigeria must, as discussed earlier in this chapter, build productive trade capacities and improve its trade logistics. Nigeria's LPI score of 2.60 is very low for its ambition. This is why significantly improving customs and trade facilitation is critical. As discussed below, Nigeria's productive and trade capacities also suffer from a lack of trade agreements with major trading blocs like the European Union. Such agreements could trigger and lock in significant trade and competitiveness reforms at home and create significant market access opportunities overseas. If there is a trade advantage anywhere, Nigeria must do everything to leverage it. Thus, Nigeria should explore and exploit trade opportunities with Commonwealth countries where the diasporic advantage is very strong, with a large diaspora of at least 17 million living abroad.[117]

EU: Nigeria Needs the Economic Partnership Agreement

For nearly three decades, the European Union's trade relations with the African, Caribbean and Pacific (ACP) countries, former European colonies, were based on unilateral preferences under the Lomé Convention, first signed in 1975. But decades later, after the rules-based WTO was created, a WTO dispute panel declared, in the *EC-Bananas case*, that the Lomé convention was incompatible with the WTO's non-discrimination rule as the convention discriminated against non-ACP developing countries.[118] The Cotonou Agreement, another preferential system, replaced the Lomé Convention in 2000 but established the framework for negotiating WTO-compatible reciprocal trade deals called the Economic Partnership Agreements (EPAs). Having already concluded a 'comprehensive' EPA negotiation with the Caribbean countries, resulting in the EU-CARIFORUM EPA, the EU started negotiating EPAs with five African regions, namely West Africa (ECOWAS), Central Africa, Eastern and Southern Africa (ESA), East African Community (EAC) and Southern African Development Community (SADC).

However, while the EPA negotiations with other African regions went on relatively smoothly, those with ECOWAS were problematic because of Nigeria's intransigence. The EU-ECOWAS EPA was very controversial in Nigeria at the policy, epistemic and business levels. In April 2012, Charles Soludo, former governor of the Central Bank of Nigeria, wrote a hard-hitting article in the Financial Times titled 'Africa needs honesty over EU trade deals', in which he argued that the EPA was 'harmful', 'intrusive' and 'unnecessary'.[119] In May 2014, at the Extra-Ordinary Session of the Conference of African Union Ministers of Trade in Addis Ababa, Ethiopia, Nigeria's then Minister of Industry, Trade and Investment, Segun Aganga, railed against the EPA, arguing that it would have a long-term negative impact on Africa's industrialisation. Nigeria's position 'is very clear', he said. Africa should not give away its 'abundant natural resources' and 'large market' by signing the agreement.[120] The Nigerian business community also opposed the agreement. At a conference organised by the *Africa Today* magazine, the then president of the Manufacturers' Association of Nigeria (MAN), Frank Jacobs, said that Nigeria 'does not need EPA until it has been adequately industrialised to trade industrial goods competitively'.[121] The public space in Nigeria, including the media, was saturated with anti-EPA sentiments and rhetoric.

These were not the views of ECOWAS itself. The conclusions of the EPA negotiations were approved by the ECOWAS 'Authority of Heads of State and Government' at their summit in Accra on 10 July 2014[122], and, at another summit held in Abuja on 15 December 2014, the Authority 'instructed' its negotiators 'to expedite actions to organise, as soon as possible, the signing of the Agreement and its ratification by all Member States.'[123] From ECOWAS's point of view, the negotiations took place on both sides 'at the levels of Experts, Senior Officials and Chief Negotiators.'[124] Although its participation was lukewarm, Nigeria did not walk away from the negotiations, which were closed in Brussels on 6 February 2014. But despite the endorsement of the agreement by the ECOWAS Heads of State and Government in July 2014, Nigeria refused to sign it. This matters because each EPA requires the signatures of all the contracting parties in each region before it can be ratified and before it can enter into force. The refusal of Nigeria to sign the EU-ECOWAS EPA has, thus, left the agreement in a doldrum. As the then Ghanaian trade minister, John Kyerematen, said out of frustration about Nigeria's intransigence, 'The agreement would be frustrated if Nigeria refused to sign.'[125]

But is the agreement such a bad thing for Nigeria? First, it is important to recognise that the EPAs are reciprocal trade agreements, which means that they involve the exchange of concessions. As Emily Jones observes in her book *Negotiating Against the Odds*, 'market access concessions are the currency of trade negotiations'.[126] Thus, unlike unilateral preferential agreements, which are one-sided, both parties have obligations under reciprocal agreements, even if developed countries are expected to give more. For instance, the EU-ECOWAS EPA says in its Preamble that it 'must' be a 'development tool' for 'increasing the production capacity and exports of West African states and supporting the structural transformation of the West African economies and their diversification and competitiveness'. Part 1 goes on to say that the parties 'undertake' to encourage improvement in the 'supply capacity and competitiveness of the production sectors of the West African region'. More specifically, on tariffs, the agreement says that products 'originating in' West Africa 'shall be imported into the EU free of customs duties' (Article 10 (1) and Annex B). The agreement also relaxes the usually stringent Rules of Origin, allowing West African countries to use materials sourced from other countries in their production without losing free access to the EU market.

One of the main challenges Nigeria faces in gaining access to the EU market is the EU's tough quality and packaging requirements, which have resulted in several Nigerian food products being banned from entering the EU on health and safety grounds. However, under the EPA, the EU undertakes to provide financial and technical support to help West African exporters meet its Sanitary and Phytosanitary (SPS) standards (Article 33), potentially removing a major non-tariff barrier to Nigeria's non-oil exports. The EU is one of Nigeria's key trading partners, with the average bilateral merchandise trade between 2017 and 2023 standing at $35 billion, which constitutes 34 per cent of Nigeria's total merchandise trade.[127]   However, nearly 99 per cent of Nigerian trade to the EU is crude petroleum. Nigeria needs to boost its non-oil exports to the EU, but significant barriers relating to standards exist. Thus, a big win for Nigeria in the EPA would be for the EU to help the country develop the critical infrastructure needed to meet EU food safety rules and standards and, at the same time, grant Nigeria deeper access to the EU market. Article 33 of the ECOWAS-EU EPA appears to commit the EU to doing this. The onus would then be on Nigeria to hold the EU to that commitment. Finally, the EU undertakes to provide funding for projects linked to trade, industry, energy and transport infrastructure in West Africa, as well as funding to cover the fiscal impact of implementing the agreement for the period of tariff dismantling (Art 60 (3)). It undertakes to help West Africa raise additional funding for the development aspect of the agreement from other donors (Article 54(4)).

What, then, are the obligations of ECOWAS under the agreement? The EU-ECOWAS EPA requires the West African party to 'reduce and eliminate customs duties' applicable to certain products 'originating in the EU' (Article 10 (2)). These cover three categories of goods. Group A applies to social goods, capital goods and specific inputs. Group B covers inputs and intermediate goods. Group C applies to final consumption goods. Under the EPA, ECOWAS member states must remove all customs duties on such goods originating in the EU within 20 years, between 2015, when the EPA was supposed to enter into force, and 2035. However, the tariff dismantling requirement does not apply to all West African products. It only covers 75 per cent of West Africa's tariff lines, i.e. product classes as defined for the purpose of customs duties. The remaining 25 per cent, under Group D, are excluded from the obligation. The Group D goods are described as 'sensitive products' for West Africa. The table below breaks down the tariff dismantling commitments and their implementation stages.

EU-ECOWAS EPA implementation stages

Group	CET	T	T+5 (2020-24)	T+10 (2025-29)	T+15 (2030-34)	T+20 (2035)
D	0					
	10					
	20		*Exclusion (i.e. no change)*			
	35					
C	5	5	5	0	0	0
	10	10	10	5	0	0
	20	20	20	10	5	0
B	0	0	0	0	0	0
	5	5	0	0	0	0
	10	10	0	0	0	0
A	0	0	0	0	0	0
	5	5	0	0	0	0

- Group D: exclusion (25% of tariff lines, covering "sensitive" locally manufactured products)
- Group C: mainly final consumption goods, e.g. watches, cameras
- Group C: mainly inputs and intermediate goods
- Group A: essential goods, basic necessities, basic raw materials, capital goods

The tariff dismantling obligation is based on the ECOWAS tariff structure. ECOWAS has five tariff bands, the fifth added at the behest of Nigeria. Only three of these tariff bands, where tariffs are already relatively low or even non-existent, are covered by the EPA tariff dismantling obligation. The three tariff bands and their current ECOWAS common external tariffs (CET) are essential social goods (0%), basic goods, basic materials, equipment, specific inputs (5%) and intermediate goods (10%). The remaining two tariff bands, where the CETs are currently very high, are excluded from liberalisation under the EPA. Specifically, products currently facing a 35 per cent CET, namely, finished products manufactured locally, such as processed meat, chocolate and printed fabrics, are excluded from liberalisation. Similarly, products currently attracting 20 per cent CET, i.e. consumer goods, such as cement, paints, perfumes and cosmetics, stationery, textiles and apparel and 'fully built cars' are excluded. Given the scope of the excluded products, ECOWAS played an active role in the EPA negotiations. Evidently, detailed haggling over market access took place, and ECOWAS secured significant protections for its industries.

However, some could argue that removing customs duties completely on 75 per cent of tariff lines, albeit over a period of 20 years, is still significant. And, particularly for Nigeria, it is arguably significant that the agreement prohibits, under Article 34, quantitative restrictions, including import bans, which are key tools in Nigeria's trade policy arsenal. In practice, however, any trade agreement that imposes a tariff dismantling obligation would also include responsive provisions that allow any of the parties to suspend or modify the commitments in response to, for instance, external shocks, fiscal losses or damage to local industries. The EU-ECOWAS EPA is not an exception in that regard. It sets out several safeguard measures. Specifically, Article 12 provides for a change in the ECOWAS tariff commitments for 'special development needs, in particular, the need to support its common sectoral policies'. Chapter 2 of the agreement makes provisions for the use of trade defence instruments, namely, anti-dumping and subsidy countervailing measures (Article 20), multilateral safeguard measures (Article 21) and bilateral safeguard measures (Article 22). These measures, which include suspension of tariff reduction or increase in customs duties, may be introduced by ECOWAS if, for instance, EU products are coming into West Africa in such large quantities as to 'cause or threaten to cause serious injuries' to domestic industries. If ECOWAS can use these flexibilities in a way consistent with the EPA, they are no doubt significant tools for mitigating any future adverse effects of the agreement.

Given the breadth of the excluded products in Group D and the responsive clauses, it is a protectionist mindset to focus on the elimination of customs duties on 75 per cent of tariff lines over 20 years. That should not overshadow the objectives of the EPA, set out in its Preamble and Part 1, and repeated throughout the agreement, about engendering improved production capacity, economic and export diversification, and international competitiveness of the West African countries, of which Nigeria would be the biggest beneficiary, enabling them to increase their non-oil exports to the EU.

The competitiveness and development elements of the EPA relate to standards and conformity assessments (chapter 3), trade facilitation and customs cooperation (chapter 5), agricultural productivity and competitiveness (chapter 6) and the development programme (Part III). The focus of the EPA development programme on 'diversifying and increasing capacities' and 'improving and reinforcing national and regional infrastructure linked to trade' clearly recognises the critical complementarity between trade and competitiveness. The key obstacles to Africa's integration into world trade, or participation in the global value chains, in terms of value-added exports, are what UNIDO described as the 'three Cs', namely, lack of enhanced competitiveness of supply capacity; lack of recognised conformity with international standards; and lack of efficient connectivity to markets.[128] The EU-ECOWAS EPA promises to address these challenges, with the EU and its Member States 'undertaking' to 'finance the development aspect of the EPA' (Chapter 6).

Nigeria has little to lose but a lot to gain from the EPA. Nigeria's main concerns are about the potential impacts of the EPA on domestic industries and on tariff revenue. However, several studies have shown that the EPA would have minimal adverse effects on Nigeria in these areas. For instance, a World Bank study found that even after the EPA's tariff dismantling obligation was fully implemented in 2035, fiscal losses in Nigeria could be expected in the magnitude of 0.8 per cent of total fiscal revenue.[129] Also, according to the study, once the EPA is fully implemented, overall tariff protection in Nigeria would reduce modestly from 11.3 to 9.2 per cent.[130] This is largely because of the number of sensitive tariff lines (25%) excluded from liberalisation under the EPA. Furthermore, the study shows that two-thirds of Nigerian manufacturing firms would experience a net increase in profitability due mainly to lower input prices.[131] In a paper by Abiodun Bankole of the Economics department of the University of Ibadan, which looked at Nigeria's application of the ECOWAS CET between 2008 and 2012, he argued that production output went up from 0.7 per cent pre-CET to 3.7 per cent after CET. As Bankole put it, 'Evidence shows a positive response of the manufacturing sector to import liberalisation in general and CET in particular'.[132] The main reason for this is lower input prices.

As of the time of writing, Nigeria is still dithering on signing the EU-ECOWAS EPA but signing and faithfully implementing the agreement would trigger significant trade and competitiveness reforms that would unlock the country's productive and trade potential. It is well known that the competitiveness of Nigeria's industries is hindered by serious supply-side constraints, including the huge infrastructure gap, high policy and regulatory costs, poor standards and conformity assessment regimes, and high trade transaction and logistics costs. The EPA gives Nigeria the opportunity to embark on far-reaching policy and institutional reforms, including in its tax and customs regimes, and to lock in these reforms while leveraging the technical and financial support and investment from the EU. If Nigeria could leverage the EPA to overcome the threefold challenges of competitiveness of supply capacity, conformity with international standards and connectivity to markets, it would reap benefits beyond increasing non-oil exports to the EU but also with other major trading nations.

United States: Decades of Missed AGOA Opportunities

In 2018, President Buhari visited the US and met President Trump in the White House during his first term. In a typical Trumpian fashion, President Trump turned to Buhari and told him that Nigeria must take down its trade barriers. He said it was important that 'we are able to sell our great agricultural products into Nigeria.'[133] Trump reminded Buhari that the US gave Nigeria 'well over $1 billion in aid every year', stressing that the amount of US aid to Nigeria 'is so large you wouldn't even believe it'.[134] In light of this, he said the trade imbalance between the two countries was unacceptable and demanded the US be treated in a 'reciprocal fashion'.[135] Indeed, as noted earlier, in his second term, President Trump deemphasised international aid by shutting down the US aid agency, USAID, and cancelling over 80 per cent of its programme. So, Nigeria should not expect what Trump called 'so large' US aid under his second term. But beyond stopping foreign aid, President Trump also unleashed the steepest tariffs in a century on other countries, including developing countries, keeping his promise to impose so-called 'reciprocal' tariffs on US trading partners to retaliate against taxes, tariffs, regulations and subsidies.[136]

On April 2, 2025, President Trump imposed two sets of tariffs on countries around the world. The first was a 10 per cent baseline tariff on all imports into the US. The second was what he called 'reciprocal tariff' based on the US trade deficits with other countries. To calculate the 'reciprocal tariff' for each country, the Trump administration took the US's trade deficit in goods with that country as a proxy for alleged unfair trade and then divided it by the amount of goods imported into the US from that country. The resulting tariff equals half the ratio between the two.[137] According to economists who spoke to the Financial Times, the formula had 'no economic rationale.'[138] However, that was the formula used to calculate the 'reciprocal tariffs' for all countries, ranging from 11 per cent to 50 per cent. Based on that formula, President Trump imposed a 14 per cent 'reciprocal tariff' on Nigeria.[139] In a subsequent post on X (formerly Twitter), the Office of the US Trade Representative (USTR) accused Nigeria of unfair trade practices against the US. The post read:

Nigeria's import ban on 25 different product categories impacts U.S. exporters, particularly in agriculture, pharmaceuticals, beverages, and consumer goods. Restrictions on items like beef, pork, poultry, fruit juices, medicaments, and spirits limit U.S. market access and reduce export opportunities. These policies create significant trade barriers that lead to lost revenue for U.S. businesses looking to expand in the Nigerian market.[140]

Indeed, in its 2025 National Trade Estimate Report on Foreign Trade Barriers submitted to the Trump administration and the US Congress, the USTR went deeper to highlight a wide range of non-tariff barriers that hindered US business interests in Nigeria. These included inconsistent application of customs regulations, lengthy clearance procedures, due to outdated paper-based manual customs procedures, cumbersome rules and procedures around import permits, widespread corruption and a lack of transparency in Nigerian procurement processes.[141]

To be sure, President Trump and the USTR were right about Nigeria's protectionism, characterised by high tariff barriers and a longstanding policy of import bans, not to mention a myriad of other non-tariff barriers, as discussed earlier in this chapter. However, the trajectory of US-Nigeria trade over the past decades shows a drastic reduction in Nigeria's trade surplus with the US. Overall, Nigeria still enjoys a trade surplus with the US on trade in goods as its goods exports to the US in 2022 totalled $4.8bn, up 38.9 per cent ($1.3bn) from 2021, while the US goods imports from Nigeria totalled $3.4bn in 2022, down 13.6 per cent ($530m) from 2021.[142] But it is worth noting Nigeria's goods exports to the US in 2022 were down by 75 per cent from its 2012 value. This is because the US dropped from being the largest importer of Nigerian oil in 2012 to being the tenth largest in 2015 as increased domestic production resulting from shale gas squeezed its demand for Nigerian oil.[143] It is, however, interesting that despite being the biggest oil producer and becoming a net oil exporter in 2022, the US still imported 8.3 million barrels a day (MBD) out of its total consumption of 20.3 mbd in 2024, 70 per cent of which came from Canada and Mexico.[144] So, America is still heavily importing oil, but not a lot from Nigeria.

That said, as noted above, Nigeria still enjoys a trade surplus with the US on goods. However, the situation is different in trade-in services. Nigeria's exports of services to the US totalled $607m in 2022, up 38 per cent ($167m) from 2021; the US services exports to Nigeria were an estimated $1.9bn in 2022, up 17 per cent ($277m) from 2021.[145] Thus, while the US has a goods trade deficit with Nigeria, it enjoys a services trade surplus with the country.

However, despite the significant fall in American demand for Nigerian oil, Nigeria could make up for that by exporting more non-oil goods to the US if, over the years, it took advantage of the export opportunities created by the US African Growth and Opportunity Act, or AGOA. The preferential trade scheme, introduced by President Bill Clinton in 2000, allows countries in sub-Saharan Africa to export products to the United States tariff-free. Nigeria is eligible for AGOA and qualifies for the scheme's textile and apparel benefits. But Nigeria failed, over AGOA's forty-three years till date, to increase its non-oil exports goods to the US. Under AGOA, Nigeria could export 6,500 products duty-free into the US market. Yet, Nigeria is Africa's least beneficiary of AGOA.[146] Nigeria's textile and clothing sector has proved incapable of exporting to the US market, while its food and agro-based sectors lack the quality infrastructure to export products that meet US standards.

In 2015, the US Congress renewed AGOA for another ten years, meaning that it was due to expire in 2025. But the future of AGOA was cast into doubt by President Trump's rumbunctious approach to international trade and his tendency to see US trade deficits with other countries as resulting from unfair trade practices. In an interview with the Financial Times, South Africa's trade minister, Parks Tau, said that Trump's tariff blitzkrieg effectively 'nullified' the AGOA. He said: 'To the extent that the executive orders said that AGOA will not be applicable, we work on the basis that it has nullified the AGOA benefits.'[147] The Nigerian Minister of Industry, Trade and Investment, Jumoke Oduwole, said that the 10 per cent blanket and 14 per cent 'reciprocal' tariffs imposed on Nigeria could potentially impact Nigeria's $6 billion annual non-oil exports to the US. She said: 'For businesses in the non-oil sector, these measures present destabilising challenges to price competitiveness and market access, especially, in emerging and value-added sectors vital to our diversification agenda.'[148] She added that SMEs building their business models around AGOA exemptions would face the pressures of rising costs and uncertain buyer commitments. Thus, while Nigeria had not maximized the AGOA opportunities for the decades that the preferential trade legislation had existed, it risked losing the US market altogether if President Trump's blanket and 'reciprocal' tariffs remain in place.

However, as noted earlier, on April 9, President Trump suspended the application of the 'reciprocal tariffs' for 90 days to allow countries that wished to negotiate with the US to do so, saying that over 75 countries had indicated that were willing to negotiate with the US. Indeed, according to the Financial Times, many countries, including South Africa, on which President Trump imposed a 30 per cent 'reciprocal tariff', were prepared to compromise. However, in May 2025, the Nigerian government unveiled a 'Nigeria First' economic policy, which instead of addressing the concerns of the US regarding trade barriers in Nigeria actually doubled down on them by favouring local companies over foreign ones.[149] Nigeria did not negotiate a deal with the US within the 90-day window, and President re-imposed a 15 per cent on the country's exports to the US. The implication is that trade relations between the US and Nigeria, under President Trump and President Tinubu, may prove difficult and challenging.

In any case, the truth is that AGOA will not be the same again. Even if President Trump were minded to renew the act, it would attract stricter conditions, such as extending tariff-free access to the US only to countries that opened their own markets to US exports and whose foreign policy was aligned with Washington's.[150] It goes without saying that if Nigeria wants to placate President Trump, known for his transactional and reciprocal approach to trade, it would not only need to review its tariff and non-tariff barriers on US products, but also buy more US exports, especially agricultural products and even weapons. In the end, however, regardless of AGOA's new status and longevity, Nigeria will not reap the benefits of the scheme and export more non-oil products to the US unless it develops the much-needed productive and trade capacities, including tackling issues related to quality and standards.

China: Beware of the Yuan Magnet

Nigeria's economic relations with China, like the wider Africa-China relations, are based on Chinese infrastructure loans and a lopsided trade in which China has huge trade surpluses. China is massively funding infrastructure projects across Africa, from railways in Kenya and hydropower stations in Ghana to rail lines, roads, bridges, airport terminals, etc, in Nigeria. In May 2019, President Buhari told the chairman of China Railway Construction Corporation, Fenjian Chen, who visited him at the State House: 'We are very grateful to China for the genuine efforts and strides to rebuild our infrastructure.'[151] In July 2020, he told the outgoing Chinese Ambassador to Nigeria, Zhou Pingjian: 'Please convey our appreciation to President Xi Jinping for the contribution of China towards reversing the infrastructure deficit we suffer in the areas of rail, roads, airports and power.'[152] The fulsome praises show how much Nigeria is indebted and beholden to China for investing in and building its infrastructure.

But all this disguises deep concerns about the fine print of Chinese loan agreements and the nature of Chinese-funded projects. The opacity of the financing terms and questions about the viability of the infrastructure projects are major concerns across Africa. Chinese loans are usually backed by African natural resources, such as a loan to Ghana repayable in refined bauxite.[153] Previously, China tied its loans to Nigeria to oil acquisitions under the oil-for-infrastructure model. But its new loan agreements with

Nigeria contain stringent waiver-of-immunity clauses. For instance, Article 8 of the railway construction contract signed in 2018 says: 'The borrower [i.e. Nigeria] hereby irrevocably waives any immunity on the grounds of sovereignty or otherwise for itself or its property in connection with any arbitration proceeding pursuant to Article 8(5) thereof with the enforcement of any arbitral award pursuant thereof'. While anti-immunity clauses are common in international commercial agreements involving a sovereign state, China has a record of aggressively enforcing such clauses. In 2018, when Sri Lanka could not service the Chinese loan that it took to build its Hambantota port, China forced its government to hand over the port and 15,000 acres of land around it for 99 years.[154]

There are also concerns about the quality and sustainability of China's infrastructure loans. In a paper for the United States Institute for Peace, Yunnan Chen, a scholar at Johns Hopkins University, said that the modus operandi of China's Export-Import (Exim) Bank is to help Chinese firms win overseas contracts, encouraging those state-owned firms to 'push economically unviable projects with the backing of Chinese state finance.'[155] In 2017, China's Minister of Foreign Affairs, Wang Yi, visited Nigeria and announced $40bn of Chinese investment in Nigeria, saying that China had already invested $45bn in the country to finance $22bn-worth of completed projects, with an additional 23bn of projects ongoing.[156] All the huge infrastructure loans raise questions about Nigeria's long-term ability to service the loans and the consequences if it couldn't. At home, China scrapped a string of infrastructure projects in its indebted regions[157] but continued to fund unsustainable infrastructure projects in Africa.

The American statesman John Adams famously said: 'There are two ways to conquer a country. One is by the sword. The other is by debt.'[158] China funds infrastructure projects in developing countries as part of its Belt and Road Initiative as a global investment and lending programme. Through the G7, the US launched the Partnership for Global Infrastructure and Investment (PGII) to developing nations as an alternative to China's Belt and Road Initiative and aims to deploy more than $600bn by 2027.[159] However, unlike the American model, which seemed to be tied to local development, China's infrastructure funds have often been criticised for supporting unsustainable projects and resulting in some countries building up unsustainable debts.[160] For example, Kenya's $5bn standard gauge railway was criticised for not being economically viable or benefiting local communities.[161] Nigeria must avoid falling into China's debt trap in the name of infrastructure development. It does not help that China's infrastructure loans are tied to projects that are only carried out by Chinese companies, using Chinese products and services and predominantly Chinese labour, while the few local workers employed in those projects are often poorly paid and badly treated.[162] Kingsley Moghalu, a former deputy governor of Nigeria's central bank, said of China's infrastructure loans to Nigeria: 'This is a rip-off. This is not a loan. Nigeria is subsiding China's export strategy.'[163]

The situation is not better with respect to trade. China imports only commodities from Africa and exports manufactured goods, while the continent records a massive trade deficit. For instance, of a total trade of $282bn in 2023, Africa's trade deficit was $64bn.[164] In relative terms, Nigeria is in a worse situation than other African countries. In 2022,

Nigeria exported $1.52bn in goods to China but imported goods worth $21.4bn, a deficit of nearly $20bn.[165] Nigeria's main exports to China were petroleum gas, crude petroleum and lead ore, while its imports from China were manufactured products, such as non-kit women's suits, rubber footwear and broadcasting equipment. In 2018, Nigeria signed a three-year Renminbi-Naira Swap Agreement worth $2.5bn, which allowed Nigeria to pay for Chinese imports without the constraints of dollar scarcity. In December 2024, Nigeria renewed the 15-billion-yuan ($2.09 billion) currency-swap deal with China[166], enabling it to bypass the use of the dollar in trading with China. Given that Nigeria is heavily import-dependent on China, the swap agreement favours China more than Nigeria as it allows China to push its manufactured products into Nigeria while it buys virtually no non-oil products from the country.

As discussed earlier, Nigeria has, so far, refused to sign the Economic Partnership Agreement with the European Union on the grounds of preventing an import surge and protecting its industries. Yet, it is relaxed about a surge of Chinese imports, which led to a trade deficit of $20bn in 2022 alone, while China has done nothing to transfer technology to Nigeria or support its industrialisation. In 2017, the then-president of Kenya, Uhuru Kenyatta, said: 'Just as Africa opens to China, China must open to Africa.'[167] That must be the thrust of Nigeria's economic diplomacy with China, a more balanced trade and economic relations, not a replication of the old imperial model, where Africa exported crude produce and imported manufactured goods. Joshua Cooper Ramo, a former foreign editor of Time magazine, once said that 'China's economic rise serves like a magnet working on grains of iron to align other nations' economic interests with the Middle Kingdom's'.[168] China is the world's second-largest economy after the US, and the world's largest manufacturing country, making up 31.63 per cent of global manufacturing out in 2024.[169] Thus, Nigeria cannot ignore China. Yet, it must seek mutually beneficial relations and avoid becoming servile to China economically.

***

The overarching argument in this chapter is that Nigeria must move away from the failed 'development path' of protectionism and import substitution and embrace an export-oriented trade policy that enables it to build its productive and trade capacities and diversify its export base from oil dependency into non-oil exports. At the heart of this is the competitiveness and productive efficiency of Nigerian industries, trade facilitation, development of customs infrastructure and promotion of trade integration through meaningful trade agreements that lock in structural reforms at home and market access abroad. The section on economic diplomacy emphasises the need for Nigeria to deepen economic integration in Africa through ECOWAS and AfCFTA, exploit the Commonwealth trade advantage, embrace the trade and competitiveness opportunities embedded in the EU Economic Partnership Agreement (EPA), negotiate a reciprocal trade deal with US so as to better utilise the trade preferences under AGOA, and ensure a more balanced economic relations with China. This chapter leads inexorably to the next one on industrialisation.

6

Industrialisation and Private Sector Development

The core argument in the preceding chapter is that Nigeria must be a serious export-oriented trading nation. But Nigeria cannot be a serious trading nation unless it has diverse and valuable products to export to the rest of the world. To quote Adam Smith in *The Wealth of Nations*, 'No nation is ever rich by the exploitation of the crude produce of the soil but the exportation of manufactures and services.'[1] However, no nation can export manufactures and services unless it is industrialised, and no nation can be industrialised without a robust and flourishing private sector. That is the logical underpinning of this chapter, which addresses the subjects of industrialisation and private-sector development in Nigeria. But, first, it is worth exploring the concept of industrialisation.

Why Industrialisation Matters

Adam Smith is right: dependence on the export of raw materials cannot make a nation rich; what can make a country rich is the ability to manufacture value-added products and/or develop quality services[2] and export them. In other words, it is the ability to industrialise and trade.

Throughout history, the world has experienced at least three waves of economic transformation. Each of these eras was characterised by industrialisation and the expansion of trade.[3] The first wave was underpinned by the Industrial Revolution of the late eighteenth and early nineteenth centuries, triggered by Britain but later followed by the rest of Europe and North America. The second wave began in the 1950s up to the early 1970s and was a product of the rise of Japan and the newly industrialised economies in East Asia, with their rapid manufacturing and export-led growth. Then, in the late 1980s, the third wave of global economic development began with the most rapid process of industrialisation to date, led particularly by China and India and more broadly by the G20-developing countries, including Brazil, Indonesia and the Philippines. The common features in the different economic phases are rapid industrial development and the exports of value-added products.

Significantly, industrialisation and export-led growth can trigger a process that enables a developing country to catch up with a developed one. As the WTO puts it, 'Once a catch-up process commences, rapid development is possible and has the potential to push incomes towards developed country levels.'[4] This is evident in the rapid economic growth of China, especially after it joined the WTO in 2001 in pursuit of its 'Going Out' policy.[5] For instance, China is now the world's largest exporter, with several other developing countries among the top twenty exporters, including Brazil, India, Malaysia, Mexico and Thailand. China's rapid industrialisation and export-led growth also helped it to reduce the proportion of its people living in extreme poverty from 60 per cent in 1990 to 12 per cent in 2010.[6] Indeed, together, China and India were responsible for lifting 1.1 billion people above the international poverty line over the past four decades as economic liberalisation in both countries generated astronomical growth, which lifted all boats.[7]

Another way of looking at the issue is to consider the counterfactual. What if a country does not industrialise and does not export value-added products but instead depends on the extraction and export of natural resources? The first problem concerns the terms of trade, i.e. the value of a country's exports, relative to that of its imports. The world prices of raw materials are lower than those of value-added manufacturing products. As Ed Conway put it in his book *Material World*, 'the price of raw materials rarely reflects their importance,' adding that '99 times out of 100 raw materials are pretty cheap.'[8] Thus, if a country only exports raw materials, such as iron ore and raw diamond and imports expensive value-added products like cars and jewels, it will, as Adam Smith postulated, be poor. That means that only countries that have the knowledge and the capacity to turn natural resources into finished products before trading it onwards stand a chance of becoming rich. Furthermore, countries that depend on exporting commodities are exposed to the vagaries of world prices. Price volatility and boom-bust cycles are the trademarks of the commodities markets.

In recent years, the commodities boom that began in 2000, fuelled by the rapid economic growth in China and other major developing countries, speculative capital flows, near-zero interest rates and quantitative easing, later unravelled as the price of oil crashed to a historic low of about \$50 per barrel in December 2014[9], putting the economies of oil-dependent countries in a precarious state. Thus, adding value to raw materials through manufacturing and exporting value-added products (and services) is the best antidote to the uncertainty and vulnerability that come with resource dependency. In addition to helping to diversify a country's export base, industrialisation can also have positive spillovers on the rest of the economy, such as the growth of the supply chain and services sector.

But comparative advantages matter. The lesson that David Ricardo taught about comparative advantage is that if a country can buy something from elsewhere for a cheaper price, instead of producing it itself, it should buy it and not attempt to produce it.[10] For instance, instead of seeking to produce vehicles, developing countries with a comparative advantage in agriculture should increase productivity and value addition in their agricultural sectors to develop vibrant and export-oriented agro-based industries, while oil-producing countries should develop their petrochemical industries and export petrochemical products, thereby diversifying their oil-based exports.[11] Thus, the message is simple. No country can be rich by exporting crude produce but by industrialising and exporting value-added products and quality services.

The Nigerian Case: Imperatives of Industrialisation

It goes without saying that Nigeria desperately needs to industrialise and diversify its economy, particularly its export base. Everyone agrees that Nigeria's economy must be rebalanced away from dependence on oil exports to value-added manufacturing exports. For decades, successive Nigerian leaders have talked about the need to industrialise and diversify the economy. But when Nigeria was awash with oil money, the country's leaders paid lip service to the structural transformation of the economy. That lethargy has now turned into desperation. The trigger is the collapsing oil prices and the realisation that, as President Buhari put it, 'The days of Nigeria as a big oil producer with plenty of money are gone.'[12]

But rhetoric is one thing; action is another. How does Nigeria intend to become an export-led industrialised nation, and would its plan, if it has any, take it there? To date, the only document that sets out Nigeria's industrial policy is the 'Nigeria Industrial Revolution Plan' (NIRP), which was published in 2014 by President Jonathan's administration and adopted by President Buhari's administration. In his book *Reclaiming the Jewel of Africa*, Dr Segun Aganga, who, as Minister of Industry, Trade and Investment, developed the NIRP, spoke glowingly about the plan, saying it 'was designed to move Nigeria from being an exporter of raw materials to an industrialised nation.'[13] The question, however, is: would the NIRP, as it is, achieve anything of the sort, that is, would it turn Nigeria into an export-led industrialised economy? The answer is no, for the reasons explained below.

The Limits of the 'Nigeria Industrial Revolution Plan'

The name of the NIRP document suggests a high level of ambition: an industrial 'revolution' plan, meaning what is expected is nothing short of a 'revolution'. But too often, in

Nigeria, the policies behind such grandiose plans fall far short of what their high-sounding titles suggest. In this case, it is doubtful that the policies set out in the NIRP would 'revolutionise' Nigeria's industrial landscape or 'rapidly build up industrial capacity and improve competitiveness in Nigeria'[14] , as the plan claims.

The first key weakness is the absence of a strong linkage between industrialisation and science and technology. All the Industrial Revolutions in history, including the three previous ones in 1784, 1870 and 1969, have one thing in common: the centrality of technology. And, today, several countries are making the digital revolution part of their manufacturing future. For instance, the UK is responding to concern about the decline of its manufacturing capacity by making emerging new technologies part of the future of its manufacturing, including Artificial Intelligence (AI), robots, additive manufacturing or 3-D printing, and the 'Internet of Things', in which machines communicate to machines.[15] In 2020, at a seminar on manufacturing excellence and the role of research and development, two senior executives of Roll Royce stressed that science and advanced technology were at the heart of manufacturing excellence. They stated that a country would only industrialise when it could achieve a step-change improvement in manufacturing through technology innovation that could transform productivity by, for instance, replacing a process that takes 46 operations with a new method that takes 21.[16]

However, as pointed out in a previous chapter, Nigeria scored -1.94 and ranked 95 out of 96 in the technology category of the 2024 Economic Complexity Index. With such an abysmally low technological base, it rings hollow to talk about industrial 'revolution' in Nigeria. It is inconceivable that Nigeria can achieve an industrial 'revolution' without first achieving a revolution in innovation and technology. In his book entitled *Dynamism*, Professor Edmund Phelps, an economics Nobel laureate, makes a distinction between 'indigenous' innovation and 'imported' innovation.[17] The former is the innovation that comes from within a country through individual creativity and investments in skills and research and development (R&D). Every country needs to promote indigenous innovation by creating a conducive environment for individual creativity to flourish and by investing heavily in skills and R&D.

But the second source of innovation, that is, 'imported' innovation, comes from exposure to the best ideas and technologies around the world. While indigenous innovation is important, internationally-driven innovation brings greater benefits. This is because a country can benefit from the transfer of ideas, know-how and technologies across borders. This aligns with David Hume's view that international trade is 'a conveyor belt for the transmission of ideas and technology across borders.'[18] Thus, a benefit of imported innovation is that domestic industries can imitate or emulate foreign companies through imports, exports and foreign direct investments (FDIs), which are usually associated with greater technological spillovers, as well as higher R&D intensity and skills enhancements.[19]

Indeed, evidence shows that nations have historically imported knowledge and technology from overseas in an effort to build out their industrial base. For instance, the Chinese bought a ThyssenKrupp steel plant in Dortmund,

Germany, and transported it brick by brick to a site in Yangtze, north of Shanghai.[20] Today, that site is the world's single biggest steelworks, and China is the world's largest steel producer.[21] The lesson here is that a country like Nigeria should do everything possible to attract foreign direct investment, whereby foreign investors are able to turn the country's natural resources into finished, exportable products. Finally, international competition is a greater source of 'imported' innovation as it puts domestic firms on their competitive toes and forces them to adapt. Thus, if Nigeria wants to develop the technological base for industrialisation, it needs an industrial policy that supports indigenous innovation but, more importantly, that takes advantage of the global diffusion of ideas, know-how and technologies through an open and competitive market economy.

However, while the NIRP contains the right buzzwords, such as 'competitiveness' and 'innovation', at its heart is an industrial policy designed to support old, struggling and uncompetitive sectors. Specifically, the policy promotes four industry groups and twenty sub-sectors that are structurally weak and technologically deficient.[22] While governments should cultivate and support winning sectors, picking 'winners' *ex-ante* is bad policy because evidence shows that such selectivity is hardly ever driven by possession of the right information and market considerations.[23] And a government that props up inefficient firms will simply perpetuate their inefficiency.

Yet, the NIRP treats virtually all sectors as the commanding heights of the economy, which the government must support and protect. The United Nations Commission on Africa (UNECA) argues that government interventions should be based on 'rigorous empirical analysis' but does not think that the NIRP meets this condition. According to the UN body, 'selecting the various sectors to be promoted appears to be based on the rule of thumb and not on known rigorous studies'[24], adding: 'The number of subsectors (20) appears on the high side to qualify for a selective trade or industrial policy.'[25]

Attempts to support a struggling industry without tackling its structural weaknesses always fail. China, which the NIRP uses as a model, is a case in point. While China is the world's largest manufacturing nation, evidence suggests that its state-led model of propping up unproductive firms is not working. According to a report in TIME magazine, China's industrial policy created 'zombie enterprises' that were churning out unwanted goods.[26] It was estimated that 3 million jobs could be cut from China's coal, steel, electrolytic, aluminium, cement and glass industries due to their inefficiency.[27] That is the danger of propping up inefficient firms. However, many of the sectors and sub-sectors selected for special treatment in the NIRP cannot survive in a competitive environment.

For instance, food processing in Nigeria has serious quality and standards problems. Cement is a highly protected, oligopolistic sector. As even the NIRP admits, 'Nigerian cement prices are currently among the highest globally'.[28] The auto industry cannot produce affordable cars, and the light manufacturing sector cannot innovate and compete. Yet, the NIRP's vertical policy interventions aim mainly to protect these struggling and unproductive sectors through the trade policy instruments of high tariffs and import bans, as well as discriminatory subsidies and public procurement.

An industrial revolution needs a consumer society.[29] Therefore, any policy to promote industrialisation cannot ignore competition and consumer welfare. Some of the key barriers to industrialisation highlighted in the NIRP are low consumer purchasing power and low patronage of 'Made-in-Nigeria' goods.[30] The first is linked, in part, to the low productivity of most Nigerian firms, which means that workers receive poor wages. It is also linked to the fact that goods produced by Nigerian companies are too expensive; again, a low productivity problem. The second is linked to the poor quality and standards of many locally made goods. The problems of low consumer purchasing power and low patronage of locally made goods pose existential challenges to industrialisation in Nigeria. It shows that Nigeria's domestic market, despite a large population of 230 million people, is not underpinned by domestic demand that is critical to driving growth, job creation and prosperity.

In November 2024, the Manufacturers Association of Nigeria (MAN) said that the inventory of unsold finished products soared to N1.24 trillion in the first half of 2024, a 357.6 per cent increase from the first half of 2023.[31] The phenomenon of unsold goods in manufacturers' warehouses was attributed to extremely weak consumer purchasing power amid escalating inflation. Diversification and development Nigeria's domestic market, through tackling the problems of weak consumer purchasing power, the high costs of goods and low quality products, both linked to a lack of productive efficiency, must be at the heart of Nigeria's industrialisation policy, for Nigeria cannot even begin to think of becoming an export-led industrial economy without vibrant homegrown industries, boosted by robust domestic demand.

In truth, it is the steady fall in prices and improvements in quality that come from higher productivity, which comes from innovation, that reduce the costs of goods and improve living standards. However, Nigerian industries have not achieved the productivity miracle through learning and experience because of the absence of innovation. Therefore, there is a need for policies to tackle problems of low productivity, lack of competitiveness and poor standards so that Nigerian companies can compete on prices and quality, which would have multiplier effects. For instance, as Nigerians earn better wages (through higher productivity) and as goods become cheaper and of better quality (through competition, productivity and innovation), consumers would have more disposable incomes and buy more things from producers, thus supporting industrial development, creating jobs and generating prosperity.

A key to industrialisation, therefore, is to ensure that any policy designed to support industrial development does not reward producers while punishing consumers but benefits businesses and consumers alike. As Adam Smith put it in *The Wealth of Nation*, 'Consumption is the sole end and purpose of all production; and the producer's interest ought to be attended to, only so far as it may be necessary for promoting that of the consumer'.[32] However, industrialisation in Nigeria is mainly seen through the prism of the producer, not that of the consumer, which is why owners of oligopolies are extremely rich while the overwhelming majority of the people are extremely poor, and consumers are fobbed off with poor-quality yet over-priced goods. The competitive market that allows efficient allocation of resources, that improves the welfare of the people and that increases real national income is patently absent. Thus, a key to industrialisation is always remembering Adam Smith's words: consumption is the sole end and purpose of all production. It is such a market-driven and consumer-focused approach that enables sustainable industrialisation.

Industries Thrive Locally When They Can Compete Globally

The foregoing is not an argument against government support for industries. Government interventions can be justified on the grounds of 'externalities', namely, to support positive externalities, such as through investments in skills and research and development, and to discourage negative ones, such as through carbon pricing that forces companies to pay for the uncompensated benefits they derive from emitting carbon.[33] Government interventions are also justified to correct market failures and provide public goods, such as building schools, hospitals and other public infrastructure.[34] Furthermore, Southeast Asian countries like South Korea successfully used government interventions, such as subsidies, to turn their domestic producers into world-class exporters. Taiwan became the world's largest producer of silicon chips of semiconductors by not only inviting Morris Chang, a Chinese American, to set up Taiwan Semiconductor Manufacturing Company (TSMC) in 1987 but also by steadily supporting the company.[35] However, such state interventions were not intended to prop up inefficient inward-looking industries but to support domestic industries with the potential to be globally competitive and export-oriented. Thus, the test is whether any government intervention is targeted and can make domestic producers globally competitive or whether it is a state largesse that simply props up inefficient ones.

So, this is not an argument for a laissez-faire approach. Every government has a task to create the policy and institutional environment that helps businesses succeed, improves their productivity and enhances their competitiveness so they can compete and thrive in the global market. In today's globalised world, any business in a traded sector that is producing only for its domestic market will struggle to survive. Unless that business is shielded from foreign competition by its government, which is not an acceptable form of government support, it will not survive exposure to foreign competition. As the saying goes, 'industries thrive locally when they can compete globally'. Indeed, a World Bank study shows that 'exporters on average are more productive, capital intensive, larger and pay higher wages than non-exporters'.[36] Exporting companies are more innovative and productive than non-exporting ones, and there is a strong nexus between innovation, productivity and prosperity. Without innovation, there can be no productivity growth; and without productivity growth, there can be no wage growth and better living standards. That is why governments should not shield industries from a productivity-enhancing competitive environment.

Unfortunately, government interventions in Nigeria are not designed to enable industries to be efficient and compete in the global market. Most economies that experience strong

GDP growth depend on strong growth in their manufacturing outputs and exports.[37] Yet, according to the NIRP, 'the Nigerian manufacturing sector has failed to undergo critical structural transformation'.[38] While the share of the manufacturing sector in the GDP rose from 8.6 per cent in 2017 to 15.7 per cent in 2023, the share of manufacturing exports in total exports (including oil and non-oil) was a minuscule 4.2 per cent in 2023.[39] Given that dire diagnosis, the government's focus should be to engineer the structural transformation of the manufacturing sector through the right supply-side incentives to improve its productivity and enhance its international competitiveness.

However, huge supply-side constraints are limiting industrial performance in Nigeria. Although Nigerian industries have firm-level technical inefficiency and other internal weaknesses, their supply-side problems result mainly from the government's policy and institutional failures. Such supply-side obstacles include high energy costs, high and multiple taxes, shortage of foreign exchange for imports, high cost of borrowing, shortage of relevant skills, and, generally, weak intermediate and backbone services or infrastructure. The coming of electricity led to a leap in industrial productivity worldwide, doubling American manufacturing productivity by 1930 and then again by 1960.[40] But electricity is a luxury in Nigeria. While Nigeria's grid electricity demand is estimated to be 20 gigawatts (GW), the country generates about 4.5GW of electricity. As a result, industries incur exorbitant costs to fuel generators to power their factories. The harsh operating environment is not conducive to industrialisation as no industry can thrive under those conditions.

To be sure, no country can industrialise without investing in its people, investing in critical infrastructure, creating a conducive environment for businesses to prosper, devolving power to regions, and boosting innovation. However, while Nigeria's industrial policy lists seven enablers, namely, infrastructure, skills, innovation, investment climate, standards, local patronage and financing, they are not the central focus of the policy. Rather, they are secondary to the overarching protectionist approach of using high tariffs and import bans to protect the twenty sectors identified as strategic in the NIRP. Nigeria's global rankings on innovation (114 out of 132 countries in 2022) and competitiveness (116 out of 141 in 2019) show a country that needs to focus on the right drivers and enablers of innovation and competitiveness, which are preconditions for industrialisation.

However, Nigeria's current industrial policy does not do that; hence, more than ten years after the NIRP was published in 2014, Nigeria is nowhere near being an export-led industrialised nation, although some would blame lack of consistency in policy implementation.[41] Yet, truth be told, the future of industrialisation in Nigeria rests on horizontal measures, focusing on infrastructure, skills, innovation, standards, access to finance, low interest rates and other supply-side measures that reduce the high input costs, in addition to a dogged commitment to developing science and technology and making Nigeria an open, competitive free-market economy.

The Imperative of Private Sector Development

While governments must create the enabling environment and incentives for industrialisation, it is, ultimately, the private sector that industrialises. It is when local and foreign investors establish viable and productive firms or invest in existing ones that industrialisation begins to take place. Foreign direct investments are particularly important because they bring in new ideas and technologies and are a key source, as discussed earlier, of imported innovation. Thus, any country that wants to industrialise should aim to attract significant foreign direct investment into different sectors of the economy, particularly manufacturing, without ignoring homegrown entrepreneurs. However, Nigeria is not attracting any significant foreign direct investment. Indeed, inflows of FDI continued to remain smaller than 1 per cent of GDP and fell to zero in 2022.[42] The 1 per cent compares unfavourably to around 1.4 per cent of GDP on average for lower-middle-income economies or 1.7 per cent of GDP for other economies in sub-Saharan Africa.[43] While there are only a few formal restrictions to foreign investment, the complex business environment and other challenges, such as insecurity, corruption, and policy-related factors like foreign exchange scarcity and policy uncertainty, negatively affect foreign investment flows into Nigeria,[44] and, indeed, led to the exit of over 70 foreign companies from Nigeria in seven years, according to BusinessDay newspaper.[45]

The truth is that local and international investors need the right business and investment conditions to invest their money and contribute to industrialisation. These conditions are not about protectionism but about relieving businesses of the policy, institutional and regulatory costs that the government itself creates. As Adam Smith said, 'Little else is requisite to carry a state to the highest degree of opulence from the lowest barbarism, but peace, easy taxes, and a tolerable administration of justice; all the rest being brought about by natural course of things.'[46] In other words, the government's role is to tackle the supply-side problems and the policy and institutional challenges that undermine the competitiveness and productivity of businesses. Thus, what is needed to promote private sector development and unlock private sector dynamism is endogenous by nature, relating to domestic governance and policy issues and measures.

According to a World Bank report titled 'Competitiveness Diagnostic Toolkit', an effective business environment requires the following: a regulatory regime that does not create unnecessary obstacles to running a business; a business-friendly tax environment; a legal framework that promotes market competition; and sound governance and capable institutions.[47] None of these is present in Nigeria. For instance, as a business newspaper put it, there are too many 'business-killing regulations'[48] in Nigeria, including high and multiple business taxes. Indeed, tax regulation is often cited as one of the significant barriers to doing business in Nigeria. For instance, according to a report by Reuters, companies in Nigeria make about 60 official tax payments per year and about 200 unofficial tax payments.[49] In its sixth trade policy review of Nigeria, published in November 2024, the WTO described the business environment in Nigeria thus: 'The investment and business environment remains complex and evenly applied. Corruption, coupled with weak enforcement of the rule of law, regulatory differences among

Nigerian's states and limited policy certainty as policies are often not fully implemented or reversed, remain significant barriers to private sector-led growth.'[50]

To be sure, Nigeria has an entrepreneurial private sector that is operating under extremely challenging environments. For instance, Nigeria's vibrant start-up ecosystem is one of Africa's largest funding destinations: two out of the four African fintech companies on CNBC's top 200 global list are Nigerian[51]. However, that distorts the true picture of the general state of private sector development in Nigeria, which is extremely business unfriendly. Yet, Nigeria can industrialise without a conducive business environment that unleashes private sector dynamism and growth.

The main global tool for assessing private sector development in any country was, until 2020, the World Bank's Doing Business Index, which started in 2003. For many years, Nigeria languished at the bottom of the index but recorded an improvement in 2018 following the Buhari government's Ease of Doing Business agenda. In the 2018 index, Nigeria moved up 24 places from 169 out of 190 in the previous year to 145. Nigeria did even better in the 2020 index, the last to be published by the World Bank, as it was ranked 131 out of 190 countries. However, of the ten areas tracked in the 2020 index, Nigeria only did relatively well in three areas, namely: getting credit (ranked 15th out of 190 countries), protecting minority investors (28), and dealing with construction permits (55).

On the other areas, Nigeria's performances were not impressive. For instance, on registering property, it ranked 183 out of 190, trading across borders (179), getting electricity (169), paying taxes (159), resolving insolvency

(148), and starting a business (105). Even its ranking of 73 out of 190 on enforcing contracts won't inspire much investor confidence, given that Nigeria only scored 8 out of 18 on the quality of the judicial process, 1 out of 6 on case management, and 0 out of 4 on court automation. Furthermore, on paying taxes, there were, according to the index, 59 tax payments per year in Nigeria, compared to an average of 37 in sub-Saharan Africa. Therefore, from a private sector development perspective, Nigeria's performances on the Doing Business Index did not point to sufficient attention being paid to the development of the private sector, especially concerning key policy, regulatory and legal issues.

The Legal Infrastructure for a Market Economy

A strong market economy comes with two sets of pre-condition. The first is an enabling macroeconomic environment. If the macroeconomic fundamentals are not conducive to fostering business profitability, savings growth and investor confidence, there won't be sufficiently high aggregate demand and aggregate supply to build and sustain a strong market economy.[52] Therefore, a strong and stable macroeconomic environment, relating to low inflation, low interest rates, stable and competitive exchange rates and a sustainable level of public debt, is a pre-condition for building a strong market economy that is driven by the private sector. However, after macroeconomics, the second pre-condition for a strong market economy is the legal, regulatory and institutional infrastructure that ensures the market operates in an efficient, fair and stable manner.[53] Even if the macroeconomic fundamentals are right, there still won't be a strong market economy or a viable commercial society unless there are strong institutional, regulatory and legal frameworks. For instance, a market economy needs an institutional infrastructure, such as market actors and service providers, to provide the market's operational basis. A market economy also needs a regulatory infrastructure with the power and responsibilities to supervise the market and promote the predictability and transparency of market operations.[54]

But of all the market infrastructure components, the most important is the legal framework. The legal infrastructure provides the underpinning of the operational and regulatory infrastructure. The legal foundations of a market economy are so pivotal because many of the drivers of economic prosperity are dependent on law: the rule of law, questions of rights, justice and fairness.[55] For instance, a wealth-creating society is impossible without property rights, contractual rights, voluntary exchange, and competition. The role of laws and legal institutions is both to facilitate efficient market transactions and to disincentive behaviours that could undermine the efficient operation of the market. As John Coates, professor of law and economics at Harvard University, rightly put it, 'without reliable law and an ability of private businesses to defend their rights, investment shrivels.'[56] Thus, the rule of law is a foundation of capitalism, ensuring protection of property rights, enforcement of contracts and vigorous market competition.[57]

What all this means is that to build a strong market economy, a country must have the right business or commercial law regime, consisting of laws protecting property rights, including intellectual property rights, laws guaranteeing the sanctity of commercial relationships, a robust competition law regime and strong and effective enforcement and adjudicative regimes. However, Nigeria lacks robust legal foundations of a market economy. The following subsections consider the legal infrastructure underpinning Nigeria's economy in three areas, namely: competition and consumer protection law, corporate governance and company law and property rights, including intellectual property.

Competition and Consumer Protection

For several decades, Nigeria did not have competition and consumer protection laws despite having an uncompetitive business environment. Indeed, this gap was recognised in the Nigeria Industrial Revolution Plan, discussed earlier. The NIRP said that 'Nigeria does not have an adequate set of policies, regulations and laws to control anti-competitive practices in industry.'[58] The NIRP identified a key competition–related problem in Nigeria, namely that 'some industrial sectors have evolved into oligopolies, with just a few companies controlling the majority of the market'[59], resulting in some product prices being among 'the highest in the world.'[60] Many developing countries, particularly South Africa, have long had a robust competition law regime to deal with such problems.[61]

However, in 2018, President Buhari signed into law the Federal Competition and Consumer Protection Act, FCCPA. But while the enactment of the FCCPA was commendable, it immediately raised questions as to whether the act could ensure a strong competition and consumer protection regime in Nigeria. The truth is that while the act has positive aspects, it is not a game changer. The first positive thing about the act is that it sets out laudable objectives. These objectives, in Part 1, section 1 (a) to (e), include to: 'promote and maintain competitive markets in the Nigerian economy; promote economic efficiency; protect and promote the interests and welfare of consumers by providing consumers with wider variety of quality products at competitive prices; and prohibit restrictive or unfair business practices which prevent, restrict or distort competition or constitute an abuse of a dominant position of market power in Nigeria.' In terms of the substantive provisions, the act contains some of the usual competition and consumer protection rules. For instance, it prohibits restrictive agreements (section 59), abuse of dominant position (section 70), monopoly and anti-competitive practices (section 76), such as price collusion. On consumer protection, the act protects a wide range of consumer rights (sections 114 to 133), even covering the remits of traditional principles of contract and sales of goods laws.

Furthermore, the act establishes the Federal Competition and Consumer Protection Commission (FCCPC) and invests it with wide-ranging powers (sections 17 and 18), including to identify and tackle 'anti-competitive, anti-consumer protection and restrictive practices.' However, there is a legitimate question as to whether the FCCPC can effectively administer and enforce the provisions of the new law. As noted earlier, a major competition challenge in Nigeria, as highlighted by the NIRP, is that 'some industrial sectors have evolved into oligopolies, with just a few companies controlling the majority of the market', resulting in the prices of some products being 'among the highest globally.' According to a World Bank report, market concentration is high in key sectors of the Nigerian economy, with other sectoral regulatory barriers creating additional barriers to competition.[62] The report adds that important incumbent companies are also often able to influence policymaking and, therefore, perpetuate existing anti-competitive policies, while unfair competitive practices and issues related to vested interests or cronyism create risks particular for new entrants. [63] The 2019 Competitiveness Report of the World Economic Forum also pointed to challenges to competition in Nigeria, saying that the level of competition is limited, especially as taxes and subsidies have a distortive effect on competition, while Nigeria ranked in the third quintile in terms of market dominance in the economy, indicating strong dominance at least in some sectors.[64]

Given the foregoing, the key test of the FCCPC's success is whether it can tackle the powerful and politically connected oligopolists. However, the omens are not good. For instance, the Commission has, since 2019, undertaken only seven investigations into both restrictive agreements and abuse of a dominant position. The number of cases is certainly negligible for an economy the size of Nigeria and for a country where anti-competitive practices, including the abuse of a dominant position, are prevalent. Thus, as the WTO puts it, 'it is too early to say whether the opportunity created to develop a more functional framework resulting from the new act will lead to significantly improved outcomes in practice.'[65] Instead of going after the major violators, the FCCPC appeared to be more preoccupied with targeting low-level offenders as it did when it shut down a

Chinese supermarket for allegedly 'discriminating against Nigerians'.[66]

But besides concerns about enforcement, certain long-standing government policies would undermine some of the objectives set out in the act. For instance, the act cannot 'promote economic efficiency' and 'protect the interests and welfare of consumers by providing consumers with a wider variety of quality products at competitive prices' when import bans and prohibit tariffs are at the heart of the government's trade policy. Any competition regime that denies market access for imports and forecloses markets to foreign competitors cannot promote economic efficiency or promote the welfare of consumers. Yet, the FCCPA is set within the economic philosophy of import-substitution and thus cannot promote economic efficiency or promote and maintain competitive markets in the Nigerian economy. It is both liberalisation and market contestability that can promote economic efficiency.

Another anti-competition provision of the act relates to price controls. Part XI of FCCPA gives the president wide-ranging powers to control the prices of goods and services. Any person who violates the president's price regulation orders can be fined up to N50million (section 90(5)) and, if it is a company, up to 10 per cent of its previous year's turnover (section 90(6)). Thus, Nigeria's first-ever competition and consumer protection legislation puts price-fixing on a statutory footing, although the practice is already prevalent among regulatory agencies in Nigeria, as the Centre for Social and Economic Rights (CSER) pointed out in a newspaper advertorial.[67] Given the above, the FCCPA 2018, Nigeria's first-ever competition and consumer protection act, is a misnomer: it is neither pro-competition nor pro-consumer.

Company Law and Corporate Governance

Like in the areas of competition and consumer protection, Nigeria had no modern company and corporate governance law for decades. The first Companies and Allied Matters Act (CAMA) was introduced in 1990. However, 30 years later, President Buhari signed a new Companies and Allied Matters Act into law in August 2020 (CAMA 2020). Some commentators hailed the enactment of the act as revolutionary.[68] However, adopting in 2020 company law principles that had existed in the companies' acts of most countries for several decades was not truly 'revolutionary.' Furthermore, the new act focuses on the incorporation and management of companies and addresses mainly procedural and administrative barriers.

To be sure, many of the business-related provisions are aimed at enhancing the ease of doing business, particularly for small companies. These include provisions that recognise single member/shareholder companies (section 18(2)) that allow for a statement of compliance signed by an applicant/agent instead of, as previously, a declaration of statement attested to by a lawyer or Notary Public (section 40(1); and that make the use of Common Seal non-mandatory (section 98). Other provisions recognise the validity of electronic signature, electronic transfer of shares and virtual meetings (section 377(2)(h)), reduce filing fees for registration of charges and exempt small companies from the requirements to appoint auditors and company secretaries (section 330). All these provisions should reduce regulatory and administrative burdens for small companies.

However, there are provisions of CAMA 2020 that are designed to protect companies and shareholders from competition. For instance, the purported attempt in section 22 to protect shareholders from the dilution of their shares by restricting who individual shareholders could initially sell their shares to is an affront to property rights. Under the UK Companies Act, a shareholder can sell their shares to a willing buyer, subject to the company's articles, not a statutory dictate.[69] Similarly, the protective shield for debtors and companies in distress under section 717, which limits the rights of creditors, goes beyond usual provisions in other companies' acts to facilitate settlements between creditors and debtors. It could create a moral hazard and, counterproductively, make it more difficult for companies to secure credit.

Overall, the business-related provisions of CAMA 2020 are good. Yet, given the weakness of state capacity in Nigeria, it is very unlikely that the Corporate Affairs Commission will be able to implement the act effectively.[70] But even if it did, CAMA 2020 will not profoundly influence the direction of corporate activities or promote entrepreneurship and economic prosperity in Nigeria. The supply-side constraints, such as overregulation, excessive and multiple taxes, high electricity costs, high interest rates, shortage of foreign exchange, etc. that undermine business competitiveness in Nigeria will not automatically disappear because of CAMA 2020. Furthermore, since the act came into force in 2020, there is no evidence that it has significantly improved the business environment in Nigeria or enhanced private sector development. More is needed beyond CAMA 2020 to achieve those outcomes.

Protection of Contractual and Property Rights

The existence of enforceable contracts and property rights is an irreducible core of a true market economy, the key driver of the wealth and prosperity of nations and people. In any society where valid contracts are not strictly adhered to or enforced or where property rights are not defended and enforced, people will lack the incentive to produce and exchange goods and services, and investors will lack the confidence to invest their money in that economy. Thus, it goes without saying that a country that does not protect contract and property rights cannot attract quality investments or engender the production and exchange of goods and services that drive economic growth and prosperity. Countries that have high scores in the contract enforcement category of the World Bank's Doing Business rankings are also the most successful economies. The same is true of countries with high scores on the International Property Rights Index (IPRI).[71] So, there is a strong correlation between robust protection and enforcement contracts and property rights and economic success and prosperity.

But commercial litigation is a nightmare in Nigeria. In a TV debate, a lawyer said that 'a case can last up to 20 years in Nigeria.[72] Furthermore, Nigeria is not a signatory to any international convention or treaty that relates to the recognition and enforcement of foreign judgments, which means that it is not bound or under compulsion to enforce a foreign judgment.[73] Even worse, Nigerian courts are not trusted to treat foreign investors fairly in cases involving them and Nigeria. For instance, in the breach of contract case between Zhongshan Fucheng Industrial Investment, a Chinese firm, and Nigeria's south-western Ogun State, the Chinese company lost its cases four times in Nigerian courts but won before arbitration tribunals in France and the United, resulting in a French court seizing three Nigerian presidential jets for the company in August 2024.[74] If Nigeria does not respect the judgments of foreign courts and its own courts do not treat foreign investors impartially, that certainly cannot boost investor confidence in Nigeria. With respect to property rights protection, Nigeria ranked 117th out of 125 countries in the 2023 International Property Rights Index.[75]

Nigerians do not *ab initio* have private property rights, given that the Land Use Act 2004 vests ownership of all urban land at the state level in the state governor, and that of all non-urban or rural land in local governments. The governor or local government chairman then has the power to grant a time-limited 'statutory rights of occupancy' in a piece of land to an individual, who can then transfer it to another person through 'deeds of assignment'. A situation in which citizens can only secure original ownership in the land at the behest of the state and only for a defined period (usually 99 years) lacks the indicia of the classical conception of property as a right, which makes the Land Use Act a breach of property rights and a disincentive to private investments.

But even more problematic are the legal institutions designed to protect the limited property rights that exist.

According to the National Content Standards in Civics and Government, property rights can be established and secured in three ways.[76] The first is the rule of physical force, a state in which brute force reigns. The second is the rule of men, which includes 'the ability of government officials and others to govern by their personal whim or desire'.[77] And the third is the rule of law, where no one is above the law, not even the state. It is universally recognised that the rule of law is the acceptable basis for organising and managing economic activities and interactions, including the creation and protection of contract and property rights, in any society.

However, both the rule of force and the rule of men compete with and often override the rule of law in Nigeria. Too often, in Nigeria, ordinary citizens are victims of the rule of force and the rule of men when it comes to land ownership but have no means of securing a legal remedy. Yet property rights offer the poor the most powerful opportunity to ascend the economic ladder, but it is not uncommon in Nigeria for the powerless to have their landed properties forcefully taken by the powerful without any recourse to legal justice.

While company laws and competition rules, discussed earlier, are critical, they are not enough to support a free market economy; they must be accompanied by robust protection and enforcement of contract and property rights. Without rules on ownership and transfer of properties, it is difficult to engage in voluntary commercial exchanges. Thus, contract and property rights provide great incentives for investment and wealth-maximising activities, which make them key legal foundations of a free market economy.

Intellectual Property Rights Protection in Nigeria

The foregoing discussion on property rights relates to physical properties, such as land and other tangible assets. However, it is also important to discuss intellectual property rights, arguably the most controversial and misunderstood of all property rights. For many people, intellectual property is obscure and distant, relating to ideas rather than tangible or physical things. Yet, intellectual property, which is about creative effort and knowledge capital, is central to all economic activities. Its scope includes patents, copyrights, trademarks, designs and performance rights.

There are three main arguments for strong protection of intellectual property rights. The first is the moral rights theory, based on the Lockean 'fruits of labour' argument.[78] John Locke argued that intellectual property is the fruit of one's labour, and everyone should be able to receive a fair recompense for the fruit of their labour. If someone created a piece of art, they should have the exclusive right to own and commercialise it. Yet, some see nothing wrong in pirating or making counterfeits of the works of others, thereby denying the creator the fruit of their labour. The second argument is based on the incentive theory.[79] The incentive theory says that intellectual property protection provides an incentive to make new inventions. For instance, if inventors cannot commercialise their patented works and protect them against unauthorised use by others, they would have no incentive to spend time and capital in inventing new drugs, new computer software, etc. Without the incentive to innovate and create new things, society will not have the high productivity and high economic growth that generate prosperity.

The third argument links strong intellectual property rights to trade and investment flows, as well as the diffusion of technology. The argument is simple. FDI flows often involve foreign investors transferring technologies to another country. But if the intellectual property in their technologies could easily be violated, that would create disincentives to trade and investment flows.[80] The ability of foreign businesses to register and enforce their intellectual property rights abroad is an incentive to FDI flows and technology transfer, while the absence of an effective intellectual property regime hinders businesses' access and operation in a market and, therefore, acts as a major disincentive to FDI flows and the transfer of technology. So, intellectual property protection matters. It is a spur for innovation and creativity and the diffusion of technologies. But how robust is Nigeria's IPR regime?

The first point is that, unlike FCCPA 2018 and CAMA 2020, most of the regulatory frameworks for intellectual property rights (IPRs) have remained unchanged in Nigeria. A new Copyright Act was enacted in 2022 to replace the Copyright Act of 2004. However, apart from that, all the other IP laws remain, so far, unchanged. These include the Patents and Design Act 1990 and the Trademarks Act 1990. The dates of these laws show that they are over 30 years old, which also means that they are not compatible with the WTO's Trade-Related Intellectual Property Rights (TRIPS) that introduced new international IP rules and entered into force in 1995. Nigeria has traditionally paid little attention to the protection of intellectual property rights. Several years ago, a Nigerian delegation to a meeting of the World

Intellectual Property Organisation, WIPO, said: 'The repeated assertion that IP could be used for the creation of wealth means nothing to the vast majority of Nigerians, whose preoccupation is not wealth creation but the struggle survival from one day to the next.'[81] That view has hardly changed. The USTR said in its 2025 National Trade Estimate Report: 'Public awareness is low regarding the role of IP in Nigeria's economy, despite the benefits Nigeria has seen from its growth as a regional hub for the African film, music and fashion industries, and despite the harm to consumers from counterfeit products.'[82] The inadequate appreciation of the benefits of IPR protection in Nigeria is certainly a key reason for poor regard and protection afforded to intellectual property rights in Nigeria.

To be sure, Nigeria is not a strong IP-producing country outside of copyrights. Indeed, it is a net importer of IP, importing around $250mn a year.[83] According to WIPO figures[84], there were only 200 patents granted to Nigerians in 2018, compared to 451 to South Africans, despite Nigeria having nearly four times the population of South Africa. The patents granted to non-residents, i.e. foreigners, in Nigeria, was 642, compared with 4,295 for South Africa, which suggests far greater foreign interest in South Africa than in Nigeria. In terms of trademark registration, the last available data for Nigeria was for 2013, when there were 4,369 trademark registrations for Nigerians and 1,048 for foreigners. But for South Africa, in 2018, there were 16,745 for residents and 15,247 for non-residents.[85] The lack of robust intellectual property protection is a key reason why foreigners are not rushing to register patents and trademarks in Nigeria. While Nigeria's new competition law, the FCCPA 2018, recognises the 'validity of a licence granted by the proprietor of a patent' (S.64), it seems to offer special protection against 'an infringement of a Nigerian patent' (S.65), which would violate WTO's non-discrimination rule.[86]

But even if Nigeria's substantive IP laws are strong, the enforcement regime is extremely weak. The government stated in the NIRP that 'Nigeria has already established the broad framework for adequate protection of IPR' but added: 'However, the enforcement of those rights is currently challenging.'[87] Indeed, the enforcement of IPR in Nigeria is extremely challenging. For instance, due to pressure from the US and indigenous lobby groups, Nigeria enacted the Copyright Act of 2004, which introduced stronger anti-piracy measures and the protection of folklore. Yet, piracy and counterfeiting remain widespread in Nigeria. Indeed, Nigeria is believed to be the largest African market for pirated products. As the USTR put it in its 2025 National Trade Estimate Report, 'counterfeit goods, including pharmaceuticals, automotive parts and other consumer goods, remain widely available in Nigeria.'[88] Neither the regulatory and enforcement agencies nor the courts robustly enforce intellectual property rights or adequately punish their infringements in Nigeria.

For instance, according to figures from the Nigerian Copyright Commission, only 23 anti-piracy operations were carried out, 48 arrests were made between 2021 and 2024, and only one conviction on copyright infringement was made in 200 and two in 2021.[89] Indeed, criminal proceedings are rare, while inspections relating to copyright infringements are very few. For instance, there were ten criminal proceedings in 2020, ten in 2021, six in 2022, and one in 2023. With respect to investigations, there were 12 in

2021, 30 in 2022, and 32 in 2023.[90] Furthermore, the average time for litigation regarding copyrights in higher courts is three years.[91] Given this litany of anomalies, there is little confidence in the Nigerian IP system.

Nigeria has a strong interest in protecting copyrights. Nigeria is well known for literature, with world-renowned writers like the literature Nobel prize winner, Wole Soyinka and Chimamanda Ngozi Adichie. The Nigerian film industry, called Nollywood, is also flourishing. The US International Trade Commission estimates that the industry contributes $600m to the Nigerian economy every year.[92] Similarly, the music industry is global. Many Nigerians have been nominated for the Grammy Award, and a few have won it.[93] Yet, despite these successes and the incentives to protect copyrights, there is hardly any copyright protection in Nigeria as books, music records and films are easily pirated or counterfeited. The story with respect to intellectual property protection is that Nigeria lacks strong IP laws and enforcement regimes. As a result, Nigeria loses the opportunity to attract high-technology goods, FDI and technology transfer. No nation has ever succeeded without a robust intellectual property regime, and Nigeria cannot be a strong market economy unless its IPR protection regime is strong. Together with a strong corporate law and a strong competition and consumer protection regime, Nigeria needs robust contract and property rights, including intellectual property rights. These are the legal foundations of a market economy, without which Nigeria cannot become an industrialised economy.

***

This chapter completes the economic part of this book and builds on chapter 4 on Nigeria's economic history and chapter 5 on the imperative of a liberal, export-oriented trade policy for Nigeria. This chapter makes the case for industrialisation in Nigeria as the only route to diversifying away from its oil dependency and escaping its vulnerability to external shocks. Nigeria must become an export-led industrial nation, with non-oil exports replacing its current dominant oil-based exports, especially in a world where future demands for oil are uncertain. However, to industrialise, Nigeria must become an open and competitive market economy, not a closed and protectionist one, and must prioritise private sector development. Nigeria must be willing to import knowledge and technology through quality foreign direct investment, on which to build an industrial base. This involves being one of the most attractive countries in the world to invest and do business. It involves removing the supply-side obstacles to unlocking private sector dynamism and ensuring that the legal foundations of a market economy, such as competition and consumer protection rules, company and corporate governance laws, and contractual and property rights, including intellectual property rights, exist and are strengthened. Put simply, Nigeria needs critical reforms that would boost investor confidence, unlock its growth potential and diversity its economy.

However, presently, Nigeria does not meet these critical pre-conditions for industrialisation. Its current industrial policy is aimed at shielding domestic industries from the competitive pressures that drive innovation and productivity. Furthermore, the legal foundations of a market economy, of a commercial society, are very weak, despite the recent enactments of competition and consumer protection rules and company and corporate governance laws. The protection and enforcement of contractual and property rights, especially intellectual property rights, still leave much to the desired. Yet, Nigeria must do the needful, as argued in the economic part of this book, to become an export-led industrialised trading nation; only then can it generate economic growth and prosperity, which, coupled with the right political institutions, as discussed in Part 1, are critical to acquiring the much-needed state capacity and government effectiveness, the subjects of Part 3 of this book and the next three chapters.

PART THREE

State Capacity and Institutional Development

7

Reversing Nigeria's Bureaucratic Deficits

Professor Paul Collier, the famous Oxford University don, ran a popular online course in 2018 titled *From Poverty to Prosperity: Understanding Economic Development.*[1] The main thrust of the course was how nations could move from poverty to prosperity and why some nations failed to make that transition. Professor Collier's starting point was that all nations were once poor, chaotic or anarchic, including Britain, which got 'pretty close to a tabula rasa of anarchy'[2] after it broke away from the Roman Empire in AD 410. His second point was that it is a 'long march' from poverty to prosperity. Then, his third point: 'Some societies have successfully managed to overcome that long march, while others are still stuck in extreme poverty'.[3] Throughout history, Professor Collier explained, poor states have ascended the path of prosperity by taking five steps. First, they have a monopoly of power within their jurisdiction by creating a professional army. Second, they build an efficient tax system to raise revenue. Third, they entrench the rule of law, including contract enforcement, to facilitate trade and business transactions, which help to grow the economy and bring in more tax revenue. Fourth, to enable even more trade, they invest in rudimentary infrastructure, such as road networks, and create efficient markets to address coordination problems. Fifth, they have a power-sharing and decentralised democracy that engenders harmony and inclusive governance.

But underpinning the above steps are four fundamental elements that any state that wants to escape poverty, chaos and anarchy must have. First, there must be rules that set out the terms of governance and the parameters of behaviours. But rules are the easiest thing to do; they can be created with a stroke of the pen. So, next, a state must build institutions. These refer to 'teams of people with a clear mandate' and the right values and motivation to make rules work. Formal institutional structures will only work if underpinned by informal ones like norms and values. The third element is a critical mass of well-informed citizens, for 'without a critical mass of support and pressure from citizens, rules and institutions become paper tigers, the rules get ignored, the institutions get overpowered.'[4] Thus, pressure from below, that is, from enlightened citizens who hold public office holders to account, is necessary for public and political institutions to work well. Finally, there is 'the authorising environment'[5], that is, leadership that brings all these together that can develop and deploy rules and institutions and mobilise an informed citizenry to transform their societies.

To sum up, for a nation to escape poverty, chaos and anarchy, it must have state capacity, including leadership and an enlightened citizenry. However, it is universally acknowledged that Nigeria lacks state capacity. For instance, according to the *Government Effectiveness Index*, 2022, Nigerian ranked 166 out of 193 countries, with a score of -

1.04.[6] It is also well known that Nigeria has, for too long, suffered from a lack of visionary and competent leadership and that its citizens do not constitute a critical mass of enlightened citizenry that can put pressure on their leaders and institutions to perform, but rather, are part of the prebendal, patronage/clientage networks that organise society from top to bottom.[7]

Nigeria Is a Fragile State

In April 2018, a joint commission of the London School of Economics and Oxford University on state fragility published a report titled *Escaping the fragility trap*.[8] The report was co-authored by Professor Collier from Oxford and Professor Tim Besley from LSE. The report listed the following as 'symptoms of fragility', that is, characteristics of a fragile state:

1. A security threat from organised non-state violence
2. The government lacks legitimacy in the eyes of many citizens
3. The state has a weak capacity for essential functions
4. The environment for private investment is unattractive
5. The economy is exposed to shocks with little resilience
6. There are deep divisions in the society

Looking at Nigeria through the prism of the above symptoms will point to one conclusion: Nigeria is a fragile state. Take insecurity. With the spread and impunity of the Boko Haram terrorists, the prevalence of bandits, kidnappers and ethnocentric militant groups, Nigeria faces multiple threats from organised non-state violence. The report states that 'lack of security lies at the heart of fragility' and that 'fragile states are ill-equipped to respond effectively to security threats.'[9] According to one Nigerian newspaper, 63,111 were killed during the eight-year government of President Buhari, and 6,931 died during the first ten months of President Tinubu's government.[10] Successive Nigerian governments have lacked legitimacy in the eyes of many Nigerians for failing to tackle unemployment, poverty, inequality and insecurity, while public officers abuse the state for personal gain.

With respect to state capacity, fragility has manifested in, among other things, the failure of the Nigerian state to deliver basic services to the citizens, with the public sector so far removed from the lives of ordinary Nigerians. Then, take the fourth symptom: an unattractive environment for private investment. As discussed in previous chapters, Nigeria is one of the worst places to do business in the world, with bureaucratic hurdles, poor infrastructure, excessive regulations, corruption and a poor rule of law environment, including weak contract and property rights enforcement. As the report notes, 'insecure property rights are both a symptom of fragility and a contributor to it.'[11] Nigeria also has the fifth symptom of fragility; its economy is exposed to shocks. A section in Dr Ngozi Okonjo-Iweala's book *Reforming the Unreformable* is titled 'Nigeria – one of the world's most volatile economies'[12], which speaks to the fact that Nigeria's economy is acutely volatile and fragile. Finally, Nigeria is a deeply divided society. The country is socially and politically divided, polarised along ethnic and religious lines, thus lacking unity and internal cohesion.

While the LSE-Oxford report does not name any country as a fragile state, the *Fragile States Index*, published annually by the Fund for Peace, does. The index considers four indicators and twelve sub-indicators, namely: Cohesion (security apparatus, divided elites, group grievance); Economic (economic decline, uneven economic development, human flight and brain drain); Political (state legitimacy, public services, human rights and the rule of law); Social and Cross-cutting (demographic pressures, refugees and IDPs, external intervention). In the 2023 Index, Nigeria was ranked 15th out of 179 countries[13], indicating that it is extremely fragile; indeed, it is more fragile than other African countries except six: Democratic Republic of Congo, Central African Republic, Chad, Ethiopia, Mali and Guinea. This is a depressing picture for Africa's largest economy and most populous country. But, as shown below, fragility and lack of state capacity permeate all aspects of Nigerian life. The next section with a discussion of the different roles of ministers and civil servants and why bureaucrats are at the heart of government effectiveness and good governance.

Beyond Ministers: Understanding the Role of Bureaucrats

The government environment is inhabited by two quite different species: ministers and civil servants. Both enjoy a symbiotic relationship, and good government depends on each fully understanding its role and playing it well. Ministers provide political leadership and policy direction: they set a clear vision, goal and objective. Civil servants turn the government or ministerial visions into workable policy that delivers worthwhile outcomes. The different characteristics, roles and relationships of ministers and civil servants are therefore indispensable to the process of government. Too often in Nigeria, public discourse focuses on ministers, the more visible of the two species, with little attention paid to the civil servants. Yet, as the political theorist Max Weber made clear, particular attention should also be paid to the civil service, because the state will not conduct its affairs without the bureaucracy. But the real concern here is not the whole of the civil service, but that tiny part known as the administrative or policy civil service. This part is usually so small that, for instance, in the UK, it is under five per cent of the whole civil service; the rest are executive or operational staff. So, who are policy civil servants? What do they do? What skills do or should they possess? And does Nigeria have this category of civil servants? But before addressing these questions, it is necessary, for context, to touch briefly on the relationship between Nigeria's civil service and its system of government.

The Nature of the Nigerian Civil Service

Nigeria practises the US-type presidential system of government but adopts the British-style permanent civil service. The US has an openly politicised senior civil service. For instance, a new US president could, broadly speaking, sack all existing senior civil servants, from deputy-director level or even lower, and nominate his own people to replace them.[14] There are approximately 1,150 to 1,250 presidentially nominated positions in the executive branch.[15] By contrast, British civil servants – senior and junior – enjoy continuity of employment or job security regardless of change of government. Nigeria inherited the British model at independence, but in the late 1980s, under the Babangida regime, there was a recommendation that the civil service should be aligned with the presidential system of government that the country practises. Consequently, Decree No 43 of 1988 abolished the post of permanent secretaries and created the political post of Directors-General, who would be appointed directly by the president and would leave office once a new president was elected, unless retained. Unsurprisingly, the reform faced stiff resistance from the civil service and was later abandoned.[16] Thus, Nigeria continues, to date, to operate the British style permanent civil service while practising the US-based presidential system of government.

To be sure, permanence is more efficient and more capable of building and maintaining trust in the process of government than any other alternative. Its key benefits are political impartiality, institutional memory and continuity. But there is also a clear division of labour that exists between ministers and civil servants in a British-style permanent civil service. Ministers bring democratic legitimacy and accountability as well as political direction and a common-sense approach to government, while civil servants bring expertise, specialist knowledge, experience in specific policy areas and objective, first-class, advice. Indeed, this division of labour – the political leadership of ministers and the expertise of civil servants – is the reason why, in the UK, ministers are seldom appointed to a particular department because they have an expertise in its work. Instead, the minister is appointed to bring a common-sense and political approach to government with expert advice provided by civil servants. For instance, Gordon Brown, who was Chancellor of the Exchequer (Finance Minister) for more than eight years before becoming prime minister in 2007, is a historian with a PhD in history. George Osborne, another former Chancellor, also studied history, while Alistair Darling, also a former Chancellor, read law and practised as a solicitor. But while they are very intelligent people, they led and were supported by Treasury civil servants with specialist knowledge and skills and experience.

In a democracy, civil servants help mediate the social contract between the government and the people. Their task is to ensure that democratically determined programmes and promises can translate from the pages of a manifesto into good policies that benefit the people on the ground. They do this by discerning the nature of the government's programme or objective, by being innovative and creative in identifying good ideas and solutions, and by advising accurately on which specific policy or decision will be most likely to achieve the policy objective. The ability of civil servants to supply the expertise, provide ministers with a range of options, give evidence-based advice or recommendations and, in the end, help ministers decide and implement policy is critical to the proper functioning of government in a liberal democracy.

However, as one senior British minister put it, 'The special tasks required of the administrative civil service to enable ministers to operate in a liberal democracy are very special indeed. And the skills involved are very great. The possession of these skills on the part of the administrative civil servants is very precious.'[17] British ministers value the possession of policy skills by their administrative civil servants so much so that they continue to invest in their development. For instance, the Fast-Stream scheme is designed to attract some of the brightest university graduates into the civil service and to provide excellent training and development for them so they can achieve rapid promotion to progress to the senior civil service. The British civil service also launched the policy profession scheme, aimed at 'the development of people with the talent and drive to reach the very highest levels of the Civil Service Policy Profession'.[18] The scheme involves sending suitable civil servants to study for the prestigious Executive Master of Public Policy, run by the London School of Economics. This focus on expertise is consistent with having a permanent civil service. The upshot is that the UK has one of the best civil services in the world.

But what is the situation in Nigeria, which, like Britain, has a permanent civil service? Does the Nigerian civil service have a core of administrative civil servants that can expertly develop policy? Evidently, that is not the case: the Nigerian civil service lacks any appreciable policy-making expertise. In an interview in the Vanguard newspaper, Philip Asiodu, a respected former permanent secretary, lamented the extinction of the administrative class in the Nigerian civil service. He said the federal character principle and quota system had 'destroyed the administrative class concept', adding that the civil service 'is no longer the destination for highfliers.'[19] The result is that, despite its 'permanent' status, the Nigerian civil service lacks the expertise and specialist knowledge that should come with such permanence. With a non-technocratic civil service, it is not hard to see why policymaking is problematical in Nigeria, as civil servants lack the technical expertise to develop successful policies.

To be sure, as noted above, ministers matter. They provide political leadership and policy direction. Indeed, the individual leadership of ministers and that of permanent secretaries can make a significant difference to policy outcomes. But ministers or even permanent secretaries cannot perform the functions of the core administrative or policy civil servants. In addition to strong leadership, the civil service also needs a cohort of experts that can develop and implement government policy effectively. However, Nigeria's civil service currently lacks such critical expertise. Ministers and civil servants are the two parts of government and the linchpins of successful policies. Unfortunately, Nigeria faces the double whammy of having incompetent ministers and non-technocratic civil servants and thus of state capacity for reasons discussed below.

The Rise of a Politicised Civil Service

The focus on the Nigerian bureaucracy in this chapter is not misplaced because, in the words of Max Weber, the state will not conduct its affairs without the bureaucracy.[20] Indeed, no country has ever succeeded without a first-class bureaucracy. But Nigeria has a mediocre bureaucracy. This was not always so. The Nigerian civil and public servants who took over from their British counterparts after Nigeria's independence in 1960 were reputed to be of top quality. Indeed, so well regarded were Nigerian civil servants that they were often seconded to other African countries to help develop and establish their civil services, and also served judges and senior administrators.[21] However, the first blow to the professionalism of the Nigerian civil servants came shortly after independence when the politicians in power began to politicise and manipulate the public servants for political advantage.[22] Subsequently, decades of military rule significantly undermined the civil service as the military used recruitments into the civil service as political tools to appease various constituencies and filled civil service positions with people who lacked requisite skills and competence.[23]

The final straw was the military's introduction, in 1979, of the Federal Character Principle, under which a quota was set for the number of public servants to be appointed from each state in Nigeria. The principle is enshrined in section 14(3) of the Constitution. But while the intention of the principle, namely, to ensure inclusive appointments into the country's public sector, was positive, the application of the principle has largely meant the abandonment of meritocracy, as the need to fill a state's quota means that anyone, regardless of competence, could be appointed even to top echelons of the public service. It is worth repeating the words of Chief Philip Asiodu, a highly respected former permanent secretary, that the federal character principle and quota system had 'destroyed the administrative class concept' and that the civil service was 'no longer the destination for high-fliers'.[24]

Indeed, as noted earlier, Nigeria lacks a professional civil service; rather, it has a politicised and mediocre one. In the UK, graduates of elite universities want to work in the civil service by choice, not because they cannot get jobs elsewhere. And private sector employees frequently seek secondment opportunities in government departments. But because of what a former Nigerian Permanent Secretary described as 'the subordination of merit to representation'[25], referring to the quota system, the civil service is unable to attract, let alone retain, competent people to make a difference.

Corruption in Public Sector Recruitment and Promotion

Another critical problem beyond the quota system is the endemic corruption in public sector recruitment and promotion, as impartial and merit-based recruitment and promotion processes are not the norm in Nigeria. In July 2024, the National Bureau of Statistics (NBS) and the United Nations Office on Drugs and Crime UNODC) published the results of a survey which showed that bribery and nepotism had almost replaced meritocracy in public-sector recruitment in Nigeria. According to the survey, nepotism and bribery in public sector recruitment and promotion were on the rise. For instance, almost half (46 per cent) of those who secured a job between 2019 and 2023 admitted that they paid a bribe to facilitate their recruitment, while 32 per cent said they were helped by a friend or a relative.[26] In other words, as the survey puts it, 'around 60 per cent, or 6 out of 10, of successful candidates for posts in the public sector between 2019 and 2023 were hired as a result of nepotism, bribery or both.'[27] Indeed, over 51 per cent of those who secured a job were not formally assessed.[28]

Bribery and nepotism also play a role in the public sector promotion processes in Nigeria, with ten per cent of those promoted between 2019 and 2023 admitting that they either resorted to bribery or nepotism or both to facilitate their promotion.[29] As the NBS and the UNODC remarked in the report, 'the selection process used to recruit public sector officials play a crucial role in shaping the culture of integrity that should drive the civil service as well as ensure that new recruits have the highest standards of professionalism and merit.'[30] With the prevalence of bribery and nepotism in public sector recruitment and promotion in Nigeria, it is little wonder that Nigeria has one of the most corrupt and incompetent civil services in the world.

The Culture of Indiscipline and Incompetence

As a result of politicisation and corruption, the Nigerian civil service or public sector faces chronic, acute challenges. Often, the Nigerian president is described as very powerful, but his power is constrained by the country's extreme bureaucratic weakness, with successive presidents frequently complaining that their policy initiatives were stymied by public servants.[31] With the absence of a competent policy cadre, the Nigerian civil service is unable to develop good policies, but it is also unable to implement the ones developed. A former British Permanent Secretary once said that policies must be 'implemented with professionalism, rigour and as much pace as is consistent with effective delivery'.[32] However, in Nigeria, the bureaucracy lacks the capacity and the motivation to ensure effective policy delivery. In 2014, the then Head of the Civil Service of the Federation (HOS), Danladi Kifasi, said the government had resorted to hiring consultants to do the tasks federal civil servants were employed to do because of poor policy delivery.[33] In various press releases from the Office of the Head of Service, words like 'habitual late coming', 'truancy', 'lukewarm and shoddy attitude to the discharge of duties', 'indiscipline', and 'corrupt practices' were used to describe Nigeria's federal civil servants.

A Bloated and Unskilled Bureaucracy

The Nigerian civil service is widely known to be bloated and inefficient. The Japanese taught the world, through their manufacturing model, that leanness helps to eradicate unproductive and wasteful activities. A bloated organisation, whether public or private, has the opposite effects. As Tunji Olaopa, then Permanent Secretary of the Federal Ministry of Communication Technology, said about the Nigerian civil service, 'there are too many people doing nothing; too many doing too little; and too few people doing too much'.[34] It is little wonder that the civil service is ineffective. Linked to that is the fact that, in today's digital age, the Nigerian civil service is still paper-pushing, with day-to-day activities in most of the ministries being paper-based, a drag on productivity and efficiency.

Added to all the above is the appalling skills level in the Nigerian public sector. In 2004, a former Head of Service, Yayale Ahmed, revealed that 'about 70 per cent of Nigeria's civil servants belong to the unskilled, non-graduate levels, while over 60 per cent are within the age brackets of 40 years and above.'[35] Nearly ten years later, indicating that nothing had changed in the interim, Dr Okonjo-Iweala, a former minister of finance, wrote in her book *Reforming the Unreformable*, published in 2012, that 'about 70 per cent of federal civil servants had no more than a high school diploma, with less than 5 per cent possessing modern computer skills.'[36] She said the bulk of her ministry's staff – 70 per cent – were lower-level administrative staff, clerks and cleaners with only high school education or the equivalent. Furthermore, only 13 per cent were graduates of universities or other tertiary institutions, and just 8 per cent had degrees related to accounting or economics.[37]

In 2019, the Blavatnik School of Government at the University of Oxford published the International Civil Service Effectiveness (InCiSE) Index.[38] The top ten best-performing civil services in the world, according to the index, were the UK, Italy, Poland, Sweden, Slovenia, Australia, Finland, Spain, Netherlands and France. These top ten countries were also among the top 20 countries on the Government Effectiveness Index, 2022, which shows that there is a strong nexus between civil service effectiveness and government effectiveness. Indeed, state capacity is largely about the effectiveness of the civil service, which is why no nation can develop beyond the capacity of its bureaucracy. But Nigeria has one of the worst civil services in the world and, consequently, one of the most ineffective governments.

Unfortunately, in a sign that Nigeria was in denial and unwilling to confront the acute weakness of its civil service, the then-retiring Head of the Civil Service of the Federation, Folasade Yemi-Esan, said in June 2024: 'Nigeria has the best civil service in the world, and I can say that confidently anywhere.'[39] Ironically, she made that comment at the same time as she revealed that hundreds of Nigerian civil servants relocated abroad without resigning their appointments and were drawing salaries from the treasury for years, aided and abetted by serving officers.[40] She later admitted that her greatest challenge as head of the civil service was the resistance to civil service reform, saying: 'Convincing them to accept better ways of doing things was a mountainous challenge. To convince civil servants to accept our reforms was a big challenge.'[41] Given the appalling situation, it stretches credulity that the head of service would describe such a corrupt civil service as the best in the world. It wasn't surprising the Yemi-Esan's comment prompted a rebuke from notable columnists, such as Simon Kolawole[42] and Fola Ojo[43], who argued that her description of the civil service was far removed from reality.

The truth is that the Nigerian civil service is broken, and Nigeria cannot succeed with such a broken bureaucracy. The success of the economy depends, in part, on a competent civil service. The private sector needs the public sector to work for it, to be an enabler of, and not a barrier to, business growth. Foreign investors want to deal with professional, efficient and transparent public servants. And citizens need the public sector to deliver critical services, in education, health and basic infrastructure. However, the private sector in Nigeria cannot depend on the public sector to create an enabling environment, while the citizens are not getting the service delivery that they are entitled to expect from the state under the social contract.

***

The solution to Nigeria's bureaucratic challenge lies in addressing all the issues raised in this chapter, specifically in professionalising and modernising the civil service and attracting some of the brightest and best Nigerians into it. Nigeria needs a competence-based system like the UK's

Fast-Stream scheme, designed to attract bright university graduates into the civil service and to provide excellent training and development for them to achieve rapid progression. The British civil service also has the policy profession scheme, aimed at 'the development of people with the talent and drive to reach the very highest levels of the Civil Service Policy Profession'.[44] Little wonder the UK has the best civil service in the world, according to the InCiSE Index. If Nigeria wants to be a successful economy and tackle its social challenges, it needs its civil service to be one of the best performing in the world. To that end, it must rebuild its civil service based on global best practices, including embedding formal, impartial and merit-based recruitment and promotion processes, with zero-tolerance for nepotism and bribery, and creating the right incentive system to reward outstanding and exemplary performances and behaviours. Nigeria also needs independent governance institutions, such as the UK Institute for Government, (IfG) that can challenge and bring the best out of government bureaucracy through independent but credible policy research and analysis, as well as challenge to the ways government works. The IfG describes its mission to 'act as a catalyst for inspiring the best in government', adding: 'We spark ideas, generate debate, challenge preconceptions, bring experience to bear and make new connections that work to improve government for the benefit of society.'[45] Nigeria needs such an institution to act as a catalyst for positive change in Nigeria's bureaucracy. The truth is that without tackling its bureaucratic deficits and addressing its weak state capacity, Nigeria would be unable to confront the critical challenge posed by the subject of the next chapter.

8

Tackling Nigeria's Endemic Corruption

The discussion in Chapter 7 on Nigeria's bureaucratic deficit covers just one aspect of the country's huge institutional weaknesses. Another is the failure to tackle endemic corruption. Every year, the Transparency International Corruption Perception Index puts Nigeria at near the bottom of the rankings. In the 2024 index, Nigeria was the world's 36th most corrupt country. It ranked 140th out of 180 countries and scored 26 out of 100 points. According to Oxfam, between 1960 and 2005, about \$20 trillion was stolen from the Nigerian treasury by public officeholders.[1] In November 2024, the World Bank said it had found \$32 million missing from a Nigerian water project, according to its Sanctions Annual Report for 2024, and believed the 'missing money might has been stolen.'[2] The bank then quickly took steps with local officials to protect the remaining funds.[3] Such is the reputation that Nigeria has globally for corruption. Indeed, the Nigerian government itself recognises the scale and spread of corruption in the country. For instance, in the National Anti-Corruption Strategy (2017 – 2020), the government states:

To the average Nigerian, corruption is essentially a public sector phenomenon, where acts of bribery, fraud, extortion, inducements, embezzlement, and influence peddling occur. There is little or no demand for accountability by the citizens, as they feel alienated from governance processes. Public resources are considered "nobody's property" and can be used at the whims of the office holder. Public office holders now "donate" budgeted classroom blocks to schools, operational vehicles to security agencies, and hospitals to communities, as though these were personal gifts to the beneficiaries. Citizens on their part see the provision of public goods and services as acts of benevolence that need to be rewarded through the ballot boxes. Thus, there are strong incentives for public officials to misuse public resources for their personal gain due to widespread ignorance, illiteracy and a culture of patronage.[4]

But this level of pervasive corruption cannot be justified considering that Nigeria has had two anti-corruption agencies, the Corrupt Practices and Other Related Offences Commission (ICPC) and the Economic and Financial Crimes Commission (EFCC), for over 20 years, and a third, the Code of Conduct Bureau (CCB), even for much longer: over 35 years.

An Acute Institutional Failure

In 2000, President Obasanjo established the ICPC, and three years later, in 2003, he established the EFCC. Earlier on, in 1989, General Ibrahim Babangida, then military head of state, established the CCB. While the CCB is tasked with fighting corruption in the public service by verifying asset declarations made by public officeholders, the ICPC is tasked with investigating citizen complaints about public corruption, whereas the EFCC, the most prominent of the three agencies, can investigate and prosecute any corruption offence independently.

Yet, despite the existence of these anti-graft agencies, Nigeria remains, as the then British prime minister David Cameron put it in 2016, two days before a global anti-corruption summit in London, a 'fantastically corrupt' country. Cameron told Queen Elizabeth II at an event to mark her 90th birthday: 'We've got leaders of some fantastically corrupt countries coming to Britain: Nigeria and Afghanistan possibly the two most corrupt countries in the world.'[5] In 2018, the then vice president, Yemi Osinbajo, described the kind of corruption in Nigeria as 'a crime against humanity', saying that some individuals 'stole $15 billion, half of the country's foreign reserves'.[6] In July 2024, a report by the United Nations Office on Drugs and Crime, based on a survey conducted by the Nigerian Bureau of Statistics (NBS), showed that Nigeria's public officials received ₦721bn ($1.3bn) bribe in 2023.[7]

In its 2024 Article IV Consultation report on Nigeria, the IMF states that 'corruption is entrenched at all levels of government activity'[8] and cites studies that show the economic benefits of tacking corruption in Nigeria. For instance, according to studies, 'reducing corruption in Nigeria to the level observed in benchmark countries (for example, Malaysia, Mongolia, Morrocco or South Africa) could boost growth by 0.5 to 1.5 percentage points annually'[9] while lowering Nigeria's level of corruption to that of South Africa could increase the amount of infrastructure obtained from each publicly invested dollar by 12 per cent.'[10] There is a multitude of agencies, policies and initiatives purportedly designed to tackle corruption in Nigeria. Yet, large-scale corruption persists. The question, therefore, is why is corruption so rife in Nigeria despite the agencies created to tackle the problem? This section explores the theoretical and practical aspects of the issue.

The Economics and Sociology of Corruption

There is a large body of knowledge on the causes of corruption, its consequences and how best to tackle it. One field of study that has explored this subject systematically, rigorously and comprehensively is economics. Since Susan Rose-Ackerman wrote *The Economics of Corruption*[11] in 1975, more than 4,000 articles have been written on the causes, costs and control of the problem.[12] In his seminal work entitled *Crime and Punishment: An Economic Approach,* the Nobel Prize-winning economist Gary Becker applied rational choice theory, an economic concept, to the analysis of crime.[13] Becker argued that all criminals are rational calculators and that they make decisions about whether or not to commit a crime based on cost-benefit analysis. First, the potential criminal calculates the expected cost of the crime. The expected costs result from multiplying the probabilities of the crime being detected and of the potential criminal being apprehended and convicted by the monetary value of the legal sanctions (e.g. a fine or a jail term or both) and the value of any non-pecuniary losses he or she might suffer (such as a loss in reputation from being branded a criminal).[14] The potential criminal would then calculate the expected benefits of the crime by multiplying the probability of success (that is, of either not being caught or, if caught, of getting away with a light fine or jail term or none at all) by the monetary (e.g. the amount of money likely to be stolen) and non-pecuniary (e.g. the social or political status that comes with being rich, albeit from stolen money) benefits of the crime. According to the Becker model, based on such explicit calculations, the rational criminal will only commit the crime if the expected costs are less than the expected benefits.[15]

The key message from the economic analysis is that an incentive system can either encourage corruption or discourage it. Steven Levitt and Stephen Dubner made this point about the power of incentives pungently in their book entitled *Freakonomics*. They argued that 'incentives are the cornerstone of modern life – and understanding them is the key to solving just about any riddle.'[16] They added: 'An incentive is a bullet, a lever, a key: an often-tiny object with astonishing power to change a situation.'[17] If the expected benefits of engaging in corrupt practices are more than the expected costs, particularly the possibility of being caught and severely punished, the rational corrupt individual will find it more rewarding to engage in such practices than to refrain from them. Therefore, the most powerful incentives to discourage corruption are strong anti-graft institutions and robust enforcement regimes. However, the benefits of corrupt practices are far greater than the costs in Nigeria simply because the possibilities of being caught and severely punished are minuscule. In part, this is because the anti-graft agencies are gravely hampered in their ability to fight corruption successfully.

First, the anti-graft agencies lack independence and are often subject to political interference, which undermines their effectiveness. For instance, as the IMF points out, 'the EFCC does not enjoy clear statutory independence, which must lead to perceptions of doubt with respect to the objectivity of its persecutions.'[18] Indeed, critics allege that successive presidents have used the EFCC to victimise political rivals and have pressured the agency to overlook alleged corruption by members of their own political parties.[19] One evidence of political interference is that every new president has dismissed the EFCC chairman appointed by his predecessor and appointed his own, suggesting that the chairman of the EFCC is a political appointee who is beholden to the president who appointed him or her. Second, leaders and operatives of the agencies have often been accused of corruption. For instance, since the inception of the EFCC, virtually all its chairmen, except the current one, have been accused of corruption. President Tinubu sacked and incarcerated the penultimate chairman, Abdulrasheed Bawa, citing 'weighty allegations of abuse of office levelled against him.'[20]

Indeed, the current EFCC chairman, Ola Olukoyede, accused his own staff of corruption. In December 2023, Olukoyede said: 'The craze and quest for gratification, bribes and other compromises by some of our investigators are becoming too embarrassing.'[21] Furthermore, the EFCC has long been criticised for its opaque handling of billions of dollars in forfeited assets. Thus, it was not surprising when, in February 2025, The Punch newspaper reported that 'EFCC battles internal scandal as operatives loot recovered assets.'[22] According to the story, 'the missing items included gold bars valued at over ₦1bn and jewellery, while between $350,000 and $400,000 had also gone missing.'[23] The fact that the agency tasked with fighting grand corruption, fraud and other major financial crimes in Nigeria is itself so corrupt points to a deep systemic rot. Yet, instead of introspecting, the EFCC tends to treat any criticism of its operation or any attempt to point out its failures as 'malice, prejudice or a naked dance to please some paymasters', as it did in response to a critical column in the Vanguard newspaper.[24]

But besides political interference and corruption, the anti-graft agencies lack the technical expertise to investigate and prosecute complex corruption cases. As a result, few cases are detected, and few investigations and arrests are converted into successful prosecutions. Too often, the EFCC accuses prominent politicians of massive corruption, only for the matter to fizzle out, either because of political pressure or because of the EFCC's lack of technical ability to pursue the cases. In February 2025, the EFCC chairman, Olukoyede, accused Nigerians of hypocrisy and doublespeak on corruption, saying Nigerians condemned corruption but defended corrupt leaders. He said: 'Everybody is crying that Nigerians are corrupt, that the system is corrupt, that corruption is killing us and destroying our system, but when we investigate high profile cases and arraign people in court, the same people will carry placards and be supporting corrupt leaders'.[25]

He was right: Nigerians are lethargic about corruption. However, it is not ordinary Nigerians that prevent successful prosecutions of public officeholders accused of corruption. Rather, it is the incompetence of the EFCC, which could not see through most investigations and prosecutions to a successful conclusion. The other reason is political interference, which often results in selective investigations and prosecutions targeted only at political opponents and those who fall out of favour with the incumbent president or his party. No anti-graft campaign can succeed without political credibility, but such credibility can be fatally damaged by perceptions of selectivity or differential treatment.

Then, there is the acute problem of a corrupt judiciary. According to the United Nations Convention Against Corruption (UNCAC), 'judges who cannot be corrupted inspire and compel corruption-free conduct in society as a whole.'[26] But that is not the case in Nigeria, where judges received the largest cash bribes in 2023.[27] The Nigerian judiciary has a penchant for acquitting people charged with corruption purely on technicalities. In 2022, the then EFCC chairman, Abdulrasheed Bawa, expressed deep frustration that several high-profile corruption cases were lost on technicalities. As he put it, 'Defendants who obviously have stolen our commonwealth and those who have aided and abetted them have been allowed to go home to enjoy their proceeds of crime on technical grounds.'[28]

Even when corrupt individuals are convicted, they are never given penalties (a fine or a jail term or both) severe enough to deter a future wrongdoer from engaging in a corrupt practice. Instead, many accused enter plea bargaining or get light fines or sentences that do not reflect the economic and moral costs of the crime committed. Consequently, people found guilty of corruption end up keeping a lot of the money they stole after the legal sanctions. In some cases, assets seized from looters were returned to them.[29] The literature on criminal price exaction shows that such a light-touch approach to penal sanctions doesn't deter criminal behaviour but rather incentivises it.[30]

But besides the economics of corruption, there is the insight from criminology. This is based on the 'fraud triangle'[31], a theory developed by Donald R. Cressey on why people commit fraud. The three elements of the triangle are opportunity, pressure and rationalisation. According to the theory, fraud or corruption occurs, firstly, because the *opportunity* to commit fraud exists, usually, in the case of public corruption, through increased government spending without strong systems and detection controls. This is particularly so in Nigeria because fiscal policy is expansionary, with billions of dollars or trillions of naira spent on contracts and procurements without strong accountability mechanisms. Thus, hugely increased spending means there is more money for corrupt politicians and officials to target.

The second element, *pressure*, also known as incentive or motivation, is another major driver of corruption in Nigeria. Politicians spend heavily to win elections in Nigeria and often loot public funds in office to recoup their election expenses, reward benefactors or godfathers who facilitated their elections, and meet endless demands for financial support from families, relatives, friends and local people, who expect such material support on the basis that one of their own is a public or political officeholder and must have access to public funds. The third element, *rationalisation*, simply refers to a person's justification for committing fraud. The key justification for corruption in Nigeria is the belief that the benefits outweigh the risk of detection: *I won't get caught*. Besides, corruptors also believe that corruption is a victimless crime, which does not have an identifiable victim, even though it hurts society and reduces the availability, quality and distribution of public services.

The foregoing leads to the sociology of corruption. This is based on the idea that social and moral incentives can also constrain corrupt behaviours. In his paper titled *Those who discourage crime*, the sociologist Marcus Felson stressed the influence of social contacts on criminality. He argued that crime would be reduced in any society where there are effective 'intimate handlers' and 'guardians'.[32] An intimate handler has an influence on an offender and can control his or her propensity to offend, and a guardian is interested in stopping a crime being committed. For instance, intimate handlers of political and public office holders include traditional rulers, religious leaders, as well as the professional bodies, social clubs and networks to which they belong. However, such intimate handlers and guardians have proved ineffectual in Nigeria. Corrupt politicians are being conferred with chieftaincy titles and other honours, and unexplained wealth is not frowned upon.

In one statement, the EFCC said: 'Across the country, the EFCC is sensitive to the unhelpful embrace and canonisation of many suspects of corruption cases. Rather than hold them at arm's length, we regularly offer them front seats in social gatherings, religious meetings, tribal festivities and other public functions.'[33] That is indicative of the failure of intimate handlers and guardians to exert moral and social influence on the behaviour of public officeholders. Indeed, even worse, corruption is so endemic in Nigeria that some of the intimate handlers and guardians are not themselves immune from it. For instance, the $2.1 billion arms purchase scandal that broke in 2014 was so sweeping that so-called pillars of integrity, such as traditional institutions, religious groups, the media and NGOs, were implicated, as prominent societal figures allegedly received a share of the loot.[34] John Egbeazien Oshodi, a US-based Police Scientist and Psychologist, argues, rightly, in an article: 'Corruption in Nigeria is not merely an individual act; it is self-replicating system, a deeply entrenched ecosystem, that has woven itself into the very structure of governance, the judiciary, the economy and even societal norms.'[35]

Yet, corruption can be successfully tackled in Nigeria. However, for that to happen, all the different types of incentives must be aligned. The economic incentives must be strong enough to deter corruption. These include tough laws and tough enforcement of laws. However, economic and legal incentives are not enough; they must be fully complemented by social and moral incentives. Corruption must be seen as a moral crime and society must frown upon it, ensuring that corrupt practices attract social opprobrium. Only through a web of economic, legal, social and moral incentives can any nation successfully tackle corruption. But none of these incentives exists in Nigeria while other institutional weaknesses create a conducive environment for corruption to thrive, as discussed below.

Corporate Governance: The Need for Credible Pillars of Integrity

The first step in tackling corruption in Nigeria is to address the issue of integrity in public and corporate life. As stated earlier, sociologists believe that corruption is likely to reduce significantly in societies that have 'pillars of integrity', that is, individuals and institutions that can create and maintain integrity. Pillars of integrity are also what the sociologist Marcus Felton calls 'intimate handlers.' These are social contacts and networks, such as professional bodies, which can influence individual behaviours by setting and enforcing ethical standards and social norms. This is why a viable Third Sector is vital in any society. As a former president of the US Council on Foundations, Jim Joseph, put it, the Third Sector is 'an intermediary space between business and government where private energy can be deployed for public good.'[36]

The robustness and mutuality of all three sectors are central to the progress of any nation, but the third sector is unique because it is 'value-driven', motivated by the desire to achieve social goals. Indeed, the biggest attraction of the Third Sector is its contribution to social capital. Jeffrey Sachs, the economist, wrote in the World Happiness Report (2015) that economic performance and social progress increase significantly in a country 'with sufficiently high-quality of social capital'[37], that is, generalised trust, high ethical behaviour, good governance, absence of corruption and high pro-sociality. However, such social capital, underpinned by high ethical behaviour, is generally lacking in Nigeria, and this gap is not filled by professional bodies that can drive ethical practices and hold public office holders, some of whom are members of those organisations, to account.

There are different types or sources of corruption in Nigeria. These include *grand corruption*, defined as 'the large-scale transfer of public resources for private interests'[38]; *political corruption*, defined as 'influence peddling on resource allocations and projects that benefit the decision maker, friends and acquittances, directing resources to special projects, and abuse of privileged information'[39]; and *administrative corruption*, defined as 'misappropriation and misuse of public funds, frauds, waste and abuse.'[40] Each of these types of corruption is perpetrated by public officials who belong to a professional body, but the professional bodies rarely sanction the behaviours of their members. Furthermore, there is also corruption in the private sector, with a rising incidence of bribery, although it is less prevalent than in the public sector, where it is twice as high.[41]

In the UK, every member of a professional organisation, such as the Bar Council or the Law Society, is required to behave in a manner that does not bring the profession into disrepute. Any member who flouts this code is likely to be struck out of the members' register, a career-destroying punitive measure and, thus, a great incentive to keep people on the straight and narrow. But that rarely happens to public officers and their private-sector collaborators found guilty of corruption or other malfeasance in Nigeria. This is because the professional bodies do not have effective codes of conduct that can constrain behaviours. Put simply, there are no guardrails or pillars of integrity that could act as a bulwark against grand, political and administrative corruption in Nigeria.

In a country that is struggling to entrench ethical practices in the public and private spheres, professional institutes, such as the Chartered Institute of Directors, Chartered Institute of Bankers and the Institute of Chartered Accountants can be true intimate handlers and pillars of integrity that can help reduce corruption in Nigeria. But that requires such professional bodies to create and enforce stringent codes of conduct and hold their members in public service, as well as in the private sector, accountable, including through disciplinary measures. But while the professional or corporate governance bodies are a good starting point in incentivising good behaviour, they won't be enough to tackle the endemic corruption in Nigeria; the other measures discussed below will also be needed.

Asset Declaration: The Global Best Practice Test

One of the most powerful tools for fighting corruption is asset declarations by public officials. The global framework for asset declarations was created by the United Nations in 2003 when it adopted the UN Convention against Corruption, to which Nigeria is a signatory.[42] In the same year, the African Union adopted the African Union Convention on Preventing and Combating Corruption, which establishes regional standards for asset declaration systems.[43] The Organisation for Economic Cooperation and Development (OECD) also developed policy principles and recommendations for public official asset declaration for its member countries. According to the OECD, there are three main aims of asset declarations.[44] First, to increase transparency and trust of citizens in public administration by disclosing information about the assets of public officers that 'show they have nothing to hide'. Second, to prevent conflict of interest and promote integrity within state institutions. Third, asset declarations are designed to monitor 'wealth variations' of individual public officers to prevent misconduct and illicit enrichment.

Most countries introduce asset declaration systems for all three reasons – transparency, conflict of interest control and wealth monitoring. Even countries with low levels of corruption, or perceptions of it, operate rigorous systems of asset declaration and disclosure based on those three principles. Yet, despite having one of the highest corruption perceptions in the world, Nigeria has one of the weakest asset declaration systems in the world. As mentioned earlier, the Code of Conduct Bureau (CCB) was established in 1989 to gather and verify asset declarations made by public officeholders. It also has the task of ensuring that public officials abide by a fourteen-point code of conduct that prohibits them from having conflicts of interest, collecting more than one official salary, holding foreign bank accounts, or accepting gifts, private loans, or kickbacks. Anyone who breaches any of the codes is reported to the attorney general for prosecution in the Code of Conduct Tribunal (CCT). But apart from the institutional weaknesses of the CCB and the CCT, the substantive asset declaration rules do not meet international standards.

Conflicts of interest control

Nigeria's asset declaration system is not designed to achieve the three objectives of transparency, conflict of interest control and wealth monitoring. For instance, conflict of interest control is hardly the aim of public official asset declaration in Nigeria given that, unlike in most countries, the Nigerian asset declaration form does not require information about potential conflicts of interest and asks no questions about gifts or benefits. Furthermore, presidents, ministers and governors often award multi-billion-naira contracts to companies in which their friends, relatives and even children have a commercial interest without any concern about violating the rules against conflicts of interest. Ethically, the president's children and other close relatives should stand down from business transactions that might create the appearance of a conflict of interest. But in Nigeria, conflict of interest is normalised.

Wealth variation monitoring

The system is hardly about monitoring wealth variations, either. There is no mandatory requirement to provide information about the sources of income, and there are no rules against unexplained wealth. Furthermore, the Constitution only requires public officers to declare their assets and those of their spouse(s) and children 'under the age of 18 years'. But corrupt public officeholders often hide assets under the names of relatives, spouses and other individuals. Hence, most countries monitor not only the wealth of a public official but also that of close relatives and household members by requesting information about the incomes and assets of close relatives, not just spouses and children under 18.

Mandatory public disclosure

Another important issue in asset declaration systems is mandatory public disclosure. As the OECD puts it, 'There is a global trend towards greater disclosure,' adding that 'there are strong reasons for disclosing the asset declarations of political officials.'[45] Transparency International also said that 'across the world, most countries expect their top leaders to publish information about their assets', adding: 'Research shows that an asset declaration open to public scrutiny is a way for citizens to ensure leaders do not abuse their power for personal gains.'[46] In Lithuania, the private interest and asset declarations of the president, prime minister, ministers, judges, parliamentarians, etc, are published annually.[47]

However, the Nigerian CCB operates in secret, and officials' asset declarations are not subject to public scrutiny. While the Constitution gives the CCB the 'power' to make declarations available for public inspection, its exercise of the power is discretionary, not mandatory. The CCB has no 'duty' to release such information, not even under the Freedom of Information Act. Indeed, the Court of Appeal ruled in March 2023 that the CCB could not publish the asset declarations of former Presidents Jonathan and Buhari.[48] The lack of mandatory public disclosure shields public officeholders from public scrutiny and undermines the true essence of asset declarations. As Paul Wolfowitz, former World Bank president said: 'Sometimes corruption is slowed by shedding light into what was previously shadowed.'[49] The IMF recommends that Nigeria should pass laws to allow public access to the asset declarations of public officeholders.[50] However, public disclosure, a common practice in liberal democracies, is a rarity in Nigeria because of official resistance to transparency and access to information. The absence of public access to the asset declarations of public officers is a major reason corruption has festered and become such a humongous monster in Nigeria.

Besides the weaknesses in rules, there are weaknesses in the enforcement capacities of the CCB and the CCT. Despite the prevalence of unexplained wealth and despite some high-profile investigations and prosecutions, the CCB has not secured any major conviction. Furthermore, the protection of Nigerian presidents, in and out of office, casts serious doubts on Nigeria's willingness to tackle corruption. Nigeria is probably the only democratic country in the world where presidents enjoy constitutional immunity in power and de facto immunity after leaving office. In 2020, the US Supreme Court held that President Donald Trump did not enjoy 'absolute immunity' from grand jury subpoenas for tax returns.[51] According to the court, 'no citizen, not even the President, is categorically above the common duty to produce evidence when called upon in a criminal proceeding.'[52] Subsequently, in November 2022, after Trump had left office, having lost his re-election bid in 2020, the Supreme Court refused to reject the request by the House Ways and Means Committee to examine his tax returns.[53] By contrast, in Nigeria, the court ruled that former Presidents Jonathan and Buhari could not be compelled to publish their asset declarations. Yet, until the anti-graft agencies and the courts can rigorously and independently enforce anti-corruption laws, including the asset declaration system, even against a former president, Nigeria will not effectively tackle corruption.

Lax Rules on Gifts to Public Officers

The Nigerian asset declaration system does not address the issue of gifts to public officers. Yet, several cases have proved conclusively that gifts to public officials are a powerful source of corruption in Nigeria. For instance, a former first lady claimed that about $32m found in her different bank accounts were 'gifts from friends and well-wishers'[54], while a former managing director of NNPC claimed that the $9.8m cash seized from his house were gifts.[55]

Gifts have a deceptive innocence because they are rooted in customs and traditions. Yet, they are also widely associated with corruption. The UN Convention Against Corruption (UNCAC) recognises the acceptance of gifts by public officials as a factor fuelling corruption.[56] As a result, gifts to public officials are tightly regulated in most countries.[57] But Nigeria has very weak rules on public officers receiving gifts. The Constitution allows a public officer to receive personal gifts or benefits from relatives or personal friends to such extent and on such occasions as are recognised by custom' (section 3 of the Fifth Schedule). No country that is serious about tackling endemic corruption should have such a nebulous provision on gifts to public officers. What does 'to such extent and on such occasions as are recognised by custom' mean? How much does it cover? $1m, $5m? Who determines what is 'recognised by custom'? Is customary law the arbiter? What about 'personal friends'?

In one instance, a judge received a gift of 500,000 naira from a lawyer appearing in a case before him and justified it as being 'in the spirit of longstanding friendship as our customs well recognises and demands.'[58] The justification technically aligned with the provision of the Fifth Schedule. But such justification would be deemed unacceptable in the UK and the US, where a lawyer could not give a gift to a judge before whom he or she is appearing, and where no public officer could receive $9.8m as gifts without declaring them and naming their donors, let alone the wife of a president or a prime minister receiving gifts totalling $32m without disclosing their sources. Nigeria must tighten its rules on gifts for public officials as it must its asset declaration system, if it seriously wants to fight corruption.

The Need to Tackle Unexplained Wealth

In addition to a robust asset declaration system and related rules on conflicts of interest and gifts to public officers, any nation that is serious about tackling corruption must have legislation against unexplained wealth. Indeed, at the international anti-corruption conference held in London in 2016, forty-one countries, including Nigeria, signed the Global Declaration Against Corruption, which requires signatory countries to create anti-graft measures, such as Unexplained Wealth Orders UWOs.[59] Since then, several countries have introduced unexplained wealth legislation.

For instance, in April 2017, the UK Parliament passed the Criminal Finance Act, which introduced the Unexplained Wealth Order. The logic of UWOs is simple. If a public officer's known source of income, such as salaries, cannot justify assets traceable to him, he should satisfactorily explain the source of the wealth or forfeit it.

However, Nigeria does not have legislation against unexplained wealth despite the prevalence of unexplained wealth in the country. As a result, given the weak investigatory and prosecutorial abilities of the EFCC, it has resorted to secret deals and plea bargaining with those accused of corruption. The EFCC always claims to have retrieved billions of dollars or trillions of naira and other assets from 'looters'[60], but the public never gets to know who the 'looters' are. In 2017, in a case instituted by the Socio-Economic Rights and Accountability Project (SERAP), the Federal High Court in Lagos ordered the government to 'immediately release to Nigerians information about the names of high-ranking public officials from whom public funds were recovered and the circumstances under which funds were recovered.'[61] The government refused to comply with the court order. But public concerns continue to dog the EFCC's opaque handling of the forfeited assets.[62]

In 2021, a senator, Ali Ndume, called for the introduction of the Unexplained Wealth Order in Nigeria, saying that plea bargaining in corruption cases incentivised more corruption.[63] In 2023, the current chairman of the EFCC, Ola Olukoyede, also called for legislation against unexplained wealth. According to him, 'treasury looters would have little cover if unexplained wealth was tackled.'[64] He said that section 7 of the EFCC Act, under which the agency carried out asset tracking and recovery, was not sufficient to deal with the problem. Nigeria signed an international agreement urging countries to create UWOs as a tool for fighting corruption. In August 2025, the EFCC chairman disclosed that many public officers had 'perfected the antics of anticipatory declaration of assets to justify their intended stealing of public funds and other acts of corruption.'[65] The best antidote is an unexplained wealth legislation.

Furthermore, Nigeria needs laws protecting whistle-blowers and witnesses. However, the Nigerian federal legislators have, so far, failed to pass the long-gestating Whistle-Blower and Witness Protection Bill into law.[66] There is no excuse for the persistent failure to enact such critical anti-corruption legislation.

Time to Reverse Burden of Proof in Corruption Cases

All the measures discussed above, taken together, should ordinarily be sufficient to tackle corruption in Nigeria. But, as also discussed, the institutional weaknesses are so acute that a more radical solution is needed. The most prominent institutional weakness is the fact that Nigeria's anti-graft agencies lack sophisticated investigatory and prosecutorial abilities, which means that they are often not a match for an accused with deep pockets. In 2009, a federal high court discharged and acquitted James Ibori, a former governor of Delta State, of 170 corruption charges brought against him by the EFCC. But the following year, the same Ibori was convicted of money laundering and sentenced to ten years' imprisonment by a High Court in England, suggesting either that the Nigerian judges were compromised or that the Nigerian prosecutors were technically ineffective.

The truth is that corruption is notoriously difficult to prosecute. The legal principle 'He who asserts must prove, not he who denies' puts excessive legal and evidential burden on the prosecution and allows the accused, who usually have limitless resources, often stolen money, to frustrate the prosecution. The court is limited to the evidence adduced by the parties and cannot inform itself by adducing its own evidence. Yet, the court must come to a decision, even if the evidence is inadequate or inconclusive. In those circumstances, the prosecution that cannot adduce probative evidence to prove its case will fail. But corruption is unlike other crimes, such as murder, where the prosecution can easily establish the two elements of a crime, namely conduct, known as *actus reus*, and intention, known as *mens rea*. As the legal dictum goes, 'the act is not guilty unless the mind is guilty'. However, if intention must be established as proof of corruption, then, given the presumption of innocence, the onus would be on the prosecution to prove, for instance, that an unexplained large sum of money found in a public officer's bank account was a product of corruption, committed with the relevant *mens rea*. With such notorious evidential difficulty, it is hard to fight corruption worldwide.

Yet, corruption is a crime that must be fought by all means because, as the Privy Council put it in one case, it is 'an evil practice which threatens the foundations of any civilised society.'[67] The then Secretary-General of the United Nations, Kofi Annan, also described corruption as 'an insidious plague that has a wide range of corrosive effects on societies.'[68] That is why the burden of proof should be reversed in corruption cases so that if someone is accused, say, of receiving a bribe or of being in possession of unexplained wealth, the onus is on him to prove that he is not guilty of the offence. For instance, if a public officer owns wealth that far exceeds his salary, the rebuttable presumption must be of illicit enrichment, and the onus is on him to rebut the presumption, not on the prosecution to prove corruption.

Many countries have reserved the burden of proof in corruption cases. Singapore, Hong Kong and Indonesia are examples of developing countries that have done so. Such reversal is common in developed countries. For instance, in 2016, the Irish Court of Appeal upheld a provision in Ireland's Prevention of Corruption Act that imposed a reverse burden of proof in corruption cases. According to the Court, the reversal of the legal burden of proof is justified 'in the unusual circumstances of the prevalence of corruption worldwide and the difficulty of proving intention, even where the circumstances are strongly suggestive of criminality.'[69] The same approach is taken in England, where the Salmon Commission said that 'the justification for reversing the onus of proof is indeed compelling in the sphere of corruption' and that such reversal 'is in the public interest and causes no injustice.'[70]

The main criticism against reversing the burden of proof in corruption cases is that it violates the presumption of innocence well-established in international conventions, such as the Universal Declaration of Human Rights and the African Charter on Human and Peoples' Rights. But this principle is not absolute. As the Irish Court of Appeal observed, Article 28 of the UN Convention on Corruption, which seems to allow the reversal of the burden of proof, is not in conflict with the UDHR's provision on the presumption of innocence.[71]

***

As argued earlier, there is a deep malaise in Nigeria's anti-graft infrastructure. Nigeria's anti-corruption laws and institutions are extremely weak. Given the structural barriers to successful investigations and prosecutions of corruption cases and given the deadly and insidious nature of corruption and the social need to stamp it out, Nigeria should be in the League of Nations that is taking bold and radical measures to fight corruption. It goes without saying that corruption has far-reaching consequences. Corruption: it damages public institutions, harms the economy and erodes the fabric of society. Economically, corruption undermines regulation that exists to protect the public interests, distorts competition or a fair market system and entrenches existing power structures and incumbents, limiting innovation and economic growth, in addition to stymying development through the plundering of a nation's resources. Socially, corruption breeds poverty. Corruption is, indeed, the most incredible machine for manufacturing poverty.[72]

Furthermore, with stolen wealth, corrupt politicians and public officials can accumulate income-yielding capital assets, acquire the best education and social standing for their children and pass on huge wealth to them. All of this increases or entrenches inequality and undermines social cohesion and social order. Then, there is the impact of corruption on politics and public institutions. Certainly, corruption undermines democracy and the rule of law and

397

reduces trust in government and the legitimacy of public institutions. Politics is highly monetised in Nigeria, and only the extremely wealthy can go into political life. Corruption distorts politics when those who have amassed wealth through illicit means can use the stolen wealth to buy political influence, muscle their way into power and determine the future direction of a country.

The Nigerian Constitution says in section 15(5) that 'The State shall abolish all corrupt practices.' But successive Nigerian governments and presidents have paid lip service to operationalising that constitutional requirement. Despite the existence of three anti-graft agencies, the first established over 30 years ago and the other two over 20 years ago, Nigeria remains an extremely corrupt country, with corruption draining billions of dollars annually from the economy and destroying the political and social fabric of the country. It is time for a radical approach built around the measures discussed in this chapter, namely, a robust asset declaration system with mandatory public disclosure, stringent rules on gifts to public officeholders, strong legislation and enforcement against unexplained wealth, and, above all, a reversal of the burden of proof in corruption cases. Nigeria cannot continue to shrug off its perception worldwide as a very corrupt country. It must frontally confront and tackle the problem. But tackling corruption in Nigeria cannot be viewed in isolation, it is related to the subject of chapter 7 and even more so to the subject of the next chapter.

9

Strengthening the Rule of Law

The final chapter in Part 3 of this book deals with the rule of law, a critical aspect of Nigeria's institutional weaknesses. The themes of the preceding two chapters, namely bureaucratic deficit and corruption, are, in a sense, rule-of-law problems. Countries that have strong rule-of-law credentials tend to have a strong bureaucracy and are more able to fight corruption, while countries that have poor rule-of-law credentials tend to have weak state bureaucracy and are less able to tackle corruption. Equally, a commitment to domestic rule of law and legality would translate into respect for international rule of law, while the reverse is also true. However, Nigeria is known for its poor commitment to the rule of international and domestic law. Nigeria is essentially a might is right country, not a rule of law country. It is a country where the powerful are above the law, and the weak cannot get justice. The 'big man' syndrome is very strong in Nigeria, and public or political office is often seen as a licence to act with impunity, given the absence of robust and effective transparency and accountability mechanisms. In his controversial book, *Nigeria and its Criminal Justice System*, the lawyer and activist Dele Farotimi says: 'Justice does not live in the Nigerian court, and you can get the court to do whatever you want as long as you know who to speak with and who to pay.'[1]

The rule of law literally means 'the law rules', and adherence to the rule of law is one of the underpinnings of a prosperous society. As the columnist Robert Shrimsley rightly put it in the Financial Times, 'Being seen as a nation which upholds the law offers economic advantages. There is value to investors in being seen as a stable nation where the law is predictably enforced.'[2] However, as the WTO noted in its latest trade policy review of Nigeria, 'weak enforcement of the rule of law' remains an 'a significant barrier to the expansion of the business and investment environment' in the country.[3] The IMF made the same point in its 2024 Article IV Consultation report on Nigeria, saying that 'strengthening the rule of law, in addition to addressing governance weaknesses and corruption vulnerabilities, will help unlock Nigeria's growth potential.'[4] Thus, this subject deserves special mention in this book, and the following sections are a window into the state of the rule of law in Nigeria, starting with some overarching principles.

Nigeria Through the Eyes of the Magna Carta

In 2015, the world celebrated the 800th anniversary of the Magna Carta, the great charter of liberty and the rule of law enacted at Runnymede in England on June 15, 1215. The charter influenced legal and constitutional developments across the English-speaking world as its provisions were incorporated into statutes and constitutions. Central to the Magna Carta are the imperatives of justice and the rule of law. Its key provisions include the principle that punishment should be in proportion to the crime committed (clause 20), the principle of fair trial (clause 39), the principle of speedy and timely justice (clause 40), and principles relating to the administration of justice, including the appointments of judges (clause 45). Chapter IV (Fundamental Rights) of the Nigerian Constitution incorporates the Magna Carta principles by providing for fair and timely hearings in both civil and criminal cases. Indeed, Nigeria's Constitution mirrors the Magna Carta ideals in many ways, especially with the provisions under Chapter II ('Fundamental Objectives and Directive Principles of State Policy') and the declaration in Section 17(1) that 'The State social order is founded on ideals of Freedom, Equality and Justice.'

However, while Nigeria reflects the letter of the Magna Carta in its constitution, it does not follow the ideals of the great charter in practice. For instance, contrary to the Magna Carta principle of fair trial in clause 39, justice is usually for the powerful and the rich in Nigeria. In their book *Nigeria: What Everyone Needs to Know*, John Campbell and Matthew Page write that Nigeria has 'a judiciary notorious for accepting bribes and awarding favourable rulings to the highest bidder.'[5] Indeed, this was borne out by a survey conducted by the National Bureau of Statistics (NBS) and the United National Office on Drugs and Crime (UNODC) in July 2024, which found that Nigerian public officials received ₦721billion in cash bribes in 2023 and that judges topped the list of the recipients.[6] In another real-life evidence, a Nigerian senator, Adamu Bulkachuwa, said in June 2023 that when his wife was President of the Court of Appeal, he influenced the court's decisions to favour his colleagues.[7] Furthermore, contrary to Clause 40 of the Magna Carta, which sets out the principle of speedy and timely justice, there is no prompt access to justice through the courts, as a court case in Nigeria can take up to 15 years to complete, with some cases even lasting longer,[8] which is, in part, due to the fact that judges are overburdened with cases and lack resources for research and digitisation in court records of proceedings.[9]

However, by far the greatest challenge is the appointment of corrupt and incompetent people as judges, contrary to clause 45 of Magna Carta, which says: 'We will appoint as justices, constables, sheriffs or other officials only men that know the law of the realm and are minded to keep it well.' In Nigeria, judges are appointed by the president or state governors based on recommendations from the National Judicial Council (NJC) and subject to approval by the Senate in the case of federal judges or state assembly in the case of state judges. However, a president or a governor can reject the recommendation of the NJC[10], which itself can be politicised. The independence of the judiciary is compromised by the fact that some judges are beholden to the president or the governor who appointed them while corrupting or politicizing the appointment process can produce poor-quality judges. For instance, in 2023, Justice Dattijo Muhammed, the second-most senior Justice of the Supreme Court, said in his valedictory speech that 'children, spouses and mistresses' of serving and retired judges were given 'undue advantage' in appointments to the judiciary.[11] He said the Supreme Court he was retiring from was not the one he had voluntarily joined and was proud to be identified with, saying 'the institution has become something else'.[12]

Formal and Substantive Elements of the Rule of Law

In 2017, President Buhari said at the national conference of the Nigerian Bar Association (NBA) that 'Rule of law must be subject to the supremacy of the nation's security and national interest'.[13] The statement provoked outrage in the Nigerian media. What the criticisms of Buhari's comments ignored was the fact that Nigeria is not a rule-of-law country and that it fails both the formal and substantive requirements of the rule of law. The formal requirements[14] state that laws must be: (a) properly promulgated, (b) clear, general and prospective – i.e. set out in advance – to enable individuals to plan their lives and (c) applied by an independent and impartial judiciary. However, advocates of the substantive, rights-based conceptions[15] of the rule of law, notably the American jurist Ronald Dworkin, argue that beyond the formal requirements, laws must also guarantee the citizens' moral rights and duties with respect to one another, as well as political rights against the state.

However, Nigeria fails both the formal and substantive tests. At the basic, formal level, law-making in Nigeria is opaque, and the emergent rules are often unclear and unstable, leaving citizens and businesses to struggle to understand what the law is and thus unable to plan their lives or activities. Even where legal rules exist and are clear, their purposes are undermined by the unlawful exercise of discretion by law enforcement agencies, who would rather take bribes than strictly apply the rules. Furthermore, the Dworkinian rights-based or substantive conception of the rule of law has little meaning in Nigeria. While the constitution sets out certain human and civil rights and freedoms, such as the right to life and the right to economic self-determination[16], the rights are not justiciable and cannot be enforced by any citizen against the state. This is because the Nigerian state and the Nigerian president are too powerful. For instance, Nigerian security agencies are known for appalling human rights abuses for which they cannot be held accountable. Any constitution that creates human and civil rights for citizens but also creates an extremely powerful state does not satisfy the rights-based conditions of the rule of law. The test of a good constitution is the extent to which it limits the exercise of executive power. As Professor Raymond Wacks, a legal theorist, put it in an article in *Counsel* magazine, 'If the rule of law means anything, it signifies a powerful check on the abuse of power', adding that 'the core of the rule of law is the constraint it imposes on unbridled power.'[17] However, the Nigerian constitution creates an executive presidency with unfettered powers.

The British jurist AV Dicey set out three fundamental principles that, beyond the formal and substantive criteria, must also underpin the rule of law.[18] The first is the absence of arbitrary power on the part of the government; in other words, nobody must be punished just at the whims of the state, and a breach of law must first be established before the ordinary courts. Second is equality before the law: no one must be above the law. As the authors of Oxford English Law put it, the rule of law means 'equality before the law or the equal subjection of all classes to the ordinary law of the land administered by the ordinary courts.'[19] Dicey's third postulation is that, under the rule of law, the right to personal liberty is protected by the courts through judicial decisions.

However, none of the Dicey principles is respected in Nigeria. Take the arbitrary use of state power. Professor Wacks states that the rule of law 'embodies the notion of legality, and the values associated with mechanisms of control over the exercise of arbitrary authority and sweeping discretion.'[20] However, in Nigeria, the state exercises arbitrary authority and sweeping discretion. Individuals are frequently detained by the state without or even against court orders. For instance, Sambo Dasuki, a former national security adviser, was detained for four years without trial despite several court orders to release him.[21] There is also no equality before the law.

In his book *The Audacity of Hope*, written before he became US president, Barack Obama said Nigeria had two sets of rules, 'one for elites and one for ordinary people'.[22] In Nigeria, a former president is treated as an 'institution' and untouchable, whereas, according to one analysis, as of 2023, 78 countries worldwide had jailed or prosecuted leaders who left office in 2000.[23] Indeed, in May 2024, a New York jury found then-former President Trump, now president again, guilty of 34-count felony charges, making him the first former US president to be convicted of a crime.[24] By contrast, a former Nigerian president cannot be questioned by a law enforcement agency, let alone prosecuted, despite allegations of massive corruption under his government.[25]

Delivering the Supreme Court ruling against President Trump in the tax returns case, Chief Justice John Roberts said: 'Two hundred years ago, a great jurist of our Court established that no citizen, not even the President, is categorically above the law.'[26] Although the Supreme Court later controversially[27] ruled in a 6-3 vote that a former president had absolute immunity from criminal prosecution for actions taken to exercise his 'core constitutional powers' and 'is entitled to at least presumptive immunity from prosecution for all his official acts, it held that the president 'enjoys no immunity from his unofficial acts.'[28] Chief Justice Roberts added: 'And not everything the president does is official. The president is not above the law.'[29] Indeed, on January 3, 2025, after Trump had been re-elected president and days before he was sworn in on January 20, a New York appeal court upheld the jury's verdict against him in the hush money case, saying that the matter involved in the case did not relate to Trump's official acts and, therefore, did not violate the Supreme Court ruling granting presidents broad immunity for their official actions.[30]

In truth, where a president's exercise of his 'official functions' conflicts with his constitutional duty to uphold the law, the exercise of the 'official functions' would inevitably be declared unlawful. For instance, embezzlement of public funds, or other abuse of power, cannot be described of the performance of an official function. But in Nigeria, whether acting officially or unofficially in office, a former president is *de facto* above the law. Yet, if, for whatever reason, a former president cannot be held accountable for what he did in office, that does not only undermine good governance but also erodes the principle of equality before the law.

Commitment to the Rule of International Law

Some scholars make an affinity argument that respect for the domestic rule of law and legality would translate into respect for the international rule of law.[31] Put simply, a government that respects its own domestic laws, constitution and judiciary is likely to honour its international obligations, whereas a government that has no respect for its own domestic laws is unlikely to see international law as anything other than a distant legal nuisance that should be ignored. Nigeria belongs to the second category; it is notorious for signing or ratifying international agreements and doing virtually nothing to implement them.

International law classifies countries as either a monist or a dualist state. A monist state treats treaties that it signs as automatically part of its domestic law with no further legislative act required, whereas as dualist state must explicitly incorporate treaties into its domestic law before they can have legal effect.[32] Nigeria is a dualist state. Section 12(1) of the Nigerian Constitution states: 'No treaty between the Federation and any other country shall have the force of law except to the extent to which any such treaty has been enacted.' Thus, Nigeria must explicitly incorporate treaties into its national laws through a legislative act before they can have legal effect domestically. As a result, international treaties are subject to domestic laws and regulations, and any dispute arising from any international treaty or agreement would only be resolved via the Nigerian court system, which, for a country that has scant regard for the rule of law, domestic or international, poses challenges for foreign investors and undermines the business environment and investor confidence in the country.

There is also the fact that while Nigeria may sign international treaties, it rarely ratifies or domesticates them. For instance, in 2020, the then Chairman of the House

Committee on Treaties, Protocols and Agreements, Ossai Ossai, said that over 400 treaties, protocols and agreements signed by successive governments in Nigeria were yet to be ratified or domesticated.[33] According to the WTO, Nigeria has concluded 31 bilateral investment treaties (BITs), of which only 15 are in force.[34] Similarly, Nigeria has 16 double taxation agreements (DTAs), only one of which entered into force in 2024.[35] Nigeria's attitude to international rule of law is not different from its attitude to domestic rule, which supports the affinity argument that its lack of commitment to the rule of law and legality at home spills over to its lack of commitment to international rule of law. Yet, without a commitment to domestic and international rule of law, Nigeria's reputation would be severely damaged internationally, as discussed in the following sections.

Nigeria and the West: What Kind of Friends Are They?

The foregoing discussion about compliance with domestic and international rule of law has implications for Nigeria's relationship with the rest of the world, particularly the developed world. In 2014, there was a diplomatic faceoff between Nigeria and the United States over the latter's refusal to sell military hardware to Nigeria to prosecute its campaign against the Boko Haram insurgents. The criticism of the US by two prominent Nigerians, General Yakubu Gowon, former head of state, and Wole Soyinka, Nobel laureate, upped the ante, with Gowon asking: 'What sort of friends are they?'[36] A similar 'unfriendly' situation arose in February 2025, when Canada denied, without explanation, visas to Nigeria's senior military officers, including the head of the military, who had wanted to attend the Invictus Games, a sports event for war veterans, held in Canada.[37] The treatment angered the Nigerian government. Nuhu Ribadu, Nigeria's national security adviser, called the decision as 'disrespectful', saying: 'Canada can go to hell'.[38] Such undiplomatic behaviours would not be expected between friendly countries. But in discussing Nigeria's relations with the West, it is important to explore the concept of 'friendship' in international relations. This is critical to understanding Nigeria's relationship with the West and vice versa.

When General Gowon posed the question, 'What sort of friends are they?', he used the word 'friends' in a diplomatic sense. But he did not say the nature of the friendship he had in mind. The truth is that friendship is an elastic term in international relations. Two states that are not at war or in conflict are 'friends', but this does not imply a close relationship. However, when used to indicate closeness, as would be the case between allies, coalition partners, strategic partners, like-minded states, and states with 'special relations', the term 'friendship' means a lot more. Friendship, in that sense, suggests the existence of an 'influence relationship' in which the states involved are accustomed to expecting and receiving a high level of responsiveness in their relationship. Influence-relationships can exist between states with widely unequal powers.

For instance, the US is often regarded as the leader of the Free World. Virtually all members of this 'alliance', which are not only Western countries, accept its implicit leadership. However, while this means that the US can exercise influence over the rest, it also means, conversely, that it is susceptible to influence in return. To be sure, under the presidency of Donald Trump, both in his first, but particularly in his second, term, America showed scant regard for the interests of its close allies.[39] However, the behaviour of the Trump administration would be regarded as an aberration because, in general, the US tends to value its allies. As Henry Kissinger, former US Secretary of State, said in his book, *Years of Upheaval*, 'We will never consciously injure the interests of our friends. We expect in return that their policies will take seriously our interests and our responsibilities.'[40] That is the nature of influence relationships: responsiveness and sensitivity even on issues of high politics, such as peace and security. For instance, in 2023, as the relationship between the West and both China and Russia became strained over trade and security matters, western leaders coined the term 'friendshoring', whereby manufacturing and supply chains are shifted away from perceived enemies and routed to countries regarded as long-term reliable business and political allies.[41] Thus, friendship in diplomatic terms means an influence relationship; it happens when countries treat each other specially and with mutual respect.

So, what kind of relationship does Nigeria have with the West? Is Nigeria truly a friend of the West and vice versa? Do they have an influence relationship? The evidence suggests otherwise. In her memoirs, The Downing Street Years, Margaret Thatcher, former British prime minister, observed that 'Nigeria's feeling towards us was volatile, even without the South African question, on which it was extremely hostile'.[42] Of course, Nigeria had its complaints against the West. For example, General Gowon referred to their tepid support during the civil war. But the civil war was *sui generis*, an issue on which Western public opinion was vehemently negative. As Alexis de Tocqueville pointed out in *Democracy in America,* public opinion is a key driver of Western foreign policy. However, since the war, many of Nigeria's actions, which did not even reflect its own public opinion, violated key Western interests and values and inflicted lasting damage on the 'friendship', if there was any.

For example, the attempt in 1984 by the General Buhari military regime to kidnap Umaru Dikko, a minister under the Shehu Shagari administration, from Britain by drugging and putting him in crates violated the international rule of law and rightly offended Britain, which imposed diplomatic sanctions on Nigeria. The annulment of the presidential election of June 12, 1993, by the General Babangida military regime was done without any regard for Western sensitivity and views, let alone those of Nigerians. Not long after that, Nigeria scored another own goal, with the killing of the writer and Ogoni rights advocated Ken Saro-Wiwa in 1995. Not even then, President Nelson Mandela's intervention, not to mention the interventions of Western leaders, stopped Sani Abacha from carrying out the killing. In a magazine interview, Baroness Lynda Chalker, the then British overseas development minister, expressed her deep concerns about the damage Nigeria's actions were doing to its international image.[43] Similarly, Chief Emeka Anyaoku, then Secretary-General of the Commonwealth, who made strenuous efforts to stop the execution of Saro-Wiwa, expressed his deep disappointment. Anyaoku said in a magazine interview that when he received the news that the

Provisional Ruling Council had confirmed the death sentence on Saro-Wiwa, 'I sent a personal message to our head of state in which I alerted him to the international perspective, and I hoped that what happened would not happen.'[44] But it was to no avail. It did not matter to the military that a Nigerian, Anyaoku, was the Secretary-General of the Commonwealth.

Although the above critical and costly errors happened under the military, the situation was not markedly different under democratic rule. Nigeria continued to score its own goals to the annoyance and frustration of its Western 'friends'. The endemic corruption, the administrative ineptitude that undermines government effectiveness, and the mishandling of the Chibok girls' abduction by the Boko Haram terrorists dealt a severe blow to Nigeria's international standing. Western countries, particularly the US, had long taken the view that corruption, insecurity and maladministration were killing the Nigerian dream. For instance, Hillary Clinton, then US Secretary of State, said that 'Nigeria has squandered oil wealth and has bred massive corruption' and that 'the Nigerian government has failed to address the underlying challenges' of insurgency.[45]

Despite Nigeria's contributions to peace-keeping operations and its positive role at the United Nations, its domestic problems and lack of regard for international rule of law continued to undermine its international peace-keeping efforts. Nigeria has yet to make the intellectual leap in recognising that a country's foreign policies straddle two environments – the domestic and the global – and that policymakers should constantly mediate between the two. This failure to understand the interface between the domestic and the international has often led Nigeria to be tetchy and defensive whenever its internal weaknesses are highlighted by outsiders, and sometimes, it reacts in a way that is counterproductive. For instance, in an article titled 'Big Country, Thin Skin'[46], the Economist magazine criticised then President Goodluck Jonathan for unleashing an angry broadside at foreign journalists and diplomats about their portrayal of Nigeria. That is clearly not how to win friends and influence people.

Of course, Western countries have their faults. They are sometimes too intolerant and impatient with Nigeria. However, they want Nigeria to succeed. It is in their strategic interest that it does. Nigeria is too important to be ignored and, indeed, too big to fail since its failure would reverberate across Africa and spill over to the rest of the world, particularly the West. However, the West is frustrated that Nigeria is not achieving its full potential due to self-inflicted internal problems. Nigeria wants to be a serious international player, and rightly so. But it needs to put its house in order and form an influence relationship with the West. It needs the West to achieve global relevance, and the West needs it as a strategic partner. Big-player ambition requires big-player thinking and action. Unfortunately, Nigeria's international reputation has not engendered such an influence relationship with many Western countries that would enable them to treat it and its citizens with the kind of respect that exists between truly friendly nations. Rather, as discussed below, Nigeria is too often treated like a pariah state while its citizens are hardly accorded decent treatment in foreign countries.

Why the West Treats Nigeria Like a 'Pariah' State

In January 2020, President Donald Trump, then still in his first term, imposed an immigrant visa ban on Nigeria,[47] describing the country as 'posing the highest degree of risk' to American national security.[48] This was followed in February 2020 by the European Union, which announced that it planned to impose visa restrictions on Nigeria.[49] But why did the US and the EU treat Nigeria with such ignominy? A good starting point is the reasons given for the actions. In his Executive Order, President Trump stated that granting immigrant entry into the US to people from Nigeria and five other countries – Burma, Eritrea, Kyrgyzstan, Sudan and Tanzania – would be 'detrimental to the interests of the US'[50] It was a national humiliation that Nigeria was branded alongside failed states like Eritrea and Sudan as a danger to the US. In the case of the EU, it imposed visa restrictions on Nigerians because Nigeria was 'failing to play its part in the return and readmission of its nationals staying illegally in Europe'.[51] The EU said that Nigerians were 'among the top ten' nationalities 'staying irregularly' and blamed Nigeria's 'non-cooperating government' for failing to tackle the problem.[52] As a result, it 'may introduce several measures to make it more difficult for Nigerians to get a Schengen visa.'[53]

In 2018, the number of Nigerians who applied for the Schengen visa to the EU was 88,587, of which 44,076, or 49.8 per cent, were rejected, 'the highest rejection rate'[54] of all other countries in need of visas. In that same year, Nigerians spent €5,315,220 on visa applications to Europe; €2,644,560 of this was spent by failed applicants. Of course, the EU welcomed the money it received from Nigerians every year, even if it rejected half of their applications. However, for those to whom visas were issued, the EU complained about the rate of 'over-stayers' and the Nigerian government's refusal to facilitate their return. International law obliges each country to accept the return of its nationals deported from a foreign country. Any country that refuses to do that is deemed 'non-cooperating' and risks facing visa sanctions. Nigeria did not create the conditions to stop its citizens from going to Europe and staying there illegally and yet refused to take them back when deported.

But if the reason given for the EU's threatened action was embarrassing for Nigeria, the reason for the US's immigrant visa ban was even more so. Essentially, the American government required all foreign countries whose nationals wanted to enter the US to share identity-management information, share national security and public-safety information, and pass a security and public-safety risk assessment. President Trump said Nigeria was among 'the worst performing in the world' in respect of these conditions. Nigeria, he said, did not comply with the established identity management and information-sharing criteria and did not share public safety and terrorism-related information. As a result, he concluded that 'Nigeria presents a high risk, relative to other countries in the world, of terrorist travel to the US.'[55]

The EU's and the US's stated reasons either portrayed Nigeria as a country that doesn't respect international law and diplomatic rules or exposed Nigeria's acute institutional weaknesses or both. In truth, it is both. For instance, why should sharing visa-related information with the US be so difficult, given how regularly and easily such information is shared by countries? That seems like a rule of law compliance problem. Of course, there are also capacity issues because it cannot be taken for granted that Nigeria has a sophisticated information management system. However, whether the problems betrayed a deliberate disregard for the international rule of law or exposed Nigeria's lack of state capacity, the truth is that they did not enhance Nigeria's international reputation and, in fact, worsened it.

Yet, beyond the stated reasons are the unstated ones. When countries have an influence relationship, as discussed in the preceding section, they do not name and shame each other as the US did when it named Nigeria in an Executive Order as a country 'posing the highest degree of risk' to America. Interestingly, in the same Executive Order, President Trump referred to five countries that did not satisfy the information-sharing criteria but which, for US foreign policy interests, warranted diplomatic engagement rather than a visa ban. That raised the question: What are the US foreign policy interests that qualified the five countries for exemption? According to President Trump, each of the countries 'provides critical counter-terrorism cooperation with the US and therefore holds strategic importance in countering malign external actors.'[56] But the Executive Order described Nigeria as 'an important strategic partner in the global fight against terrorism.'[57] So, why was Nigeria not accorded the same treatment extended to the five countries excluded from the visa ban?

In truth, Nigeria suffered from such acute negative perceptions that it was not seen as deserving of any special favours beyond routine diplomatic practices. And the strongest negative perception is of endemic corruption. As noted in chapter 8, in 2016, the then British Prime Minister David Cameron described Nigeria as 'a fantastically corrupt country'. In governmental and diplomatic circles across the world, Nigeria is seen as a very corrupt nation. In their book titled Nigeria: What Everyone Needs to Know, John Campbell and Matthew Page, the former US Ambassador to Nigeria, said: 'Official corruption is more than conventional in Nigeria; it is endemic and has saturated Nigeria's political culture.'[58] They added: 'If Nigeria is a democracy, it is also a kleptocracy.'[59] It is hard to imagine that such a country would be treated with respect internationally beyond normal diplomatic niceties. Another negative perception is of deepening insecurity.

In 2018, when President Buhari visited the White House, President Trump strongly condemned the burning of churches and killing of Christians by Boko Haram and the marauding herdsmen, saying: 'We gonna be working on that problem, and working on that problem very, very hard because we can't allow that to happen.'[60] Then, there is, as discussed earlier, the disregard for domestic rule of law. With such negative perceptions, Nigeria has few true friends in government and diplomatic circles around the world. It is hard to think of Western presidents, diplomats and policymakers who think that Nigeria deserves special favours or deferential treatment. At the heart of it all is the perception of widespread corruption and disregard for domestic and international rule of law, a problem that Nigeria must tackle head-on if it is to improve its standing in the world.

***

All the problems discussed in this chapter and in the previous two chapters, which all form Part 3 of this book, are interrelated. The bureaucratic deficit, corruption and the absence of the rule of law are interconnected products of Nigeria's institutional failure and acute lack of state capacity. Where a country lacks state capacity, where it suffers institutional failure, corruption, and the absence of rule are inevitable. But unless these problems are comprehensively and decisively tackled, Nigeria cannot even begin to address, let alone tackle the social challenges discussed in Part 4 of this book and its two chapters.

PART FOUR

Nigeria's Social Challenges

10

Extreme Poverty and Inequality

The Nigerian Constitution states in section 14(2)(b): 'The security and welfare of the people shall be the primary purpose of government'. But successive Nigerian governments have failed to give effect to the constitutional provision. Most Nigerians continue to suffer from debilitating insecurity and deteriorating welfare in terms of unemployment, poverty and inequality. Poverty and inequality in Nigeria are truly troubling, especially because Nigeria is not following the global trends in the reduction of poverty and inequality. The World Bank made this point as far back as 2015 when it said that the poverty rate in Nigeria 'remains very high at more than 60 per cent of the population' and 'there is little evidence of recent progress in poverty reduction', which 'is at odds with the general international trend of poverty reduction'.[1] On the twin problem of inequality, the World Bank said that the concentration of households in the middle of the Nigerian income distribution had diminished, with 'increased clustering in the highest and lowest deciles'.[2]

Thus, the upper and lower classes are growing, while the middle class is shrinking, a situation that has increasingly become worse, with a widening gap between the rich and the poor. Nigeria scored 35.1 per cent in the 2022 Gini coefficient, the measure of wealth distribution, and ranked 11th in West Africa and 100th out of 163 countries globally.[3]

According to Oxfam, the combined wealth of Nigeria's five richest men is $29.9 billion,[4] whereas 63 per cent of the Nigerian population are multidimensionally poor.[5] Research by Enhancing Financial Innovation and Access, EFInA, a financial-inclusion outfit, showed that 62 per cent of adult Nigerians earn less than ₦100,000 (about $64.70) per month, with an average income of around ₦31,000 (about $20.00)[6], which confirms that, despite multi-trillion-naira annual federal budgets, economic prosperity and wealth are not widely shared and enjoyed in Nigeria.

Section16 (2)(c) of the Nigerian Constitution mandates that the State 'shall direct its policy towards ensuring that the economic system is not operated in such a manner as to permit the concentration of wealth or the means of production and exchange in the hands of few individuals or of a group.' But Nigeria is an 'extractive' state where a small group of elite dominates and exploits the people. Despite the above constitutional provision, crony capitalism and corruption have allowed the concentration of wealth in the hands of a few individuals. In its 2019 Inequality Index, Oxfam ranked Nigerian 157th out of 189 countries where the gap between the rich and the poor has worsened and ranked Nigeria 157th out of 158 countries on the 2022 Commitment to Reducing Inequality Index, with respect to commitment to reducing inequality with respect to education, health, social protection, taxation and workers' rights.[7]

Nigeria's leaders are tellingly relaxed about the widening inequality in the country. For instance, in 2014, then-President Jonathan was livid when the World Bank listed Nigeria among the five poorest nations. He retorted: 'If you talk about ownership of private jets, Nigeria will be among the first 10 countries, yet they are saying that Nigeria is among the five poorest nations.'[8] Jonathan was measuring the wealth of Nigeria and the prosperity of Nigerians by the number of billionaires who owned private jets. It did not bother him that while some Nigerians owned private jets, several million wallowed in extreme poverty.

The poverty situation is particularly dire. In 2018, the Brookings Institution named Nigeria as the 'poverty capital of the world'.[9] According to the Institution, Nigeria overtook India as the world's poverty capital, with 87 million people in extreme poverty compared with India's 73 million. Furthermore, the report said that 'extreme poverty in Nigeria is growing by six people every minute.'[10] Then, in 2019, the World Bank warned that unless Nigeria urgently undertook radical reforms, the number of its citizens living in extreme poverty could rise by more than 30 million by 2030, adding that the country would then account for 25 per cent of the world's total population of the extremely poor.[11] In 2022, the National Bureau of Statistics (NBS) published Nigeria's Multidimensional Poverty Index (MPI) in conjunction with international bodies such as the United Nations Development Programme (UNDP), the United Nations Children's Fund (UNICEF), and the Oxford Poverty and Human Development Initiative (OPHI). The index showed that 133 million Nigerians, or 63 per cent of the country's population, are multidimensionally poor, meaning that they suffer high deprivations with respect to sanitation, healthcare, food security, and housing.[12]

Nigeria Defies Positive Global Trends

Yet, poverty and inequality are falling around the world. The World Data Lab, a think-tank, shows that more than half the world's population is now middle class. Specifically, as of 2018, 3.6 billion people qualified as middle class, i.e. those living on up to $110 a day.[13] The ranks of the middle classes are being swelled by rising incomes in Asia, with 9 in ten of the new entrants into middle classes coming from China, India and south and east Asia. Even more striking, while one person escapes extreme poverty every second, according to the analysis, five people are entering the middle classes every second, with a projection that, by 2030, the middle classes will have expanded by 1.7bn to 5.3bn people.[14] Indeed, globally, the proportion of living in extreme poverty fell from 59 per cent in 1950 to 8.5 per cent in 2024, despite a tripling of the world population.[15] The upshot of the astonishing reduction in poverty and the steep rise in the number of the middle classes is that global inequality has fallen sharply, leading to dramatic improvements in human welfare.[16] But Nigeria is not following this global trend. Rather, the country appears to be stuck in the extreme poverty trap, with predictions that the situation could get even worse, especially as, according to the Brookings Institution, 'extreme poverty in Nigeria is growing by six people every minute.'[17]

The issues are complex, but without a doubt, unemployment is the primary source of poverty. But poverty is also rife among those who are employed. This is known as 'in-work poverty' and arises when people are in low-productivity jobs and earn poor wages or are self-employed but cannot make ends meet, which is the case with most self-employed in Nigeria. The high cost of living is another cause of poverty, which is a problem, particularly for those with low earnings. Then, there is the problem of the informal economy. According to the IMF, the informal sector accounted for 65 per cent of Nigeria's 2017 GDP.[18] However, the informal economy does not enable people to escape poverty because the informal sector imposes constraints, such as a lack of access to finance. Finally, there is an acute mismatch between graduate skills and the needs of industries. Such a mismatch is a barrier to growth and productivity and a major cause of unemployment, low wages and poverty.

Given the universal nature of the problems, the solutions are also universal in nature. Across the world, a vast array of tools has been developed to tackle poverty and inequality. These include (i) boosting employment through generating growth and attracting foreign direct investment, (ii) increasing incomes by paying a national living wage, (iii) taking measures to reduce the cost of living, such as the prices of food, fuel and transport (iv) helping people to move from informal into formal work, with possible tax incentives, (v) providing appropriate and targeted welfare support to the most vulnerable, (vi) enabling people to escape poverty through better education and training, and (vii) promoting an entrepreneurial society by incentivising self-employment.

The Nigerian Constitution envisages a welfare state. It requires the State to 'direct its policies towards ensuring that suitable and adequate shelter, suitable and adequate food, reasonable national minimum living wage, old age care and pensions, and unemployment, sick benefits and welfare of the disabled are provided for all citizens' (section 16(2)(d)). As noted in Chapter 10, South Africa has one of the most generous social safety nets in the world, with a welfare state that has raised millions out of indigence. By contrast, Nigeria has no safety net for its citizens, and no Nigerian government has attempted to fulfil the constitutional requirement for a welfare state. For instance, there is no unemployment benefit in Nigeria, and there is no minimum 'living' wage. In truth, however, a welfare state is not deliverable without a growing economy and without, as discussed above, a growing middle class and a flourishing private sector to create such an economy and generate the tax revenues needed to fund a welfare state. The UK funds its welfare system through tax revenues generated from a growing economy, a robust private sector and a large and growing middle class.

Furthermore, while welfare in the form of income transfers, known as the 'pockets' approach, may have a role, what is more sustainable is the 'prospects' approach that helps people protect themselves against poverty by earning good income through paid jobs or self-employment. In the UK, for instance, the focus has shifted away from welfare and benefits to promoting employment to tackle poverty, requiring those receiving benefits to do enough to get jobs.[19] One of the flagship anti-poverty programmes in OECD countries is called NEET (Not in Education, Employment or Training), which is designed to reduce the number of people who are NEET through apprenticeships, traineeships and work experience.[20]

The above shows that tackling poverty and inequality requires a coherent strategy. Indeed, a study by the John

Rowntree Foundation in the UK, which reviewed existing evidence of poverty reduction in many countries, found that most of the countries that have reduced poverty have anti-poverty strategies.[21] The study, however, also shows that anti-poverty strategies are more likely to succeed if they have the following characteristics: (i) political commitment, (ii) clear lines of responsibility and accountability for delivery, (iii) links to wider economic policy, (iv) the creation of dedicated institutions or systems of governance to support the strategy, (v) all-government approach, that is, coordination across government, (vi) effective implementation, (vii) the involvement of external stakeholders, and (viii) an effective system of monitoring and review, including measuring results against objectives.[22]

None of the above exists in Nigeria. The government's National Social Investment Programme is not a coherent anti-poverty and anti-inequality strategy. Despite the trillions of naira purportedly spent through the programme, poverty and inequality remain rife in Nigeria. Marred by allegations of misappropriation and embezzlement of funds, the programme had to be suspended by the current government. So, Nigeria needs coherent and credible anti-poverty and anti-inequality strategies. But without a robust economy underpinned by strong private sector and middle classes, Nigeria cannot even begin to tackle unemployment, poverty and inequality.

Poor and Unpaid Wages Deepen Poverty in Nigeria

Another aspect of poverty and inequality in Nigeria is the phenomenon of poor and unpaid wages. To appreciate the importance of this, one needs to understand the role that wages play in wealth creation. Wages are significant because they are a determinant of wealth. The two dimensions of wealth are income from labour and income from capital. The former includes wages, salaries and other labour-related earnings or remuneration, and the latter consists of rent, dividends, interest, profits, capital gains, royalties, etc. But income from capital, i.e., from savings, investment, properties, etc, is usually the biggest and most sustainable source of wealth. The generations that save, invest and acquire capital assets are richer and wealthier than those that do not. Yet, unless someone benefits from an inheritance, income from labour is the only means by which he or she can start to accumulate such capital in the first place. Even if a person wants to take a loan from the bank to build up assets, he or she needs a salary or a wage as a critical test of creditworthiness. Thus, what someone earns can determine what he or she owns. This is why wage inequality is a major cause of wealth inequality, as Thomas Piketty argues in his book *Capital in the Twenty-First Century*.

Piketty argues that inequalities in income from capital grow largely because of inequalities in income from labour, especially as some people get disproportionately high remunerations and allowances while others earn very low wages that may not even be paid. Unfair wealth inequality arises when those who undeservingly receive high salaries and allowances use their huge earnings to accumulate capital while the low-wage earners have no means of doing so. Piketty argues that the capital/income ratio is at the heart of wealth inequality.[23] This is because as the rate of return on capital increases, the owners of capital become richer and wealthier, and the gap between them and those who have no assets becomes wider.

The key message here is that capital accumulation, through saving, investing, acquiring assets, etc, is a principal means of tackling inequality in society. For this reason, several decades ago, the then British Prime Minister, Margaret Thatcher, promoted the idea of a property-owning democracy by encouraging tenants in council flats to buy them with government support[24]. Indeed, in many Western countries, the emergence of a propertied middle class became a significant development of the 20th century[25]and a key antidote to wealth inequality. But an economy made up largely of an underclass of 'working poor' will never be able to tackle inequality because the people don't earn enough even for subsistence let alone to acquire capital assets. Such wealth inequality or concentration is incompatible with the principles of social justice fundamental to modern democratic societies. Hence, low wages and unpaid wages are enemies of social progress.

In Nigeria, the political class garner a disproportionate share of the national income, with Nigerian federal legislators believed to be among the highest earning in the world. In 2018, a Nigerian senator, Shehu Sani, revealed that every senator gets ₦13.5 million monthly for operational costs and a monthly salary of ₦1.5 million.[26] But the minimum wage was, as of July 2024, only ₦30,000 per month. According to an analysis by the BBC, it would take a Nigerian on the minimum wage 'approximately 722 years and 3 months to earn what a senator receives in a year!'[27] In August 2024, a current senator, Sumaila Kawu, disclosed that his total monthly take-home was ₦21 million.[28] With their huge salaries, coupled with money stolen from the state treasury, Nigerian politicians are able to accumulate capital assets across the country and overseas, thereby raising their capital/income ratios, while the poor workers on low wages are condemned to a low capital/income ratio as they do not earn enough to own anything of value. Despite its profligacy, the Nigerian government has always refused to pay workers a reasonable minimum wage, let alone a living wage, an antidote to extreme poverty.[29] Yet, according to a survey by the National Bureau of Statistics, poverty is so rife in Nigeria that, amid high inflation and food insecurity, 62.4 per cent of Nigerians could not afford enough food to eat in 2023, with several skipping meals, some even for a whole day.[30] Such a decimation of living standards is unjustified in any society.

The Case for a Living Wage

In Nigeria, the minimum wage has never changed for several years. From 2011 to 2018, the minimum wage stood at ₦18,000 per month for seven years until it was changed to ₦30,000 in 2018. And the ₦30,000 minimum wage remained in place for six years until July 2024. Negotiations for a new minimum wage, conducted by a 37-man Tripartite Committee, lasted six months and deadlocked several times. Initially, the labour unions asked for the unrealistic amount of ₦615,000 per month but later reduced their demand to ₦250,000 per month. On its part, the government offered ₦62,000 per month, which the unions rejected. However, in July 2024, the government and the unions announced that they had agreed to a new minimum wage of ₦70,000 per month. But while the new amount more than doubles the old

₦30,000 per month, it would translates into about ₦2,333 a day, which leaves on the minimum wage living well below the poverty line, which is $2.00 (₦3,250) per day.

In an analysis by the research and intelligence group, SB Morgen termed the Jollof Rice Index, a family on the minimum wage of ₦30,000 ($18.87) a month would spend 67 per cent of their income on a single pot of jollof rice while with the proposed minimum wage of ₦70,000 ($44,03) a month, the proportion of income on a single pot of the Nigerian favourite meal would fall to 30 per cent.[31] But, as the research group put it, that is 'a single mean in a month of meals.'[32] The implication is that the new minimum wage of ₦70,000 per month will do little to reduce extreme poverty, not least with inflation skyrocketing at well over 30 per cent. Furthermore, with only eight per cent of the adult working population employed in the public sector and nine per cent employed private sector, while the remaining 83 per cent were 'employed' in the informal sector, the coverage of the minimum wage is extremely small, as 83 per cent of the adult working population will not receive the minimum, which is even the more reason those few wage workers should be paid a living wage so that they can earn enough to look after the unemployed members of their family.

The Nigerian Constitution calls for a 'living wage'. Section 16(2)(d) requires the state to 'direct its policy towards ensuring that suitable and adequate shelter, suitable and adequate food, a reasonable national minimum living wage, old age care and pensions, unemployment, sick benefits, and the welfare of the disabled are provided for all citizens.' Given that the Nigerian state does not provide any basic amenities for the citizens and does not provide any safety net, a living wage becomes even more imperative.

The Oxford Dictionary defines a living wage as 'a wage that is high enough to maintain a normal standard of living.' In many countries, the focus has shifted away from the minimum wage, which is the lowest hourly wage, to the living wage, which allows a worker to maintain a normal standard of living, such as being able to afford adequate shelter, food, and other necessities. For instance, the UK introduced the living wage in 2016[33], and in March 2024, the ILO endorsed living wages, saying that 'decent wages are central to economic and social development and to advance social justice. They also play an essential role in reducing poverty and inequality and ensuring a decent and dignified life.'[34] There are usually concerns about inflation, but there is little evidence that paying the living wage has triggered inflation; rather, it is inflation and the cost-of-living crisis that, in part, make the payment of the living wage a necessity. With the cost-of-living crisis decimating lives, Nigeria needs to pay workers a decent living wage, which should be between ₦120,000–₦150,000 per month.

The Phenomenon of Unpaid Wages

But low wages are only one part of the problem; another is unpaid wages. A report in the Vanguard newspaper stated that 26 states owed workers unpaid salaries, some for several months.[35] Many of the states also owed unpaid pensions, subjecting pensioners, many of them old and indigent, to financial pains. Yet, Nigeria ratified the ILO's Protection of Wages Convention (1949), Article 12(1), which states:

'Wages shall be paid regularly.' The persistent non-payment of workers' salaries is a flagrant violation of the letter and the spirit of that provision. The twin evils of low and unpaid wages are major contributors to poverty and inequality in Nigeria, and they must be tackled as part of a coherent and credible strategy to address the social challenges.

The dearth of true philanthropic giving in Nigeria

Nigeria operates rentier or crony capitalism whereby most Nigerian billionaires derived their wealth from patronage and favouritism by the state. Yet, as a former chairman of the Federal Inland Revenue Service (FIRS) noted, 'over 6,772 billionaires don't pay tax.'[36] Furthermore, great personal wealth has not translated into wealth for the wider society. Kingsley Moghalu, a former governor of the Central Bank of Nigeria, put it pointedly in an article: 'Let's get it straight: Dangote's wealth is personal to him. It hasn't made Nigerians broadly richer on any significant scale.'[37] Unlike in the US, where the wealthy generally give back to society, there is no culture of philanthropic giving among the wealthy in Nigeria. Will Hutton notes in his book, *The State We're In*: 'Although the value system formally celebrates individual rights, competition and the primacy of markets, there is also a powerful impulse towards charity and solidarity in US culture, signalling the co-existence of a more altruistic cooperative tradition.'[38] Such a culture of philanthropic giving is not entrenched in Nigeria. Thus, poverty and inequality in Nigeria cannot be discussed without mentioning the failure of those enriched by Nigeria's extractive state to give back to help tackle poverty.

Population explosion: A driver of poverty

The elephant in the room is overpopulation. Poverty in Nigeria is inextricably linked to the population growth rate. While the developed world is fretting about population decline, the opposite problem exists in Nigeria. For Nigeria, the projection is about population explosion. Nigeria is currently the world's sixth most populous country, with a population of about 227 million. However, according to the United Nations, Nigeria's population will reach 400 million by 2050, overtaking the United States to become the third-largest country in the world.[39] Then, by 2100, Nigeria is projected to overtake China to become the world's second most populous country after India.[40] Given Nigeria's exponential population growth to date, that is not an outlandish projection. For instance, at independence in 1960, Nigeria's population was 46 million, while that of Britain was 52 million. But by 2023, Nigeria's population had grown astronomically to 216 million, while Britain's grew modestly to only 68 million.

Social scientists would argue that nations with wealthier and more educated people tend to have smaller populations than those with relatively poor and illiterate people. A Financial Times editorial put it this way. 'Lower fertility rates can reflect economic success: wealthier, freer women generally chose to have fewer children, instead spending more time and effort on just one or two.'[41] Poor women, with little or no voice, hardly have the luxury of thinking of such family planning. Religion and tradition also play an important role. Predominantly Christian countries, which practise monogamy, are more likely to have smaller families than countries with large numbers of Muslims and traditional believers, who practise polygamy. For instance, a Muslim parliamentarian took his four wives to the Nigerian House of Representatives and declared that he had 27 children and was expecting more.[42] So, Nigeria's exponential population growth can be explained in terms of poverty, illiteracy, religion, tradition and lack of gender equality.

But whatever the causes, the consequences, unless the growth rate is slowed, is deepening poverty and related social challenges. When a country's population grows faster than, or even level-pegs with, its economy, the result is a decline in per capita income, the true measure of prosperity. Falling per capita income means that more people are thrown into poverty. Nigeria's population has been growing at an average annual rate of about 3 per cent, with roughly 5.5 million people added to the population every year. However, with an average annual economic growth rate of 2.6 per cent, Nigeria's economy has not grown fast enough to outstrip the rate of population growth. This has resulted in a very low per capita income. For instance, Nigeria's per capita income was approximately $3,223 in 2014.[43] However, ten years later, in 2024, it fell precipitously to $877, according to the IMF, and dipped further to $835 in 2025[44], showing a deepening erosion of living standards in Nigeria.

Nigerian politicians and officials often see the country's population and demography as advantages, given the potential benefits of a large internal market and a young population, with an average age of about 18.6 years, among the lowest in the world. However, Nigeria's population and demography can only be beneficial if the large population can contribute to economic expansion and the young population is productive. But Nigeria's population and demography have proved to be of little benefit to the country for two reasons. First, given the high poverty level (38.9 per cent of the population are below the poverty line in 2023) and, thus, the low disposable incomes and purchasing powers, Nigeria's large population is not supporting economic growth. Nigeria has a large population, but it doesn't have a large consumer market to the extent that, as noted in Chapter 6, there is very low consumer purchasing power, resulting in large stocks of unsold manufactured products.

Many foreign companies that invested in Nigeria hoping its large population would create a wave of demand for their products, found that the population was too poor to do so. As Aubrey Hruby, a senior fellow at the Atlantic Council, a US think-tank, put it in the Financial Times, 'The bigger question is if the middle class will ever materialise or is Nigeria becoming home to institutionalised poverty,'[45] adding: 'People always say it's a market of 200million, but 85 million live in abject poverty.'[46] The truth is that without a robust middle class that can provide a stable consumer base to support industrial development, a large population is of little value to Nigeria.

Second, Nigeria's young population is largely unproductive. As a result, Nigeria is not harnessing the demographic dividend where a large working-age population leads to higher productivity and accelerated growth. For instance, the average productivity of a Nigerian worker is $3.24/hr, compared with $19.68/hr in South Africa.[47] According to the World Bank, the productivity gap between Nigeria and comparator countries 'reflects both its relatively low physical and human capital stocks and the inefficiency with which inputs are transformed into outputs.'[48] In other words, the level and quality of education and skills in Nigeria are appallingly low. The following statistics from the World Bank's 2019 Nigeria Economic Update put the human capital situation in sharp focus.[49] About 50 per cent of Nigerian workers have only primary education or less; 30 per cent never attended school; just 20 per cent of Nigerian adults aged 18-37 years who completed primary school can read; among workers aged 15-24, only 59 per cent of women are literate compared to men: less than half completed secondary school; only 51 per cent of Nigeria's estimated labour force of 90 million are literate. Nigeria performs woefully in the Human Development Index, ranked 161st out of 189 countries in the 2023 Index.

Nigeria's large and growing population has not proved to be a blessing. Thomas Malthus, the 18th-century economist, famously warned in his 1789 treatise *Essay on the Principle of Population* that unfettered population growth could trigger acute poverty. In his 1968 book *The Population Bomb*, Paul Ehrlich made the same point, predicting that an exponential growth in population would lead to widespread famine and social disruption. However, others, such as the 17th-century philosopher William Petty, argued that the more people there were in the world, the more likely they were to come up with clever ideas to resolve their problems.[50] Indeed, today, despite the world's population being 8 billion, hunger and famine have not been a widespread issue. The share of undernourished people around the world fell from around 65 per cent in 1950 to under 10 per cent by 2010, largely because of the increased cross yields resulting from cheap, widespread fertilisers.[51]

However, while the world has avoided the Malthusian predictions due to ingenuity in agricultural production and productivity and the free markets that have ensured that basic food commodities are accessible globally[52], the story is somewhat different for Nigeria. Population explosion has driven famine and hunger in Nigeria in the face of food insecurity. First, this is because Nigeria has not achieved the transformation in agricultural production and productivity needed to feed its people, and second, it is because, for protectionist reasons, it misguidedly continued to ban food imports, as discussed in Chapter 4. Furthermore, economic growth has not outpaced population growth in Nigeria. Instead of driving economic productivity and prosperity, Nigeria's large and young population is fuelling and deepening poverty.

The Prevalence of Modern Slavery in Nigeria

In 2017, *The Sunday Times*, a British newspaper, published a story captioned 'Nigerian agents to snare slavers at UK airports.'[53] According to the story, 'Nigerian anti-trafficking officials have been posted at British airports to combat gangs trading human slaves.'[54] The phenomenon of human slavery in Nigeria is frequently reported in Western media. But it reached such an alarming scale that the British government had to resort to recruiting and sending officials of Nigeria's National Agency for the Prohibition of Trafficking in Persons (Naptip) to UK airports to help stop Nigerians selling other Nigerians as slaves to buyers in Britain and other European countries. Julie Okah-Donli, then director-general of Naptip, was quoted as saying to the human traffickers: 'If we miss you here in Nigeria at departure, we will not miss you as you arrive at your destination.'[55]

Human trafficking from Nigeria to Europe increased eight-fold between 2014 and 2016. According to the 2016 Global Slavery Index, Nigeria came second after Albania for trafficking humans to the UK.[56] In 2015, the UK government introduced the Modern Slavery Act, which raised the sentence for slavery and exploitation offences from 14 years to life. The act also created the office of an independent anti-slavery commissioner. But as soon as the first anti-slavery tsar, Kevin Hyland took office, he declared Nigerian trafficking as his 'top priority'.[57] He said it was 'deeply concerning' that hundreds of Nigerians were brought into the UK every year for prostitution, domestic servitude and forced labour.[58] In February 2025, ten years after Kevin Hyland made that statement, Nigeria's anti-human-trafficking agency, Naptip, raised concern that human trafficking had become widespread across Nigeria. The agency's Zonal Commander, Ganiu Aganran, said: 'In Nigeria now, there is no state that is not endemic in trafficking in persons and illegal migration,' adding: 'Even all the local government areas across the country are now endemic in trafficking in persons and illegal migration.'[59] So, the phenomenon of human trafficking and slavery has grown, and not abated, in Nigeria.

Without a doubt, human slavery in Nigeria is driven by poverty, greed and government failure. At its heart, there are economic factors. As the UK anti-slavery commissioner pointed out, the Nigerian slave traders 'are earning a fortune trading in people's lives',[60] which motivates them to look for more vulnerable Nigerians that they can trade as a commodity. This is not without a historical precedent. In his book *Empire*, Niall Ferguson said that 'supplying slaves to Europeans and Arab traders was Africa's biggest source of income'[61], and, as a result, 'Africans were simply capturing and selling one another.'[62] But for that history to repeat itself in the twenty-first century and for Nigeria to be at the forefront of modern slavery is beyond belief. Yet, the truth is that economic decline, growing population, rising poverty and moral decadence in Nigeria, coupled with the insatiable demand for slave workers in Europe, are driving a massive increase in the despicable act of human trading in Nigeria.

The Nigerian government is, of course, culpable. First, it has failed to generate economic prosperity and ensure social justice to improve the well-being of ordinary Nigerians, who are driven by poverty into the hands of human traffickers. Poverty is pushing vulnerable Nigerians into the hands of modern slave traders. Second, as discussed earlier, the lack of state capacity has led to government failure to protect the weak and the vulnerable. Despite the existence of Naptip, Nigeria has failed to tackle the scourge of modern slavery due to chronic institutional deficiency and corruption. Nigeria has consistently remained a Tier-2 country, meaning that while its government has made some efforts, it still fails to meet the minimum standards for the elimination of trafficking.[63] Human traffickers are criminal networks operating with impunity, but they won't thrive without government ineffectiveness, including the collusion or connivance of corrupt law enforcement officers. But Nigeria loses any claim to civilisation if it becomes a hub of modern slavery and human trafficking in the twenty-first century and does not create the social, economic and institutional conditions that eradicate the cruel practices.

11

Insecurity in Nigeria: A Hobbesian State of Nature

This chapter focuses on the last of the social challenges addressed in Part 4 of this book. However, one cannot isolate insecurity from the other social challenges for, in part, it is a consequence of unemployment, poverty and inequality. Certainly, it is impossible to talk about the causes of insecurity in Nigeria without mentioning joblessness, poverty and inequality, caused by economic and social failures. There is a strong interconnectedness or cause-and-effect relationship between the social forces in the sense that there can be no economic and social development without security, and there can be no security without development. But the starting point in looking at the pervasive insecurity in Nigeria is an understanding of the social contract, a concept that defines the relationship between the state and the citizen.

Violation of the Social Contract

Insecurity in Nigeria is a function of the lack of government effectiveness or state capacity, a failure of the state to fulfil the most critical aspect of its social contract with the people. In *Leviathan,* Thomas Hobbes described the state of nature without a powerful government as a 'war of all against all', where human life was 'solitary, poor, nasty, brutish and short'.[1] To avoid that, men submitted themselves to the authority of the state in return for protection from arbitrary violence of nature.[2] John Locke reached the same conclusion in his *The Second Treatise of Civil Government* but from a different premise. In his view, the state of nature was not inherently barbaric, but predicated on the successful pursuit of life, liberty and property. However, even in that perfect state of liberty, one could not prevent interference from others without resorting to self-help, which may lead to a state of perpetual war. To prevent that, men surrendered the freedom to protect themselves to the government under a social contract for state protection.[3]

Whichever justification is preferred, whether the Hobbesian or the Lockean, the point is that civil governments have their roots in an implied social contract, under which they protect the lives, property and general well-being of citizens in return for their submission to the authority of the state. It is from this philosophical standpoint that the universal credo is derived, namely, that the first duty of a government is to protect the lives and property of its citizens.

However, the brutal state of nature that Hobbes describes in *Leviathan* exists in Nigeria, with the spread and impunity of Islamist insurgents, terrorists, bandits, killer-herdsmen, kidnappers and militants of diverse types. Nigerians elected General Buhari as president in 2015, in part because of his military background and the belief that he would tackle insecurity in Nigeria head-on. Indeed, during his campaign, he vowed that, if elected, he would 'spare no effort' to defeat terrorism and insurgency in Nigeria. But during his eight years in power, an estimated 63,000 people were killed through non-state violence, while hundreds of thousands were internally displaced.[4] According to the Global Terrorism Index, Nigeria was the third least peaceful country in the world in 2020, with Boko Haram listed as the fourth deadliest terrorist group in the world, while marauding killer-herdsmen were responsible for 26 per cent of terror-related deaths in Nigeria in 2019.

Insecurity remained widespread under Buhari's successor, President Tinubu, with the rise of kidnapping for ransom, including school children. For instance, in a report, the National Bureau of Statistics said that Nigerians made ₦2.3 trillion ransom payments from May 2023 to August 2024 under Tinubu, with 65 per cent of households affected by kidnapping incidents having to resort to paying ransoms to secure the release of victims.[5] According to the report, an estimated 52 million crime incidences were experienced by households nationally during the period.[6] In April 2025, dozens of Christians were killed in a spate of pre-Easter attacks on communities in Nigeria's Middle Belt Plateau State by Islamist Fulani herdsmen,[7] while 16 Fulani hunters were killed in a gruesome attack in Uromi, Edo State, heightening tensions across the country.[8] According to Senator Ali Ndume, there were 252 Boko Haram attacks from November 2024 to April 2025, leading to 380 deaths in Borno State, his home state.[9] In a spate of devastating attacks between June 8 and 14 2025, over 218 people were killed and over 6,000 displaced in Benue State, with the deadliest being on June 13 when more than 100 people were massacred by Fulani militia in the Yelewata community, which had sheltered over 400 internally displaced persons.[10]

The 'Yelewata massacre', as the media dubbed the mass killings, shook Nigeria, but that ignored the fact that, according to a security report, 1,043 people were killed in Benue between May 2023, when Tinubu became president, and May 2025, when he was two years in office.[11] Thus, the stark reality is that insecurity has remained a hydra-headed, intractable problem under successive governments in Nigeria, inflicting immeasurable costs on the country.

The Economic and Social Costs of Insecurity

It is obvious that widespread insecurity has inflicted huge economic and social costs on Nigeria. The combination of economic fragility and national insecurity is deadly for any nation. As the BBC once put it, 'Nigeria's insecurity has added to its economic woes, hindering foreign investment.'[12] There is a strong relationship between Nigeria's Terrorism Index and FDI inflows, with FDIs falling as terrorism rises.[13] In one of its World Investment Reports, the United Nations Conference on Trade and Development (UNCTAD) noted that foreign investors were avoiding the oil sector, partly due to security challenges. Indeed, widespread insecurity contributed to the challenging operating environment that triggered the exit of many foreign companies from Nigeria.

Besides the negative impact on the inflow and retention of investment, insecurity in Nigeria is disrupting economic activities in other areas. For instance, it is estimated that 80 per cent of Nigeria's crude oil is stolen through organised crude oil theft, while pipeline vandalism, militancy and piracy have also prevented Nigeria from meeting its OPEC oil production quota and generating more foreign exchange.[14] There is also the theft of electricity cables, which further hampers the availability of electricity in Nigeria. Then, there is the huge impact of insecurity on food security. In an editorial titled *The looming hunger, poverty time bomb*, the Vanguard newspaper said that 'The widespread hunger verging on famine has been exacerbated by an escalation of insecurity across the land', adding that 'the entire food belts of Nigeria have been under siege by violent armed groups', resulting in the displacements of 'many farming communities'.[15] The newspaper warned that 'Insecurity is fuelling poverty and hunger in a way never seen before, not even during the Nigerian Civil War.'[16] Thus, insecurity is further damaging Nigeria's fragile economy and making lives unbearable for Nigerians who are not only being starved for lack of food security but are also being killed, maimed and displaced in their hundreds of thousands.

Drivers of Insecurity in Nigeria

As stated earlier, widespread poverty, inequality, perceived injustices, and government failure are the main causes of insecurity in Nigeria. When millions of youths are unemployed and poor, with no prospect of a better life through decent living, they are pawns in the hands of unscrupulous people. In Nigeria, politicians weaponise security for political and personal gains and often lure unemployed youth into political thuggery, while criminal kingpins hire jobless youth for their criminal activities. At a conference in Abuja in January 2025, Rotimi Chibuike Amaechi, a former governor of Rivers State, said: 'The politician is there in Nigeria to steal, maim, and kill to remain in power.'[17] He was right. Most Nigerian politician would steal, maim and kill, not only to remain in power but also to gain power in the first place. And they use illiterate, jobless, and poor youths as thugs to achieve their nefarious political ambitions. As the columnist Simon Kolawole rightly put it: 'Conventional wisdom is: if you control the streets, you control the thugs; if you control the thugs, you control the ballot; if you control the ballot, you control power.'[18]

But poverty and political thuggery alone do not explain violence in Nigeria. Communal crises contribute to the high rate of violence, and they are driven by battles over access to resources, such as land, oil and water. Long-standing local grievances arising from environmental degradation caused by oil exploration in the Niger Delta or from the perception of state neglect are also a major source of violence, fueling militancy and armed banditry across Nigeria.[19]

However, ultimately, insecurity in Nigeria is a product of state fragility, which manifests in the weaknesses of its security forces. Even though Nigeria has an overcentralized political system, it lacks the monopoly of legitimate and organised violence within its territory. Exploiting the weaknesses of the Nigerian state, terrorists, bandits, Islamists, and militants have taken control of large, ungoverned spaces. Furthermore, as discussed below, the government's mishandling of the challenging security issues made matters worse.

The Herder/Farmer Conflicts

No other security challenge generated so much political tension in Nigeria than the herder/farmer conflicts. This was because of widespread perception that the government of President Buhari took sides in the conflicts. Specifically, many Nigerians believed that Buhari, a Fulani, supported the Fulani herders against the Middle-Belt farmers. In 2019, the Buhari government announced that it would create rural grazing areas, otherwise known as 'RUGA settlements' across Nigeria. The government said the RUGA plan was 'to resolve the farmer/herder conflicts'.[20] The proposed RUGA settlements were not ordinary ranches but special communities for the herders, with 'necessary and adequate basic amenities, such as schools, hospitals, road networks, etc.', for which the government allocated an initial sum of ₦12 billion for a pilot project.[21] However, the public outcry was so deafening that the government had to abandon the plan. Instead of stopping the incessant killing of innocent farmers by criminal herders and giving justice to the victims, the Buhari government wanted to appease the herders by creating cattle colonies in the same states where they had killed and maimed thousands of people in genocidal-type attacks.

But the issues are complex, and any analysis of the herder/farmer conflict must begin with a proper understanding of its nature. Those sympathetic to the herdsmen's case often cite environmental challenges, such as desertification and drought, caused by climate change, which have reduced the supplies of grass and water for their cattle. They argue that the herdsmen's desperate search for water and grazing areas led them to migrate across states, bringing them into regular conflicts with farmers.[22] However, while the environmental challenges faced by the herders are undeniable, the violent nature of the clashes, with trails of destruction, rape and murders in several communities across Nigeria, cannot simply be the consequence of those challenges. Environmental and economic hardships cannot explain why the herder-farmer clashes have taken the forms of invasions of communities, seizures of farmlands and massacre of innocent farmers.

Conceptually, one can describe the herder/farmer clashes as a conflict of two rights, the herders' right to freedom of movement and the farmers' right to peaceful enjoyment of their private property. If the conflict is about competing rights, then the solution should be straightforward. Competing rights are not new. But where freedom of movement and property rights clash, the latter tends to prevail because everyone has the right to peaceful enjoyment of their property. Thus, the herders cannot enter other people's private farmlands to feed their cattle without negotiations and agreements with the owners of the farms, and the government has a duty to protect the farmers against any violation of their property rights.

However, the herders are Nigerians and should enjoy freedom of movement in any public space, as opposed to private lands, subject to state or local government regulation of the use of public spaces. Nigeria is a single market and, like every single market, such as the United States, citizens are entitled to move freely from state to state to look for jobs, buy and sell goods and engage in social intercourse, provided they do not violate private property rights. In the

US, the Constitution protects commercial and social intercourse between citizens of different states under the 'Commerce Clause', which allows Congress to regulate to protect interstate commerce (Article I, Section 8, Clause 3). But to preserve the principle of federalism, the US Supreme Court held in *US vs Lopez* that Congress could only use the Commerce Clause power to regulate 'activities which have a substantial relation to interstate commerce'[23], meaning that such regulation must not undermine the constitutional rights of the states to govern their affairs in the spirit of true federalism.

What the foregoing means, therefore, are the following: 1) herders should negotiate with and compensate farmers if they wish to graze their cattle in their farmlands; 2) herders, individually or with the support of their state governments, should negotiate with other state governments to create ranches in those states, 3) in the spirit of promoting interstate commercial and social intercourse, the states so approached to create ranches should respond cooperatively, subject to compensation and other reasonable conditions they may wish to impose, and 4) while the federal government should facilitate interstate commerce, it must not undermine the principle of federalism, which means it must negotiate with, and not bully, states to provide lands for ranches. State governments own the land in their states under the Land Use Act. The Federal Government should respect the provisions of the act.

But that spirit of consultation and negotiation has been lacking in the herder/farmer issue. The herders have behaved like the imperialists who secured trade routes in other countries through 'gunboat diplomacy' rather than through negotiations. In like manner, the herders invaded communities, appropriated their farmlands, and displaced their people. The government's seeming complicity or tacit condonement did not help matters. In 2005, the UN General Assembly recognised the 'Responsibility to Protect' in case of genocide, ethnic cleansing, and massive violence. But the Buhari government did nothing to protect the oppressed farming communities. Rather, every step it took appeasing the armed Fulani herders. Even more troubling, the military was allegedly complicit. In 2018, General Theophilus Danjuma, a former Chief of Army Staff and Minister of Defence, urged Nigerians to defend themselves because 'the armed forces are not neutral', adding that 'they collude with the armed bandits that kill the people; they facilitate their movement.'[24] The military denied complicity, but the perception of bias was strong. The government must protect the lives and property and find legitimate and lasting solutions to the deadly clashes between herders and farmers.

Military/Civilian Conflicts

Like the herder/farmer conflicts, military/civilian conflicts are becoming a dangerous phenomenon in Nigeria. There have been several instances of civilian gangs ambushing and killing soldiers and policemen and of the military responding disproportionately by attacking and killing hundreds of civilians.[25] For instance, in 2018, civilian gangs ambushed and killed 48 soldiers in Zari village in Borno State; in March 2020, at least 50 Nigerian soldiers were killed in an ambush in Gorgi, Yobe State; then, in June 2022, 34 soldiers (and eight policemen) were also killed after being ambushed by gunmen in the Shiroro area of Niger State; one year later, in the same Shiroro area, another 36 soldiers were killed in twin attacks; and in August 2023, another 36 were killed in Chukuba, Niger State. Then, in March 2024, seventeen soldiers, including four officers, were ambushed and killed in the Okuama community of Ughelli South Local Government Area of Delta State, with six policemen also killed in the same month in Delta State.

When soldiers and policemen, who are symbols of state authority, become frequent targets of civilian attacks, it is a sign of anarchy, an indication that citizens are rebelling against the state and that the state lacks a monopoly on the use of organised violence within its territory. Nigeria must be the only country in the world where civilians ambush and kill soldiers and policemen with such impunity. In several other countries, it is almost a taboo to criticise the military, not because a law prohibits it but because, by convention, based on genuine respect for the military, people revere members of the armed forces. For instance, in the US and the UK, there are many charities established to support serving soldiers, veterans and their families. But such public affections for the military and the police hardly exist in Nigeria.

So, why are military-civilian relations so bad in Nigeria that civilians frequently ambush and kill soldiers? There are three main causes. First, as discussed in Chapters 1 and 2, Nigeria is not a nation-state. It is a state but not a nation-state, with a shared purpose and a strong sense of unity and oneness. It is hard to imagine citizens of a truly unified nation regularly ambushing and killing its soldiers and policemen. Second, even though Nigeria is a state with all the paraphernalia of statehood, it is, as discussed in Chapter 7, a fragile state. It lacks the capacity to tackle security threats from organised non-state violence. And third, the military and the police have not endeared themselves to the Nigerian people. There is mutual distrust, even hostility, between the security forces and many people who see them as oppressive agents of an uncaring state. These three points need further elucidation.

Take the first point. There is a difference between a state and a nation. A state is a mere political entity with a settled population, a defined territory, a government and instruments of coercion. But a nation is more than that. A nation has internal cohesion and stability because all its people have a shared sense of nationhood, of undivided common national identity and of belonging. But Nigeria lacks a centripetal force that pulls everyone towards unity; rather, it has a centrifugal force that pushes its people away from unity. Power is concentrated at the centre, while the core ethnic identities remain powerless, at the regions. But in any country where there is a mismatch of power and identity, disharmony and instability are inevitable. The central government, though powerful, won't have legitimacy in the eyes of many people and can't secure their voluntary compliance.

The truth is that many communities across Nigeria see the Nigerian state as responsible for their problems, whether environmental degradation or other forms of state neglect; yet, at the same time, they believe the Nigerian state, represented by the Federal Government, is too far removed from them. As a result, there are deep-seated grievances in communities across Nigeria against the Nigerian state, whose agents, such as soldiers and policemen, are considered legitimate targets for attacks. As discussed in an earlier chapter, the most viable solution to the mismatch or misalignment of power and identity is to move the structure of power towards the structure of identities. That means decentralising power and devolving it to regional governments. The first solution to the military/civilian conflicts in Nigeria, therefore, is to remove the sources of local grievances against the central government by devolving responsibilities and powers to regional governments that can tackle local issues and be held accountable for doing so.

The second point is that even though a political leviathan, Nigeria is a fragile state, as discussed in Chapter 7. Indeed, according to the Fragile State Index (2023), published by the Fund for Peace, Nigeria ranked only 15th out of 179 countries in terms of state capacity, which means that it is extremely fragile. One of the categories measured in the index is cohesion, which is divided into three sub-categories: security apparatus, factionalised elites and group grievance. Nigeria performs abysmally on all these elements. A key characteristic of a fragile state is that it cannot respond effectively to security challenges. There is a serious problem with military capability in Nigeria. The Australian military defines 'military capability' as 'the ability to achieve a desired effect in a specific operating environment'.[26] The spread and impunity of terrorists, insurgents, bandits and militants in Nigeria is a strong indication that the Nigerian military has not sufficiently demonstrated the capability to achieve the specific objective of defeating insurgency and other forms of organised non-state violence.

Yet, the military's weakness is not due to poor funding or equipment. According to Global Firepower's 2024 Military Strength Ranking, Nigeria has the fourth most powerful armed forces in Africa after Egypt, Algeria and South Africa in terms of budget, manpower and equipment, and, globally, ranks 39th out of 145 countries surveyed.[27] However, having sufficient material resources is not a guarantee of success. There are non-material factors that can affect military capability. In a study, Temitope Abiodun, a scholar at the Institute for Peace and Strategic Studies (IPSS), University of Ibadan, found stark evidence of a mismatch of funding for Nigeria's military, which is about $2bn annually, and its performance.[28] The topmost reason for the underperformance, according to the study, is corruption, with military personnel enriching themselves 'by diverting public funds meant to fight terror and insecurity.'[29] Politics, bad leadership and poor governance in the military hierarchy also play a role. While the top officers enrich themselves, the soldiers on the battlefield are neglected, engendering low morale among the rank and file.[30] Thus, the Nigerian military has huge resources – generous budgets, large manpower and sophisticated equipment – but lacks the right ethos, training, leadership, organisation and governance. As a result, it lacks, seemingly, the basic military intelligence and capability to prevent its men from being easily ambushed and killed by civilian gangs.

But the third factor is also important. The Nigerian military has failed to endear themselves to the people. Decades of military rule and dictatorship made the military unpopular. Apart from the negative impacts the military has, corporately, had on Nigeria's political and institutional development, they have not, at the individual level, been good at building healthy relations with the civilian population. Military courtesy is legendary, but it is hardly extended to *bloody civilians*.[31] Instances of soldiers physically abusing civilians are common in Nigeria.

In their seminal report on state fragility, Professors Paul Collier and Tim Besley wrote: 'Each interaction between the security forces and a citizen is a "teachable moment" that either increases or reduces trust in government.'[32] Given the prevalence of insecurity in Nigeria, the military and, to a lesser extent, the police are ubiquitous, which brings them into physical contact with aggrieved communities, including armed militants. But the military rarely handles such interactions tactfully; often, they are heavy-handed, leaving negative 'teachable moments' that breed mistrust, even hatred, and that portray them as oppressive agents of an overbearing state. In their book *Nigeria: What Everyone Needs to Know*, John Campbell and Matthew Page wrote that the Nigerian military 'sees collective punishment of civilian communities as a legitimate and effective military tactic.'[33] There have been many examples of such extreme overreaction, which heightened tension.

For instance, hundreds of civilians were killed in the Odi community in Bayelsa State in 1999 after locals killed some policemen. Two years later, in Zaki Biam in Benue State, the army killed more than one hundred civilians after civilian gangs killed about 19 soldiers. In 2009, over eight hundred people were killed after a military crackdown on Mohammed Yusuf, a former Boko Haram leader, and his followers in Maiduguri, and in 2015, at least 350 Shiites were killed by soldiers in Zaria after a clash with members of the Shia sect. These incidents pale into insignificance in terms of the number of casualties when compared with the deaths of several thousand detainees at the Giwa Barracks and other army-controlled detention centres from late 2011 to date.[34] Frequently, the military clamped down on legitimate protests at the orders of the government and sometimes brutalised and killed protesters, as happened during the #EndSARS protests in October 2020, when, according to Amnesty International, at least 56 people died across the country.[35]

For several years, Amnesty International accused the Nigerian military of human rights violations[36], which they denied, and for many years, the US refused to sell military equipment to Nigeria, citing the military's human rights abuses. In 2015, after Nigeria's persistent complaint that the US had refused to sell military hardware to fight the Boko Haram terrorists, the then US Ambassador, James Entwistle, said: 'Before we share equipment with any country, we look at a couple of things. Does it make sense in terms of the country's needs? The second thing we look at is the country's human rights situation?'[37] Entwistle implied that, on human rights grounds, Nigeria was not eligible for American military hardware. And it is, in part, because of the Nigerian military's human rights abuses that military/civilian relations are so bad in Nigeria. Evidently, therefore, Nigeria must tackle the problem of military/civilian conflicts at its roots. That means forging genuine nationhood, building an effective and functioning state, including the state security apparatus, and reorienting the security forces to endear themselves to the people.

Nigeria Needs Regional Police, Not State Police

Although Nigeria claims to practise US-style presidential system, it does not practise US-style federalism. Unusual for a supposed federal system, policing is centralised in Nigeria, with a unitary police force based in the federal capital, Abuja, and headed by the Inspector-General of Police, who appoints a police commissioner for each of Nigeria's 36 states. In other words, while the Constitution vests the executive powers of a state in the governor, it strips the governor of direct control of the police. Section 214 (1) of the Constitution states: 'There shall be a police force for Nigeria, which shall be known as the Nigeria Police Force, and subject to the provisions of this section, no other police force shall be established for the Federation or any part thereof.' The implication of the centralisation of policing is that while a governor is the Chief Executive and Chief Security officer of his state, he has no direct and effective means of maintaining law and order in his state.

For several years, many Nigerians called for the establishment of state police so that each state could have its own police force. In February 2024, Nigeria's new president, Tinubu, announced that he would work with state governors and the National Assembly to start the process of establishing state police. In May 2024, speakers of Nigeria's 36 State Houses of Assembly issued a communique after a meeting in Abuja supporting the creation of state policy.[38] And in December 2024, after a meeting of the National Economic Council, it was disclosed that 33 of Nigeria's 36 states had formally supported the creation of state police.[39] The endorsement of speakers of the state houses of assembly and the support of most of the state governors were significant because it meant that if the National Assembly amended the Constitution to create state police, that amendment would be ratified by at least 24 of the 36 state assemblies, as required under the Constitution. Given that the president would almost certainly assent to such a constitutional amendment bill, Nigeria would invariably establish state police, with each state having its own police force.

The acknowledgement by the Federal Government that Nigeria cannot continue to have a unitary police force that purports to 'police' the entire country with orders from the centre is a positive development. It is long overdue that policing should be decentralised in Nigeria. However, it is also important to recognise the challenges and risks of having state police in Nigeria and the need to consider a better alternative, which is regional police. The truth is that, in the Nigerian context, regional police offer greater advantages than, and avoid many of the risks of, state police.

The first challenge with state police in Nigeria is funding. Some may point out that each of America's fifty states has a police force. However, it is worth noting that even the smallest American state, Rhode Island (population: 1,096 million), with a GDP of $55.6bn, is richer than each of Nigeria's 36 states, except Lagos State, with a ₦41trn ($102bn) GDP in 2023. Rivers State has the second highest GDP: ₦7.96trn ($19.72bn). The truth is that none of Nigeria's states, apart from Lagos, can properly fund and run a police force. Most of the states cannot survive without the monthly allocations from the Federation Account, and virtually all of them still borrow heavily to cover their recurrent expenses. For instance, according to the National Bureau of Statistics, Lagos State, the richest state in Nigeria, recorded the highest domestic debt with ₦996.44 billion and the highest external debt with US$1.26 billion in Quarter 3 of 2023.[40] Unless the revenue-sharing formula is changed so that states get at least 35 per cent, instead of the current 26.7 per cent, from the Federation Account, most states in Nigeria will not be able to fund a police force. To ignore the question of the proper funding of state police forces in Nigeria is to set them up to fail. Maintaining a professional and well-functioning police force is expensive, and therefore, creating state police must not be based on some sentimental attachment to the idea, while ignoring the stark reality.

Currently, many state governments support armed vigilante groups to tackle insecurity. Yet, there has been no appreciable improvement in the security situation in those states. Leaving states to create their police forces without proper funding would merely result in the proliferation of glorified vigilante groups. However, instead of creating five, six or seven separate police forces within a region, the states in each region can pool their resources and establish a strong and powerful regional police force. What Nigeria needs is formidable regional police with devolved commands and extensive reach across a region, not a mushrooming of under-resourced, badly trained and poorly remunerated state *police forces*.

Apart from funding challenges, state police will be politicised and abused in Nigeria. No constitutional safeguards will stop state governors from hijacking state police for political ends. For instance, state governors have hijacked the State Independent Electoral Commission,

SIEC, such that no local government election is free and fair in Nigeria. One of the key findings in the Uwais Report is that the Executive arm of government, both at the federal and state levels, has always controlled and manipulated the electoral bodies and security agencies to gain electoral advantage. The Report highlighted concerns about executive interference in the operational activities of the police such that the police were unable to remain neutral, impartial and non-partisan in the conduct of elections.[41] In a country where politics is a high-stakes, do-or-die, winner-takes-all affair, nothing will stop state governors from hijacking state police during elections.[42] Put simply, state police, in the hands of state governors, will completely destroy local democracy in Nigeria.

By contrast, regional police will be less easy to manipulate. This is because each region's police force will be jointly run by the states in the region. Given that no geopolitical zone is likely to be controlled by one single political party, the possibility of a region's police force being commandeered by one state governor is remote because governors from the other party or parties will not consent to the police being hijacked for political ends by another governor. In the UK, ministers have oversight over the territorial police forces, but the police are operationally independent from the government. This will be easier to achieve under regional police than under state police in Nigeria. Regional police will have in-built checks and balances that can be strengthened constitutionally.

Finally, in the Nigerian context, regional police are better than state police because, in Nigeria, insecurity is not contained within a state; it spreads within a region. The economist Charles Tiebout argues that where there are possibilities of significant inter-jurisdictional externalities or spillovers, it is better to create institutions with inter-jurisdictional or inter-territorial reach.[43] Thus, given the significant security externalities or spillovers in Nigeria, strong and powerful regional police would be better able to deal with the problem, including through intra-regional intelligence gathering, than siloed state police.

There are no political or constitutional obstacles to creating regional police. Politically, state governors within each of Nigeria's six geopolitical zones are already working together and meeting regularly to promote the development of their regions. Furthermore, there are already regional security outfits, such as the Western Nigeria Security Network (WNSN), codenamed *Amotekun*, established by the governments of the six South-West geopolitical zones in January 2020, as well as the South-East regional security outfit, called *Ebube Agu*, established by governors of the five South-East states in April 2021. Therefore, politically, regional police forces can be created if the governors of each geo-political zone agree to do so.

Constitutionally, there are also no obstacles. If the constitution can be amended to create state police, then it can be amended to recognise the current six geopolitical zones and create six regional police forces. The six geopolitical zones are already the de facto structure for allocating political and developmental resources in Nigeria. Furthermore, the six geopolitical zones have been recognised statutorily as the National Assembly passed regional development commission bills, named after the zones, which have become law. Thus, it follows that, as part of restructuring Nigeria and giving the country a new political and constitutional settlement, a new Constitution can create six regional police forces based on the six geopolitical zones. While state police are desirable in principle, they face, in practice, huge challenges, notable among which are funding, politicalisation and limitations in dealing with the intra-regional nature of insecurity in Nigeria. By contrast, regional police would overcome, to a significant extent, the challenges of funding, politicisation and negative inter-jurisdictional externalities.

***

Tackling insecurity and the other social challenges discussed in Part 4 of this book – unemployment, poverty and inequality – is, ultimately, the main purpose of government. Every government exists to secure the lives and property of its citizens and to improve their well-being. After all, as Aristotle put it, politics is 'primarily concerned with the development and actualisation of human flourishing'[44], the pursuit of the higher good of living well. Or, as Niall Ferguson said in his book *Civilisation*, 'The success of a civilisation is measured not just in its aesthetic achievements but also, and surely more importantly, in the duration and quality of life of its citizens.'[45] Thus, no nation is civilised without social progress, without tangible improvements in the well-being and living standards of its citizens. But Nigeria faces acute social challenges, as discussed in Part 4 of this book, precisely because it has not met the preconditions for tackling those social challenges. Those preconditions are the subjects discussed in the preceding Parts 1, 2 and 3, namely political governance, economic governance and state capacity. Yet, the truth is that if Nigeria does not tackle its political malfunction, including its weak state capacity, it cannot tackle its economic challenges and without tackling its economic challenges it cannot address its multifaceted social challenges. This book, in its entirety, sets out how Nigeria can tackle its political, economic and social challenges so that it can become the great nation that it has the potential to become rather than remaining, as it currently is, a sleeping or troubled giant.

PART FIVE

Conclusion and the Way Forward

Conclusion

Change Eludes Nigeria, But It Must Happen

It is easier to catch the wind than to bring about transformative change in Nigeria. Going by the theories of change, Nigeria should long ago have undergone root and branch political, economic and social reforms that will turn its fortunes around and make it a united, stable and prosperous nation. In his book *The Rise and Decline of Nations*, the American economist and sociologist Mancur Olson argued that if a country did not undergo a systemic shock over time, it could suffer institutional sclerosis as excessive stasis makes the status quo acceptable and change impossible.[1] However, Olson also posited that systemic shocks or existential crises would jolt a country out of a state of sclerosis and trigger fundamental reforms.[2] The logic of this theory is that when a major crisis pushes a country into a *There-Is-No-Alternative (TINA)* moment, an inflection point, radical change is inevitable. In other words, major crises tend to trigger fundamental reforms because they make the status quo unsustainable. Indeed, many transformative changes have emerged from the ashes of a crisis. In a seminal book titled *The Political Economy of Policy Reform*, edited by the economist John Williamson, there are real-world examples of thirteen countries, such as Chile and Poland, where radical reforms occurred in the aftermath of crises.[3] In their influential book *Why Nations Fail*, Daron Acemoglu and James Robinson describe how 'critical junctures', defined as major events or confluence of factors that could disrupt an existing order, led to major institutional shifts and caused a sharp turn in the trajectory of many nations.[4] But in Nigeria, critical junctures and existential crises are not a prologue to radical reform. Hence, despite having faced, and still facing, existential crises, Nigeria defies the theories of change.

In its over sixty years as an independent country, Nigeria has had a devastating civil war; it has had economic and debt crises that forced it to seek international debt relief; it remains one of the world's most volatile and fragile economies; it is deeply polarised politically and socially, with a total absence of unity and internal cohesion; it is gripped by debilitating insecurity; above all, it lacks state capacity to tackle any of its challenges. These are elements that should have delegitimised and swept away the existing order and forced Nigeria's leaders and citizens to concede the case for fundamental change. However, Nigeria tends to show a stubborn insouciance in the face of a major crisis and learns nothing from it. For instance, many of the grievances and schisms that led to the civil war nearly sixty years ago are still present today, deepening disharmony and instability in the country. Instead of negotiating a new political and constitutional settlement to unite its ethnically diverse people and forge genuine nationhood, Nigeria continues with the status quo, with business as usual.

But why has radical change eluded Nigeria? Political economists advance a taxonomy of three factors, known as the *3-I framework*[5], for understanding policy developments and change and why there may be resistance to them. The first is ideas; the second is institutions; the third is interests. The hypothesis is that each or a combination of these factors determines whether and to what extent policy reform or change happens in a country.

Take ideas. They refer to beliefs about what ought to be. Typically, ideas flow from intellectuals, visionary leaders and the dominant values and cultures in society. In his recent book *Growth: A Reckoning*, Daniel Susskind talks about 'the infinite universe of ideas'[6], saying that the power of ideas should not be underappreciated. He is right; ideas matter. But change only happens in society when ideas lead to a normative consensus and political momentum in favour of a particular cause of action. As Cass Sunstein, the American legal scholar, put it in his book *Why Change Happens*: 'What is needed is some kind of movement, initiated by people who say that they disapprove of the existing norm and succeeding when some kind of tipping point is reached.'[7] Once that happens, he adds, 'change is inevitable'.[8] But there is no normative consensus for change in Nigeria. If there is any, it has failed to reach the tipping point, the critical mass, needed to make change inevitable.

It is worth stating that while crisis is a necessary condition for change, it is never a sufficient condition: there must be a consensus. But why is a consensus or a critical mass for change unreachable in Nigeria even though the status quo is not sustainable? The answer lies mainly in the fact that Nigeria is a deeply polarised country, fractured along ethnic, regional and political lines. Ethnic division and political polarisation are deeply entrenched countervailing forces against the emergence of any consensus for change in

Nigeria. If the South supports a proposition, the North is bound to oppose it, and vice versa, however sensible the proposition may be; if a major political party favours a particular change, another major party is likely to reject it. Nothing illustrates this better than the clamour for political restructuring. The North largely regards political restructuring as the South's agenda. As a result, even though two conferences and one committee produced reports on political restructuring, there has been no national consensus to implement their recommendations.

In 2005, President Obasanjo's government spent over ₦1billion to organise the National Political Reform Conference, attended by about 400 delegates. But Obasanjo jettisoned the conference report apparently because he could not build a national consensus for its implementation. About ten years later, President Jonathan set up the 2014 National Conference, attended by about 500 delegates and believed to have gulped about ₦7billion naira.[9] But the then main opposition party, All Progressives Congress (APC), rejected the conference and refused to participate in it. Jonathan lost power in the following year's general election and his successor, President Buhari of the APC, vowed that he would not read the report of the conference, let alone implement it.[10] Buhari was pandering to the prejudice of the North, his ethnic group and political base, which was not enthusiastic about restructuring. He was also playing partisan politics, refusing to give legitimacy to the report of a conference organised by his political opponents, the People's Democratic Party (PDP).

However, as the 2019 general election loomed, Buhari's party, APC, could not resist the intense agitations for political restructuring. So, in 2017, the party inaugurated a restructuring committee headed by then-Kaduna State governor, Nasir El-Rufai. But, although some governors from the main opposition PDP participated in the El-Rufai committee, the party itself refused to endorse it[11], again reflecting the general unwillingness of politicians to cooperate across party lines. Nevertheless, in January 2018, after nearly six months of gathering evidence across Nigeria, the El-Rufai committee submitted a four-volume report to the party's National Working Committee. But President Buhari refused to recognise the report of the committee established by his own party, which was itself split between its Northern and Southern elements on the issue of restructuring. Thus, ethnic division and political polarisation are major factors preventing the emergence of a normative consensus for the much-needed fundamental change in Nigeria.

But there are also deeply entrenched institutional barriers to change. Existing institutions, such as a country's constitution and governance structure, can constrain policy choices and change. This is particularly so when existing institutions create path dependency[12], whereby a country is unwilling to move away from its past even though the past is hindering the future. The truth is that Nigeria is trapped in an inertia-inducing path dependency. It is unwilling to break free from the paths imposed by critical junctures in its past. These critical junctures resulted from decades of colonial rule as well as decades of military rule. For instance, the colonialists cobbled Nigeria together from disparate centuries-old kingdoms with no attempt to forge them into a cohesive nation, resulting in a structural imbalance that continues to foster inter-ethnic tension and disunity. Then, the military intervened shortly after independence and terminated the parliamentary system and replaced it with the expensive, corruption-prone and centralising presidential system; scrapped the four semi-autonomous regional governments and created thirty-six mostly unviable state governments; and enacted a constitution that gives the central government and the president enormous and unfettered powers over the diverse peoples of Nigeria and their resources, a constitution that entrenches a perverse form of democracy.[13] Yet, while these colonial- and military-era political and governance structures are obstacles to Nigeria's unity, stability and progress, the country has refused to make the critical path-switching decision to restructure itself.

There is a view that the dramatic change needed to transform Nigeria can only happen under a military regime. Indeed, in 2021, a senior lawyer, Robert Clarke, controversially called for military intervention, saying that the military should dissolve the current 36 states and replace them with six states.[14] His view was that a civilian administration lacked the willingness and courage to restructure Nigeria. Senator Opeyemi Bamidele, then Chairman of the Senate Committee on Judiciary, Human Rights and Legal Matters, buttressed this view when he said: 'We cannot afford to do away with the current Constitution because it would be an invitation to anarchy. The only way a constitution could be suspended is if there is a military coup. Only the military can suspend the Constitution.'[15] In other words, radical constitutional or structural changes can only occur under the military, not under a civilian government.

But where does that leave Nigeria's future if transformative change cannot happen under civil rule? Many countries have changed their constitutions and systems of government through the democratic process. By contrast, self-reinforcing path dependency makes structural changes through the democratic process virtually impossible in Nigeria.

But at the heart of all this is vested interests, entrenched and powerful forces against change. Whether it is the failure to reach a normative consensus for change or the failure of existing institutions to facilitate the process of change, it is simply the case that vested interests who benefit from the current situation, from the status quo, are still able to resist and prevent change. These vested interests are not necessarily in government, but they are powerful and influential enough to hold sway over those in government, both in the political and economic realms. John Maynard Keynes famously said that ideas ruled the world and could overcome vested interests. As he put it, 'The ideas of economists and political philosophers are more powerful than is commonly understood. Indeed, the world is ruled by little else.'[16] While that is generally true, Nigeria is not ruled by ideas. Where the ideas for change exist, the forces of conservatism and the status quo continue to oppose change. With respect to institutions, the economics Nobel laureate Douglass North posited that institutions could shape human behaviour and influence political and economic choices and change.[17] But in Nigeria, existing institutions have only produced path dependency and have created powerful vested interests that continue to thwart change. The political and economic incentives that the existing structures create for the powerful vested interests make changing the structures, perverse as they are, almost impossible.

Yet, despite the seemingly insurmountable obstacles, transformative change is not inevitable in Nigeria. However, certain conditions must be present for such change to happen. First, there must be visionary leadership. In any country where there has been transformative change, a visionary leader led and drove the process, overcoming resistance, to forge a national consensus for change. Two notable examples of such transformational leaders are Lee Kuan Yew and Nelson Mandela. As the first prime minister of Singapore, Yew took a sleepy port town and transformed it into one of the world's wealthiest countries; he took a country blighted by racial, religious and language divisions and forged it into a new nation with a shared sense of purpose. Mandela took South Africa, a country fractured by decades of apartheid and segregation, and led a unity government that negotiated and produced an enduring political and constitutional settlement, creating a new country from the old. Through the powers of narrative, signalling actions and institution-building, Lee Kuan Yew and Nelson Mandela were able to transform their respective countries.

The ancient philosopher Cicero says that 'those who govern a country should be the best and the brightest of the land,' adding that 'if leaders don't have a thorough knowledge of what they are talking about, their speeches will be a silly prattle of empty words and their actions will be dangerously misguided.'[18] Plato makes the same point in *The Republic*, saying that 'those with the most intelligence should rule a nation'.[19] Finally, Socrates advocates rule by 'philosopher-king', saying that the best form of government is one in which a leader combines political power with moral and intellectual powers, in which rulers are also philosophers.[20]

It is evident from the foregoing that those great philosophers attached great importance to the quality of those who rule nations. However, Nigeria has never had a leader who can be described as one of 'the best and the brightest in the land' or as one of 'those with the most intelligence'. Indeed, in Nigeria, rulers are never philosophers, and philosophers are never rulers. Matthew Parris, a prominent London Times columnist, said that, in every government, there must be 'the presiding intellect with the intelligence to grasp the problem, the concentrating sense of moral purpose'[21] to drive through change. However, to date, Nigeria has never had competent and visionary political leaders with a purposive, problem-solving and progress-creating mindset.

In their joint report entitled *Escaping the Fragility Trap*, Professors Paul Collier and Tim Besley wrote that 'Good leaders change policies, but great leaders build institutions.'[22] To date, Nigeria has lacked good leaders, let alone great ones. Instead, Nigerian leaders tend to personalise power and govern wilfully, impervious to the need for a fundamental change. That was the case with President Buhari, who, in his eight years in power, rejected calls for structural political and economic reforms. Thus, what Nigeria needs, as a first step towards transformative change, is a political leader who has the right vision for a new future for Nigeria and who can build a national consensus for that vision and assemble the best teams to deliver the vision.

Yet, there is another pre-condition for transformative change in Nigeria: an enlightened and active citizenry. The quality of a country's governance is directly proportional to the quality of its people. In the context of governance, 'people' encompasses both leaders and the wider citizenry. Both are important if a country must succeed. The preceding discussion focuses on leaders, those with the power and authority to run a country, and the core argument is that successive Nigerian leaders have failed the country. But Nigerian citizens are complicit in the failure. In a democracy, it is the duty of citizens to protect against bad leadership, first, by electing the right people to power and, second, by putting pressure on those elected to perform and implement a transformative change. Historically, given the fact that powerful vested interests will not willingly allow institutional changes that will reduce their economic privileges or erode their political power, radical change always happened through pressure from the people, resulting in a critical juncture that disrupted the existing balance of political or economic power in a nation.[23]

But Nigerian citizens do not perform either of the two critical duties of citizens. On the first duty, elections in Nigeria are largely shaped by ethnic, regional and religious considerations, not by ideologies or the vision that a party or a candidate has for the country's future. Given the level of poverty in the country, most Nigerian voters are, indeed, far from being independent; rather, they are part of, and manipulated by, the patronage/clientage networks that organise society from top to bottom.[24] The result is that most of those elected to power are self-serving, lacking integrity, competence and vision.

The second duty of the citizens, holding elected leaders to account, is as important as the first. This is because democracy is not just about elections; it is also about what happens between elections, that is, the extent to which citizens can hold elected politicians accountable and ensure that they govern well. After all, a representative democracy entails an agency relationship in which the elected government becomes the agent of the people, working for and accountable to them; that relationship is rooted in the concept of the social contract. So, the duty to put pressure on elected politicians to perform is as important as the duty to elect the right people in the first place. But just as the latter is neglected in Nigeria, so is the former often shirked.

In any country, democracy and good governance are predicated upon the existence of guardrails: a feisty press, a vibrant civil society, an unbound judiciary, an enlightened and demanding citizenry and vigilant pillars of integrity. But Nigeria lacks robust institutions of checks and balances; it lacks powerful countervailing forces against arrogant executive action. Once elected, a determined government can do what it will without let or hindrance. In his book *Enemies of Society*, Paul Johnson argues that the true essence of democracy is 'the ability to remove a government without violence, to punish political failure by votes.'[25] However, in Nigeria, democracy does not guarantee the removal of a bad government by votes, as elections are almost always rigged, which makes elections in Nigeria a 'collective celebration of popular powerlessness', as one scholar puts it.[26]

Furthermore, given the abysmally low voter turnouts, often well below 30 per cent, it is evident that the mass of the population simply lacks the inclination to demand radical change. In the developed world, the middle classes are usually the bulwark against bad governance through the exercise of their voting power and their agitations. But Nigeria's eviscerated middle classes simply want to go about their daily business rather than agitate for change. While part of the attentive public[27], particularly the commentariat and Twitterati, are active on social media, the popular movement behind every major change is lacking on the ground. Nigerians are not what the New York Times columnist Thomas Friedman called 'the square people', that is, people who demonstrate in public squares 'aspiring to a higher standard of living and liberty'.[28]

Even when protests become inevitable, ethnic and regional polarisations make them ineffective. Some Nigerians will oppose a national protest simply because it is directed at a president that comes from their ethnic group or region. For instance, during the #RevolutionNow protest organised by the activist Omoyele Sowore in 2019, nine Northern groups declined to join the protest, saying it was not in the North's best interests,[29] presumably because a northerner, Buhari, was the president. In the 2024 #EndBadGoverance protest, there was also a strong North-South divide, with the North embroiled in violent protest while the South, particularly the Southeast, was eerily quiet. This prompted two editorials in BusinessDay, one titled 'Beyond the protest: A nation fractured'[30]; the other titled 'Beyond the protest: Can we stitch a fractured nation back together?'[31] In both editorials, the newspaper lamented the lack of national cohesion and the deep-seated regional disparities in the approach to national protests.

The Nigerian state is, in any case, always too willing to unleash the instruments of repression – the military and the police – against any protest, often killing some protesters, as was the case during the popular #EndSARS protest in 2020.[32] In the July 2024 #EndBadGoverance protest, provoked by widespread hunger caused by the harsh economic policies of the Tinubu administration[33], the government did everything to frustrate the protest, including unleashing state security agents, which led to several deaths.[34]

In their paper titled *Democracy, Development and Conflict*, Paul Collier and Dominic Rohner argued that there is likely to be an increase in protests in countries with poor economic conditions, where poverty and inequality are rife because democracy generates 'technical repression in regression.'[35] However, although poverty and inequality are rife in Nigeria, protests are not common because the citizens are less prone to take to the streets but also because, despite being a democracy, there is no regression in repression.[36] Yet, the powerful forces against change in Nigeria can only be dislodged by more powerful counterforces, among which is a critical mass of enlightened citizens who can stand against the status quo and demand change instead of passive, compliant and alienated citizens.

Ultimately, however, an appeal must be made to the good senses of all Nigerians because genuine transformative change will only happen when all Nigerians, leaders and followers alike, vested interests and patriots alike, act in the national interest. The national interest encompasses the interests of Nigeria as a country and of the Nigerian people as a whole. Those acting in the national interest would be primarily concerned about the strength, security and survival of Nigeria as a nation; its unity and internal cohesion; its economic prosperity and the wellbeing of all its citizens; and whether it is a fair, just and equitable society.

Those issues inevitably raise the following questions: can Nigeria's current political and governance structure enable the country to become the united, stable and prosperous nation that it should be? If not, then what should a new political and governance structure look like? In answering the second question, and in designing a new political and constitutional settlement, anyone acting in the national interest would be guided by the framework proposed by the political philosopher John Rawls for creating a just society that maximizes mutual benefits for all.

In his book *A Theory of Justice*, Professor Rawls develops conceptual tools for creating a just society.[37] He calls the first the 'original position'. And the basic question is, if a rational person has a blank canvas to create a new society, what kind of society would he create? Rawls answers this question with his second concept, the 'veil of ignorance'. People would create a fair society from a position of ignorance about their role in that society. The logic goes thus. By imagining they might not be the beneficiaries of a future society they are creating, people would create a society that is fair, just and equitable. Put differently, when acting under the veil of ignorance, people are likely to act with the best of motives, not selfishly. For instance, the drafters of the American Constitution wanted to create a just society for future generations of Americans. George Mason asked at the

Constitutional Convention: 'Shall any man be above justice?' The answer was a resounding no. The result was a constitution that treated everyone equally before the law. Thus, as Chief Justice John Roberts said in a Supreme Court judgement in 2020, 'no citizen, not even the President, is categorically above the law.'

The Way Forward

It is possible to think about the future of Nigeria through the metaphorical veil of ignorance and design a political and constitutional settlement that will transform the country. This requires leaders and citizens who, shorn of self-centeredness, can imagine a just, well-ordered, peaceful and prosperous country and create a new political and governance structure, a new constitutional settlement, that will ensure that Nigerians of all ethnicities and religions live peaceably and cooperatively together; that political, economic and social institutions work effectively and harmoniously to deliver peace, security and prosperity; and that governance is responsive and accountable through effective checks and balances.

In August 2024, Dr Ngozi Okonjo-Iweala, a two-time Finance Minister in Nigeria and current Director-General of the WTO, gave a speech titled 'A social contract for Nigeria's future' at the annual conference of the Nigerian Bar Association. She called for a social contract with the following elements: a shared understanding that Nigeria must prioritise the security of lives, property and national assets; ensuring that the basic organs of the economy are left to work; and provision of basic infrastructure services and a social safety net to catch segments of society that are vulnerable. She was certainly right that Nigeria needs a social contract. What she missed out, however, was the need for political restructuring and a new political and constitutional settlement. A social contract cannot exist in a vacuum. It can only exist as part of a negotiated political and constitutional settlement. Furthermore, a social contract cannot work within the current political and governance structure in Nigeria. Therefore, creating a social contract for Nigeria's future must involve a holistic political restructuring of the country.

As noted in Chapter 3, nearly 50 billion naira was expended on so-called constitutional amendments by each of the nine National Assemblies since Nigeria returned to civil rule in 1999, but the exercise resulted in just five inconsequential alterations that do nothing to address Nigeria's deeply flawed political and governance structures. Yet, the fundamental truth is that a new Nigeria cannot be achieved through tinkering at the edges of constitutional reform; it requires fundamental institutional and structural changes. Furthermore, as the failures of past political and constitutional conferences show, a new political and constitutional settlement cannot be the preserve of one political party or one ethnic group. Indeed, the political restructuring proposed in this book can only happen through a Government of National Unity. In every country where a radical political restructuring has taken place, it was delivered by a Government of National Unity as was the case in South Africa, where Mandela led a unity government that created a new political and constitutional settlement, and in Northern Ireland, where the rival parties united to create the

Good Friday Agreement. So, restructuring Nigeria cannot be the exclusive preserve of one party; it needs a cross-party, cross-ethnic and cross-society consensus. That requires a president, in particular, and a political class, in general, that can build a national consensus across political parties, across ethnic and regional boundaries and across society at large. It requires visionary and competent political leadership, with a long-term horizon.

The task of creating a new Nigeria that will bring about political, economic and social transformations is urgent. This book stresses that urgency and calls for its actualisation. The themes are political restructuring underpinned by a new political and constitutional settlement and a new Constitution for Nigeria; economic restructuring anchored on a new trade and industrial model that will turn Nigeria into an open, competitive market economy, and an export-led industrial nation; and the need to build state capacity through bureaucratic and institutional development to tackle the social challenges of unemployment, poverty, inequality and insecurity. The goal must be to have a Nigeria that is politically stable, economically prosperous, socially cohesive, open and outward-looking. Nigeria must discard its extractive political and economic institutions that concentrate political and economic powers in the hands of a small group of elites and create a pluralistic society, with inclusive institutions, that political power and economic opportunities and prosperity are widely shared across society.

Those aspirations cannot be achieved under the current political and governance structures. That is why Nigeria needs, as a starting point, a new political and constitutional order; then, it must create a robust market economy structure by making a policy shift away from protectionism to free market policies to turn its economy into an open, competitive and export-oriented one. And it must build state capacity, underpinned by strong formal and informal institutions of governance, including the bureaucracy. These are the critical steps towards political, economic and social transformations, and towards Nigeria's unity, stability and progress. It is a task that calls for every leader, every citizen, every vested interest to slay their shibboleths. It is a task that calls for every Nigerian to act in the national interest. Only then can a new Nigeria, united, stable and prosperous, emerge, not only as the true giant of Africa but also as a global powerhouse. This book charts a path to that national renewal, that critical transformation.

NOTES

Introduction

[1] Peter Hicks, 'Sleeping with China and Napoleon', Napoleon.org: https://www.napoleon.org/en/history-of-the-two-empires/articles/ava-gardner-china-and-napoleon/
[2] Dike Onwuamaeze, 'World Bank: Nigeria Stuck in Lower Middle Income Economy Below Libya, Gabon', ThisDay, July 7, 2025: middle-income-economy-below-libya-gabon/
[3] Adam Smith, The Wealth of Nations (1776), Wordsmith Edition, 9 July 2012.
[4] The LSE-Oxford Commission on State Fragility, Growth and Development, 'Escaping the Fragility Trap', April 2018, p.59.
[5] Wayne Booth, The Rhetoric of Fiction, Second Edition, University of Chicago Press, 1983.

Chapter 1: A political history of Nigeria

[1] Niall Ferguson, Empire, Penguin Books, 2004, p224.
[2] John, E Flint, Sir George Goldie and the Making of Nigeria (London, 1960).
[3] Ibid.
[4] Encyclopedia Britannica, 'Shaw, Flora (1852–1929)': https://www.encyclopedia.com/women/encyclopedias-almanacs-transcripts-and-maps/shaw-flora-1852-1929#.
[5] Chinua Achebe, There Was a Country, Penguin, 2012, p.2
[6] Obafemi Awolowo, Path to Nigerian Freedom, Faber & Faber, 1947, pp 47-49.
[7] Wole Soyinka, 'Between Nation Space and Nationhood', a lecture at the Centenary Birthday Celebration of Chief Obafemi Awolowo, March 3, 2009: https://www.nas-int.org/between-nation-space-and-nationhood/
[8] Fola Ojo, 'United States of Nigeria is phantasm', Punch, April 19, 2024: https://punchng.com/united-states-of-nigeria-is-phantasm/.

9 James Hubbard, The United States and the End of British Colonial Rule in Africa, 1941-1968, McFarland & Co, 2010.
10 Ibid.
11 Ibid.
12 Nnamdi Azikiwe, Speech to the Congress of the National Council of Nigeria and the Cameroons, May 12, 1953: https://guardian.ng/features/ziks-voice-that-voided-planned-secession-by-the-north-in-1953/.
13 Ibid.
14 The economic and social advancements of the South-West of Nigeria, relative to the other regions, are still attributed to the performance of Chief Obafemi Awolowo as Premier of Western Region from 1954 to 1960.
15 Hansard, "Nigeria Independence Bill debates, 15 July 1960: https://hansard.parliament.uk/commons/1960-07-15/debates/daa5ea6e-3c95-4e39-9bff-b363300deaa9/NigeriaIndependenceBill.
16 Chinua Achebe, There Was a Country, p.50.
17 Ibid, p52
18 Hansard, "Nigeria Independence Bill debates, 15 July 1960: https://hansard.parliament.uk/commons/1960-07-15/debates/daa5ea6e-3c95-4e39-9bff-b363300deaa9/NigeriaIndependenceBill.
19 Chinua Achebe, There Was a Country, p43.
20 Chinua Achebe, There Was a Country, p51.
21 Ibrahim I Babangida, A Journey in Service, Bookcraft, 2025, p.41..
22 Ibid, p.45.
23 Ibid
24 Ibid. p.42.
25 Ibid. p.39.
26 Ibid.
27 Ibid.
28 Adewale Ademoyega, Why We Struck: The Story of the First Nigerian Coup. Ibadan: Evans Brothers, 1981.
29 Olu Fasan, 'A Journey in Service: Warts and all, Babangida enriches Nigerian history,' BusinessDay, March 3, 2025: https://businessday.ng/opinion/article/a-journey-in-service-warts-and-all-babangida-enriches-nigerian-history/?amp.
30 For instance, he was accused of refusing to put the January 15, 1966, coup plotters on trial, presumably because most of

them were his fellow Igbos. See
https://dailytrust.com/january-15-1966-coup/.
[31] Ibrahim I Babangida, A Journey in Service, Bookcraft, 2025, p.75.
[32] Ibid. p.62
[33] Ibid. p.45.
[34] Colin Legum of The Observer newspaper (UK) was said to be the first to the killings of the Igbos in the North as 'a pogrom'. See Achebe, There Was a Country, p.82.
[35] Ibrahim I Babangida, A Journey in Service, Bookcraft, 2025, p.61.
[36] Ibid. p.62.
[37] Ibid. p.63.
[38] This is one of Chinua Achebe's theories for why the war could not be averted. Ibid, p120.
[39] Ibrahim I Babangida, A Journey in Service, Bookcraft, 2025, p.62.
[40] The Aburi Accord was brokered in Aburi, Ghana, at a conference chaired by the then military head of state of Ghana, Lt.-General J.A. Ankrah, and attended by Lt-Col. Yakubu Gowon and Lt-Col. Odumegwu Ojukwu.
[41] For instance, Ojukwu believed the Aburi Accord mandated a confederation, i.e. a loose federation, for Nigeria, while Gowon insisted that the accord favoured a strong united Nigerian federal state. In an interview in June 2025, General Gowon said: 'I don't know what accord he (Ojukwu) was reading,' adding that 'my understanding was not his understanding.' See Timilehin Babatope, 'Why Aburi Accord failed, by Gowon,' The Nation, June 19, 2025: https://thenationonlineng.net/why-aburi-accord-failed-by-gowon/.
[42] Contrary to the view, held by some Igbos, that Chief Awolowo told Ojukwu that the Yoruba would follow suit if the Igbo declared secession, but reneged on the vow, Awolowo said no such thing. Based on the transcript of the meeting between Awolowo and Ojukwu in May 1967, before the war started, Awolowo made strenuous effort to persuade Ojukwu not to declare secession. See Odia Ofeimun, 'Awolowo and the forgotten documents of the civil war', Vanguard, November 10, 2012:

https://www.vanguardngr.com/2012/11/awolowo-and-the-forgotten-documents-of-the-civil-war-by-odia-ofeimun-3/.

[43] Ibrahim Babangida, 'I still carry a bullet of the Civil War as a permanent reminder …', Twitter, https://twitter.com/General_Ibbro/status/561121795558744064.

[44] Emeka Odumegwu-Ojukwu, Because I am Involved, Spectrum, 1989.

[45] Ibid.

[46] Hansard, 'Nigeria Independence Bill, July 15, 1960, column 1794.

[47] Ibid. Arthur Creech-Jones's speech at column 1815.

[48] Clifford D. May, 'Nigerian ruler tells Diplomats why he took over', New York Times, January 5,1884: https://www.nytimes.com/1984/01/05/world/nigerian-ruler-tells-diplomats-why-he-took-over.html.

[49] Ibid.

[50] Ibrahim I Babangida, A Journey in Service, Bookcraft, 2025, p.281

[51] Kingsley Obiejesi, 'The people Buhari jailed in 1984 are APC kingspins today, laments Kukah', ICiR, December 11, 2017: https://www.nytimes.com/1984/01/05/world/nigerian-ruler-tells-diplomats-why-he-took-over.html.

[52] The Cable, 'Rewind: Dogonyaro's coup speech that overthrew Buhari on August 27, 1985': https://www.thecable.ng/flashback-coup-speech-overthrew-buhari-august-27-1985/.

[53] Ibrahim I Babangida, A Journey in Service, Bookcraft, 2025, p.118.

[54] Chinedu Asadu, 'Buhari: I ended up in jail after jailing many for corruption', The Cable, December 7, 2017: https://www.thecable.ng/buhari-ended-jail-jailing-many-corruption/

[55] Ibrahim I Babangida, A Journey in Service, Bookcraft, 2025, p.120.

[56] Ibid. p.259.

[57] Ibid. p.262.

[58] Kenneth Noble, 'Nigerians vote but choices are limited', The New York Times, December 15, 1991: https://www.nytimes.com/1991/12/15/world/nigerians-vote-but-choices-are-limited.html.

59 Inaugural Address of President John F. Kennedy, January 20, 1961: https://www.jfklibrary.org/archives/other-resources/john-f-kennedy-speeches/inaugural-address-19610120.
60 Ibrahim I Babangida, A Journey in Service, Bookcraft, 2025, p. 267.
61 Ibid.
62 Ibid. p.269.
63 Ibid.
64 Ibid. p.268.
65 Ibid.
66 Ibid.
67 Ibid. p. 274
68 The Cable, 'FLASHBACK: Why we annulled June 12, by IBB', The Cable, June 12, 2017:
https://www.thecable.ng/flashback-annuled-june-12-ibb/
69 Ibid.
70 New York Times, 'A court in Nigeria declares interim government is illegal', NYT, November 11, 1993:
https://www.nytimes.com/1993/11/11/world/a-court-in-nigeria-declares-interim-government-is-illegal.html.
71 Ngozi Okonjo-Iweala, Reforming the Unreformable: Lessons from Nigeria, The MIT Press, 2012, p.84.
72 Law Mefor, 'Abacha loot: Who will recover loot of other Nigerian leaders', The Cable, November 8, 2023:
https://www.thecable.ng/abacha-loot-who-will-recover-loot-of-other-nigerian-leaders/.
73 Isiaka Wakili, 'Presidency: Those Behind June 12 Annulment Angry with Buhari', Daily Trust, June 11, 2018:
https://dailytrust.com/presidency-those-behind-june-12-annulment-angry-with-buhari/.
74 The Cable, 'FLASHBACK: Why we annulled June 12, by IBB', The Cable, June 12, 2017:
https://www.thecable.ng/flashback-annuled-june-12-ibb/
75 Abdulrahman Zakariyau, 'FG voided June 12 to avoid paying Abiola N45bn – Lamido,' The Punch, May 14, 2025:
https://punchng.com/fg-voided-june-12-to-avoid-paying-abiola-n45bn-lamido/
76 Ibid.
77 Ibrahim Babangida, 'We annulled June 12 elections to avoid violent coup', Interview with Arise TV, August 6, 2021:

https://www.arise.tv/ibb-we-annulled-june-12-elections-to-avoid-violent-coup/.

[78] Ibrahim I Babangida, A Journey in Service, Bookcraft, 2025, p.272

[79] Ibid. p. 274.

[80] Ibid. p.282.

[81] Ibid. p.281.

[82] Ibid. p.275.

[83] Ibid.

[84] Ibid.

[85] Ibid. p.276.

[86] Ibid. p.277.

[87] Ibid. p.287.

[88] Ibid.

[89] Vanguard, 'PRIMORG's Agbonsuremi criticises Babangida's memoir over June 12 annulment,' News, March 7, 2025: https://www.vanguardngr.com/2025/03/ibbs-book-backlash-criticism-over-june-12-annulment-persist/.

[90] Olu Fasan, 'June 12 annulment: Babangida's breathtaking cowardice demythifies him!' Vanguard, March 6, 2025: https://www.vanguardngr.com/2025/03/june-12-annulment-babangidas-breathtaking-cowardice-demythifies-him-by-olu-fasan/.

[91] Seun Adeuyi, 'IBB Didn't deny power transfer oath with Abacha when I asked him – Pro-June 12 General,' Daily Trust, March 1, 2025: https://dailytrust.com/ibb-didnt-deny-power-transfer-oath-with-abacha-when-i-asked-him-pro-june-12-general/.

[92] Ibid.

[93] Saawua Terzungwe, 'Stop tarnishing our father's image, Abacha family tackles IBB,' Daily Trust, March 9, 2025: https://dailytrust.com/stop-tarnishing-our-fathers-image-abacha-family-tackles-ibb/.

[94] Ibid.

[95] Simon Kolawole, 'June 12, IBB and the missing persons,' The Cable, February 22, 2025: https://www.thecable.ng/june-12-ibb-and-the-missing-persons/.

[96] Uwais Report: Report of the Electoral Reform Committee, Vol 1, Main Report, December 2008, p.102.

[97] John Campbell and Matthew Page. Nigeria: What Everyone Needs To Know, Oxford University Press, 2018, p.109.

98 Ishaya Bamaiyi, 'How we tried to stop Obasanjo in 1999', Nigerian Tribune, April 1, 2017: https://tribuneonlineng.com/tried-stop-obasanjo-1999-bamaiyi/.
99 Wole Mosadomi, 'How we formed PDP military wing – IBB', Vanguard, March 12, 2017: https://www.vanguardngr.com/2017/03/formed-pdp-military-wing-ibb/.
100 Reuters, 'Yar'Adua declared winner of Nigeria poll "charade"', Reuters, August 9, 2007: https://www.reuters.com/article/idUSL21496329/.
101 Abdul-Rahman Abubakar, et al. 'Yar'Adua Admits Election Flaws', Daily Trust, May 30, 2007: https://allafrica.com/stories/200705300320.html.
102 You Tube, 'Obama delivers a message to the Nigerian people', The Obama White House, March 23, 2015: https://www.youtube.com/watch?v=zxk9mxURChw.
103 Ngozi Okonjo-Iwaela, Fighting Corruption Is Dangerous, The MIT, 2018, p.126.
104 Ibid.
105 Samuel Ogundipe, 'How Obama plotted my defeat in 2015 — Goodluck Jonathan,' Premium Times, November 20, 2018: https://www.premiumtimesng.com/news/headlines/296675-how-obama-plotted-my-defeat-in-2015-goodluck-jonathan.html?tztc=1.
106 LSE, 'Nigeria's 2015 General Elections: giving democracy a chance', a lecture by Professor Attahiru Jega, November 10, 2015: https://www.lse.ac.uk/Events/2015/11/20151110t1830vSZT/Nigerias-2015-General-Elections.
107 EU-EOM, Final Report on Nigeria's 2019 general elections: https://eeas.europa.eu/sites/eeas/files/nigeria_2019_eu_eom_final_report-web.pdf, p.21
108 See 'Nigeria's 2023 elections: Preparations and priorities for electoral integrity and inclusion,' Chatham House, January 17, 2023: https://www.chathamhouse.org/events/all/research-event/nigerias-2023-elections-preparations-and-priorities-electoral-integrity.
109 Ijeoma Opara, 'Obasanjo asks INEC to cancel results in areas where BVAs, servers failed', ICiR, February 27, 2023:

https://www.icirnigeria.org/obasanjo-asks-inec-to-cancel-results-in-areas-were-bvas-servers-failed/.

[110] Ibid.

[111] EU-EOM, Final Report on Nigeria's 2023 general elections: https://www.eeas.europa.eu/eom-nigeria-2023/european-union-election-observation-mission-nigeria-2023-final-report_en, p.6.

[112] Ibid, p.47.

[113] US Bureau of Democracy, Human Rights and Labour, 2023 Country Reports on Human Rights Practices: Nigeria, p.22: https://www.state.gov/reports/2023-country-reports-on-human-rights-practices/nigeria/.

[114] BBC, The Reith Lecture 2019: Jonathan Sumption – Law's Expanding Empire: https://www.youtube.com/watch?v=GhCmCARiXoo

[115] The Economist Intelligence Unit, Democracy Index 2022: https://www.eiu.com/n/campaigns/democracy-index-2022/, p.67.

[116] Ibid, p.56.

[117] Denis Derbyshire and Ian Derbyshire, Political Systems of the World, Chambers, 1993.

[118] British High Commission, Abuja, 'Statement from the British and other embassies at the beginning of 2019 election campaign', published on November 18, 2018: https://www.gov.uk/government/news/statement-on-the-occasion-of-the-beginning-of-2019-election-campaigns.

[119] See 'Corruption in Nigeria: Patterns and Trends,' UNODC/NBS, July 2024: https://www.unodc.org/conig/uploads/documents/3rd_national_corruption_survey_report_2024_07_09.pdf.

[120] Claire Mom, 'Nigerian politicians can buy everybody to get into office, says Achike Udenwa,' The Cable, March 2, 2025: https://www.thecable.ng/nigerian-politicians-can-buy-everybody-to-get-into-office-says-achike-undenwa/.

[121] Brainy Quotes, Tom Stoppard: https://www.brainyquote.com/quotes/tom_stoppard_105453.

[122] Daily Post, 'I helped PDP rig elections – Ibrahim Mantu confesses [Video]': https://dailypost.ng/2018/03/30/helped-pdp-rig-elections-ibrahim-mantu-confesses-video/.

[123] Ibid.

[124] Adeleke Alade, 'I rigged elections under Amaechi – Rivers APC's Okocha, The Punch, October 3, 2024: https://punchng.com/i-rigged-elections-under-amaechi-rivers-apcs-okocha/#. See video here: https://www.youtube.com/watch?v=Xm2bBPfWmUo.

[125] Seye Olumide, Gbenga Salau, et al. '2027: Opposition kicks as Tinubu hails defections, APC endorsement,' The Guardian, May 23, 2025: https://guardian.ng/politics/2027-opposition-kicks-as-tinubu-hails-defections-apc-endorsement/.

[126] Stephen Angbulu, 'Ganduje backs one-party system as three Kebbi senators join APC,' The Punch, May 10, 2025: https://punchng.com/ganduje-backs-one-party-system-as-three-kebbi-senators-join-apc/.

[127] Olu Fasan, 'One-party state: Political parties are just special purpose vehicles in Nigeria,' BusinessDay, May 19, 2025: https://businessday.ng/pro/article/one-party-state-political-parties-are-just-special-purpose-vehicles-in-nigeria/.

[128] Will Hutton, The State We're In, Jonathan Cape, 1995, p.17

[129] Ibid.

[130] Olusegun Aganga, Reclaiming the Jewel of Africa, Practical Inspiration Publishing, 2023, p.7.

Chapter 2: The Restructuring Debate

[1] The core North consists of the following states: Jigawa, Kaduna, Kano, Katsina, Kebbi, Sokoto and Zamfara – they make up the current North-West of Nigeria.

[2] John D. Fage and T. C. McCaskie, 'The Jihad of Usman dan Fodio', Encyclopedia Brittanica, June 28, 2024: https://www.britannica.com/place/western-Africa/The-jihad-of-Usman-dan-Fodio.

[3] Niall Ferguson, Empire, Penguin, 2004, p.239

[4] Chris Brown (ed), Political Restructuring in Europe – Ethical perspectives, Routledge, 1994.

[5] Chinua Achebe, There Was a Country, p.51.

[6] Keating, Michael, State and Nation in the United Kingdom: The Fractured Union (Oxford, 2021; online edn, Oxford Academic, 20 May 2021), https://doi.org/10.1093/oso/9780198841371.001.0001.

[7] Sunday Times, 'Revealed: Our Disunited Kingdom', Sunday Times (London), January 24, 2021.

[8] Ibid.

[9] Alex Massie, 'The UK is, in a quite literal sense, dying', Sunday Times, January 24, 2021: https://www.thetimes.co.uk/article/scottish-independence-attracts-young-voters-who-just-dont-feel-british-ch2k3jpvd.

[10] Financial Times, 'Is the UK heading for break-up?', FT, April 2, 2021: https://www.ft.com/content/ff6c0f6b-2d65-4a4e-bbba-878e2260cf3e.

[11] Gordon Brown, Interview with BBC's political editor, Laura Kuenssberg, January 20, 2020: https://www.bbc.co.uk/news/av/uk-politics-51179863.

[12] John Major, Article in Financial Times, March 26, 2021: https://johnmajorarchive.org.uk/2021/03/26/sir-john-majors-article-in-the-financial-times-26-march-2021/.

[13] Lord Owen, Article in The Times, May 9, 2015: https://www.thetimes.co.uk/article/could-the-way-forward-point-to-a-federal-uk-33z73fkf8fr.

[14] Mark Drakeford, 'Union of UK over', South Wales Argus, March 4, 2021: https://www.southwalesargus.co.uk/news/19137368.mark-drakeford-declares-union-united-kingdom-over/

[15] UK Parliament, 'A new constitutional convention for the UK?', Report: https://publications.parliament.uk/pa/cm201213/cmselect/cmpolcon/371/37105.htm

[16] The UK Prime Minister's website has used the phrase 'countries within a country' to describe the UK. See: https://webarchive.nationalarchives.gov.uk/ukgwa/20080909013512/http://www.number10.gov.uk/Page823

[17] Omoniyi Ibietan, 'API's Nigeria Social Cohesiveness survey: A scary report spiced with hope', Premium Times, October 7, 2022: https://www.premiumtimesng.com/opinion/contributors/558474-apis-nigeria-social-cohesion-survey-a-scary-report-spiced-with-hope-by-omoniyi-ibietan.html?tztc=1.

[18] Muhammadu Buhari, Statement on inclusiveness at a meeting in the US, in 2015: https://www.youtube.com/watch?v=Mm_VEkxyiKw.

[19] Muhammadu Buhari, Interview with Arise News, June 10, 2021: https://www.arise.tv/arise-news-exclusive-interview-with-president-muhammadu-buhari/.

[20] Ibid.

[21] Cletus Ukpong, 'Umar to Buhari: You'll destroy Nigeria with lopsided appointments', Premium Times, May 30, 3020: https://www.premiumtimesng.com/news/headlines/395471-umar-to-buhari-youll-destroy-nigeria-with-lopsided-appointments.html.

[22] Ibid.

[23] For instance, Senator Ali Ndume, a critic of the lopsidedness of President Tinubu's political appointments hailed his appointment of 12 Northerners as chairmen of federal agencies. See Saawua Terzungwe, 'Tinubu's inclusion of 12 northerners in new appointments good omen – Ndume,' Daily Trust, May 24, 2025: https://dailytrust.com/tinubus-inclusion-of-12-northerners-in-new-appointments-good-omen-ndume/.

[24] Olu Fasan, 'Yorubanisation of Tinubu's government: Nigeria's fate is now in Yoruba hands,' Vanguard, November 21, 2024:

[25] Ugboji Egbujo, 'Is Tinubu Settling Scores,' Vanguard, October 26, 2024: https://www.vanguardngr.com/2024/10/is-tinubu-setting-scores/.

[26] Seye Olumide, 'Afenifere chides Tinubu over lopsided federal appointments in favour of Yoruba,' The Guardian, November 2, 2024: https://guardian.ng/news/afenifere-chides-tinubu-over-lopsided-federal-appointments-in-favour-of-yoruba/.

[27] John Campbell and Matthew Page, Nigeria: What Everyone Needs to Know, Oxford University Press, 2018, p.72

[28] Saxone Akhaine, 'Buhari has mismanaged Nigeria's diversity, says Col Abubakar Umar', The Guardian, July 8, 2021: https://guardian.ng/news/buhari-has-mismanaged-nigerias-diversity-says-col-abubakar-umar/.

[29] Ibrahim Babangida, 'A Journey in Service,' Bookcraft, 2025, p.99

[30] Ibid, p.271.

[31] This is revealed in Bisi Akande, My Participations: An Autobiography, Roving Heights Books, 2021.

[32] Muhammed Babangida, 'Transcript of El Rufai's controversial statement about Peter Obi, Tinubu, CAN, 2023 elections', Premium Times, June 8, 2023: https://www.premiumtimesng.com/regional/nwest/603360-transcript-of-el-rufais-controversial-statement-about-peter-obi-tinubu-can-2023-elections.html?tztc=1.
[33] Ibid.
[34] Edwin Clark, 'Open Letter to Obasanjo', BusinessDay, December 29, 2021: https://businessday.ng/news/article/for-the-record-edwin-clarks-open-letter-to-obasanjo/.
[35] Sadik Oyeleke, 'Open letter: I don't hate Niger Delta, Obasanjo replies Clark', Punch, December 28, 2021: https://punchng.com/open-letter-i-dont-hate-niger-delta-obasanjo-replies-clark/.
[36] Ibid.
[37] Ibid
[38] Sam Eyoboka, 'Who owns the oil, Okogie asks', Vanguard, December 32, 2021: https://www.vanguardngr.com/2021/12/who-owns-the-oil-okogie-asks/.
[39] Ibid.
[40] For instance, the attempt by the Tinubu administration to allocate the share of VAT due to states based on 60 per cent derivation formula, as opposed to the existing 20 per cent, was vehemently rejected by the North, which argued it would disadvantage them.
[41] Robert Keohane, After Hegemony: Cooperation and Discord in World Political Economy, Princeton, 1984.
[42] Chris Brown (ed), Political Restructuring in Europe
[43] Escaping the Fragility Trap, p.59.
[44] Ibid.
[45] Blavatnick, 'Anyaaku calls for restructuring of Nigeria', Blavatnick School of Government, Oxford, November 2, 2012: https://www.bsg.ox.ac.uk/news/anyaoku-calls-restructuring-nigeria.
[46] Gbenga Salau and Ijeoma Opara, 'Anyaoku urges return to regional government', The Guardian, October 22, 2015: https://guardian.ng/news/anyaoku-urges-return-to-regional-govt/.
[47] The Nation, 'Anyaoku advocates geo-political zones as federating units', The nation, February 2, 2016:

https://thenationonlineng.net/anyaoku-advocates-geo-political-zones-as-federating-units/.

[48] Emeka Anyaoku, 'Whither Nigeria?: The Need for Restructuring and National Dialogue', Premium Times, March 7, 2021: https://www.premiumtimesng.com/opinion/447386-whither-nigeria-the-need-for-restructuring-and-national-dialogue-by-emeka-anyaoku.html.

[49] Muyiwa Adeyemi and Ayodele Afolabi, 'Anyaoku, Afe Babaloa call for new constitution to save Nigeria', The Guardian, October 22, 2023: https://guardian.ng/news/anyaoku-afe-babalola-call-for-new-constitution-to-save-nigeria/.

[50] Ibid.

[51] Subair Mohammed and Segun Kasali, 'Restructuring: Nigeria has only two options – Anyaoku', Nigerian Tribune: https://tribuneonlineng.com/restructuring-nigeria-has-only-two-options-anyaoku/.

[52] Johnbosco Agbakwuru, 'Anyaoku-led The Patriots meets Tinubu, calls for 'new democratic constitution', Vanguard, August 9, 2024: https://www.vanguardngr.com/2024/08/anyaoku-led-the-patriots-meets-tinubu-calls-for-new-democratic-constitution/.

[53] Kunle Oderemi, 'Anyaoku, other eminent citizens set for three-day constitutional conference,' Nigerian Tribune, July 14, 2025

[54] Emeka Anyaoku, 'Wither Nigeria?', March 7, 2021.

[55] John Campbell and Matthew page, Nigeria: What Everyone Needs to Know, p.86.

[56] Obafemi Awolowo, The Peoples Republic, Oxford University Press, 1968.

[57] Paul Collier, Lef Behind: A New Economics for the Neglected Places, Allen Lane, June 2024.

[58] See The King's Speech 2024, Gov.UK, July 17, 2024: https://www.gov.uk/government/speeches/the-kings-speech-2024.

[59] UNPO, 'Self-determination', The Unrepresented Nations and Peoples Organisation, 2017: https://unpo.org/article/4957.

[60] See, for example, Right of Peoples to Self-determination, UN General Assembly 42/95: https://www.un.org/unispal/document/auto-insert-186526/

[61] Alberto Alesina, 'The size of countries: Does it matters? Jospeh Schumpeter Lecture', Journal of the European Economic Association 1, no2-3: 301-316.

[62] Ibid.

[63] Chinua Achebe, There Was a Country, p.74

[64] Joshua Keating, 'Scotland's independence leader on how Margaret Thatcher helped Scottish nationalism' Foreign Policy Magazine, April 9, 2013: https://foreignpolicy.com/2013/04/09/scotlands-independence-leader-on-how-margaret-thatcher-helped-scottish-nationalism/

[65] Ibid.

[66] Ibid, p.167.

[67] Katy Balls and Michael Gove, 'I will die protecting this country': Kemi Badenoch on where she plans to take the Tories, The Spectator, December 14, 2024: https://www.spectator.co.uk/article/i-will-die-protecting-this-country-kemi-badenoch-on-where-she-plans-to-take-the-tories/.

[68] One of such strident criticisms was an article by the columnist Simon Kolawole titled 'The Kemi Badenoch Complex', published in ThisDay on December 22, 2024: https://www.thisdaylive.com/index.php/2024/12/22/the-kemi-badenoch-complex//

[69] Sam Francis, 'Badenoch stands by Nigeria comments after criticism,' BBC, December 11, 2024: https://www.bbc.co.uk/news/articles/cx2ygwxn9kzo.

[70] Paul Collier, 'From poverty to prosperity', seminar slides with author.

[71] John Naisbitt, Megatrends: Ten New Directions Transforming our Lives, Grand Central Publishers, 1982.

[72] David Pilling, 'Africa's voters are ready for democracy', Financial Times, august 9, 2017: https://www.ft.com/content/8a28ec8a-7ce8-11e7-ab01-a13271d1ee9c.

[73] Olu Fasan, 'Restructuring: Is Nigeria's problem the Constitution or its operators? Vanguard, August 28, 2025.

[74] Premium Times, 'Nigeria at 60: Buhari's Independence Day Speech [Full Text]', October 1, 2020: https://www.premiumtimesng.com/news/top-news/417759-nigeriaat60-buharis-independence-day-speech-full-text.html?tztc=1.

75 Henry Umoru, 'Adesina's Book: Your 8-year rule, unjust, filled with bigotry, nepotism, Clark knocks Buhari', Vanguard, January 18, 2024: https://www.vanguardngr.com/2024/01/adesinas-book-your-8-year-rule-unjust-filled-with-bigotry-nepotism-clark-knocks-buhari/.

76 Ibid.

77 Steve Levitt and Stephen Dubner, Freakonomics: A rogue economist explores the hidden side of everything, Penguin, 2006.

78 Daron Acemoglu and James Robinson, Why Nations Fail: The Origins of power, prosperity and poverty, Profile Books, 2013.

79 Ibrahim Wuyo, 'Those calling for restructuring naïve, dangerous, says Buhari', Vanguard, June 20, 2021: https://www.vanguardngr.com/2021/06/those-calling-for-restructuring-naive-dangerous-says-buhari/.

80 Johnbosco Agbakwuru, 'Restructuring: My problem with South-East — Buhari', Vanguard, January 5, 2022: https://www.vanguardngr.com/2022/01/restructuring-my-problem-with-south-east-buhari/.

81 John Owen Nwachukwu, 'Restructuring: What Buhari told Nigerians in diaspora', Daily Post, November 13, 2018: https://dailypost.ng/2018/11/13/restructuring-buhari-told-nigerians-diaspora/.

82 Keith Richburg, 'French President's Term Cut to Five Years', Washington Post, September 24, 2000: https://www.washingtonpost.com/archive/politics/2000/09/25/french-presidents-term-cut-to-five-years/c988b212-2e37-4e49-818f-7a33862f32f5/.

83 See The King's Speech 2024, Gov.UK, 17 July 2024: https://www.gov.uk/government/speeches/the-kings-speech-2024.

84 Ibid.

85 Ian Macleod MP, 'Nigeria Independence Bill debate', Hansard, July 15, 1960.

86 RW Apple Hr., 'Nigerian Tribal Issue Remains', The New York Times, January 13, 1970: https://www.nytimes.com/1970/01/13/archives/nigerian-tribal-issue-remains-lagos-must-attempt-a-reconciliation.html.

[87] Speech by Major-General Yakubu Gowon Declaring a Twelve State Structure for Nigeria – May 1967, reproduced in Vanguard, September 30, 2019: https://www.vanguardngr.com/2010/09/speech-by-major-general-yakubu-gowon-declaring-a-twelve-state-structure-for-nigeria-may-1967/.

[88] ThisDay, 'Despite NDDC, Senate Approves New Development Commission for South-south Zone,' October 3, 2024: https://www.thisdaylive.com/index.php/2024/10/03/despite-nddc-senate-approves-new-development-commission-for-south-south-zone/.

[89] Ibid.

[90] Waziri Adio, 'On the Proposed Budget and Related Matters,' ThisDay, December 29, 2024: https://www.thisdaylive.com/index.php/2024/12/29/on-the-proposed-budget-and-related-matters/.

[91] Premium Times, 'NDDC has 13,000 doubtful projects despite receiving N6 trillion allocation in 19 years – Malami,' September 2, 2021: https://www.premiumtimesng.com/news/headlines/482638-nddc-has-13000-doubtful-projects-despite-receiving-n6-trillion-allocation-in-19-years-malami.html?tztc=1

[92] BBC, 'NDDC: Buhari order of forensic audit of Niger Delta Development Commission make Nigerians hail,' October 18, 2019: https://www.bbc.com/pidgin/tori-50094359.

[93] Tunji Oyeyemi, 'Buhari Receives Forensic Audit Report of NDDC,' Federal Ministry of Information and National Orientation, Press Release, September 3, 2021: https://fmino.gov.ng/buhari-receives-forensic-audit-report-of-nddc/

[94] EFCC, 'Bawa Charges NDDC, Ministry of Niger Delta on Prudent Use of Government Resources,' EFCC website, September 14, 2022: https://www.efcc.gov.ng/efcc/news-and-information/news-release/8479-bawa-charges-nddc-ministry-of-niger-delta-on-prudent-use-of-government-resources#

[95] World Bank, Enabling Sustained Recovery in the North East Nigeria Project Report, 2021.

[96] Ibid.

[97] Paul Dada, 'Presidency clears air over Niger Delta Ministry,' PM News, October 24, 2024:

https://pmnewsnigeria.com/2024/10/24/presidency-clears-air-over-niger-delta-ministry/.

[98] See The King's Speech 2024, Gov.UK, July 17, 2024: https://www.gov.uk/government/speeches/the-kings-speech-2024.

[99] Matthew Ochei, '10 nations should be created out of Nigeria – Asagba of Asaba', Punch, January 21, 2024: https://punchng.com/10-nations-should-be-created-out-of-nigeria-asagba-of-asaba/.

Chapter 3: The Imperative for a New Political Settlement

[1] BusinessDay, 'Nigeria needs economic restructuring not political restructuring', Editorial, July 31, 2020: https://businessday.ng/editorial/article/nigeria-needs.-economic-not-political-restructuring/.

[2] The Nation, 'Osinbajo: Nigeria needs diversification not restructuring,' News, July 11, 2016: https://thenationonlineng.net/osinbajo-nigeria-needs-diversification-not-restructuring/.

[3] Will Hutton, The State We're In, pgxii.

[4] Daron Acemoglu and James Robinson, Why Nations Fail, Profile Books, 2013.

[5] Douglass North, Institutions, Institutional Change and Economic Performance, Cambridge University Press, 1991.

[6] Will Hutton, The State We're In, Preface.

[7] DfID, The Politics of Poverty: Elites, Citizens and States, Findings from ten years of DfID-funded research on Governance and Fragile States, 2001-2010, A Synthesis Paper, UK Department for International Development, 2010, p.2.

[8] Ibid.

[9] Encyclopaedia Britannica, Federalism, May 8, 2024: https://www.britannica.com/topic/federalism.

[10] Campbell and Page, p.87.

[11] Ibid.

[12] Ibid.

[13] See also, Eric Teniola, 'The supreme powers of the President,' Vanguard, August 27, 2025.

[14] Aganga, p.13.

15 Ibid.

16 See Olusegun Adeniyi, 'The Road to Constitutional Dictatorship,' ThisDay, March 20, 2025: https://www.thisdaylive.com/index.php/2025/03/20/the-road-to-constitutional-dictatorship/.

17 Jemilat Nasiru, 'Rivers' emergency rule against spirit of federalism, says Soyinka,' The Cable, March 23, 2025: https://www.thecable.ng/rivers-emergency-rule-against-spirit-of-federalism-says-soyinka/.

18 Mansur Abubakar, 'Outrage as Nigeria changes national anthem', BBC Africa, May 29, 2024: https://www.bbc.co.uk/news/articles/c3gg7z0n4jxo#.

19 Ahmed Sahabi, 'Gumi to Tinubu: Remove Wike as FCT minister or we won't be on same page', The Cable, October 19, 2023: https://www.thecable.ng/gumi-to-tinubu-remove-wike-as-fct-minister-or-we-wont-be-on-same-page/.

20 Encyclopaedia Britannica, Federalism, May 8, 2024.

21 Charles Tiebout, 'A Pure Theory of Local Expenditures', Journal of Political Economy, Vol 64, No5, 1965.

22 Richard Musgrave, 'Economics of Fiscal Federalism', Nebraska Journal of Economics and Business, Vol.10, No4 (Autumn 1971).

23 The European Union defines the principle of subsidiarity in Article 5(3) of the Treaty on the European Union as ensuring that decisions are taken at the closest possible level to the citizen: https://eur-lex.europa.eu/EN/legal-content/glossary/principle-of-subsidiarity.html.

24 BudgIT, 'Oronsaye Report: What does this mean?', Tweet, February 27, 2024: https://twitter.com/BudgITng/status/1762368468433707284.

25 Ayodele Oluwafemi, 'Tinubu directs full implementation of Oronsaye report to cut size of government', The Cable, February 26, 2024: https://www.thecable.ng/tinubu-directs-full-implementation-of-oronsaye-report-to-cut-size-of-government/

26 Oska Kurer, John Stuart Mill on Democratic Representation and Centralisation, Cambridge University Press, 2009.

27 Gissur Erlingsson and Jorgen Odalen, 'A normative Theory of Local Government: Connecting Individual Autonomy and Local Self-determination with Democracy', Journal of Local Self-Determination, 15(2), April 2017.

[28] Robert Gannett Jr, 'Tocqueville and Local Government: Distinguishing Democracy's Second Track', The Review of Politics, Vol 67, No4 (Autumn 2005).

[29] World Bank, 'Poverty: Overview', Apr 02, 2024: https://www.worldbank.org/en/topic/poverty/overview.

[30] Wikipedia, 'Home Rule in the United States': https://en.wikipedia.org/wiki/Home_rule_in_the_United_State

[31] See 'An introduction to the Localism Act', Local Government Association, https://www.local.gov.uk/introduction-localism-act#

[32] Campbell and Page, p.97.

[33] Ibid.

[34] Clifford, Ndujihe, 'Undemocratic LGAs: 19 states run 433 councils with caretaker committee', Vanguard, May 18, 2024: https://www.vanguardngr.com/2024/05/undemocratic-lgas-19-states-run-433-councils-with-caretaker-committee/.

[35] Ibid.

[36] The Cable, 'Buhari blows hot, accuses governors of misappropriating LG allocations,' December 1, 2022: https://www.thecable.ng/buhari-blows-hot-accuses-governors-of-stealing-lga-allocations/.

[37] Sunday Isuwa, 'Governors Have 'Killed' Local Government System – Senate,' May 15, 2024: https://leadership.ng/governors-have-killed-local-government-system-senate/

[38] Halimah Yahaya, 'Buhari signs Executive Order on financial autonomy for state legislature, judiciary,' Premium Times, May 23, 2020: https://www.premiumtimesng.com/news/headlines/394155-buhari-signs-executive-order-on-financial-autonomy-for-state-legislature-judiciary.html.

[39] Bolanle Olabimtan. 'Supreme court nullifies executive order empowering FG to deduct from state funds,' The Cable, February 11, 2022: https://www.thecable.ng/breaking-scourt-nullifies-executive-order-empowering-fg-to-deduct-from-state-funds/.

[40] QueenEsther Iroanusi, 'https://www.premiumtimesng.com/news/headlines/514547-breaking-senate-passes-bill-to-grant-lg-financial-administrative-autonomy.html,' Premium Times, March 1, 2022:

https://www.premiumtimesng.com/news/headlines/514547-breaking-senate-passes-bill-to-grant-lg-financial-administrative-autonomy.html.

[41] Dyepkazah Shibayan, 'FG sues governors, seeks FULL autonomy for LGs,' The Cable, May 26, 2024: https://www.thecable.ng/fg-sues-governors-seeks-full-autonomy-for-lgs/.

[42] Ikechukwu Nnochiri, 'Supreme Court grants financial autonomy to Local Governments,' Vanguard, July 11, 2024: https://www.vanguardngr.com/2024/07/breaking-supreme-court-grants-financial-autonomy-to-local-governments/.

[43] Ikechukwu Nnochiri, 'Supreme Court grants financial autonomy to Local Governments,' Vanguard, July 11, 2024

[44] Ibid.

[45] See Patrick S. Hodge, 'The scope of judicial law-making in constitutional law and public law,' The Supreme Court UK: https://www.supremecourt.uk/docs/judicial-law-making-in-constitutional-law-and-public-law-paper.pdf.

[46] Owei Lakemfa, 'Supreme Court weakens federalism, strengthens unitary system,' Vanguard, July 15, 2024: https://www.vanguardngr.com/2024/07/supreme-court-weakens-federalism-strengthens-unitary-system-by-owei-lakemfa/amp/.

[47] See David Feldman, 'English Public Law, Oxford University Press, 2004, p437.

[48] John Akubo, 'Senate condemns flawed LG elections across Nigeria,' The Guardian, October 10, 2024: https://guardian.ng/news/senate-condemns-flawed-lg-elections-across-nigeria/.

[49] See Mohammadu Lawal Uwais, CJN, 'Attorney-General of Lagos State vs Attorney-General of the Federation, Supreme Court Judgement, December 10, 2004: http://www.nigeria-law.org/LawReporting/2004/.

[50] Saawua Terzungwe, 'LG autonomy: Senate to amend constitution to institutionalise S/Court judgement,' Daily Trust, October 10, 2024: https://dailytrust.com/lg-autonomy-senate-to-amend-constitution-to-institutionalise-s-court-judgement/.

[51] Ismael Uthman and Olufemi Adediran, 'S'Court's judgment fails to seal LG autonomy seven months after verdict,' The Punch, February 23, 2025: https://punchng.com/scourts-

judgment-fails-to-seal-lg-autonomy-seven-months-after-
verdict/.

[52] Abiodun Nejo, 'Nobody can revisit Supreme Court ruling
on LG Autonomy — AGF,' Punch, October 22, 2024:
https://punchng.com/nobody-can-revisit-supreme-court-ruling-
on-lg-autonomy-agf/.

[53] Ibid.

[54] Abiodun Nejo, 'Nobody can revisit Supreme Court ruling
on LG Autonomy — AGF,' Punch, October 22, 2024:
https://punchng.com/nobody-can-revisit-supreme-court-ruling-
on-lg-autonomy-agf/.

[55] 'Laolu Afolabi and Deborah Musa, 'LG autonomy: FG
threatens contempt suit against errant govs,' December 13,
2024: https://punchng.com/lg-autonomy-fg-threatens-
contempt-suit-against-errant-govs/.

[56] Ibid.

[57] See OECD, Competitive Regional Cluster – National Policy
Approach, OECD Review of Regional Innovation, 2007.

[58] Gilles Duranton and William R Kerr, 'The Logic of
Agglomeration,' Working Paper 16-037, Harvard Business
School, 2015.

[59] Dirisu Yakubu, 'Tinubu gets bill on regional government
next week', The Punch, June 8, 2024:
https://punchng.com/tinubu-gets-bill-on-regional-govt-next-
week/.

[60] Ben Ezeamalu, 'Nigeria: Is the north afraid of regional
restructuring?' The Africa Report, June 11, 2024:
https://www.theafricareport.com/351426/nigeria-is-the-north-
afraid-of-regional-restructuring/.

[61] See, for instance, Agency Report, 'Agbakoba seeks return to
regional govt, faults agitation for new states,' Punch, July 14,
2024: https://punchng.com/agbakoba-seeks-return-to-regional-
govt-faults-agitation-for-new-states/.

[62] See 'Regionalism, parliamentary system not solutions for
Nigeria – Emir of Kano, Sanusi,' Vanguard, June 14, 2024:
https://www.vanguardngr.com/2024/06/regionalism-
parliamentary-system-not-solutions-for-nigeria-emir-of-kano-
sanusi/.

[63] Muyiwa Adeyemi and Sodiq Omolaoye, 'Lawmakers push
for 31 new states amid N11.47tr debt by existing ones,' The
Guardian, February 7, 2025:

https://guardian.ng/news/lawmakers-push-for-31-new-states-amid-n11-47tr-debt-by-existing-ones/.

64 Ibid.

65 Chris Moffat, 'House of Reps Committee Rejects 31 States Creation Proposal,' Channels TV, February 21, 2025: https://www.channelstv.com/2025/02/21/house-of-reps-committee-rejects-31-states-creation-proposal/.

66 Bernd Hayo and Stefan Voigt, 'Determinants of Constitutional change: Why do countries change their form of government?', Journal of Comparative Economics, Vol 38, Issue 3, September 2010, pp 283-305.

67 Ibid.

68 Ibrahim Babangida, 'A Journey in Service', Bookcraft, 2025, p.122.

69 Chris Akor, 'Parliamentarism can offer Nigeria an escape from bad government and weak institutions (1)', BusinessDay, September 24, 2020: https://businessday.ng/columnist/article/parliamentarism-can-offer-nigeria-an-escape-from-bad-governance-and-weak-institutions-1/.

70 Olu Fasan, 'Okonjo-Iweala's reflections on the challenges of fighting corruption in Nigeria', Africa at LSE blog, May 30, 2018: https://blogs.lse.ac.uk/africaatlse/2018/05/30/okonjo-iwealas-reflections-on-the-challenges-of-fighting-corruption-in-nigeria/.

71 Aganga, p.32

72 Ibid, p.168

73 OECD, Trust in Government survey, 2022: https://data.oecd.org/gga/trust-in-government.htm.

74 Richard McManus and Gulcin Ozkan, 'Who does better for the economy? Presidents versus Parliamentary Democracies', Discussion Papers in Economics, University of York, No17/03, February 22, 2017.

75 Ibid.

76 Bakare Majeed, '60 Nigerian lawmakers want presidential system abolished, transition to parliamentary system', Premium Times, February 14, 2024: https://www.premiumtimesng.com/news/top-news/668409-breaking-60-nigerian-lawmakers-want-presidential-system-abolished-transition-to-parliamentary-system.html?tztc=1.

[77] Arise News, 'Ooni of Ife, Bishop Onaiyekan Add Voices to Calls for Nigeria's Return To Parliamentary System', Arise News, March 10, 2024: https://www.arise.tv/ooni-of-ife-bishop-onaiyekan-add-voices-to-calls-for-nigerias-return-to-parliamentary-system/

[78] Vanguard, 'Regionalism, parliamentary system not solutions for Nigeria – Emir of Kano, Sanusi,' News, June 14, 2024: https://www.vanguardngr.com/2024/06/regionalism-parliamentary-system-not-solutions-for-nigeria-emir-of-kano-sanusi/.

[79] Mumini Abdulkareem, 'Shettima, Fashola fault call for parliamentary system,' Daily Trust, June 2, 2024: https://dailytrust.com/shettima-fashola-fault-call-for-parliamentary-system/.

[80] Ibid.

[81] Olu Fasan, 'Emir Sanusi's misguided intervention on regionalism, parliamentary system,' BusinessDay, July 1, 2024: https://businessday.ng/opinion/article/emir-sanusis-misguided-intervention-on-regionalism-parliamentary-system/.

[82] EU-EOM, Final report on Nigeria's 2023 general elections.

[83] Uwais Report: Report of the Electoral Reform Committee, Vol 1, Main Report, December 2008, p.5.

[84] Ibid.

[85] Chinagorom Ugwu, 'Jega asks Tinubu to review appointment of partisan individuals as INEC officials', Premium Times, November 28, 2023: https://www.premiumtimesng.com/news/top-news/647102-jega-asks-tinubu-to-review-appointment-of-partisan-individuals-as-inec-officials.html?tztc=1.

[86] Uwais Report, p25.

[87] Ibid, p63.

[88] Ibid, p144.

[89] Ibid, p.116

[90] EU-EOM, Final report on Nigeria's 2023 general elections, p.12.

[91] Colins Okeke, 'Post-2023: How to improve Nigeria's Electoral Processes and Institutions Using the Uwais Committee Report', Olisa Agbakoba Law (OAL) publication, May 3, 2023: https://oal.law/post-2023-how-to-improve-

nigerias-electoral-processes-and-institutions-using-the-uwais-committee-report/.

[92] Ibid.

[93] Uwais Report, p.25

[94] Ibid, p.55.

[95] For instance, in the 2023 presidential election, Atiku Abubakar, a former vice-president, attempted to succeed President Buhari, a fellow Northerner, after his eighth years in power. But he faced resisted from the South, which insisted on power shift, and he lost the election.

[96] Taiwo Amodu, 'Tinubu is an emperor, will be difficult to dislodge in 2027 — Sule Lamido,' Nigerian Tribune, August 31, 2024: https://tribuneonlineng.com/tinubu-has-become-an-emperor-that-will-be-difficult-to-dislodge-in-2027-ex-jigawa-gov-sule-lamido/.

[97] '2023: Full text of Pius Anyim's speech on Igbos political interest', Vanguard, December 21, 2020: https://www.vanguardngr.com/2020/12/2023-full-text-of-pius-anyims-speech-on-igbos-political-interest/

[98] Daily Trust, '2023 Presidency - No Need for Zoning, Mamman Daura Says', July 29, 2020: https://allafrica.com/stories/202007290206.html.

[99] Escaping the fragility trap, p.69

[100] According to one academic study, there are eight key characteristics of a representative democracy, namely: universal participation, political equality, political competition and choice, political accountability, transparency in government, majority rule, civil liberties/equality of opportunity, and rule of law. Details available here: https://quizlet.com/89824486/key-characteristics-of-representative-democracy-flash-cards/.

[101] Olusegun Aganga, Reclaiming the Jewel of Africa, Practical Inspiration Publishing, 2023, p.7

[102] See https://data.worldbank.org/indicator/eg.elc.accs.zs

[103] See https://data.unicef.org/country/nga/.

[104] Ngozi Okonjo-Iweala (2018) "Fighting Corruption Is Dangerous", The MIT Press, at page 54.

[105] John Campbell and Matthew Page, ' Nigeria: What everyone needs to know, Oxford University Press, 2018, p.106.

[106] See Press freedom in Nigeria: The spiral of repression continues in 2024, Media Foundation for West Africa, April 10, 2024: https://mfwa.org/press-freedom-in-nigeria-the-spiral-of-repression-continues-in-2024/.

[107] Olu Fasan, 'Fight for a free press in Nigeria, it's the bulwark against bad government,' BusinessDay, August 9, 2021: https://businessday.ng/columnist/article/fight-for-a-free-press-in-nigeria-its-the-bulwark-against-bad-government/.

[108] Olusola Oludiran, 'One year after: How the media, press freedom fared under President Tinubu,' Nigeria Democratic Report, May 29, 2024: https://www.ndr.org.ng/one-year-after-how-the-media-press-freedom-fared-under-president-tinubu/.

[109] Nigerian Guild of Editors, Press Statement, November 14, 2024: https://ngeditors.org.ng/press-statement/.

[110] Financial Times, 'The UK should not treat journalists like spies,' The FT View, July 28, 2021: https://www.ft.com/content/35d86be0-1327-474e-b184-6067d28dd8b4.

[111] Martin Bright, Letters to the Editor, The Times, August 15, 2021: https://www.thetimes.com/uk/healthcare/article/times-letters.

[112] John Ademola Yakubu, 'Trends in Constitution-making in Nigeria', Transnational Law and Contemporary Problems, 423, 2000.

[113] Ibrahim Babangida, A Journey in Service, Bookcraft, 2025, p.256.

[114] Ibid. p.258.

[115] Campbell and Page, p.87.

[116] Ibid.

[117] Will Hutton, The State We're In, p.288.

[118] John Campbell and Matthew Page, Nigeria: What Everyone needs to Know, p86

[119] Olusegun Aganga, Reclaiming the Jewel of Africa, p7

[120] Abraham Ogbodo, 'Back again to the unending search,' Nigerian Tribune, January 10, 2025: https://tribuneonlineng.com/back-again-to-the-unending-search/.

[121] Agency Report, 'NASS has no power to give Nigeria new constitution — Omo-Agege', Premium Times, December 2, 2020: https://www.premiumtimesng.com/news/top-

news/429146-nass-has-no-power-to-give-nigeria-new-constitution-omo-agege.html.

[122] Nigerian Tribune, 'It is too late to push for a new Constitution, says Senator Bamidele', News report, June 4, 2021: https://tribuneonlineng.com/it-is-too-late-to-push-for-a-new-constitution-says-senator-bamidele/.

[123] Sunday Aborisade, 'Forcing NASS to produce new constitution, invitation to anarchy –Senate', Punch, June 5, 2021: https://punchng.com/forcing-nass-to-produce-new-constitution-invitation-to-anarchy-senate/.

[124] Olusola Oludiran, 'How Olisa Agbakoba, SAN, spoke truth to power in an audacious manner', Nigeria Democratic Report, December 17, 2023: https://www.ndr.org.ng/how-olisa-agbakoba-san-spoke-truth-to-power-in-an-audacious-manner/

[125] Escaping the fragility trap, p.57.

Chapter 4: Nigeria's Economic History

[1] Hume, Political Essays, Of the Jealousy of Trade (Chapter 8), Cambridge University Press, 1994, p.329: https://davidhume.org/texts/empl2/jt.

[2] Ibid, p.330.

[3] Okonjo-Iweala, reforming the Unreformable, p.3.

[4] Ibid, see also note 2 of Chapter 1 for a definition of Dutch Disease.

[5] BBC, 'Africa Debate: Will Africa ever benefit from its natural resources?', BBC News, October 15, 2012: https://www.bbc.co.uk/news/world-africa-19926886.

[6] Collins Olayinka, 'At 80 Gowon Explains – "Nigeria's Problem Is Not Money, but How to Spend It"', The Guardian, October 19, 2014: https://allafrica.com/stories/201410202349.html.

[7] David Landes, The Wealth and Poverty of Nations, Abacus, 1998, p499.

[8] Olusegun Aganga, Reclaiming the Jewel of Africa, Practical Inspiration, 2023, p.166.

[9] Wole Oyebade, '17 FG airports not viable, may shut down over losses', The Guardian, May 11, 2020: https://guardian.ng/news/17-fg-airports-not-viable-may-shut-down-over-losses/

[10] Abimbola Adelakun, '15 useless airports and Nigeria's concrete democracy', Punch, November 9, 2023: https://punchng.com/15-useless-airports-and-nigerias-concrete-democracy/

[11] Jeffrey Herbst and Adebayo Olukoshi. 'Nigeria: Economic and Political Reforms at Cross Purposes' in Stephen Haggard and Steven Webb (eds) Voting for Reforms, Oxford University Press, 1999, pp467-471.

[12] Ibrahim Babangida, A Journey in Service, Bookcraft, 2025, p.154.

[13] Ibid.

[14] Ibid. p.164.

[15] Lolade Akinmurele, 'Inside IBB's controversial economic reforms,' BusinessDay, February 21, 2025: https://businessday.ng/pro/article/inside-ibbs-controversial-economic-reforms/.

[16] BusinessDay, 'The Babangida Confession,' The Editorial Board, March 3, 2025: https://businessday.ng/editorial/article/the-babangida-confession/.

[17] US Department of State, 1996 Country Reports: On Economic Policy and Trade Practices, January 20, 2021: https://1997-2001.state.gov/issues/economic/trade_reports/africa96/nigeria96.html.

[18] The Gurdian newspaper, Nigeria, December 18, 2003.

[19] Olu Fasan, 'Nigeria's Import Restrictions: A Bad Policy That Harms Trade Relations', Africa at LSE blog, August 17, 2015: https://blogs.lse.ac.uk/africaatlse/2015/08/17/nigerias-import-restrictions-a-bad-policy-that-harms-trade-relations/.

[20] See 'What you need to know about CBN's lifting of Forex restrictions on 43 items,' CBN's Corporate Communications Department, 13 October 2023: https://www.cbn.gov.ng/Out/2023/CCD/FAQ%20on%20Removal%20of%20FOREX%20Restriction%20-%2043%20Items.pdf. ON 43 ITEMS

[21] Charles Soludo, 'Avoiding the Mistakes of the Old Buharinomics', Special Report, Vanguard, November 21, 2015: https://www.vanguardngr.com/2015/11/avoiding-the-mistakes-of-the-old-buharinomics/.

22 Samuel Akpan, 'President now mandated to name cabinet within 60 days as Buhari signs amended bills into law', The Cable, March 17, 2023: https://www.thecable.ng/president-now-mandated-to-name-cabinet-within-60-days-as-buhari-signs-amended-bills-into-law/.

23 Benjamin Cohen, 'The triad and the Unholy Trinity: Problems of International Monetary Cooperation', in Jeffrey Frieden and David Lake, International Political Economy: Perspectives on global power and wealth, Routledge, 2000, p.245.

24 K Akintoye, 'Buhari Rejects Devaluation, Says "I Won't Kill The Naira"', Channels TV, January 26, 2016: https://www.channelstv.com/2016/01/28/buhari-rejects-devaluation-says-i-wont-kill-the-naira/.

25 Niran Adedokun, 'The personal change that Buhari needs', The Cable, June 2, 2016: https://www.thecable.ng/personal-change-buhari-needs/.

26Muhammed Sagagi, 'What We Told President Buhari: Reflections On The Work Of The Presidential Economic Advisory Council (PEAC) (I)', Daily Trust, December 27, 2023: https://dailytrust.com/what-we-told-president-buhari-reflections-on-the-work-of-the-presidential-economic-advisory-council-peac-i/.

27 President Buhari's Budget Statement to the National Assembly, December 14, 2016.

28 Ibid.

29 The Economist said: 'The hit list appears to have been drawn up by someone wandering around a home and a building site and randomly pointing at item'. See Toothpick Alert: https://www.economist.com/middle-east-and-africa/2015/07/04/toothpick-alert.

30 Okechukwu Enelamah, Interview with BBC HARDtalk programme, October 8, 2016: https://www.bbc.co.uk/programmes/b07xy26k.

31 The research and analysis were undertaken by Lolade Akinmuerele, Wasiu Alli and Eniola Olatunji, See, 'Three Charts show Nigeria is not import-dependent', BusinessDay, January 15, 2024: https://businessday.ng/news/article/three-charts-show-nigeria-is-not-import-dependent/.

32 World Bank, 'Trade Statistics by Country/Region': https://wits.worldbank.org/countrystats.aspx?lang=en.

[33] World Bank, 'Trade Flows', https://wits.worldbank.org/CountryProfile/en/Country/WLD/Year/2015/TradeFlow/EXPIMP/Partner/by-country.

[34] WTO, Trade Policy review of Nigeria, Report By the Secretariat, October 9, 2024: https://www.wto.org/english/tratop_e/tpr_e/s462_e.pdf.

[35] Encyclopedia Britanica, 'price-specie-flow adjustment mechanism,' https://www.britannica.com/topic/price-specie-flow-adjustment-mechanism.

[36] According to the Nigerian Economic Summit Group (NESG), foreign investment flows fell by 26.7% to $3.9bn in 2023 from $5.3bn in 2022. There was a mass exodus of foreign-owned firms, such as GlaxoSmithKline and Unilever, from Nigeria.

[37] Chinwe Michael and Folake Balogun, '70 firms exited Nigeria in 7 years on FX, power,' BusinessDay, November 4, 2024: https://businessday.ng/pro/article/70-firms-exited-nigeria-in-7-years-on-fx-power/.

[38] Kingsley Nwezeh, 'Ribadu: Buhari's Administration Bankrupted Nigeria', ThisDay, November 14, 2023: https://www.thisdaylive.com/index.php/2023/11/14/ribadu-buharis-administration-bankrupted-nigeria.

[39] Johnbosco Agbakwuru, 'Tinubu inherited dead economy: Presidency tackles New York Times,' Vanguard, June 17, 2024: https://www.vanguardngr.com/2024/06/tinubu-inherited-dead-economy-presidency-tackles-new-york-times/.

[40] David Pilling and Aanu Adeoye, 'Will shock therapy revive Nigeria's economy — or sink it further?' Financial Times, July 10, 2024: https://www.ft.com/content/137058b2-d48a-4adf-91f1-e25494350e6e.

[41] WTO, Trade Policy review of Nigeria, Report By the Secretariat, October 9, 2024: https://www.wto.org/english/tratop_e/tpr_e/s462_e.pdf.

[42] Okonjo-Iweala, Fighting Corruption is Dangerous, p.27

[43] John Canpbell and Matthew Page, Nogeria: What everyone needs to know, Oxford, 2019, p.53.

[44] Ibid.

[45] Bola Tinubu, 'Removal of Oil Subsidy: President Jonathan breaks social contract with the people', PM News, January 11, 2012: https://pmnewsnigeria.com/2012/01/11/removal-of-oil-

subsidy-president-jonathan-breaks-social-contract-with-the-people/.

[46] Ibid.

[47] Ibid.

[48] Ibid.

[49] Ayoola Babalola, 'Fayemi apologises to Jonathan, says political interest fuelled subsidy protest in 2012', Peoples Gazette, September 5, 2023: 231.
https://gazettengr.com/fayemi-apologises-to-jonathan-says-political-interest-fueled-subsidy-protest-in-2012/.

[50] Terhemba Daka, 'I delayed removal of petrol subsidy for Tinubu, APC to win election', The Guardian, June 27, 2023: https://guardian.ng/news/i-delayed-removal-of-petrol-subsidy-for-tinubu-apc-to-win-election-says-buhari/.

[51] Ibid.

[52] Taiwo Oyedele and Ayo Akinduyile, 'Fuel subsidy in Nigeria – Issues, challenges and the way forward', PwC Nigeria, May 2023:
https://www.pwc.com/ng/en/publications/fuel-subsidy-in-nigeria-issues-challenges-and-the-way-forward.html.

[53] Peter Uzoho, 'Nigeria Imports Refined Petroleum Products Worth $28bn Yearly, Says Energy Consultant', ThisDay, May 24, 2022:
https://www.thisdaylive.com/index.php/2022/05/24/nigeria-imports-refined-petroleum-products-worth-28bn-yearly-says-energy-consultant.

[54] Faith Esifiho, '150,000 bpd Port Harcourt Refinery Complex to begin mid-2025,' BusinessDay, November 26, 2024: https://businessday.ng/news/article/150000-bpd-port-harcourt-refinery-complex-to-begin-mid-2025/.

[55] Mary Izuaka, 'Warri Refinery begins operation, says NNPC,' Premium Times, December 30, 2024:
https://www.premiumtimesng.com/news/top-news/764346-warri-refinery-begins-operation-says-nnpc.html.

[56] Dare Olawin, 'NNPCL slams Rivers community leader, insists Port Harcourt refinery operational,' The Punch, November 29, 2024: https://punchng.com/nnpcl-slams-rivers-community-leader-insists-port-harcourt-refinery-operational/.

[57] Ibid.

[58] Abubakar Ibrahim, 'Is Port Harcourt refinery a blending plant?,' BusinessDay, November 27, 2024: https://businessday.ng/pro/article/explainer-is-port-harcourt-refinery-the-same-as-blending-plant/.

[59] Victor AhiumaYoung, 'Blending at Port Harcourt Refinery is no crime – NNPC,' Vanguard, December 5, 2024: https://www.vanguardngr.com/2024/12/blending-at-port-harcourt-refinery-is-no-crime-nnpc/#.

[60] News report, 'NNPC invites Obasanjo to inspect refineries amid controversy over $2bn expenditure, Vanguard, January 2, 2024: https://www.vanguardngr.com/2025/01/nnpc-invites-obasanjo-to-inspect-refineries-amid-controversy-over-2bn-expenditure/.

[61] Ibid.

[62] Adekunle Agbetiloye, 'Nigeria's NNPC considers refinery sale despite billions spent on repairs,' Business Insider Africa, July 12, 2025.

[63] ThisDay, 'Refineries and the option to sell,' Editorial, July 20, 2025.

[64] See Tinubu's presidential election manifesto, 'Renewed Hope,' at p.37.

[65] Ibid.

[66] Dare Olawin, 'Dangote refinery to supply 25 million litres of petrol daily,' Punch, September 3, 2024: https://punchng.com/dangote-refinery-to-supply-25-million-litres-of-petrol-in-september/#.

[67] Arise News, 'Dangote: Our Refinery Will Eliminate All Petrol Queues in Nigeria,' September 3, 2024: https://www.arise.tv/dangote-our-refinery-will-eliminate-all-petrol-queues-in-nigeria/#

[68] BusinessDay, 'Dangote refinery attains peak PMS production of 33m litres a day,' News, February 6, 2025: https://businessday.ng/news/article/dangote-refinery-attains-peak-pms-production-of-33m-litres-a-day/?amp.

[69] Oladehinde Oladipo, 'Explainer: Separating fact from fiction in NMDPRA's claims against Dangote refinery,' BusinessDay, July 19, 2024: https://businessday.ng/energy/oilandgas/article/explainer-separating-fact-from-fiction-in-nmdpras-claims-against-dangote-refinery/.

[70] Aanu Adeoye, 'Nigeria's Dangote refinery embroiled in billionaire's feud with government,' Financial Times, July 30, 2024: https://www.ft.com/content/290d6195-5f46-4548-944c-107d49e3f07d.

[71] See Bayo Onanuga, 'Breaking: President Tinubu offers lifeline to Dangote Refinery, NNPC to sell crude to it in Naira,' X (formerly Twitter): https://x.com/aonanuga1956/status/1817936972867866818.

[72] Isaac Anyaogu, 'Nigeria's local currency crude sales fall short of target, Dangote refinery says,' Rueters, November 22, 2024: https://www.reuters.com/business/energy/nigerias-local-currency-crude-sales-fall-short-target-dangote-refinery-says-2024-11-22/#.

[73] Emmanuel Addeh, 'Dangote Refinery Imports One-third of Its Crude Supply from US,' ThisDay, June 9, 2025: https://www.thisdaylive.com/2025/06/09/dangote-refinery-imports-one-third-of-its-crude-supply-from-us/#.

[74] Dare Olawin and Damilola Aina, 'Dangote blames crude shortage as imports from US surge,' The Punch, June 20, 2025: https://punchng.com/dangote-blames-crude-shortage-as-imports-from-us-surge/

[75] See Full text of President Bola Tinubu's speech at the 2025 budget presentation to the joint National Assembly, BusinessDay, December 18, 2024: https://businessday.ng/opinion/article/full-text-of-the-president-bola-tinubus-speech-at-the-2025-budget-presentation-to-the-joint-national-assembly/.

[76] Gift ChapiOdekina, 'Reps probe IOCs over alleged sabotage of Dangote refinery,' Vanguard, July 18, 2024: https://www.vanguardngr.com/2024/07/reps-probe-iocs-over-alleged-sabotage-of-dangote-refinery/.

[77] Daily Trust, 'Nigerians: Our hopes dashed over Dangote fuel price', September 20, 2024: https://dailytrust.com/nigerians-our-hopes-dashed-over-dangote-fuel-price/#.

[78] Dare Olawin, 'Dangote price slash: Marketers with imported fuel fear losses,' The Punch, February 7, 2025: https://punchng.com/dangote-price-slash-marketers-with-imported-fuel-fear-losses/.

[79] ThisDay, 'Dangote, NNPC petrol price war thickens amid concerns, Business News, March 9, 2025:

https://www.thisdaylive.com/index.php/2025/03/09/dangote-nnpc-petrol-price/.

80 Okonjo-Iweala, Fighting Corruption is Dangerous, pp27-54.

81 Ibid, p54.

82 Ibid, p.39.

83 Ibid.

84 FocusNGR, 'Subsidy: "My Friend Got Tired of Making Money from Fuel Subsidy" -Former Governor Reveals', FocusNGR News, June 27, 2023: https://focusngr.wordpress.com/2023/06/27/subsidy-my-friend-got-tired-of-making-money-from-fuel-subsidy-former-governor-reveals/.

85 Wale Igbintade, 'Nigeria Lost $450m to Petrol Subsidy Fraud in Six Years, Bawa Reveals in His Book,' ThisDay, June 8, 2025: https://www.thisdaylive.com/2025/06/08/nigeria-lost-450m-to-petrol-subsidy-fraud-in-six-years-bawa-reveals-in-his-book/.

86 Simon Kolawole, 'Sleaze in the season of subsidy,' ThisDay, June 8, 2025: https://www.thisdaylive.com/2025/06/08/sleaze-in-the-season-of-subsidy/.

87 IMF, 'Transcript of African Department April 2024 Press Briefing', April 19, 2024: https://www.imf.org/en/News/Articles/2024/04/19/tr041924-transcript-of-afr-presser.

88 Aanu Adeoye, 'Nigeria's economic crisis puts fuel subsidies removal under scrutiny', Financial Times, February 26, 2024: https://www.ft.com/content/29752a06-adea-4175-b278-22e0632c375a.

89 BBC Africa, 'How FG plan to share N50,000 to help 100,000 homes for states across Nigeria?', June 28, 2024: https://www.bbc.com/pidgin/articles/cw0y57jnd8wo.

90 Abubakar Ibrahim, 'Petrol subsidy nears N1trn monthly, bigger than when Tinubu came', BusinessDay, February 16, 2024: https://businessday.ng/energy/oilandgas/article/petrol-subsidy-nears-n1trn-monthly-bigger-than-when-tinubu-came/.

91 Bunmi Aduloju, 'El-Rufai: FG paying more money on petrol subsidy than before', The Cable, April 15, 2024: https://www.thecable.ng/el-rufai-fg-paying-more-money-on-petrol-subsidy-than-before/

[92] Aanu Adeoye, 'Nigeria's economic crisis puts fuel subsidies removal under scrutiny', Financial Times, February 26, 2024: https://www.ft.com/content/29752a06-adea-4175-b278-22e0632c375a.
[93] See IMF (2024), IMF Country Report No. 24/102, p. 5
[94] Ibid. See also WTO (2024), Trade Policy Review (Nigeria) – Report by the Secretariat, p. 20, October 9, 2024: https://www.wto.org/english/tratop_e/tpr_e/s462_e.pdf.
[95] The Economist: https://www.economist.com/middle-east-and-africa/2019/05/30/muhammadu-buhari-has-big-ambitions-for-nigerian-manufacturing.
[96] Aanu Adeoye and Joseph Cotterill, 'Bet on Nigerian recovery draws investors seeking to dodge trade wars, Financial Times, March 18, 2025: https://www.ft.com/content/5b5a4a67-cc17-419e-96d6-4f7ba7c3be7d.
[97] Olayemi Cardoso, 'Depleted foreign reserves used to settle debts, not defend Naira', Vanguard, April 17, 2024: https://www.vanguardngr.com/2024/04/depleted-foreign-reserves-used-to-settle-debts-not-defend-naira-cardoso/.
[98] Ogaga Ariemu, 'CBN spent $8bn on Naira defence against dollar at FX market – Rewane,' Daily Post, February 23, 2025: https://dailypost.ng/2025/02/23/cbn-spent-8bn-on-naira-defence-against-dollar-at-fx-market-rewane/.
[99] Busola Aro, 'CBN sells FX to BDCs at N1,251/$', The Cable, March 25, 2024: https://www.thecable.ng/cbn-sells-fx-to-bdcs-at-n1251/.
[100] See Nigeria's 2024 Article IV Consultation report, published in May 2024: https://www.imf.org/en/Publications/CR/Issues/2024/05/08/Nigeria-2024-Article-IV-Consultation-Press-Release-Staff-Report-Staff-Statement-and-548726.
[101] Josephine Okojie, 'Rising costs push manufacturing exports down 62% in 4yrs', BusinessDay, April 8, 2024: https://businessday.ng/real-sector/article/rising-costs-push-manufacturing-exports-down-62-in-4yrs/.
[102] Aanu Adeoye and Madeline Speed, 'Currency crisis pushes consumer groups from Nigeria,' Financial Times, April 14, 2024: https://www.ft.com/content/a4f91e34-bd11-408d-989c-e56ecd3b0fc7.

[103] Tunde Oso, 'Economic Crisis: Huge job losses as 16 multinationals exit Nigeria in 3 years,' Vanguard, July 7, 2024: https://www.vanguardngr.com/2024/07/economic-crisis-huge-job-losses-as-16-multinationals-exit-nigeria-in-3-years/.

[104] Ibid.

[105] Babajide Komolafe, Godwin Oritse and Gabriel Ewepu, 'Why exporters are struggling — Investigation,' Vanguard, November 4, 2024: https://www.vanguardngr.com/2024/11/why-exporters-are-struggling-investigation/#.

[106] Ibid.

[107] WTO (2024), Trade Policy Review (Nigeria) – Report by the Secretariat, p. 17, October 9, 2024: https://www.wto.org/english/tratop_e/tpr_e/s462_e.pdf.

[108] Ibid. See also Chijioke Ohuocha, 'Nigeria Central Bank sets limits on oil firms' FX transfer from crude, Reuters, February 15, 2024: https://www.reuters.com/world/africa/nigeria-central-bank-sets-limits-oil-firms-fx-transfers-crude-2024-02-15/#.

[109] See Nigeria's 2024 Article IV Consultation report, published in May 2024: https://www.imf.org/en/Publications/CR/Issues/2024/05/08/Nigeria-2024-Article-IV-Consultation-Press-Release-Staff-Report-Staff-Statement-and-548726.

[110] Ibid.

[111] Okonjo-Iweala, Reforming the Unreformable, p.20

[112] Ibid.

[113] Aganga, p.166.

[114] The Economist, 'Nigeria's high-cost oil industry in decline', March 23, 2024: https://www.economist.com/middle-east-and-africa/2024/03/21/nigerias-high-cost-oil-industry-is-in-decline

[115] Zainab Usman, 'Africa's petrostates are missing out on the oil boom – and it matters', Financial Times, August 20, 2024.

[116] Aanu Adeoye, 'African countries seek $5bn for new fossil fuel project lender,' Financial Times, October 13, 2024: https://www.ft.com/content/4dee2177-053b-48d0-8210-2e58e2f61809.

[117] WTO (2024), Trade Policy Review (Nigeria) – Report by the Secretariat, p. 84, October 9, 2024: https://www.wto.org/english/tratop_e/tpr_e/s462_e.pdf.

[118] Ibid. See also Nigeria Extractive Industries Transparency Initiative (NEITI), NEITI 2021 Audit Report: https://neiti.gov.ng/cms/wp-content/uploads/2024/04/2021-Simplified-OIL-GAS-REPORT.pdf.

[119] The FT View, 'Shock therapy alone will not cure Nigeria's economic ills,' Financial Times, July 17, 2024.

[120] 'Lunch with the FT: Tony Elumelu,' Financial Times, August 10 and 11, 2024.

[121] Ijeoma Nwogwugwu, 'Will Kyari Address the Elephant in the Room?', ThisDay, May 9, 2024: 258.
https://content.thisdaylive.com/index.php/2020/03/16/will-kyari-address-the-elephant-in-the-room/.

[122] Ibid.

[123] Oladehinde Oladipo, 'Nigeria is world's second most expensive country to produce oil', BusinessDay, February 26, 2024: 260.   https://businessday.ng/energy/article/nigeria-is-worlds-second-most-expensive-country-to-produce-oil/.

[124] John Campbell and Matthew Page, Nigeria: What Everyone Needs to Know, Oxford University Press, 2018, p61.

[125] Zainab Usman, 'Africa's petrostates are missing out on the oil boom – and it matters', Financial Times, August 20, 2024.

[126] Holly Ellyatt, 'Global oil demand to peak around 2040 or "much sooner", IMF says', CNBC, February 6, 2020: https://www.cnbc.com/2020/02/06/global-oil-demand-to-peak-around-2040-imf-says.html.

[127] Ibid.

[128] See BP Energy Outlook 2023 Edition (BP, 2023).

[129] Ed Conway, Material World: A Substantial Story of our Past and Future, Penguin, 2023, p.342.

[130] Ibid.

[131] Simon Kuper, 'Will China win the clean-energy era?' FT Magazine, November 21 2024: https://www.ft.com/content/525e557d-d571-4581-a0da-5db860a33513.

[132] See Nigeria's 2024 Article IV Consultation report, published in May 2024: https://www.imf.org/en/Publications/CR/Issues/2024/05/08/Nigeria-2024-Article-IV-Consultation-Press-Release-Staff-Report-Staff-Statement-and-548726.

[133] Ibid, p.73

[134] Ibid.

[135] Jamie Smyth and Myles McCormick, 'US shale sector in peril as oil price plunge rattles drillers,' Financial Times, April 10, 2025: https://www.ft.com/content/cd7c043a-1983-4106-b4f9-13d66f951faf.

[136] Ibid.

[137] World Economic Forum, 'Norway's Sovereign Wealth Fund', 263.

https://www.weforum.org/agenda/2022/09/norways-massive-sovereign-wealth-fund-sets-net-zero-goal/.

[138] Okonjo-Iweala, Fighting Corruption is Dangerous, p61.

[139] WTO (2024), Trade Policy Review (Nigeria) – Report by the Secretariat, p. 6, October 9, 2024: https://www.wto.org/english/tratop_e/tpr_e/s462_e.pdf.

[140] President Buhari's speech at COP26: https://statehouse.gov.ng/news/at-cop26-president-buhari-pledges-net-zero-emissions-by-2060-says-nigeria-will-maintain-gas-based-energy-transition/.

[141] Agora Policy, 'Climate change poses great risks to Nigeria': https://leadership.ng/climate-change-poses-grave-risks-to-nigeria-agora-policy/.

[142] Ibid.

[143] Daisy Donne, 'The Carbon Brief Profile: Nigeria', Carbon Brief, February 17, 2023: https://www.carbonbrief.org/the-carbon-brief-profile-nigeria.

[144] WTO (2024), Trade Policy Review (Nigeria) – Report by the Secretariat, p. 89, October 9, 2024: https://www.wto.org/english/tratop_e/tpr_e/s462_e.pdf.

[145] International Energy Agency, https://www.iea.org/data-and-statistics/data-tools/greenhouse-gas-emissions-from-energy-data-explorer.

[146] Nigerian Tribune, 'FG's unfulfilled EV promise', Editorial, April 11, 2024: 270.   https://tribuneonlineng.com/fgs-unfulfilled-ev-promise/

[147] Kieran Smith and Jim Pickard, 'UK government considers 'flexibilities' to help carmakers hit EV targets,' Financial Times, November 17, 2024: https://www.ft.com/content/675a60c9-8cfe-42b9-8d2b-532c47be430d.

[148] See World Bank Group, Global Flaring and Methane Reduction Partnership (GFMR):

https://www.worldbank.org/en/programs/gasflaringreduction#
7.
[149] Campbell and Page, p.170.
[150] Joshua Odeyemi, 'Climate Change: Nigeria Lost 35%
Mangrove Cover In 20 Years – USAID,' Daily Trust, July 18,
2024: https://dailytrust.com/climate-change-nigeria-lost-35-
mangrove-cover-in-20-years-usaid/.
[151] Ibid. USIAD, Press Release, July 18, 2024:
https://www.usaid.gov/nigeria/press-release/jul-18-2024-
usaid-and-sdn-host-mangroves-dialogues-address-climate-
change-nigeria.
[152] President Buhari's speech as COP26.
[153] Ahmed Oluwasanjo, 'I won't solve climate change as
president unless funded by Western nations: Tinubu,' People's
Gazette, October 17, 2022: https://gazettengr.com/i-wont-
solve-climate-change-as-president-unless-funded-by-western-
nations-tinubu/.
[154] See Olu Fasan, 'Tinubu says climate change is not
Nigeria's problem. What a smart aleck!', BusinessDay,
October 31, 2022:
https://businessday.ng/columnist/article/tinubu-says-climate-
change-is-not-nigerias-problem-what-a-smart-aleck/.
[155] Attracta Mooney and Kenza Bryan, 'Developing nations
brand $300bn deal on climate change an "illusion"' Financial
Times, November 25, 2024.
[156] Rachel Millard and Rob Rose, 'Global jobs market shaken
by green transition,' Financial Times, September 12 2024:
https://www.ft.com/content/a15badc1-93ba-4a3a-b763-
66b183d93f67.
[157] Olu Fasan, 'COP28: Tinubu's hypocrisy and wishful
thinking on climate change,' BusinessDay, December 18,
2023: https://businessday.ng/columnist/article/cop28-tinubus-
hypocrisy-and-wishful-thinking-on-climate-change/.
[158] See 'Press Release: President Tinubu Establishes
Committee to Oversee Green Economic Initiatives, Appoints
Chief Ajuri Ngelale as Special Envoy on Climate Action,'
State House: May 19, 2024:
https://statehouse.gov.ng/news/president-tinubu-establishes-
committee-to-oversee-green-economic-initiatives-appoints-
chief-ajuri-ngelale-as-special-envoy-on-climate-action/.

[159] Johnbosco Agbakwuru, 'German firm to build renewable energy, decarbonization tech in evergreen city — Presidency,' Vanguard, August 1, 2024: https://www.vanguardngr.com/2024/08/german-firm-to-build-renewable-energy-decarbonization-tech-in-evergreen-city-presidency/#

[160] UN Climate Press Release, 'COP28 Agreement Signals "Beginning of the End" of the Fossil Fuel Era,' UN, December 13, 2023: https://unfccc.int/news/cop28-agreement-signals-beginning-of-the-end-of-the-fossil-fuel-era.

[161] Adeyinka Adedipe, 'Edo refinery gets operational licence from NMDPRA,' Punch, August 20, 2024: https://punchng.com/edo-refinery-gets-operational-licence-from-nmdpra/#.

[162] Udeme Akpan, 'South Korean investors to construct 4 refineries in Nigeria – FG,' Vanguard, October 9, 2024: https://www.vanguardngr.com/2024/10/south-korean-investors-to-construct-4-refineries-in-nigeria-fg/.

[163] See President Trump's inaugural address on January 20, 2025: https://www.whitehouse.gov/remarks/2025/01/the-inaugural-address/.

[164] Edward White, 'China's accelerating green transition,' FT, September 26, 2024: https://www.ft.com/content/4afdd319-230f-4763-8107-d8a43308dcfc.

[165] Michael Pooler, 'Brazil wants to be a climate champion and an oil giant. Can it be both?' FT, September b16, 2024: https://www.ft.com/content/8d25d4d5-0258-4676-81ab-30bb711f4fd2,

[166] Attracta Mooney, et al. 'Russia urges Donald Trump to remain in Paris agreement at upside-down COP29,' Financial Times, November 17, 2024: https://www.ft.com/content/d8fd9c52-c12b-4909-9d31-6ef0c81250c9.

[167] Aanu Adeoye, 'Nigeria's plan to boost delta drilling sparks anger,' Financial Times, January 27, 2025: https://www.ft.com/content/39ef75ff-8abd-4bbd-935d-e3e7afb008b1.

[168] Kenza Bryan, 'UK government's climate action plan is unlawful, High Court rules,' Financial Times, May 3, 2024: https://www.ft.com/content/f57e608b-f230-44c9-97f8-44c5c60f3ccb.

[169] Campbell and Page, p.171.

[170] James Lovelock, The Revenge of Gaia, Penguin, 2007, p,15.

[171] Emmanuel Addeh, 'In Key Policy Shift, US Halts Plan to Pressure Nigeria, Others to Jettison Fossil Fuels,' ThisDay, March 10, 2025: https://www.thisdaylive.com/index.php/2025/03/10/in-key-policy-shift-us-halts-plan-to-pressure-nigeria-others-to-jettison-fossil-fuels/.

[172] Ibid.

[173] Adrien Bilal & Diego R. Känzig, 'Does Unilateral Decarbonization Pay For Itself?' National Bureau of Economic Research, Working Paper 33364, January 2025: https://www.nber.org/papers/w33364.

[174] See Nigeria's 2024 Article IV Consultation report, published in May 2024: https://www.imf.org/en/Publications/CR/Issues/2024/05/08/Nigeria-2024-Article-IV-Consultation-Press-Release-Staff-Report-Staff-Statement-and-548726.

[175] Tim Harford, 'The selfish guide to decarbonising,' Financial Times, February 28, 2025: https://www.ft.com/content/2284bb0c-03d4-478d-9783-7cbf3908ff92.

[176] Onyinye Nwachukwu, 'Presidency queries FIRS boss Babatunde Fowler over tax revenues', BusinessDay, August 19, 2019: https://businessday.ng/lead-story/article/presidency-queries-firs-boss-babatunde-fowler-over-tax-revenues/.

[177] Ibid.

[178] IMF, 'Nigeria: 2019 Article IV Consultation – Press Release': https://www.imf.org/en/Publications/CR/Issues/2019/04/01/Nigeria-2019-Article-IV-Consultation-Press-Release-Staff-Report-and-Statement-by-the-46726/.

[179] IMF, 'Transcript of Africa Regional Economic Outlook', October 13, 2023: https://www.imf.org/en/News/Articles/2023/10/13/tr101323-transcript-of-africas-regional-economic-outlook/.

[180] Gregory Kronstein, 'Taxes: Are paying, should pay more', FBNQuest, August 26, 2016: https://fbnquest.com/taxes-are-paying-should-pay-more/.

[181] IMF Country Focus, 'Nigeria: Mobilizing Resources to Invest in People', April 3, 2019: https://www.imf.org/en/News/Articles/2019/04/01/na040219-nigeria-mobilizing-resources-to-invest-in-people#.

[182] Kemi Adeosun, 'All Change!!! Nigeria is not an oil economy', The Guardian, November 7, 2017: https://guardian.ng/opinion/all-change-nigeria-is-not-an-oil-economy/.

[183] FIRS, 'Going after billionaire tax defaulters': FIRS website: https://www.firs.gov.ng/firs-going-after-billionaire-tax-defaulters/.

[184] State House, 'Tinubu inaugurates Presidential Committee on Fiscal Policy and Tax reforms': https://statehouse.gov.ng/news/mr-presidents-address-at-the-inaugural-meeting-of-the-presidential-committee-on-fiscal-policy-and-tax-returns/.

[185] Economic Confidential, 'Tinubu, Bill Gates Propose Digital Identity Platform for Seamless Tax Collection', April 29, 2024: https://economicconfidential.com/2024/04/tinubu-bill-gates-tax/.

[186] Matthew Keep, 'Tax Statistics: an overview', House of Commons Library, March 28, 2024, pp.22-23.

[187] Martin Wolf, 'Boris Johnson's promise to 'level up' will be hard to keep', Financial Times, February 13, 2020: https://www.ft.com/content/011b0c62-4cf1-11ea-95a0-43d18ec715f5.

[188] ILO Terms of Reference, 'A Rapid Diagnostic Assessing the Impact of Covid-19 on enterprises and workers in the informal economy in Nigeria', 2021.

[189] Aganga, p.88.

[190] Sunday Aborisade and Juliet Akoje, 'Tinubu Writes National Assembly, Presents Four Tax Reform Bills,' ThisDay, October 4, 2024: https://www.thisdaylive.com/index.php/2024/10/04/tinubu-writes-national-assembly-presents-four-tax-reform-bills/.

[191] Johnbosco Agbakwuru, 'New tax laws 'll ease burden on Nigeria's poor – Oyedele,' Vanguard, June 27,2025: https://www.vanguardngr.com/2025/06/new-tax-laws-ll-ease-burden-on-nigerias-poor-oyedele/.

[192] Chiamaka Enendu, 'Nigeria's major tax overhaul explained,' BBC News, June

26, 2025: https://www.bbc.co.uk/news/articles/czdvnmz0j9go.
[193] WTO (2024), Trade Policy Review (Nigeria) – Report by the Secretariat, p.50, October 9, 2024: https://www.wto.org/english/tratop_e/tpr_e/s462_e.pdf.
[194] Deji Elumoye and Olawale Ajimotokan, 'For Broader Consultation, NEC Advises Tinubu to Withdraw Tax Reform Bills,' ThisDay, November 1, 2024: https://www.thisdaylive.com/index.php/2024/11/01/for-broader-consultation-nec-advises-tinubu-to-withdraw-tax-reform-bills/.
[195] See the communique of the Nigeria Governors' Forum on the Twitter feed here: https://x.com/NGFSecretariat/status/1879915873533571505.
[196] Ibid.
[197] See the presidency statement welcoming the governors' proposals on Bayo Onanuga's Twitter feed here: https://x.com/aonanuga1956/status/1880281296892751987.
[198] Press Release, 'President Tinubu: New Tax Laws, the way Forward for Nigeria's Prosperity,' State House, Abuja, June 26, 2025:
[199] Ibid.
[200] Oluwole Crowther, 'Ten charts that define Tinubu's two years in office', BusinessDay, May 29, 2025: https://businessday.ng/pro/article/ten-charts-that-define-tinubus-two-years-in-office/.
[201] Ngozi Okonjo-Iweala, 'Point of View: Nigeria's Shot at Redemption', Finance and Development Quarterly, December 2008, Vol 45, No4: https://www.imf.org/external/pubs/ft/fandd/2008/12/okonjo.htm.
[202] Humeleng Makgetta, 'Innovations got Successful Societies: Interview with Obadiah Mailafia', Princeton University, August 28, 2009.
[203] Okonjo-Iweala, Reforming the Unreformable, Chapter 6 'Obtaining Debt Relief'.
[204] Ibid.
[205] Daniel Adaji, 'Nigeria becomes World Bank's IDA third-largest debtor, owes $16.5bn,' Punch, September 3, 2024: https://punchng.com/nigeria-becomes-world-banks-ida-third-largest-debtor-owes-16-5bn/#.

206 Premium Times, 'Senate to probe N30trillion "Way and Means" obtained by Buhari's administration from CBN': https://www.premiumtimesng.com/news/headlines/672433-senate-to-probe-n30trn-ways-and-means-obtained-by-buhari-administration-from-cbn.html?tztc=1.

207 Charles Soludo, 'Avoiding the Mistakes of the "Old" Buharinomics', Vanguard, November 21, 2015: https://www.vanguardngr.com/2015/11/avoiding-the-mistakes-of-the-old-buharinomics/.

208 Wasiu Alli, 'Nigeria's public debt rises by N12.6trn in three months on naira depreciation,' BusinessDay, November 12, 2024: https://businessday.ng/news/article/nigerias-public-debt-rises-by-n12-6trn-in-three-months-on-naira-depreciation/.

209 The Cable, 'America should be in jail if borrowing is a crime, says Tinubu', October 21, 2022: https://www.thecable.ng/just-in-america-should-be-in-jail-if-borrowing-is-a-crime-says-tinubu/.

210 See 'Banking on Borrowing,' SBM Intelligence, May 20, 2025: https://sbmintelligence.substack.com/p/bankingborrowing?utm_source=substack&utm_medium=email

211 Camillus Eboh, 'Nigeria's Senate approves President Tinubu's $21 billion
external borrowing plan,' Reuters, July 23, 2025

212 Tope Omogbolagun & Godsgift Onyedinefu, 'Tinubu's new loans push debt to N183trn,' BusinessDay, May 28, 2025: https://businessday.ng/news/article/tinubus-new-loans-push-debt-to-n183trn/.

213 Dirisu Yakubu, 'Tinubu seeks N'Assembly's nod for $347m external loan,' The Punch, July 23, 2025: https://punchng.com/tinubu-seeks-nassemblys-nod-for-347m-external-loan/

214 Opinion Nigeria, 'Bayo Onanuga replies critics, says 'No sin in borrowing',
Opinion Nigeria, June 2, 2025: https://www.opinionnigeria.com/bayo-onanuga-replies-critics-says-no-sin-in-borrowing/

215 Roger Aliaga-Diaz and Josh Hirt, 'Why the US dollar remains a reserve currency leader', Vanguard, UK, May 1, 2024: https://www.vanguard.co.uk/professional/insights-

education/insights/why-the-us-dollar-remains-a-reserve-currency-leader.

[216] Wasiu Alli, 'Debt service-to-revenue ratio jumps 162% amid FX, subsidy reforms,' BusinessDay, November 13, 2024: https://businessday.ng/business-economy/article/debt-service-to-revenue-ratio-jumps-162-amid-fx-subsidy-reforms/.

[217] Wasilat Azeez, 'KPMG: Nigeria may spend over 100% of its revenue on debt servicing in 2023', The Cable, May 19, 2023: https://www.thecable.ng/kpmg-nigeria-may-spend-over-100-of-its-revenue-on-debt-servicing-in-2023/.

[218] Samuel Nwite, 'Nigeria's Debt-to-GDP ratio surpasses 50% for the first time,' Tekedia, July 1, 2024: https://www.tekedia.com/nigerias-debt-to-gdp-ratio-surpasses-50-for-the-first-time/.

[219] Dr Okonjo-Iweala made this comment as the Keynote speaker at the 2024 Annual Conference of the Nigerian Bar Association in August 2024.

[220] Oluwatobi Ojabello and Wasiu Alli, 'Fiscal instability: Behind the ticking time bomb of Nigeria's debt,' BusinessDay, August 5, 2024: https://businessday.ng/business-economy/article/fiscal-instability-behind-the-ticking-time-bomb-of-nigerias-debt/#.

[221] Simon Kuznets, 'Economic Growth and Income Inequality', American Economic Review 45, No1 1955:1-28.

[222] David Pilling, The Growth Delusion: The Wealth and Well-being of Nations, Bloomsbury Publishing, 2018.

[223] For instance, Bhutan developed the Gross National Happiness (GNH) as an alternative to the GDP on the basis that the GDP alone does not tell the whole story about social progress and happiness.

[224] See also Daniel Susskind, Growth: A reckoning, Allen Lane, 2024.

[225] Chris Giles, 'The perils in the search for the perfect GDP alternative,' Financial Times, November 27, 2024: https://www.ft.com/content/3a03880d-c287-4b1f-9ab9-78a7b05c669f.

[226] David Susskind, Growth: A Reckoning, Allen Lane, 2024.

[227] Shekhar Aiyar, 'Global inequality is narrowing – and that is cause for celebration,' Financial Times, August 13, 2024.

[228] World Bank, The Nigeria Economic Report 2014, https://www.worldbank.org/en/country/nigeria/publication/nig

eria-economic-report-improved-economic-outlook-in-2014-and-prospects-for-continued-growth-look-good.

[229] Ibid.

[230] Okonjo-Iweala, Reforming the Unreformable, p.135.

[231] Sola Fajan, "Industrial relations in the oil industry in Nigeria, Working Paper, International Labour Office, 2005.

[232] WTO (2024), Trade Policy Review (Nigeria) – Report by the Secretariat, p. 12, October 9, 2024: https://www.wto.org/english/tratop_e/tpr_e/s462_e.pdf.

[233] Luis Aguilar Luna and Deborah Winkle, Linking Export Activities to Productivity and Wage Rate Growth, Policy Research Working Paper, 10737, World Bank, March 26, 2024.

[234] Ed Conway, Material World, Penguin, p.274.

[235] Pauk Krugman, The Age of Diminished Expectations, The MIT Press, 1997.

[236] IMF (2021), IMF Country Report No. 21/34, p. 26.

[237] World Bank, 'Nigeria Economic Update: Jumpstarting Inclusive Growth - Unlocking the Productive Potential of Nigeria's People and Resource Endowments', World Bank, 2015, p.2

[238] Ibid, p.29

[239] PwC, 'The Africa Business Agenda: Changing Gear', A PwC report, 6th edition, May 2017, p.27.

[240] World Bank, Nigeria Economic Update 2015, p.43.

[241] Ibid, p.34

[242] Thomas Piketty, Capital in the 21st Century, p.21.

[243] World Bank, Nigeria Economic Report 2015, p.10.

[244] Onyinye Nwachukwu, Hope Moses-Ashike and Faith Omoboye, 'IMF/World Bank Meetings: Nigeria's productivity hinges on improved electricity supply – W'Bank,' BusinessDay, October 28, 2024: https://businessday.ng/business-economy/article/imf-world-bank-meetings-nigerias-productivity-hinges-on-improved-electricity-supply-wbank/.

[245] The Economist, 'Why the AI revolution is leaving Africa behind,' July 25, 2024: https://www.economist.com/middle-east-and-africa/2024/07/25/why-the-ai-revolution-is-leaving-africa-behind.

[246] David Pilling, 'Can AI help Africa close the development gap?' Financial Times, October 17, 2024.

247 The Economist, 'Why the AI revolution is leaving Africa behind,' July 25, 2024: https://www.economist.com/middle-east-and-africa/2024/07/25/why-the-ai-revolution-is-leaving-africa-behind.
248 Piketty, p.71.
249 Cited in John Campbell and Matthew Page Nigeria: What Everyone Needs to Know, Oxford, 2018, p.156.
250 Aart Kraay and David McKenzie, 'Do Poverty Traps Exist? Assessing the
Evidence,' Journal of Economic Perspectives—Volume 28, Number 3—Summer 2014—Pages 127–148.
251 Ibid.
252 Boeri, Tito, and others (eds), Brain Drain and Brain Gain: The Global Competition to Attract High-Skilled Migrants (Oxford, 2012; online edn, Oxford Academic, 20 Sept. 2012), https://doi.org/10.1093/acprof:oso/9780199654826.001.0001, accessed 17 Apr. 2025.
253 Olusegun Aganga, Reclaiming the Jewel of Africa, Practical Inspiration Publisher, 2023, p.207.
254 John Campbell and Mattew Page, Nigeria: What Everyone Needs to Know, Oxford University Press, p156.
255 Bhagwati, Jagdish. "Borders beyond Control." Foreign Affairs, vol. 82, no. 1, 2003, pp. 98–104. JSTOR, https://doi.org/10.2307/20033431. Accessed 25 Apr. 2025.
256 Financial Times, 'Remittance crackdown is a tax on the poor,' The FT View, June 15, 2025: https://www.ft.com/content/fe31c1d1-e686-4617-9cf2-d4f7f154b2dd
257 Temitayo Jaiyeola, Dayo Adenubi and Amarachi Orjiude, 'Nigerians in Diaspora remit $65.34bn in three years,' The Punch, August 23, 2021: https://punchng.com/nigerians-in-diaspora-remit-65-34bn-in-three-years/.
258 See National Diaspora Policy, available at: https://nidcom.gov.ng/national-diaspora-policy/.
259 The risk of overreliance on remittances is highlighted by President Trump's
plan to impose a levy on remittances from the US, which was criticised a s tax on
the poor. See Financial Times, 'Remittance crackdown is a tax on the poor,' The FT View, June 15, 2025: https://www.ft.com/content/fe31c1d1-e686-4617-9cf2-

d4f7f154b2dd

260 Olusegun Aganga, Reclaiming the Jewel of Africa, Practical Inspiration Publisher, 2023, p.208.
261 See National Diaspora Policy, available at: https://nidcom.gov.ng/national-diaspora-policy/.
262 Ibid.
263 Ibid.
264 Olusegun Aganga, Reclaiming the Jewel of Africa, Practical Inspiration Publisher, 2023, p.18.
265 Ed Conway, Material World, Penguin, p201.
266 John Campbell and Mattew Page, Nigeria: What Everyone Needs to Know, Oxford University Press, p49.
267 Ibid.
268 WTO (2024), Trade Policy Review (Nigeria) – Report by the Secretariat, p. 76, October 9, 2024: https://www.wto.org/english/tratop_e/tpr_e/s462_e.pdf.
269 Damilola Odifa, 'Agric plans without smallholder farmers as focus show less chance for impact', BusinessDay, December 14, 2022: https://businessday.ng/agriculture/article/agric-plans-without-smallholder-farmers-as-focus-show-less-chance-for-impact/.
270 Sean Woolfrey, Philomena Apiko and Kesa Pharatlhatlhe, 'Nigeria and South Africa: Shaping prospects for the African Continental Free Trade Area', Discussion Paper No242, European Centre for Policy Development and Management, February 2019, p.10.
271 WTO (2024), Trade Policy Review (Nigeria) – Report by the Secretariat, p. 9, October 9, 2024: https://www.wto.org/english/tratop_e/tpr_e/s462_e.pdf.
272 Ibid.
273 Voice of Nigeria, 'Only 2.5% Of Nigeria's Arable Land Is Used for Agriculture -Buhari', VON, January 10, 2022: https://von.gov.ng/only-2-5-of-nigerias-arable-land-is-used-for-agriculture-buhari/.
274 Timothy Obiezu, 'Nigeria Unveils Massive Pile of Rice Marking Production Progress', January 18, 2022: https://www.voanews.com/a/nigeria-unveils-massive-pile-of-rice-marking-production-progress-/6402059.html.
275 Josephine Okojie, 'Insufficient rice trails decade-long trillion-naira interventions', BusinessDay, April 29, 2024:

https://businessday.ng/news/article/insufficient-rice-trails-decade-long-trillion-naira-interventions/.

[276] David Pilling, 'Why small is not beautiful when it comes to development', Financial Times, November 5, 2023: https://www.ft.com/content/90b13a05-0d91-4aac-9faf-738900c1389c.

[277] Press release, '25 million Nigerians at high risk of food insecurity in 2023', UNICEF, January 16, 2023: https://www.unicef.org/press-releases/25-million-nigerians-high-risk-food-insecurity-2023.

[278] SBM Intelligence, 'Starving and stunted,' SBM, November 28, 2024: https://medium.com/@sbmintel/starving-and-stunted-3ce6b0bfb3df.

[279] Gov.UK, 'United Kingdom Food Security Report 2021: Theme 2: UK Food Supply Sources', October 5, 2023: https://www.gov.uk/government/statistics/united-kingdom-food-security-report-2021/united-kingdom-food-security-report-2021-theme-2-uk-food-supply-sources.

[280] Michael Pooler, 'Brazil to scrap import tariffs on basic foods,' Financial Times, March 7, 2025: https://www.ft.com/content/7605b78d-610e-4dea-b253-e75a3d816cde.

[281] Ruth Tene Nasta, 'Nigeria opts for massive food importation to ease cost of living crisis,' BusinessDay, July 8, 2024: https://businessday.ng/news/article/fg-suspends-duty-on-rice-wheat-others-approves-n2tn-package-to-tackle-food-inflation/.

[282] Punch, 'FG, implement duty-free food imports now,' The Punch Editorial Board, October 27, 2024: https://punchng.com/fg-implement-duty-free-food-imports-now/.

[283] Alan Beattie, 'Open markets have delivered unmatched levels of food security,' Financial Times, September 3, 2024.

[284] David Pilling and Aanu Adeoye, 'Will shock therapy revive Nigeria's economy — or sink it further?' Financial Times, July 10, 2024: https://www.ft.com/content/137058b2-d48a-4adf-91f1-e25494350e6e.

[285] Financial Times, 'Shock therapy alone will not cure Nigeria's economic ills,' The FT View, July 16, 2024: https://www.ft.com/content/86fd53bd-9adb-47f4-8e4e-589f80ecf190.

[286] Aanu Adeoye and Jospeh Cotterill, 'Nigeria's economy 30% bigger after GDP
Recalculation,' Financial Times, July 22, 2025:
[287] Ibid.
[288] Wasiu Alli, 'Nigeria remains fourth largest economy in Africa despite
rebasing,' BusinessDay, July 21, 2025.
[289] Dike Onwuamaeze, 'World Bank: Nigeria Stuck in Lower Middle Income Economy Below Libya, Gabon,' ThisDay, July 7, 2025.

Chapter 5: Towards a welfare and prosperity trade agenda

[290] See Herbst, Jeffrey and Olukoshi, Adebayo. "Nigeria: Economic and Political Reforms at Cross Purposes" in Haggard, Stephen and Webb, Steven (eds) Voting for Reforms, Oxford University Press, 1999.
[291] Olu Fasan, 'Love it or hate it, the IMF is a force for good,' BusinessDay, January 18, 2016:
https://businessday.ng/columnist/article/love-it-or-hate-it-the-imf-is-a-force-for-good/.
[1] Quoted in Clive Schmitthoff, Schmitthoff's Export Trade: The Law and Practice of International Trade, Stevens & Sons, 9th Edition, 1990.
[2] Okonjo-Iweala, Reforming the Unreformable, p.61.
[3] President Buhari's 2017 Budget Speech.
[4] Ibid.
[5] David Clayton and David Higgins, 'The ineffectiveness of 'Buy British' campaigns', LSE Business Review bogs, May 11, 2017:
https://blogs.lse.ac.uk/businessreview/2017/05/11/the-ineffectiveness-of-buy-british-campaigns/.
[6] See Douglas Irwin, 'The rise and fall of import substitution', World Development, Volume 139, March 2021.
[7] See Arnaud Costinot and Ivan Werning, 'The Lerner Symmetry Theorem: Generalisations and Qualifications', National Bureau of Economic Research, Working Paper 23427, May 2017: https://www.nber.org/papers/w23427.
[8] Martin Wolf, 'Tariffs are bad policy, but good politics,' Financial Times, June 11, 2024:

https://www.ft.com/content/497ca6af-1565-443a-ad18-3e9180d04d5e.

[9] Ibid.

[10] Soamiely Andriamanajara, et al, 'Assessing the Economic Impacts of an Economic Partnership Agreement in Nigeria', Policy Research Working Paper 4920, World Bank, April 2009.

[11] Martin Wolf, 'Tariffs are bad policy, but good politics,' Financial Times, June 11, 2024: https://www.ft.com/content/497ca6af-1565-443a-ad18-3e9180d04d5e.

[12] Vince Cable, 'Industrial policy must be practical not performative,' Financial Times, January 2, 2025: https://www.ft.com/content/aac3c1e5-e2fb-4341-89ce-6c4433f8e800.

[13] World Bank, 'Nigeria Economic Report, 2014.

[14] See Mohammed Bin Rashid School of Government (2024), Global Economic Diversification Index 2024. Viewed at: www.economicdiversification.com.. See also WTO (2024), Trade Policy Review (Nigeria) – Report by the Secretariat, p. 14, October 9, 2024: https://www.wto.org/english/tratop_e/tpr_e/s462_e.pdf.

[15] See WTO (2024), Trade Policy Review (Nigeria) – Report by the Secretariat, October 9, 2024: https://www.wto.org/english/tratop_e/tpr_e/s462_e.pdf.

[16] BusinessDay, 'Non-oil exports to drive Nigerian economy soon – NEPC', July 31, 2016: https://businessday.ng/exclusives/article/non-oil-exports-to-drive-nigerian-economy-soon-nepc/.

[17] Ibid.

[18] Finn Tarp, et al. Made in Africa: Learning to compete in industry, Brookings Institution Press, 2016, p.201.

[19] WTO, Trade Policy Review of Nigeria, Report of the Secretariat, WT/TPR/S/356, World Trade Organisation, May 9, 2017, p.7.

[20] See Nigeria - Merchandise Trade (% Of GDP), Trading Economics: https://tradingeconomics.com/nigeria/merchandise-trade-percent-of-gdp-wb-data.html#.

[21] Hutton, The State We're In, p.80.

[22] Abdulkareem Mojeed, 'Over 76% of Nigeria's agricultural commodities rejected by EU— NAFDAC', Premium Times, August 10, 2021: https://www.premiumtimesng.com/agriculture/478500-over-76-of-nigerias-agricultural-commodities-rejected-by-eu-nafdac.html?tztc=1.
[23] See WTO (2024), Trade Policy Review (Nigeria) – Report by the Secretariat, p.52, October 9, 2024: https://www.wto.org/english/tratop_e/tpr_e/s462_e.pdf.
[24] Ibid.
[25] See Trade Policy of Nigeria 2023- 2027, Federal Ministry of Industry, Trade and Investment, January 2023 p.18.
[26] See WTO (2024), Trade Policy Review (Nigeria) – Report by the Secretariat, pp.51-53, October 9, 2024: https://www.wto.org/english/tratop_e/tpr_e/s462_e.pdf.
[27] Okonjo-Iweala, Reforming the Unreformable, p.61.
[28] See WTO (2024), Trade Policy Review (Nigeria) – Report by the Secretariat, p.50, October 9, 2024: https://www.wto.org/english/tratop_e/tpr_e/s462_e.pdf.
[29] Olu Fasan, 'In defence of globalisation: The moral and liberal case,' BusinessDay, October 22, 2014: https://businessday.ng/analysis/article/in-defence-of-globalisation-the-moral-and-liberal-case/.
[30] On the Allison bureaucratic model, see Brent Durbin, 'Bureaucratic Politics Approach', Encyclopedia Brittanica: https://www.britannica.com/topic/bureaucratic-politics-approach.
[31] Interview by the author.
[32] Paul Krugman, Pop Internationalism, The MIT Press, 1997, p.25.
[33] WTO, 'DDG Agah stresses importance of open and predictable markets to foster economic recovery.' November 11, 2020: https://www.wto.org/english/news_e/news20_e/ddgya_11nov20_e.htm.
[34] Trade Policy of Nigeria, 2023-2027, Federal Ministry of Industry, Trade and Investment, January 2023, p.4.
[35] Ibid.
[36] Ibid. see also WTO (2024), Trade Policy Review (Nigeria) – Report by the Secretariat, p.6, October 9, 2024: https://www.wto.org/english/tratop_e/tpr_e/s462_e.pdf.

37 WTO, Trade Policy Review of Nigeria, WTO document, WT/TPR/M/147 of 14 June 2005.

38 WTO, Trade Policy Review of Nigeria, 2017.

39 WTO (2024), Trade Policy Review (Nigeria) – Report by the Secretariat, p.50, October 9, 2024: https://www.wto.org/english/tratop_e/tpr_e/s462_e.pdf.

40 Ibid, p8.

41 Ibid.

42 Ibid, p.6.

43 Hume, Of the Jealousy of Trade.

44 Christian Appolos, 'NECA rejects new 4% customs levy, warns of economic devastation,' Nigerian Tribune, February 9, 2025: https://tribuneonlineng.com/neca-rejects-new-4-customs-levy-warns-of-economic-devastation/.

45 Anozie Egole, 'Fresh price hike looms as NPA plans 15% tariff increase,' The Punch, February 7, 2025: https://punchng.com/fresh-price-hike-looms-as-npa-plans-15-tariff-increase/.

46 Abdullateef Aliyu, Eugene Agha, Peter Moses & Philip Shimnom Clement, 'Manufacturers, others decry new 4% levy on imports', Daily Trust, February 10, 2025: https://dailytrust.com/manufacturers-others-decry-new-4-levy-on-imports/.

47 Tobi Awodipe, 'MAN, NECA warn of NPA, Customs charges' impact on businesses, Nigerians,' The Guardian, February 10, 2025: https://guardian.ng/news/man-neca-warn-of-npa-customs-charges-impact-on-businesses-nigerians/.

48 WTO (2024), Trade Policy Review (Nigeria) – Report by the Secretariat, p51, October 9, 2024: https://www.wto.org/english/tratop_e/tpr_e/s462_e.pdf.

49 General Agreement on Tariffs and Trade, GATT, 1994, Article VI.I.

50 Ibid, Article IV.2.

51 Ibid, Article VI.3.

52 See WTO document WT/TPR/M/39/Add.1, 12 November 1998.

53 WTO, Trade Policy Review of Nigeria, 2017.

54 WTO (2024), Trade Policy Review (Nigeria) – Report by the Secretariat, p51, October 9, 2024: https://www.wto.org/english/tratop_e/tpr_e/s462_e.pdf.

55 Ibid, p.51.

[56] Okonjo-Iweala, Reforming the Unreformable, p.68.

[57] Enk von Uexkull, et al. 'ECOWAS Economic Partnership Agreement with the EU and Nigeria Trade and Development', World Bank, September 30, 2014, p.15.

[58] Ibid.

[59] Jagdish Bhagwati and T.N Srinivasan, 'Smuggling and trade policy' in J Jagdish Bhagwati and T.N Srinivasan, 'Smuggling and trade policy' in J, Bhagwati (ed) Illegal Transactions in International Trade, Studies in International Economics, 1974, pp27-38.

[60] Neil Munshi, 'Smuggled rice makes mockery of Nigerian quest to boost farming', Financial Times, June 6, 2019: https://www.ft.com/content/c2636fca-86b0-11e9-97ea-05ac2431f453.

[61] J, Bhagwati (ed) Illegal Transactions in International Trade, Studies in International Economics, 1974, p.32.

[62] Ibid, p.33.

[63] Sean Woolfrey, Philomena Apiko and Kesa Pharatlhatlhe, 'Nigeria and South Africa: Shaping prospects for the African Continental Free Trade Area', Discussion Paper No242, European Centre for Policy Development and Management, February 2019, p.14.

[64] Olu Fasan and Stephen Woolcock, 'Exploring Innovative Approaches for Unlocking the WTO Doha Development Agenda Impasse', Commonwealth Secretariat, 2013: https://www.academia.edu/8532294/Exploring_Innovative_Approaches_for_Unlocking_the_WTO_Doha_Development_Agenda_Impasse.

[65] Ibid.

[66] WTO (2024), Trade Policy Review (Nigeria) – Report by the Secretariat, p42, October 9, 2024: https://www.wto.org/english/tratop_e/tpr_e/s462_e.pdf.

[67] See 2025 National Trade Estimate Report on Foreign Trade Barriers, USTR, p.276: https://ustr.gov/sites/default/files/files/Press/Reports/2025NTE.pdf

[68] WTO (2024), Trade Policy Review (Nigeria) – Report by the Secretariat, p42, October 9, 2024: https://www.wto.org/english/tratop_e/tpr_e/s462_e.pdf. p.40.

[69] See 2025 National Trade Estimate Report on Foreign Trade Barriers, USTR, p.276:

https://ustr.gov/sites/default/files/files/Press/Reports/2025NTE
.pdf
[70] Ibid.
[71] WTO (2024), Trade Policy Review (Nigeria) – Report by
the Secretariat, p8, October 9, 2024:
https://www.wto.org/english/tratop_e/tpr_e/s462_e.pdf.
[72] Logistics Performance Index (LPI) 2023:
https://lpi.worldbank.org/international/global.
[73] John S. Odell, Negotiating the World Economy, Cornell
University Press, 2000. P.15.
[74] Ibid.
[75] EIU, 'Business Environment Rankings – Assessing the most
improved places for doing business', EIU, 2024.
[76] Ibid.
[77] Peter Navarro, 'Donald Trump's tariffs will fix a broken
system,' Financial Times, April 7, 2025:
https://www.ft.com/content/f313eea9-bd4f-4866-8123-
a850938163be.
[78] Financial Times, 'Why Vietnam should revamp its
economic model,' The FT View, June 19, 2025.
[79] Financial Times, 'Trump's self-defeating tariffs on south-
east Asia,' The FT View, April 8, 2025:
https://www.ft.com/content/c592bf92-7da3-408a-904d-
72d5c8f26f52.
[80] Andy Bounds, 'Donald Trump sparks race for trade deals to
counter US tariffs,' Financial Times, January 27, 2025:
https://www.ft.com/content/f33f3d35-3f49-4a48-97dd-
fcddd3b02e32.
[81] Christine Lagarde and Ursula von der Leyen, 'Europe has
got the message on change,' Financial Times, January 32,
2025: https://www.ft.com/content/fba6b27a-3a72-4451-8c75-
ea8533c62681.
[82] David Pilling, 'Can international aid survive in a crumbling
world order?' Financial Times, March 4, 2025:
https://www.ft.com/content/b3667445-a242-46fb-bcb3-
0a21386ce355.
[83] Ibid.
[84] Humeyra Pamuk, 'Trump administration scraps over 80% of
USAID programs, top diplomat Rubio says,' Reuters, March
10, 2025: https://www.reuters.com/world/us/trump-

administration-scraps-over-80-usaid-programs-top-diplomat-rubio-says-2025-03-10/.

[85] Olivia O'Sullivan &Jerome Puri, 'First USAID closes, then UK cuts aid: what a Western retreat from foreign aid could mean,' Chatham House, March 5, 2025: https://www.chathamhouse.org/2025/03/first-usaid-closes-then-uk-cuts-aid-what-western-retreat-foreign-aid-could-mean.

[86] Kat Lay, "This will cost lives': cuts to UK aid budget condemned as 'betrayal' by international development groups, 'The Guardian, March 2, 2025: https://www.theguardian.com/global-development/2025/mar/02/this-will-cost-lives-cuts-to-uk-aid-budget-condemned-as-betrayal-by-international-development-groups.

[87] David Pilling, 'Can international aid survive in a crumbling world order?' Financial Times, March 4, 2025: https://www.ft.com/content/b3667445-a242-46fb-bcb3-0a21386ce355.

[88] Olu Fasan, 'AfCFTA: Africa is moving too slowly towards a single market,' Africa At LSE Blog, February 11, 2019: https://blogs.lse.ac.uk/africaatlse/2019/02/11/afcfta-africa-is-moving-too-slowly-towards-a-single-market/.

[89] David Pilling, 'The foreign powers competing to win influence in Africa,' Financial Times, August 23, 2024: https://www.ft.com/content/a811400c-6c1f-4970-b1a9-4e9d28efa62e.

[90] Wamkele Mene, 'Helping to create a single integrated market across Africa is in the west's interests,' Financial Times, August 15, 2014: https://www.ft.com/content/2b867f0f-522e-47e4-b619-aa3b728a7cfd.

[91] The FT View, 'The middle-power competition in Africa,' Financial Times, August 29, 2024: https://www.ft.com/content/e4c11faa-cc9d-4341-84e8-e6348dc92fb5.

[92] Wamkele Mene, 'Helping to create a single integrated market across Africa is in the west's interests,' Financial Times, August 15, 2014: https://www.ft.com/content/2b867f0f-522e-47e4-b619-aa3b728a7cfd.

93 Ibid.
94 Ibid.
95 James Shikwati, 'AfCFTA: A beacon of hope or a failed project?' Friedrich Naumann Foundation for Freedom, April 2, 2024: https://www.freiheit.org/sub-saharan-africa/beacon-hope-or-failed-project.
96 Aanu Adeoye, 'Unfree movement — why can't Africans travel around Africa?,' Financial Times, December 18, 2024: https://www.ft.com/content/3685de67-c99f-4904-871d-4522478589b3.
97 Ibid.
98 Ibid.
99 Tunji Oyeyemi, 'Free Trade Must Also Be Fair Trade, Says President Buhari as Nigeria Signs African Free Trade Agreement', Press Release: https://fmino.gov.ng/free-trade-must-also-be-fair-trade-says-president-buhari-as-nigeria-signs-african-free-trade-agreement/.
100 Leke Baiyewu, 'AfCFTA: Poor policies may cause Nigeria nightmare, says FG', Punch, October 27, 2019: https://punchng.com/afcfta-poor-policies-may-cause-nigeria-nightmare-says-fg/.
101 Wamkele Mene, 'Helping to create a single integrated market across Africa is in the west's interests,' Financial Times, August 15, 2014: https://www.ft.com/content/2b867f0f-522e-47e4-b619-aa3b728a7cfd.
102 Gbenga Salau, 'Four years on: Why AfCFTA's impact on Nigeria's trade integration, economic growth remains lean,' The Guardian, January 25, 2025: https://guardian.ng/features/four-years-on-why-afcftas-impact-on-nigerias-trade-integration-economic-growth-remains-lean/#.
103 Ibid.
104 Oluseyi Awojulugbe, 'Emefiele: More items will face forex ban, AfCTA won't stop us', The Cable, August 19, 2019: https://www.thecable.ng/emefiele-more-items-forex-ban-afcta/.
105 United Nations, 'World Economic Situation and Prospects: March 2024 Briefing, No. 179,' UNDESA, February 29, 2024.
106 Okonjo-Iweala, Reforming the Unreformable, p.65.

[107] WTO (2024), Trade Policy Review (Nigeria) – Report by the Secretariat, p.50, October 9, 2024: https://www.wto.org/english/tratop_e/tpr_e/s462_e.pdf.

[108] Ibid.

[109] Meran Hulse, 'Regional Powers and Leadership in Regional Institutions: Nigeria in ECOWAS and South Africa in SADC', KFG Working Paper No. 76 | November 2016.

[110] Commonwealth Secretariat, 'The Commonwealth in the Unfolding Global Trade Landscape: Prospects, Priorities, Perspectives', The Commonwealth Trade Review, 2015.

[111] Ibid, p52.

[112] Ibid, p54.

[113] Ibid, p54.

[114] Ibid, p65.

[115] Trade Policy of Nigeria, 2023-2027, Federal Ministry of Industry, Trade and Investment, January 2023, p17.

[116] Ibid, p23.

[117] WTO (2024), Trade Policy Review (Nigeria) – Report by the Secretariat, p.50, October 9, 2024: https://www.wto.org/english/tratop_e/tpr_e/s462_e.pdf.

[118] See DS27: European Communities – Regime for the Importation, Sale and Distribution of Bananas, 1997: https://www.wto.org/english/tratop_e/dispu_e/cases_e/ds27_e.htm.

[119] Charles Soludo, 'Africa needs honesty over EU trade deals', Financial Times, April 10, 2012: https://www.ft.com/content/106452b4-8233-11e1-9242-00144feab49a.

[120] Phillip Oladunjoye, 'EPA: African leaders align with Nigerian position', Tralac, May 5, 2014: https://www.tralac.org/news/article/5600-epa-african-leaders-align-with-nigeria-s-position.html.

[121] David Ogah, 'Manufacturers Kick Against Implementation of EPA In Nigeria', The Guardian, August 15, 2015: https://guardian.ng/business-services/manufacturers-kick-against-implementation-of-epa-in-nigeria/.

[122] See Final Communique, 45th Ordinary Session of the Authority of ECOWAS Heads of State and Government, 10 July 2014, paras 15-20.

[123] See Final Communique, 46th Ordinary Session of the Authority of ECOWAS Heads of State and Government, 15 December 2014, Abuja, para 15.

[124] Ibid.

[125] Olu Fasan, 'EU-Africa trade relations: Why Africa needs the economic partnership agreements', International Growth Centre, 26 March 2018: https://www.theigc.org/blogs/eu-africa-trade-relations-why-africa-needs-economic-partnership-agreements.

[126] Emily Jones, 'Negotiating Against the Odds,' Commonwealth Secretariat, April 2013.

[127] WTO (2024), Trade Policy Review (Nigeria) – Report by the Secretariat, p.50, October 9, 2024: https://www.wto.org/english/tratop_e/tpr_e/s462_e.pdf.

[128] UNIDO, 'UNIDO activities in Standards, Metrology, Testing and Quality (SMTQ), Thematic Evaluation Report', 2010.

[129] Soamiely Andriamanajara, et al, 'Assessing the Economic Impacts of an Economic Partnership Agreement in Nigeria', Policy Research Working Paper 4920, World Bank, April 2009.

[130] Ibid.

[131] Ibid.

[132] Abiodun Bankole, et al, 'ECOWAS Trade Liberalisation Scheme (ETLS) and its Impact on Intra-Regional Trade', Journal of West African Integration. January 2012, p12.

[133] Trump White House Archives, 'Remarks by President Trump and President Buhari of the Federal Republic of Nigeria in Joint Press Conference', April 18, 2018: https://trumpwhitehouse.archives.gov/briefings-statements/remarks-president-trump-president-buhari-federal-republic-nigeria-joint-press-conference/.

[134] Ibid.

[135] Ibid.

[136] Aime Williams, et al. 'Donald Trump unveils 'reciprocal' tariff plan to hit trade partners, 'Financial Times, February 14, 2025: https://www.ft.com/content/3cc5ecae-0a51-422c-b617-17030b96e506.

[137] See USTR, 'Reciprocal Tariff Calculations,' https://ustr.gov/issue-areas/reciprocal-tariff-calculations.

[138] Robin Harding, et al. 'Donald Trump defies market tumult as tariffs take effect,' Financial Times, April 9, 2025: https://www.ft.com/content/81cbdcdf-aafa-411e-8458-4af2b2b186d0.

[139] See list of 'reciprocal tariffs by country here: https://www.whitehouse.gov/wp-content/uploads/2025/04/Annex-I.pdf.

[140] Nkiruka Nnorom, with agency reports, 'Tariff war: US slams Nigeria over import ban on 25 items,' Vanguard, April 9, 2025: https://www.vanguardngr.com/2025/04/tariff-war-us-slams-nigeria-over-import-ban-on-25-items/.

[141] See USTR 2025 National Trade Estimate Report on Foreign Trade Barriers, USTR, pp 275-280: https://ustr.gov/sites/default/files/files/Press/Reports/2025NTE.pdf.

[142] USTR, 'Nigeria: AGOA Status', 2024, https://ustr.gov/countries-regions/africa/nigeria

[143] Campbell and Page, p.61.

[144] Alan Beattie, 'How to deal with Donald Trump's tariff threats,' Financial Times, November 26, 2024: https://www.ft.com/content/d077ab84-aa15-4b66-a9cc-42e98d2ddc90.

[145] USTR, 'Nigeria: AGOA Status', 2024.

[146] The Nation, 'Nigeria is Africa's least beneficiary of AGOA', December 21, 2015: https://thenationonlineng.net/nigeria-is-africas-least-beneficiary-of-agoa-2/.

[147] FT, 'Trade Minister Parks Tau urges African pivot to China in wake of Trump tariffs,' Biz News, April 6, 2025: https://www.biznews.com/global-citizen/ft-parks-tau-african-pivot-china.

[148] James Emejo and Michael Olugbode, 'Oduwole: Trump's Tariff to Impact $6bn Annual Exports to US,' ThisDay, April 7, 2025: https://www.thisdaylive.com/index.php/2025/04/07/oduwole-trumps-tariff-to-impact-6bn-annual-exports-to-us/.

[149] Anthony Ailemen, 'Tinubu to sign Executive Order prioritising local Industry as FEC unveils "Nigeria First" policy,' BusinessDay, May 5, 2025: https://businessday.ng/news/article/tinubu-to-sign-executive-

order-prioritising-local-industry-as-fec-unveils-nigeria-first-policy/.

[150] Andres Schipani and David Pilling, 'Joe Biden embarks on first and final Africa trip as US president with Angola visit,' Financial Times, December 2, 2024: https://www.ft.com/content/c2068ee9-bff0-430f-8539-701819994fd3.

[151] Omololu Ogunmade, 'China Responsible for Infrastructure Strides in Nigeria, Says Buhari', ThisDay, May 11, 2019: https://www.thisdaylive.com/index.php/2019/05/11/china-responsible-for-infrastructure-strides-in-nigeria-says-buhari/.

[152] State House statement, 'President Buhari lauds outgoing ambassador, says China plays a great role in reversing Nigeria's infrastructure deficit', https://statehouse.gov.ng/news/president-buhari-lauds-outgoing-ambassador-says-china-playing-great-role-in-reversing-nigerias-infrastructural-deficit/.

[153] Jonas Nyabor, 'Ghana: Chinese loans take centre stage in restructure talks', The Africa Report, June 21, 2023: https://www.theafricareport.com/311884/ghana-chinese-loans-take-centre-stage-in-restructure-talks/.

[154] Maria Abi-Habib, 'How China got Sri Lanka to cough up a port', New York Times, June 25, 2018: https://www.nytimes.com/2018/06/25/world/asia/china-sri-lanka-port.html.

[155] Yunnan Chen, 'China's role in Nigerian railway development and implications for security and development', United States Institute of Peace, Special Report 423, April 2018.

[156] Construction Overview, Oxford Business Group, The Nigeria Report, 2019. 188.

[157] Joe Leahy, et al, 'China's treatment of local debt 'ulcer' threatens growth target', Financial Times, March 13, 2024: https://www.ft.com/content/901bc68e-ad35-42eb-97e0-542c631b9033.

[158] John Adam, 'There are two ways to conquer and enslave a nation. One is by the sword. The other is by debt', Goodreads, https://www.goodreads.com/quotes/697421-there-are-two-ways-to-conquer-and-enslave-a-nation.

[159] Andres Schipani, 'The US-backed railway sparking a battle for African copper,' Financial Times, August 21, 2024:

https://www.ft.com/content/cb2823c7-f451-4bc9-959e-
ec7e07384a31.
160 Ibid.
161 Ibid.
162 Yun Sun, 'Africa in China's Foreign Policy', Brookings,
April 2014
163 Kingsley Moghalu, Comment on China's loans to Nigeria,
X (formerly Twitter):
https://x.com/MoghaluKingsley/status/1295270237613498371
.
164 Oyintarelado Moses, '10 Charts to Explain 22 Years of
China-Africa Trade, Overseas Development Finance and
Foreign Direct Investment', BU Global Development Policy
Centre, April 2, 2024: https://www.bu.edu/gdp/2024/04/02/10-
charts-to-explain-22-years-of-china-africa-trade-overseas-
development-finance-and-foreign-direct-investment/.
165 Philip Shimnom Clement, 'Nigeria, China Trade Deficit
Stands At $18bn — NEPC', Daily Trust, May 14, 2024:
https://dailytrust.com/nigeria-china-trade-deficit-stands-at-
18bn-nepc/.
166 Anthony Osae-Brown and Phila Siu, 'China and Nigeria
Renew Currency Swap to Boost Bilateral Trade,' Bloomberg,
December 27, 2024:
https://www.bloomberg.com/news/articles/2024-12-27/china-
and-nigeria-renew-currency-swap-to-boost-bilateral-trade.
167David Pilling and Adrienne Klasa, 'Kenya president urges
rebalance of China-Africa trade', Financial Times, May 14,
2017: https://www.ft.com/content/947ea960-38b2-11e7-821a-
6027b8a20f23.
168 Joshua Cooper Ramo, 'The Beijing Consensus', The
Foreign Policy Centre, May 2004.
169 World Population Review, 'Manufacturing by Country
2024,' https://worldpopulationreview.com/country-
rankings/manufacturing-by-country.

Chapter 6: Industrialisation and private sector development

1 Adam Smith, The Wealth of Nations (1776), Wordsmith
Edition, 9 July 2012.

[2] Some resource-based countries like Dubai, Saudi Arabia and Norway have managed to become wealthy without manufacturing base but by developing massive services sectors, such as tourism (in the case of Dubai) or have invested heavily in overseas assets and built-up massive reserves to diversify their sources of income.
[3] See the WTO World Trade Report 2014 for a more detailed discussion of the three waves of economic development.
[4] Ibid.
[5] Hongying Wang, 'A Deeper Look at China's "Going Out" Policy', Centre for International Governance Innovation, March 8, 2016: https://www.cigionline.org/publications/deeper-look-chinas-going-out-policy/.
[6] WTO World Trade Report 2014.
[7] Shekhar Aiyar, 'Global inequality is narrowing – and that is cause for celebration,' Financial Times, Agust 13, 2024.
[8] Ed Conway, Material World, Penguin, 2023, p52.
[9] World Bank, The impact of the 2014-16 oil price collapse, Global Economic Prospects, Special Focus, January 2018.
[10] Karl, Montevirgen. 'Comparative advantage.' Encyclopedia Britannica, June 11, 2024: https://www.britannica.com/money/comparative-advantage.
[11] Campbell and Page, Nigeria: What everyone needs to know, p.173.
[12] Levinus Nwabughiogu, 'The days of Nigeria as a big oil producer with plenty of money are gone – Buhari', Vanguard, February 25, 2016: https://www.vanguardngr.com/2016/02/days-nigeria-was-big-oil-producer-gone-buhari/.
[13] Aganga, Reclaiming the Jewel of Africa, p69.
[14] Nigeria Industrial Revolution Plan, 2015, p.5.
[15] See HM Government, 'Industrial Strategy White Paper', 2017, p36.
[16] Seminar presentation with the author.
[17] Edmond Phelps, et al, Dynamism: The values that drive innovation, job satisfaction and economic growth, Harvard University Press, 2020.
[18] David Hume, Of Jealousy of Trade.
[19] Razeen Sally, Trade Policy, New Century: The WTO, FTAs and Asia Rising, The Institute of Economic Affairs, 2008.

[20] Ed Conway, Material World, Penguin, 2023, p.207.

[21] Ibid.

[22] The four sectors are agro allied, metals and solid minerals, oil and gas, and construction, light manufacturing and services. The subsectors include food processing, textiles, cement, petrochemicals. These subsectors have proved inefficient for decades.

[23] Shantayanan Devarajan, 'Three reasons why industrial policy fails', Brookings, January 14, 2016: https://www.brookings.edu/articles/three-reasons-why-industrial-policy-fails/.

[24] UNECA, Economic Report on Africa 2015: Industrialising Through Trade, Part 2, Industrial-Trade Nexus, 2015, p86.

[25] Ibid.

[26] Hannah Beech, 'How China Is Getting in the Way of Its Own Economy', March 10, 2016: https://time.com/4253757/how-china-is-getting-in-the-way-of-its-own-economy/.

[27] Ibid.

[28] Nigeria Industrial Revolution Plan, 2015, p.44.

[29] Niall Ferguson, Civilisation: The Six Killer Apps of Western Power, Penguin Books, 2011, pp196-255.

[30] Nigeria Industrial Revolution Plan, 2015, p.18.

[31] David Olujinmi, 'Unsold goods in manufacturers' warehouses jump 87% as sales drop,' BusinessDay, November 18, 2024: https://businessday.ng/companies/article/unsold-goods-in-manufacturers-warehouses-jump-87-as-sales-drop/#.

[32] Adam Smith on consumption as the only end and purpose of production. See The Wealth of Nations, 1776, IV. viii.49.

[33] Martin Wolf, 'How not to do industrial policy, Financial Times, June 18, 2024: https://www.ft.com/content/a1a99a43-eca1-42ac-942b-30351daba248.

[34] Ibid.

[35] Ed Conway, Material World, Penguin, 2023, p.108.

[36] Claudia Berg, et al, Exports and Labour Demand: Evidence from Egyptian Firm-level Data, Policy Research Working Paper 10213, World Bank, 2022, p.4.

[37] Will Hutton, The State We're IN, p.67.

[38] Nigeria Industrial Revolution Plan, 2015, p9.

³⁹ WTO (2024), Trade Policy Review (Nigeria) – Report by the Secretariat, p.91, October 9, 2024: https://www.wto.org/english/tratop_e/tpr_e/s462_e.pdf.
⁴⁰ Ed Conway, Material World, Penguin, 2023, p.256.
⁴¹ Understandably, the argument of the originators of the NIRP would be that if the policy had been consistently implemented by successive governments, it would have achieved some of its goals and move Nigeria towards industrialisation. But that defence cannot override criticisms of some of the NIRP's underlying policy prescriptions.
⁴² WTO (2024), Trade Policy Review (Nigeria) – Report by the Secretariat, p.91, October 9, 2024: https://www.wto.org/english/tratop_e/tpr_e/s462_e.pdf.
⁴³ Ibid.
⁴⁴ Ibid.
⁴⁵ Chinwe Michael & Folake Balogun, '70 firms exited Nigeria in 7 years on FX, power,' BusinessDay, November 4, 2024: https://businessday.ng/pro/article/70-firms-exited-nigeria-in-7-years-on-fx-power/.
⁴⁶ Quote expanded on in Timothy Besley and Torsten Persson, Pillars of Prosperity: The Political Economics of Development Clusters, Princeton University Press, 2011.
⁴⁷ Thomas Farole Reis and Jose Guilherme, Trade Competitiveness Diagnostic Toolkit, World Bank, 2012.
⁴⁸ BusinessDay, 'With the economy in ruins, business-killing regulations should go', The Editorial Board, August 5, 2020: https://businessday.ng/editorial/article/with-the-economy-in-ruins-business-killing-regulations-should-go/.
⁴⁹ Reuters, 'Nigeria aims to cut number of taxes to fewer than 10 – official,' Reuters, October 24, 2023: https://www.reuters.com/markets/rates-bonds/nigeria-aims-cut-number-taxes-fewer-than-10-official-2023-10-24/#
⁵⁰ WTO (2024), Trade Policy Review (Nigeria) – Report by the Secretariat, p.91, October 9, 2024: https://www.wto.org/english/tratop_e/tpr_e/s462_e.pdf.
⁵¹ See Nigeria's 2024 Article IV Consultation report, published in May 2024: https://www.imf.org/en/Publications/CR/Issues/2024/05/08/Nigeria-2024-Article-IV-Consultation-Press-Release-Staff-Report-Staff-Statement-and-548726.

[52] Ravi Gulhati, The Making of Economic Policy in Africa (EDI Seminar Series), World Bank, 1990.

[53] Stephen Copp (ed) The Legal Foundations of Free Markets, The Institute of Economic Affairs, 2008.

[54] Ibid.

[55] Ibid, p19.

[56] John Coates, 'Trump's legal attacks threaten the very basis of sound investment,' Financial Times, April 10, 2025: https://www.ft.com/content/cc498e08-7765-45ee-bfa3-5520e754f325.

[57] Ibid.

[58] Nigeria Industrial Revolution Plan, 2015, p.18

[59] Ibid, p.18

[60] Ibid, p.44.

[61] For instance, Post-apartheid South Africa has had a robust Competition Act and competition authority since 1988, see the Competition Act of 1988.

[62] World Bank Group (2020), 'Country Private Sector Diagnostics: Creating Markets in Nigeria,' World Bank, 2020. See also WTO (2024), Trade Policy Review (Nigeria) – Report by the Secretariat, p.91, October 9, 2024: https://www.wto.org/english/tratop_e/tpr_e/s462_e.pdf.

[63] Ibid.

[64] See World Economic Forum (2019), The Global Competitiveness Index Report, 2019. See also WTO (2024), Trade Policy Review (Nigeria) – Report by the Secretariat, p.91, October 9, 2024: https://www.wto.org/english/tratop_e/tpr_e/s462_e.pdf.

[65] WTO (2024), Trade Policy Review (Nigeria) – Report by the Secretariat, p.64, October 9, 2024: https://www.wto.org/english/tratop_e/tpr_e/s462_e.pdf.

[66] Olu Fasan, 'Closure of KFC, Chinese supermarket: Stop the enforcement by jungle justice!', BusinessDay, May 13, 2024: https://businessday.ng/columnist/article/closure-of-kfc-chinese-supermarket-stop-the-enforcement-by-jungle-justice/.

[67] Chronicle, 'Government Institutions' Unhealthy Fixation with Price Fixing', Advertorial, Centre for Social and Economic Rights (CSER), September 4, 2020: https://www.chronicle.ng/news/government-institutions-unhealthy-fixation-with-price-fixing/.

⁶⁸ Davidson Iriekpen, 'Revolutionary Highlights of CAMA 2020', ThisDay, August 16, 2020: https://www.thisdaylive.com/index.php/2020/08/16/revolutionary-highlights-of-cama-2020/.
⁶⁹ See Part 17 of (UK) Companies Act 2006.
⁷⁰ Sonnie Ekwowusi, 'Reforming the Corporate Affairs Commission', ThisDay, August 12, 2020: https://www.thisdaylive.com/index.php/2020/08/12/reforming-the-corporate-affairs-commission/.
⁷¹ International Property Rights Index, 2023: https://www.internationalpropertyrightsindex.org/.
⁷² Channels TV, 'A Court Case Can Last Up To 20 Years,' Experts Discuss Tinubu's 8-Point Agenda', https://www.youtube.com/watch?v=t1XVDnziYuo.
⁷³ Oyetola Muyiwa Atoyebi, 'The Recognition and Enforcement of Foreign Judgements In Nigeria', Law Pavilion Blog, July 19, 2023: https://lawpavilion.com/blog/the-recognition-and-enforcement-of-foreign-judgements-in-nigeria/.
⁷⁴ Wedaeli Chibelushi, 'France seizes three Nigerian jets for Chinese firm,' BBC News, August 16, 2024: https://www.bbc.co.uk/news/articles/cdjwlrx8n8xo.
⁷⁵ International Property Rights Index, 2023.
⁷⁶ Foundation for Teaching Economics, 'Property Rights and Rule of Law': https://fte.org/teachers/teacher-resources/lesson-plans/is-capitalism-good-for-the-poor-2/lesson-2-property-rights-and-the-rule-of-law/
⁷⁷ Ibid.
⁷⁸ Reto Hilty, et al, 'Intellectual Property Justification for Artificial Intelligence' in Jyh-An Lee (ed), Artificial Intelligence and Intellectual Property, Oxford Academic, 25 February 2021.
⁷⁹ David Bainbridge, Intellectual Property, Pitman Publishing, 1922.
⁸⁰ C Fink and CA Primo Braga, 'How Stronger Protection of Intellectual Property Rights Affects International Trade Flows' in Fink, C and Maskus, KE (eds.) (2005) Intellectual Property and Development: Lessons from Recent Economic Research (The World Bank/Oxford University Press).
⁸¹ See WIPO document PCIPD/4/3 Pro.2 at p.45.

[82] See USTR,2 025 National Trade Estimate Report on Foreign Trade Barriers, USTR, p.275: https://ustr.gov/sites/default/files/files/Press/Reports/2025NTE.pdf.

[83] See WTO (2024), Trade Policy Review (Nigeria) – Report by the Secretariat, p.64, October 9, 2024: https://www.wto.org/english/tratop_e/tpr_e/s462_e.pdf.

[84] WIPO, IP Facts and Figures, 2018.

[85] Ibid.

[86] There are two main WTO non-discrimination rules. The first is the Most-Favoured-Nation ('MFN') rule which requires Members to accord the most favourable tariff and regulatory treatment given to the product of any one Member to the 'like products' to all other Members. The second is the National Treatment principle which forbids WTO from discriminating between imports and 'like domestic products', meaning that imported goods should not be treated less favourably to similar domestic ones.

[87] Nigeria Industrial Revolution Plan, 2015, p.65.

[88] See USTR,2 025 National Trade Estimate Report on Foreign Trade Barriers, USTR, p.275: https://ustr.gov/sites/default/files/files/Press/Reports/2025NTE.pdf.

[89] See WTO (2024), Trade Policy Review (Nigeria) – Report by the Secretariat, p.72, October 9, 2024: https://www.wto.org/english/tratop_e/tpr_e/s462_e.pdf.

[90] Ibid.

[91] Ibid.

[92] Campbell and Page, p.166.

[93] Sunday Adeniyi, known professional as King Sunny Ade is the first Nigerian to be nominated for a Grammy Award; Damini Ebunoluwa Ogulu, known professionally as Burna Boy, is the first Nigerian-born musician to win a Grammy.

Chapter 7: Nigeria's Bureaucratic Deficit

[1] Paul Collier, 'From poverty to prosperity: Understanding economic development', 2018: https://www.edx.org/learn/economics/university-of-oxford-from-poverty-to-prosperity-understanding-economic-development.

2 Ibid. Lecture slides with author.

3 Ibid.

4 Ibid.

5 Ibid.

6 Government Effectiveness Index:
https://www.theglobaleconomy.com/rankings/wb_government
_effectiveness/.

7 Campbell and Page, p.90.

8 Paul Collier and Timothy Besley, 'Escaping the Fragility
Trap', LSE-Oxford Commission on State Fragility, Growth
and Development, April 2018.

9 Ibid, p.50

10 Vanguard, 'Insecurity: 63,111 persons killed in Buhari's
eight years', May 20, 2023:
https://www.vanguardngr.com/2023/05/insecurity-63111-
persons-killed-in-buharis-eight-years/.

11 Escaping the Fragility Trap, p.41

12 Okonjo-Iweala, Reforming the Unreformable, p.20.

13 Fragile States Index Annual Report 2023, The Fund for
Peace, p.7.

14 Jack Queen and Daniel Wiessner, 'Explainer: Are Trump's
mass firings of federal workers legal?' Reuters, February 13,
2025: https://www.reuters.com/world/us/are-trumps-mass-
firings-federal-workers-legal-2025-02-13/.

15 Ibid.

16 See Ogochukwu E.S. Nebo and Nnamani, Desmond
Okechukwu, 'Civil Service Reforms and National
Development in Nigeria,' South American Journal of
Management Volume 1, Issue 2, 2015

17 See Speech by Cabinet Minister Oliver Letwin at the
Institute for Government on
17 September 2012:
https://www.civilservant.org.uk/library/2012_letwin_speech.p
df.

18 See UK Civil Service Policy Profession:
https://www.gov.uk/government/organisations/civil-service-
policy-profession.

19 Philip Asiodu, 'How corruption hit civil service', Vanguard,
August 10, 2015: https://www.vanguardngr.com/2015/08/how-
corruption-hit-civil-service-asiodu/.

[20] Helen Constas, 'Max Weber's two conceptions of bureaucracy', America Journal of Sociology, Vol 63, No4, January 1958.
[21] Okonjo-Iweala, Reforming the Unreformable, p.52.
[22] Achebe, There Was a Country, p.51.
[23] Okonjo-Iweala, Reforming the Unreformable, p.53.
[24] Philip Asiodu, 'How corruption hit civil service', Vanguard, August 10, 2015: https://www.vanguardngr.com/2015/08/how-corruption-hit-civil-service-asiodu/.
[25] Tunji Olaopa, 'The Centenary of the Nigerian Civil Service', Premium Times, February I, 2014: https://www.premiumtimesng.com/opinion/154385-centenary-nigerian-civil-service-tunji-olaopa.html?tztc=1.
[26] See 'Corruption in Nigeria: Patterns and Trends,' UNODC/NBS, July 2024: https://www.unodc.org/conig/uploads/documents/3rd_national_corruption_survey_report_2024_07_09.pdf.
[27] Ibid. p.122.
[28] Ibid.
[29] Ibid. p.131.
[30] Ibid. p.122.
[31] For instance, in a speech on civil service reform, then President said: 'Rather than being a source of innovation or productivity, our civil service has been turned to a haven for primitive accumulation and recycling of outdated ideas', cited in Okonjo-Iweala, Reforming the Unreformable, p.54.
[32] Martin Donnelly, 'Senior civil servant calls for more assertiveness in Whitehall', Financial Times, June 30, 2014: https://www.ft.com/content/7e75d64a-0037-11e4-8aaf-00144feab7de.
[33] BusinessDay, 'Human Development in the civil service', Editorial, September 18, 2014: https://archive.businessday.ng/editorial/article/human-development-in-the-civil-service/.
[34] Tunji Olaopa, 'The Centenary of the Nigerian Civil Service', Premium Times, February 1, 2014.
[35] Iyefu Adoba, 'Nation's civil servants ageing', ThisDay, June 18, 2004: https://allafrica.com/stories/200406180837.html.
[36] Ibid.
[37] Okonjo-Iweala, Reforming the Unreformable, p.52.

38 The International Civil Service Effectiveness (INCiSE) Index, 2019, Blavatvik School of Government, Oxford University: https://www.bsg.ox.ac.uk/about/partnerships/international-civil-service-effectiveness-index-2019.

39 'Nigeria's civil service best in the world – Yemi-Esan,' Vanguard, June 22, 2024: https://www.vanguardngr.com/2024/06/nigerias-civil-service-best-in-the-world-yemi-esan/.

40 Premium Times, 'Tinubu orders sanction of civil servants drawing salaries after relocating abroad,' Agency Report, June 23, 2024: https://www.premiumtimesng.com/news/top-news/706179-tinubu-orders-sanction-of-civil-servants-drawing-salaries-after-relocating-abroad.html.

41 Philip Shimnom Clement, 'My biggest challenge in service was workers' resistance to reforms – Yemi-Esan,' Daily Trust, September 28, 2024: https://dailytrust.com/my-biggest-challenge-in-service-was-workers-resistance-to-reforms-yemi-esan/.

42 Simon Kolawole, 'The world's best civil service,' The Cable, June 29, 2024: https://www.thecable.ng/the-worlds-best-civil-service/.

43 Fola Ojo, 'Nigeria's uncivil service: Dead workers drawing living wages,' Punch, June 28, 2024: https://punchng.com/nigerias-uncivil-service-dead-workers-drawing-living-wages/.

44 UK Civil Service's Policy Profession Scheme: https://lsedesignunit.com/LSEConnectWinter2015/html5/index.html?page=24&noflash

45 See Institute for Governance – Vision and values: https://www.instituteforgovernment.org.uk/about-us/mission/vision-and-values

Chapter 8: Tackling endemic corruption in Nigeria

1 Oxfam International, 'Nigeria: extreme inequality in numbers,' https://www.oxfam.org/en/nigeria-extreme-inequality-numbers.

2 Oluwatosin Ogunjuyigbe, 'CBN to refund $22m as World Bank detects $32m unaccounted funds in water project,'

BusinessDay, November 17, 2024:
https://businessday.ng/business-economy/article/cbn-to-
refund-22m-as-world-bank-detects-32m-unaccounted-funds-
in-water-project/.
[3] Ibid.
[4] Cited in Nigeria's 2024 Article IV Consultation report,
published in May 2024, at p68:
https://www.imf.org/en/Publications/CR/Issues/2024/05/08/Ni
geria-2024-Article-IV-Consultation-Press-Release-Staff-
Report-Staff-Statement-and-548726.
[5] BBC, 'David Cameron calls Nigeria and Afghanistan
"fantastically corrupt"', BBC News, May 1o, 2016:
https://www.bbc.co.uk/news/uk-politics-36260193.
[6] Yemi Osinbajo, 'Close To $15Billion, More Than Half of
Nigeria's Current Foreign Reserves, Was Lost To Fraudulent
Security Equipment Spending', The Office of the Vice
President, May 2, 2016: https://www.yemiosinbajo.ng/close-
to-15billion-more-than-half-of-nigerias-current-foreign-
reserves-was-lost-to-fraudulent-security-equipment-spending/.
[7] See 'Corruption in Nigeria: Patterns and Trends,'
UNODC/NBS, July 2024:
https://www.unodc.org/conig/uploads/documents/3rd_national
_corruption_survey_report_2024_07_09.pdf.
[8] See Nigeria's 2024 Article IV Consultation report, published
in May 2024:
https://www.imf.org/en/Publications/CR/Issues/2024/05/08/Ni
geria-2024-Article-IV-Consultation-Press-Release-Staff-
Report-Staff-Statement-and-548726.
[9] Ibid, p.63.
[10] Ibid.
[11] Susan Rose-Ackerman, 'The economics of corruption',
Journal of Public Economics, Volume 4, Issue 2, February
1975, pp. 187-203.
[12] See Susan Rose-Ackerman (ed), International Handbook on
the Economics of Corruption, Edward Elgar Publishing, 2007.
[13] Gary Becker, 'Crime and Punishment: An Economic
Approach', Journal of Political Economy, Vol 76, No2, March-
April 1968, pp.169-217.
[14] Ibid.
[15] Ibid.

[16] Steve Levitt and Stephen Dubner, Freakonomics: A rogue economist explores the hidden side of everything, Penguin, 2006.

[17] Ibid.

[18] See Nigeria's 2024 Article IV Consultation report, published in May 2024, at p68: https://www.imf.org/en/Publications/CR/Issues/2024/05/08/Nigeria-2024-Article-IV-Consultation-Press-Release-Staff-Report-Staff-Statement-and-548726.

[19] Campbell and Page, p.104.

[20] Vanguard, 'Tinubu suspends Bawa over weighty allegations of office abuse', News, June 14, 2023: https://www.vanguardngr.com/2023/06/tinubu-suspends-bawa-over-weighty-allegations-of-office-abuse/.

[21] Abiodun Sanusi, 'EFCC investigators taking bribes embarrassing — Chairman', Punch, January 18, 2024: https://punchng.com/efcc-investigators-taking-bribes-embarrassing-chairman/.

[22] Godfrey George et al. 'https://punchng.com/efcc-battles-internal-scandals-as-operatives-loot-recovered-assets/,' The Punch, January 25, 2025: https://punchng.com/efcc-battles-internal-scandals-as-operatives-loot-recovered-assets/.

[23] Ibid.

[24] Dele Oyewale, 'Olukoyede's record-breaking strides in EFCC and Olu Fasan's errors of analysis,' The Cable, February 15, 2025: https://www.thecable.ng/olukoyedes-record-breaking-strides-in-efcc-and-olu-fasans-errors-of-analysis/. This was a rejoinder to Olu Fasan, 'EFCC's failure: Olukoyede's blame-shifting is mere shadow-boxing,' Vanguard, February 13, 2025: https://www.vanguardngr.com/2025/02/efccs-failure-olukoyedes-blame-shifting-is-mere-shadow-boxing-by-olu-fasan/.

[25] Vanguard, 'Nigerians condemn corruption but defend corrupt leaders – EFCC chairman Olukoyede, News, February 1, 2025: https://www.vanguardngr.com/2025/02/nigerians-condemn-corruption-but-defend-corrupt-leaders-efcc-chairman-olukoyede/.

[26] See UN Guide for Anti-Corruption Policies, United Nation, 2003: https://www.unodc.org/pdf/crime/corruption/UN_Guide.pdf.

27 Nduka Orjinmo, 'Nigerian Officials Took $1.3 Billion in Bribes in 2023, NBS Says,' Bloomberg UK, July 11, 2024: https://www.bloomberg.com/news/articles/2024-07-11/nigerian-officials-took-1-3-billion-in-bribes-in-2023-nbs-says.

28 EFCC, 'Corruption cases should no longer be lost on technical grounds – BAWA', EFCC Media & Publicity, May 23, 2022: https://www.efcc.gov.ng/efcc/news-and-information/news-release/8040-corruption-cases-should-no-longer-be-lost-on-technical-grounds-bawa.

29 Adekunle Sulaimon, 'Loot recovered under Buhari returned to owners -Ex-presidential aide, Obono-Obla,' Punch, June 30, 2024: https://punchng.com/loot-recovered-under-buhari-returned-to-owners-ex-presidential-aide-obono-obla/.

30 RP Adelsten, 'The negotiated guilty plea: a framework for analysis', New York University Law Review, 53(4), 783-833, 1978.

31 Van Akkeren, J. (2023). Fraud Triangle: Cressey's Fraud Triangle and Alternative Fraud Theories. In: Poff, D.C., Michalos, A.C. (eds) Encyclopedia of Business and Professional Ethics. Springer, Cham. https://doi.org/10.1007/978-3-030-22767-8_216.

32 Marcus Felson, 'Those who discourage crime', Journal of Crime and Place, Vol4, 1995.

33 Dele Oyewale, 'Olukoyede's record-breaking strides in EFCC and Olu Fasan's errors of analysis,' The Cable, February 15, 2025: https://www.thecable.ng/olukoyedes-record-breaking-strides-in-efcc-and-olu-fasans-errors-of-analysis/.

34 Olu Fasan, 'Armsgate: The scandal that ravages Nigeria's critical institutions', BusinessDay, January 25, 2016: https://businessday.ng/columnist/article/armsgate-the-scandal-that-ravages-nigerias-critical-institutions/.

35 John Egbeazien Oshodi, 'Olukoyede's Challenge, Fasan's Concerns, And Nigeria's Reality: A Psychologist's Take on Corruption,' Modern Ghana, February 15, 2025: https://www.modernghana.com/news/1379989/olukoyedes-challenge-fasans-concerns-and-niger.html.

36 See 'Third Sector – Marketing Dictionary', Monash Business School,

https://www.monash.edu/business/marketing/marketing-
dictionary/t/third-sector.

[37] John Helliwell, et al (eds), 'World Happiness Report (2015),
United Nations, 2015: https://s3.amazonaws.com/happiness-
report/2015/WHR15_Sep15.pdf.

[38] Ngozi Okonjo-Iweala, 'Fighting Corruption Is Dangerous,
The MIT Press, 2018. See also William Dorintinsky and
Shilpa Pradham, 'Exploring Corruption in Public Financial
Management' in the many Faces of Corruption: Tracking
Vulnerabilities at the Sector Level, edited by J. Edgardo
Campos and Sanjay Pradhan, 267-294, World Bank, 2007,
cited in Okonjo-Iweala, Fighting Corruption Is Dangerous,
2018.

[39] Ibid.

[40] Ibid.

[41] See 'Corruption in Nigeria: Patterns and Trends,'
UNODC/NBS, July 2024:
https://www.unodc.org/conig/uploads/documents/3rd_national
_corruption_survey_report_2024_07_09.pdf.

[42] United Nations Convention against corruption:
https://treaties.un.org/Pages/ViewDetails.aspx?src=TREATY&
mtdsg_no=XVIII-14&chapter=18&clang=_en

[43] African Union Convention on Preventing and Combatting
Corruption: https://au.int/en/treaties/african-union-convention-
preventing-and-combating-corruption.

[44] OECD, Asset Declaration for Public Officials: A Tool to
Prevent Corruption, OECD Publishing, 2011.

[45] Ibid.

[46] Transparency International, 'Holding politicians to account:
Asset Declaration', January 17, 2013,
https://www.transparency.org/en/news/holding-politicians-to-
account-asset-declarations.

[47] OECD, 'Asset Declaration in Lithuania', OECD 2011.

[48] Ameh Ejekwonyilo, 'Appeal Court dismisses request for
disclosure of Jonathan, Buhari, others' assets declarations',
Premium Times, March 15, 2024:
https://www.premiumtimesng.com/news/headlines/677915-
appeal-court-dismisses-request-for-disclosure-of-jonathan-
buhari-others-assets-declarations.html?tztc=1.

[49] Françoise Grouigneau and Richard Hoult of Les Echos,
'Interview with Paul Wolfowitz - full transcript', Financial

Times, October 29, 2006:
https://www.ft.com/content/3836c4c4-6787-11db-8ea5-0000779e2340.
[50] See Nigeria's 2024 Article IV Consultation report, published in May 2024, at p.71:
https://www.imf.org/en/Publications/CR/Issues/2024/05/08/Nigeria-2024-Article-IV-Consultation-Press-Release-Staff-Report-Staff-Statement-and-548726.
[51] Devin Dwyer, 'Supreme Court rejects Trump claim of "absolute immunity" from grand jury subpoena for tax returns', ABC News, June 10, 2020:
https://abcnews.go.com/Politics/scotus-rules-trump-financial-records-subpoenas/story?id=71382157.
[52] Ibid.
[53] Chris Stein, 'US supreme court allows Congress to view Trump's tax returns', The Guardian, November 22, 2022:
https://www.theguardian.com/us-news/2022/nov/22/supreme-court-trump-tax-returns-congress-house.
[54] The Cable, 'Patience Jonathan: It took me 15 years to save up the $15m frozen by EFCC', The Cable, October 20, 2016:
https://www.thecable.ng/patience-jonathan-it-took-me-15-years-to-save-up-the-15m-frozen-by-efcc/.
[55] Wale Odunsi, 'Yakubu refuses to disclose donors of $9.8m "gift"', Daily Post, March 12, 2017:
https://dailypost.ng/2017/03/12/yakubu-refuses-disclose-donors-9-8m-gift/.
[56] See Article 15 of the UN Convention Against Corruption.
[57] LexisNexis, 'Gifts and hospitality policy—government officials', 2024:
https://www.lexisnexis.co.uk/legal/precedents/gifts-hospitality-policy-government-officials.
[58] Alabi Williams, 'My lord, tell me when a gift is not a bribe', The Guardian, February 26, 2017:
https://guardian.ng/opinion/my-lord-tell-me-when-a-gift-is-not-bribe/.
[59] Gov.UK, 'Anti-Corruption Summit: London 2016', May 12, 2016: https://www.gov.uk/government/topical-events/anti-corruption-summit-london-2016.
[60] Soni Daniel, 'EFCC recovers $2.9b looted cash in 2 years', Vanguard, November 8, 2017:

https://www.vanguardngr.com/2017/11/efcc-recovers-2-9b-looted-cash-2-years/.
[61] Press Release, 'Court orders Nigerian govt to disclose names of suspected looters', Premium Times, July 5, 2017: https://www.premiumtimesng.com/news/top-news/235938-court-orders-nigerian-govt-disclose-names-suspected-looters.html?tztc=1.
[62] Campbell and Page, p.104.
[63] News Agency of Nigeria, 'Ndume calls on Buhari to sign Unexplained Wealth Order', published in The Guardian, November 8, 2021: https://guardian.ng/news/ndume-calls-on-buhari-to-sign-unexplained-wealth-order/.
[64] EFCC, 'Olukoyede seeks legislation against unexplained wealth', EFCC, December 15, 2023: https://www.efcc.gov.ng/efcc/news-and-information/news-release/9670-olukoyede-seeks-legislation-against-unexplained-wealth.
[65] See, 'How Public Officers Make Fraudulent Anticipatory Declaration of Assets - Olukoyede,' EFCC, August 12, 2025.
[66] See Nigeria's 2024 Article IV Consultation report, published in May 2024, at p.71: https://www.imf.org/en/Publications/CR/Issues/2024/05/08/Nigeria-2024-Article-IV-Consultation-Press-Release-Staff-Report-Staff-Statement-and-548726.
[67] Lord Templeman's statement while giving the judgement of the Privy Council in Attorney-General for Hong Kong v Reid [1994]AC 324 at 330.
[68] UN Press Statement, 'Secretary-General lauds adoption by General Assembly of United Nations Convention Against Corruption', UN, October 31, 2003: https://press.un.org/en/2003/sgsm8977.doc.htm.
[69] PILA Bulletin, 'Irish Court of Appeal upholds reversal of burden of proof in corruption cases', Public International Law Alliance, October 12, 2016: https://www.pila.ie/resources/bulletin/2016/10/12/irish-court-of-appeal-upholds-reversal-of-burden-of-proof-in-corruption-cases.
[70] Law Commission, 'Legislating the criminal code: corruption', Gov.UK website, March 3, 1998: https://www.gov.uk/government/publications/legislating-the-criminal-code-corruption.

[71] However, the Irish Supreme Court later nullified the ruling od the Irish Appeal Court on the ground that reversal of burden of proof in corruption cases undermined the presumption of innocence. See: https://www.irishlegal.com/articles/supreme-court-reverse-burden-of-proof-undermined-allegedly-corrupt-councillor-s-presumption-of-innocence. But there are many countries where such reversal is deemed legal.

[72] Aganga, Reclaiming the Jewel of Africa, p.211.

Chapter 9: Strengthening the Rule of Law

[1] Dele Farotimi, Nigeria and its Criminal Justice, Farotimi Publishers, 2024, Chapter 1.

[2] Robert Shrimsley, 'Britain will not thrive in a might is right world,' Financial Times, Friday, 14 February 2025: https://www.ft.com/content/eadeb257-de36-4748-a6ea-1bd76806b8a0.

[3] WTO (2024), Trade Policy Review (Nigeria) – Report by the Secretariat, p.91, October 9, 2024: https://www.wto.org/english/tratop_e/tpr_e/s462_e.pdf.

[4] See Nigeria's 2024 Article IV Consultation report, published in May 2024, at p.21: https://www.imf.org/en/Publications/CR/Issues/2024/05/08/Nigeria-2024-Article-IV-Consultation-Press-Release-Staff-Report-Staff-Statement-and-548726.

[5] Campbell and Page, Nigeria, p.105.

[6] See 'Corruption in Nigeria: Patterns and Trends,' UNODC/NBS, July 2024: https://www.unodc.org/conig/uploads/documents/3rd_national_corruption_survey_report_2024_07_09.pdf.

[7] Ameh Ejekwonyilo, 'Ex-senator under fire after confessing to influencing wife's decisions as appeal court judge', Premium Times, June 13, 2023: https://www.premiumtimesng.com/news/604233-ex-senator-under-fire-after-confessing-to-influencing-wifes-decisions-as-appeal-court-judge.html?tztc=1.

[8] Olisa Agbakoba, 'Nigeria's court procedural landscape is sluggish and inefficient and needs Reform,' Olisa Agbakoba Legal, OAL, November 8, 2022: https://oal.law/nigerias-court-

procedural-landscape-is-sluggish-and-inefficient-and-needs-reform/.

9 See Nigeria's 2024 Article IV Consultation report, published in May 2024, at p.70:
https://www.imf.org/en/Publications/CR/Issues/2024/05/08/Nigeria-2024-Article-IV-Consultation-Press-Release-Staff-Report-Staff-Statement-and-548726.

10 See Nigeria's 2024 Article IV Consultation report, published in May 2024, at p.70:
https://www.imf.org/en/Publications/CR/Issues/2024/05/08/Nigeria-2024-Article-IV-Consultation-Press-Release-Staff-Report-Staff-Statement-and-548726.

11 Donatus Anichukwueze, 'Full Text of Justice Dattijo's Speech on CJN's Powers, State of The Judiciary, Other Matters', Channels TV, October 27, 2023:
https://www.channelstv.com/2023/10/27/full-text-of-justice-dattijos-speech-on-cjns-powers-state-of-the-judiciary-other-matters/.

12 Ibid.

13 Olalekan Adetayo, 'Buhari says rule of law must be subject to national interest', Punch, August 27, 2018:
https://punchng.com/buhari-says-rule-of-law-must-be-subject-to-national-interest/.

14 Paul Craig, Formal and Substantial Conceptions of the Rule of Law: An Analytical Framework, Oxford University Research Archive, ORA, 2017.

15 Kai Mollar, 'Dworkin's Theory of Rights in the Age of Proportionality', Law Society Economy Working Papers, London School of Economics Research Online, 2017.

16 See Chapter IV (Fundamental Rights) of Nigeria's 1999 Constitution, as amended.

17 Raymond Wacks, 'The rule of law misconstrued?' Counsel magazine, November 2024, p38.

18 David Feldman (ed) English Public Law, Oxford University Press, 2004, pp. 34-35.

19 Ibid, p.34.

20 Raymond Wacks, 'The rule of law misconstrued?' Counsel magazine, November 2024, p37.

21 The Cable, 'Dasuki regains freedom after four years in custody', News report, December 24, 2019:

https://www.thecable.ng/breaking-dasuki-regains-freedom-after-four-years-in-custody/.

[22] Barack Obama, The Audacity of Hope, Canongate, 2007, p.319.

[23] Jon Henley, 'From Trump to Sarkozy: the political leaders who have been prosecuted', The Guardian, April 9, 2023: https://www.theguardian.com/us-news/2023/apr/09/presidents-pms-political-leaders-prosecuted-jailed.

[24] See Luc Cohen, et al. 'Donald Trump becomes first US president convicted of a crime', Reuters, May 31, 2024: https://www.reuters.com/legal/jurors-begin-second-day-deliberations-trump-hush-money-trial-2024-05-30/.

[25] Ikechukwu Amaechi, 'Why Buhari must be put on trial!', Vanguard, August 17, 2023: https://www.vanguardngr.com/2023/08/why-buhari-must-be-put-on-trial-by-ikechukwu-amaechi/.

[26] Chris Winters, 'SCOTUS: Trump Is Not Above the Law', Yes Magazine, July 9, 2020: https://www.yesmagazine.org/opinion/2020/07/09/supreme-court-trump-tax-returns.

[27] For instance, in his book 'The Challenges of Democracy and the Rule of Law, Jonathan Sumption, a former Justice of the UK Supreme Court, criticised the US Supreme Court decision on the basis that the decision failed to explain how the interpretation of 'official functions' is to be reconciled with a president's constitutional duty to uphold the law.

[28] Stefanie Palmer, 'US Supreme Court says Donald Trump immune for 'official acts' as president,' Financial Times, July 2, 2024: https://www.ft.com/content/3aee93fb-9bae-4783-be01-d471f99d16a6.

[29] Ibid.

[30] Ben Protess and Kate Christobek, 'Judge Upholds Trump's Conviction but Signals No Jail Time,' The New York Times, January 3, 2025: https://www.nytimes.com/2025/01/03/nyregion/trump-sentencing-hush-money-case-ny.html.

[31] A-M Slaughter, 'International Law and International Relations theory: A Dual Agenda', American Journal of International Law, Vol 87, Issue 2 (April 1993), 205-239

[32] Carolyn Dubey, 'General Principles of International Law: Monism and Dualism', International Judicial Monitor, 2014,

Winter Issue:
http://www.judicialmonitor.org/archive_winter2014/generalpri
nciples.html.
[33] Alex Enumah, 'FG Yet to Ratify over 400 Treaties,
Protocols, Agreements', ThisDay, January 8, 2020:
https://www.thisdaylive.com/index.php/2020/01/08/fg-yet-to-
ratify-over-400-treaties-protocols-agreements/.
[34] WTO (2024), Trade Policy Review (Nigeria) – Report by
the Secretariat, p.91, October 9, 2024:
https://www.wto.org/english/tratop_e/tpr_e/s462_e.pdf.
[35] Ibid.
[36] Emeka Omeihe, 'Gowon, Soyinka and US,' The Nation,
December 8, 2014: https://thenationonlineng.net/gowon-
soyinka-us/.
[37] Wycliffe Muia, 'Nigeria angered after military chief denied
Canada entry,' BBC News, February 15, 2025:
https://www.bbc.com/news/articles/c17eky00r5ro.
[38] Ibid.
[39] For instance, Donald Trump threated to acquire Greenland,
which belongs to Denmark, by force and to take control of the
Panama Canal. He also threatened to annex Canada and make
it the 51st of the US and said he would rename the Guld of
Mexico and call it Gulf of America, ignoring the feeling and
sensitivity of Mexico. See: Christine Murray and Ilya
Gridneff, 'Mexico's president calls for parts of US to be
renamed 'Mexican America', Financial Times, January 8,
2025: https://www.ft.com/content/c8702574-fd47-4cfb-b047-
63e76786ff48.
[40] Henry Kissinger, Years of Upheaval, Little Brown US,
1989.
[41] Leo Lweis, 'Why it's hard to be a friend of America,'
Financial Times, January 2, 2024:
https://www.ft.com/content/ddd79f43-b56d-45e0-8282-
38b8f0f9feb9.
[42] Margaret Thatcher, The Downing Street Years, Happer
Collins Publishers, 1993.
[43] Baroness Chalker's interview with Marketfinder
International Magazine, June/July 1995 edition, pp42-45.
[44] Emeka Anyaoku's interview with the African Expatriate
Magazine, June/July 1996 edition, pp18-22.

[45] Jeffrey Gettleman, 'Two Sides of Nigeria Addressed by Clinton,' New York Times, August 12, 2009: https://www.nytimes.com/2009/08/13/world/africa/13diplo.html.

[46] The Economist, 'Big country, thin skin,' February 13, 2014: https://www.economist.com/baobab/2014/02/13/big-country-thin-skin.

[47] The visa ban was later revoked by President Joe Biden in January 2021. See: Proclamation on Ending Discriminatory Bans on Entry to The United States: https://www.whitehouse.gov/briefing-room/presidential-actions/2021/01/20/proclamation-ending-discriminatory-bans-on-entry-to-the-united-states/.

[48] Quinn Owen, 'Trump administration expands travel ban to Nigeria and 5 other countries,' ABC News, January 31, 2020: https://abcnews.go.com/Politics/trump-administration-expands-travel-ban-nigeria-countries/story?id=68677970.

[49] Shkurta Januzi, 'EU Plans to Impose Visa Restrictions on Nigerians,' Schengen News, February 21, 2020: https://schengen.news/eu-plans-to-impose-visa-restrictions-on-nigerians/.

[50] Proclamation 9983 of January 31, 2020: https://www.govinfo.gov/content/pkg/FR-2020-02-05/pdf/2020-02422.pdf.

[51] Shkurta Januzi, 'EU Plans to Impose Visa Restrictions on Nigerians,' Schengen News, February 21, 2020: https://schengen.news/eu-plans-to-impose-visa-restrictions-on-nigerians/.

[52] Ibid.

[53] Ibid.

[54] Ibid.

[55] Proclamation 9983 of January 31, 2020: https://www.govinfo.gov/content/pkg/FR-2020-02-05/pdf/2020-02422.pdf.

[56] Ibid.

[57] Ibid.

[58] John Campbell and Matthew Page, Nigeria: What Everyone Needs to Know, Oxford, 2018. P101.

[59] Ibid. p2.

[60] The Cable, 'Trump to Buhari: America won't accept killing of Christians in Nigeria,' April 30, 2018:

https://www.thecable.ng/breaking-america-wont-accept-killing-of-christians-says-trump/.

Chapter 10: Extreme Poverty and Inequality

[1] World Bank, 'Poverty Reduction in Nigeria in the last Decade', Report, October 13, 2016.
[2] World Bank, 'Social Protection Project, Nigeria', Report No PIDC22018, March 13, 2015. .
[3] Ode Uduu, 'Nigeria's Wealth Inequality Score is 35.1 and its 11th in West Africa,' Ode Uduu, 'Nigeria's Wealth Inequality Score is 35.1 and its 11th in West Africa,' Dataphyte, August 25, 2022: https://www.dataphyte.com/latest-reports/nigerias-wealth-inequality-score-is-35-1-and-its-11th-in-west-africa/.
[4] Oxfam, 'Nigeria: extreme inequality in numbers,' https://www.oxfam.org/en/nigeria-extreme-inequality-numbers.
[5] NBS, 'Nigeria Launches its Most Extensive National Measure of Multidimensional Poverty.,' Press Release, November 17, 2022: https://nigerianstat.gov.ng/news/78#
[6] See A2F 2023 Financial Inclusion Factsheet, EFinA, December 2, 2023: https://a2f.ng/a2f-2023-financial-inclusion-state-factsheet/.
[7] Oxfam, 'The Commitment to Reducing Inequality Index 2022', Research Report, October 11, 2022: https://policy-practice.oxfam.org/resources/the-commitment-to-reducing-inequality-index-2022-621419/..
[8] Fredrick Nwabufo, 'Jonathan: Private jets show Nigeria is not poor', May 1, 2014: https://www.thecable.ng/nlc-president-asks-jonathan-to-get-his-men-out-of-abuja/.
[9] Homi Kharas, et al, The start of a new poverty narrative, Brookings, June 19, 2018: https://www.brookings.edu/articles/the-start-of-a-new-poverty-narrative/.
[10] Ibid.
[11] World Bank, Nigeria Economic Update, Fall 2019.
[12] National Bureau of Statistics, Nigeria launches its Most Extensive National Measure of Multidimensional Poverty, NBS Press Release, 17 November 2022.
[13] John Aglionby, 'More than half the world's population is now middle class', Financial Times, September 30, 2018:

https://www.ft.com/content/e3fa475c-c2e9-11e8-95b1-d36dfef1b89a.

[14] World Data Lab, 'The World of Tomorrow in Data', 2018: https://worlddata.io/the-world-of-tomorrow-in-data/.

[15] Martin Wolf, 'The case for persisting with foreign aid,' Financial Times, February 11, 2025: https://www.ft.com/content/3e470e39-ba59-443f-a717-78debb5edca2.

[16] Shekhar Aiyar, 'Global inequality is narrowing – and that is cause for celebration,' Financial Times, August 13, 2024.

[17] Homi Kharas, et al, The start of a new poverty narrative, Brookings, June 19, 2018: https://www.brookings.edu/articles/the-start-of-a-new-poverty-narrative/.

[18] Bank of Industry, 'Economic Development through the Nigerian Informal Sector: A BOI perspective', BOI Blogs: https://www.boi.ng/economic-development-through-the-nigerian-informal-sector-a-boi-perspective/.

[19] For instance, the UK has pursued a welfare-to-work policy since 2015, See, 'Welfare-to-work', House of Commons Work and Pensions Committee report, 14 October 2015. The unemployed must prove that they are spending at least 35 hours a week looking for work.

[20] OECD, Youth not in employment, education or training (NEET). OECD Data, 2023.

[21] Donald Hirsch, 'Strategies against poverty: A shared roadmap', Joseph Rowntree Foundation, December 13, 2004: https://www.jrf.org.uk/work/strategies-against-poverty-a-shared-road-map.

[22] Ibid.

[23] Piketty, Capital, p.15.

[24] See Matthew Francis, 'A crusade to enfranchise the many: Thatcherism and the property-owning democracy', Twentieth Century British History, Vol 23, Issue 2, June 2012, pp275-297.

[25] Piketty, Capital, p.47.

[26] BBC, 'Nigerian senator 'busts open' $37,500 expenses payments', BBC Africa, March 12, 2018: https://www.bbc.co.uk/news/world-africa-43377690.

27 BBC, 'Nigerian senator salary calculator: How do you compare?', BBC Africa, April 1, 2018: https://www.bbc.co.uk/news/world-africa-43516825.
28 Tope Omogbolagun, 'I get N21m monthly as take home, Kano lawmaker reveals,' The Punch, August 14, 2024: https://punchng.com/i-get-n21m-monthly-as-take-home-kano-lawmaker-reveals/.
29 Olu Fasan, 'A living wage is an antidote to poverty; it's time Nigeria paid it,' BusinessDay, May 20, 2024: https://businessday.ng/columnist/article/a-living-wage-is-an-antidote-to-poverty-its-time-nigeria-paid-it/.
30 Joy Jimoh, '62.4 % Nigerian households' food insecure – NBS,' BusinessDay, November 21, 2024: https://businessday.ng/news/article/62-4-nigerian-households-food-insecure-nbs/
31 See 'The SBM Jollof Index: Unbounded Set', July 25, 2024: https://www.sbmintel.com/2024/07/the-sbm-jollof-index-unbounded-set/.
32 Ibid.
33 See the UK National Living Wage, GOV.UK: https://www.gov.uk/government/publications/national-minimum-wage-and-national-living-wage-low-pay-commission-remit-2024/national-minimum-wage-and-national-living-wage-low-pay-commission-remit-2024-html-version.
34 See ILO, 'ILO reaches agreement on the issue of living wages,' Press Statement, March 15, 2024: https://www.ilo.org/resource/news/ilo-reaches-agreement-issue-living-wages.
35 Victor Ahiuma-Young, 'BLEAK MAY DAY: 26 states' workers owed salaries', Vanguard, May 1, 2016: https://www.vanguardngr.com/2016/05/bleak-may-day-26-states-workers-owed-salaries/.
36 FIRS, 'Going after billionaire tax defaulters': FIRS website: https://www.firs.gov.ng/firs-going-after-billionaire-tax-defaulters/.
37 Kingsley Moghalu, 'Beyond Dangote Refinery: We need prosperity for Nigerians,' BusinessDay, July 25, 2024: https://businessday.ng/opinion/article/beyond-dangote-refinery-we-need-prosperity-for-nigerians/.

[38] Will Hutton. The State We're In, Jonathan Cape, 1995, p.261.

[39] UNPF, 'United Nations Population Fund Country programme document for Nigeria', Technical Report, February 3, 2023: https://nigeria.unfpa.org/en/publications/united-nations-population-fund-country-programme-document-nigeria.

[40] Ibid.

[41] Financial Times, 'A slow population decline is nothing to fear', The FT View, June 4, 2021: https://www.ft.com/content/a5b0a0d1-943a-44f8-be5d-b3d3fc458008.

[42] Channels TV, 'Rep shows off his four wives, declares he has 27 children', You Tube: https://www.youtube.com/watch?v=RG_ybSn5Mh4.

[43] Wasiu Alli, 'Nigerians' per capita income hits 20-year low on weak economy,' BusinessDay, November 4, 2024: https://businessday.ng/business-economy/article/nigerians-per-capita-income-hits-20-year-low-on-weak-economy/.

[44] Wasiu Alli, 'Nigeria's GDP per capita down to $835 in 2025 – IMF,' BusinessDay, February 6, 2025: https://businessday.ng/business-economy/article/nigerias-per-capita-income-down-to-835-in-2025-imf/.

[45] Madeline Speed, Aanu Adeoye and Mercedes R Madeline Speed, Aanu Adeoye and Mercedes Ruehl, 'The Singaporean firm betting on Nigeria amid multinationals' "exodus",' Financial Times, June 19, 2024: https://www.ft.com/content/84a7ba8a-de53-4d4e-b21a-22042c7b27da.

[46] Ibid.

[47] PwC, The Africa Business Agenda, p.27.

[48] World Bank, Nigeria Economic Update, Fall 2019, p.43

[49] Ibid.

[50] Ed Conway, Material World, Penguin, 2023, p.276.

[51] Ibid, p.173.

[52] Alan Beattie, 'Open markets have delivered unmatched levels of food security,' Financial Times, September 3, 2024.

[53] John Ungoed-Thomas and George Arbuttnott, Nigerian agents to snare slavers at UK Airports, Sunday Times, July 30, 2017: https://www.thetimes.co.uk/article/nigerian-agents-to-snare-slavers-at-uk-airports-ktsfqpgfm

[54] Ibid.

[55] Akinola Ajibola, 'Human Trafficking: NAPTIP Operatives to Work at UK Airports', Channels TV, July 10, 2017: https://www.channelstv.com/2017/07/10/human-trafficking-naptip-operatives-to-work-at-uk-airports/.

[56] See Patrician Hynes, et al, 'Vulnerability to Human Trafficking: A Study of Viet Nam, Albania, Nigeria and the UK', Report of Shared Learning Event held in Hanoi, Viet Nam, December 6-7, 2017.

[57] BBC, 'Nigeria trafficking "top priority", Commissioner says', BBC Africa, June 17, 2015: https://www.bbc.co.uk/news/uk-33159899.

[58] Ibid.

[59] Femi Akinyemi, 'Human trafficking, illegal migration endemic in Nigeria — NAPTIP,' Nigerian Tribune, February 1, 2025: https://tribuneonlineng.com/human-trafficking-illegal-migration-endemic-in-nigeria-naptip/.

[60] BBC, 'Nigeria trafficking "top priority", Commissioner says', BBC Africa, June 17, 2015: https://www.bbc.co.uk/news/uk-33159899.

[61] Niall Ferguson, Empire, p.74.

[62] Ibid.

[63] US Bureau of African Affairs, '2023 Trafficking in Persons Report: Nigeria', Office to Monitor and Combat Trafficking in Persons, 2023: https://www.state.gov/reports/2023-trafficking-in-persons-report/nigeria#report-toc__exec-summary.

Chapter 11: Insecurity: A Hobbesian State of Nature

[1] Tom Sorrell, 'Leviathan: work by Hobbes', Encyclopedia Britannica, May 17, 2024: https://www.britannica.com/topic/Leviathan-by-Hobbes.

[2] Ibid.

[3] John Locke (Author), Marck Goldie (Editor), Second Treatise of Government and A letter Concerning Toleration, Oxford World's Classics, Oxford University Press, First Edition, 2016.

[4] Vanguard, 'Insecurity: 63,111 persons killed in Buhari's eight years', News Report, May 20, 2023:

https://www.vanguardngr.com/2023/05/insecurity-63111-persons-killed-in-buharis-eight-years/.

[5] Joy Jimoh, 'Nigerians pay N2.3trn as ransom in 12 months-NBS survey,' BusinessDay, December 17, 2024: https://businessday.ng/news/article/nigerians-pay-n2-3trn-as-ransom-in-12-months-nbs-survey/.

[6] Ibid.

[7] Release International, 'Dozens of Christians slaughtered in attacks in Nigeria,' Release, April 11, 2025: https://releaseinternational.org/dozens-of-christians-slaughtered-in-attacks-in-nigeria/.

[8] Mansur Abubakar & Abubakar Maccido, ''How I survived Nigeria attack that killed my 16 friends', BBC News, April 4, 2025: https://www.bbc.co.uk/news/articles/cgrgwxxw2kro.

[9] Sunday Aborisade and Linus Aleke, 'Borno Senator Ndume Reveals 380 Casualties in 252 Boko Haram Attacks Between November 2024 and April 2025,' Arise News, April 14, 2025: https://www.arise.tv/borno-senator-ndume-reveals-380-casualties-in-252-boko-haram-attacks-between-november-2024-and-april-2025/.

[10] Open Doors, 'More than 218 killed in latest spate of deadly attacks in Nigeria,'
Open Doors, June 19, 2025: https://www.opendoorsuk.org/news/latest-news/nigeria-deadly-attacks/

[11] Mansur Abubakar, 'What is behind the wave of killings in central Nigeria?' BBC, June 16, 2025: https://www.bbc.co.uk/news/articles/clyznnl4mddo.

[12] BBC, 'Why Nigeria's economy is in such a mess', BBC Africa, February 27, 2023: https://www.bbc.co.uk/news/world-africa-68402662.

[13] See Iyaji Danjuma, 'Insurgency, Political Risk and Foreign Direct Investment Inflows in Nigeria: A Sectoral Analysis', CBN Journal of Applied Statistics, Vol 12. No 2 (December 2021).

[14] Aganga, Reclaiming the Jewel of Africa, p.166.

[15] Vanguard, 'The looming hinger, poverty bomb', Vanguard Editorial, April 25, 2019: https://www.vanguardngr.com/2019/04/the-looming-hunger-poverty-time-bomb/.

[16] Ibid.

[17] Deborah Sanusi, 'Nigerian politicians in office to kill, steal, remain in power -Amaechi,' The Punch, January 30, 2025: https://punchng.com/nigerian-politicians-in-office-to-kill-steal-remain-in-power-amaechi/.

[18] Simon Kolawole, 'Making Sense of Amaechi's Confessions,' ThisDay, February 2, 2025: https://www.thisdaylive.com/index.php/2025/02/02/making-sense-of-amaechis-confessions/.

[19] Campbell and Page, Nigeria, pp.132 and 133.

[20] Tunji Oyeyemi, 'Ruga Settlement is to Resolve Farmer/Herder conflicts – Presidency', Press Release, Federal Ministry of Information and National Orientation, June 30, 2019: https://fmino.gov.ng/ruga-settlement-is-to-resolve-farmer-herder-conflicts-presidency/.

[21] Ibid.

[22] The Crisis Group, The Climate Factor in Nigeria's Farmer-Herder violence: https://nigeriaclimate.crisisgroup.org/.

[23] Jon E Anderson, 'United States v. Lopez (1995)', Encyclopedia Britannica, April 19, 2024: https://www.britannica.com/topic/United-States-v-Lopez.

[24] Dyepkazah Shibayan, 'Danjuma asks Nigerians to defend themselves against killers, says "armed forces not neutral"', The Cable, March 24, 2018: https://www.thecable.ng/danjuma-asks-nigerians-defend-killers/.

[25] Abimbola Adelakun, 'Okuama: Beyond the talk of reprisals', Punch, March 21, 2024: https://punchng.com/okuama-beyond-the-talk-of-reprisals/.

[26] Wikipedia, 'Military capability', https://en.wikipedia.org/wiki/Military_capability#.

[27] See Global Firepower, '2024 Military Strength Ranking', GFP, https://www.globalfirepower.com/countries-listing.php.

[28] Temitope Abiodun, 'Why there is a mismatch between funding for Nigeria's military and its performance', The Conversation, November 18, 2020: https://theconversation.com/why-theres-a-mismatch-between-funding-for-nigerias-military-and-its-performance-149554.

[29] Ibid.

[30] Ibid.

[31] Olu Fasan, 'The military's past, present and future', BusinessDay, March 2, 2015:

https://businessday.ng/columnist/article/the-militarys-past-present-and-future/.

[32] Collier and Besley, 'Escaping the fragility trap', p.18.

[33] Campbell and Page, Nigeria, p.138.

[34] Ibid, 139.

[35] Amnesty International, '#EndSARS: Investigate killings of protesters', Press Statement: https://www.amnesty.org.uk/urgent-actions/endsars-investigate-killings-protestors#.

[36] Amnesty International, 'Human Rights in Nigeria Report 2023': https://www.amnesty.org/en/location/africa/west-and-central-africa/nigeria/report-nigeria/.

[37] Austin Ajayi, 'Why Nigerian military has difficulty getting arms from America — U.S. govt', Premium Times, October 9, 2014: https://www.premiumtimesng.com/news/headlines/169264-why-nigerian-military-has-difficulty-getting-arms-from-america-u-s-govt.html?tztc=1.

[38] Idowu Bankole, '36 States Assembly Speakers back state police', Vanguard, May 16, 2024: https://www.vanguardngr.com/2024/05/36-states-assembly-speakers-back-state-police/.

[39] Yakubu Mohammed, 'Nigeria moves closer to state policing as majority of governors agree,' Premium Times, December 13, 2024: https://www.premiumtimesng.com/news/top-news/761022-nigeria-moves-closer-to-state-policing-as-majority-of-governors-agree.html.

[40] National Bureau of Statistics, Nigerian Domestic and Foreign Debt, Q3 2022, published in January 2023.

[41] Uwais Report, p.140.

[42] Simon Kolawole, 'Announcing the arrival of state police', The Cable, May 18, 2024: https://www.thecable.ng/announcing-the-arrival-of-state-police/

[43] Robert Inman and Daniel Rubinfeld, 'Economics of Federation', Oxford Handbook of Law and Economics, 2014.

[44] Kevin M Cherry, Plato, Aristotle and the Purpose of Politics, Cambridge University Press, 2012.

[45] Niall Ferguson, Civilisation, Penguin, 2012, p3.

Conclusion: Change is elusive in Nigeria, but must happen

[1] Mancur Olson, 'The Rise and Decline of Nations – Economic, Growth, Stagfaltion, and Social Rigidities, Yale University Press, 1984.
[2] Ivo Bischoff, 'A Broader View on Mancur Olson's Theory of Institutional Sclerosis', Southern Economic Journal, 74(1), July 2007, pp34-49.
[3] John Williamson (ed), The Political Economy of Policy Reform, Peterson Institute for International Economics, January 1994.
[4] Daron Acemoglu and James Robinson, Why Nations Fail, Profile Books, 2013.
[5] 'Understanding Policy Development and Choices Through the "3-I" Framework: Interests, Ideas and Institutions', https://policyreadinesstool.com/strategies/.
[6] Daniel Susskind, Growth: A Reckoning, Allen Lane, April 2024.
[7] Cass Sunstein, How Change Happens, The MIT Press, April 2019.
[8] Ibid.
[9] BBC, 'Analysis: What did Nigeria's National Conference Achieve?', BBC Africa, August 24, 2014: https://www.bbc.co.uk/news/world-africa-28929532.
[10] Henry Umoru and Levinus Nwabughiogu, 'Buhari: Confab report is for the archives', Vanguard, June 4, 2016: https://www.vanguardngr.com/2016/06/buhari-confab-report-archives/.
[11] Chijioke Jannah, 'Restructuring: PDP reveals what APC plans to do with El-Rufai committee's report', Daily Post, January 31, 2018: https://dailypost.ng/2018/01/31/restructuring-pdp-reveals-apc-plans-el-rufai-committees-report/.
[12] Caroline Banton, 'What is Path Dependency? Definition, Effects and Examples', Investopedia, November 29, 2021: https://www.investopedia.com/terms/p/path-dependency.asp.
[13] For instance, under Nigeria's constitution, anyone can become president of Nigeria even if he received only 30 per cent of the total votes cast, provided he secured the highest

votes among all the contestants. The electoral system can produce a president with a very weak mandate and legitimacy.
[14] The Whistler, 'Clarkes calls for military takeover', News report, November 25, 2016: https://thewhistler.ng/clarke-calls-for-military-takeover/.
[15] Sunday Aborisade, 'Forcing NASS to produce new constitution, invitation to anarchy –Senate', June 5, 2021: https://punchng.com/forcing-nass-to-produce-new-constitution-invitation-to-anarchy-senate/.
[16] JM Keynes, The General Theory of Interest, Employment and Money, London: Macmillan, 1936, p.383.
[17] Douglas North, Institutions, Institutional Changes and Economic Performance, Cambridge University Press, 1991.
[18] Monte Bute, 'How to run a country: Cicero gives us 10 lessons for modern leaders', Minesota Reformer, March 2022: https://minnesotareformer.com/2022/03/24/how-to-run-a-country-cicero-gives-us-10-lessons-for-modern-leaders/.
[19] James Orr, An Analysis of Plato's Republic, Routledge, 2017.
[20] Lane, Melissa. 'Philosopher king'. Encyclopedia Britannica, 5 Feb. 2024, https://www.britannica.com/topic/philosopher-king.
[21] Matthew Parris, 'War refugees are being let down at the top,' The Times, April 1, 2022: https://www.thetimes.com/world/russia-ukraine-war/article/war-refugees-are-being-let-down-at-the-top-t3q67n8xq.
[22] Collier and Besley, Escaping the fragility trap, p.30.
[23] Daron Acemoglu and James Robinson, Why Nations Fail, Profile Books, 2013.
[24] Campbell and Page, Nigeria, p.90.
[25] Paul Johnson. Enemies of Society. Atheneum, 1977.
[26] 697.   Ivan Krastev, 'From politics to protest', Journal of Democracy, October 2014: https://www.journalofdemocracy.org/wp-content/uploads/2014/10/Krastev-25-4.pdf
[27] 698.   The 'attentive public' refers to that proportion of the people in mass society who hold articulate, informed and coherent attitudes about public policy issues. It excludes, at the top, those who make, or participate in making policy, and excludes those at the bottom, the mass public, who do not hold

consistent and coherent views about policy. See Graham Evans and Jeffrey Newnham, The Penguin Dictionary of International Relations, Penguin Books, 1998, p.38.

[28] Thomas Friedman, 'The Square People, Part 1', The New York Times, May 13, 2014: https://www.nytimes.com/2014/05/14/opinion/friedman-the-square-people-part-1.html.

[29] PM News, '#RevolutionNow: 9 northern groups pull out of Aug 22 protest,' August 21, 2019: https://pmnewsnigeria.com/2019/08/21/revolutionnow-9-northern-groups-pull-out-of-aug-22-protest/.

[30] BusinessDay, 'Beyond the protests: A nation fractured,' The Editorial Board, August 8, 2024: https://businessday.ng/columnist/article/beyond-the-protests-a-nation-fractured/.

[31] BusinessDay, 'Beyond the protests: Can we stitch a fractured nation back together?' The Editorial Board, August 12, 2024: https://businessday.ng/columnist/article/beyond-the-protests-can-we-stitch-a-fractured-nation-back-together/.

[32] Amnesty International, '#EndSARS: Investigate killings of protesters', Press Statement: https://www.amnesty.org.uk/urgent-actions/endsars-investigate-killings-protestors#.

[33] Premium Times, '#EndBadGovernanceInNigeria Protests Day 3 (LIVE UPDATES), August 3, 2024: https://www.premiumtimesng.com/news/top-news/720463-endbadgovernanceinnigeria-protests-day-3-live-updates.html.

[34] Olajide Omojolomoju, Solomon Odeniyi and Nathaniel Shaibu, 'Hunger protest: 17 feared killed as firms, others count huge losses,' The Punch, August 2, 2024: https://punchng.com/hunger-protest-17-feared-killed-as-firms-others-count-huge-losses/.

[35] Paul Collier and Dominic Rohner, Democracy, Development and Conflict, Journal of the European Economic Association, Vol. 6, No 2/3 (April-May 2008).

[36] See Olu Fasan, 'Economics of protests: Why Nigeria should be having more demonstrations,' BusinessDay, August 26, 2019: https://businessday.ng/columnist/article/economics-of-protests-why-nigeria-should-be-having-more-demonstrations/.

[37] John Rawls, A Theory of Justice, Revised Edition, Harvard University Press, 1999.

Selective Bibliography

Acemoglu, Daron and Robinson, James, Why Nations Fail: The origins of power, prosperity and poverty, Profile Books, 2013.

Achebe, Chinua, *There Was a Country: A Personal History of Biafra*, London: Penguin, 2013.

A Carl LeVan and Patrick Ukata, The Oxford Handbook on Nigerian Politics, OUP, Oxford, 2021.

Adedeji, Adebayo (ed). Nigerian Administration and its Political Setting. Routledge, 2023.

Ademoyega, Adewale, *Why We Struck: The Story of the First Nigerian Coup*. Ibadan: Evans Brothers, 1981.

Adejumobi, Said (ed), Governance and Politics in Post-Military Nigeria: Changes and Challenges. National Research Working Group (NRWG), 2010.

Adeniyi, Olusegun. *Against the Run of Play: How an Incumbent President Was Defeated in Nigeria*, Lagos: Prestige/ThisDay Press, 2017.

Adeniyi, Olusegun. *Power, Politics, and Death: A Front Row Account of Nigeria under the Late President Yar'Adua.* Lagos: Prestige, 2011.

Adeniyi, Olusegun, The Last 100 Days of Abacha: Political Drama in Nigeria Under One of Africa's Most Corrupt and Brutal Military Dictatorships, Bookhouse Company, 2015.

Aganga, Olusegun. *Reclaiming the Jewel of Africa: A blueprint for taking Nigeria and Africa from potential and prosperity.* Practical Inspiration Publishing, 2023.

Asiodu, Philip. Essays on Nigerian Political Economy. Victoria Island: Sankore Publishers, 1993.

Awolowo, Obafemi, *Path to Nigerian Freedom*, Faber & Faber, 1947.

Ayandele, E.A, The Educated Elite in the Nigerian Society, Ibadan University Press, 1974.

Babangida, B. Ibrahim, A Journey in Service: An Autobiography, Bookcraft, 2025

Bamaiyi, Ishaya, Vindication of a General, Daybis Limited (Ibadan), 2017.

Bayne, Nicholas and Woolcock, Stephen. The New Economic Diplomacy: Decision-making and negotiations in international economic relations. Fourth Edition, Routledge, 2017.

Campbell, John and Page, Matthew, *Nigeria: What Everyone Needs To Know*, Oxford University Press, 2018.

Collier Paul and Bexley Timothy (Authors). *Escaping the Fragility Trap*, LSE-Oxford Commission on State Fragility, Growth and Development, April 2018.

Collier Paul, Left Behind: A New Economics for Neglected Places, Allen Lane, June 2024.

Collier, Paul. The Bottom Billion: Why the poorest countries are failing and what can be done about it. Oxford University Press, 2008.

Conrad, Joseph. Heart of Darkness, London, 1973.

Conway, Ed. Material World: A Substantial Story of our Past and Present, Penguin, 2023

Diamond, Jared. Collapse: How Societies Choose to Fail or Succeed, New York, 2005.

Derbyshire, D and Derbyshire, I, *Political Systems of the World*, Chambers, 1993.

Falola, Toyin and Matthew Heaton, *A History of Nigeria*, New York: Cambridge University Press, 1999.

Falola, Toyin and Julius Ihonvbere, The Rise and Fall of Nigeria's Second Republic, 1979 -84. Zed Books Ltd, 1985.

Ferguson, Niall, Empire, *Penguin Books*, 2003.

Ferguson, Niall. Civilisation: The Six Killer Apps of Western Power, Penguin Books, 2012.

Flint, John, E., Sir George Goldie and the Making of Nigeria, London, 1960.

Gould, Michael. The Biafran War: The Struggle for Modern Nigeria. I.B. Tauris, 2013.

Hubbard, James, *The United States and the End of British Colonial Rule in Africa, 1941-1961*, McFarland, 2010.

Hutton, Will. The State We're In, Jonathan Cape, London, 1995.

Jones, L Ella and Edwards, R. Grace (eds). Nigeria: Economic, Political and Social Issues. Nova Science Publishers Inc, 2008

Joseph, A. Richard. Democracy and Prebendal Politics in Nigeria: The Rise and Fall of the Second Republic, Cambridge University Press, 2014.

Jonathan, E. Goodluck, My Transition Hours, Ezekiel Press, 2018.

Landes, David. The Wealth and Poverty of Nations, Abacus, 1998.

Levan, Carl and Ukata, Patrick (eds), The Oxford Handbook of Nigerian Politics, Oxford University Press, 2018.

Madiebo, A Alexander, The Nigerian Revolution and the Biafran War, Fourth Dimension Publishing Co, 2000.

Maier, Karl, This House Has Fallen: Nigeria in Crisis, Basic Books, 2002.

Muffett, D.J.M., Empire Builder Extraordinary: Sir George Goldie – His Philosophy of Government and Empire, Douglas, Isle of Man, 1978.

North, Douglass. Institutions, Institutional Changes and Economic Performance, Cambridge University Press, 1991.

Obasanjo Olusegun, *My Command: An account of the Nigerian Civil War 1967-1970*. Oxford: Heinemann, 1980.

Odumegwu-Ojukwu, Emeka, *Because I am Involved*, Spectrum, 1989.

Okonjo-Iweala, Ngozi. *Reforming the Unreformable: Lessons from Nigeria.* The MIT Press, 2012.

Okonjo-Iweala, Ngozi. *Fighting Corruption Is Dangerous: The Story Behind the Headlines,* The MIT Press, 2018.

Pilling, David. The Growth Delusion: The Wealth and Wellbeing of Nations, Bloomsbury Publishing, 2018.

Rawls, John. A Theory of Justice, Revised Edition, Harvard University Press, 1999.

Rose-Ackerman, Susan (ed). International Handbook on the Economics of Corruption, Edward Elgar Publishing, 2007.

Sally, Razeen. Trade Policy, New Century: The WTO, FTAs and Asia Rising, The Institute of Economic Affairs, 2008.

Shagari, Shehu. Beckoned To Serve, Heinemann Educational Books (Nigeria), 2001.

Siollun, Max. What Britain Did to Nigeria: A short history of conquest and rule, Hurst, 2021.

Smith Adam, *The Wealth of Nations* (1776), Wordsworth Edition, 2012.

Soyinka, Wole. The Open Sour of a Continent: A Personal Narrative of the Nigerian Crisis, Oxford University Press, USA, 1997.

Sunstein, Cass. How Change Happens, The MIT Press, 2019.

Susskind, Daniel. Growth: A reckoning, Allen Lane, 2024.

Uwais Report: Report of the Electoral Reform Committee, Vol 1, Main Report, December 2008.

Williams, Gavin. State and Society in Nigeria, Malthouse Press, 2019

Acknowledgements

From start to finish, I owe everything about this book to God Almighty. The conception, writing and publication of this book would not have been possible without the grace of God, and I give all the glory, honour and thanks to Him. I am grateful to my church in London, New Wine Church, whose 3Ds vision to help people discover, develop and deploy their God-given talents has always been an inspiration to me. I thank Pastor Kola Taiwo, the Senior Pastor of New Wine Church, and the entire leadership of the church for their prayers and support.

Of course, God works through humans, and there are many people and institutions that played key roles in the emergence of this book. First, I owe a debt of gratitude to Vanguard and BusinessDay, two of Nigeria's most popular and highly respected newspapers, whose platforms I used, as a weekly columnist for over ten years, to explore some of the ideas in this book. Being a weekly columnist enabled me to immerse myself in the political, economic and social affairs of Nigeria; to research, think and share ideas about the country's present challenges and future direction. All that gave me the impetus to develop those ideas further and to write this book.

But I cannot talk about Vanguard and BusinessDay without paying great tribute to their publishers and editors who gave me those opportunities in the first place. In October 2014, the then Editor of BusinessDay, Phillip Isakpa, invited me to write for the newspaper. That invitation was at the instance of the Publisher, Frank Aigbogun, a celebrated former Editor of Vanguard. I am grateful to them for their confidence in me. Over the years, I worked with many Editors in BusinessDay, but, apart from Mr Isakpa, the current Editor, Tayo Fagbule, stands out for his professionalism and creativity. He is a great encourager who never stopped complimenting my writing. Thank you! Then, there is Chris Akor, BusinessDay's Op-Ed Editor for many years, with whom I had a great relationship. That relationship transcended his time in the newspaper and remains till today. I am grateful to him. My thanks also go Daniel Obi, BusinessDay's Marketing and Brands Editor, who, as far back as 2019, urged me to write this book 'for posterity', and was willing to invest time and effort in it. But the timing was not right. I thank him for his encouragement and support.

In October 2018, the Editor of Vanguard, Eze Anaba, invited me to join the newspaper as a weekly columnist. That relationship brought me into contact with the newspaper's legendary Publisher, Mr Sam Amuka, fondly called Uncle Sam, whose support has been valuable beyond estimation. Uncle Sam played a critical role in the publication of this book, connecting me with key individuals in Nigeria. Mr Anaba, a current two-term President of the Nigerian Guild of Editors, was also always a phone call away. I owe both Uncle Sam and Mr Anaba a huge debt. Every writer, however brilliant and experienced, needs good editors, and I had them in Vanguard. Mike Ebonugwu, Features Editor, and Udo Ibuot, Chief Sub-Editor, received my articles every week and gave them a good editorial treatment. I thank them.

A former President and Publisher of the Washington Post, Philip L. Graham, reportedly described journalism as the 'first rough draft of history'. I agree. And this book draws heavily from news stories written by journalists from all over the world. But instead of merely citing the newspapers or other publications in which the news stories or reports appeared, I deliberately credited, in the extensive endnotes and index, the individual journalists and writers who wrote the stories or the articles. This is because I want them to be part of the history that this book represents. I pay tribute to all the journalists.

In 2022, while still writing the manuscript, I enrolled for a two-year part-time Diploma in Creative Writing at the University of Oxford's Department for Continuing Education (Conted). The course gave me the opportunity to think, read and write. I received a lot of encouragement and support from the brilliant tutors and from my fellow students. I am particularly grateful to Dr John Ballam, the course director, as well as Jeremy Hughes and Frank Egerton, both of whom taught long fiction and offered good advice on the book. My gratitude also goes to my fellow students who were really good company throughout the course. Some of them couldn't wait to attend the book launch. Thank you all!

Coming back to the publication of the book, I am grateful to my publisher, Penguin Publishers, for their support in getting this book published. After initially working with Ryan Chase, a literary agent and author consultant, who got the project off the ground, I was introduced to Josh Baker, the Lead Project Manager, who ably coordinated the editing, proofreading and formatting of the manuscript. Following Mr Baker's promotion, he was replaced by Danny Brown, an experienced and personable project manager, who navigated the book through to publication, including ably handling the publicity campaign. I am grateful to the Penguin team. I am also enormously indebted to Robert Jarocki, an experienced professional cover designer with Reedsy Publishing, for designing the cover of this book. Mr Jarocki's flexibility, creativity and speed are impressive. My gratitude also goes to the indexers at PDF Index Generator, led by Hesham Gneady, for creating a comprehensive index for the book. I feel fortunate that my book ended up in such capable hands.

I am also immensely fortunate that the book received great endorsements and praises from prominent and highly reputable people. I am extremely grateful to Professor Sir Paul Collier, a world-renowned economist and expert on Africa, and Professor Pat Utomi, a famous Nigerian political economist, for taking the time to read the manuscript and write the forewords to the book. Unusually, the book has two forewords, but that's because each of the two foreword writers brings a unique perspective that enriches the book. I owe them huge debt of gratitude. My enormous gratitude also goes the David Pilling, Africa Editor of the Financial Times, and Alex Vines, Director of Africa Programme at Chatham House, who, despite their busy schedules, found the time to read the manuscript and endorse the book. I am indebted to them.

On a personal level, I thank Mr Yemi Akeju, whose company, Ideas Communications, runs the prestigious

Nigeria Media Merit Awards (NMMA) annually in Nigeria. Mr Akeju, and his wife, Bola, have been my stalwart supporters for decades, and are great supporters of this book. I am eternally grateful for their longstanding and continued love and support.

Last but not least, my family. My wife, Adedoyin, and my children, Oluwatomi, Oluwatoyosi and Oluwatoni, have always been a great source of inspiration and motivation. Thank you for your understanding, tolerance and, above all, best wishes.

Index

594

597

Uwais, Muhammadu Lawal, 40, 141
Uwais Report, 141–144, 460

Vanguard, xxi, 65, 121, 204–205,
    364, 379, 432, 445
Voigt, Stefan, 133

Wacks, Raymond, 404
Warri Refinery, 192, 197
Weber, Max, 361, 365
Welfare and Prosperity, 260, 262,
    264, 266, 268, 270, 272, 274, 276,
    278, 280
Western Nigeria, 38, 72, 461
Western Sahara, 85
Whistle-blowers, protection of, 156,
    394
Williams, Akintola, 79
Williams, Ishola, 35
Williams, Rotimi, 114, 161
Williamson, John, 465
    *The Political Economy of Policy
    Reform*, 465
Wolf, Martin, 226
World Bank, 106, 119, 151, 174, 181,
    216, 232–233, 237–239, 242, 244,
    246, 248, 259, 263–264, 278, 306,
    330, 334–335, 340, 344, 373, 389,
    421–423, 436–437

Yakubu, Mahmood, Professor, 42, 44
Yar' Adua, Shehu Musa, 24, 32,
    39–40, 47, 67, 69, 140, 145
Yar' Adua, Umaru Musa, 140, 145
Yelewata community, 443
Yemi-Esan, Folasade, 370
Yew, Lee Kuan, 90–91, 472
Yi, Wang, 314
Yoruba, 3, 12–13, 63–65, 84, 86, 89,
    94, 116, 134, 136, 145–146, 150
'Yoruba Lokan', 150
Yuan Magnet, 313
Yuguda, Isa, 198
Yusuf, Mohammed, 455

Zaki Biam, 455
Zhongshan Fucheng Industrial
    Investment, 345

About the Author

Dr Oluseto (Olu) Fasan is a lawyer, political economist, academic, policy analyst and writer. He was called to the English Bar, at the Inner Temple, in 2001 and later obtained a master's (with Distinction) in international political economy and a PhD in International Economic and Trade Law from the London School of Economics (LSE). He taught International Political Economy, International Trade and Economic Diplomacy at LSE, in addition to being a Visiting Fellow at the International Trade Policy Unit in the Department of International Relations. He was also a researcher with the International Growth Centre (IGC), jointly run by LSE and Oxford University. Dr Fasan worked at the World Trade Organisation (WTO) in Geneva and consulted for the Commonwealth Secretariat. For nearly 15 years, he was a senior policy adviser with the UK Government, working in a range of policy areas, including regulatory reform, trade, energy and climate change and industrial strategy. A dedicated writer, Dr Fasan has written widely in peer-reviewed academic journals and was a weekly columnist for two of Nigeria's most popular newspapers, Vanguard and BusinessDay, for over ten years. To further explore and develop his creative writing skills, Dr Fasan obtained a Diploma in Creative Writing from Oxford University in 2024. He is a Fellow of the Royal Society for the Encouragement of Arts, Manufactures and Commerce (RSA). He lives in London.